Fatal Revenant

THE LAST CHRONICLES
OF THOMAS COVENANT

STEPHEN DONALDSON

Fatal Revenant

GOLLANCZ

LONDON

The right of Stephen R. Donaldson to be identified as the
author of this work has been asserted by him in accordance
with the Copyright, Designs and Patents Act 1988.

First published in Great Britain in 2007 by Gollancz
An imprint of the Orion Publishing Group
Orion House, 5 Upper St Martin's Lane, London WC2H 9EA
An Hachette Livre UK Company

This edition published in Great Britain in 2008 by Gollancz

A CIP catalogue record for this book is
available from the British Library

ISBN 978 0 57508 2 380

1 3 5 7 9 10 8 6 4 2

Printed in the UK by CPI William Clowes
Beccles NR34 7TL

The Orion Publishing Group's policy is to use papers that
are natural, renewable and recyclable products and
made from wood grown in sustainable forests. The logging and
manufacturing processes are expected to conform to the
environmental regulations of the country of origin.

www.orionbooks.co.uk

ACKNOWLEDGMENTS

As this saga goes along, I have more and more people to thank. Members of Kevin's Watch have been generous and diligent. John Eccker has demonstrated once again that he is indispensable: a friend, a gentleman, and an unfailing aid. Robyn Butler has contributed more than I had any right to ask. And Jennifer Christensen, the notorious Cameraman Jenn, has been a 'power reader' of the most useful sort.

TABLE OF CONTENTS

WHAT HAS GONE BEFORE

As a young man – a novelist, happily married, with an infant son, Roger – Thomas Covenant is inexplicably stricken with leprosy. In a leprosarium, where the last two fingers of his right hand are amputated, he learns that leprosy is incurable. As it progresses, it produces numbness, often killing its victims by leaving them unaware of injuries which have become infected. Medications arrest the progress of Covenant's affliction; but he is taught that his only real hope of survival lies in protecting himself obsessively from any form of damage.

Horrified by his illness, he returns to his home on Haven Farm, where his wife, Joan, has abandoned and divorced him in order to protect their son from exposure.

Other blows to his emotional stability follow. Fearing the mysterious nature of his illness, the people around him cast him in the traditional role of the leper: a pariah, outcast and unclean. In addition, he discovers that he has become impotent – and unable to write. Grimly he struggles to go on living; but as the pressure of his loneliness mounts, he begins to experience prolonged episodes of unconsciousness, during which he appears to have adventures in a magical realm known only as 'the Land'.

In the Land, physical and emotional health are tangible forces, made palpable by an eldritch energy called Earthpower. Because vitality and beauty are concrete qualities, as plain to the senses as size and colour, the well-being of the physical world has become the guiding precept of the Land's people. When Covenant first encounters them, in *Lord Foul's*

Bane, they greet him as the reincarnation of an ancient hero, Berek Halfhand, because he, too, has lost half of his hand. Also he possesses a white gold ring – his wedding band – which they know to be a talisman of great power, able to wield 'the wild magic that destroys peace'.

Shortly after he first appears in the Land, Covenant's leprosy and impotence disappear, cured by Earthpower; and this, he knows, is impossible. And the mere idea that he possesses some form of magical power threatens his ability to sustain the stubborn disciplines on which his survival depends. Therefore he chooses to interpret his translation to the Land as a dream or hallucination. He responds to his welcome and health with Unbelief: the harsh, dogged assertion that the Land is not real.

Because of his Unbelief, his initial reactions to the people and wonders of the Land are at best dismissive, at worst despicable (at one point, overwhelmed by his reborn sexuality, he rapes Lena, a young girl who has befriended him). However, the people of the Land decline to punish or reject him for his actions. As Berek Halfhand reborn, he is beyond judgment. And there is an ancient prophecy concerning the white gold wielder: 'With the one word of truth or treachery,/he will save or damn the Earth.' Covenant's new companions in the Land know that they cannot make his choices for him. They can only hope that he will eventually follow Berek's example by saving the Land.

At first, such forbearance conveys little to Covenant, although he cannot deny that he is moved by the ineffable beauties of this world, as well as by the kindness of its people. During his travels, however, first with Lena's mother, Atiaran, then with the Giant Saltheart Foamfollower, and finally with the Lords of Revelstone, he learns enough of the history of the Land to understand what is at stake.

The Land has an ancient enemy, Lord Foul the Despiser, who dreams of destroying the Arch of Time – thereby destroying not only the Land but the entire Earth – in order to escape what he perceives to be a prison. Against this evil stands the Council of Lords, men and women who have dedicated their lives to nurturing the health of the Land, to studying the lost lore and wisdom of Berek and his long-dead descendants, and to opposing Despite.

Unfortunately these Lords possess only a small fraction of the power of their predecessors. The Staff of Law, Berek's primary instrument of Earthpower, has been hidden from them. And the lore of Law and Earthpower seems inherently inadequate to defeat Lord Foul. Wild magic rather than Law is the crux of Time. Without it, the Arch cannot be destroyed; but neither can it be defended.

Hence both the Lords and the Despiser seek Thomas Covenant's allegiance. The Lords attempt to win his aid with courage and compassion: the Despiser, through manipulation. And in this contest Covenant's Unbelief appears to place him on the side of the Despiser.

Nevertheless Covenant cannot deny his response to the Land's apparent transcendence. And as he is granted more and more friendship by the Lords and denizens of the Land, he finds that he is now dismayed by his earlier violence towards Lena. He faces an insoluble conundrum: the Land cannot be real, yet it feels entirely real. His heart responds to its loveliness – and that response has the potential to kill him because it undermines his necessary habits of wariness and hopelessness.

Trapped within this contradiction, he attempts to escape through a series of unspoken bargains. In *Lord Foul's Bane*, he grants the Lords his passive support, hoping that this will enable him to avoid accepting the possibilities – the responsibilities – of his white gold ring. And at first his hopes are realised. The Lords find the lost Staff of Law; their immediate enemy, one of Lord Foul's servants, is defeated; and Covenant himself is released from the Land.

Back in his real world, however, he discovers that he has in fact gained nothing. Indeed, his plight has worsened: he remains a leper; and his experience of friendship and magic in the Land has weakened his ability to endure his outcast loneliness on Haven Farm. When he is translated to the Land a second time, in *The Illearth War*, he knows that he must devise a new bargain.

During his absence, the Land's plight has worsened as well. Decades have passed in the Land; and in that time Lord Foul has gained and mastered the Illearth Stone, an ancient bane of staggering power. With it, the Despiser has created an army which now marches to overwhelm the Lords of Revelstone. Although the Lords hold the Staff of Law, they lack sufficient might to withstand the evil horde. They need the strength of wild magic.

Other developments also tighten the grip of Covenant's dilemma. The Council is now led by High Lord Elena, his daughter by his rape of Lena. With her, he begins to experience the real consequences of his violence: it is clear to him – if to no one else – that she is not completely sane. In addition, the army of the Lords is led by a man named Hile Troy, who appears to have come to the Land from Covenant's own world. Troy's presence radically erodes Covenant's self-protective Unbelief.

Now more than ever Covenant feels that he must resolve his conundrum. Again he posits a bargain. He will give the defenders of the Land his active support. Specifically, he will join Elena on a quest to discover the source of EarthBlood, the most concentrated form of Earthpower. But in return he will continue to deny that his ring holds any power. He will accept no responsibility for the ultimate fate of the Land.

This time, however, the results of his bargain are disastrous. Using the Illearth Stone, Lord Foul slaughters the Giants of Seareach. Hile Troy is only able to defeat the Despiser's army by giving his soul to Caerroil Wildwood, the Forestal of Garroting Deep. And Covenant's help enables Elena to find the EarthBlood, which she uses to sever one of the necessary boundaries between life and death. Her instability leads her to think that the dead will have more power against Lord Foul than the living. But she is terribly wrong; and in the resulting catastrophe both she and the Staff of Law are lost.

Covenant returns to his real world knowing that his attempts to resolve his dilemma have served the Despiser.

Nearly broken by his failures, he visits the Land once more in *The Power that Preserves*, where he discovers the full cost of his actions. Dead, his daughter now serves Lord Foul, using the Staff of Law to wreak havoc. Her mother, Lena, has lost her mind. And the defenders of the Land are besieged by an army too vast and powerful to be defeated.

Covenant still has no solution to his conundrum: only wild magic can save the Land – and he cannot afford to accept its reality. However, sickened at heart by Lena's madness, and by the imminent ruin of the Land, he resolves to confront the Despiser himself. He has no hope of defeating Lord Foul, but he would rather sacrifice himself for the sake of a magical, but unreal, place than preserve his outcast life in his real world.

Before he can reach the Despiser, however, he must first face dead Elena and the Staff of Law. He cannot oppose her; yet she defeats herself when her attack on him draws an overwhelming response from his ring – a response which also destroys the Staff.

Accompanied only by his old friend, the Giant Saltheart Foamfollower, Covenant finally gains his confrontation with Lord Foul and the Illearth Stone. Facing the full force of the Despiser's savagery and malice, he at last finds the solution to his conundrum, 'the eye of the paradox': the point of balance between accepting that the Land is real and insisting that it is not. On that basis, he is able to combat Lord Foul by using the dire might of the Illearth Stone to trigger the wild magic of his ring. With that power, he shatters both the Stone and Lord Foul's home, thereby ending the threat of the Despiser's evil.

When he returns to his own world for the last time, he learns that his new-found balance benefits him there as well. He knows now that the reality or unreality of the Land is less important than his love for it; and that knowledge gives him the strength to face his life as a pariah without fear or bitterness.

THE SECOND CHRONICLES OF THOMAS COVENANT

For ten years after the events of *The Power that Preserves*, Covenant lives alone on Haven Farm, writing novels. He is still an outcast, but he has one friend, Dr Julius Berenford. Then, however, two damaged women enter his life.

His ex-wife, Joan, returns to him, violently insane. Leaving Roger with her parents, she has spent some time in a commune which has dedicated itself to the service of Despite, and which has chosen Covenant to be the victim of its evil. Hoping to spare anyone else the hazards of involvement, Covenant attempts to care for Joan alone.

When Covenant refuses aid, Dr Berenford enlists Dr Linden Avery, a young physician whom he has recently hired. Like Joan, she has been badly hurt, although in entirely different ways. As a young girl, she was locked in a room with her father while he committed suicide. And as a teenager, she killed her mother, an act of euthanasia to which she felt compelled by her mother's illness and pain. Loathing death, Linden has become a doctor in a haunted attempt to erase her past.

At Dr Berenford's urging, she intrudes on Covenant's treatment of his ex-wife. When members of Joan's commune attack Haven Farm, seeking Covenant's death, Linden attempts to intervene, but she is struck down before she can save him. As a result, she accompanies him when he is returned to the Land.

During Covenant's absence, several thousand years have passed, and the Despiser has regained his power. As before, he seeks to use Covenant's wild magic in order to break the Arch of Time and escape his prison. In *The Wounded Land*, however, Covenant and Linden soon learn that Lord Foul has fundamentally altered his methods. Instead of relying on armies and warfare to goad Covenant, the Despiser has devised an attack on the natural Law which gives the Land its beauty and health.

The overt form of this attack is the Sunbane, a malefic corona around the sun which produces extravagant surges of fertility, rain, drought and pestilence in mad succession. So great is the Sunbane's power and destructiveness that it has come to dominate all life in the Land. Yet the Sunbane is not what it appears to be. And its organic virulence serves primarily to mask Lord Foul's deeper manipulations.

He has spent centuries corrupting the Council of Lords. That group now rules over the Land as the Clave; and it is led by a Raver, one of the Despiser's most ancient and potent servants. The Clave extracts blood from the people of the Land to feed the Banefire, an enormous blaze which purportedly hinders the Sunbane, but which actually increases it.

However, the hidden purpose of the Clave and the Banefire is to inspire from Covenant an excessive exertion of wild magic. And towards that end, another Raver afflicts Covenant with a venom intended to cripple his control over his power. When the venom has done its work, Covenant will be unable to defend the Land without unleashing so much force that he destroys the Arch.

As for Linden Avery, Lord Foul intends to use her loathing of death against her. She alone is gifted or cursed with the health-sense which once informed and guided all the people of the Land by enabling them to perceive physical and emotional health directly. For that reason, she is uniquely vulnerable to the malevolence of the Sunbane, as well as to the insatiable malice of the Ravers. The manifest evil into which she has been plunged threatens the core of her identity.

Linden's health-sense accentuates her potential as a healer. However, it also gives her the capacity to possess other people; to reach so deeply into them that she can control their actions. By this means, Lord Foul intends to cripple her morally: he seeks to transform her into a woman who will possess Covenant in order to misuse his power. Thus she will give the Despiser what he wants even if Covenant does not.

And if those ploys fail, Lord Foul has other stratagems in place to achieve his ends.

Horrified in their separate ways by what has been done to the Land, Covenant and Linden wish to confront the Clave in Revelstone; but on their own, they cannot survive the complex perils of the Sunbane. Fortunately they gain the help of two villagers, Sunder and Hollian. Sunder and Hollian have lived with the Sunbane all their lives, and their experience enables Covenant and Linden to avoid ruin as they travel.

But Linden, Sunder, and Hollian are separated from Covenant near a region known as Andelain, captured by the Clave while he enters Andelain alone. It was once the most beautiful and Earthpowerful place in the Land; and he now discovers that it alone remains intact, defended from the Sunbane by the last Forestal, Caer-Caveral, who was formerly Hile Troy. There Covenant encounters his Dead, the spectres of his long-gone friends. They offer him advice and guidance for the struggle ahead. And they give him a gift: a strange ebony creature named Vain, an artificial being created for a hidden purpose by ur-viles, former servants of the Despiser.

Aided by Waynhim, benign relatives – and ancient enemies – of the ur-viles, Covenant hastens towards Revelstone to rescue his friends. When he encounters the Clave, he learns the cruellest secret of the Sunbane: it was made possible by his destruction of the Staff of Law thousands of years ago. Desperate to undo the harm which he has unwittingly caused, he risks wild magic in order to free Linden, Sunder and Hollian, as well as a number of *Haruchai*, powerful warriors who at one time served the Council of Lords.

With his friends, Vain, and a small group of *Haruchai*, Covenant sets out to locate the One Tree, the wood from which Berek originally fashioned the Staff of Law. Covenant hopes to devise a new Staff with which to oppose the Clave and the Sunbane.

Travelling eastward towards the Sunbirth Sea, Covenant and his companions encounter a party of Giants, seafaring beings from the homeland of the lost Giants of Seareach. One of them, Cable Seadreamer, has had a vision of a terrible threat to the Earth, and the Giants have sent out a Search to discover the danger.

Convinced that this threat is the Sunbane, Covenant persuades the Search to help him find the One Tree; and in *The One Tree*, Covenant, Linden, Vain and several *Haruchai* set sail aboard the Giantship Starfare's Gem, leaving Sunder and Hollian to rally the people of the Land against the Clave.

The quest for the One Tree takes Covenant and Linden first to the land of the *Elohim*, cryptic beings of pure Earthpower who appear to understand and perhaps control the destiny of the Earth. The *Elohim* agree to reveal the location of the One Tree, but they exact a price: they cripple Covenant's mind, enclosing his consciousness in a kind of stasis, purportedly to protect the Earth from his growing power, but in fact to prevent him from carrying out Vain's unnamed purpose. Guided now by Linden's determination rather than Covenant's, the Search sets sail for the Isle of the One Tree.

Unexpectedly, however, they are joined by one of the *Elohim*, Findail, who has been Appointed to bear the consequences if Vain's purpose does not fail.

Linden soon finds that she is unable to free Covenant's mind without possessing him, which she fears to do, knowing that she may unleash his power. When events force her to a decision, however, she succeeds at restoring his consciousness – much to Findail's dismay.

At last, Starfare's Gem reaches the Isle of the One Tree, where one of the *Haruchai*, Brinn, succeeds at replacing the Tree's Guardian. But when Covenant, Linden, and their companions approach their goal, they learn that they have been misled by the Despiser – and by the *Elohim*. Covenant's attempt to obtain wood for a new Staff of Law begins to rouse the Worm of the World's End. Once awakened, the Worm will accomplish Lord Foul's release from Time.

At the cost of his own life, Seadreamer succeeds at making Linden aware of the true danger. She in turn is able to forestall Covenant. Nevertheless the Worm has been disturbed, and its restlessness forces the Search to flee as the Isle sinks into the sea, taking the One Tree beyond reach.

Defeated, the Search sets course for the Land in *White Gold Wielder*. Covenant now believes that he has no alternative except to confront the Clave directly, to quench the Banefire, and then to battle the Despiser; and Linden is determined to aid him, in part because she has come to love him, and in part because she fears his unchecked wild magic.

With great difficulty, they eventually reach Revelstone, where they are rejoined by Sunder, Hollian and several *Haruchai*. Together the Land's few defenders give battle to the Clave. After a fierce struggle, the companions corner the Raver which commands the Clave. There Seadreamer's brother, Grimmand Honninscrave, sacrifices his life in order to make possible the 'rending' of the Raver. Then Covenant flings himself into the Banefire, using its dark theurgy to transform the venom in his veins so that he can quench the Banefire without threatening the Arch. The Sunbane remains, but its evil no longer grows.

When the Clave has been dispersed, and Revelstone has been cleansed, Covenant and Linden turn towards Mount Thunder, where they believe that they will find the Despiser. As they travel, still followed by Vain and Findail, Linden's fears mount. She realises that Covenant does not mean to fight Lord Foul. That contest, Covenant believes, will unleash enough force to destroy Time. Afraid that he will surrender to the Despiser, Linden prepares herself to possess him again, although she now understands that possession is a greater evil than death.

Yet when she and Covenant finally face Lord Foul, deep within the Wightwarrens of Mount Thunder, she is possessed herself by a Raver; and her efforts to win free of that dark spirit's control leave her unwilling to interfere with Covenant's choices. As she has feared, he does surrender, giving Lord Foul his ring. But when the Despiser turns wild magic against Covenant, slaying his body, the altered venom is burned out of Covenant's spirit, and he becomes a being of pure wild magic, able to sustain the Arch despite the fury of Lord Foul's attacks. Eventually the

Despiser expends so much of his own essence that he effectively defeats himself; and Covenant's ring falls to Linden.

Meanwhile, she has gleaned an understanding of Vain's purpose – and of Findail's Appointed role. Vain is pure structure: Findail, pure fluidity. Using Covenant's ring, Linden melds the two beings into a new Staff of Law. Then, guided by her health-sense and her physician's instincts, she reaches out with the restored power of Law to erase the Sunbane and begin the healing of the Land.

When she is done, Linden fades from the Land and returns to her own world, where she finds that Covenant is indeed dead. Yet she now holds his wedding ring. And when Dr Berenford comes looking for her, she discovers that her time with Covenant and her own victories have transformed her. She is now truly Linden Avery the Chosen, as she was called in the Land: she can choose to live her old life in an entirely new way.

THE LAST CHRONICLES OF THOMAS COVENANT

In Book One, *The Runes of the Earth*, ten years have passed for Linden Avery; and in that time, her life has changed. She has adopted a son, Jeremiah, now fifteen, who was horribly damaged during her first translation to the Land, losing half of his right hand and – apparently – all ordinary use of his mind. He displays a peculiar genius: he is able to build astonishing structures out of such toys as Tinkertoys and Lego. But in every other way, he is entirely unreactive. Nonetheless Linden is devoted to him, giving him all of her frustrated love for Thomas Covenant and the Land.

In addition, she has become the Chief Medical Officer of a local psychiatric hospital, where Covenant's ex-wife, Joan, is now a patient. For a time, Joan's condition resembles a vegetative catatonia. But then she starts to punish herself, punching her temple incessantly in an apparent effort to bring about her own death. Only the restoration of her white gold wedding band calms her, although it does not altogether prevent her violence.

As the story begins, Roger Covenant has reached twenty-one, and has come to claim custody of his mother: custody which Linden refuses, in part because she has no legal authority to release Joan, and in part because she does not trust Roger. To this setback, Roger responds by kidnapping his mother at gun-point. And when Linden goes to the hospital to deal with the aftermath of Roger's attack, Roger takes Jeremiah as well.

Separately Linden and the police locate Roger, Joan and Jeremiah. But while Linden confronts Roger, Joan is struck by lightning, and Roger opens fire on the police. In the ensuing fusillade, Linden, Roger and – perhaps – Jeremiah are cut down; and Linden finds herself once again translated to the Land, where Lord Foul's disembodied voice informs her that he has gained possession of her son.

As before, several thousand years have passed in the Land, and everything that Linden knew has changed. The Land has been healed, restored to its former loveliness and potency. Now, however, it is ruled by Masters, *Haruchai* who have dedicated themselves to the suppression of all magical knowledge and power. And their task is simplified by an eerie smog called Kevin's Dirt, which blinds the people of the Land – as well as Linden – to the wealth of Earthpower all around them.

Yet the Land is threatened by perils which the Masters cannot defeat. *Caesures* – disruptions of time – wreak havoc, appearing and disappearing randomly as Joan releases insane blasts of wild magic. In addition, one of the *Elohim* has visited the Land, warning of dangers which include various monsters – and an unnamed *halfhand*. And the new Staff of Law that Linden created at the end of *White Gold Wielder* has been lost.

Desperate to locate and rescue Jeremiah, Linden soon acquires companions, both willing and reluctant: Anele, an ancient, Earthpowerful, and blind madman who claims that he is 'the hope of the Land', and whose insanity varies with the surfaces – stone, dirt, grass – on which he stands; Liand, a naïve young man from Mithil Stonedown; Stave, a Master who distrusts Linden, and wishes to imprison Anele; a small group of ur-viles, artificial creatures that were at one time among Lord Foul's most dire minions; and a band of Ramen, the human servants of the Ranyhyn, Earthpowerful horses that once inhabited the Land. Among the Ramen, Linden discovers that the Ranyhyn intend to aid her in her search for her son. And she meets Esmer, the tormented and powerful descendant of the lost *Haruchai* Cail and the corrupted *Elohim* Kastenessen.

From Esmer, Linden learns the nature of the *caesures*. She is told that the ur-viles intend to protect her from betrayal by Esmer. And she finds that Anele knows where the Staff of Law was lost thousands of years ago.

Because she has no power except Covenant's ring, which she is only able to use with great difficulty – because she has no idea where Lord Foul has taken Jeremiah – and because she fears that she will not be able to travel the Land against the opposition of the Masters – Linden decides to risk entering a *caesure*. She hopes that it will take her into the past, to the time when her Staff of Law was lost, and that Anele will then be able to guide her to the Staff. Accompanied by Anele, Liand, Stave, the ur-viles, and three Ramen – the Manethrall Mahrtiir and his two Cords, Bhapa and Pahni – Linden rides into the temporal chaos of Joan's power.

Thanks to the theurgy of the ur-viles and to the guidance of the Ranyhyn, she and her companions emerge from the *caesure* more than three thousand years in their past, where they find that the Staff has been hidden and protected by a group of Waynhim. When she reclaims the Staff, however, she is betrayed by Esmer: using powers inherited from Kastenessen, he brings a horde of Demondim out of the Land's deep past to assail her. The Demondim are monstrous beings, the makers of the ur-viles and Waynhim, and they attack with both their own fierce lore and the baleful energy of the Illearth Stone, which they siphon through a *caesure* from an era before Thomas Covenant's first visit to the Land.

Fearing that the attack of the Demondim will damage the integrity of the Land's history, Linden uses Covenant's ring to create a *caesure* of her own. That disruption of time carries her, all of her companions, and the Demondim to her natural present. To her surprise, however, her *caesure* deposits her and everyone with her before the gates of Revelstone, the seat of the Masters. While the Masters fight a hopeless battle against the Demondim, she and her companions enter the ambiguous sanctuary of Lord's Keep.

In Revelstone, Linden meets Handir, called the Voice of the Masters: their leader. And she encounters the Humbled, Galt, Branl and Clyme:

three *Haruchai* who have been maimed to resemble Thomas Covenant, and whose purpose is to embody the moral authority of the Masters. Cared for by a mysterious – and oddly comforting – woman named the Mahdoubt, Linden tries to imagine how she can persuade the Masters to aid her search for Jeremiah, and for the salvation of the Land. However, when she confronts Handir, the Humbled and other Masters, all of her arguments are turned aside. Although the Masters are virtually helpless against the Demondim, they refuse to countenance Linden's desires. Only Stave elects to stand with her: an act of defiance for which he is punished and spurned by his kinsmen.

The confrontation ends abruptly when news comes that riders are approaching Revelstone. From the battlements, Linden sees four Masters racing to reach Lord's Keep ahead of the Demondim. With the Masters are Thomas Covenant and Jeremiah. And Jeremiah has emerged enthusiastically from his unreactive passivity.

PART I

*'lest you prove
unable to serve me'*

Chapter One:

Reunion

In sunshine as vivid as revelation, Linden Avery knelt on the stone of a low-walled coign like a balcony high in the outward face of Revelstone's watchtower.

Implacable as the Masters, Stave of the *Haruchai* stood beside her: he had led her here in spite of the violence with which his kinsmen had spurned him. And at the wall, the young Stonedownor, Liand, stared his surprised concern and incomprehension down at the riders fleeing before the on-rush of the Demondim. Like Stave, if by design rather than by blows, he had abandoned his entire life for Linden's sake; but unlike the former Master, he could not guess who rode with the *Haruchai* far below him. He could only gaze urgently at the struggling horses, and at the leashed seethe of theurgy among the monsters, and gape questions for which he seemed to have no words or no voice.

At that moment, however, neither Liand nor Stave impinged on Linden's awareness. They were not real to her.

Near Liand, Manethrall Mahrtiir studied the exhausted mounts with Ramen concentration while his devoted Cords, Bhapa and Pahni, protected mad, blind Anele from the danger of a fall that he could not see.

With Linden, they had crossed hundreds of leagues – and many hundreds of years – to come to this place at this time. In her name, they had defied the repudiation of the Masters who ruled over the Land.

But none of her companions existed for her.

To the north lay the new fields which would feed Revelstone's inhabitants. To the south, the foothills of the Keep's promontory tumbled towards the White River. And from the southeast came clamouring the mass of the Demondim, vicious as a host of doom. The monsters appeared to melt and solidify from place to place as they pursued their prey: four horses at the limits of their strength, bearing six riders.

Six riders. But four of them were Masters; and for Linden, they also did not exist. She saw only the others.

In the instant that she recognised Thomas Covenant and Jeremiah, the meaning of her entire life changed. Everything that she had known and understood and assumed was altered, rendering empty or unnecessary or foolish her original flight from the Masters, her time among the Ramen, her participation in the horserite of the Ranyhyn. Even her precipitous venture into the Land's past in order to retrieve her Staff of Law no longer held any significance.

Thomas Covenant was alive: the only man whom she had ever loved.

Her son was free. Somehow he had eluded Lord Foul's cruel grasp.

And Jeremiah's mind had been restored. His eager encouragement of the Masters and their mounts as they struggled to outrun the horde showed clearly that he had found his way out of his mental prison; or had been rescued—

Transfixed, she stared at them past the wall of her vantage point, leaping towards them with her gaze and her health-sense and her starved soul. Moments ago, she had seen only the ruinous advance of the Demondim. But now she was on her knees, struck down by the miraculous sight of her adopted son and her dead lover rushing towards Revelstone for their lives.

Already her arms ached to hold them.

For two or three heartbeats, surely no more than that, she remained kneeling while Liand tried to find his voice, and Stave said nothing, and Mahrtiir murmured tensely to his Cords. Then she snatched up the Staff and surged to her feet. Mute and compelled, she flung herself back into the watchtower, intending to make her way down to the open gates; to greet Jeremiah and Covenant with her embrace and her straining heart.

But the chambers within the tower were crowded with tall mounds of firewood and tubs of oil. At first, she could not locate a stairway. And when she discovered the descent, the Masters refused to let her pass. One of them stood on the stair to forbid her.

'We prepare for battle,' he informed her curtly. His people had already refused her claims on them. 'You will be endangered here.'

He did not add, And you will impede our efforts. Nor did she pause to heed him, or to contest the stair. *Linden, find me.* Her need for haste was too great. In all of her years with her son, she had never seen him react to people and events around him; had never seen an expression of any kind on his slack features. Riding towards Revelstone, however, his face shone with excitement as he waved his arms, urging his companions forward.

She wheeled away from the stair; ran for the suspended wooden bridge which linked the tower to the battlements of Revelstone.

Stave came to guide her. He had not wiped the blood from his mouth and chin. Dark stains marked his tunic. But his hurts did not slow him. And Mahrtiir accompanied him, with Bhapa, Pahni, and Liand grouped around Anele at his back.

They were her friends, but she hardly noticed them.

Fearless with urgency, she followed Stave and Mahrtiir across the unsteady span above the courtyard between the watchtower and Revelstone's inner gates. Gripping the Staff hard in one hand, she pursued her guides into the sudden gloom of the Keep's lightless passages.

She did not know the way. She had spent too little time here to learn even a few of Revelstone's complex intersections and halls. And she required illumination. If she had been willing to move more slowly, using only her enhanced senses, she could have trailed Stave's hard shape and Mahrtiir's more legible tension through the wrought gutrock. But she had to *hurry*. Instinctively, irrationally, she felt that her own rush to meet them might enable Jeremiah and Covenant to reach the comparative safety of the massive interlocking gates, the friable sanctuary of the Masters. As the reflected sunshine behind her faded, and the darkness ahead deepened, she called up a gush of flame from one iron heel of the Staff. That warm light, as soft and clean as cornflowers, allowed her to press Stave and the Manethrall to quicken their pace.

Nearly running, they descended stairways apparently at random, some broad and straight enough to accommodate throngs, others narrow spirals delving downward. Her need for haste was a fever. Surely she could reach the cavernous hall within the gates ahead of Jeremiah and Covenant and their small band of Masters?

Her friends followed close behind her. Anele was old; but his intimacy with stone, and his decades among the mountains, made him sure-footed: he did not slow Liand and the Cords. And after them came the three Humbled, Galt, Clyme and Branl, maimed icons of the Masters' commitments. They were as stubborn and unreadable as Stave; but Linden did not doubt that they intended to protect her – or to protect against her. The Masters had rejected Stave because he had declared himself her ally; her friend. Naturally they would not now trust him to fill any of their self-assigned roles.

Fervidly she tried to cast her health-sense farther, striving to penetrate Revelstone's ancient rock so that she might catch some impression of the Vile-spawn. How near had they come? Had they overtaken Covenant and Jeremiah? But she could not concentrate while she dashed and twisted down the passages. She could only chase after Stave and Mahrtiir, and fear that her loved ones had already fallen beneath the breaking tsunami of the Demondim.

But they had not, she insisted to herself. They had *not*. The Demondim had withdrawn their siege the previous day for a reason. Possessed by some fierce and fiery being, Anele had confronted the Vile-spawn; and they had responded by allowing Linden and those with her to escape – and then by appearing to abandon their purpose against Lord's Keep. Why had they acted thus, if not so that Jeremiah and Covenant might reach her? If they desired Jeremiah's death, and Covenant's, they could have simply awaited their prey in front of Revelstone's gates.

Jeremiah and Covenant were not being hunted: they were being *herded*.

Why the Demondim – and Anele's possessor – might wish her loved ones to reach her alive, she could not imagine. But she strove to believe that Covenant and Jeremiah would not fall. The alternatives were too terrible to be endured.

Then Linden saw a different light ahead of her: it spilled from the courtyard into the Keep. A moment later, Stave and Mahrtiir led her down the last stairs to the huge forehall. Now she did not need the Staff's flame; but she kept it burning nonetheless. She might require its power in other ways.

The time-burnished stone echoed her boot heels as she ran into the broad hall and cast her gaze past the gates towards the courtyard and the passage under the watchtower.

Beyond the sunshine in the courtyard, the shrouded gloom and angle of the wide tunnel obscured her line of sight. She felt rather than saw the open outer gates, the slope beyond them. With her health-sense, she descried as if they were framed in stone the four Masters astride their labouring horses. Covenant clung to the back of one of the *Haruchai*. Jeremiah balanced precariously behind another.

The mustang that bore her son was limping badly: it could not keep pace with the other beasts. And Covenant's mount staggered on the verge of foundering. All of the horses were exhausted. Even at this distance, Linden sensed that only their terror kept them up and running. Yet somehow they remained ahead of the swarming Demondim. If the monsters did not strike out with the might of the Illearth Stone, the riders would reach the outer gates well before their pursuers.

The fact that the Vile-spawn had not already made use of the Stone seemed to confirm Linden's clenched belief that Jeremiah and Covenant were being herded rather than hunted.

She wanted to cry out her own encouragement and desperation; wanted to demand why the Masters had not organised a sally to defend her loved ones; wanted to oppose the horde with Law and Earthpower in spite of the distance. But she bit down on her lip to silence her panic. Jeremiah and Covenant would not hear her. The *Haruchai* could not combat the Demondim effectively. And she did not trust herself to wield power when the people whom she yearned to save were between her and the horde.

Grimly she forced herself to wait, holding her fire over her head like a beacon, nearly a stone's throw from the courtyard so that the Keep's defenders would have room in which to fight if the monsters could not be prevented from passing the gates.

Abruptly the Masters and their horses surged between the outer gates into the dark tunnel. Hooves clanged on the worn stone as first Covenant and then Jeremiah fell into shadow.

A heartbeat later, ponderous as leviathans, the outer gates began to close.

The heavy stone seemed to move slowly, far too slowly to close out the rapacity of the monsters. Through her fear, however, Linden realised that the Demondim had once again slackened their pace, allowing their foes to escape. She felt the impact as the gates thudded together, shutting out the Vile-spawn; plunging the tunnel into stark blackness.

Then the riders reached daylight in the courtyard, and she saw that all six of them were safe. She did not know how far they had fled the Demondim; but she recognised at once that none of them had suffered any harm.

The mounts had not fared so well. Like their riders, the horses were uninjured. But their terror had driven them to extremes which might yet kill them: they had galloped hard and long enough to break their hearts. Yet they did not stop until they had crossed the courtyard and passed between the inner gates. Then, as those gates also began to close, shutting out the last daylight, Jeremiah's mount stumbled to its knees; fell gasping on its side with froth and blood on its muzzle. Jeremiah would have plunged to the stone, but the Master with him caught him and lifted him aside. The horse bearing Covenant endured only a moment longer before it, too, collapsed. But Covenant and his fellow rider were able to leap clear.

When the inner gates met and sealed like the doors of a tomb, the flame of the Staff was the only light that remained in the forehall.

The Ramen protested at the condition of the horses; but Linden ignored them. She had already begun to rush forward, avid to clasp her loved ones, when Covenant yelled as if in rage, 'Hellfire, Linden! *Put that damn thing out!*'

She stopped, gasping as though his vehemence had snatched the air from her lungs. Her power fell from her, and instant darkness burst over her head like a thunderclap.

Oh, God—

Just be wary of me. Remember that I'm dead.

If she could have found her voice, or drawn sufficient breath, she might have cried out at the Despiser, You *bastard*! What have you *done*?

A hand closed on her arm. She hardly heard Stave as he urged her softly, 'A moment, Chosen. Handir and others approach, bearing torches among them. You need only constrain yourself for a moment.'

He could still hear the mental speech of the Masters, although they now refused to address or answer him in that fashion.

At once, she rounded on Stave. Behind him, Liand and the Ramen were whispering, perhaps asking her questions, but she had no attention to spare for them. Gripping Stave as he gripped her, she demanded, 'Your senses are better than mine.' Like their preternatural strength, the vision of the *Haruchai* had always exceeded hers. 'Can you *see* them?' See *into* them? 'Are they all right?'

In the absence of the Staff's flame, she knew only blackness and consternation.

'They appear whole,' the former Master answered quietly. 'The ur-Lord has ever been closed to the *Haruchai*. Even the Bloodguard could not discern his heart. And his companion' – Stave paused as if to confirm his perceptions – 'is likewise hidden.'

'You can't see *anything?*' insisted Linden. Even Kevin's Dirt could not blind the Masters—

Stave may have shrugged. 'I perceive his presence, and that of his companion. Nothing more.'

'Chosen,' he asked almost immediately, 'is the ur-Lord's companion known to you?'

Linden could not answer. She had no room for any questions but her own. Instead she started to say, Take me to them. She needed to be led. Covenant's shout had shattered her concentration: she might as well have been blind.

But then the torches that Stave had promised appeared. Their unsteady light wavered towards her from the same passage which had admitted her and her companions to the forehall.

A few heartbeats later, the Voice of the Masters, Handir, entered the hall. A coterie of *Haruchai* accompanied him, some bearing fiery brands. As they moved out into the dark, the ruddy light of the flames spread along the stone towards the gates. It seemed to congeal like blood in the vast gloom.

Now Linden could see the faces of her companions, confused by erratic shadows. None of them had the knowledge or experience to recognise Covenant and Jeremiah. Perhaps as a reproach to Linden, Handir had called the newcomers 'strangers'. Nevertheless Mahrtiir and his Cords may have been able to guess at Covenant's identity. The Ramen had preserved ancient tales of the first Ringthane. But Liand had only his open bafflement to offer Linden's quick glance.

Apparently none of the Masters had done her friends the courtesy of mentioning Covenant's name aloud. And of course even the Masters could only speculate about Jeremiah.

Then the light reached the cluster of horses and their riders within the gates; and Linden forgot everything except the faces that she loved more dearly than any others she had ever known.

Unconscious that she was moving again, she hurried towards them, chasing the limits of the ambiguous illumination.

The inadequacy of the torches blurred their features. Nevertheless she could not be mistaken about them. Every flensed line of Covenant's form was familiar to her. Even his clothes – his old jeans and boots, and the T-shirt that had seen too much wear and pain – were as she remembered them. When he held up his hands, she could see that the right lacked its last two fingers. His strict gaze caught and held the light redly, as if he were afire with purpose and desire.

And Jeremiah was imprinted on her heart. She knew his gangling teenaged body as intimately as her own. His tousled hair and slightly scruffy cheeks, smudged here and there with dirt or shadows, could belong to no one else. He still wore the sky-blue pyjamas with the mustangs rampant across the chest in which she had dressed him for bed days or worlds earlier, although they were torn now, and stained with grime or blood. And, like Covenant's, his right hand had been marred by the amputation of two fingers, in his case the first two.

Only the eagerness which enlivened the muddy colour of his eyes violated Linden's knowledge of him.

The light expanded as more torches were lit. Holding brands high, the Humbled followed her, joined by her friends; followed as if she pulled them along behind her, drawing their fires with her. Now she could see clearly the cut in Covenant's shirt where he had been stabbed, and the old scar on his forehead. Flames lit his eyes like threats; demands. His appearance was only slightly changed. After ten years and more than three millennia, the grey was gone from his hair: he looked younger despite his gauntness. And the marks of the wounds that he had received while Linden had known him were gone as well, burned away by his consummation in wild magic. Yet every compelling implication of his visage was precious to her.

Nevertheless she did not approach him. Deeper needs sent her hastening towards Jeremiah.

She was still ten paces from her son, however, when Covenant snapped harshly, 'Don't *touch* him! Don't touch *either* of us!'

Linden did not stop. She could not. Long days of loss and alarm impelled her. And she had never before seen anything that resembled consciousness in Jeremiah's eyes. Had never seen him react and move as he did now. She could not stop until she flung her arms around him and felt his heart beating against hers.

At once, his expression became one of dismay; almost of panic. Then he raised his halfhand – and a wave of force like a wall halted her.

It was as warm as steam: except to her health-sense, it was as invisible as vapour. And it was gone in an instant. Yet she remained motionless as if he had frozen her in place. The shock of his power to repulse her deprived her of will and purpose. Even her reflexive desire to embrace him had been stunned.

At a word from Mahrtiir, Bhapa and Pahni moved away to help the Masters tend the horses. The Manethrall remained behind Linden with Liand, Anele and Stave.

'He's right,' said Jeremiah: the first words that Linden had ever heard him utter. His voice sounded as unsteady as the torchlight, wavering between childhood and maturity, a boy's treble and a man's baritone. 'You can't touch either of us. And you can't use that Staff.' He grinned hugely. 'You'll make us disappear.'

Among the shadows cast by the flames, she saw a small muscle beating like a pulse at the corner of his left eye.

Linden might have wept then, overwhelmed by shock and need. Suddenly, however, she had no tears. The Mahdoubt had told her, *Be cautious of love. It misleads. There is a glamour upon it which binds the heart to destruction.* And days ago Covenant had tried to warn her through Anele—

Between one heartbeat and the next, she seemed to find herself in the presence, not of her loved ones, but of her nightmares.

In the emptiness and silence of the high forehall, the old man asked plaintively, 'What transpires? Anele sees no one. Only Masters, who have promised his freedom. Is aught amiss?'

No one answered him. Instead Handir stepped forward and bowed to Covenant. 'Ur-Lord Thomas Covenant,' he said firmly, 'Unbeliever and Earthfriend, you are well come. Be welcome in Revelstone, fist and faith – and your companion with you. Our need is sore, and your coming an unlooked-for benison. We are the Masters of the Land. I am Handir, by right of years and attainment the Voice of the Masters. How may we serve you, with the Demondim massed at our gates and their malice plain in the exhaustion of your mounts?'

'*No*,' Linden said before Covenant – or Jeremiah – could respond. 'Handir, stop. *Think* about this.'

She spoke convulsively, goaded by inexplicable fears. 'The Demondim *allowed* us to escape yesterday. Then they pulled back so that' – she could not say Covenant's name, or Jeremiah's, not now; not when she had been forbidden to touch them – 'so that these people could get through. Those monsters *want* this.' Her throat closed for a moment. She had to swallow grief like a mouthful of ashes before she could go on. 'Otherwise they would have used the Illearth Stone.'

The Demondim had not planned this. They could not have planned it. They had not known that she would try to protect the Land by snatching them with her out of the past. If Anele had not been possessed by a being of magma and rage, and had not encountered the Vile-spawn—

Surely Covenant and Jeremiah would not be standing in front of her, refusing her, if some powerful enemy had not willed it?

Turning from the Voice of the Masters to Covenant, she demanded, 'Are you even real?'

The Dead in Andelain were ghosts; insubstantial. *They* could not be touched—

Covenant faced her with something like mirth or scorn in his harsh gaze. 'Hell and blood, Linden,' he drawled. 'It's good to see you haven't changed. I knew you wouldn't take all this at face value. I'm glad I can still trust you.'

With his left hand, he beckoned for one of the Humbled. When Branl stepped forward holding a torch, Covenant took the brand from him.

Waving the flame from side to side as if to demonstrate his material exist-ence, Covenant remarked, 'Oh, we're real enough.' Aside to Jeremiah, he added, 'Show her.'

Still grinning, Jeremiah reached into the waistband of his pyjamas and drew out a bright red toy racing car – the same car that Linden had seen him holding before Sheriff Lytton's deputies had opened fire. He tossed it lightly back and forth between his hands for a moment, then tucked it away again. His manner said as clearly as words, See, Mom? *See?*

Linden studied his pyjamas urgently for bullet holes. But the fabric was too badly torn and stained to give any indication of what happened to him before he had been drawn to the Land.

None of the Masters spoke. Apparently they understood that her questions required answers.

Abruptly Covenant handed his torch back to Branl. As Branl with-drew to stand with Galt and Clyme, Covenant returned his attention to Linden.

'This isn't easy for you. I know that.' Now his voice sounded hoarse with disuse. He seemed to pick his words as though he had difficulty remembering the ones he wanted. 'Trust me, it isn't easy for us either.

'We're here. But we aren't *just* here.' Then he sighed. 'There's no good way to explain it. You don't have the experience to understand it.' His brief smile reminded her that she had rarely seen such an expression on his face. Roger had smiled at her more often. 'Jeremiah is *here*, but Foul still has him. *I'm* here, but I'm still part of the Arch of Time.

'You could say I've folded time so we can be in two places at once. Or two realities.' Another smile flickered across his mouth, contradicted by the flames reflecting in his eyes. 'Being part of Time has some advantages. Not many. There are too many limitations, and the strain is fierce. But I can still do a few tricks.'

For a moment, his hands reached out as if he wanted something from her; but he pulled them back almost at once.

'The problem with what I'm doing,' he said trenchantly, 'is that you've got too much power, and it's the wrong kind for me. Being in two places at once breaks a lot of rules.' This time, his smile resembled a grimace. 'If you touch either one of us – or if you use that Staff – you'll undo the fold. Time will snap back into shape.

'It's like your son says,' he finished. 'We'll disappear. I'm not strong enough to keep us here.'

'Your son?' Liand breathed. 'Linden, is this your *son?*'

'Liand, no,' Mahrtiir instructed at once. 'Do not speak. This lies beyond us. The Ringthane will meet our questions when greater matters have been resolved.'

Linden did not so much as glance at them. But she could no longer look at Covenant. The torchlight in his eyes, and his unwonted smiles, daunted her. She understood nothing. She wanted to scoff at the idea of folding time. Or perhaps she merely yearned to reject the thought that she might undo such theurgy. How could she bear to be in his presence, and in Jeremiah's, without touching them?

As if she were turning her back, she shifted so that she faced only her son.

'Jeremiah, honey—' she began. Oh, Jeremiah! Her eyes burned, although she had no tears. 'None of this makes sense. Is he telling the truth?'

Had her son been restored to her for *this*? And was he truly still in Lord Foul's grasp, suffering the Despiser's wealth of torments in some other dimension or manifestation of time?

She was unable to see the truth for herself. Covenant and her son were closed to her, as they were to Stave and the Masters.

An *Elohim* had warned the Ramen as well as Liand's people to *Beware the halfhand.*

Jeremiah gazed at her with a frown. He seemed to require a visible effort to set aside his excitement. 'You know he is, Mom.' His tone held an unexpected edge of reproach; of impatience with her confusion and yearning. 'He's *Thomas Covenant.* You can see that. He's already saved the Land twice. He can't be anybody else.'

But then he appeared to take pity on her. Ducking his head, he added softly, 'What you can't see is how much it hurts that I'm not *just* here.'

For years, she had hungered for the sound of her son's voice; starved for it as though it were the nurturance that would give her life meaning. Yet now every word from his mouth only multiplied her chagrin.

Why could she not weep? She had always shed tears too easily. Surely her sorrow and bafflement were great enough for sobbing? Still her eyes remained dry; arid as a wilderland.

'All you have to do is trust me,' Covenant put in. 'Or if you can't do that, trust *him*.' He nodded towards Jeremiah. 'We can do this. We can make it come out right. That's another advantage I have. *We* have. We know what needs to be done.'

Angry because she had no other outlet, Linden wheeled back to confront the Unbeliever. 'Is that a fact?' Her tone was acid. She had come to this: her beloved and her son were restored to her, and she treated them like foes. 'Then tell me something. Why did the Demondim let you live? Hell, why have they left any of us alive? It was just yesterday that they wanted to kill us.'

Jeremiah laughed as if he were remembering one of the many jokes that she had told him over the years; jokes with which she had attempted to provoke a reaction when he was incapable of any response. The muscle at the corner of his left eye continued its tiny beat. But Covenant glared at her, and the fires in his gaze seemed hotter than any of the torches.

'Another trick,' he told her sourly. 'An illusion.' He made a dismissive gesture with his halfhand. 'Oh, I didn't have anything to do with what happened yesterday.' Despite its size, the forehall seemed full of *halfhands*, the Humbled as well as Covenant and Jeremiah. 'That's a different issue. But they let Jeremiah and me get through because' – Covenant shrugged stiffly – 'well, I suppose you could say I put a crimp in their reality. Just a little one. I'm already stretched pretty thin. I can't do too many things at once. So I made us look like *bait*. Like we were leading them into an ambush. Like there's a kind of power here they don't understand. That's why they just chased us instead of attacking. They want to contain us until they figure out what's going on. And maybe they like the idea of trapping all their enemies in one place.'

Again he smiled at Linden, although his eyes continued to glare. 'Are you satisfied? At least for now? Can I talk to Handir for a minute? Jeremiah and I need rest. You have no idea of the strain–'

He sighed heavily. 'And we have to get ready before those Demondim realise I made fools out of them. Once that happens, they're going to unleash the Illearth Stone. Then hellfire and bloody damnation won't be something we just talk about. They'll be *real*, and they'll be *here*.'

Apparently he wanted Linden to believe that he was tired. Yet to her ordinary eyes he looked potent enough to defeat the horde unaided.

And her son seemed to *belong* with him.

She could not identify them with her health-sense. Jeremiah and Covenant were as blank, as isolated from her, as they would have been in her natural world. Yet there she would have been able to at least *touch* them. Here, in the unrevealing light of the torches, and fraught with shadows, Jeremiah seemed as distant and irreparable as the Unbeliever, in spite of his obvious alert sentience.

If Covenant could do all of this, why had he told her to *find* him?

Bowing her head, Linden forced herself to take a step backwards, and another, into the cluster of her friends. She ached for the comfort of their support. She could discern them clearly enough: Liand's open amazement, his concern on her behalf; Mahrtiir's rapt eagerness and wonder and suspicion; Anele's distracted mental wandering. Even Stave's impassivity and his ruined eye and his new hurts felt more familiar to her than Covenant and Jeremiah, her loved ones. Yet the complex devotion of those who stood with her gave no anodyne for what she had gained and lost.

Linden, find me.

Be cautious of love.

She needed the balm of touching Covenant; of hugging and *hugging* Jeremiah, running her fingers through his hair, stroking his cheeks– But she had been refused. Even the warm clean fire of the Staff of Law had been forbidden to her.

Covenant nodded with an air of satisfaction. Then both he and Jeremiah turned to the Voice of the Masters.

'Sorry about that. I didn't mean to keep you waiting.' For a moment, Covenant's voice held an unwonted note of unction, although he suppressed it quickly. 'You know Linden. When she has questions, she insists on answers.' He grinned as if he were sharing a joke with Handir. 'You have to respect that.'

Then he swallowed his smile. 'You said we're well come. You have no idea how well come we are.

'You speak for the Masters?'

Abruptly Linden swung away from them. She could no longer bear the sight of her son's eagerness and denial. She wished that she could close her ears to the sound of Covenant's voice.

In the light of the torches, her friends studied her. Liand's curiosity and puzzlement had become alarm, and Mahrtiir glowered. Stave's single eye regarded her with characteristic stoicism. Anele's moonstone blindness shifted uncertainly around the great hall as though he were trying to recapture an elusive glimpse of significance.

Because her nerves burned for human contact – for any touch which might reassure her – she hooked her arms around Liand's and Mahrtiir's shoulders. At once, Liand gave her a hug like a promise that she could rely on him, whatever happened. And after an instant of hesitation, Mahrtiir did the same. Through his dislike of impending rock and the lack of open skies, she tasted his readiness to fight any foe in her name.

With senses other than sight, she felt Handir bowing to Covenant a second time, although the Voice of the Masters had never bowed to her.

'I am Handir,' he began again, 'by right of—'

'Of years and attainment,' interrupted Covenant brusquely. 'The Voice of the Masters.' Now his manner seemed to betray the exertion he had claimed; the difficulty of folding time. 'I heard you the first time.

'Handir, I know you're worried about the Demondim. You should be. You and your people can't hold out against them. Not if they use the Stone. But they're unsure of themselves right now. By hell, Foul himself is probably having fits.' Grim pleasure glinted through the impatience in Covenant's tone. 'They'll realise the truth eventually. But I've been pretty clever, if I do say so myself.' With her peripheral vision, Linden saw Jeremiah's nod, his happy grin. 'I think we might have a day, or even two, before the real shit hits the fan.'

To her friends, Linden murmured, 'Don't say anything. Just listen.' She could not bear to be questioned. Not now. She was in too much pain. 'That's Thomas Covenant and my son. My Jeremiah. I *know* them.

'But there's something wrong here. Something dangerous. Maybe it's just the strain of what they're doing.' Being in two places at once? 'Maybe that's making them both a little crazy.' Or maybe the Despiser had indeed *done* something. Maybe the *Elohim* had sought to warn the Land against *the halfhand* for good reason. 'Whatever it is, I need your help.

'Mahrtiir, I want Bhapa and Pahni to stay with Liand and Anele.'

Liand opened his mouth to protest, but Linden's grip on his shoulder silenced him. 'The Masters won't threaten you,' she told him. 'I trust them that far,' in spite of what the Humbled and Handir had done to Stave. They were *Haruchai*. 'But I have to be alone, and I'll feel better if Bhapa and Pahni are with you.' She had seen Ramen Cords fight: she knew what Bhapa and Pahni could do. 'Whatever is going on here, it might have consequences that we can't imagine.' *Don't* touch *him! Don't touch* either *of us!* To Mahrtiir, she added, 'They should be safe enough in Liand's room.'

In response, the Manethrall nodded his assent.

'Anele is confused,' the old man informed the air of the forehall. 'He feels Masters and urgency, but the cause is hidden. The stone tells him nothing.'

Linden ignored him. Covenant was still speaking to Handir.

'What Jeremiah and I want right now is a place where we can rest without being disturbed. Some food, and maybe some springwine, if you've got it. We have to gather our strength.'

Linden tried to ignore him as well. 'As for you,' she continued to Mahrtiir, 'I need you to guide me out of here. To the plateau.' He and his Cords had spent the night there. He would know the way. 'I can't *think* like this. I need daylight.'

She might find what she sought in the potent waters of Glimmermere. The lake could not give her answers, but it might help her to remember who she was.

The Manethrall nodded again. When he left her so that he could speak to Pahni and Bhapa, she turned to Stave. The tasks that she had in mind for him would be harder—

Meeting his gaze with her dry, burning eyes, she said, 'I want you to find the Mahdoubt for me. Please.' *Be cautious of love.* 'I need to talk to her.' That strange, kindly woman had given Linden a hint of what was in store. If Linden probed her directly, she might say more. 'And keep the Humbled away from me. If you can. I can't face their distrust right now.'

Her memories of Glimmermere – of Thomas Covenant as he had once been – were private and precious. She could not expose them, or herself, to anyone: certainly not to the demeaning suspicions of Branl, Galt or Clyme.

Stave did not hesitate. 'Chosen, I will,' he said as if obstructing the actions of the Masters were a trivial challenge.

At least he was still able to hear his people's thoughts—

Behind Linden, Covenant appeared to be nearing the end of his exchange with Handir. His voice had become a hoarse rasp, thick with effort. Yet when she glanced at him at last, Linden saw that he was smiling again.

At Covenant's side, Jeremiah seemed hardly able to contain his anticipation. The only sign that he might still be in Lord Foul's power was the rapid beating at the corner of his eye.

'I know what to do,' Covenant assured the Voice of the Masters. 'That's why we're here. When we're done, your problems will be over. But first I'll have to convince Linden, and that won't be easy. I'm too tired to face it right now.

'Just give us a place to rest. And keep her away from us until I'm ready. We'll take care of everything else.' Darkly he avowed, 'I know a trick or two to make the Demondim and even the almighty Despiser wish they had never come out of hiding.'

In spite of her clenched dismay, Linden found herself wondering where he had learned such things. How much of his humanity had he lost by his participation in Time? What had the perspective of eons done to him? How much had he changed?

And how much pain had her son suffered in the Despiser's grasp? How much was he suffering at this moment? If even the tainted respite of being in two places at once filled him with such glee—

In many ways, she had never truly known him. Yet he, too, may have become someone she could no longer recognise.

She needed to *do* something. She needed to do it *now*. If she waited for Covenant to explain himself, she would crumble.

While Handir replied to the ur-Lord, the Unbeliever, the Land's ancient saviour – while the Voice of the Masters promised Covenant everything that he had requested – Linden strode away into the shadows of the forehall, trusting Mahrtiir to claim a torch and catch up with her before she lost herself in darkness.

Chapter Two:

Difficult Answers

How Stave accomplished what she had asked of him, Linden could not imagine. Yet when Mahrtiir led her at last past the switchbacks up through the long tunnel which opened onto the plateau above and behind Revelstone – when they finally left gloom and old emptiness behind, and crossed into sunshine under a deep sky stained only by Kevin's Dirt – she and the Manethrall were alone. The Humbled had not followed them. In spite of Stave's severance from his people, he had found some argument which had persuaded the Masters to leave her alone.

Here she could be free of their distrust; of denials that appalled her. Here she might be able to think.

Covenant and Jeremiah had been restored to her. And they would not allow her to touch them. They had been changed in some quintessential fashion which excluded her.

And Kevin's Dirt still exerted its baleful influence, slowly leeching away her health-sense and her courage – and she had been ordered not to use the Staff of Law. Both Covenant and her son had assured her that its power would undo the theurgy which enabled their presence. In dreams, Covenant's voice had told her, *You need the Staff of Law*. Through Anele, he had said, *You're the only one who can do this*. Yet now she was asked to believe that if she drew any hint of Earthpower from the warm wood, she would effectively erase Covenant and Jeremiah. The two people in all of life whom she had most yearned to see – to have and hold – would vanish.

She believed them, both of them. She did not know whether or not they had told the truth: she believed them nonetheless. They were Thomas Covenant and Jeremiah, her son. She could not do otherwise.

She had repeatedly insisted that she could not be compared to the Land's true heroes; and now the greatest of them had come.

And he had asked the Masters to keep her away from him until he was ready to talk. *I'm too tired—* But she did not protest. While she could still think and choose – while she could still determine her own actions – she meant to make use of the time.

As Mahrtiir had guided her up through the Keep, she had resolved to find some *answers*.

She was on her way to Glimmermere because she had once been there with Thomas Covenant: a brief time of unconstrained love after the defeat of the na-Mhoram and the quenching of the Banefire. She hoped to recapture at the eldritch lake some sense of what she and Covenant had meant to each other; of who she was. But now she had another purpose as well. The strange potency of Glimmermere's waters might give her the power to be heard—

With Mahrtiir beside her and the Staff hugged in her arms, she walked steadily – grim and dry-eyed, as though she were not weeping inside – out of Revelstone onto the low upland hills which rumpled the plateau between Lord's Keep and the jagged pinnacles of the Westron Mountains.

Here she could see the handiwork of Sunder and Hollian, who had accepted the stewardship of the Land thirty-five centuries ago. When she had walked into these hills with Thomas Covenant, the Sunbane had still ruled the Upper Land; and a desert sun had destroyed every vestige of vegetation. She and Covenant had crossed hard dirt and bare stone baked by the arid unnatural heat of the sun's corona. But now—

Ah, now there was thick grass underfoot, abundant forage for herds of cattle and sheep. With her health-sense, she could see that the gentler slopes ahead of her were arable. Revelstone was nearly empty, and its comparatively few inhabitants were easily fed by the fields to the north of the watchtower. At need, however, crops could be planted here to support a much larger population. And there were trees– God, there were *trees*. Rich stands of pine and cedar accumulated off to her right until they grew so thickly that they obscured her view of the mountains

in that direction. And ahead of her, clumps of delicate mimosa and arching jacaranda punctuated the hillsides until the slow rise and fall of the
slopes seemed as articulate as language. Everywhere spring gave the air
a tang which made all of the colours more vibrant and filled each scent
with burgeoning.

Under the Sunbane's bitter curse, she had seen nothing here that was
not rife with pain – until she and Covenant had reached the mystic
lake which formed the headwater of the White River. Now everywhere
she looked, both westward and around the curve of the sheer cliffs towards the north, the plateau had been restored to health and fertility.
Somehow Linden's long-dead friends had taught themselves how to
wield both Earthpower and Law. While they lived, Sunder and Hollian
had made luxuriant and condign use of the Staff. The beauty which
greeted Linden's sore heart above and behind Lord's Keep was one result
of their labours.

Poor Anele, she thought as she walked towards the first trees. It was
no wonder that his parents had filled him with astonishment; or that
he had been daunted. Throughout their long lives, he had known the
harsh after-effects of the Sunbane – and had seen those enduring blights
transformed to health. In his place, Linden, too, might have felt overwhelmed by their example.

Yet neither Anele nor the restoration of these hills dominated her
thoughts. At her side, the Manethrall lost some of his severity as he
regained the wide sky and the kindly hills; but if he had spoken to
her, she might not have heard him. While she walked, the prospect of
Glimmermere filled her with memories of Thomas Covenant.

When the threat of the Banefire had been extinguished, she had joined
him in the private chambers which had once been High Lord Mhoram's
home. At that time, she had feared that he would reject her; scorn
her love. Earlier his intention to enter alone and undefended into the
inferno of the Clave's evil had appalled her, and she tried to stop him by
violating his mind, *possessing* him. That expression of her own capacity
for evil might have destroyed the bond between them. Yet when they
were alone at last, she had learned that he held nothing against her; that
he forgave her effortlessly. And then he had taken her to Glimmermere,
where the lake had helped her to forgive herself.

She wanted to hold onto that memory until she reached the upland tarn and could endeavour once again to wash away her dismay.

Don't touch him! Don't touch either of us!

She had risked the destruction of the world in order to retrieve the Staff of Law so that she might have some chance to redeem her son; yet both Jeremiah and Covenant had appeared through no act or decision or hazard of hers. For years and *years* she had striven to free Jeremiah from the chains of his peculiar disassociative disorder; yet he had reclaimed his mind in her absence, while Lord Foul tormented him. She had used all of her will and insight in an attempt to sway the Masters, and had won only Anele's freedom and Stave's friendship – at the cost of Stave's violent expulsion from the communion of his people. And she had brought the Demondim to this time, recklessly, when Revelstone had no defence.

Like Kevin's Dirt, shame threatened to drain her until she was too weak to bear the cost of her life. Without the Staff's fire to sustain her, she clung to her best memories of Covenant's love – and to the possibilities of Glimmermere – so that she would not be driven to her knees by the weight of her mistakes and failures.

But those memories brought others. Alone with her, Covenant had spoken of the time when he had been the helpless prisoner of Kasreyn of the Gyre in *Bhrathairealm*. There the thaumaturge had described the value and power of white gold; of the same ring which now hung uselessly on its chain around her neck. *In a flawed world*, Kasreyn had informed Covenant, *purity cannot endure. Thus within each of my works I must perforce place one small flaw, else there would be no work at all.* But white gold was an alloy; inherently impure. *Its imperfection is the very paradox of which the Earth is made, and with it a master may form perfect works and fear nothing.*

The flaw in Kasreyn's works had permitted the Sandgorgon Nom to escape the prison of Sandgorgons Doom. Without it, Covenant, Linden and the remnants of the Search might not have been able to breach Revelstone in order to defeat the Clave and quench the Banefire. But that was not the point which Covenant had wished Linden to grasp. Long centuries earlier, his friend Mhoram had told him, *You are the white gold.* And in the Banefire, Covenant himself had become a kind of alloy, an admixture of wild magic and the Despiser's venom; capable of perfect power.

At the time, he had wanted Linden to understand why he would never again use his ring. He had become too dangerous: he was human and did not trust himself to achieve any perfection except ruin. With his own strict form of gentleness, he had tried to prepare her for his eventual surrender to Lord Foul.

But now she thought that perhaps his words three and a half thousand years ago explained his unexpected appearance here. He had been transformed in death: Lord Foul had burned away the venom, leaving Covenant's spirit purified. As a result, he may have become a kind of perfect being—

—who could wield wild magic *and fear nothing.*

If that were true, he had come to retrieve his ring. He would need the instrument of his power in order to transcend the strictures imposed on him by his participation in the Arch of Time. Without his ring, he would only be capable of what he called *tricks.*

But why, then—? Linden's heart stumbled in pain. Why did he and Jeremiah refuse her touch?

She believed that she understood why her Staff threatened them. If Covenant had indeed *folded time,* he could only have done so by distorting the fundamental necessities of sequence and causality; the linear continuity of existence. Therefore the force of her Staff would be inherently inimical to his presence, and to Jeremiah's. It would reaffirm the Law which he had transgressed. He and Jeremiah might well disappear back into their proper dimensions of reality.

But how could her touch harm him, or her son? Apart from her Staff, she had no power except his wedding band.

If he wanted his ring back, why did he require her to keep her distance?

She groaned inwardly. She could not guess her way to the truth: she needed answers that she could not imagine for herself. As she and the Manethrall gradually turned their steps northwestward with the potential graze lands and fields of the lowest hillsides on their left and the gathering stands of evergreen on their right, she spoke to him for the first time since they had left the forehall.

'Could you see them?' she asked without preamble. 'Covenant and my son? Is there anything that you can tell me about them?'

For some reason, Anele had seemed unaware of their presence.

Mahrtiir did not hesitate. 'The sight of the sleepless ones is not keener than ours,' he avowed, 'though we cannot resist the diminishment of Kevin's Dirt.' Scowling, he glanced skyward. 'Yet the Unbeliever and your child are closed to us. I can descry nothing which you have not yourself beheld.'

'Then what do you think I should do?' Linden did not expect guidance from him. She merely wished to hear the sound of his voice amid the distant calling of birds and the low rustle of the trees. 'How can I uncover the truth?'

Just be wary of me.

She needed something akin to the fierce simplicity with which Mahrtiir appeared to regard the world.

He bared his teeth in a smile like a blade. 'Ringthane, you may be surprised to hear that I urge caution. Already I have dared a Fall – aye, and ridden the great stallion Narunal – in your name. Nor would I falter at still greater hazards. Yet I mislike any violation of Law. I was the first to speak against Esmer's acceptance by the Ramen, and the last to grant my trust. Nor does it now console me that he has justified my doubts. I judge that I did wrongly to turn aside from them.

'The Unbeliever and his companion disturb me, though I cannot name my concern. Their seeming is substantial, yet mayhap they are in truth spectres. These matters are beyond my ken. I am able to counsel only that you make no determination in haste.'

The Manethrall paused for a long moment, apparently indecisive; and Linden wondered at the emotion rising in him. As they passed between mimosas towards the steeper hills surrounding Glimmermere, he cleared his throat to say more.

'But know this, Linden Avery, and be certain of it. I speak for the Ramen, as for the Cords in my care. We stand with you. The Ranyhyn have declared their service. Stave of the *Haruchai* has done so. I also would make my meaning plain.

'It appears that the Unbeliever has come among us, he who was once the Ringthane, and who twice accomplished Fangthane's defeat, if the tales of him are sooth. Doubtless his coming holds vast import, and naught now remains as it was.' Mahrtiir's tone hinted at battle as he pronounced, 'Yet the Ramen stand with you. We cannot do less than the Ranyhyn have done. To him they reared when he was the Ringthane, but to you they gave unprecedented homage, bowing their heads. And they are entirely true. If you see peril in the Unbeliever's presence, then we will oppose it at your side. Come good or ill, boon or bane, we stand with you.'

Then the Manethrall shrugged, and his manner softened. 'Doubtless Liand will do the same. For the Demondim-spawn, either Waynhim or ur-vile, I cannot speak. But I have no fear that Stave will be swayed by the Unbeliever. He has withstood the judgment of the sleepless ones, and will no longer doubt you. And Anele must cling to the holder of the Staff. He cannot do otherwise.'

Mahrtiir faced her with reassurance in his eyes. 'When you are summoned before the Unbeliever, consider that you are not alone. We who have elected to serve you will abide the outcome of your choices, and call ourselves fortunate to do so.'

I seek a tale which will remain in the memories of the Ramen when my life has ended.

Under other circumstances, Linden might have been moved by his declaration. But she was too full of doubt; of thwarted joy and unexplained bereavement. Instead of thanking him, she said gruffly, 'It isn't like that. I'm not going to oppose him.' Them. 'I can't. He's Thomas Covenant.

'I just don't understand.'

Then she looked away; quickened her pace without realising it. Her impatience for the cleansing embrace of Glimmermere was growing. And her dilemma ran deeper than the Manethrall seemed to grasp.

If both Covenant and Jeremiah were here – and they indeed had *something wrong* with them – she could imagine conditions under which she might be forced to choose between them. To fight for one at the expense of the other.

If that happened, she would cling to Jeremiah, and let Thomas Covenant go. She had spent ten years learning to accept Covenant's death – and eight of those years devoting herself to her son. Her first loyalty was to Jeremiah. Even if Covenant truly knew how to save the Land—

The Mahdoubt had warned her to *Be cautious of love.*

God, she did not simply need answers. She needed to wash out her mind. *Just be wary of me. Remember that I'm dead.* She had been given too many warnings; and she comprehended none of them.

Fortunately the high hills which cupped Glimmermere's numinous waters were rising before her. She could not yet catch the scent of their magic: the mild spring breeze carried it past the hilltops. And the lake itself was hidden from sight and sound on all sides except directly southward, where the White River began its run towards Furl Falls. Nevertheless she knew where she was. She could not forget the last place where she and Covenant had known simple happiness.

She wanted to run now, in spite of the ascent, but she forced herself to stop at the base of the slope. Turning to Mahrtiir, she asked, 'You've been here already, haven't you?' He and his Cords had spent the previous afternoon and night among these hills with the Ranyhyn. 'You've seen Glimmermere?'

She expected a prompt affirmative; but the Manethrall replied brusquely, 'Ringthane, I have not. By old tales, I know of the mystic waters. But my Cords and I came to these hills to care for the Ranyhyn – and also,' he admitted, 'to escape the oppression of Revelstone and Masters. Our hearts were not fixed on tales.

'However, the Ranyhyn parted from us when we had gained the open sky. Galloping and glad, they scattered to seek their own desires. Therefore we tended to our refreshment with *aliantha* and rest, awaiting your summons. We did not venture towards storied Glimmermere.'

In spite of her haste, Linden felt a twist of regret on his behalf. 'Why not?'

'We are Ramen,' he said as if his reasons were self-evident. 'We serve the Ranyhyn. That suffices for us. We do not presume to intrude upon other mysteries. No Raman has beheld the tarn of the horserite, yet we feel neither regret nor loss. We are content to be who we are. Lacking any clear cause to approach Glimmermere, I deemed it unseemly to distance ourselves from Revelstone and your uncertain plight.'

She sighed. Now she understood the blind distress of Mahrtiir and his

Cords when she had met them in the Close. But she had scant regard to spare for the Manethrall's strict pride. Her own needs were too great.

'All right,' she murmured. 'Don't worry about it.

'I'm going on ahead. I want you to stay here. I need to be alone for a while. If the Masters change their minds – if the Humbled decide that they have to know what I'm doing – try to warn me.' Glimmermere's potency might muffle her perception of anything else. 'When I come back, we'll talk about this again.

'I think that you'll want to see the lake for yourself.'

She held his gaze until he nodded. Then she turned to stride up the hillside without him.

Almost at once, he seemed to fall out of her awareness. Her memories of Covenant and Glimmermere sang to her, dismissing other considerations. At one time, she had been loved here. That experience, and others like it, had taught her how to love her son. She needed to immerse herself in Earthpower and clarity; needed to recover her sense of her own identity. Then she could try to make herself heard; heeded.

She was breathing hard – and entirely unconscious of it – as she passed the crest of the hill and caught sight of the lake where Thomas Covenant had given her a taste of joy; perhaps the first joy that she had ever known.

In one sense, Glimmermere was exactly as she remembered it. The lake was not large: from its edge, she might have been able to throw a stone across it. On all sides except its outlet to the south, it was concealed by hills as though the earth of the plateau had cupped its hands in order to isolate and preserve its treasure. And no streams flowed into it. Even the mighty heads of the Westron Mountains, now no more than a league distant, sent their rivers of rainfall and snow-melt down into the Land by other routes. Instead Glimmermere was fed by hidden springs arising as if in secret from the deep gutrock of the Land.

The surface of the water also was as Linden remembered it: as calm and pure as a mirror, reflecting the hills and the measureless sky perfectly; oblivious to distress. Yet she had not been here for ten long years, and she found now that her human memory had failed to retain the lake's full vitality, its untrammelled and untarnishable lucid purity. Remembering Glimmermere without percipience to refresh her recall, she had been unable to preserve its image undimmed. Now she was shocked almost breathless by the crystalline abundance and promise of the waters.

Taken by the sight, she began to jog down the hillside. She knew how cold the water would be: she had been chilled to the core when Covenant had called her into the lake. And now there was no desert sun to warm her when she emerged. But she also knew that the cold was an inherent aspect of Glimmermere's power to cleanse; and she did not hesitate. Covenant and Jeremiah had been returned to her, but she no longer knew them – or herself. When she reached the edge of the lake, she dropped the Staff of Law unceremoniously to the grass; tugged off her boots and socks, and flung them aside; stripped away her grass stained pants as well as her shirt as if by that means she could remove her mortality; and plunged headlong into the tonic sting of memory and Earthpower.

In the instant of her dive, she saw that she cast no reflection on the water. Nothing of her interrupted Glimmermere's reiteration of its protective hills and the overarching heavens. The clustered rocks around the deep shadow of the lake's bottom looked sharp and near enough to break her as soon as she struck the surface. But she knew that she was not in danger. She remembered well that Glimmermere's sides were almost sheer, and its depths were unfathomable.

Then she went down into a fiery cold so fierce that it seemed to envelop her in liquid flame.

That, too, was as she remembered it: inextricable from her happiness with Covenant; whetted with hope. Nevertheless its incandescence drove the breath from her lungs. Before she could name her hope, or seek for it, she was forced gasping to the surface.

For a brief time, no more than a handful of heartbeats, she splashed and twisted as if she were dancing. But she was too human to remain in the lake: not alone, while Covenant's recalled love ached within her. Scant moments after she found air, she swam to the water's edge and pulled herself naked up onto the steep grass. There she rested in spite of the wet cold and the chill of spring, giving herself time to absorb, to recognise, Glimmermere's effects.

Closing her eyes, she used every other aspect of her senses to estimate what had become of her.

The waters healed bruises: they washed away the strain and sorrow of battle. She needed that. They could not undo the emotional cost of the things which she had suffered, but they lifted from her the long physical weariness and privation of recent days, the visceral residue of her passage through *caesures*, the tangible galls of her fraught yearning for her son. The eldritch implications of Glimmermere renewed her bodily health and strength as though she had feasted on *aliantha*.

As cold as the water, Covenant's ring burned between her breasts.

But the lake did more. The renewed accuracy with which she was able to perceive her own condition told her that the stain of Kevin's Dirt had been scrubbed from her senses. And when she reached beyond herself, she felt the ramified richness of the grass beneath her, the imponderable life-pulse of the undergirding soil and stone. She could not detect Mahrtiir's presence beyond the hills: his emanations were too mortal to penetrate Glimmermere's glory. Yet spring's fecundity whispered to her along the gentle breeze, and the faint calling of the birds was as eloquent as melody. The wealth of the lake was now a paean, a sun-burnished outpouring of the Earth's essential gladness, as lambent as Earthpower, and as celebratory as an aubade.

In other ways, nothing had changed. Her torn heart could not be healed by any expression of this world's fundamental bounty. Covenant and Jeremiah had been restored to her – and they would not let her touch them. That hurt remained. Glimmermere held no anodyne for the dismay and bereavement which had brought her here.

Nevertheless the lake had given her its gifts. It had made her stronger, allowing her to feel capable again; more certain of herself. And it had erased the effects of Kevin's Dirt, when she had been forbidden to do so with the Staff of Law.

She was as ready as she would ever be.

Steady now, and moving without haste, she donned her clothes and boots; retrieved her Staff. Then she climbed a short way up the hillside, back towards Revelstone, until she found a spot where the slope offered a stretch of more level ground. There she planted her feet as though her memories of Thomas Covenant and love stood at her back to support her. Facing southward across the hillside, she braced the Staff in the grass at her feet and gripped it with one hand while she lifted the white gold ring from under her damp shirt with the other and closed it in her fist.

She took a deep breath; held it for a moment, preparing herself. Then she lifted her face to the sky.

She had ascended far enough to gain a clear view of the mountainheads in the west. Clouds had begun to thicken behind the peaks, suggesting the possibility of rain. It would not come soon, however. The raw crests still clawed the clouds to high wisps and feathers that streamed eastward like fluttering pennons. As Glimmermere's waters flowed between the hills into the south, they caught the sunshine and glistened like a spill of gems.

Now, she thought. Now or never.

With her head held high, she announced softly, 'It's time, Esmer. You've done enough harm. It's time to do some good.

'I need answers, and I don't know anyone else who can give them to me.'

Her voice seemed to fall, unheard, to the grass. Nothing replied to her except birdsong and the quiet incantations of the breeze.

More loudly, she continued, 'Come on, Esmer. I know you can hear me. You said that the Despiser is hidden from you, and you can't tell me where to find my son, but those seem to be the *only* things that you don't know. There's too much going on, and all of it matters too much. It's time to pick a side. I need *answers*.'

Still she had no reason to believe that he would heed her. She had no idea what his true powers were, or how far they extended. She could not even be sure that he had returned to her present. He may have sought to avoid the pain of his conflicting purposes by remaining in the Land's past; in a time when he could no longer serve either Cail's devotion or Kastenessen's loathing.

Hell, as far as she knew, he had arrived to aid and betray her outside the cave of the Waynhim before his own birth. And he had certainly brought the Demondim forward from an age far older than himself. But his strange ability to go wherever and whenever he willed reassured her obliquely. It was another sign that the Law of Time retained its integrity.

No matter which era of the Earth Esmer chose to occupy, his life and experience remained consecutive, as hers did. His betrayal of her, and of the Waynhim, in the Land's past had been predicated on his encounters with her among the Ramen only a few days ago. If he came to her now, in his own life he would do so after he had brought the Demondim to assail her small company. The Law of Time required that, despite the harm which Joan had wrought with wild magic.

Even if he did hear her, however, he had given her no cause to believe that he could be summoned. He was descended – albeit indirectly – from the *Elohim*; and those self-absorbed beings ignored all concerns but their own. Linden was still vaguely surprised that they had troubled to send warning of the Land's peril.

Nevertheless Esmer's desire to assist her had seemed as strong as his impulse towards treachery. The commitments that he had inherited from Cail matched the dark desires of the *merewives*.

He might yet come to her.

She was not willing to risk banishing Covenant and Jeremiah with the Staff. And she was not desperate enough to chance wild magic. But she had found her own strength in Glimmermere. She had felt its cold in the marrow of her bones. When a score of heartbeats had passed, and her call had not been answered, she raised her voice to a shout.

'Esmer, God *damn* it! I'm keeping score here, and by my count you still *owe* me!' Even his riven heart could not equate unleashing the Demondim – and the Illearth Stone – with serving as a translator for the Waynhim. 'Cail was your *father*! You can't deny that. You'll tear yourself apart. And the Ranyhyn trust me! You love them, I *know* you do. For their sake, if not for simple fairness—!'

Abruptly she stopped. She had said enough. Lowering her head, she sagged as if she had been holding her breath.

Without transition, nausea began squirming in her guts.

She knew that sensation; had already become intimately familiar with it. If she reached for wild magic now, she would not find it: its hidden place within her had been sealed away.

She felt no surprise at all as Esmer stepped out of the sunlight directly in front of her.

He was unchanged; was perhaps incapable of change. If she had glimpsed him from a distance, only his strange apparel would have prevented her from mistaking him for one of the *Haruchai*. He had the strong frame of Stave's kinsmen, the brown skin, the flattened features untouched by time. However, his gilded cymar marked him as a being apart. Its ecru fabric might have been woven from the foam of running seas, or from the clouds that fled before a thunderstorm, and its gilding was like fine streaks of light from a setting sun.

But he stood only a few steps away; and at this distance, his resemblance to his father vanished behind the dangerous green of his eyes and the nausea he evoked as though it were an essential aspect of his nature. His emanations were more subtle than those of the Demondim, yet in his own way he seemed more potent and ominous than any of the Vilespawn.

By theurgy if not by blood, he was Kastenessen's grandson.

For a moment, nausea and perceptions of might dominated Linden's attention. Then, belatedly, she saw that he was not alone.

A band of ur-viles had appeared perhaps a dozen paces behind him: more ur-viles than she had known still existed in the world; far more than had enabled her to retrieve the Staff of Law. Only six or seven of those creatures had lived to reach the ambiguous sanctuary of Revelstone and the plateau. Yet here she saw at least three score of the black Demondim-spawn; perhaps as many as four. None of them bore any sign that they had endured a desperate struggle for their lives, and hers.

And on either side of the ur-viles waited small groups of Waynhim. The grey servants of the Land numbered only half as many as the ur-viles; yet even they were more than the mere dozen or so that had accompanied her to Lord's Keep. Like the ur-viles, they showed no evidence that they had been in a battle.

What—? Involuntarily Linden took a startled step backwards. Esmer—?

Millennia ago, he had brought the Demondim out of the Land's ancient past to assail her.

In alarm, she threw a glance around the surrounding hills – and found more creatures behind her. These, however, she recognised: twelve or fourteen Waynhim and half that many ur-viles, most of them scarred by the nacre acid of the Demondim, or by the cruel virulence of the Illearth Stone. They had formed separate wedges to concentrate their strength.

And both formations were aimed at Esmer. The battered loremaster of the ur-viles pointed its iron jerrid or sceptre like a warning at Cail's son.

Esmer, what have you *done*?

Where else could he have found so many ur-viles, so many Waynhim, if not in a time before she and Covenant had faced the Sunbane? A time when the ur-viles had served Lord Foul, and the Waynhim had defended the Land, according to their separate interpretations of their Weird?

Instinctively Linden wanted to call up fire to protect herself. But the creatures at her back had supported her with their lives as well as their lore when no one else could have aided her. They intended to defend her now, although they were badly outnumbered. And the force of her Staff would harm them. For their sake – and because there were Waynhim among the ur-viles with Esmer – she fought down her fear.

As she mastered herself, all of the Demondim-spawn began to bark simultaneously.

Their raucous voices seemed to strike the birdsong from the air. Even the breeze was shocked to stillness. Guttural protests as harsh as curses broke over her head like a prolonged crash of surf. Yet among the newcomers appeared none of the steaming ruddy iron blades which the ur-viles used as weapons. None of them resembled a loremaster. And neither they nor the Waynhim with them stood in wedges to focus their power.

Then Linden understood that the newcomers did not mean to strike at her. They were not even prepared to ward themselves. Their voices sounded inherently hostile; feral as the baying of wild dogs. Nevertheless no power swelled among them. Their yells were indistinguishable from those of her allies.

And Esmer himself sneered openly at her apprehension. A sour grin twisted his mouth: the baleful green of disdain filled his gaze.

'God in Heaven,' Linden muttered under her breath. Trembling, she forced herself to loosen her grip on the Staff; dropped Covenant's ring back under her shirt. Then she met Esmer's eyes as squarely as she could.

'So which is it this time?' She almost had to shout to make herself heard. Aid and betrayal. 'I've never seen so many—'

She was familiar with Esmer's inbred rage at the *Haruchai*. He had nearly killed Stave with it. If Hyn's arrival, and Hynyn's, had not stayed his hand—

Because of the Haruchai, *there will be endless havoc!*

The Masters would not expect an assault from the direction of the plateau.

If the Waynhim condoned – or at least tolerated – the presence of the ur-viles, she could be sure that she was not in danger. Perhaps the Masters and Revelstone were also safe. Yet she could not imagine any explanation for Esmer's actions except treachery.

Fervently she hoped that Mahrtiir would not rush to her aid. She trusted him; but his presence would complicate her confrontation with Esmer.

However, Kevin's Dirt had blunted the Manethrall's senses. And the Demondim-spawn were able to disguise their presence. If the shape of the hills contained the clamour – or if the sound of the river muffled it – he might be unaware of what transpired.

'"Keeping score"?' replied Esmer sardonically. '"Count"? Such speech is unfamiliar to me. Nonetheless your meaning is plain. In the scales of your eyes, if by no other measure, my betrayals have outweighed my aid. You are ignorant of many things, Wildwielder. Were your misjudgments not cause for scorn, they would distress me.'

She had often seen him look distressed when he spoke to her.

'Stop it, Esmer,' she ordered flatly. 'I'm tired of hearing you avoid simple honesty.' And she was painfully aware of her ignorance. 'I called you because I need *answers*. You can start with the question I just asked. Why are these creatures here?'

A flicker that might have been uncertainty or glee disturbed the flowing disdain in his eyes. 'And do you truly conceive that I have come in response to your summons? Do you imagine that you are in any fashion capable of commanding me?'

Around Linden, the ur-viles and Waynhim yowled and snarled like wolves contending over a carcass. She could hardly recognise her own thoughts. As if to ready a threat of her own, she clenched her fists. 'I said, *stop* it.'

She wanted to be furious at him. Ire would have made her stronger.

But her writhen nausea described his underlying plight explicitly. He could not reconcile his conflicting legacies, and behind his disdain was a rending anguish.

More in exasperation than anger, she continued, 'I don't care whether I actually summoned you or not. If you aren't going to answer my questions,' if he himself did not constitute an answer, 'go away. Let your new allies do whatever they came to do.'

Neither Esmer's expression nor his manner changed. In the same mordant tone, he responded, 'There speaks more ignorance, Wildwielder. These makings are not my "allies". Indeed, their mistrust towards me far surpasses your own.'

He heaved a sarcastic sigh. 'You have heard me account for my actions, and for those of the ur-viles and Waynhim as well. Still you do not comprehend. I have not garnered these surviving remnants of their kind from the abysm of time in order to serve me. Nor would they accept such service for any cause. I have enabled their presence here, and they have accepted it, so that they may serve you.'

'*Serve* me?' Linden wanted to plead with the Demondim-spawn to lower their voices. Their shouting forced her to bark as roughly as they did. 'How?'

Did they believe that less than a hundred Waynhim and ur-viles would suffice to drive back the Demondim? When that horde could draw upon the immeasurable bane of the Illearth Stone?

'Wildwielder,' Esmer rasped, 'it is my wish to speak truly. Yet I fear that no truth will content you.

'Would it suffice to inform you, as I have done before, that these creatures perceive the peril of my nature, and are joined in their wish to guard against me? Would it appease you to hear that they now know their kindred accompanying you have discovered a purpose worthy of devoir, and that therefore they also desire to stand with you?'

'Oh, I can believe that,' she retorted. The ur-viles at her back had already shown more selfless devotion than she would have believed possible from the Despiser's former vassals. The Waynhim had demonstrated that they were willing to unite with their ancient enemies for her sake. And none of the creatures on the hillside had raised anything more than their voices against each other. 'But you're right. I'm not "content".

'Why did you bring them here? What do you gain? Is this something that Cail would have done, or are you listening to Kastenessen?'

In response, a brief flinch marred Esmer's disdain. For an instant, he gave her the impression that he was engaged in a fierce battle with himself. Then he resumed his scorn.

God, she wished that the Demondim-spawn would *shut up*—

'It is your assertion that I am in your debt,' Esmer said as if he were jeering. 'I concur. Therefore I have gathered these makings from the past, for their kind has perished, and no others exist in this time. They retain much of the dark lore of the Demondim. They will ward you, and this place' – he nodded in the direction of Revelstone – 'with more fidelity than the *Haruchai*, who have no hearts.'

Covenant had said that he did not expect the horde to attack for another day or two. Could so many ur-viles and Waynhim working together contrive a viable defence? If she ended the threat of the Illearth Stone?

She had already made her decision about the Stone. Its powers were too enormous and fatal: she could not permit them to be unleashed. Nonetheless she shook her head as though Esmer had not affected her.

'That tells me what they can do,' she replied through the tumult of barking. 'It doesn't tell me why you brought them here. With you, every-thing turns into a betrayal somehow. What kind of harm do you have in mind this time?'

He gave her another exaggerated sigh. 'Wildwielder, it is thought-less to accuse me thus. You have been informed that "Good cannot be accomplished by evil means", yet you have not allowed the ill of your own deeds to dissuade you from them. Am I not similarly justified in all that I attempt? Why then do you presume to weigh my deeds in a more exacting scale?'

Linden was acutely aware that the 'means' by which she had reached her present position were questionable at best: at worst, they had been actively hurtful. She had used Anele as if he were a tool; had violated Stave's pride by healing him; had endangered the Arch of Time simply to increase her chances of finding her son. But she did not intend to let Esmer deflect her.

She met his disdain with the fierceness of Glimmermere's cold and strength. 'All right,' she returned without hesitation. 'We're both judged by what we do. I accept that. But I take risks and make mistakes because I know what I want, not because I can't choose between help and hurt. If you want me to believe you, answer a straight question.'

She needed anything that he could reveal about Covenant and Jeremiah; needed it urgently. But first she had to break down his scorn. It protected his strange array of vulnerabilities. He would continue to evade her until she found a way to touch his complex pain.

'You don't want to talk about what you've just done,' she said between her teeth. 'That's pretty obvious. Tell me this instead.

'Who possessed Anele in the Verge of Wandering? Who used him to talk to the Demondim? Who filled him with all of that fire? Give me a name.'

Covenant and Jeremiah had been *herded*– If she knew who wished them to reach her, she might begin to grasp the significance of their arrival.

The abrupt silence of the Waynhim and ur-viles seemed to suck the air from her lungs: it nearly left her gasping. Their raucous clamour was cut off as if they were appalled. Or as if—

Trying to breathe again, she swallowed convulsively.

—as if she had finally asked a question that compelled their attention.

Now Esmer did not merely flinch. He almost appeared to cower. In an instant, all of his hauteur fled. Instead of sneering, he ducked his head to escape her gaze. His cymar fluttered about him, independent of the breeze, so that its sunset gilding covered him in disturbed streaks and consternation.

Together all of the Demondim-spawn, those behind him as well as those with Linden, advanced a few steps, tightening their cordon. Their wide nostrils tasted the air wetly, as though they sought to detect the scent of truth; and their ears twitched avidly.

When Esmer replied, his voice would have been inaudible without the silence.

'You speak of Kastenessen.' He may have feared being overheard. 'I have named him my grandsire, though the Dancers of the Sea were no get of his. Yet they were formed by the lore and theurgy which he gifted to the mortal woman whom he loved. Therefore I am the descendant of his power. Among the *Elohim*, no other form of procreation has meaning.'

The ur-viles and Waynhim responded with a low mutter which may have expressed approval or disbelief. Like them, if in an entirely different fashion, the *merewives* were artificial beings, born of magic and knowledge rather than of natural flesh.

Kastenessen, Linden thought. New fears shook her. She believed Esmer instinctively. Kastenessen had burned her with his fury in the open centre of the Verge of Wandering. And yesterday he had influenced the Demondim, persuading them to alter their intentions.

'That's why you serve him,' she murmured unsteadily. *I serve him utterly.* 'You inherited your power from him.'

His power – and his hunger for destruction.

'As I also serve you,' he told her for the second time.

Kastenessen. The name was a knell; a funereal gong adumbrating echoes in all directions. Her nausea was growing worse. The *Elohim* had forcibly Appointed Kastenessen to prevent or imprison a peril *in the farthest north of the world*. But now he had broken free of his Durance. When Lord Foul had said, *I have merely whispered a word of counsel here and there, and awaited events*, he may have been speaking of Kastenessen.

She knew how powerful the *Elohim* could be, any of them—

Kastenessen had provided for her escape from the horde. Had he also enabled Covenant and Jeremiah to reach her? Did he want all three of them alive?

Still scrambling to catch up with the implications of Esmer's revelation, she mused aloud, 'So when Anele talks about *skurj*—'

'He names the beasts' – Esmer shook his head – 'nay, the monstrous creatures of fire which Kastenessen was Appointed to contain. They come to assail the Land because he has severed or eluded the Durance which compelled him to his doom.'

Behind the Mithil's Plunge, Anele had referred to Kastenessen. *I could have preserved the Durance!* he had cried. *Stopped the* skurj. *With the Staff! If I had been worthy.*

Did you sojourn under the Sunbane with Sunder and Hollian, and learn nothing of ruin?

According to Anele – or to the native stone that he had touched behind the Plunge – the *Elohim* had done nothing to secure Kastenessen's imprisonment.

Aching for Anele's pain, and for her own peril, Linden asked Esmer softly, 'What about this morning? The Demondim *let* Covenant and my son reach Revelstone.' Covenant had given her an explanation. She wanted to know if he had told the truth. 'Was that Kastenessen's doing too?'

'You do not comprehend,' Esmer protested dolefully; as regret-ridden as the wind that drove seafarers into the Soulbiter. 'Your ignorance precludes it. Do you not know that the Viles, those beings of terrible and matchless lore, were once a lofty and admirable race? Though they roamed the Land widely, they inhabited the Lost Deep in caverns as ornate and majestic as castles. There they devoted their vast power and knowledge to the making of beauty and wonder, and all of their works were filled with loveliness. For an age of the Earth, they spurned the heinous evils buried among the roots of Gravin Threndor, and even in the time of Berek Lord-Fatherer no ill was known of them.'

Esmer's ambiguous conflicts had grown so loud that Linden could not shut them out. They hurt her nerves like the carnage before Revelstone's gates, when the Demondim had slaughtered so many Masters and their mounts.

She had asked about Kastenessen – about Covenant – and Esmer talked of Viles.

'Yet a shadow had already fallen upon them,' Cail's son continued, 'like and unlike the shadow upon the hearts of the *Elohim*. The corruption of the Viles, and of their makings, the Demondim, transpired thus.'

Wait, she wanted to insist. Stop. That isn't what I need to know. But the accentuation of Esmer's manner held her. He was right: her ignorance precluded her from asking the right questions – and from recognising useful answers.

'Many tales are told,' said Esmer, 'some to conceal, some to reveal. Yet it is sooth that long before the Despiser's coming to the littoral of the Land, he had stretched out his hand to awaken the malevolence of Lifeswallower, the Great Swamp, as it lurked in the heart of Sarangrave Flat, for he delights in cruel hungers. And from that malevolence

– conjoined with the rapacity of humankind – had emerged the three Ravers, *moksha, turiya* and *samadhi*. By such means was the One Forest decimated, and its long sentience maimed, until an *Elohim* came to preserve its remnants.

'Awakened to themselves,' Esmer explained as though the knowledge grieved him, 'the trees created the Forestals to guard them, and bound the *Elohim* into the Colossus of the Fall as an Interdict against the Ravers, repulsing them from the Upper Land.

'Later the Despiser established Ridjeck Thome as his seat of power, though he did not then declare himself to human knowledge. There he gathered the Ravers to his service when the Colossus began to wane. And with his guidance, they together, or some among them, began cunningly to twist the hearts of the sovereign and isolate Viles. Forbidden still by the Colossus, the Ravers could not enter the Lost Deep. Instead they met with Viles that roamed east of Landsdrop, exploring the many facets of the Land. With whispers and subtle blandishments, and by slow increments, the Ravers obliquely taught the Viles to loathe their own forms.

'Being Ravers, the brothers doubtless began by sharing their mistrust and contempt towards the surviving mind of the One Forest, and towards the Forestals. From that beginning, however, the Viles were readily led to despise themselves, for all contempt turns upon the contemptuous, as it must.'

Esmer had raised his head: he faced Linden as steadily as he could. But his eyes were the fraught hue of heavy seas crashing against each other, and his raiment gusted about him in the throes of a private storm.

'In that same age,' he went on, 'as the perversion of the Viles progressed, *samadhi* Raver evaded the Interdict by passing beyond the Southron Range to taint the people who gave birth to Berek Lord-Fatherer. By his influence upon their King, *samadhi* instigated the war which led Berek through terrible years and cruel bloodshed to his place as the first High Lord in the Land.

'Among the crags of Mount Thunder, Berek had sworn himself to the service of the Land. But he was new to power, and much of his effort was turned to the discovering of the One Tree and the forming of the Staff of Law. He could not halt all of humankind's depredations against the forests. And as the trees dwindled, so the strength of the Colossus was diminished.

'Nonetheless in the time of High Lord Damelon the Interdict endured. When the Viles turned their lore and their self-loathing to the creation of the Demondim in the Lost Deep, the Ravers were precluded from interference.'

Esmer nodded as if to himself. His gaze drifted away from Linden. He may have been too absorbed in his tale, in rue and old bitterness, to remember that he was not answering her. Nevertheless the Waynhim and ur-viles heeded him in utter silence, as if their Weird hinged on his words. For their sake, and because she could not evaluate his reasons for speaking, she swallowed her impulse to interrupt him.

'And the Viles were too wise to labour foolishly, or in ignorance. They did not seek to renew their own loathing, but rather to render it impotent. Therefore the Demondim were spawned free of their creators' stain. Though they lacked some portion of the Viles' majesty and lore, they were not ruled by contempt. Instead they were a stern race, holding themselves apart from the Viles in renunciation.

'Yet across the years the Demondim also were turned to abhorrence. Dwelling apart from the Viles, they made their habitation in proximity to the Illearth Stone and other banes. And the evil within the Sarangrave called to them softly, as it had to the Viles. When at last the Demondim ventured to seek the source of that call, they entered the Lower Land and Sarangrave Flat, and there they met the fate of their makers, for the Ravers gained power over them also.'

Complex emotions seemed to tug like contrary winds at Esmer's cymar, and his voice resembled the threat of thunder beyond the Westron Mountains. '*Moksha* Jehannum took possession of their loremaster, and *turiya* with him, luring the Vile-spawn to self-revulsion. Though the loremaster was later slain by the *krill* of Loric Vilesilencer, the harm was done. The Demondim also learned the loathing of trees, and so came to loathe themselves. Thus they met the doom of their makers, and the labours which created the ur-viles and the Waynhim began.

'Unlike the Viles, however, the Demondim were seduced to the Despiser's service. Their makers had created within them an aspect of mortality and dross, and they were unable to perceive that the Despiser's scorn towards them exceeded their own. Nor was their desire to follow the dictates of their loathing restricted by the Interdict. They acted upon the Upper Land while the Ravers were hidden from the Council of Lords, and the Despiser himself remained unknown.

'Throughout the years of Loric Vilesilencer and High Lord Kevin, the Demondim pursued evil in the Land, until at last they participated in the treachery which broke Kevin Landwaster's resolve and led him to the Ritual of Desecration. That the Demondim themselves would also perish in the Ritual, they could not foresee, for they did not comprehend the disdain of their master. Therefore they were unmade.'

The listening creatures had moved still closer. They seemed to hear Esmer with their nostrils as much as their ears. And as they approached, more and more of the Waynhim were mingled among the ur-viles. For the moment, at least, they had set aside their long enmity.

'For millennia thereafter,' Esmer sighed, 'the ur-viles likewise served the Despiser and opposed the Lords, following in the steps of their makers, though the Waynhim chose another path. Yet the Demondim had accomplished both less and more than their purpose. The ur-viles and Waynhim were entirely enfleshed. For that reason, their blindness exceeded that of the Demondim – as did their inadvertent capacity for wisdom. Being imprisoned in mortality, they became heir to a power, or a need, which is inherent in all beings that think and may be slain. By their very nature, they were compelled to reconsider the significance of their lives. Flesh and death inspired the ur-viles and Waynhim to conceive differing Weirds to justify themselves – and to reinterpret their Weirds as they wished. In consequence, their allegiances were vulnerable to transmutation.'

Linden recognised aspects of truth in what he said, but that did nothing to relieve her distress. Her mouth was full of bile and illness, and she did not know how much longer she could contain her nausea. Esmer's conflicts aggravated it. The Demondim-spawn may have understood his intent: she did not.

'Why are you telling me this?' she asked abruptly. 'It isn't what I need. I have to know why the Demondim didn't kill Jeremiah and Covenant. You said that Kastenessen convinced those monsters to let me escape. Did he do the same for my son and Covenant?'

A flare of anger like a glimpse of the Illearth Stone showed in Esmer's eyes. 'And are you also ignorant,' he retorted, 'that the *Cavewights* were once friendly to the people of the Land? I wish you to grasp the nature of such creatures. You inquire of Kastenessen, and I reply. That which appears evil need not have been so from the beginning, and need not remain so until the end.

'Doubtless your knowledge of Viles and Demondim and ur-viles has been gleaned from the *Haruchai*.' He had recovered his scorn. 'Have they also informed you that when both the Viles and the Demondim had been undone, the ur-viles retained the lore of their making? Do you comprehend that the ur-viles continued to labour in the Lost Deep when all of their creators had passed away? Though the Waynhim did not arrogate such tasks to themselves, the ur-viles endeavoured to fashion miracles of lore and foresight which would alter the fate of their kind, and of the Land, and of the very Earth.'

He had shaken Linden again. Holding the Staff in the crook of her arm, she pushed her fingers through the damp tangles of her hair: she wanted to push them through her thoughts in an effort to straighten out the confusion of Esmer's indirect answers.

'Wait a minute,' she protested with her hands full of uncertainty. 'Stave said—'

He had said, *Much of the black lore of the Viles and the Demondim endured to them – and much did not. Both Waynhim and ur-viles continued to dwindle. They created no descendants, and when they were slain nothing returned of them.*

Esmer snorted. 'The *Haruchai* speak of that which they know, which is little. The truth has been made plain to you, for you have known Vain. You cannot doubt that the ur-viles pursued the efforts of their makers.

'At the same time, however, more of these creatures' – he gestured around him – 'came into being, both ur-viles and Waynhim. For that reason, I have been able to gather so many to your service.'

Linden tried to interrupt him again; slow him down so that she could think. He overrode her harshly. Twisted by the contradictory demands of his heritage, he may still have been trying to answer her original question.

'But the ur-viles have created other makings also. They did not cease their labours when they had formed Vain, for they were not content. Their reinterpretation of their Weird was not yet satisfied. Therefore they have made—'

Suddenly he stopped as if he had caught himself on the edge of a precipice. Chagrin darkened his gaze as he stared at her, apparently unable or unwilling to look away.

'Made what?' Linden breathed softly. His manner alarmed her.

The ur-viles and Waynhim crowded closer. Ripples of dark power ran among them as if they were sharing intimations of vitriol; nascent outrage.

Linden unclosed the Staff from the crook of her arm and wrapped both of her hands around it. She had too many fears: she could not allow them to daunt her. 'Made what?' she repeated more strongly.

Esmer's green eyes seemed to spume with anger or dread as he pronounced hoarsely, 'Manacles.'

She gaped at him in surprise. What, *manacles? Fetters?*

'Why?' she demanded. 'Who are they for?' Or what?

Which of the powers abroad in the Land did the ur-viles hope to imprison?

He shook his head. At the same time, the creatures started barking again, arguing incomprehensibly in their guttural tongue. Some of them made gestures that may have been threats or admonitions. Force rolled through them, small wavelets of energy like ripples spreading outward from the impact of their inhuman emotions; but they did not seek to concentrate it.

Linden wanted to cover her ears. 'What are they saying?' Her voice held an involuntary note of pleading. 'Esmer, tell me.'

At once, the froth of waves seemed to fill his eyes, concealing their deeper hues. 'They have heard me. They acknowledge my intent, though you do not. Now some debate the interpretation of their Weirds. Others demand that I explain their purpose further.' He folded his arms like bands across his chest. 'But I will not. The debt between us I have redeemed, and more. In this, there is no power sufficient to compel me.'

Around him, the shouting of the creatures subsided to an angry mutter. Or perhaps their low sounds expressed resignation rather than ire.

Manacles—? In frustration, Linden wanted to hit him with the Staff. He still had not answered her question about his grandsire – or shed any light on the conundrum of Covenant and Jeremiah.

Struggling to keep her balance amid a gyre of information and implications which she did not know how to accommodate, she retreated to surer ground.

'All right. Forget the manacles. I don't need to know.' Not now, when she had so many more immediate concerns. 'Tell me something I can understand. How did you convince your ur-viles and Waynhim to come with you?' She knew why her own small band had combined their efforts against the Demondim. Even now, however, she could not be certain that the truce between them would hold. And those with Esmer had not shared in her battles. 'They've been enemies for thousands of years. Why have they set that aside?'

Esmer raised one hand to pinch the bridge of his nose. Closing his eyes, he massaged them briefly with his fingertips. As he did so, he replied in a tone of exaggerated patience, as if he had already answered her question in terms that even a child could comprehend.

'To the ur-viles, I offered opportunity to see fulfilled the mighty purpose which they began in the making of Vain. To the Waynhim, I promised a joining with their few kindred, that they might be powerful in the Land's service.' Then he lowered his hand, letting her see the wind-tossed disturbance in his eyes. 'And of both I required this covenant, that they must cease all warfare between them.'

As if in assent, the creatures fell silent again.

Before Linden could ask another question, Esmer added, 'Wildwielder, you exhaust my restraint. You have demanded answers. I have provided them, seeking to relieve the darkness of my nature. But one of the *Haruchai* approaches from that place' – again he indicated Revelstone – 'and I will not suffer his presence. I cannot. Already my heart frays within me. Soon it will demand release. If I do not depart, I will wreak—'

He stopped. His expression and his green eyes seemed to beseech her for forbearance.

But her nausea and distress were too great. Her son and Thomas Covenant had refused to let her hold them. They might as well have rejected her years of unfulfilled love. Instead of honouring Esmer's appeal, she said grimly, 'If you didn't insist on doing harm, you wouldn't need relief.'

For an instant, he looked so stricken that she thought he might weep. But then, as if by an act of will, he recovered his scorn. 'If I did not insist upon aiding you,' he told her acidly, 'I would not be required to commit harm.'

He had told her the history of the Viles and Demondim in order to justify himself: she believed that, although it may have been only part of the truth. He wanted her to trust that the creatures which he had brought forward from the past would serve her. At the same time, he was plainly trying to warn her—

But she could not afford to think about such things now. He was about to depart: she would not be able to stop him. And she still had learned nothing about Covenant and Jeremiah.

'All right,' she said again, trying to speak more quickly. 'I accept your explanation. I accept' – she gestured around at the ur-viles and Waynhim – 'all of them. You're trying to help me, even though I don't understand it. But I still need answers.

'You said that there's a shadow on the hearts of the *Elohim*. What does that *mean?*' She meant, What does Kastenessen have to do with Covenant and my son? But Esmer had already evaded that question. 'Why didn't they stop Kastenessen from breaking free?'

Esmer groaned as if she endangered his sanity. Gritting his teeth, he said, 'The *Elohim* believe that they are equal to all things. This is false. Were it true, the Earth entire would exist in their image, and they would have no need to fear the rousing of the Worm of the World's End. Nonetheless they persist in their belief. That is shadow enough to darken the heart of any being.

'They did not act to preserve Kastenessen's Durance because they saw no need. Are you not the Wildwielder? And have you not returned to the Land? The *skurj* are mindless beasts, ravaging to feed. Kastenessen's will rules them, but they cannot harm the *Elohim*. And you will oppose both Kastenessen and his monsters. What then remains to cause the *Elohim* concern? They have done that which they deem needful. They have forewarned the people of the Land, speaking often of the peril of the halfhand when the *Haruchai* have effaced any other knowledge or defence. Their Würd requires nothing more. While you endure, they fear no other threat.'

Linden flinched. She should have been prepared for Esmer's assertion. Since their first meeting millennia ago, the *Elohim* had distrusted and disdained Thomas Covenant. They had been convinced even then that she, not Covenant, should be the one to hold and use white gold. And later, just a few days ago, Esmer had said, *You have become the Wildwielder, as the* Elohim *knew that you must.*

Nevertheless he filled her with dismay.

'Wait a minute,' she protested. 'You have to tell me. What's "the peril of the halfhand"? You can't mean the Humbled. They don't have any power — and they don't *want* to threaten the Land. And you can't mean my son. That poor boy has been Lord Foul's prisoner ever since he came here. He doesn't have a ring, or a staff, or lore.' He retained only his racecar, pitiable and useless. 'He has power now, but he must be getting it from someone else.

'No.' She shook her head in denial. 'You're talking about Thomas Covenant. But how is *he* dangerous? My God, Esmer, he's already saved the Land *twice*. And he's probably been holding the Arch of Time together ever since Joan started her *caesures*. Why do the *Elohim* think that *anybody* has to *beware the halfhand?*'

'Wildwielder.' Esmer seemed to throw up his hands in disgust or apprehension. 'Always you persist in questions which require no response, or which serve no purpose, or which will cause my destruction. You waste my assistance, when any attempt at aid or guidance is cruel to me. Do you mean to demand the entire knowledge of the Earth, while the Land itself is brought to ruin, and Time with it?'

'It's not that simple!' she snapped urgently. 'Practically everything is being hidden from me,' and not only by Cail's son. 'When I do learn something, it isn't relevant to my problems. Even with the Staff, I might as well be blind.

'You've at least got *eyes*. You see things that I can't live without. You're in my debt. You said so. Maybe that's why these ur-viles and Waynhim are here. Maybe it isn't. But if I'm asking the wrong questions, whose fault is that? I've got nothing *but* questions. How am I supposed to know

which are the right ones? How can I help *wasting* you when you won't
tell me what I need to know?"

Esmer's sudden anguish was so acute that it seemed to splash against
her skin like spray; and the doleful green of his gaze cried out to her.
In response, her stomach twisted as though she had swallowed poison.
Another mutter arose from the watching creatures, a sound as sharp as
fangs. The air felt too thick to breathe: she had difficulty drawing it into
her lungs.

As if the words were being wrung from him by the combined insistence of the Waynhim and ur-viles, he hissed, 'You must be the first to
drink of the EarthBlood.'

For a moment longer, he remained in front of her, letting her see that
his distress was as poignant as a wail. Then he left.

She did not see him vanish. Instead he seemed to sink back like a
receding wave until he was gone as if he had never been there at all,
leaving her with the fate of the Land on her shoulders and too little
strength to carry it alone.

The abrupt cessation of her nausea gave her no relief at all.

Chapter Three:

Love and Strangers

Linden hardly saw the ur-viles and Waynhim disperse, withdrawing apparently at random across the hillsides. With Esmer gone, they seemed to have no further purpose. They kept their distance from Glimmermere. And none of them headed towards Revelstone. As they drifted away, small clusters of Waynhim followed larger groups of ur-viles, or chose directions of their own. Soon they were gone, abandoning her to her dilemmas.

You must be the first to drink of the EarthBlood.

In the west, a storm-front continued to accumulate behind the majesty of the mountains. Leery of being scourged by winds and rain and hostility, she peered for a moment at the high threat of the thunderheads, the clouds streaming past the jagged peaks. But she saw nothing unnatural there: no malice, no desire for pain. The harm which had harried her return to the Verge of Wandering – malevolence that she now believed had arisen from Kastenessen's frustration and power – was entirely absent. When this storm broke over the plateau, it would bring only torrents, the necessary vehemence of the living world. And when it passed, it would leave lucent and enriched the grass-clad hillsides, the feather-leaved swaths of mimosa, the tall stands of cedar and pine.

Aching, she wished that she could find ease in such things. But Thomas Covenant and Jeremiah had refused to let her touch them; and Esmer had foiled her efforts to find out what was *wrong* with them. Her fear that they had been herded towards her remained unresolved.

Covenant had claimed responsibility for that feat – but how could she know whether his assertions were even possible? How did his place in the

Arch of Time enable him to violate time's most fundamental strictures? Had he indeed become a being of pure paradox, as capable of saving or damning the Earth as white gold itself?

And Jeremiah had not simply recovered his mind: he appeared to have acquired the knowledge and understanding of a fifteen-year-old boy, even though he had been effectively absent from himself for ten of those years. That should have been enough for her. It was more, far more, than she could have hoped for if she had rescued him with her own strength and determination; her own love.

But he and Covenant had denied her. Her son had gained power – and had used it to repel her. They kept their distance even though every particle of her heart and soul craved to hold them in her arms and never let them go. And they claimed that they had good reason for doing so. Instead of relief, joy, or desire – the food for which her soul hungered – she felt only an unutterable loss.

Don't touch *him! Don't touch* either *of us!*

Faced with Esmer's surprises and obfuscations, she had failed to ask the right questions; to make him tell her *why* Covenant and her son were so changed. Now she had no choice except to wrest understanding from Covenant himself. Or from Jeremiah. Somehow.

Keep her away from us until I'm ready.

Her heart was full of pain, in spite of Glimmermere's healing, as she turned at last to ascend the hillside towards Revelstone. How had the man whom she had loved here, in this very place, become a being who could not tolerate the affirmation of Law? And where had Jeremiah obtained the lore, the magic, or the need to reject her yearning embrace?

She did not mean to wait until Covenant decided that he was *ready*. She had loved him and her son too long and too arduously to be treated as nothing more than a hindrance.

But first she hoped to talk to the Mahdoubt. The older woman had been kind to Linden. She might be willing to say more about her strange insights. In any case, her replies could hardly be less revealing than Esmer's—

As Linden reached the crest of the hills which cupped and concealed Glimmermere, the southeastward stretch of the upland plateau opened before her. Distraught as she was, she might still have lingered there for a moment to drink in the spring-kissed landscape: the flowing green of the grass, the numinous blue of the jacarandas' flowers, the yellow splash of blooms among the mimosas. But Manethrall Mahrtiir stood at the foot of slope below her, plainly watching for her return. And in the middle distance, she saw Stave's solitary figure striding purposefully towards her. Their proximity drew her down the hillside to meet them.

She wanted a moment alone with Mahrtiir before Stave came near enough to overhear her.

The Manethrall studied her approach as though he believed – or feared – that she had been changed by Glimmermere. He must have noticed the sudden silence of the birds— She felt his sharp gaze on her, searching for indications that she was unharmed.

He was unaware of what had transpired: she could see that. Both Esmer and the Demondim-spawn were able to thwart perception. And the bulk of the hill must have blocked the noises of her encounter with them. If Mahrtiir had felt their presence, he would have ignored her request for privacy.

Yet it was clear that he retained enough discernment, in spite of Kevin's Dirt, to recognise that *something* had happened to her or changed for her. As she neared him, he bowed deeply, as if he felt that he owed her a new homage. And when he raised his eyes again, his chagrin was unmistakable, in spite of his fierce nature.

'Ringthane—' he began awkwardly. 'Again you have surpassed me. You are exalted—'

'No, Mahrtiir.' Linden hastened to forestall his wonder. She was too lost, and too needy, to bear it. 'It isn't me. It's Glimmermere. That's what you're seeing.' She attempted an unsuccessful smile. 'You don't need to stay away from it. As soon as you touch the water, you'll know what I mean. It belongs to the Land. To everyone. You won't feel like an intruder. And it cleans away Kevin's Dirt.

'I can't use my Staff right now.' She frowned at the wood in frustration. 'You know that. I can't protect us from being blinded, any of us. But as long as we can go to Glimmermere—'

When they knew the truth, Liand, Bhapa and Pahni would be delighted. Anele, on the other hand— Linden sighed. He would avoid the lake strenuously. He feared anything that might threaten his self-imposed plight. And his defences were strong. He would use every scrap of his inborn might to preserve the peculiar integrity of his madness.

As Stave came closer, she promised the Manethrall quietly, 'You'll get your chance. I'll make sure of it.'

The Raman bowed again. 'My thanks, Ringthane.' Wryly he added, 'Doubtless you have observed that the pride of the Ramen runs hotly within me. I do not contain it well.'

Hurrying to put the matter behind her, Linden said again, 'Don't worry about it. I respect your pride. It's better than shame. And we have more important problems.'

Mahrtiir nodded. He may have thought that he knew what she meant.

A moment later, Stave reached the Manethrall's side. He, too, bowed as if in recognition of some ineffable alteration, an elevation at once too subtle and too profound for Linden to acknowledge. 'Chosen,' he said with his familiar flatness, 'the waters of Glimmermere have served you well. You have been restored when none could have known that you had been diminished.'

He had cleaned the blood from his face, but he still wore his spattered tunic and his untended bruises as if they were a reproach to the Masters. His single eye gave his concentration a prophetic cast, as if in losing half of his vision he had gained a supernal insight.

Did he see her accurately? Had she in fact gleaned something sacramental from the lake? Something untainted by her encounter with Esmer's ambiguous loyalties?

She shrugged the question aside. It could not change her choices – or the risks that she meant to take.

Without preamble, she replied, 'I was just about to tell Mahrtiir that something happened after I—' She had no words adequate to the experience. 'I wanted to talk to somebody who could tell me what's going on, so I called Esmer.' Awkwardly she explained, 'I have no idea what he can and can't do. I thought that he might be able to hear me.'

While Stave studied her, and Mahrtiir stared with open surprise, she described as concisely as she could what Cail's son had said and done.

'Ur-viles,' the Manethrall breathed when she was finished, 'and

Waynhim. So many – and together. Have these creatures indeed come to your aid? Do they suffice against the Teeth of the Render?'

Stave appeared to consult the air. With his tongue, he made a sound that suggested vexation. 'The actions of these Demondim-spawn are unexpected,' he said aloud, 'but no more so than those of their makers. If the spirit of Kastenessen is able to possess our companion Anele, much is explained.'

Our companion— Linden could not remember hearing Stave speak the old man's name before. Apparently the former Master had extended his friendship to include all of her comrades.

'For that reason, however,' he continued, 'the peril that the same spirit moves Esmer, and with him the ur-viles and Waynhim, cannot be discounted.

'Did Esmer reveal nothing of the ur-Lord, or of your son?'

'No,' she muttered bitterly. 'I asked him whether Kastenessen helped Covenant and Jeremiah reach Revelstone, but he just changed the subject.'

Mahrtiir opened his mouth, then closed it again grimly. Stave had more to say.

'I mislike this confluence. Plainly the return of the Unbeliever from the Arch of Time holds great import. It appears to promise that the Land's redemption is at hand. Yet his account of his coming troubles me. That he is able to cast a glamour of confusion upon the Demondim, I do not greatly question. However, his avowal concerning distortions of the Law of Time—' He hesitated momentarily, then said, 'And Esmer's grandsire connives with Demondim while Esmer himself removes Waynhim and ur-viles from their proper time.

'Chosen, here is cause for concern. It cannot lack meaning that such divergent events have occurred together.'

'Stave speaks sooth, Ringthane,' the Manethrall said in a low growl. 'Esmer has been altered by your return to the Land. He is not as he was when he first gained the friendship of the Ramen. Had he answered you, his words would have held too much truth and falsehood to be of service.'

Linden agreed; but the thought did not comfort her. She had suffered too many shocks.

Jeremiah is here, *but Foul still has him.*

What you can't see is how much it hurts that I'm not just here.

What were Esmer's surprises – or his betrayals – compared to that?

Fiercely she set aside her failures. Supporting her resolve, if not her heart, on the Staff of Law, she met Stave's flat gaze.

'I'm worried about the same things. Maybe Covenant can explain them.' Or perhaps the Mahdoubt might share her obscure knowledge. 'Is he ready to see me yet? Has something else happened? I wasn't expecting you so soon.'

'There is no new peril,' replied the *Haruchai*. 'The Demondim remain in abeyance, without apparent purpose. But the ur-Lord has indeed announced his readiness to speak with you. I have been instructed to summon you.'

His manner suggested that he disliked being 'instructed' by either Covenant or the Masters.

'Then let's go.' At once, Linden started into motion. 'Foul still has my son.' Somehow. 'If I don't do something about that soon, it's going to tear me apart.'

Lord's Keep was at least a league away.

Stave and the Manethrall joined her promptly, walking at her shoulders like guardians. She set a brisk pace, borne along by Glimmermere's lingering potency; but they accompanied her easily. Either one of them could have reached Revelstone far more swiftly without her—

As they followed low valleys among the hills and trees, Linden asked Stave, 'Did you find the Mahdoubt? Will she talk to me?'

The *Haruchai* shook his head. 'It is curious. It appears that the Mahdoubt has departed from Revelstone. How she might have done so is unclear. Demondim in abundance guard the gates, the passage to the plateau is watched, and Lord's Keep has no other egress. Yet neither the Masters nor those who serve the Keep can name her whereabouts.

'I was shown to her chambers, but she was not there. And those who have known her cannot suggest where she might be found.' He paused for a moment, then added, 'Nor are they able to account for her. Indeed, they profess to know nothing certain of her. They say only that she conveys the sense that they have always known her – and that she seldom attracts notice.'

Stave shrugged slightly. 'In the thoughts of the Masters, she is merely a servant of Revelstone, unremarkable and unregarded. To me, also, she has appeared to be entirely ordinary. Yet her absence now demonstrates our error. At a time of less extreme hazard, the Masters would seek to grasp her mystery. While Revelstone remains besieged, however, their attention is compelled by the Demondim.'

'I also was baffled by her,' Mahrtiir put in. 'In some fashion, she appeared to alter herself from moment to moment, yet I could not be certain of my sight. Another woman inhabited her place, or she herself inhabited—' He muttered in irritation. 'I do not comprehend it.'

'Me neither,' Linden admitted. But she swallowed her disappointment. If the Mahdoubt had not warned her to *Be cautious of love*, she would never have thought to ask for the older woman's guidance.

'All right,' she went on. 'Since that doesn't make any sense, maybe you can tell me something that does. How did you convince the Humbled to leave me alone? If they don't trust me, shouldn't they be guarding me?'

Stave considered briefly before saying, 'Other concerns require precedence. A measure of uncertainty has been sown among the Masters. They know nothing of the peril which Esmer has revealed. But they have heard Anele speak of both Kastenessen and the *skurj*. And they are chary of the Demondim. That such monsters front the gates of Revelstone, holding among them the might of the Illearth Stone, and yet do nothing, disturbs the Masters. In addition, the Unbeliever's presence is' – he appeared to search for a description – 'strangely fortuitous. It is difficult to credit.

'Your power to create Falls, or to efface the ur-Lord by other means, troubles the Masters deeply. However, I have reminded the Humbled that your love for both the Unbeliever and the Land is well known – and that your son will be lost by any act of theurgy. Further, I have assured them that you are not a woman who will forsake those companions who remain in Revelstone. This your fidelity to Anele confirms.

'Also' – Stave shrugged eloquently – 'the Humbled will not willingly forego their duty to the Halfhand, regardless of their disquiet. Therefore they heeded my urging.'

Stave's tone reminded Linden that the Humbled would not otherwise have listened to him.

'They are fools,' growled Mahrtiir.

'They are *Haruchai*,' Stave replied without inflection. 'I thought as they do. Had I not partaken of the horserite, I would do so still.'

He deserved gratitude, especially because of his own bereavement; and Linden thanked him as well as she could. Then she asked a different question. 'You mentioned the *skurj*. Why didn't you say anything about them before we came here?'

'Chosen?' Stave cocked an eyebrow at her question.

'You've heard Anele talk about them. You were there when that *Elohim* appeared in Mithil Stonedown,' warning Liand's people *that a bane of great puissance and ferocity in the far north had slipped its bonds, and had found release in Mount Thunder*. 'And you told me yourself that "Beasts of Earthpower rage upon Mount Thunder". But you haven't said anything else.'

Until now, she had not needed to know more—

'Your people are the Masters of the Land. If something that terrible has been set loose,' something which resembled fiery serpents with the jaws of krakens, something capable of devouring stone and soil, grass and trees, 'someone must have at least *noticed*. I assume that the Masters can't fight the *skurj*, but they must be watching, studying, trying to understand.'

Now Stave nodded. 'There has been misapprehension between us. The Masters have no knowledge of the *skurj* which has not been gleaned from Anele. We—' He stopped himself. 'They have beheld no such evil upon the Land. If the *skurj* have come, they have done so recently, or without exposing themselves to the awareness of the Masters.

'When I spoke of "beasts of Earthpower", I should perhaps have named the Fire-Lions of Mount Thunder. I did not because I believed them unknown to you. Their life within Gravin Threndor is ancient, far older than the history of Lords in the Land. They came first to human knowledge in the time of Berek Halfhand, the Lord-Fatherer, who called upon them to destroy the armies of his foes. So the tale was later told to the Bloodguard during the time of Kevin Landwaster. Indeed, it has been sung that the Landwaster himself once stood upon the pinnacle of Gravin Threndor and beheld the Fire-Lions. Thereafter, however, they were not again witnessed until the time of the Unbeliever's first coming to the Land, when he called upon Gravin Threndor's beasts for the salvation of his companions.'

'So it is remembered among the Ramen,' Mahrtiir assented, 'for Manethrall Lithe accompanied the Ringthane and his companions into the Wightwarrens, though we loathe the loss of the open sky. She it was who guided the defenders of the Land from those dire catacombs to the slopes of Gravin Threndor. She witnessed the Ringthane's summoning of the Fire-Lions – and of the Ranyhyn who bore the Ringthane's companions to safety.'

'That also the *Haruchai* have not forgotten,' said Stave. 'The courage of the Raman enabled hope which would otherwise have been lost utterly.'

Linden bit her lower lip and waited for Stave to continue his explanation.

'Now, however,' he said, 'the Fire-Lions are restive. After millennia of concealed life, they may be observed at any time rampaging upon the slopes of Mount Thunder. They present no peril to the Land, for they are beings of Earthpower, as condign after their fashion as the Ranyhyn. But the cause of their restlessness must be a great peril indeed. When the unnamed *Elohim* spoke of "a bane of great puissance and ferocity" from the far north which had "found release" in Mount Thunder, no Master knew the form or power of that evil, though all presumed it to be the source of the Fire-Lions' unrest.

'Upon that occasion, the *Elohim* also named the *skurj*.'

'As they did among the Ramen also,' Mahrtiir put in.

The *Haruchai* nodded again. 'And Anele has indeed uttered that name repeatedly. But his words revealed nothing of what the *skurj* might be, or of the Fire-Lions' unrest. Only when he spoke in the Close did he declare beyond mistake that Kastenessen had been Appointed to contain the *skurj*, that he has now broken free of his Durance, and that therefore the *skurj* are a present danger to the Land.

'For that reason, we' – again he stopped himself – 'the Masters, and I as well, conceive that the *skurj* are not the bane which has been released in Mount Thunder. The Fire-Lions have been too long restless, and such devouring harm as Kastenessen was Appointed to imprison would surely have become manifest to our senses. Rather I deem, as do the Masters, that the bane of which the *Elohim* spoke, and the cause of the Fire-Lions' unrest, is Kastenessen himself. We surmise that when he had broken free of his Durance, he came alone to Mount Thunder, preceding his former prisoners. Those creatures are the *skurj*, as Anele has plainly proclaimed. Only now does Kastenessen summon them to his aid.'

Kastenessen again, Linden thought darkly. She did not doubt Stave: his explanation fit Anele's cryptic references to the *skurj*, the Durance, and the Appointed. Nor did she doubt that when Lord Foul had *whispered a word of counsel here and there, and awaited events*, he had been speaking to Kastenessen. He may even have told Kastenessen how to shatter or evade his Durance.

Whether or not the Despiser had also advised Esmer, she could not begin to guess.

But Lord Foul had Jeremiah. Her son had constructed images of Revelstone and Mount Thunder in her living room. And the Masters had reason to think that Kastenessen now inhabited Mount Thunder.

Perhaps he was also responsible for Kevin's Dirt—

Such speculations left her sick with frustration. They were too abstract: she needed a concrete explanation for what had happened to Covenant and Jeremiah. And she feared the storm of her own emotions when she stood before them again. If they still rejected her touch, she might not be able to think at all.

Still searching for some form of insight, she asked Stave what he remembered of the *Elohim*'s portentous visit to Mithil Stonedown. Surely he had heard or understood more than Liand was able to recall?

He replied with pronounced care, as though she had asked him to touch on subjects that would cause her pain.

'I can add little to that which the Ramen have revealed, or to the Stonedown's memory of the event. I saw the *Elohim* for what he was, oblique and devious. Such names as *merewives*, Sandgorgons and *croyel* were known to me, as they are to you, though they conveyed naught to the Stonedownors. Also the *Haruchai* have heard it said, as you have, that there is a shadow upon the heart of the *Elohim*.

'But of the *skurj* we knew nothing. The Masters do not grasp the purpose of the *Elohim*'s appearance, for they cannot comprehend his warning against the halfhand. Indeed, they honour those who have been titled

Halfhands, both Berek Lord-Fatherer and ur-Lord Thomas Covenant the Unbeliever. The Humbled are a token of that honour, as they are of the fault which doomed the Bloodguard.'

A premature twilight dimmed the air as Linden and her companions strode among the low hills. She had been on the plateau longer than she realised. The sun was not yet setting; but the peaks of the Westron Mountains reached high, and the dark clouds behind them piled higher still. She seemed to cross into shadow as Stave answered her.

'Yet, Chosen—' The *Haruchai* hesitated, apparently uncertain that he should continue. However, he had declared his loyalty to her. His tone remained dispassionate as he said, 'I have been cast out from the Masters, but they cannot silence their thoughts. They merely refuse to heed me if I do not speak aloud. For that reason, I know that they are disturbed by the knowledge that your son also is a halfhand.'

Linden flinched involuntarily; but she did not interrupt.

'In the time of the new Lords,' Stave continued, 'the Unbeliever was considered by some the reincarnation of Berek Heartthew, for their legends said that Berek would one day return. It may be that the *Elohim* fear the Unbeliever because his presence, the rebirth of High Lord Berek's potent spirit, will dim their own import in the Earth. Or it may be that the *Elohim* seek to warn the Land against your son, seeing in him a peril which is hidden from us.'

No, stop, Linden protested inwardly. I can't think— Without noticing what she did, she dragged her fingers roughly through the tangles of her hair: she needed that smaller hurt to contain her larger shock. What, you suspect that *my son* is a threat to the Land? *Now* what am I supposed to do? Jeremiah had recovered his mind. *He had recovered his mind.* How could she bear to believe that he had become dangerous? That the *Elohim* saw danger in him?

Or in Covenant—?

Where had Jeremiah's mind been while she had tried and failed for years to reach it?

After a moment, Mahrtiir said gruffly, 'This gains nothing, Stave. That we have cause for concern is plain enough. But the youth is no son of ours. We cannot gaze upon him as the Ringthane must. And the burden of determination is not ours, for we hold neither white gold nor the Staff of Law. She will speak with the Unbeliever and her son, and her wisdom and valour will guide her. The speculations of the Masters – mere imaginings, for the truth remains shrouded – serve only to tarnish her clarity.'

The Manethrall's words offered Linden a way to calm her turmoil. He was right: she could not guess the truth of Jeremiah's condition – or of Covenant's. She needed to fight her impulse to jump to conclusions.

'She will learn what she can,' Mahrtiir said, 'and do what she must. This the Ramen understand, who have spent their lives in the service of the Ranyhyn. But the Masters have lost such wisdom, for they conceive themselves equal to that which they serve. Among your people, you alone recognise their fault' – the Manethrall grinned sharply – 'humbling my pride as you do so, for the Ramen also are not without fault. We have permitted ourselves to forget that at one time, when the Bloodguard had ended their service to the Lords, some few of them chose instead to serve the Ranyhyn among the Ramen. Foolishly we have nurtured our disdain towards the sleepless ones across the centuries, and so we have proffered distrust where honour has been earned.

'Together we must now be wary that we do not teach the Ringthane to share our ancient taints. We may be certain that she will serve the Land and her own loves. No other knowledge is required of us.'

Although her heart trembled, Linden pushed aside the warning of the *Elohim*. She could not afford to be confused by fears that had no name.

She and her companions were nearing the wide passage that angled down into Lord's Keep. There she stopped so that she would not be overheard by the Masters who presumably guarded the passage. Resting her free hand on Stave's shoulder, she turned to meet the Manethrall's whetted gaze.

'Thank you,' she said gravely. 'That helps.' Then she faced Stave. 'And thank you. I need to know anything that you can tell me. Even if it makes me crazy.' She grimaced ruefully. 'But Mahrtiir is right. I can't think about everything right now. We have too many problems. I need to take them as they come.

'We're running out of time. I know that. Those Demondim aren't going to wait much longer.' And when they resumed their siege, they would unfurl the full virulence of the Illearth Stone from its source in the deep past. 'But I can't worry about them yet.' She knew what she had to do. 'First I need to talk to Covenant and Jeremiah.'

The gloom on the upland continued to darken as storm clouds hid the sun.

'I hope that you'll forgive me,' she told Stave. 'There might be things that I can't talk about in front of you.' Not until she knew more about the Unbeliever and her son – and about where she stood with them. 'If you can still hear the Masters' thoughts, I have to assume that they can hear yours. And if they even half believe that Jeremiah is a threat—' She swallowed a lump of distress. 'I can't take the chance that they'll get in my way.'

Stave faced her stolidly. 'No forgiveness is needful. I do not question you. The Masters are indeed able to hear my thoughts – should they deign to do so. Speak to me of nothing which may foster their opposition.'

Mutely Mahrtiir gave the former Master a deep Ramen bow. And Linden squeezed his shoulder. She wanted to hug him – to acknowledge his understanding as well as his losses – but she did not trust herself. Her emotions gathered like the coming storm. If she could not emulate his stoic detachment when she confronted Covenant and her son – and if they still refused her touch – she would be routed like a scatter of dried leaves.

Millennia ago, Covenant had promised that he would *never use power again*. But he was using power now: he was folding time. He might ask for his ring. Why else had he come so unexpectedly? He might demand—

And somehow Jeremiah had obtained his own magic.

If either of them accepted Linden's embrace now, she would certainly lose control of herself. And she feared the costs of her vulnerability.

At the end of the long tunnel down into the ramified convolutions of Revelstone, Linden, Stave, and Mahrtiir were met by Galt of the Humbled. He greeted them with a small inclination of his head, hardly a nod, and announced that he would guide the Chosen to speak with ur-Lord Thomas Covenant.

Linden paused to address Mahrtiir and Stave again. 'I have to do this alone.' Her voice was tight with trepidation. 'But I hope that you'll stay nearby, Stave.

'Mahrtiir, it might be a good idea to take Liand and the others to Glimmermere. Drink the water. Go swimming. Anele won't, but the rest of you will be better off.' Unnecessarily she added, 'There's a storm coming, but it doesn't feel like the kind of weather that can hurt you.'

When the Manethrall had bowed to her and walked away, she returned her attention to Galt.

'All right,' she said softly. 'Let's do this. I'm tired of waiting.'

Saying nothing, the Humbled led her and Stave into the intricate gutrock of Revelstone's secrets.

The way had been prepared for her, by the Masters if not by Revelstone's servants. Torches interspersed with oil lamps lit the unfamiliar halls, corridors, stairs. Some of the passages were blunt stone: others, strangely ornate, elaborated by Giants for reasons entirely their own. But the inadequate illumination left the details caliginous, obscure.

As Galt guided her downward and inward, she sensed that he was taking her towards the Keep's outer wall where it angled into the northwest from the watchtower. The complications of his route – abrupt turns, ascents instead of descents, corridors that seemed to double back on themselves – might have confused her; but her refreshed percipience protected her from disorientation. Concentrating acutely, she felt sure that she was nearing her destination when the Humbled steered her into a plain hallway where there were no more lamps or torches after the first score or so paces.

Beside the last lamp, a door indistinguishable from the one to Linden's quarters defined the wall of the corridor. She wanted to pause there, rally her courage, before she faced the uncertain possibilities behind the door. But when Galt knocked, a stone-muffled voice called promptly, 'Come in.'

Even through the barrier of rock, she seemed to recognise Covenant's stringent tone; his harsh commandments.

Without hesitation, Galt pressed the door open and gestured for Linden to enter.

Even then she might have faltered. But from beyond the doorway, she heard the faint crackle and snap of burning wood, saw firelight reflect redly off the stone. And there was another glow as well: not the flame of lamps or torches, but the tenebrous admixture of the fading day.

Such homely details steadied her. Very well: Thomas Covenant and her son were still human enough to want a fire against the residual chill of the stone, and to leave their windows open for the last daylight. She would be able to bear seeing them again.

Even if they still refused her touch—

For a brief moment, she braced herself on Stave's inflexible aura. Then she left him in the corridor. Biting her lip, she crossed the threshold into the chambers that the Masters had made available to Covenant and Jeremiah.

As she did so, Galt shut the door. He remained outside with Stave.

She found herself in a room larger than her own small quarters. A dozen or more people could have seated themselves comfortably around the walls: she saw almost that many stone chairs and wooden stools. Among them, a low table as large as the door held the remains of an abundant repast – bread and dried fruit, several kinds of cured meat, stew in a wide stoneware pot, and clay pitchers of both water and some other drink which smelled faintly of *aliantha* and beer. The floor was covered to the walls by a rough flaxen rug raddled to an ochre like that of the robe of the old man who should have warned her of her peril.

A large hearth shining with flames occupied part of the wall to her left. Above it hung a thick tapestry woven predominantly in blues and reds which must have been bright until time had dimmed their dyes. The colours depicted a stylised central figure surrounded by smaller scenes; but Linden recognised nothing about the arras, and did not try to interpret it.

Four other doors marked the walls. Three of them apparently gave access to chambers that she could not see: two bedrooms, perhaps, and a bathroom. But the fourth stood open directly opposite her, revealing a wide balcony with a crenellated parapet. Beyond the parapet, she could see a sky dimmed by late afternoon shadows.

On this side, Revelstone faced somewhat east of north. Here the cliffs which protected the Keep's wedge and the plateau cut off direct sunshine. From the balcony, the fields that fed Revelstone's inhabitants would be visible. And off to the right, along the wall towards the southeast, would be at least a glimpse of the massed horde of the Demondim.

Then Thomas Covenant said her name, and she could no longer gaze anywhere except at him – and at her son.

Her pulse hammered painfully in her chest as she stared at Covenant and Jeremiah. They were much as she had seen them in the forehall; too explicitly themselves to be anyone else despite their subtle alterations. Jeremiah sprawled with the unconsidered gracelessness of a teenager in one of the stone chairs, grinning with covert pleasure or glee. Although Lord Foul must have tortured him – must have been torturing him at this moment – his features retained their half undefined youth. But the imminent drooling which had marked his slack mouth for years was gone. An insistent tic at the corner of his left eye contradicted his relaxed posture.

His eyes themselves were the same muddy colour that they had always been: the hue of silted water. But now they focused keenly on his adoptive mother. He watched her avidly, as if he were studying her for signs of acceptance, understanding, love.

If Linden had seen him so in their lost life together, she would have wept for utter joy; would have hugged him until her heart broke apart and was made new. But now her fears – for him, of him – burned in her gaze, and the brief blurring of her vision was not gladness or grief: it was trepidation.

Tell her that I have her son.

He was closed to her, more entirely undecipherable than the *Haruchai*. Her health-sense could discern nothing of his physical or emotional condition. Past his blue pyjamas with their rearing horses, she searched his precious flesh for some sign of the fusillade which had ended her normal life. But the fabric had been torn in too many places, and his exposed skin wore too much grime, to reveal whether or not he had been shot.

Shot and healed.

To her ordinary sight, he looked well; as cared for and healthy as he had been before Roger Covenant took him. She did not know how that was possible. During their separation, he had been in the Despiser's power. She could not imagine that Lord Foul had attended to his needs.

Covenant claimed that he had *folded time*, that he and Jeremiah were *in two places at once. Or two realities.* But she had no idea how such a violation of Time had restored her son's physical well-being. Or his mind.

Covenant himself was sitting on a stool near Jeremiah. Her former lover had tilted the stool back on two legs so that he could lean against the wall. Lightly held by his left hand, a wooden flagon rested in his lap.

He, too, was smiling: a wry twist of his mouth etiolated by an uncharacteristic looseness in his mouth and cheeks. His gaze regarded her with an expression of dull appraisal. He was exactly the same man whom she had known for so long in the Land: lean to the point of gauntness; strictly formed; apt for extreme needs and catastrophes. The pale scar on his forehead suggested deeper wounds, hurts which he had borne without flinching. And yet he had never before given her the impression that he was not entirely present; that some covert aspect of his mind was fixed elsewhere.

His right arm hung, relaxed, at his side. Dangling, the fingers of his halfhand twitched as though they felt the absence of the ring that he had worn for so long.

'I'm sorry, Mom,' Jeremiah said, grinning. 'You still can't touch us.' He seemed to believe that he knew her thoughts. 'You've changed. You're even more powerful now. You'll make us vanish for sure.'

But he had misinterpreted her clenched frown, her deep consternation. She had forgotten nothing: his prohibition against contact held her as if she had been locked in the manacles of the ur-viles. Nevertheless her attention was focused on Covenant. The smaller changes in him seemed less comprehensible than her son's profound restoration.

Covenant nodded absently. 'Glimmermere,' he observed. 'I'm pretty damn strong, but I can't fight *that*.' His tongue slurred the edges of his words. 'Reality will snap back into place. Then we're *all* doomed.'

Was he—?

In a flat voice, a tone as neutral as she could make it, Linden asked, 'What are you drinking?'

Covenant peered into his flagon. 'This?' He took a long swallow, then set the flagon back in his lap. 'Springwine. You know, I actually forgot how good it tastes. I haven't been' – he grimaced – 'physical for a long time.' Then he suggested, 'You should try it. It might help you relax. You're so tense it hurts to look at you.'

Jeremiah started to giggle; stopped himself sharply.

Linden stepped to the edge of the table, bent down to a pitcher that smelled of treasure-berries and beer. The liquid looked clear, but its fermentation was obvious. Somehow the people of the Land had used the juice of *aliantha* to make an ale as refreshing as water from a mountain spring.

The Ramen believed that *No servant of Fangthane craves or will consume* aliantha. *The virtue of the berries is too potent.*

Facing Covenant again, she said stiffly, 'You're drunk.'

He shrugged, grimacing again. 'Hellfire, Linden. A man's got to unwind once in a while. With everything I'm going through right now, I've earned it.

'Anyway,' he added, 'Jeremiah's had as much as I have—'

'I have not,' retorted Jeremiah cheerfully.

'—and *he's* not drunk,' Covenant continued. 'Just look at him.' As if to himself, he muttered, 'Maybe when he swallows it ends up in his other stomach. The one where he's still Foul's prisoner.'

Linden shook her head. Covenant's behaviour baffled her. For that very reason, however, she grew calmer. His strangeness enabled her to reclaim a measure of the professional detachment with which she had for years listened to the oblique ramblings of the psychotic and the deranged: dissociated observations, warnings, justifications, all intended to both conceal and expose underlying sources of pain. She did not suddenly decide that Covenant was insane: she could not. He was too much himself to be evaluated in that way. But she began to hear him as if from a distance. As if she had erected a wall between him and her denied anguish – or had hidden her distress in a room like the secret place where her access to wild magic lurked.

Her tone was deliberately impersonal as she replied, 'You said that you wanted to talk to me. Are you in any condition to explain things?'

'What,' Covenant protested, 'you think a little alcohol can slow me down? Linden, you're forgetting who I *am*. The keystone of the Arch of Time, remember? I know everything. Or I can, if I make the effort.'

He seemed to consider the air, trying to choose an example. Then he turned his smeared gaze towards her again.

'You've been to Glimmermere. And you've talked to Esmer. Him and something like a hundred ur-viles and Waynhim. Tell me. Why do *you* think they're here? I don't care what he said. He was just trying to justify himself. What do *you* think?'

Disturbed by his manner, Linden kept her reactions to herself. Instead of answering, she said cautiously, 'I have no idea. He took me by surprise. I don't know how to think about it.'

Covenant snorted. 'Don't let him confuse you. It's really pretty simple. He likes to talk about "aid and betrayal", but with him it's mostly betrayal. Listening to him is a waste of time.'

While Covenant spoke, Jeremiah took his racecar from the waistband of his pyjamas and began to roll the toy over and around the fingers and palm of his halfhand as if he were practising a conjuring trick; as if he meant to make the car vanish like a coin from the hand of a magician.

Covenant's awareness of her encounter with Esmer startled Linden; but she clung to her protective detachment. 'You know what he said to me?'

You must be the first to drink of the EarthBlood. Did Covenant understand what Esmer meant?

'Probably,' Covenant drawled. 'Most of it, anyway. But it's better if you tell me.'

He was Thomas Covenant: she did not question that. But she did not know how to trust him now. Carefully she replied, 'He said that the ur-viles and Waynhim want to serve me.'

'How?' Suddenly he was angry. 'By joining up with all those Demondim? Hell and blood, Linden. Use your brain. They were *created* by the Demondim, for God's sake. Even the Waynhim can't forget that, no matter how hard they try. They were *created* evil. And the ur-viles have been Foul's servants ever since they met him.'

'They made Vain,' she countered as if she were speaking to one of her patients. Without the ur-viles, her Staff of Law would not exist.

'And you think that's a *good* thing?' Covenant demanded. 'Sure, you stopped the Sunbane. But it would have faded out on its own after a while. It needed the Banefire. And since then mostly what that thing you insist on carrying around has done is make my job a hell of a lot harder.

'Damn it, Linden, if you hadn't taken my ring and made that Staff, I would have been able to fix everything *ages* ago. I could have stopped time around Foul right where he was when you left the Land. Then Kastenessen would still be stuck in his Durance, and the *skurj* would still be trapped, and Kevin's Dirt wouldn't exist, and Foul wouldn't have been able to find that chink in Joan's mind, and we wouldn't have *caesures* and Demondim and ur-viles and Esmer and the bloody Illearth *Stone* to worry about. Not to mention some of the *other* powers that have noticed what's happening here and want to take advantage of it.

'Hellfire, I know you like that Staff. You're probably even proud of it. But you have *no idea* what it's costing me.' He glanced over at Jeremiah. 'Or your son.'

Jeremiah nodded without raising his eyes from the racecar tumbling in his halfhand.

'What do you think I'm *doing* here?' Covenant finished. 'I'm still trying to clean up your mess.'

Linden flinched in spite of her self-discipline. He held her responsible—? She wanted to protest, But you said—!

In her dreams, he had told her, *You need the Staff of Law.*

And through Anele, he had urged her to *find* him. *I can't help you unless you find me.*

Yet he was the one who had found her.

'It's awful, Mom,' Jeremiah said softly as if he were talking to his car. 'There aren't any words for what it feels like. Words aren't strong enough. The Despiser is ripping me to pieces. And I can't stop him. Covenant can't stop him. He just keeps hurting me and laughing like he's never had so much fun.'

Oh, my son!

Linden bit her lip and forced herself to face Covenant again. She was beginning to understand why he had warned her to be wary of him. The man whom she had loved would never have held her accountable for consequences which she could not have foreseen.

Nevertheless the discrepancy between her recollections and his attitudes helped her to regain her balance. In a moment, the impact of his recrimination was gone; hidden away. She would consider it later. For the present, she stood her ground.

As she had so often with her patients, she responded to his ire by trying to alter the direction of their interaction, attempting to slip past his defences. She hoped to surprise some revelation from him which he could or would not offer voluntarily.

Instead of defending herself, she asked mildly, as if he had not hurt her, 'How did you get that scar on your forehead? I don't think you ever told me.'

Covenant's manner or his mood was as labile as Esmer's. His anger seemed to fade into a brume of springwine. Rubbing at his forehead with his halfhand, he grinned sheepishly. 'You know, I've forgotten. Isn't that weird? You'd think I'd remember what happened to my own body. But I've been away from myself for so long—' His voice faded to a sigh. 'So full of time—' Then he seemed to shake himself. Emptying his flagon with one long draught, he refilled it and set it in his lap again. 'Maybe that's why this stuff tastes so much better than I remember.'

Linden paid no attention to his reply: she heeded only his manner. Deliberately casual, she changed the subject again.

'Esmer mentioned manacles.'

His response was not what she expected. 'Exactly,' he sighed as if he were drowsy with drink. 'And who do you think they're for? Not you. Of course not. Those ur-viles are here to serve you.' His tone scarcely hinted at sarcasm. 'No, Linden, the manacles are for me. That's why Esmer brought his creatures here. That's how they're going to help their makers. And Foul. By stopping me before we can do what we have to do to save the Land.'

Although she tried to conceal her reaction, she flinched. What she knew of the ur-viles and Waynhim led her to believe that they were her allies; that she could rely on them. But what she knew of Esmer urged doubt. The creatures that had enabled her to retrieve the Staff of Law and reach Revelstone had clearly accepted the newcomers. But if both groups wished to serve her because they felt sure that she would fail the Land – if their real purpose, and Esmer's, hinged on stopping Covenant—

She could not sustain her detachment in the face of such possibilities. They were too threatening; and the truth was beyond her grasp. She had no sortilege for such determinations. The Demondim-spawn had done so much to earn her trust– If she had not witnessed Esmer's conflicted treachery, she might have concluded that Covenant was lying.

Trembling inside, she turned away from her former lover. Her lost son was here as well. Even if he, too, blamed her for the Land's plight, she yearned to talk to him.

He had regained his mind at the cost of more torment than he could describe.

Carefully she leaned the Staff against the wall near the hearth. Although she craved its comforting touch, she wanted to show Jeremiah that he was in no danger from her. Then she took one of the stools and placed it so that she could sit facing him. Leaning forward with her elbows braced on her knees, she focused all of her attention on him; closed her mind to Thomas Covenant.

'Jeremiah, honey,' she asked quietly, intently, 'were you shot?'

Jeremiah wrapped his hand around his toy. For a moment, he appeared to consider trying to crush the racecar in his fist; and the pulse at the corner of his eye became more urgent. But then he returned the car to the waistband of his pyjamas. Lifting his head, he faced Linden with his soiled gaze.

'You really should ask *him*, Mom.' Her son nodded towards Covenant. 'He's the one with all the answers.' He shrugged uncomfortably. 'I'm just here.'

As if he were speaking to himself, Covenant murmured, 'You know, that tapestry is pretty amazing. I think it's the same one they had in my room the first time I came here. Somehow it survived for seven thousand years. Not to mention the fact that it must have been old when I first saw it.'

Linden ignored the Unbeliever. 'Jeremiah, listen to me.' Intensity throbbed in her voice: she could not stifle it. 'I need to know. Were you shot?'

Could she still attempt to save his former life? Was it possible that he might return to the world in which he belonged?

'Maybe they didn't keep it in the Hall of Gifts,' Covenant mused. 'There was a lot of damage when we fought Gibbon. Maybe they stored the tapestry in the Aumbrie. That might explain why it hasn't fallen apart.'

Jeremiah hesitated briefly before he replied, 'I'm not sure. Something knocked me down pretty hard, I remember that. But there wasn't any pain.' Reflexively he rubbed at the muscle beating in the corner of his eye. 'I mean, not at first. Not until Lord Foul started talking—

'It's strange. Nothing *here*' – he pressed both palms against his chest – 'hurts. In *this* time – or this version of reality – I'm fine. But that only makes it worse. Pain is worse when you have something to compare it to—'

Covenant was saying, 'That's Berek there in the centre. The o-*rigi*-nal Halfhand. He's doing his "beatitude and striving" thing, peace in the midst of desperate struggle. Whatever *that* means. And the rest tells his story.'

Linden's gaze burned. If she could have lowered her defences – if she could have borne the cost of her emotions, any of them – she would have wept. Jeremiah conveyed impressions which made her want to tear at her own flesh for simple distraction, so that she would feel some other suffering than his.

Her voice threatened to choke her as she asked, 'Do you know where you are? In that other reality?'

'That Queen there,' Covenant explained, 'turned against her King when she found out he was human enough to actually like power. And Berek was loyal to her. He fought on her side until the King beat him. Cut his hand in half. After which Berek tried to escape. He ran for Mount Thunder. That scene shows his despair. Or maybe it was just self-pity. And in that one, the Fire-Lions come to his rescue.'

Jeremiah shook his head. 'It's dark.' Like Linden, he seemed to ignore Covenant. 'Sometimes there's fire, and I'm in the middle of it. But there isn't really anything to see. It could be anywhere.'

'So you don't know where Lord Foul is?' she insisted. 'You can't tell me where to look for you?'

Until she found him, she could do nothing to end his torture.

'It all started there,' Covenant went on, 'the whole history of the Lords with their grand ideals and their hopeless mistakes. Even Foul's plotting started there – in the Land, anyway. Not directly, of course. Oh, he sent out a shadow to help the King against Berek. But he didn't show himself then. For centuries, the Lords were too pure to feel Berek's despair. Just remembering Berek's victories was enough to protect Damelon – and Loric too, at least for a while. Foul couldn't risk anything overt until

Kevin inherited a real talent for doubt from his father. But even that was Foul's doing. He used the Viles and the Demondim to undermine Loric's confidence, plant the seeds of failure. By the time Kevin became High Lord, he was already doomed.'

'I'm sorry, Mom.' Jeremiah's tone was like his eyes: it suggested solid earth eroded by the irresistible rush of his plight. 'I want to help you. I really do. I want you to make it stop. But as far as I know, I just fell into a pit, and I've been there ever since. It could be anywhere. Even Covenant doesn't know where I am.'

Linden clenched herself against the distraction of Covenant's obscure commentary. She needed all of her strength to withstand the force and sharpness of her empathy for her son.

'Poor Kevin,' Covenant sighed unkindly. 'He didn't recognise Foul because no one in the Land knew who the Despiser was. No one told Berek, and his descendants didn't figure it out for themselves. While Foul was hard at work in Ridjeck Thome and Kurash Qwellinir, the Lords didn't even know he existed. Kevin actually let him join the Council, and *still* no one saw the truth.

'I suppose it's understandable,' the older man added. 'Foul confused the hell out of them. Of course, he didn't use his real name. That would have been too obvious. He called himself a-Jeroth until it was too late for anyone to stop him. And he's pretty damn good at getting what he wants by misdirection. He always *acts* like he's after something completely different.'

Gritting her teeth, Linden continued her questions. 'That's all right, honey,' she assured Jeremiah. 'Maybe you can tell me something else that might help me.

'I don't understand why' – she swallowed convulsively – 'why that other reality doesn't show. You said that you're fine here. How is that possible, if Foul is still torturing you?'

Despite the damage to his pyjamas, he seemed entirely intact.

'It's sort of funny,' remarked Covenant. 'Do you know the real reason Kevin let Foul talk him into the Ritual of Desecration? It wasn't because Foul defeated him. Kevin hated that, but he could have lived with it. He still had enough of Berek's blood in him. But Foul beat him before the war even started. What really broke him is that he let his best friends, his most loyal supporters, get killed in his place.'

'He's doing it,' Jeremiah answered. Again he nodded towards Covenant. 'He's doing something with time to protect me while I'm here.' The boy's gaze slipped out of focus as if he were concentrating on his other self in its prison. 'He's keeping me whole. That's another reason you can't touch me. He's using more power for me than he is for himself. A lot more.'

Covenant's voice held a hint of relish as he explained, 'The Demondim invited him to a parley in Mount Thunder. Naturally he suspected it was a trap. He didn't go. But then he felt ashamed of himself for thinking that way, so he sent his friends instead. And of course it *was* a trap. His friends were slaughtered.

'That,' Covenant finished in a tone of sodden triumph, 'is what made Kevin crazy enough to think he had something to gain by desecrating the Land. Losing the war just confirmed his opinion of himself. The legends all say he thought the Ritual would destroy Foul, but that's a rationalisation. The truth is, he wanted to be punished, and he couldn't think of anything else bad enough to give him what he deserved.'

Linden wished that she did not believe Jeremiah. Everything that he said – everything that happened in this room – was inconceivable to her. She had not forgotten his unaccountable theurgy. And the Ranyhyn had shown her horrific images of her son *possessed*— But of course she did believe him. How could she not? He was her *son*, speaking to her for the first time in his life. His presence, and his healed mind, were all that enabled her to retain some semblance of self-control.

And because she believed Jeremiah, she could not doubt Covenant. He knew too much.

At last she brought herself to her most urgent question.

'Jeremiah, honey, I don't understand any of this. It's incredible – and wonderful.' It was also terrible. Yet how could she regret anything that allowed him to acknowledge her? 'But I don't understand it.

'How did you get your mind back? And when? How long have you been—?'

'You mean,' he interrupted, 'how long have I been able to talk?' Now he did not meet her gaze. Instead he looked at Covenant as if he needed help. 'Since we came to the Land.'

'Linden,' Covenant suggested, his voice sloppy with springwine, 'you should ask him where his mind has been all this time. He made it pretty obvious that he always *had* a mind. Where do you suppose it was?'

Linden kept her eyes and her heart fixed on her son. 'Jeremiah? Can you tell me?'

So far, he had revealed nothing that might aid her.

He twitched his shoulders awkwardly. The tic of his eye increased its thetic signalling. 'It's hard to explain. For a while' – he sighed – 'I don't know how long, I was sort of hiding. It was like a different version of being in two places at once. Except the other place wasn't anywhere in particular. It was just *away*.' Flames empty of daylight gave his face a ruddy flush, made him look feverish. 'It was safe.

'But then you gave me that racecar set with all the tracks and pylons. When it was done – when you gave me enough pieces, and they were all connected in the right shapes – I had a' – he clung to Covenant with his eyes – 'a loop. Like a worm that eats its own tail. I guess you could call it a door in my mind. I went through it. And when I did that, I came here.

'I don't mean "here" the way I am now.' He seemed to grope for words. 'I wasn't a prisoner. I wasn't even physical. And I didn't come *here* – I mean to Revelstone – very often. There wasn't anybody I could talk to. But I was in the Land. I'm not sure when. I mean when in relation to now. Mostly I think it was a long time ago. But I was here pretty much whenever you put me to bed.

'The only people I could talk to – the only people who knew I was there – were powers like the *Elohim* and the Ravers. There were a few wizards, something like that. I met some people who called themselves the Insequent. And there was him.' Jeremiah clearly meant Covenant. 'He was the best. But even he couldn't explain very much. He didn't know how to answer me. Or I didn't know how to ask the right questions. Mostly we just talked about the way I make things.

'Once in a while, people warned me about the Despiser. Maybe I should have been scared. But I wasn't. I had no idea what they meant. And I never met him. He stayed away.'

Linden reeled as she listened. Insequent? If she had tried to stand, she would have staggered. *Ravers?* But she held herself motionless; allowed no flicker of her face or flinch of her muscles to interrupt her son.

He had known Covenant for a long time; perhaps since he had first completed his racetrack construct. – the best.

'But Mom,' Jeremiah added more strongly, 'it was *so* much better than where I was with you. I loved being in the Land. And I loved it when people knew I was there. Even the Ravers. They would have hurt me if they could – but *they knew I was there*. I don't remember feeling *real* before I started coming here.'

She did not realise that tears were spilling from her eyes, or that a knot of grief and joy had closed her throat, until Jeremiah said, 'Please don't cry, Mom. I didn't mean to upset you.' Now he sounded oddly distant, almost mechanical, as if he were quoting something – or someone. His tic lost some of its fervour; and as the flames in the hearth slowly dwindled, the hectic flush faded from his cheeks. 'You said you didn't understand. I'm just trying to explain.'

For his sake, Linden mastered herself. 'Don't worry about me, honey.' Sitting up straight, she wiped her eyes on the sleeve of her shirt. 'I cry too easily. It's embarrassing. I'm just so glad—!' She sniffed helplessly. 'And sad too. I'm glad you haven't been alone all this time, even if you couldn't talk to me.' When he had crafted Revelstone and Mount Thunder in her living room, he had known exactly what he was doing. 'And I'm sad' – she swallowed a surge of empathy and outrage – 'because this makes being Foul's prisoner so much worse. Now there's nowhere you can be safe.

'I swear to you, honey. I'm never going to stop searching for you. And when I find out where you are, there isn't anything in this world that's going to prevent me from rescuing you.'

Jeremiah squirmed in his chair, apparently embarrassed by the passion of her avowal. 'You should talk to *him* about that.' Again he meant Covenant. 'He can't tell you where I am. Lord Foul has me hidden somehow. But he knows everything else. If you just give him a chance—'

Her son's voice trailed away. His gaze avoided hers.

For a long moment, Linden did not move. In spite of his discomfort, she probed him with every dimension of her senses, trying to see past the barriers which concealed him. Yet her percipience remained useless with him. He was sealed against her.

The ur-Lord has ever been closed to the Haruchai. *And his companion is likewise hidden.*

'All right,' she told Jeremiah finally. 'I'll do that.'

Slapping her palms on her thighs in an effort to shift her attention, she rose to her feet and retrieved the Staff. With its clean wood almost delitescent in her hands, its lenitive powers obscured, she took a few steps across the fading light of the room so that she could confront Covenant directly.

Her detachment was gone; but she had other strengths.

When Covenant dragged his gaze up from his flagon, she began harshly, 'You're the one with all the answers. Start by telling me why you're *doing* this. I mean to *him*.' She indicated Jeremiah. 'He hurts worse when he feels it like this,' from the outside. He had said so. 'If you really have the answers, you don't need him. You're making him suffer for nothing.'

After everything that he had already endured—

'For God's sake,' she protested, 'he's just a *boy*. He didn't choose any of this. *Tell* me you have a good reason for causing him more pain.'

Covenant's mien had a drowsy cast in the dying firelight. He seemed to be falling asleep where he sat. In a blurred voice, he replied as if his reasons should have been obvious to her, 'I did it so you would trust me.

'I know how this looks to you, Linden. I know I'm not the way you remember me. Too much has happened. And I'm under too much strain—' He lifted his shoulders wearily. 'I knew how you would react when you saw how much I've changed. So I tried to think of something – I don't know what to call it – something to demonstrate my good faith.

'I wanted to show you I can give him back. I have that much power. And I know how to do it. If you just trust me.'

'But he—' she objected, trying to find words for her dismay.

'—isn't any worse off than he was before,' Covenant sighed. 'Not really. If you think what I've done is so terrible, ask him if he regrets being here. Ask him if he regrets *anything*.'

Before Linden could turn to her son, Jeremiah said, 'He's right, Mom. I don't regret it, any of it. If he hadn't brought me with him, I wouldn't be able to see you. We couldn't talk. I wouldn't know you're trying so hard to rescue me.'

Jeremiah's response struck her indignation to dust. For at least half of his life, he had given her no direct sign that he was aware of her protective presence – yet now he was willing to endure torments and anguish so that he could speak to her. She had not lavished her love on him in vain.

While she struggled with her emotions, Covenant continued, 'I can see what happened to you. That hole in your shirt makes it pretty obvious. And I know you're worried about him. I can understand that.' He sounded strangely like a man who was trying to convince himself. 'Unfortunately I can't tell you if he was shot. I would if I could. But I wasn't there. I'm not part of that reality.'

Slowly Linden regained her resolve. She had lost her detachment, and Jeremiah had rendered her protests meaningless. But she was still herself; still able to think and act. And Covenant's answers disturbed her. They were like a song sung slightly out of tune: instead of soaring, they grated.

She took a moment to turn away and toss another couple of logs onto the fire. She needed better light. Her health-sense was useless: she had to rely on ordinary sight and hearing.

As the new wood began to blaze, she faced the Unbeliever once more. 'All right,' she said unsteadily. 'You can't tell me if Jeremiah was shot. You can't tell me where he is. What *can* you tell me?'

Covenant squinted vaguely at the rising flames. 'What do you want to know?'

Linden did not hesitate. 'It was Kastenessen who convinced the Demondim to let my friends and me reach Revelstone. You said that you and Jeremiah were able to get here because you tricked them.' *I put a crimp in their reality.* 'But how can I be sure that *that* wasn't Kastenessen's doing too?'

Earlier she had believed that Covenant and Jeremiah were being herded rather than pursued.

She expected a flare of anger; but Covenant only peered into his flagon as though its contents meant more to him than her implied accusation. 'Because he didn't know we were coming. He couldn't. I didn't start on all this – what we're doing now – until I knew you were safe.

'When he realised we were on our way here—' Covenant offered her a slack smile. 'That made him mad as hell. He was beside himself.' Turning his head, he winked at Jeremiah. 'Practically in two places at once.' When Jeremiah grinned, Covenant returned his attention to his flagon. 'But you have to remember– He can't *communicate* with those damn monsters. The only way he can talk to them is through the old man.' Covenant shrugged. 'Since yesterday, that poor lunatic hasn't been available.'

Abruptly Linden sagged. Hardly aware of what she did, she sank into a chair. Relief left her weak. Deep in her heart, she had been so afraid– Now Covenant had given her a reason to believe in him.

But he was not done. While she tried to gather herself, he said, 'You might ask why I didn't make us just appear *here*.' He sounded dull with drink; sleepy; almost bored. 'Riding in ahead of the Demondim was pretty risky. But I wanted a chance to mess with their reality. They can use the damn Illearth Stone whenever they want. I had to make sure they didn't attack too soon.

'And I was afraid of you.' He drank again, unsteadily. A little spring-wine sloshed down his cheeks. 'If we took you by surprise – if you didn't see us coming – you might do something to erase us. I couldn't take that chance.' He nodded towards Jeremiah. 'This isn't something I could do twice. Kastenessen knows about us now. Hellfire, Linden, Foul himself knows. Neither of them would have any trouble stopping us. Not when I'm stretched this thin.'

By degrees, Linden's weakness ebbed. At last, something made sense to her. She could follow Covenant's explanation. Only the imprecise pitch of his voice inhibited her from believing him completely.

Because of his strangeness, she found an unforeseen comfort in the knowledge that he had reason to fear her.

When he was done, she nodded. 'All right. I get that. But I had to ask. I'm sure you understand.'

For a moment, Jeremiah turned his grin on her. But Covenant did not reply. Instead he replenished his flagon.

With an effort, she mustered a different question. She had so many– If she did not keep him talking, he might drink himself to sleep.

'So what's it like?' she asked quietly. 'Being part of the Arch of Time?'

'I'm sorry, Linden.' He raised his flagon as if he were driving himself towards unconsciousness. 'It's like Jeremiah's pain. There aren't any words for it. It's too vast, and I'm everywhere at once.

'I feel like I know the One Forest and the Worm of the World's End and even,' he drawled, 'poor ol' Lord Foul better than I know myself. If you asked me the names of all the Sandgorgons – or what Berek had for breakfast the day he turned against his King – I could probably tell you. If I didn't have to work so hard just to stay where I am. And,' he concluded, 'if I actually cared about things like that.'

Studying him closely – the increasing looseness of his cheeks, the deepening glaze in his eyes, the mounting slur of his speech – Linden said, 'Then I'll try to be more specific. I don't understand why the *caesures* haven't already destroyed everything.

'Joan's using wild magic. And she's out of her mind, you know that. God, Covenant, it seems to me that just one Fall ought to be enough to undo the whole world. But she's made dozens of them by now. Or hundreds.' Ever since Linden had restored her wedding band. 'How can the Arch survive that? How can you? Why hasn't everybody and everything that's ever existed already been sucked away?'

Surely Anele, a handful of ur-viles and Kevin's Watch were not the only victims of Joan's agony?

Covenant lifted his unmaimed hand and peered at it; extended his fingers as though he meant to enumerate a list of reasons. But then he appeared to forget what he was doing, or to lose interest in it. Returning his hand to his lap and the handle of his flagon, he answered dully, 'Because the Law of Time is still fighting to protect itself. Because *I'm* still fighting to protect it. And because *caesures* have limits. They wouldn't be so easy to make if the Laws of Death and Life hadn't been damaged. Before that, everything was intact. So there's a kind of barrier in the Land's past. It restricts how far back the *caesures* tend to go.

'Joan's too far gone to know what she's doing. She can't sustain anything. So most of her *caesures* don't last very long. If they aren't kept going by some other power – like the Demondim – they fade pretty quickly. And they don't usually reach as far back as the Sunbane. That gives the Law of Time a chance to reassert itself. It gives me room to work.'

Covenant's air of drowsiness grew as he continued, 'Plus her *caesures* are localised. They only cover a certain amount of ground, and they move around. She's too crazy to make them do anything else. Wherever they are at a particular moment, every bit of time in that precise spot happens at once. For the last three millennia, anyway. But since they're moving, they give those bits of time back as fast as they pick up new ones.'

Abruptly his head dropped, and Linden feared for a moment that he had fallen asleep. But then he seemed to rally. His head jerked up. He widened his eyes to the firelight; blinked them several times; stared at her owlishly.

'But the *real* reason,' he continued, 'is what the Lords called "the necessity of freedom".' For some reason, he sounded bitter. 'Wild magic is only as powerful as the will, the determination, of the person it belongs to. The rightful white gold wielder.

'In the wrong hands, it's still pretty strong. Which is why *you* can create Falls with it' – the statement was a sneer— 'and why Foul was able to kill me. But it doesn't really come alive until the person it belongs to *chooses* to use it. Foul might not even have been able to kill me if I hadn't given him my ring voluntarily. And I did not choose to destroy the Arch.' Covenant's tone suggested that now he wondered why he had bothered to choose at all. 'Since he wasn't the rightful wielder, the power he unleashed only made me stronger.

'Well,' he snorted, 'Joan *is* the rightful wielder of her ring. But she isn't choosing anything. All she's really trying to do is scream. *Turiya* has her. He feeds her pain. But that only aggravates her craziness. He can't make her *choose* because she's already lost. Oh, he could force her to hand her ring to someone else. But it wouldn't be *her* choice. And the ring wouldn't belong to whoever got it.'

Covenant drank again, and his manner resumed its drift towards somnolence. 'For what Foul really wants, Joan and her ring are pretty much useless. They're just a gambit. A ploy. The danger is real enough, but it won't set him free. Or help him accomplish any of his other goals. He's counting on you for that. It's all about manipulating you so you'll serve him.'

The idea made Linden wince. His other goals– Through Anele, the

Despiser had suggested that he did not merely wish to escape the Arch of Time. *There is more*, he had said, *but of my deeper purpose I will not speak.*

'Serve him how?' Fear which she could not suppress undermined her voice.

'You'll have to ask *him*,' Covenant said through a yawn. 'He hides from me in all kinds of ways. I can't tell where he's keeping Jeremiah, or where he is himself, or what he thinks you're going to do. All I know for sure is, the danger's real. And I can stop it.'

In spite of her concern, Linden recognised her cue: she was supposed to ask him how. He had blamed her for everything that had happened since she had formed her Staff. Now he would offer to ease her guilt and responsibility.

She assumed that he wanted his ring. How else could he possibly intervene in the Despiser's designs? Surely he needed his instrument of power? It belonged to him.

Like Joan, he could not exert wild magic without his ring.

With it a master may form perfect works and fear nothing.

But she was not ready for that. Not yet. She could not rid herself of the sensation that he was speaking off-key; that his attitude or his drinking obliquely falsified whatever he said. And the fact that he had not already asked for his ring – or demanded it – troubled her. So far, he had given her explanations which made sense. Nevertheless, instinctively, she suspected him of misdirection. In spite of her relief, her apprehension was growing.

Instead of following his lead, she said, 'Wait a minute. You're getting ahead of me. I think I understand why the *caesures* haven't destroyed everything. But are you also saying that they *won't*? That they *can't* break the Arch?'

Covenant's head lolled towards Jeremiah. 'I told you she was going to do this,' he remarked. 'Didn't I tell you she was going to do this?'

Jeremiah grinned at him. 'That's my Mom.'

Nodding, the Unbeliever faced Linden again. 'You're just like I remember you. You never let anything go.'

He spread his hands as if to show her that he was helpless. 'Oh, eventually they'll destroy everything. You've been through two of them now.

You know what they're like. Part of what they do is take you inside the mind of whoever created them. You've been in Joan's mind. You should ask that callow puppy who follows you around what it's like being in *your* mind.'

Before she could react to his sarcasm, he added, 'Another part, the part that feels like hornets burrowing into your skin, is time itself. It's all those broken moments being stirred together.

'And *another* part – the part that's just freezing cold emptiness for-ever—' Covenant made a visible effort to appear earnest. 'Linden, that's the future. The eventual outcome of Joan's craziness. Even that probably won't bring down the Arch. But there won't be anything left inside it. No Land, no Earth, no beings of any kind, no past or present or future. No *life*. Just freezing cold emptiness that can't escape to consume eternity because it's still being contained.'

Involuntarily Linden shivered. She remembered too well the feature-less wasteland within the Falls, gelid and infinitely unrelieved. She herself had created an instance of that future – and she could not claim the excuse that she had not known what she was doing.

'All right,' she acceded. 'I think I understand.' Instead of probing him further, she gave him the question that he had tried to prompt from her. 'But how can you stop any of this? You said that you know what to do. What do you mean?'

Wild magic was the keystone of the Arch of Time. How could he step out of his position within its structure – exist *in two places at once* – and wield power, any kind of power, without causing that structure to crumble?

Earlier in the day, Esmer had said, *That which appears evil need not have been so from the beginning, and need not remain so until the end.* Had he intended his peroration about the Viles and their descendants as a kind of parable? An oblique commentary on the discrepancy between who Covenant was and how he behaved?

'Hell and blood, Linden,' Covenant slurred. 'Of *course* I know what to do. Why else do you suppose I'm here? You can't possibly believe I'm putting myself through all this' – he gestured vaguely around the room – 'not to mention everything I have to do to protect the Arch – just because I want to watch you try to talk yourself out of trusting me.'

'Then tell me.' Tell me that you want your ring. Tell me what I can do to rescue my son. 'Tell me how you're going to save the Land.'

She wanted to speak more strongly; ached for the simple self-assurance to jar him out of his lethargy. But he baffled her. And the eroded look in Jeremiah's eyes seemed to leach away her determination. She had no firm ground under her: yearning weakened her wherever she tried to place her feet.

Covenant squinted, apparently trying to bring his glazed vision into focus. 'That depends on you.'

'*How?*' She gripped the Staff with both hands so that they would not quaver. 'All I have is questions. I don't have any answers.'

'But you have this one,' he said like a sigh. His gaze drifted to the hearth; filled itself with reflected flames. 'That ring under your shirt belongs to me. Are you going to give it to me or not?'

Linden lowered her head to hide her sudden chagrin. She had expected his request; had practically demanded it. But now she realised that she did not know how to respond. How could she make such a choice? His ring was all that she had left of the man whom she had loved: it meant too much to her. And she *wanted* it; wanted every scrap of power or effectiveness that she could obtain. Through Anele, Covenant himself had told her that she would need it.

But if Covenant had indeed been perfected in death, so that he could wield wild magic without fear, she had no right to refuse him. He might be capable of re-creating the entire Earth in any image that he desired. If she kept his wedding band, she would bear the blame for all of the Land's peril and Jeremiah's suffering and her own plight.

'Just hand it over,' Covenant continued as reasonably as his sleepy voice allowed. 'Then you can stop worrying about everything. Even Jeremiah. I'm already part of the Arch. With my ring, there won't be anything I can't do. Send the Demondim back where they belong? No problem. Finish off Kastenessen so he and the *skurj* and Kevin's Dirt can't bother us anymore? Consider it done. Create a cyst in time around Foul to make him helpless forever? I won't even break a sweat.

'All you have to do,' he insisted with more force, 'is stop dithering and give me the damn ring. You'll get your son back, and your troubles will be over.'

He held out his halfhand, urging her to place his ring in his palm.

The Thomas Covenant who had spoken to her in her dreams would not have asked for his ring in that way. He would have explained more and demanded less; would have been more gentle—

Almost involuntarily, she looked to Jeremiah for help, guidance. But his attention was focused on Covenant: he did not so much as glance at her.

And in the background of Covenant's voice, she heard Roger saying outside Joan's room in Berenford Memorial, *It belongs to me. I need it.*

Once before, Linden had restored a white gold ring. Directly or indirectly, that mistake had led her to her present straits. It had made possible her son's imprisonment in agony.

'Covenant, this is hard for me.' A tremor of supplication and dread marred her voice: she could not control it. 'I need to know more about what it *means*.

'You swore to me. After the Banefire. You swore that you were never going to use power again.'

'That was then.' His brief intensity faded as the springwine seemed to renew its numbness. 'This is now. In case you haven't noticed, everything's changed. Just being here uses staggering amounts of power. And how do you suppose I stopped Foul after I surrendered my ring? For something like forever, I've done nothing *but* use power.'

Linden could not argue with him. But his response was not enough. 'Then tell me this,' she said, groping for knowledge that might shed light on her dilemma. 'Where did Jeremiah get the force to push me away?' As far as she knew, her son had no lore – and no instrument of theurgy. His only inherent magic was his need for her; his ability to inspire her love. 'When did he become powerful?'

'Oh, that.' Covenant flapped his halfhand dismissively. 'He has talents you can't imagine. All he needs is the right stuff to work with. In this case, folding time – being in two places at once – I'm bending a lot of Laws. There's bound to be a certain amount of leakage. Think of it like blood from a wound. Your kid is using it. As long as I can keep him here – as long as you don't *erase* us' – for an instant, his eyes flickered redly – 'he's pretty strong.'

Again his voice conveyed the impression that it was out of tune; that he could not find the right notes for what he said.

Without looking away from Covenant, Jeremiah put in, 'I've been visiting the Land for a long time, Mom. I learned a lot about magic. But it didn't do me any good until Covenant brought me here.' His smile was not for Linden. 'I mean to Revelstone. Until he gave me my mind back.

'I can't make something out of nothing. But when I have the right materials, I can build all kinds of doors. And walls.'

Both of them were trying to reassure her, but her alarm increased nonetheless. She could not doubt them, and did not know how to believe them. Her son had become a kind of mage, incomprehensible to her. And Covenant sounded—

Doom seemed to ride on all of her choices, and she had not been convinced.

'So what happens,' she asked, still trembling, 'if I don't give up your ring? What will you do if I refuse? Take it?'

Had he changed that much?

If she spurned Covenant's aid, she might spend days or weeks or months hunting for Jeremiah's prison. She would almost certainly fail to reach him in time to save his tortured mind.

Covenant dropped his hand; looked down to drink from his flagon, then turned his head to meet Jeremiah's silted gaze. 'I told you that, too, didn't I?' His voice was full of dreary bitterness. 'I told you she wouldn't trust me.'

Jeremiah nodded. 'Yes, you did.'

Still facing the boy, Covenant informed Linden sourly, 'Of *course* I'm not going to take it. I can't get that close to you. But I *know* you, so I came prepared. I still know what to do.'

Slowly he swung back towards her; but he did not meet her gaze. His head hung at a defeated angle, and the firelight cast shadows across his eyes. A faint red heat like embers glowed in the depths of his darkened eyes.

'If you won't let me have my ring, what *will* you do? What do you think you can accomplish? You've got Esmer and a hundred or so ur-viles on one side, and the Demondim with the Illearth Stone on the other. Kevin's Dirt is going to blind you over and over again. You don't know where to look for Jeremiah. Joan will keep making *caesures*. Kastenessen

and the *skurj* are out there, not to mention the *Elohim* and who knows
how many other powers. The Masters don't like you, and your only
friends are three Ramen, a crazy old man, a kid who's as ignorant as a
stone and one outcast *Haruchai*.

'What exactly do you propose to do about all that?'

Linden hardly knew how to face him; yet she did not fall or falter.
Instead she held up her head, drew back her shoulders. If Covenant
thought to daunt her with his recitation of dangers, he had forgotten
their time together; forgotten who she had become. And he could not
weaken her by disdaining her friends. She knew them better than he
did.

He was asking her about decisions which she had already made.

Searching his hidden eyes for embers, she announced as though she
were certain, 'I'll put a stop to the Demondim. Then I'm going to take
my friends and ride like hell to Andelain. I want to talk to the Dead.
They helped you once when you had no idea how to save the Land.
Maybe they'll do the same for me.'

And it was conceivable that the *krill* of Loric still remained where
Sunder had left it, stabbed deep into the blasted tree stump of Caer-
Caveral's body. Such a weapon might enable her to channel the com-
bined force of Covenant's ring and the Staff of Law safely.

Groaning, Jeremiah buried his face in his hands as if he were ashamed
of his mother.

'Hellfire!' Abruptly Covenant slammed the front legs of his stool
down onto the floor. With his halfhand, he covered his eyes as if to mask
a burst of flame. Then he dragged his touch down his features; and as he
did so, every vestige of his drunkenness was pulled away. Almost without
transition, he became the man who had ridden a failing horse into the
forehall of Revelstone: commanding and severe, beyond compromise.

Through his teeth, he rasped, 'Linden Avery, you damn idiot, that is
a truly terrible idea.'

'Is it?' She held his glare without flinching; did not let her son's reaction diminish her. 'Tell me why.'

Vehemently Covenant flung his flagon against the wall. The wood
cracked: chips and splinters fell to the floor: springwine splashed across
the rug. 'Oh, I'll tell you,' he growled. 'Bloody damnation, Linden! And

I won't even mention the fact that you have no idea how powerful the Demondim really are, or what you'll have to go through just to slow them down. And I won't talk about the Dead because they don't really exist anymore. Not the way you remember them. Too many Laws have been broken. The *definitions* are blurred. Spirits as vague as the Dead can't hold themselves together. They certainly can't give you *advice*.

'No, ignore all that.' With both hands, he seemed to ward off wasted explanations. 'Going to Andelain is a terrible idea because that's where Kastenessen is. And he commands the *skurj*.'

Linden stared at him, stricken mute by the force of his revelations. Every solution that she had imagined for her dilemma – and for Jeremiah's—

'You'll recognise them when you see them,' continued Covenant trenchantly. 'Foul showed you what they're like.' Dire serpents of magma with the crushing jaws of krakens and the destructive hunger of *kresh*: monsters which emerged from chancres to devour the earth. 'But he didn't tell you they serve Kastenessen now because that sonofabitch set them free.

'He hasn't brought very many of them down from the north yet. But he can get more whenever he wants them. And he always knows where you are. He can feel you through that loony old man. So no matter what you try to do, the *skurj* will be in your way. He'll send them wherever you are, and they'll eat you alive. You may think you're powerful enough to take care of yourself, but you've never fought those monsters before. And your friends don't have any magic. They don't have any lore. You'll lose them all.'

Harshly Covenant finished, 'Going to Andelain right now is just about the only purely suicidal thing you could do.'

Without lifting his face from his hands, Jeremiah muttered in a muffled voice, 'He's telling the truth, Mom. I swear to God, I don't know why you have so much trouble believing him. He's the only real friend I've ever had. Can't you understand that?'

He had called Covenant *the best*— For that alone, Linden owed Covenant a debt too vast to be repaid.

Now it seemed that all of her choices and desires had been wrong from the beginning. Misguided and fatal.

And yet—

Her heart could not be torn in so many directions and remain whole.

—her impression of disharmony persisted. Covenant was like a man who knew the words but could not remember the song. Her nerves were unable to discern truth or falsehood. And she trusted Jeremiah. Nevertheless her instincts cried at her that she was being misled in some way.

Her Staff was the only thing that still belonged to her beyond question. Holding it tightly, she asked in a small voice, 'What should we do instead?'

Covenant sighed as though he had gained an important concession; and his ire seemed to fall away. More quietly, he answered, 'Like I said, I know another way to make this mess turn out right.' Again his eyes gave out a brief red glint like a glimpse of ready embers. 'But I don't exactly enjoy being treated this way. Like I'm some damn Raver in disguise. Sure, I'm not how you remember me. But I deserve better than this. I've given you a lot here, even if you don't realise it.

'I need something in return. A *little* bit of trust.

'Meet us up on the plateau tomorrow. Maybe an hour after dawn. Over on the south edge, near Furl Falls. Then I won't have to explain what I'm going to do. I can show you.'

Studying him for some hint of what had caused that momentary molten gleam in his eyes, Linden observed cautiously, 'You don't think that I'll approve of what you're planning.'

He sighed again. 'I don't know. You might. You might not. It depends on how badly you want to get your son back in one piece.'

There Linden found a small place of clarity in the wide landscape of her hurt and self-doubt. She recognised emotional blackmail when she heard it. Perhaps Covenant was as benign as Jeremiah believed, and as necessary; but to suggest that her love for her son could be measured by her acquiescence to Covenant's desires was patently manipulative.

No doubt inadvertently, he restored her conviction that there was something wrong with him; or in him.

Jeremiah had raised his head to watch her in the firelight as though his life depended on her. He seemed to plead with her mutely, beseeching her to let Covenant prove himself.

The need in her son's muddied eyes tapped a source of tears that she was barely able to contain. He had already endured too much— No matter what she thought of Covenant, she did not know how to refuse Jeremiah.

Stiffly she rose to her feet.

'All right,' she said to Covenant. 'I'll meet you there.' If she did not concede at least that much, she might never learn the truth. 'You can show me what you have in mind.'

Then, for the last time in that room, she stood her ground. 'But you should know—' *Do something they don't expect.* 'Between now and then, I'm going to use the Staff.

'I'm telling you because I don't want to take you by surprise. And I'll stay as far away as I can. I don't mean to threaten you.' She absolutely did not wish to disrupt the theurgy which enabled their presence. 'But there are some things about our situation that I *do* understand. I won't shirk them.'

She did not wait for Covenant's reply. She had come to the end of her self-control. 'Jeremiah, honey,' she said thickly, 'I'll see you in the morning.' On the verge of weeping, she promised, 'And I'll find a way to help you. Even if I'm too confused to make the right choices.'

In response, Jeremiah offered her a smile that filled her throat with grief. At once, she headed for the door as if she had been routed, so that he would not see her lose herself.

Chapter Four

A Defence of Revelstone

In the corridor outside Covenant's rooms, Linden found Stave waiting for her.

He stood among the three Humbled as though they were all still Masters together; as though his true purposes were in tune with theirs. But as soon as she emerged from the doorway, he moved towards her like a man who meant to catch her before she collapsed. The tumult of her emotions, the torn gusts of confusion and dismay and sorrow, must have been as plain as wind-whipped banners to his senses. Ignoring Clyme, Galt and Branl, he gripped her quickly by one arm and guided her along the passage, away from bewilderment and loss.

Without his support, she might have fallen. Tears crowded her heart: she could hardly contain them. Only Stave's firm hand, and her clenched grasp on the Staff of Law, enabled her to take one step after another, measuring her paltry human sorrows and needs against Revelstone's bluff granite.

She was not Anele: she had no friend in stone. Lord's Keep had never offered her anything except distrust, imprisonment, bloodshed, malice. She could only be consoled by grass and trees; by Andelain's loveliness and Glimmermere's lacustrine potency; by the unharmed rightness of the Land.

Or by her son, who sided with Covenant.

Nevertheless she allowed Stave to steer her through Revelstone's convoluted intentions towards the rooms which his kinsmen had set aside for her. Where else could she go? The clouds brewing over the upland held no malevolence; but they would bring darkness with them, concealment and drenching rain. Her own storm was already too much for her.

Be cautious of love. There is a glamour upon it which binds the heart to destruction.

Covenant and Jeremiah were altered almost beyond recognition. They had not simply refused Linden's touch: they had rebuffed her heart.

Why had Covenant sounded false when he so obviously wished to persuade her, win her confidence? God, she thought, oh, God, he might have been a ventriloquist's dummy, his every word projected onto him, off-key and stilted, from some external source.

From Jeremiah? From the power, the *leakage*, that her son had acquired by being in two places at the same time? Or were they both puppets? The playthings of beings and forces which she could not begin to comprehend?

Or were they simply telling her as much of the truth as they could? Did the fault lie in her? In her reluctance to trust anyone who contradicted her? In her unwillingness to surrender Covenant's ring?

Anele had said that the stone of the Close spoke of *Thomas Covenant, whose daughter rent the Law of Death, and whose son is abroad in the Land, seeking such havoc that the bones of the mountains tremble to contemplate it. For the wielder also this stone grieves, knowing him betrayed.*

Covenant and Jeremiah were the two people whom she had loved most in all the world. Now she felt that they had broken her.

But she was not broken. She knew that, even though her distress filled her with unuttered wailing. She was only in pain; only baffled and grieved, flagrantly bereft. Such things she understood. She had spent the past ten years studying the implications of what she had learned from Thomas Covenant and the Despiser. Her former lover's attempts to manipulate her now might hurt like a scourge, but they could not lash her into surrender.

Her desire to weep was merely necessary. It did not mean that she had been undone. When Stave brought her at last to her rooms and opened the door for her, she found the strength to swallow her grief so that she could speak.

'We need to talk,' she said, hoarse with self-restraint. 'You and me. Mahrtiir and Liand. All of us. Can you get them for me? If Covenant is right, the Demondim won't attack before tomorrow. We should have time.'

The *Haruchai* appeared to hesitate. 'Chosen,' he replied after a moment, 'I am loath to leave you thus.'

'I understand.' With the sleeve of her shirt, she rubbed some of the tears from her face. 'I don't like sending you away. But I'm in no condition to go with you. And we *need* to talk. Tomorrow morning, Covenant wants to show me how he plans to solve our problems. But there's something that I have to do first. I'm going to need all of you,' every one of her friends. 'And—' She paused while she struggled to suppress a fresh burst of sorrow. 'And you should all hear what Covenant and Jeremiah told me.'

Stave would stand by her to the best of his abilities; but he could not give her solace.

He nodded without expression. 'As you wish.' Then he bowed to her and obeyed.

Still stifling sobs, Linden entered her rooms and closed the door.

She felt that she had been absent from her small sanctuary for a long time, and did not know what to expect. Who would provide for her, if the Mahdoubt had left Revelstone? During the day, however, more firewood had been piled beside the hearth, and the lamps had been refilled and lit. In addition, a fresh tray of food awaited her. It was as bountifully laden as Covenant's had been: like his, it included pitchers of water and springwine.

The Masters may well have elected to side with the Unbeliever, but clearly the servants of Revelstone made no distinction between their guests.

Clinging to the Staff, Linden poured a little springwine into a flagon and drank it. When she could feel that small hint of *aliantha* extend its delicate nourishment through her, she went into her bedroom and opened the shutters to look out at the weather.

A light drizzle was falling from the darkened sky: the seepage of leaden clouds. It veiled the Westron Mountains, and she was barely able to see the foothills far below her, the faint hue of the White River some distance off to her right. Behind the spring rain, dusk had closed over Revelstone. Full night would cover the plateau and the Keep and the threatening horde of the Demondim before Stave returned with her friends.

The thought of darkness disturbed her. Dangers which she did not know how to confront lurked where there was no light. Abruptly she closed the shutters, then returned to her sitting room, to the kind illumination of the lamps, and knelt to build a fire in the hearth.

The wood took flame quickly, aided by a splash of oil from one of the lamps. Soon a steady blaze began to warm the room.

But light and heat alone could not denature the midnight in her mind. Her head was full of echoes. *I deserve better than this. That's my Mom.* They repeated themselves obsessively, feeding her tears. *Pain is worse when you have something to compare it to. I need something in return.* Their reiteration was as insistent and compulsory as keening. A little *bit of trust. Ask that callow puppy who follows you around—*

The sound of Covenant's voice, and of Jeremiah's, haunted her.

Trying to protect herself, she went back into her bedroom and stretched out fully dressed on her strict bed. Hugging the Staff against her chest, she concentrated as well as she could on the numinous wood's cleanliness.

She had never seen Berek's original Staff of Law, but she knew enough to be sure that hers was not identical to his. His had been crafted by lore and earned wisdom from a limb of the One Tree: she had formed hers with urgency and wild magic, melding Findail and Vain. And her own understanding of Law might well differ from Berek's. For all she knew, the two Staffs had little in common except the iron heels which Berek had forged. The magic which had transformed Vain's forearm may have arisen from the Worm of the World's End rather than from the One Tree.

Nonetheless her Staff was a tool of Earthpower, as Berek's had been, and she had fashioned it in love and yearning to sustain the beauty of the Land. Somehow it would aid her to discover the truth, to rescue her son, and to oppose the Despiser.

With the Staff resting against her exhausted heart, she hardly noticed as she drifted into sleep.

When the sound of knocking at her door awakened her, she sat up suddenly, startled. She could not guess how much time had passed; could scarcely believe that she had fallen asleep. Momentarily befuddled, she thought, Shock. Nervous prostration. The prolonged difficulties of the day had drained her—

Almost at once, however, she remembered her friends. Surging out of bed, she hurried to the door.

Until she saw Stave standing there, with Mahrtiir and Liand behind him, and Pahni, Bhapa and Anele as well, she did not realise that she had feared some other arrival: a new summons from Covenant and Jeremiah, perhaps; or one of the Masters come to inform her that the Demondim had begun their attack.

Awkwardly, as if she suspected that they might vanish into one of her uninterpretable dreams, she urged her companions to enter. Then she scanned the hall for some sign of the Humbled; for any indication of trouble. But the passageway outside her door was empty. The smooth stone walls held no hint of distress.

Breathing deeply to clear the alarm from her lungs, she closed the door, latched it and turned to face the concern of her friends.

She was glad to see that they emanated health and vigour, in spite of their concerned expressions. The diminishment of Kevin's Dirt had been replaced by a vitality so acute that it seemed to cast a palpable penumbra around all of them except Anele and Stave himself. Now she knew what the former Master and Mahrtiir had discerned in her when she had returned from Glimmermere. The eldritch strength of the waters had washed away their bruises and their weariness and perhaps even their doubts. And she perceived with relief that the lake's effects would last longer than the relatively evanescent restoration which she had performed with her Staff earlier in the day. Kevin's Dirt would not soon regain its power over them.

For Liand even more than for the Ramen, the experience of Glimmermere must have been like receiving an inheritance; a birthright which should have belonged to him throughout his life, but which had been cruelly denied.

By comparison, Stave's impassivity resembled a glower. Anele murmured incomprehensibly to himself, apparently lost in his private dissociation: the effect of standing on wrought stone. Yet his blind eyes seemed to regard Linden as though even in his madness he could not fail to recognise the significance of what had happened to her.

In simple relief, Linden would have liked to spend a little time enjoying the presence of her friends. She could have offered them food and
drink and warmth, asked them questions; distracted herself from her
personal turmoil. But they were clearly alarmed on her behalf. Although
the Ramen said nothing, Pahni's open worry emphasised Mahrtiir's fierce
anger, and Bhapa frowned anxiously.

Liand was less reticent. 'Linden,' he breathed softly, fearfully. 'Heaven
and Earth! What has befallen you? If the Masters plunged a blade into
your heart, I would not think to see you so wounded.'

Involuntarily Linden ducked her head as if she were ashamed. His
immediate sympathy threatened to release tears which she could not
afford. Already the consequences of her encounter with Covenant and
Jeremiah resembled the leading edge of the fury which had flailed her
after the horserite. If that storm broke now, she would be unable to
speak. She would only sob.

'Please don't,' she replied, pleading. 'Don't look so worried. I understand. If I were you, I would probably do the same. But it doesn't help.'

Stave folded his arms over his chest as if to close his heart. 'Then
inform us, Chosen. What form of aid do you require? Your anguish is
plain. We who have determined to stand at your side cannot witness
your plight and remain unmoved.'

In response, Linden jerked up her head, taken aback by a sudden rush
of insight. Perhaps unwittingly, Stave reminded her that behind their
stoicism the *Haruchai* were an intensely passionate people.

The bond joining man to woman is a fire in us, and deep, Brinn had told
her long ago. The Bloodguard had broken their Vow of service to the
Lords, he had explained, not merely because they had proven themselves
unworthy, but more because they had abandoned their wives *in the name
of a chosen fidelity* which they had failed to sustain. The sacrifices that
they had made for their Vow had become too great to be endured.

For the same reason, thousands of years later, Brinn and Cail had
withdrawn their service to Thomas Covenant. In their eyes, their seduction by the Dancers of the Sea – their vulnerability to such desires – had
demonstrated their unworth. *Our folly must end now, ere greater promises
than ours become false in consequence.*

—and remain unmoved. Shaken by memory and understanding,

Linden realised abruptly that Stave had made a similar choice when he had declared himself her friend. He had recanted his devotion to the chosen service of the Masters.

Liand had glimpsed the truth when he had suggested that the Masters feared grief. As a race, Stave and his kinsmen had already known too much of it.

Mourning for the former Master, Linden felt her own sorrow recede. It did not lose its force: perhaps it would not. Nevertheless it seemed to become less immediate. Stave's words and losses had cleared a space in which she could control her tears, and think, and care about her friends.

'You're already helping,' she told Stave as firmly as she could. 'You're here. That's what I need most right now.'

There would be more, but for the moment she had been given enough.

When the *Haruchai* nodded, accepting her reply, she turned to Manethrall Mahrtiir and his Cords.

'I know that being surrounded by stone like this is hard for you,' she began. A faint quaver betrayed her fragility. However, she anchored herself on Mahrtiir's combative glare; clung to the insight which Stave had provided for her.

As she did so, she discovered that she could see more in the auras of the Ramen – and of Liand as well – than magically renewed vitality and protective concern. Beneath the surface, their emotions were complicated by hints of a subtler unease. Something had happened to trouble them since she had parted from Mahrtiir.

'But we have a lot to talk about,' she continued. 'When we're done, I won't ask you to stay. We'll get together again in the morning.'

Bhapa inclined his head as though he were content with whatever she chose to say. But Pahni still stared at Linden with shadows of alarm in her dark eyes. She rested one of her hands on Liand's shoulder as if she had come to rely on his support – or as if she feared for him as well as for Linden. And Mahrtiir remained as watchful as a raptor, searching Linden as though he expected her to name her enemies; his prey.

The Manethrall's manner suggested unforeseen events. Yet his reaction to them tasted of an eagerness which his companions did not share.

His manner strengthened Linden's ability to hold back the effects of her confrontation with Covenant and Jeremiah.

Finally she shifted her gaze to Liand's, addressing him last because his uncomplicated concern and affection touched her pain directly.

'Liand, please don't ask me any questions.' He also seemed privately uneasy, although he conveyed none of the Manethrall's eagerness – and little of Pahni's fear. 'I'll tell you everything that happened. I'll tell you what I plan to do about it. But it will be easier for me if I can just talk. Questions make it harder for me to hold myself together.'

Liand mustered a crooked smile. 'As you wish. I am able to hold my peace, as you have seen. Yet allow me to say,' he added with a touch of rueful humour, 'that since my departure from Mithil Stonedown, no experience of peril and power, no discovery or exigency, has been as unexpected to me as this, that I must so often remain silent.'

Damn it, Linden thought as her eyes misted, he's doing it again. The unaffected gallantry of his attempt to jest undermined her self-control. Striving to master her tears again, she turned her back and pretended to busy herself at the hearth; prodded the logs with the toe of her boot although they plainly did not require her attention.

Over her shoulder, she said thickly, 'Sit down, please. Have something to eat. It's been a long day. I want to tell you about Covenant and Jeremiah, and that's going to be hard for me. But there's no hurry.' If the Demondim did not strike unexpectedly, she intended to wait until the next morning to confront the horde. 'We can afford a little time.'

She meant to speak first. Surely then she would be able to put her pain behind her and listen more clearly to the tales of her friends? But she had one question which could not wait.

With her nerves as much as her ears, she heard her friends shift their feet, glance uncertainly at each other, then begin to comply with her request. Stave remained standing by the door, his arms folded like bars across his stained tunic. But Liand and Pahni urged Anele into a chair and seated themselves beside him. At once, the old man reached for the tray of food and began to eat. At the same time, Bhapa and Mahrtiir also sat down. The older Cord did so with deliberate composure. In contrast, Mahrtiir was tangibly reluctant: he appeared to desire some more active outlet for his emotions.

While her companions settled themselves, poured water or springwine into flagons, took a little food, Linden gathered her resolve. Facing the wall beside the hearth, nearly resting her forehead on the blunt stone, she said uncomfortably, 'There's something that I have to know. And I need the truth. Please don't hold anything back.

'It's about the *caesures*. About what you felt going through them. I've already asked Liand about the first one.' In the cave of Waynhim, he had told her only that he had felt pain beyond description; that he would have broken if the black lore of the ur-viles had not preserved him. 'Is there anything else that any of you can tell me? I mean about being in that specific Fall?'

A moment of fretted silence seemed to press against her back. Then the Manethrall replied stiffly, 'Ringthane, the pain was too great to permit clear perception. Within the *caesure* was unspeakable cold, a terrible whiteness, agony that resembled being flayed, and fathomless despair. As the Stonedownor has said, we were warded by the theurgy of the ur-viles. But the Ranyhyn also played a part in our endurance. That they did not lose their way in Time diminished a measure of our suffering.'

Linden heard the faint rustle of bodies as her friends looked at each other and nodded. With her health-sense, she recognised that Liand, Pahni and Bhapa agreed with Mahrtiir's assessment.

'What about you, Stave?' she asked. He had emerged from the Fall apparently unscathed. 'What was it like for you?'

The *Haruchai* did not hesitate. 'As the Manethrall has said, both the ur-viles and the Ranyhyn served us well. We rode upon a landscape of the purest freezing while our flesh was assailed as though by the na-Mhoram's *Grim*. Also there stood a woman among rocks, lashing out in anguish with wild magic. Towards her I was drawn to be consumed. However, *turiya* Herem held her. He is known to me, for no *Haruchai* has forgotten the touch of any Raver. Therefore I remained apart from her, seeking to refuse the doom which befell Korik, Sill, and Doar.'

Remained apart– Linden thought wanly. *Damn*, he was strong. From birth, he had communicated mind to mind; and yet he had retained more of himself in the Fall than anyone except Anele. Even she, with the strength of the ur-viles in her veins, had been swept into Joan's madness.

Stave's severance from his people must have hurt him more than Linden could imagine.

But she could not afford to dwell on the prices that her friends paid to stand at her side: not now, under these circumstances. She had her own costs to bear.

'All right,' she said after a moment of silence. 'That was the first one. What about the second?' The *caesure* which she had created, bringing herself and her companions back to their proper time – and displacing the Demondim. 'It must have been different. I need to know *how* it was different.'

Mahrtiir spoke first. 'For the Ramen, the distinction was both subtle and profound. Again we were assailed by a white and frozen agony which we were unable to withstand. The ur-viles no longer warded us. We lack the strength of the *Haruchai*. And we did not bear the Staff of Law on your behalf.' Liand had served Linden in that way, freeing her to concentrate on wild magic. 'Yet the certainty of the Ranyhyn seemed greater, and their assurance somewhat diminished our torment. This, we deem, was made possible by the movement of time within the *caesure*, for we did not seek to oppose the current of the whirlwind.'

Linden nodded to herself. Yes, that made sense. Days ago, she had chosen to believe that the temporal tornado of any Fall would tend to spin out of the past towards the future. Mahrtiir confirmed what she had felt herself during her passage from the foothills of the Southron Range three thousand years ago to the bare ground before the gates of Revelstone.

Cautiously, approaching by increments the question which Covenant had advised her to ask, she said, 'What about you, Stave? Can you offer anything more?'

The former Master did not respond immediately. Behind his apparent dispassion, he may have been weighing risks, striving to gauge the effect that his answer might have on her. When he spoke, however, his tone revealed none of his calculations.

'To that which the Manethrall and I have described, I will add one observation. Within the second Fall, the woman possessed by despair and madness was absent. Rather I beheld you mounted upon Hyn. Within you blazed such wild magic that it was fearsome to witness. As in the first passage, I was drawn towards the mind of the wielder. But again I remained apart.'

So. Twice Stave had preserved his separate integrity. Like the Ramen, he could not tell Linden what she needed to know.

—ask that callow puppy—

Liand did not deserve Covenant's scorn.

She continued to face the wall as though she wished to muffle her voice; conceal her heart. 'And you, Liand? You were carrying the Staff. That must have made a difference.'

By its very nature, the Staff may have imposed a small pocket of Law on the swirling chaos of the *caesure*.

'Linden—' the young man began. But then he faltered. His reluctance scraped along the nerves of her back and scalp, the skin of her neck. But percipience alone could not tell her why he was loath to speak, or what he might reveal.

'Please,' she said softly, almost whispering. 'I need to know.'

She felt him gather himself – and felt the Ramen regard him with a kind of apprehension. Stave gazed steadily at the Stonedownor. Only Anele continued to eat and drink as though he were oblivious to his companions.

'Then I must relate,' Liand answered unsteadily, 'that within the *caesure* I rode Rhohm upon an endless plain of the most bitter emptiness and cold. About me, I felt a swarm of stinging hornets, each striving to pierce and devour me, though they were not visible to my sight. And at the same time—' Again he faltered. But the underlying bedrock of his dignity and courage supported him. 'At the same time,' he repeated more firmly, 'it appeared to me that I was contained within you – that I sat upon Hyn rather than Rhohm, and that from my heart arose a conflagration such as I have never known. There none of my desires or deeds was my own. In some form, I had ceased to exist, for my thoughts were your thoughts, my pain was yours, and no aspect of Liand son of Fostil remained to me.'

Before Linden could press him, he added, 'You need not name your query. You wish to hear what it is that I beheld within you.

'Our conjoining was severed when we emerged from the Fall, and I became myself again. Yet while we were one, I participated in your love for your son, and for Thomas Covenant. I was filled with your fear and pain, your extremity and desperation. I shared your resolve, which is greater than valour or might.' Liand did not hesitate now, or hold back. 'And I saw that you have it within you to perform horrors. You have known the blackest cruelty and despair, and are able to inflict your full dismay upon any who may oppose you.

'This is the knowledge that you seek,' he concluded, 'is it not?'

Facing the unwritten stone, Linden groaned to herself: she may have groaned aloud. Was Covenant Jeremiah's puppet? Were they both puppets? Or did the fault lie in her? Liand, she believed, had answered those questions. In Covenant's name, she had prevailed against *moksha* Jehannum and the Sunbane; but Liand seemed to say that she had never truly healed the capacity for evil which Lord Foul's servants had exposed in her. Her inability to understand or trust Covenant and Jeremiah now was her failure, not theirs.

Softly, speaking more to the wall than to Liand, she breathed, 'And yet you're still my friend.'

'How could I be otherwise?' returned the Stonedownor. 'It is possible that your loves will bind your heart to destruction, as the Mahdoubt has warned. It may be that you will repeatedly seek to accomplish good through evil means, as you have done before. But I am myself now, and I am not afraid. I no longer retain all that I have known of you. Yet I have known your loves, and in their name, I am proud to be both your companion and your friend.'

Helplessly Linden sagged forward, bracing her forehead against the cool stone. A cloudburst of weeping advanced on her across the convoluted terrain of her confusion; and she could not bear it. Covenant had as much as said that he did not trust her – and Liand had told her that the Unbeliever had good reason for his caution – and yet she heard nothing in Liand's tone except unalloyed candour. He was proud—

She might not have been able to fend off her grief; but abruptly Anele spoke. 'Anele has been made free of *them*,' the old man announced with unmistakable satisfaction. 'And' – he turned his head from side to side in a way that suggested surprise – 'the dark things, the creatures lost and harsh, demanding remembrance– Anele no longer fears them. He has been spared much.'

The unexpected sound of his voice helped her to step back once more from her clamouring emotions.

He sat on wrought stone, with his bare feet on the polished granite of the floor. As a result, he was in one of the more coherent phases of his madness. He may have understood more than he appeared to grasp. Indeed, he may have been trying in his distorted fashion to reassure Linden.

To some extent, at least, he had already demonstrated the truth of his assertion that he was *the Land's last hope.* He had made possible the recovery of the Staff.

'For my part,' Mahrtiir put in while Linden mastered herself, 'I aver that there is no surprise in the knowledge which the Stonedownor has gleaned.' The Manethrall's voice was gruff with unaccustomed tenderness. 'Breathes there a being in the Land, or upon the wide Earth, who does not nurture some measure of darkness? Surely Esmer would not be drawn to you as he is, did he not behold in you an aspect of his own torment. And has it not been repeated endlessly of the white gold wielder that he will save or damn the Land? That which Liand has witnessed in you alters nothing.'

Bracing herself on the strength of her friends, Linden set aside her bewilderment and loss; her self-doubt. She could not forget such things. They would affect all of her choices and actions. But the faith of her friends restored her ability to contain herself; to say what needed to be said.

When she had wiped her face once more with the sleeve of her shirt, she turned back towards Stave, Liand, Anele and the Ramen.

'Thank you,' she said quietly. 'All of you. The things that I have to tell you are hard for me.' And she still needed to hear what had happened to her companions while she had been with Covenant and Jeremiah. 'But I think I can do it now' – she attempted a smile – 'without being too messy about it.'

Summoning her frayed courage, she pulled a chair close to the table so that she would be able to reach the tray of food. When she had seated herself, poured a flagon of springwine, and taken a few swallows, she met the expectant stares of her friends and began.

She said nothing about Esmer: she trusted that Mahrtiir had told the tale of Esmer's recent appearance. Embarrassed on Covenant's behalf, she made no mention of his drinking. And she glossed over his apparently aimless comments about Berek Halfhand and Kevin Landwaster. In retrospect, Covenant's description of Kevin seemed whetted with foreboding. With so much peril crowding around her and her companions, Linden heard prophecy in Kevin's plight. *He wanted to be punished*– But on that subject, she swallowed her fears.

Everything else, however, she conveyed with as much clarity as she could command: Covenant's strangeness, and Jeremiah's; the self-absorbed and stilted relationship between them; the discrepancy between them and her memories of them; the oblique inadequacy and occasional scorn of their answers. Hugging the Staff to her chest, she admitted that Covenant had asked for his ring – and that she had not complied. With difficulty, she acknowledged that the blame for her reluctance and distress might lie in her. And she finished by telling her friends that Covenant had asked her for *something in return*. A little *bit of trust*.

Then I won't have to explain what I'm going to do. I can show you.

'There's only one other thing that I can tell you,' she concluded thinly. 'They don't love me anymore. They've changed too much. That part of them is gone.'

Finally a wash of lassitude seemed to carry away her last strength. The effort of holding her emotions at bay had wearied her; and she found that she needed the sustenance of *aliantha* in springwine – and needed as well at least a modicum of numbness. When she had emptied half of her flagon, she took a little fruit and chewed it listlessly. As she did so, she kept her head down, avoiding the uncertainty and trepidation of her friends.

For a long moment, they faced her in silence. They had stopped eating: they seemed almost to have stopped breathing. Then Liand asked cautiously, 'If the Unbeliever seeks your aid in his intent, will you give it?'

Linden jerked up her head. She had not considered the possibility– But of course Liand's question made sense. Why else had Covenant come here, bringing Jeremiah with him? Certainly he wanted his ring. However, he was prepared for the chance – the likelihood? – that she would refuse: he had said so. Then why had he asked for a show of trust?

I know another way to make this mess turn out right. He and Jeremiah could have simply dismissed her and put his other plans into effect – unless those plans required her participation.

Meet us up on the plateau tomorrow.

'I have to,' she answered slowly. 'I already know that I won't like what they want me to do. But if I don't cooperate, I'll never learn the truth. About either of them.'

In fact, she could not imagine refusing them. They wanted her aid in some way. They had reason to be afraid of her. And they would not let her touch them.

The truth had become as vital to her as her son's life.

Liand nodded. Although he frowned darkly, he accepted her reasoning.

After another moment, Stave unfolded his arms if he were readying himself for combat. 'You have informed the ur-Lord that you intend to make use of the Staff. What will you attempt?'

Linden pressed her cheek against the comforting strictures of the Staff. 'I'll tell you,' she promised. 'Before you go,' before she was left alone with her mourning, 'we'll make our own plans. But this whole day' – she grimaced – 'has taken a lot out of me. I need a little time.'

Across the table, she faced Liand and the Ramen. 'And you have something to tell me. I can feel it. Something happened to you – something more than Glimmermere. If you're willing to talk about it, I want to hear what it was.'

At once, as if she had prodded a forgotten worry, Mahrtiir, Bhapa, Pahni and Liand became restless. Anele appeared unaware that Linden had spoken, and Stave betrayed no reaction. But hesitation clouded the eyes of the others. None of them looked at her directly. Liand studied his hands, Bhapa frowned at the hearth as though the flames puzzled him, and Pahni focused her attention anxiously on Liand. Only Mahrtiir conveyed a sense of anticipation; but he closed his eyes and scowled fiercely, apparently attempting to conceal what he felt.

Then, however, the Manethrall opened his eyes to meet Linden's gaze. 'We scruple to reply,' he said roughly, 'because we have no wish to augment the burdens which you must bear. Yet I deem it false friendship to withhold what has transpired. Therefore I will answer.

'When I parted from you, some time passed while I gathered together the Cords, the Stonedownor and Anele so that I might guide them to Glimmermere. Together we traversed the impending stone until at last we regained the open sky of the plateau.

'There we beheld rainfall upon the mountains, and a storm gathering. But we have no fear of the world's weather. Rather we rejoiced that we were freed from stone and constraint. And we had grown eager for the sight of Glimmermere. Therefore we made haste among the hills, that we might gain the eldritch tarn swiftly.

'As we did so, Anele appeared to accompany us willingly' – Liand and Pahni nodded in confirmation – 'though you had informed us that he would eschew the waters. He spoke constantly to himself as we hastened—' For a moment, Mahrtiir dropped his gaze as if he felt a touch of chagrin. 'It may be that we should have attended to his words. You have informed us that his madness is altered by that which lies beneath his feet. Some insight might have been gleaned from him.' Then the Manethrall looked at Linden again. 'But we have grown accustomed to his muttering, which is largely incomprehensible to us. And our eagerness distracted us. We were grateful only that he kept pace without urging.'

Linden stared at him. The grass. Damn it, she thought, the *grass*. The region above Revelstone was not as lush as the Verge of Wandering, but its emerald and fertile greensward resembled the tall grass of that valley. And she had given not one moment's consideration to how walking across the upland might affect the old man. She had been so shaken by her meeting with Esmer – and so apprehensive about talking to Covenant and Jeremiah—

'I made the same mistake,' she admitted to assuage her own chagrin. 'We've all had a lot on our minds. Please go on.'

'Nonetheless,' Mahrtiir asserted severely, 'the old man was altered. Failing to observe him clearly, we failed both him and you.

'I will not prolong my preamble. Together we gained the shores of the tarn. There we cast no reflection upon the waters, although Anele's image was plainly visible. True to your word, he would not partake of Glimmermere's benison. When we drank, however – when we had bathed and been transformed—'

Abruptly the Manethrall stopped, caught by a resurgence of his earlier reluctance.

Leaning forward earnestly, Liand explained on Mahrtiir's behalf, 'Linden, Anele spoke to us. He has not done so ere now. Always his moments of clear speech have been directed to you, or have been uttered in your name.' Bewilderment filled the Stonedownor's face. 'Upon the verges of Glimmermere, however, he addressed each of us in turn. And his manner of speaking—'

When Liand stumbled, Mahrtiir forced himself to resume. His voice was husky as he said, 'Ringthane, it appeared to us that his voice resembled his fashion of speech when he accosted you in the Verge of Wandering, before fire and fury possessed him, and he was struck down for your preservation. And his words held such gentleness and sorrow that our hearts were wrung to hear him.'

Linden blinked in shock. Was it possible? Had Covenant spoken to her friends through Anele? Had they heard his voice? Felt his love? *While she had been alone with him and her son, struggling to make sense of their strangeness, their disturbing evasions, their glimpses of scorn?*

Oh, Linden. I'm so glad to see you.

Covenant had claimed or implied that he was exercising his relationship with Time for several different purposes at once, simultaneously making himself and Jeremiah manifest in Revelstone, seeking the means to oppose Kastenessen, and defending the Arch against Joan's *caesures*. Could he also have taken possession of Anele; addressed her friends with 'gentleness and sorrow'?

Or—

Not to mention some of the other powers that have noticed what's happening here and want to take advantage of it.

—were there other beings at work? Forces other than Kastenessen and the Demondim and Esmer and the *Elohim*? Was some foe whom she had never met endeavouring to manipulate her friends?

Linden, find me. I can't help you unless you find me.

Oh, God, she thought; groaned. Who's doing this? How many lies have we been told?

Nevertheless this new surprise galvanised her. Her lassitude vanished: even her inward storm was pushed aside. Throughout her encounter with Covenant, he had sounded subtly false; insidiously out of tune. If Jeremiah had become so much more than the boy whom she had known, Covenant had seemed to be less than himself. The voice that had spoken to her through Anele – like the voice in her dreams – had felt far more *true* than Covenant himself did.

You need the ring.

Dreaming, she had heard Covenant urge her to trust herself.

'Tell me,' she told the Manethrall and Liand intently. 'If that was Covenant – or even if it just *sounded* like him – I need to know what he said.'

The words themselves might reveal who had spoken them.

In a formal tone, Mahrtiir responded, 'First he addressed us generally. His words were these.' Then he altered his voice to produce an unexpected imitation of Covenant's. '"I can only say all of this once. And I can't explain it. As soon as he notices what I'm doing, he'll stop me. If I even start to say his name, he'll stop me before I can finish.

'"She can do this. Tell her I said that. It's hard now. And it's going to get harder. She'll have to go places and do things that ought to be impossible. But I think she can do it. And there's no one else who can even make the attempt."'

The Manethrall paused. When Liand and the Cords nodded, confirming his recitation, he resumed.

'Anele's possessor then spoke to Liand, saying, "I wish I could spare you. Hell, I wish any of us could spare you. But I can't see any way around it. What you need is in the Aumbrie. Stave will show you where that is, whether the Masters want him to or not. You'll know what you're looking for when you touch it."'

The *Aumbrie?* Linden gripped the Staff; stifled an interruption. The Aumbrie of the *Clave?* She had never seen that hidden storeroom herself. But she had heard from Covenant that Vain had found his way to the Aumbrie, seeking the iron bands which had formed the heels of Berek's original Staff of Law.

'To me,' Mahrtiir was saying, 'Anele next addressed himself.' Linden felt the veiled knife-edge of the Manethrall's eagerness as he quoted, '"You'll have to go a long way to find your heart's desire. Just be sure you come back. The Land needs you."'

Hurrying past his excitement as if he considered it unseemly, Mahrtiir said, 'Last Anele named the Cords. He said, "In some ways, you two have the hardest job. You'll have to survive. And you'll have to make them listen to you. They won't hear her. She's already given them too many reasons to feel ashamed of themselves."

'We thronged with questions at his words,' the Ramen leader admitted; and Liand nodded vigorously. 'We would have urged explanations, though he had said that he could not provide them. But then Anele appeared to grow faint, as though a sudden ailment, or perhaps an undetected forbidding, had fallen upon him. Expressing regret, he fell to the grass, and his eyes rolled as though he had been taken by a seizure.

'The moment was brief,' finished the Manethrall. 'He roused himself shortly and became as he had been before, distracted and incomprehensible. To us, it appeared that he was unaware of his words. We surmise that his unnamed foe had indeed become cognisant of him, and had roughly imposed incoherence upon him.

'That is our tale, Ringthane. While we pondered what we had heard, the first of the rain began to fall. Desiring shelter more for the old man than for ourselves, we departed from Glimmermere. Stave met us returning towards Revelstone and guided us hither.'

Pahni continued to rest one hand on Liand's shoulder, keeping her eyes downcast in an effort to mask her alarm. And Bhapa had lapsed into a reverie: he seemed to study the hearth without seeing it, as if he sought the meaning of Anele's words behind the restless dance and gutter of the flames.

But when the Manethrall was done, Liand asked at once, 'Is it conceivable, Linden? Was Thomas Covenant indeed able to address us through Anele while he was also present with you?'

Linden held Mahrtiir's discomfited gaze for a moment, thanking him with her eyes. Then she faced Liand's question.

'I don't know.' Her alarm had become a kind of courage. Upon occasion, she had experienced a similar reaction during emergency surgeries. At those times, when detachment and training failed her, her own fear had enabled her to proceed. Under the right circumstances, dread and even inadequacy became as compelling as valour. 'Covenant says that he and Jeremiah are "in two places at once". It's three if you count taking possession of Anele. I don't know how he can do any of that.

'And he's *dead*.' She forced herself to say this. 'I watched Lord Foul kill him.' Through Anele, he had urged her, *Just be wary of me*. 'I don't know how it's possible for him to have *any* physical form. He told me himself that too many Laws have been broken for the Dead to hold themselves together.

'But he did say that there are "other powers", enemies or beings that we don't know about. And he gave me such a strong impression of' – she could not say the word *falsehood* aloud, not speaking to her friends about Thomas Covenant – 'of discrepancy. Like all of the pieces didn't fit. Or I didn't understand them well enough to put them together.'

Her Jeremiah had been a wizard at such things, making the pieces fit—

'For all I know,' she sighed, 'Covenant never said a word to me until today,' and every voice in her dreams, every word in Anele's mouth, had belonged to someone else. 'I can't even begin to guess whether he actually talked to the four of you. And I certainly can't tell you what any of it means.'

'Then, Chosen,' Stave put in flatly, 'my question stands. If it remains your purpose to exert the Staff, though such forces may dismiss the Unbeliever and your son, what will you attempt to accomplish?'

Steadying herself on a kind of daring and indomitable trepidation, Linden answered him as plainly as she could.

'Covenant wants me to meet him near Furl Falls about an hour after dawn.' She had explained this earlier: she repeated it more for her own sake than to remind her friends. 'But I'm not willing to wait that long. I have to do something about the Demondim. I want Revelstone to have a fighting chance if Covenant fails – or even if he just makes a mistake.'

The Demondim were reputed to be profoundly lorewise. Surely no perceptual *trick* would baffle them for long?

'Those creatures can use the Illearth Stone,' Linden went on unsteadily. 'Once they decide to attack, they can probably tear this whole place apart in a matter of hours. The Masters won't stand a chance.

'I want to prevent that.'

Before Stave or Mahrtiir could object, she explained, 'Covenant agrees with the Masters. The Demondim are using a *caesure* to draw power directly from the Stone, even though it was destroyed a long time ago. I can't feel the Fall – they're masking it somehow – but it has to be there,' in the midst of the horde. 'And if it's there, the Staff of Law can unmake it.

'I'm going to study those monsters,' she said directly to the former Master, knowing that he would not be able to conceal what he heard from his kinsmen, 'until I locate their *caesure*.' She no longer cared what the Masters might think of her intentions. 'And when I can feel it,' when her health-sense had identified the precise miasmic *wrongness* of the Fall, 'I'm going to erase it.'

As if she were not afraid, she concluded, 'Without the Illearth Stone, they're just Demondim.' Hideously potent in themselves: more than a match for the Masters. But they would need days rather than mere hours to overwhelm Revelstone. 'And maybe I'll be able to cut down their numbers without using more power than Covenant can withstand.'

Stave showed no reaction; made no comment. He may have been content to accept any of her decisions. But Bhapa turned from his study of the flames to regard her with surprise and hope. Pahni raised her head with an air of hesitation, almost of timidity, as though she felt abashed in Linden's presence. And Liand gazed at Linden as if she had once again justified his faith in her.

However, the Manethrall's emanations were more complex. Linden might have expected his heart to leap at the prospect of combat; but he made a visible effort to swallow his anticipation.

'Ringthane,' he said carefully, 'it is a bold stroke, and I applaud. But I must inquire when you will make the attempt. It is plain to all who behold you that you are weary beyond measure. Will you not eat and rest to refresh yourself? If you sleep, you need not fear that the bale of Kevin's Dirt will reclaim you. The benison of Glimmermere will not fade so swiftly.

'If you will heed me, I urge that you will be better able to confront the Teeth of the Render when your strength has been restored.'

Liand and Pahni nodded in unison; and Stave said stolidly, 'The Manethrall's counsel is apt. You require slumber. If it is your wish, I will gather our companions and awaken you in the hour before dawn. You will have time enough to confront the Demondim before the ur-Lord desires your presence at Furl Falls.'

Linden would have preferred immediate action. She would have chosen anything that promised to distract her from the poignant throb of her meeting with Jeremiah and Covenant. But she did not argue. 'All right,' she sighed. 'That makes sense. I'm not sure how much sleeping I can do. But I'll eat as much as I can stomach. And maybe some of this springwine will help.'

Certainly she wanted numbness—

In addition, she found now that she wanted to be alone. She had reached the end of her capacity for words. The emotions which remained to her were voiceless; too private to be shared. Long ago, she had loved a man and adopted a son. She did not know how to grieve for them in the presence of her friends.

'In the meantime,' she added, 'you should get some rest yourselves. God knows what's going to happen tomorrow. It could be hard on all of us.'

'As you say, Chosen.' Stave moved at once to the door.

Mahrtiir and Bhapa rose promptly to follow his example. They were Ramen, uncomfortable under the monumental constraint of the Keep. They would find a night on the plateau preferable to being confined in Revelstone, regardless of the weather.

But Liand remained seated. Anele continued to munch distractedly at the tray of food. And Pahni lingered at Liand's side. Her hand on his arm gently advised him to stand, but she did not insist.

Liand dropped his gaze for a moment, then looked at Linden again. 'Linden—' he began awkwardly. 'It saddens me that you must be alone with all that has transpired. You asked that I do not question you, and I have complied. But now I must speak. Is it well that no companion remains with you at such a time?'

'It is her wish,' stated the *Haruchai*. And Mahrtiir commanded Pahni, 'Bring the Stonedownor and Anele, Cord. When we have delivered them to Liand's chambers, we will seek a less constrained place of rest.'

Obediently Pahni left her seat. Taking Anele's hand, she brought him to his feet. Yet she continued to watch Liand, plainly hoping that he would join her.

Linden covered her face, threatened once more by Liand's candour. As gently as she could, she told him, 'You don't need to worry. Sure, this is hard.' Anele had said as much, in Covenant's voice or someone else's. 'But I've known worse.' She had survived the Sunbane and Rant Absolain's malice, the na-Mhoram's *Grim* and the Worm of the World's End. She had been possessed by a Raver, and had confronted the Despiser. And her son was *here*. His mind had been restored to him. If he and Covenant truly did not love her, she might spend the whole night crying, but she would not lose herself. 'I have the Staff of Law. And if that's not enough, I have something even more precious. I've got friends.

'Go on,' she said quietly. 'Take care of Anele. Try to get some sleep. I'll see you early tomorrow.'

Liand studied her for a long moment, obviously striving to see past her words into the condition of her spirit. Then he stood up and offered her a lopsided smile. 'Linden, you surpass me – continually, it seems. As you say, we will gather upon the morrow. And we who name ourselves your friends with pride will hope to see that you have found a measure of solace.'

She could not match his smile; but perhaps he did not expect that of her. Or perhaps Pahni's soft gaze was enough for him. When he had joined the young Cord and Anele, Stave opened the door. Together, the *Haruchai* and Mahrtiir ushered their companions out into the corridor, leaving Linden alone with her thoughts and her desire to weep and her growing terror.

She did not believe that she would sleep. The events of the day had worn her nerves raw. And the prospect of dreaming frightened her. If she heard Covenant's voice – his voice as she remembered it rather than as it was now – she might lose the last of her frayed resolve. An old paresis lurked in the background of her pain, and it meant death.

But she had underestimated her hunger and fatigue. Her nap before her friends had arrived was not enough: she needed more. When she had eaten her fill, and drunk a flagon of springwine, she found it difficult to hold up her head. Her eyes seemed to fall closed of their own accord. Instead of spending the night as she had imagined, striving to make sense of Esmer and Covenant and her son, she went almost helplessly to her bed.

As soon as she took off her clothes and stretched out under the blankets, she sank into a sleep as empty and unfathomable as the loneliness between the stars. If she dreamed or cried out, she did not know it.

One short night was not enough. She needed whole days of tranquillity and balm. Nevertheless she was awake and dressed, as ready as she would ever be, when a knock at her door announced that her friends had returned for her. Some unconscious awareness of time had roused her so that she could try to prepare herself.

She had opened her shutters briefly to look out at the weather. A drenching rain fell steadily, obscuring any hint of dawn's approach; and the damp breeze brought memories of winter from the ice-clogged peaks to the west. The prospect of being soaked and chilled felt like foreboding as she closed the shutters and left the lingering embers in the hearth in order to answer the summons of her friends and Revelstone's need.

Stave stood outside with the Ramen, Liand, and Anele. Liand and Anele wore woollen cloaks, heavy and hooded, although the Ramen and the former Master apparently disdained such protections. But over one arm, Stave carried a cloak for Linden.

Her companions offered her a subdued greeting which she hardly returned: she had already begun to sink into herself, focusing her concentration on the friable structure of her resolve – and on her percipience itself, striving to sharpen her health-sense so that she might be able to penetrate the mystic obfuscations of the Demondim. Distractedly she accepted the cloak from Stave, shrugged it over her shoulders. Clinging to the Staff, she nodded to indicate that she was as ready as she would ever be.

She can do this. Tell her I said that.

Flanked by Stave and Mahrtiir, with the Cords, Liand, and Anele behind her, she set out to confront the innominate powers of the Vilespawn.

Although she had not said so, she wanted to reach the highest possible vantage above the horde. There distance and rain might conceal her from the monsters until she was prepared to unfurl the Staff's fire. But Stave appeared to grasp her unspoken desires. Without a word, he led her where she needed to go.

Tense and determined, her small company passed along the intricate passages of the Keep to the wide tunnel which led like a road towards the upland. And as they rounded the last switchback, they began to splash through streams of rainwater. Below them, the streams were diverted into culverts and drains; and Linden wondered obliquely how the *Haruchai* had contrived to block those waterways when the Sandgorgon Nom had used Glimmermere's outflow to extinguish the lingering inferno of the Banefire, three and a half thousand years ago. Since then, however, the drains and channels had obviously been re-opened so that accumulating torrents would not flood into the Keep.

As she ascended, Linden seemed to struggle against a current of memories: Covenant's extravagant bravery when he had quenched the theurgy of the Banefire; her own weakness and Nom's blunt strength. But then she slogged out of the tunnel into the open rain, and the downpour forced her attention back to the present. It impelled her to pull up her hood and huddle into her cloak; required her to forget who she had been and remember who she was.

There's no one else who can even make the attempt.

From the shelter of the tunnel, she and her companions turned north and east across the hills towards the promontory of Revelstone. Almost at once, the rain soaked into her cloak. Darkness covered the world, blotting out every horizon: she could only guess where she placed her feet. Nevertheless she sensed that the worst of the storm had passed; that the rainfall was beginning to dwindle as the laden clouds drifted eastward.

Stave and the Manethrall steered her in a northerly curve towards the jut of the plateau, seeking, perhaps, to avoid an unseen hill or some other obstacle. Slowly water seeped through her cloak into her clothes: it dripped from her legs into her boots. By degrees, the chill of night and spring and damp leached the warmth from her skin. More and more, she yearned to draw on the invigorating fire of the Staff. She wanted to banish cold and fear and her own mortality so that she might feel equal to what lay ahead of her.

But if she did so, she would forewarn the Demondim. Knowing that she meant to release Law and Earthpower, Covenant might muster enough of his inexplicable puissance to protect himself and Jeremiah. But the Vile-spawn would recognise their danger. And they would not need prescience to guess her purpose. They would ramify their defences, creating cul-de-sacs and chimeras of lore to baffle her health-sense so that she could not identify their *caesure*. Or perhaps they would preempt her by unleashing the full evil of the Illearth Stone—

She knew that bane too well to believe that she could stand against it: not without wild magic. And she trembled to think what might happen to Covenant and her son – or indeed to the hidden Fall of the Demondim – if she were compelled to unveil the force of Covenant's ring. *It's hard now. And it's going to get harder.* Covenant and Jeremiah might not simply vanish: they might cease to exist in any meaningful form. And the *caesure* of the Demondim might grow vast enough to devour the whole of Lord's Keep.

Her own fears as much as the cold and rain filled her with shivering, imminent fever, as she restrained her wish for the Staff's warmth and consolation. Instead she let her companions lead her to her destination as if she were more blind than Anele, and had far less fortitude.

Immersed in private dreads, she did not sense the presence of the Masters until she neared the rim of Revelstone high above the courtyard and watchtower that guarded the Keep's gates.

Two of them awaited her. By now, she knew them well enough to recognise Handir and Galt, although she could scarcely discern their shapes in the darkness; certainly could not make out their features. No doubt the other Humbled, Branl and Clyme, had remained with Covenant and Jeremiah.

Galt and the Voice of the Masters stood between her and the cliff-edge of her intent.

She was not surprised to find them in her way. Doubtless they had read her intentions in Stave's mind. And she was confident that they had informed the ur-Lord– If she had not sunk so far into herself, she might have expected to encounter the Masters earlier.

Perhaps she should have been grateful that only two of Stave's kinsmen had come to witness her actions; or to oppose them.

'Chosen,' Handir said when Linden and her friends were near enough to hear him easily through the rain, 'the Unbeliever requests that you refrain from your intent. He requests it. He does not command it. In this, he was precise. He acknowledges the merit of your purpose. But he conceives that the peril is too great.

'Having been forewarned, he asserts that he will be able to refuse banishment. That is not his concern. Rather he fears what will transpire should you fail. Provoked, the Demondim will draw upon the full might of the Illearth Stone. From such an assault, only ruin can ensue. The ur-Lord's design for the salvation of the Land is fragile, easily impeded. If he is assailed by the Demondim, he will be unable to perform what he must.

'For that reason and no other, he asks that you turn aside from your intent and await the revelation of his purposes at Furl Falls.'

'And if the Chosen does not fail?' countered Stave before Mahrtiir could retort. 'Are the Masters not thereby greatly aided in their service to both Lord's Keep and the Land?'

The Voice of the Masters did not reply. Instead Galt stated, 'Her failure is certain. Our discernment exceeds hers, yet we cannot determine how the Fall of the Demondim is concealed. And if she draws upon Earthpower to enhance her sight, she will be revealed, and the horde will strike against her. Therefore she cannot achieve her aim.

'It is the ur-Lord, the Unbeliever, the rightful wielder of white gold who requests her compliance. How may any refusal be justified?'

Linden stepped closer. She was beyond persuasion: fear and determination and even bafflement had made her as unwilling to compromise as the Masters themselves. Covenant's indirect appeal and Galt's reasoning were like the rain: they could fall on her, soak into her clothes, fill her mortal heart with shivering; but they could not deflect her.

Handir had not bowed to her. She gave him no greeting of her own. Ignoring Galt, she asked abruptly, 'Did he tell you what this design of his is?'

'No,' Handir answered as though her question had no relevance. 'We cannot aid him, and so he did not speak of it. He asked only that we keep the ancient promise of the *Haruchai* to preserve Revelstone.'

'Then,' she said softly, as if she wished only Handir and the rain to hear her, 'it seems to me that you still don't understand what Brinn did against the Guardian of the One Tree.' If the Master did not consider the specific nature of Covenant's purpose germane, he could not say the same of the example upon which his people had founded their Mastery. 'I tried to explain it yesterday, but I probably wasn't clear.

'Brinn didn't beat *ak-Haru Kenaustin Ardenol* by defeating him. He beat him by *surrendering*. He couldn't stop the Guardian from throwing him off a cliff, so he took *Kenaustin Ardenol* with him when he fell.'

'This you have—' Handir began; but Linden did not let him interrupt her.

'Doesn't that strike you as a rather un-*Haruchai* thing to do? In your whole history, have your people ever considered trying to solve a problem by surrendering to it?'

That may have been why Covenant had asked the *Haruchai* not to accompany him while he and Linden went to confront Lord Foul. The ancestors of the Masters might have sacrificed their lives to prevent him from giving his ring to the Despiser. Indeed, Covenant may have decided on his own course because he had witnessed Brinn's victorious defeat.

'So where do you suppose Brinn got the idea? How did he even think of it?' She suspected that Handir knew the answer – that his ancestors had heard it from Cail, and that it was the underlying reason for their repudiation of Brinn's companion – but she did not pause for his reply. 'I'll tell you. He got it because he already thought of himself as a failure. He and Cail were seduced by the *merewives*. They *surrendered*. They proved that they were unworthy before Brinn fought the Guardian of the One Tree.'

He had said, *Our folly must end now*– But no *Haruchai* except Cail had harkened to him.

Still softly, almost whispering, Linden finished, 'Brinn became your *ak-Haru*, your greatest hero, *because* he was a failure. He believed the worst about himself, and he understood surrender.'

If the Masters had heeded Brinn's example, they would have chosen their Humbled, not by victory, but by defeat.

'It may be so,' Handir admitted after a moment's silence. 'We have not yet determined our stance towards you. But we have become the Masters of the Land, and the import of the Unbeliever's presence among us is plain. Lords whom the Bloodguard honoured believed that Thomas Covenant was Berek Earthfriend come again. They sacrificed much in his name, trusting that he would save rather than damn the Land. And he has twice justified their faith.

'We know nothing of the rebirth of ancient legends. But we are

Haruchai and will not turn aside from ourselves. Therefore we also will place our faith in the Halfhand. Where he is concerned, we discount the warning of the *Elohim*, for they are arrogant and heartless, and their purposes are often cruel.'

'All right.' Linden looked away from the sound of Handir's voice. 'You didn't hear Cail, you didn't hear Stave, and you won't hear me.' *You'll have to make them listen to you*, but that was not her task. 'You've made that obvious enough.' When she directed her attention past him and the grass-cloaked rim of Revelstone, she could feel the distant moiling of the Demondim. Through the rain, she tasted their opalescence and vitriol, their ravenous hunger for harm, as well as their wary defences and apparent confusion. 'But we're still your guests, and Covenant didn't *command* you to stop me. So unless you have something else to say, I want to get started before those monsters notice me.'

Even if the Demondim could not feel her presence, they might detect the proximity of the Staff of Law.

Handir appeared to hesitate. Then Linden felt rather than saw him move until he no longer stood between her and the horde.

Do something they don't expect.

At once, she dropped to her hands and knees as if she were sinking back into herself; into her concentration and dismay. She no longer regarded Handir and Galt, or her friends, or the clammy grasp of the rain on her back. If anyone spoke to her, she did not hear. By touch, she crawled through the drenched grass towards the extreme edge of Revelstone's promontory. She did not know what the limits of the Vile-spawn's perceptions might be; but she hoped to expose as little of herself as possible.

Then she found it: the outermost rim of the cliff, where the grass and soil of the plateau fell away from their foundation of stone. With little more than her head extended beyond the edge, she cast her health-sense downward.

At first, the rain seemed to plunge past her into a featureless abyss, black and primitive as terror. But as she focused her percipience, she saw with every sense except vision the shaped, deliberate surface of Revelstone's prow directly below her; the walled and open courtyard; the massed bulk of the watchtower. For a moment, she distracted herself by noticing the presence of Masters within the tower. Then she looked farther.

The crown of the watchtower partially blocked her view of the Demondim. However, only a small portion of the horde was obscured: in spite of the rain and the darkness, she could discern most of the forces gathered beyond the Keep's outer gates. When she had attuned herself to the roil and surge of the horde's hatred, its dimensions became clear.

Veiled by rainfall, fiery opalescence seethed in chaotic waves and spatters from edge to edge of the Demondim formation. And through the stirred turmoil of the monsters' might, amid the randomness of their black vitriol, she caught brief hints and glimpses, as elusive as phosphenes, of the dire emerald which emanated from the Illearth Stone. That evil was muffled, muted; banked like embers in ash. But she knew it intimately and could not be mistaken.

Yet of the *caesure* which the Vile-spawn used to reach the Illearth Stone, she saw no sign.

To her taut nerves, the confusion and uncertainty of the monsters seemed as loud as the blaring of battle-horns. But as she studied what she felt and heard and tasted – seeking, seeking – she began to think that their display of bewilderment was *too* loud. Surely if such lorewise creatures were truly baffled, chary of destruction, their attention would resemble hers? They would search actively for comprehension and discernment. Yet they did not. Rather their behaviour was like the wailing of confounded children: thoughtless; apparently incapable of thought.

Galvanised by a small jolt of excitement, Linden pushed her perceptions further, deeper. As she did so, she became certain that the Demondim were putting on a *show* of confusion, that their obvious disturbance was a ruse. It was one of the means by which they concealed their doorway to the Illearth Stone.

According to Covenant, he had *put a crimp in their reality. I made us look like* bait. But Linden was no longer convinced that the Vile-spawn feared an ambush. They had some other reason for withholding their attack.

For a time, uncertainty eroded her concentration, and her sense of the horde became blurred, indefinite; as vague and visceral as the wellsprings of nightmares. Instead of continuing to search for some glimpse of the *caesure*, she felt Kevin's Dirt overhead, high among the clouds. Independent of wind and weather, it spread a smear of doubt across her health-sense; numbed her tactile connection to the Land's true life.

If Covenant had lied—

Mahrtiir had assured her that Kevin's Dirt could not blind her while the effects of her immersion in Glimmermere lingered. Stave had implied that he held the same belief. Nevertheless she seemed to grow weaker by the moment, losing focus; drifting out of tune with the recursive emanations of the horde. She would never be able to identify the Fall unless she awakened the fire of Law to sharpen her perceptions.

Two days ago, the Masters had been able to descry the *caesure's* presence because the Demondim had not yet adopted their tactics of concealment. If she had been aware then of any Fall other than her own – and if she had been stronger—

She had missed that opportunity. It would not come again.

Surely it was Covenant who had told her that she needed the Staff of Law?

Yet any premature use of Earthpower would trigger the defences and virulence of her foes.

Trust yourself. You're the only one who can do this.

Her time with Thomas Covenant long ago had taught her to ignore the dictates of panic.

All right, she told herself. All right. So she could not guess how the Demondim had decided on their present stratagems. So what? She had come to the rim of Revelstone to attempt a kind of surgery; and surgery demanded attention to what was immediately in front of her. The underlying motivations of the monsters were irrelevant. At this moment, under these circumstances, Kastenessen's and even Covenant's designs were irrelevant. Her task was simply and solely to extirpate the cancer of the horde's access to the Illearth Stone. For the surgeon in her, nothing else mattered.

With assiduous care, Linden Avery the Chosen reclaimed her focus on the manipulative masque of the Demondim.

She had spotted quick instances of the Stone's green and lambent evil earlier: she saw more of them now. But they were widely scattered throughout the horde; brief as single raindrops; immediately absorbed.

And they were in constant motion, glinting like fragments of lightning reflected on storm-wracked seas. When she had studied them for a time, she saw that they moved like the whirling migraine miasma of a *caesure*—

Then she understood why she could not discern the Fall itself. Certainly the Demondim concealed it with every resource at their command. Behind their feigned confusion, they seethed with conflicting energies and currents, seeking to disguise the source of their might. But still they exerted that might, using it to obscure itself. Each glimpse and flicker of the Illearth Stone was so immediate, immanent and compelling that it masked the disruption of time which made it possible.

Linden understood – but the understanding did not help her. Now that she had recognised what was happening, she could focus her health-sense past the threat inherent in each individual glint of emerald; and when she did so, she saw hints of time's enabling distortion, the swirl of instants which severed the millennia between the horde and the Stone. But those hints were too brief and unpredictable. Their chaotic eva-nescence obscured them. They were like haemorrhaging blood-vessels in surgery: they prevented her from seeing the precise place where her scalpel and sutures were needed.

There she knew the truth. The task that she had chosen for herself was impossible. She was fundamentally inadequate to it. The tactics of the Demondim were too alien for her human mind to encompass: she could not find her way through the complex chicanery and vehemence of the monsters. She would not be able to unmake the *caesure* unless she found a way to grasp what all of the Demondim were thinking and doing at every moment.

Therefore—

Groaning inwardly, she retreated a little way so that she could rest her forehead on the wet grass. She wanted to console herself with the sensation of its fecund health, its fragile and tenacious grip on the aged soil of the plateau; its delicate demonstration of Earthpower. Even the chill of the rain contradicted in some fashion the hurtful machinations of the Demondim, the savage emerald of the Stone, the quintessential *wrong* of the *caesure*; the impossibility of her task. Rain was appropriate; condign. It fell because the earth required its natural sustenance. Such things belonged to the organic health of the world. They deserved to be preserved.

She could not cut the *caesure* away as she had intended. Therefore she would have to approach the problem in a less surgical – and far more hazardous – manner. She would have to risk a direct assault on the monsters, hoping that they would strike back with the force of the Illearth Stone. Then, during the imponderable interval between the instant of their counterattack and the moment when she was incinerated, she would have to locate the horde's now-unveiled Fall; locate and extinguish it. If she survived long enough—

She had no reason to believe that she could succeed. The challenge would be both swift and overwhelming. And if she effaced the *caesure*, she would be no closer to rescuing Jeremiah or relieving the Land's other perils. If she failed, she might not live long enough to see Revelstone destroyed because of her.

In her son's name, she had twice risked absolute ruin. But now the question of his survival had become far more complex. In spite of the fact that he remained Lord Foul's prisoner, he was here. He had regained his mind. And Covenant, whose every word disturbed her, had averred that his own plans would free Jeremiah at last—

Covenant was concerned that an assault by the horde might prevent him from carrying out his designs. If she confronted the Demondim directly, she might do more than cause a catastrophe for the Land: she might cost her son his only real chance to live.

And yet – and yet—

The Demondim were *here*. The power of the Illearth Stone was *here*. Kastenessen and the *skurj* were already at work, seeking the destruction of the Land. And somewhere the Worm of the World's End awaited wakening. How could she turn her back on any immediate threat when she did not understand Covenant, and the Masters had no effective defence?

Trapped in her dilemma, she was conscious of nothing except the ravening powers of the horde and the extremity of her hesitation. She did not feel the rain falling on her back or the dampness of the grass. And she did not sense Stave's approach. Until he said, 'Attend, Chosen,' she had forgotten that she was not alone.

He had said those exact words twice before, both times in warning – and both because either Esmer or the ur-viles had taken her by surprise.

Dragging herself up from the grass, she braced her doubts on the Staff of Law and climbed to her feet.

As if without transition, Liand reached her side and took hold of her arm so that she would not stumble or fall as she turned to find herself peering dumbly into the black face of the ur-viles' loremaster.

The creature's nostrils gaped, scenting her through the rain. Behind the storm-clouds, dawn had reached the Upper Land, and the sun drove a dim illumination into the dark; just enough light to reveal the dire shape of the loremaster. Now that she was aware of the creature, she felt rain spatter against its obsidian flesh, run down its torso and limbs – and hiss into steam as droplets struck the blade of molten iron gripped in its fist.

Behind the larger creature stood a packed wedge of Demondim-spawn, as black as ebony and midnight, and as ominous. Even the Waynhim scattered among them seemed as dark as demons. As far as she could tell, those few creatures that had accompanied her here had joined the larger force which Esmer had delivered beside Glimmermere. And they all seemed to be muttering imprecations as they crowded close to each other and Linden, aiming their combined might through the loremaster and its hot blade.

When it smelled her attention, the loremaster lifted its free hand and held its ruddy knife over its palm, apparently offering to cut itself on her behalf.

This same creature had behaved in the same fashion when she was preparing herself for her first experience of a *caesure*; when she had been sick with fear and the after-effects of the horserite. At that time, a much smaller wedge of ur-viles had healed her, giving her the strength to find her way through Joan's madness; to reach the Land's past and the Staff of Law.

Now the loremaster appeared to be making a similar offer—

Yesterday Esmer had said to her, *I have enabled their presence here, and they have accepted it, so that they may serve you. They will ward you, and this place – Revelstone – with more fidelity than the* Haruchai, *who have no hearts.*

Covenant had jeered at Esmer's assertion. He had warned her that the manacles of the ur-viles were intended for him. *They've been Foul's servants ever since they met him.* And she had her own reasons for wondering what secret purpose lay behind the assistance of the ur-viles. Esmer's involvement cast doubt in all directions.

'Linden' – the rain muffled Liand's voice – 'your distress is plain. You fear that you will fail. But here is aid. Few of these creatures are those that have served you with both lore and valour. Yet those ur-viles are here, and the Waynhim with them. It may be that they will strengthen you to succeed.'

He gave his faith too easily— Covenant would have mocked him for it.

Out of the dim dawn, Mahrtiir added, 'The Ramen have long known some few of these ur-viles. They have acted for our benefit. And they have succoured Anele.'

Stave said nothing. He had felt Esmer's fury and might therefore suspect the motives of the ur-viles.

When she did not respond, the Stonedownor turned to Handir. 'You speak for the Masters,' he said more strongly. 'What is your word now? I have learned that in their time your kind fought long and bitterly against such creatures. Also the Unbeliever desires the Chosen to desist. Will you permit her to be aided now?'

For a long moment, Linden heard nothing except the harsh invocations – or imprecations – of the Demondim-spawn. Then Handir replied dispassionately, 'From Stave, we have received one account of these creatures, and from the ur-Lord, another. We cannot discern the sooth of such matters. Yet here we need make no determination. Waynhim now stand among the ur-viles. In the name of their ancient service to the Land, we honour the Waynhim as we do the Ranyhyn. While they participate in the actions of these ur-viles, we will not hinder them.'

Covenant had discounted the Waynhim as though their long devotion meant nothing.

Still the loremaster extended its open palm; poised its blade to shed its own blood.

Trust yourself.

Until now, she had accomplished almost nothing that had not been made possible by the ur-viles – and the Waynhim.

Holding her breath, Linden opened her hand and proffered it to the loremaster.

Swift as a striking snake, as if it feared that she might change her mind, the creature flicked at her with its eldritch dagger, slicing a quick line of blood across the base of her thumb. Then the loremaster cut itself and reached out to clasp her hand so that its acrid blood mingled with hers.

Involuntarily all of her muscles clenched, anticipating a rush of strength and exaltation that would lift her entirely out of herself; elevate her doubts to certainty and power.

In the Verge of Wandering, the loremaster's ichor had changed her, transcending her sickness and dread; her sheer mortality. It transformed her again now – but in an entirely different way. The wedge in front of her, more than a hundred creatures all chanting together, had called a new lore to her aid; had given her a new power. Instead of strength like the charging of Ranyhyn, she felt an almost metaphysical alteration, at once keener and more subtle than simple health and force and possibility. The creatures had not made *her* stronger: they had augmented her health-sense, increasing its range and discernment almost beyond comprehension.

Now she could have pierced the closed hearts of the Masters, if she had wished to do so. Hell, she could have *possessed* any one of them– Or she could have searched out the mysteries locked within the Demondim-spawn themselves. They had given her the power to lay bare the complex implications of their Weird. Or she might have been able to discern the causes of Covenant's strangeness, and Jeremiah's. Certainly she could have identified the nature of her son's unforeseen power—

But she found that she had no desire for any of those things; no desire and no time. The same given percipience which made them possible also made her aware that her enhancement would be ephemeral. She had perhaps a dozen heartbeats, at most two dozen, in which to exercise her whetted perceptions.

And she was already able to descry every single one of the Demondim far below her. The ur-viles and Waynhim had been formed by Demondim: they understood their makers. They had given her the capacity to penetrate all of the defences which the horde had raised against her.

That was enough. She did not need more.

With Stave and Liand beside her, she turned to face the cliff and the siege again. There she raised the Staff high in both hands, gripping her own blood and that of the loremaster to the surface of the incorruptible wood.

Now she beheld plainly all that was required of her. The opalescent surges and cross-currents of the monsters' subterfuge were clear, as etched and vivid as fine map-work. And they were transparent. Through them, disguised and concealed by them, she found the means by which the Demondim deployed the Illearth Stone. With all of her senses, she watched baleful green glints swirl and spit, many thousands of them, outlining precisely the mad hornet-storm of time that allowed the horde to exert the Stone's evil.

While her heart beat towards the instant when her transcendental percipience would fail, she reached through the veil of emerald to the horde's *caesure*.

It was as obvious to her now as the Fall which Esmer had summoned to the Verge of Wandering on her behalf; as unmistakable as the chaos which she herself had ripped in time. Fed by the insight, lore, and vitriol of the wedge at her back, her health-sense at last recognised the exact location and shape, as specific as a signature, of the monsters' Fall. Each piece of time that Joan shattered with wild magic had its own definitive angles, texture, composition; its own place in the wilderland of rubble at Joan's feet. With the telic power of the ur-viles and Waynhim in her veins, Linden was able to name unerringly the unique substance which Joan had destroyed to form this particular *caesure*.

When she was utterly certain of what she *saw*, she called forth a blaze as bright and cleansing as sunfire from the Staff. In an instant, she had surrounded herself with brilliance and flame, lighting the proud jut of Revelstone as if she had effaced the storm and the gloom, the shroud of rain; as if she had pierced with Earthpower and Law even the vile fug of Kevin's Dirt.

For perhaps as long as a heartbeat, she considered hurling her fire directly against the Illearth Stone. Through the open door of the Fall, she could have striven to excise the Stone's perversion at its source. Then she rejected the idea. If she failed – if she proved inadequate to that unfathomable contest – she would lose her opportunity to unmake the Fall. And if she did not fail, she would alter the Land's past so profoundly that the Arch of Time itself might break.

Instead, risking everything, she took a moment to search through the rampant insanity of the *caesure* for Joan, hoping somehow to soothe that tormented woman. In spite of the danger, she spent precious seconds seeking to send care and concern through the maelstrom created by Joan's pain.

Then she had to stop. She had no more time.

Relinquishing thoughts of Joan, Linden exerted all of her bestowed percipience to concentrate the energies of the Staff. And when she had summoned enough conflagration to reach the heavens, she sent a prodigious wall of fire crashing down like a tsunami on the horde's Fall.

That *caesure* was huge, even by the measure of the one which she had created. And it had been nurtured as well as controlled and directed with every resource of cunning and lore that the Demondim could command. It was defended now by the entire virulence and will of the monsters. The woman whom she had been before the loremaster had shared its blood with her would not have been able to overcome such opposition.

As the bestowed potency of her health-sense faltered and failed, however, she heard the horde's feigned confusion become a feral roar of rage; and she knew that she had succeeded.

Chapter Five:

'I know what to do'

Sinking under a sudden wave of exhaustion, Linden might have fallen if Stave and Liand had not caught her; upheld her. As rain and faint dawn returned to the promontory of Lord's Keep, their gloom filled her heart: as damp as tears, and blocked from the sun by the receding storm.

She felt a kind of grief, the consequences of self-expenditure, as though her success were a complex failure. She had missed her chance to learn the truth about the Demondim-spawn. More than that, she had let slip an opportunity to understand the changes in Jeremiah and Covenant. If only the gift of the wedge had lasted longer—

She had sacrificed her own concerns for the safety of Revelstone. The loss of augmented percipience and blazing Law seemed to blind her.

Nevertheless a grim and satisfied part of her knew what she had accomplished, and how. That was *aid*, she thought as she blinked at the rain. Out of the Land's past, Esmer had brought ur-viles and Waynhim to *serve* her in the truest sense of the word.

So where was his betrayal? How did the presence and assistance of the Demondim-spawn endanger her, or the Land? Had Esmer simply intended to repay a perceived debt? Was that possible?

Linden could not believe that he had come to the end of his self-contradictions.

Still the ur-viles and Waynhim had given her more help than she could have expected or imagined. And in so doing, they had made themselves vulnerable to her. While their bestowed percipience had endured, she could have probed their deepest and most cherished secrets. They had trusted her—

She did not comprehend what motivated them; but she was no longer able to doubt them. Esmer's intentions were not theirs. When he betrayed her, he would do so through his own deeds, not through the presence or purposes of the Demondim-spawn.

Until her first rush of weariness passed, she did not notice that Liand was speaking to her, murmuring his astonishment.

'Heaven and Earth, Linden.' His voice was husky with wonder. 'I know not how to name what you have wrought. Never have I witnessed such fire. Not even in the course of our flight from the Demondim—' She felt his awe through his grasp on her arm. 'For a moment while you dazzled me, I seemed to stand at the side of the Land's redemption.'

Earlier he had told her, *You have it within you to perform horrors.* But she had not done so here: of that she was certain. Instead she had struck an important blow in Revelstone's defence.

Sighing to herself, she began to struggle against her fatigue. So much remained to be done—

'You have extinguished the Fall,' Stave announced as if she had asked for confirmation. 'The bale of the Illearth Stone is now absent from this time.' Then he added, 'Thus the Demondim are enraged. Already they assail the Keep. If the Masters wish to preserve Revelstone, a long and arduous battle awaits them. Yet you have made it conceivable that they will prevail.'

Dully Linden tried to think of some other way that she might oppose the horde. In spite of Stave's attempt to reassure her, she was not confident that his kinsmen could hold off the Demondim for long. But she had already spent all of her resources. Only the support of her friends and the nourishing touch of the Staff kept her on her feet. And Covenant wanted her to meet him near Furl Falls: a walk of, what, close to two leagues? If she did not rally soon, her friends would have to carry her.

Long ago, the Unhomed had designed Revelstone to withstand the enemies of the Old Lords. In her weakness, Linden could only hope that the ancient granite would prove to be as obdurate as the men who warded it.

With an effort, she turned her attention outward; towards the people and creatures gathered around her.

She was not surprised to find that most of the Demondim-spawn had already dispersed, leaving no trace of themselves in the dawn or the rain. But she felt a small frisson of anticipation when she saw that the loremaster still stood nearby with a wedge at its back. The formation held no more than half a dozen creatures – but they were all Waynhim.

The loremaster's knife had disappeared. Instead, with both hands the black creature offered her an iron bowl.

As soon as she heard the muted guttural voices of the Waynhim, and caught the dust-and-mildew scent of *vitrim*, her heart lifted. The creatures understood the effects of their earlier gift. Now they sought to restore her. The Waynhim chanted, summoning and concentrating their lore, in order to multiply the lenitive potency of the liquid in the bowl.

At once, she reached for the bowl, eager for sustenance; for any theurgy which might revive her.

As she swallowed the dank fluid in long gulps, she recognised its distilled virtue. It was stronger than any *vitrim* she had ever tasted. In an instant, it seemed to spangle like sunshine through her veins and along her nerves as if it were a form of hurtloam. It was not, of course: it was not organic or natural in any useful sense. Like the ur-viles and Waynhim themselves, the beverage had been created of knowledge and might which were alien to Earthpower or Law. Nonetheless it met her needs. It did more than give back the energy and courage which she had expended against the horde's *caesure*: in some fashion, it restored her sense of her self.

With gratitude in her eyes and appreciation in her limbs, she bowed deeply as she returned the bowl to the loremaster. Then she looked as closely as she could at the creature and its companions. Earlier she had given no consideration to the chance that her efforts against the horde might harm the Demondim-spawn. Now she felt chagrin at her thoughtlessness. A few short days and several millennia ago, she had seen that the Waynhim were damaged by their stewardship of the Staff—

Once again, they had aided her in spite of their own peril.

The artificial nature of the creatures confused her health-sense. Yet she detected no injury in the loremaster, or in its small wedge. The attitudes of the Waynhim suggested fatigue and strain, but nothing more.

Perhaps they had been protected by the fact that every aspect of her power had been directed away from them.

'Thank you,' she said to the loremaster's eyeless face and slitted mouth. 'I don't know why you turned your back on Lord Foul. I'll probably never understand it. But I want you to know that I'm grateful. If you can ever figure out how to tell me what you need or want from me, I'll do it.'

The loremaster gave no sign that it had heard her. It had put its bowl away somewhere within itself. The Waynhim behind it had stopped chanting. A moment after she fell silent, the creatures loped away, taking no apparent notice of Handir and Galt, or of the Ramen and Anele. Soon they seemed to dissolve into the dark air and the rain, and Linden lost sight of them.

She no longer needed Stave's support, or Liand's. She was strong enough to face her friends – and almost eager to meet with Jeremiah and Covenant. Briefly she considered expending some of her new vitality against the Demondim. Then she shrugged the idea aside. She did not know what Covenant's intentions might require of her, or how much power she would be asked to wield.

She had done what she could for Revelstone. The Masters would have to do the rest.

When she looked towards Mahrtiir and his Cords, they bowed in the Ramen style. 'That was well done, Ringthane,' said Mahrtiir gruffly. 'Your tale grows with each new deed – and will doubtless expand in the telling. We are honoured that it has been granted to us to accompany you.'

Bhapa nodded his earnest agreement, and Pahni smiled gravely. Yet it seemed to Linden that the young woman's attention was fixed more on Liand than on her.

Without warning, Anele remarked, 'Such power becomes you.'

He stood with thick wet grass under his feet, but his voice was not Covenant's – or any other voice that she recognised. It was deep and full, rich with harmonics which she had not heard before. Apparently the force that had silenced Covenant – or Covenant's imitator – the previous day still allowed other beings to inhabit the old man.

'But it will not suffice,' he continued. 'In the end, you must succumb. And if you do not, you will nonetheless be compelled to accept my aid, for which I will demand recompense.'

His moonstone eyes glowed damply in the crepuscular air.

'Anele?' Quickly Linden focused her revitalised senses on him. 'Who are you now?' But she could perceive nothing except his age and frailty, and his heritage of Earthpower. Even his madness was masked, at least for the moment. 'Who's speaking?'

Anele replied with an incongruously gallant bow. 'Lady,' the stranger in him answered, 'we will meet at our proper time – if you do not fail the perils which have been prepared for you. But you would do well to heed my words.'

An instant later, the old man's derangement closed like a shutter on the being who had possessed him. Either the stranger had made a hasty departure, or some force had expelled him.

'Did you hear that?' Linden asked her friends unsteadily. 'Did it sound familiar? Have you heard that voice before?'

Liand shook his head; and the Manethrall stated without hesitation, 'We have not. The distinction cannot be mistaken. Some new being has spoken.'

Oh, shit! she thought in sudden anger. *Another* one? How many were there? How many of them were her enemies? And how much longer would Anele have to suffer such violations?

When would his pain become great enough to merit healing?

It will not suffice.

Covenant had referred to '*other* powers' – And Jeremiah had mentioned a race called 'the Insequent'. Those people were – or had been – lorewise enough to recognise and respond to her son's disembodied presence.

The possibility that Linden's situation might be even more complicated and treacherous than she had realised made her stomach clench. Hell and damn! she muttered to herself as if she were Covenant. This is getting ridiculous. How was she supposed to find her way when she knew so little about what was really going on?

—the perils which have been prepared for you.

Abruptly she wheeled on the Voice of the Masters. 'Are Covenant and my son still here?' she demanded in alarm. 'Did I banish them?'

This is bad enough. Tell me that I haven't made it worse.

Handir's mien tightened slightly, but he betrayed no other reaction. 'The ur-Lord and his companion remain. They were forewarned of your power, and have endured it.' A moment later, he added, 'They have departed from their chambers, proceeding towards the upland and Furl

Falls.' The moisture on his face seemed to increase the severity of his gaze. 'If you have no wish to delay them, we must set forth.'

In response, Mahrtiir growled softly. 'If the ur-Lord is delayed, let him be delayed. She is the Ringthane and has demonstrated her worth. Do you question this?'

Torn between relief that she had not erased Covenant and Jeremiah, anger on Anele's behalf, and anxiety about what lay ahead of her, Linden made a placating gesture towards the Manethrall. 'You're right,' she told Handir. 'We should go. Covenant says that he can save us. I don't want to keep him waiting.'

She did not fear that he would attempt *the salvation of the Land* without her. She had some innominate role to play in his designs. But they would be dangerous: she was sure of that. How could they be otherwise, when she had resisted his desire for his ring?

Whatever happened, she meant to protect her son.

Beckoning for her friends to join her, she walked away from the savagery of the Demondim to keep her promise to Covenant and Jeremiah.

As she trod the sodden grass, the rainfall slanting into her face continued its gradual decline. Behind her, the storm-front blocked the rising sun. But a cold wind was rising, sweeping down onto the plateau from the distant mountains. Its taste and touch implied that it would increase. Already it slapped the dwindling rain at her. Soon the droplets would begin to sting when they struck her skin.

Her cloak was soaked, and most of her clothes were damp. If she remained exposed to the weather, the wind would gradually chill her until she lost the effects of the loremaster's *vitrim*. Nevertheless she strode towards the west with determination in her strides and a semblance of clarity in her heart. She feared so many things that she could not name them all; but wind and rain and cold were not among them.

Now Stave, Handir and Galt guided her along the south-facing rim of the great Keep, avoiding the centre of the promontory. Doubtless this was the most direct path towards Furl Falls. Liand walked steadily at her side, his face set against the weather. Occasionally his attention turned towards Pahni as if every sight of her took him by surprise. Even more than the Ramen, however, he seemed settled in his distrust of Covenant

– and of Jeremiah. He had not been raised on legends of the Ringthane who had refused to ride the Ranyhyn. And he knew nothing of Covenant's victories over the Despiser – or of their terrible cost – apart from what he had heard from Linden. For him, the situation was comparatively simple. His loyalty belonged to Linden.

She felt a desire to stop and talk to him; to explain how Covenant had earned her love and gratitude, and why she was prepared to sacrifice anything and everything for Jeremiah. She wanted Liand to understand why she intended to give Covenant as much help as she could, in spite of his strangeness and his scorn and his oblique cruelty. But she resisted the impulse. Covenant had avowed that he knew how to retrieve the Land from Lord Foul's malice. Liand would learn the truth soon enough: Linden herself would learn it. Then she would no longer feel a need to justify her choices.

Instead of speaking, she tightened her grasp on the Staff; confirmed with her free hand that the immaculate circle of Covenant's ring still hung on its chain under her shirt. For Revelstone's sake, she had already missed one opportunity to explore Covenant's motives and Jeremiah's plight: she would not miss another.

Because she restrained herself, she and her companions walked in silence. The Ramen had a clearer sense than Liand did of what was at stake, for the Land if not for her: they were enclosed in a tight, expectant concentration. And Stave was *Haruchai*, too self-contained for unnecessary conversation. Only Anele spoke; but his incoherent mumbling conveyed nothing.

Then Stave touched Linden's arm. When she glanced at him, she saw that Galt and the Voice of the Masters had turned their steps away from the line of the cliff, angling across a low rise. In that direction, by her estimate, lay the opening of the tunnel which emerged from Revelstone. Presumably Handir and the Humbled aimed to intercept Covenant and Jeremiah there.

With her companions, she followed the two Masters.

Clouds still occluded the dawn, but the thin grey light was enough. From the top of the rise, Linden could see the wide mouth of the Keep gaping to the rain. Just outside the tunnel, Covenant and Jeremiah stood facing towards her; obviously waiting for her.

They were accompanied by Clyme and Branl, as well as by perhaps twenty other Masters.

Vaguely Linden wondered if these *Haruchai* were all that could be spared from the defence of Revelstone. She still had no idea how many of Stave's kinsmen occupied Lord's Keep.

Covenant did not appear to look at her: he held his head down as if he were lost in contemplation. But Jeremiah waved with the enthusiasm of an excited boy.

The sight of his eagerness smote Linden deeply. She should have been delighted; should have felt unalloyed joy at his conscious and willing presence, his show of gladness. But she could not forget that it was *his* power which had prevented her from touching him in the forehall.

He and Covenant remained impenetrable to her senses.

Involuntarily her heart tightened, and her face settled into a grim frown, as she strode down the hillside to meet the two people whom she most loved – and whom she most wanted to trust.

At her approach, Covenant glanced up once, briefly, then began to walk away from the throat of Revelstone, heading towards Furl Falls. But Jeremiah called happily, 'Hi, Mom! It's time to get started!' before he moved to join Covenant.

Her son's tattered pyjamas were drenched, but he did not appear to feel the cold. She still did not know whether he had been shot.

The Masters arrayed themselves protectively around the Unbeliever and Jeremiah without impeding Linden's approach. In a few moments, she caught up with them.

Stave walked like a guardian between her and them. Rain pricked at her face and hands. The wind had teeth now, biting through her cloak into her clothes.

Covenant was closer to her, between Stave and Jeremiah. Carefully neutral, as if she were speaking to the weather rather than to Covenant, she said, 'I think that I understand why you didn't want to tell me what you're planning.' *I deserve better than this. I need something in return.* 'But why did we have to come out here?' She gestured vaguely at the rain. *A little bit of trust.* 'Why couldn't you show me inside? And why did you have to wait until now?'

Covenant seemed distracted, his thoughts elsewhere. But he did not pretend that he had not heard her. 'It isn't going to be easy,' he said absently. 'We don't just need distance from the Demondim. We need a smoke-screen. Like the Earthpower coming out of Glimmermere. If they catch even a whiff of what we're doing—' For a moment, his voice faded. Then he added, 'But that's not the only problem. There are other forces that might try to stop us. We needed time to prepare for them.'

'What "forces"?' asked Linden. 'You said something like that last night, but you didn't explain.'

He kept his head down, studying the soaked grass. 'Well, Kastenessen for one. Who knows what the hell Esmer is going to do?' He glanced over at Jeremiah. 'And you're forgetting that those ur-viles have manacles.'

Linden missed a step. She could no longer conceive any ill of the Demondim-spawn. After what she had just experienced, his suspicions sounded absurd.

'But if I were you,' he went on before she could pursue the subject, 'I'd be more worried about the *Elohim*. They've never trusted me. You remember *that*.

'Of course,' he said sourly, 'you have my ring, which suits them just fine. But that doesn't mean they won't try to interfere. They haven't spent all this time warning people to "beware" of me just for fun.'

'I've met them,' Jeremiah offered. 'I think they just don't like it when somebody else is more important than they are.'

By slow degrees, dawn leaked though the receding storm; dissolved the darkness over the plateau. Now stands of trees were visible on either side of the route chosen by the Masters: copses of mimosa and wattle, clustered cedars, all dark, shrouded with rain and full of implied secrets. Any number of lorewise beings could have concealed themselves there, and Linden would have caught no hint of them.

She shook her head. 'I don't understand. If Kastenessen wants to stop you, why would the *Elohim* want the same thing?' Esmer had told her that they expected her to deal with Kastenessen and the *skurj*. *Are you not the Wildwielder? What then remains to cause the* Elohim *concern?* 'They Appointed him to stop the *skurj*. In fact, they *forced* him. They made him a prisoner. Why would they want what *he* wants now?'

'You're right,' replied Covenant sharply. 'You *don't* understand. Especially Kastenessen.'

With elaborate patience, he explained, 'You need to realise that he didn't *break* his Durance. He didn't have that much actual power. No, he *slipped out*. Which he managed to do by becoming part *skurj* himself.' While Linden stared at him, Covenant muttered as if to himself, 'He probably got the idea from Foul. The Despiser loves shit like that.'

Then he resumed his explanation. 'Oh, the effect was the same. No more Durance. But the point is, it was hideously painful. Merging with the *skurj*, even a little bit— It was more painful than you can imagine. Hell and blood, Linden, it probably makes what Jeremiah is going through feel like a picnic.'

'He's right, Mom,' Jeremiah put in with as much earnestness as his excitement allowed. He was tossing his racecar back and forth between his hands as he walked, catching it deftly with his remaining fingers. '*I saw it*. Before you came to the Land. It's horrible. If I ever have to choose' – he shuddered dramatically – 'I'll stay where I am.'

Still studying the rain-matted grass, Covenant nodded. 'Now Kastenessen is *all* pain. It's made him completely insane. There's nothing else left. And rage is his only outlet. Everything he does is just another way of screaming.

'But he can't rage hard enough to stop the pain. No one can. Not for long, anyway. So he does what any lunatic does in his situation. He causes himself *more* pain, trying to make his rage more powerful. Being part *skurj* isn't excruciating enough, so he surrounds himself with them, he makes them carry out his rage. And when that doesn't work, he maims—'

Covenant's voice trailed away.

'Maims what?' Linden asked at once.

'Him*self*, of course,' the Unbeliever snorted. 'It doesn't matter what he hurts. All that matters is pain and rage. He's a walking, talking *apotheosis* of pain, and nothing is going to make him sane again. I intend to put him out of his misery, but he just doesn't understand. He can't. His pain is all he's got. He's terrified of losing it. That's why he wants to stop me.

'If he figures out what's about to happen, he'll go berserk. He can't bring the *skurj* against us fast enough to make a difference. But he's still *Elohim*. He can show up anywhere in a heartbeat. And you do not want to fight that kind of power.'

Abruptly Covenant stopped; turned so that Linden was forced to face him. Again she saw a glimpse of embers in the depths of his eyes, ruddy and threatening. The strict lines of his visage seemed to challenge her. While Stave watched him warily, and her friends crowded close to hear him, the Unbeliever told her harshly, 'That's what *I've* been doing all night.' He seemed to suggest that she had been wasting her time on trivialities. 'Distracting Kastenessen. Confusing him with tricks, like I did to the Demondim.'

'All right.' Linden struggled to absorb Covenant's description. 'Now it makes even less sense. If you're right about Kastenessen' – if his condition resembled Joan's – 'how can the *Elohim* possibly want what he wants?'

'Damnation.' Covenant wiped at the rain on his face; rubbed the hint of fire out of his eyes. 'They have different reasons. Kastenessen is just screaming. He hurts, and he wants to fill the world with it. The *Elohim* don't trust *me*. They never have. As far as they're concerned, the fact that I'm part of the Arch – that I can do the things I do – is a disaster.

'Time is too important to them. Their immortality depends on it. They don't want anybody who even *remembers* what death means to have the kind of power I do. So they don't want me to stop Foul. They're afraid I might change the shape of the Arch. The shape of their Würd. They're afraid of what that might cost them.

'Of course, they're wrong. I'm not here to change Time. I protect it. That's my *job*. But they don't believe me.'

'He's right, Mom,' Jeremiah said again. But he sounded far away, hidden behind Covenant.

A sharp gust snatched back the hood of Linden's cloak, flung rain into her face. Among the trees, the wind droned with trepidation.

Turning as if in disgust, Covenant strode away. 'Come on,' he demanded before Linden could try to understand him. 'I can't keep this up indefinitely. And I can't do it without you.'

Linden nearly stumbled in surprise. Until that moment, he had not acknowledged that she was important to him; that he sought anything from her except his ring.

She hastened to catch up with him again. But when she did so, she found that he had silenced her. *I can't do it*— Realities seemed to shift around her, veering from one uncertainty to another. Over the plateau, the rain declined to a thin drizzle that would have felt as soothing as mist if it had not been driven by the wind. Through the gloom, the advance of daylight gave definition to the landscape, clarifying the contours of the hills, distancing the darkness among the trees. Yet she hardly noticed such things. *I can't—*

But first I'll have to convince Linden— When she had resisted his desire for his ring, however, he had insisted on nothing except *a* little *bit of trust.* From that, Liand had inferred that Covenant still had a use for her. But Covenant himself had said nothing of the kind.

Until now.

As he or the Masters led her past a cluster of gnarled and arching jacarandas, Linden caught sight of a river in the distance ahead. There Glimmermere's out-flow gathered rain and small streams in its accelerating rush towards Furl Falls. The wind stung her eyes, forced her to shade them with her free hand. But when she had blinked the blur from her vision, she saw the river clearly. Along the watercourse, the hills seemed to bow down in homage to Glimmermere's waters. Apart from a few knaggy firs clinging to the rim of the cliff, there were no trees. From the vicinity of the falls, nothing would obstruct her view for a long stone's throw in any direction.

The terrain offered that advantage. Findail's kind, and Kastenessen's, could appear anywhere, flowing up from the ground without warning, or materialising along the rough wind. And Esmer had inherited some of their abilities. But other foes would be plainly visible. Even the Demondim – and they could not reach the plateau without first defeating Revelstone.

In spite of Covenant's warnings, however, Linden was only vaguely troubled by the possibility of an attack. She still felt sustained by *vitrim*. At need, she might find a way to defend herself and her companions without endangering Covenant and Jeremiah. Under the circumstances, she was more afraid of Covenant's manner – and of Jeremiah's strange powers.

I can't do it—

Neither the Unbeliever nor her son loved her. Covenant had been profoundly altered by his millennia in the Arch of Time. And Jeremiah's heart was fixed on the man who had made it possible for him to be here.

He was the best. —the only real friend—

And he needed her– Did he have a *design for the salvation of the Land?* A plan that included her? Good. But if he did not, she still intended to learn the truth about him. And about her tormented son.

Gripping her courage, she descended the last slopes towards the vicinity of Furl Falls.

Covenant brought her within a dozen strides of the riverbank, then stopped. 'This'll do,' he said stiffly to Jeremiah. 'Don't you think?'

Jeremiah tossed his racecar into the air as if he were testing the force of the wind. Then he tucked the bright red toy into the waistband of his pyjamas. 'It feels right. If we can't do it here, we probably can't do it at all.'

Covenant nodded. The wind rumpled his hair and tugged at his clothes, making him look as wild and driven as a prophet.

Without apparent hurry, the Masters positioned themselves in an arc that enclosed Covenant, Jeremiah, and Linden's small company between the riverbank and the edge of the cliff. At the same time, Galt joined Branl, Clyme and Handir in front of Covenant. He was the ur-Lord, the reincarnation of Berek Halfhand. The Voice of the Masters and the Humbled stood with him. And Linden did not doubt that they remained suspicious of her. They distrusted Earthpower and loss—

Gusts flicked her tresses across her eyes. Pulling back her wet hair, she risked taking a step closer to Covenant. If he wanted a 'smoke-screen' to disguise his actions, he had chosen his destination well. Glimmermere's outflow still held a measure of its eldritch vitality: its supernal energies sang to her senses. But it was much diluted; too weak to banish him and her son.

'All right,' she said against the wind. 'We're here. What are you going to do?'

'Enjoy the view,' he replied acidly. Her question appeared to offend him. Or perhaps he felt threatened by her nearness. But then he relented. 'I'm sorry. You're right. We should get started. I'm just about at the end of what I can do.

'But don't ask me to explain it.' His gaze held hers for an instant, then shied away. During that moment, however, she saw no fire in his eyes. Instead she seemed to detect a transitory glint of anticipation or fear. 'I haven't got the time or the energy. And I'm tired of the way you look at me. Like I'm about to rape somebody. Do what I tell you, and I'll show you how I'm going to save all of us.'

A little *bit of trust*. Slowly Linden nodded her acquiescence. What else could she do? She needed answers; needed to understand– If she refused Covenant now, she might lose her only chance to redeem her son.

At once, he commanded, 'Then make your friends stand back. They're in the way. This doesn't include them.'

Before she could reply, Mahrtiir stepped forward. Ominously relaxed, Stave balanced his weight on the balls of his feet. Liand curled his hands into fists at his sides.

'You are the Unbeliever,' the Manethrall rasped. 'Once you were the Ringthane. In this, we do not doubt you. But we stand with Linden Avery. That which falls to her will fall to us as well, for good or ill.'

From his place between Pahni and Bhapa, Anele announced firmly, 'I no longer fear the ur-viles.'

Instantly angry, Covenant snapped, 'Hellfire, Linden! This is *important*. I need your goddamn friends to *get out of my way*.'

His eyes remained shrouded, revealing nothing.

'Linden,' said Liand softly. The mounting moan of the wind snatched at his voice. 'I mislike this. How is it that a man who once loved you spurns your friends?'

As if to protect her, Stave placed himself squarely between Linden and Covenant. His single eye regarded her intently.

'Chosen, the Masters will support the ur-Lord in this. If you do not oppose him, they will not oppose you. But he is the Unbeliever, the Illender. The Giants have named him Earthfriend and Rockbrother. The Lords of old entrusted him with the Land's doom. If he requests it of them, the Masters will aid him.'

Linden heard him. The Masters would use force– And they were too many: Stave, Liand, and the Ramen could not fight them. She would lose everything that might be gained by cooperating with Covenant.

She might cost Jeremiah his redemption.

I can't do it without you.

The boy moved so that she could see him past Stave and Covenant. His young face wore an expression of pleading which was almost desperation.

'Please, Mom,' he said tensely. 'We need this. It has to be just you.'

His tic signalled to her in a code that she could not decipher.

—*if you do not fail the perils which have been prepared for you.*

Deliberately Linden turned away from Covenant and Jeremiah and the assembled Masters. With a gesture, she gathered her friends around her. *Vitrim* and the Staff of Law gave her the strength to say, 'Listen. I know how you feel. I don't like this any better than you do. But it's a risk that we have to take. Covenant says that he can save the Land.' He can save *my son.* 'If he fails, I'm not exactly helpless. And you won't be far away.

'I'm not asking you to trust him. Hell, I'm not even asking you to trust *me.*' She smiled grimly. 'I just think that we can't afford to miss this chance.'

One by one, she looked around at the people who had chosen to share her fate.

Liand ducked his head as if he were abashed. Mahrtiir glared at her, fierce with disapproval. Stave's scarred visage revealed nothing. Bhapa frowned like a man who agreed absolutely with his Manethrall. But Pahni's gaze was fixed on Liand as though she feared for him; wanted him to comply with Covenant's demand. And Anele's blind eyes watched the north as if it held secrets that only he could discern.

At last, Stave said flatly, 'I see no other road.' And Mahrtiir muttered, 'Nor do I.'

Liand flung a look like an appeal at Linden, but he did not protest. Instead he went abruptly to help Pahni draw Anele away from Covenant and Jeremiah; away from Linden.

With a tight shrug, Bhapa joined Mahrtiir and Stave as they retreated perhaps a dozen paces. There Linden's companions stood in a loose cluster, holding themselves in abeyance.

All of her friends except the old man followed Linden with their eyes as she faced Covenant and Jeremiah again.

More angrily than she intended, she asked; demanded, 'Are you satisfied?' She felt an inexplicable bereavement, as if like Kastenessen she had maimed herself with her own pain.

She wanted to add, I remember a time when you weren't like this. But she also recalled vividly that he had rejected the company of the

Haruchai when he had left Revelstone to seek out the Despiser. He had always been severe in his purposes – and stubbornly determined to spare as many people as possible from sharing the price of his actions.

He may have been trying to spare her friends, despite his ire and scorn—

The Unbeliever did not reply directly. He seemed to be in a hurry now, driven to complete his purpose. Instead of answering her, he pointed at a spot on the grass one long stride in front of him and ordered, 'Stand there. And don't *touch* us. Don't let that damn *Staff* touch us. If we feel even a *reminder* of power from you, this whole thing is going to unravel.'

The wind raised an unsteady wailing among the distant trees. It cut at the wet grass; lashed fine spray from the surface of the river. For a moment, it whipped at Linden's eyes, blinding her with tears. If for no other reason than because Covenant was afraid of her, she wanted to call up Earthpower and Law. Then she would learn the truth in an instant—

—and she would sacrifice her best opportunity to succour Jeremiah. Perhaps her only opportunity.

Rubbing moisture from her eyes with the back of her hand, she moved to stand where her former lover had indicated. There she planted one heel of the Staff near her boots and hugged the incorruptible wood against her chest.

At once, Covenant and Jeremiah separated. Her son came to stand in front of her scarcely more than an arm's length away. His smile may have been intended to reassure her; but the frantic twitching at the corner of his eye made him appear feverish with excitement or dread. His muddy gaze seemed to blur in the wind, losing definition as the air whipped past him.

At the same time, Covenant positioned himself directly behind Linden, facing her and Jeremiah. Like her son, he stood nearly close enough to reach out and touch her.

I can't do it—

Jeremiah glanced past her towards Covenant; nodded at what he saw. His smile fell away, replaced by an expression of intent concentration. His mouth moved as if he were speaking, although he made no sound that she could hear. Still he and Covenant were closed to her health-sense. She felt the knotted anxiety and frustration of her friends more acutely than the presence of Covenant or Jeremiah. Only ordinary sight assured her that her son and his companion in fact stood near her.

I can't—

The Masters tightened their cordon, perhaps preparing to intervene if they saw any sign of her power – or if her friends attempted to intrude.

Slowly, and apparently in unison, Jeremiah and Covenant began to raise their arms, holding their fingers splayed. For an instant, Jeremiah's hands seemed to point straight at Covenant's through Linden's shoulders. But their arms continued to rise until together the two men implied an arch over her head.

—the perils which have been prepared—

Without warning, Anele proclaimed, 'I have said that I no longer fear the ur-viles! Did you not heed me?'

At the edge of her vision, Linden caught a glimpse of blackness to the north, upstream beside the river. Instinctively she turned to squint across the wind in that direction.

A tight black wedge of ur-viles had appeared with startling sudden-ness. They might have been translated from some other realm of exist-ence, although Linden knew that they had only concealed themselves until they were ready to be noticed. Their loremaster brandished an iron jerrid or sceptre fraught with vitriol: the entire formation was a seethe of power, bitter and corrosive. And the wedge seemed *huge*– Every ur-vile that she and Esmer had brought to this time must have joined together, united by some new interpretation of their Weird. Scores of glowing blades flashed among them, as cruel as lava, and as fatal.

They charged towards the poised arc of Masters, running hard. In seconds, they would be near enough to strike. Yet Linden believed instantly that their assault was not intended for the *Haruchai*. Handir and his kinsmen merely stood in the way.

The point of the wedge was aimed straight at her – or at Covenant and Jeremiah. The loremaster's weapon spat acrid theurgy and ruin as the creatures rushed forward.

They had created manacles—

Frozen with shock, she had stared at them for two quick heartbeats, or three, before she realised that there were no Waynhim among them. She saw no Waynhim anywhere. Apparently the ancient servants of the Land had declined to participate in the actions of their black kindred. But if they had not chosen to join the ur-viles, they also did not interfere.

What had their complex intentions required of them now?

If the manacles were intended for Covenant, and the ur-viles were trustworthy, then he was not.

If. If. If.

But the Demondim-spawn could not tell Linden how to reach her son.

Liand and Bhapa shouted warnings. Jeremiah dropped his arms, plainly stricken with dismay. At Linden's back, Covenant snarled, 'Hell and *blood!*' Then he yelled at the Masters, '*Stop them! We've been betrayed!*'

The *Haruchai* had already spun to face the wedge. At Covenant's command, they moved to intercept the ur-viles.

They were potent and supremely skilled. Nevertheless they were too few to do more than slow the advance of the creatures.

Linden had time to think, Betrayed. Yes. But not by the ur-viles. Suddenly her guts were filled with the nausea that bespoke Esmer's nearness.

Looking around wildly, she saw him step out of the air on the far side of the river.

His cymar hung loosely along his limbs as if he were impervious to the tangling wind. She could hardly make out his features. In spite of the distance, however, the dangerous and fuming green of his eyes blazed vividly, as incandescent and unclean as small emerald suns tainted by despair.

In a mounting roar, he shouted, 'You have given birth to havoc, *Haruchai*, Bloodguard, treachers! Now bear the blame for the Land's doom!'

Everything happened too quickly: Linden could not react to it. Ignoring Esmer, the ur-viles and the Masters flung themselves towards each other. Vitriol frothed and spattered on the blades of the creatures: the loremaster's jerrid gathered gouts of darkness. But none of the weapons struck as the *Haruchai* spread out swiftly to challenge the wedge along its edges. Linden's companions sprang forward to ward her, Stave and Mahrtiir first among them. And Esmer—

Cail's son made a savage gesture with one hand; gave a howl like a great blaring of horns. Instantly all of the earth under the feet of the ur-viles and the Masters erupted.

Grass and soil spattered upwards like oil on hot iron. Gouts of sodden loam and rocks and roots and grass-blades burst into the air and were immediately torn to chaos by the wind. Ur-viles and *Haruchai* alike were scattered like withered leaves: they could not keep their feet, hold their formations; summon their power. Linden half expected to see them tumble away, hurled across the hillside by Esmer's violence. But they only fell, and were tossed upwards, and fell again, pummelled by a hurtling rain of stones and dirt.

Yet the ground where she stood with Jeremiah and Covenant remained stable. Shock and incomprehension held her friends motionless, but Esmer's puissance did not threaten them.

He spared them deliberately: Linden could not believe otherwise. *Aid and betrayal.* He must have wanted Covenant and Jeremiah to succeed—

Abruptly Covenant yelled, '*Now*, Jeremiah!'

The boy shrugged off his chagrin. Instantly obedient, he repulsed Linden's companions with a flick of his hand. Then he raised his arms as he had before; swung them upwards until once again they and Covenant's suggested an arch over Linden's head. Jeremiah resumed his voiceless incantation. Covenant may have done the same.

For a brief moment, a piece of time too slight to be measured by the convulsive labour of her heart, Linden felt power gather around her: the onset of an innominate theurgy. From Jeremiah, it seemed to be the same force which had stopped her in the forehall, but multiplied a hundredfold. From Covenant, however, it had the ferocity of running magma. If it continued, it would scorch the cloak from her back, char away her clothes until her flesh bubbled and ran.

Liand and Pahni may have shouted her name: even Stave may have called out to her. But their voices could not penetrate the accumulating catastrophe.

Then Linden heard and saw and felt and tasted a tremendous concussion. Lightning completed the arch over her head, striking like the devastation of worlds from Jeremiah's fingertips to Covenant's.

After that, Covenant and Jeremiah, all of her friends, Esmer, the geyser-scattered ur-viles and *Haruchai*, the gradual slopes on either side of the watercourse, the whole promontory of Revelstone: everything vanished. The fierce arc of lightning lingered momentarily, burned onto her retinas. The Earthpower of Glimmermere's outflow persisted. But such things faded; and when they did, everything that she knew – perhaps everything that she had ever known – was gone.

Chapter Six:

Interference

The shock was too great. Linden was too human: no aspect of her body or her mind had been formed to accommodate such a sudden and absolute transition.

The sheer sensory excess of her original translation to the Land had left her numbed and dissociated; hardly able to react. And her passages through *caesures* had been bearable only because she had been protected by power, the ur-viles' and her own.

This was utterly different. In some ways, it was worse. In a small fraction of an instant, everything that she could see and feel and understand and care about vanished—

—or was transformed.

She hardly noticed that she staggered, instinctively trying to regain her balance on different ground; scarcely realised that the gloom and the battering wind were gone, replaced by dazzling whiteness and sharp cold. The chill in her lungs was only another version of her icy garments. She did not seem to have gone blind because the sunlight was too intense, but rather because her optic nerves simply could not accept the change. If the Staff of Law had not remained, unaltered and kindly, in her embrace, she might have believed that she had been snuffed out. Every neuron in her body except those that acknowledged the Staff refused to recognise where and who she was.

But then she heard Covenant pant as if he were enraged, 'Hellfire! Hell and blood!' and she knew that she was not alone.

An autonomic reflex shut her eyes against the concussive dazzling that seemed to fill the whole inside of her head like the clamour of great incandescent bells. And a different kind of visceral reflex caused her to reach for the fire of the Staff. She wanted to wall herself off with Earthpower from the incomprehensible change which had come over the world.

At once, however, Covenant yelled, 'Don't even *think* about it! God *damn* it, Linden! Don't you understand that you can still erase me? I'm still folding time, and it's *fragile*. If you use that Staff, you'll be stuck here *alone*, you'll be *helpless* while Foul destroys everything!'

Cowed by his anger, and belatedly afraid, she snatched herself back from the strength of Law. Gripping the Staff in one hand, she held it away from her so that its dangerous succour would not rest so close to her heart.

She felt Covenant's fury change direction. Muttering, 'Hellfire and bloody damnation,' he turned his back on her. His steps crunched through a brittle surface as he increased the distance between them.

With her eyes closed and her entire sensorium stunned, she could not find any sign of Jeremiah's presence.

Or of the Masters. Or of her friends. Somehow she had left them behind. The nausea with which Esmer afflicted her was gone. The ur-viles could conceal themselves whenever they wished.

But Jeremiah—

Now she wanted to open her eyes, look around frantically for her son. But she could not. Not yet. The brightness was too concentrated to be borne; or she was too vulnerable to it. She might damage her retinas—

Covenant? she asked, demanded, pleaded. Where are we? What have you done? But her voice refused to respond.

What have you done with Jeremiah?

'*Damn* it!' Covenant shouted abruptly. '*Show* yourself!' His anger carried away from her. 'I know you're here! This whole place *stinks* of you! And' – he lowered his voice threateningly – 'you do *not* want me to force you. That's going to hurt like hell.'

'And do you not fear that I will reveal you?' answered a light voice.

Cupping her free hand over her eyes, Linden began blinking furiously, trying to accustom herself to the cold white glare so that she could see. She had never heard that voice before.

'*You*,' Covenant snorted. 'You wouldn't dare. You'll be caught in the crossfire. You'll lose everything.'

'Perhaps you speak sooth—' the stranger began.

Covenant insisted, 'So what the hell are you doing? Damn it, we're not *supposed* to be here.'

'—yet my knowledge suffices,' the other voice continued calmly, 'to intervene in your designs. As you have seen.'

Linden fought the stricken numbness of her senses; and after a moment, she found that she could discern the new arrival. He stood a few paces beyond Covenant. Even through the confusion of cold and dazzling, he appeared to be an ordinary man. If he moved, his steps did not crunch as Covenant's did. Nevertheless his aura seemed comparatively human.

And yet— And yet—

Something about the man conveyed an impression of slippage, as if in some insidious, almost undetectable fashion he was simultaneously in front of and behind himself; and on both sides—

Perhaps he had simply stepped out of hiding when Covenant demanded it.

'You didn't have to show me,' retorted Covenant bitterly. 'I already know what you can do. Hellfire, I already know what you're *going* to do. What I don't know is why you put me *here*. This is the wrong time. Not to mention the wrong damn *place*.'

'The *Elohim* would have done so, if I did not.' The stranger sounded amused.

The *Elohim*—? Still blinking urgently, Linden made slits of her fingers; tried to force herself to see through the hurtful brilliance. By slow degrees, her health-sense adjusted to the changed world. Spring had inexplicably become winter—

Covenant swore between his teeth. 'No, they wouldn't. That's why I brought *her*. As long as they think she's the Wildwielder, she protects me.

'Anyway,' he growled, 'you hate them. You people might as well be that "darkness" they keep talking about, that shadow on their hearts. So why are you doing their dirty work?'

'It pleases me to usurp them, when I may.' Now the man's tone suggested satisfaction; smugness. 'Also I do not desire the destruction of the Earth. The peril of your chosen path I deemed too great. Therefore I have set you upon another. It is equally apt for your purpose. And its hazards lie within the scope of my knowledge. It will serve me well.'

Covenant, Linden tried to say, listen to me. Where is Jeremiah? What have you done to my son? But the cold scraped at her throat with every breath, making the muscles clench. She was involuntarily mute; helpless.

'No,' Covenant snapped, 'it isn't *equally* damn *apt*. It's a bloody disaster. You people are such infernal meddlers. I wish you would find something else to do. Go start a war with somebody, leave the rest of us alone.'

The stranger laughed. 'When such powers are joined in the hands of one who is constrained by mortality, unable to wield both together?' His tone was ambiguous, a mixture of scorn and regret. 'When the *Elohim* as a race gnash their teeth in frustration and fear? My gratification is too great to be denied. If ever she obtains that which will enable her to bear her strengths, your chagrin will provide my people with vast amusement.'

He did not sound amused.

'Amusement, hell,' growled Covenant. 'If *that* ever happens – which it won't – your people will be frantically trying to stop her, just like everybody else. Only in their case, it'll be sheer greed. They'll want all that power for themselves.

'Oh, that's right,' he added suddenly, mocking the newcomer. 'I forgot. Your people hardly ever agree on anything. Half of them will be after her power. Half of them will be busy at something completely loony, like trying to make friends with the damn Worm of the World's End. And half of them will be doing the only thing they're really good at, which is watching the rest of the world go by and wishing they were *Elohim*.'

At last, the stabbing glare was blunted enough to let Linden make out blurred details through the slits between her fingers. Gradually her health-sense approached clarity. The sun shone hard on a wide field of snow; snow so pristine and untrampled that it reflected and concentrated the light cruelly. Once, she guessed, it would have covered her knees. But it had fallen some time ago. Days of hard sunshine had melted its surface often enough to compact the snow and form an icy crust. As her vision improved, she could see the scars which Covenant's boots had gouged in the snow, leading away from her. But he and his companion or antagonist remained indistinct: they were no more than blots on her straining sight.

The surrounding silence was sharper than the chill, and more ominous.

She did not know where she was. She could be sure only that she was still in the Land. Even through the snow and her freezing boots, she felt its characteristic life-pulse, its unique vitality. But this place was not familiar in any other way.

'Covenant.' Her voice was a hoarse croak, raw with cold. 'Where's Jeremiah?'

Instead of responding to Covenant's gibes, the stranger said, 'She requires your consolation.' Now he sounded impatient with Covenant. 'Doubtless your merciful heart will urge you to attend to her. I will abide the delay.'

The imprecise stain of Covenant's shape appeared to gesture in Linden's direction. 'Ignore her. She always thinks what she wants is more important than what anybody else is doing. She's lost here without me. We're too far from her time. And she can't get back without me. She can wait until I'm done with you.'

Too far—

She should have been shocked.

—from her time.

Covenant had removed her from Revelstone, from the upland plateau, from her friends – and from the time in which she belonged.

And she can't get back—

But the incomprehensible jolt of her dislocation was fading as her senses reasserted themselves. She could not be shocked again, or paralysed: not while Jeremiah was missing. At that moment, nothing else mattered.

Don't you understand that you can still erase me?

Covenant had cause to fear her. She could compel answers—

Squeezing her eyes shut to dismiss tears of pain, Linden opened them again; dropped her hand. 'Covenant!' she gasped harshly as she took a couple of unsteady steps towards him. Her boots broke through the stiff crust and plunged into snow deep enough to reach her shins. 'Catch!'

In desperation and dismay, she flung the Staff of Law straight at him.

Panic flared in his eyes. Cursing, he jumped aside.

As he stumbled away, one heel of the Staff jabbed through the ice two or three paces beyond him. Then the wood fell flat. Almost immediately, its inherent warmth melted the crust. In a small flurry of snow, the shaft sank out of sight.

'Hellfire!' Covenant panted. 'Hellfire. Hellfire.'

Linden stamped forward another step, then stopped as she saw the newcomer clearly for the first time.

He was moving over the fierce whiteness of the snow. And he was closer to the Staff than she was. When he stooped to retrieve it, she could not stop him. Helplessly she watched him lift it in both hands, examine it from end to end.

With her heart hammering, she clutched at the cold circle of Covenant's ring: her only remaining instrument of power.

A moment later, the stranger moved again. She feared that he would withdraw, but he did not. Instead he came towards her as if he were gliding over the surface of the ice.

He was wrapped from head to foot in russet cloth: it covered him like a winding sheet. His hands and feet were bound. Even his head was bound, even his eyes, so that only the blunt protrusion of his nose and the hollow of his mouth indicated that his face had any features at all. Soon he stood before Linden, holding the Staff in shrouded hands.

'Lady,' he said, 'that was foolish. Yet it was also clever. Already the wisdom of my intervention is manifest.' He paused, obviously studying the Staff. Then he announced, 'Sadly, it is incomplete. Your need is great. You will require puissance. I return this implement of Law to you with my thanks for the knowledge of its touch.'

Formally he proffered the Staff to Linden.

With her pulse pounding, Linden released the ring and snatched up her Staff.

Then the stranger touched the spot where Covenant's ring lay hidden under her clothes. 'That is another matter altogether. I have dreamed of such might—' The light voice softened with awe and envy – and with compassion. 'It is a heavy burden. It will become more so. And it is not for me. Therefore I am grieved. Yet I am also gladdened to learn that I have not dreamed in vain.'

Linden ignored him. She had no attention to spare for anything except Jeremiah's absence. And she had seen Covenant's fright. She still had power over him.

Driving her boots into the ice and snow, she surged towards her former lover.

'Understand this!' she shouted as she floundered closer to him. 'You want something. I don't know what it is, but you want it badly. And I can keep you from getting it. You *need* me.' Her hands itched, eager for fire, where they gripped the Staff. 'So answer the damn question. *Where is my son?*'

For an instant, crimson glinted in Covenant's eyes. Then it vanished, replaced by an expression that may have been alarm. 'You'll be lost—' he began.

'I don't *care*! Without Jeremiah, nothing that you do means anything to me!'

He flinched; looked away. 'Oh, well. He'll be here.' His tone may have been intended to placate her. 'Esmer helped us get away, but now he's trying to hold onto your kid. Life would be *so* much easier if he would just make up his mind. But we were ready for him. And the ur-viles have re-grouped. That's lucky for us. Esmer can't fight them and keep his grip on your kid at the same time.' Covenant appeared to study the air. 'He'll show up pretty soon. The power we used to slip past time ties us together.'

Aid and betrayal.

Linden was not sure that she believed him. Nevertheless his reply seemed to drain the strength from her limbs; the anger. At the same time, her overwrought nerves finally awoke to the cold. Her cloak had been drenched, and her clothes were wet. God, she was freezing– Winter and ice surrounded her. Wherever she was – and when – this was the coldest time of the year; too cold even for snow.

She had no idea what was going on, or how to understand it. Pretty soon– Deliberately she looked around, hoping to see something that she could recognise; something that would make sense of her situation.

But there was nothing familiar here except Covenant. She stood in ice and snow in the flat bottom of a wide valley surrounded by steep, snow-clad hills, all so white and bright and difficult to gaze upon that they might have been featureless. Sunlight as bitter and cutting as the snow poured down on her from a sky made pale by cold. And the sky held no suggestion of Kevin's Dirt, or of any other taint. Nothing defined this place except the marks of her boots, and of Covenant's, and the pain in her lungs. Without her health-sense, she would not have known north from south.

Covenant had told the truth. She was *too far from her time.*

If she did not find a source of heat soon, she would start to die. She was already shivering. That would grow worse; become uncontrollable. Then would come drowsiness. Soon the cold itself would begin to feel like warmth, and she would be lost.

'All right,' she said, trembling. 'Assume that I believe you. I can't survive this. If I don't use the Staff—' Her voice shook. 'As far as I can see, the cold doesn't bother you,' either Covenant or the stranger. 'But it's going to kill me.'

I can't do it without you.

'Oh, that.' Covenant had recovered his air of superiority. 'I'm doing so many things here, I forget how frail you are. Of course I don't want you to freeze.'

With his right hand, he made a quick gesture that seemed to leave a memory of fire in the air; and at once Linden felt warmth wash through her. In an instant, her clothes and her cloak were dry: even her socks and the insides of her boots were dry. Almost without transition, she rebounded from harsh cold to a sustaining anger like an aftertaste of the gift which the Waynhim and the loremaster had given her.

'Better?' asked Covenant with mordant sweetness. 'Can I finish my conversation now?'

Linden blinked – and found the stranger standing nearby. The swaddled man's head shifted from side to side, directing hidden eyes back and forth between Covenant and Linden. When he was satisfied with the sight, he said, 'There is no need for haste. I mean to accompany you for some little while. We may converse at leisure. And' – now the light voice was arch, almost taunting – 'we have not been introduced.'

'You don't need a damn introduction,' growled Covenant. 'You know who she is. And you sure as hell know who *I* am.'

'But she does not know us,' said the stranger, chuckling. 'Would you prefer that I speak on your behalf?'

'Hellfire!' Covenant snapped at once. 'Don't even *try* it. I've already warned you.' Then he sighed. Apparently trying to mollify the newcomer, he began, 'Linden, this is—'

'Proceed with caution, Halfhand,' the man interrupted sharply. 'If you step aside from the path which I have offered to you, the *Elohim* will assuredly intervene.'

'Why?' Covenant demanded in surprise. 'Why the hell would they bother? She's *here*, isn't she? That's all they care about. And you're going to humiliate them. Eventually, anyway. Why should they give a damn if I mess with you? Hell, I'd expect them to *thank* me.'

He was part of the Arch of Time. And he had suggested that he knew – or could know – everything that had ever happened. Could he see the future as well? Or was his vision constrained by the present in which he had reified himself?

Now it was the stranger who sighed. 'The *Elohim* are haughty in all sooth. They decline to profit by the knowledge which may be gleaned from humiliation. Yet among them there are matters which outweigh even their own meritless surquedry. They will act to preserve the integrity of Time. They must.'

'But they haven't been humiliated *yet*,' countered Covenant. 'How does what I tell her about you threaten Time?'

With a show of patience, the newcomer explained, 'Because she is *here*. In this circumstance, her mind cannot be distinguished from the Arch of Time. Do you dare to acknowledge that you do not comprehend this? Her place lies millennia hence. She has experienced the distant outcome of events which transpire in this present. If she is given knowledge which she cannot possess by right of that experience – knowledge which may alter her understanding of her own past – a paradox akin to the paradox of wild magic will ensue. Her every deed will have the power of wild magic to undo Time.

'Yet if she acts freely, without incondign comprehension or suasion, her deeds will do no harm. That I will ensure. Therefore you must permit her to command – aye, and to make demands – as she chooses.' Again the man sighed. 'I have said that I do not desire the destruction of the Earth. If you are wise – if wisdom is possible for one such as you – you also will not desire it.'

Linden's impatience for Jeremiah mounted. She could not understand what Covenant and the wrapped man were talking about; and she was sure that they would not explain themselves. They both had something to gain by mystifying her.

Nonetheless their attitudes confirmed that they had reason to fear her. That was a form of power which she could use.

Covenant was saying sourly, 'Of *course* I don't desire it. Hell and blood! Why didn't you just say so? All this beating around the bush is giving me a headache.'

Turning to Linden, he indicated the stranger with an exasperated gesture. 'Linden, he's the Theomach. That's really all I can tell you about him. Except you've probably noticed that he's crazy. His whole damn race is crazy.'

Linden nodded to herself. The stranger, the Theomach, had challenged Covenant to introduce him as a kind of test.

'I don't care,' she replied with her own acid sweetness. 'None of this makes sense to me. And you both know that. I want you to stop treating me as if I weren't here.

'While we're waiting for Jeremiah—' She faltered. 'He *is* coming, isn't he?' Both Covenant and the Theomach nodded. Tightening her grip on herself, she continued, 'Then tell me. How did you *do* that? I didn't feel a *caesure*.' She would not have failed to recognise any disruption of time that arose from white gold. 'How did we get here?'

Give me something that I can understand.

Perhaps Covenant was free to go wherever he wished. But surely the fact that he had brought her with him endangered Time?

Covenant muttered an obscenity under his breath. 'You're right. We didn't break through time. We didn't threaten the Arch. Instead we sort of slipped between the cracks. It's like folding time. But it takes a *lot* more power. That's why I couldn't do it alone. Being in two places at once is hard enough. Moving us this far into the past really ought to be impossible.'

'Indeed,' remarked the Theomach casually.

'But your kid has his own magic now,' Covenant continued. 'I told you that.' *Think of it like blood from a wound.* 'When we work together, we can do some pretty amazing things. Like slip through cracks in time. Or make doors from one place to another.'

I can build all kinds of doors. And walls. In the Land, Jeremiah's talent for constructs had taken an entirely new form.

'All right.' Linden shook her head in astonishment at what her son had become. 'All right. I'll assume that that makes sense.' What choice did she have? 'I'll try, anyway. So where are we? And when?'

And why? What could Covenant – or Jeremiah – possibly do *here* that would save the Land?

Scowling, Covenant looked around. Then he said, 'Let's go up there.' He nodded towards one of the hills bordering the valley on the south. 'Right now, we're in the middle of nowhere. If we want to accomplish anything, we have a lot of ground to cover.' He glared at the Theomach. 'We might as well get started. You'll understand better when you can see farther.'

Before Linden could ask about Jeremiah, the Theomach put in, 'Your son will appear at the Halfhand's side. No movement in this time will delay him.'

Swearing to himself again, Covenant began to pound through the ice and snow. The Theomach followed without waiting for Linden to make up her mind. As the stranger stepped lightly over the crust, he said to Covenant, 'If you will but consider the path which I have opened to you, you will recognise that you have no cause for anger. True, I have presented new obstacles. But others I have removed. And my path is indeed less perilous.'

When Covenant did not respond, the Theomach said sharply, 'I do not speak of *her* peril, Halfhand. I speak of yours.'

—the perils which have been prepared for you.

Behind them, Linden straggled into motion. She did not intend to be left behind when Jeremiah might rejoin Covenant at any moment. Bracing herself on the Staff, she fought the crust and the cloying snow in an effort to keep pace.

'Fuck that,' Covenant rasped. 'Fuck you and your fake concern. I can handle my *perils*. But it galls the hell out of me that you think you have the right to interfere.'

'Now you are dishonest,' replied the Theomach with a mocking laugh. 'It is not my interference that "galls" you. It is your powerlessness to prevent me.'

Again his movements conveyed an eerie sense of slippage. He seemed to accompany himself across the dazzling field as if the theurgy which kept him from breaking through the ice caused him to shift subtly between different places in time and space.

'Believe that if you can,' Covenant retorted. 'What I have in mind for you is going to be worse than "the destruction of the Earth". I'm going to make you and all your people and even the damn *Elohim* irrelevant.'

Lightly the Theomach answered, 'You are welcome to the attempt.'

'What, you think I can't do it? Hellfire. You aren't paying attention. I know more about what's going to happen to you than *you* do. And I guarantee you won't like it.'

For some reason, the Theomach did not respond. Covenant may have surprised or shaken him.

Linden floundered after them. The soles of her boots gripped the buried snow well enough; but each step was an awkward hesitation-and-plunge as the ice held her weight for an instant and then broke. Soon she had to pant for air, and each breath drew scalding cold deeper into her lungs. Only the warmth of Covenant's magic and her desire for Jeremiah kept her going.

If her son appeared, as she had been promised—

The first slopes of the hills seemed far away. And they would not be easy to climb. The pale uninterrupted blue of the sky felt as wide as her incomprehension, and as empty. The white glitter of the field was empty as well, undefined by any trees or shrubs. Even *aliantha* did not grow in this place. She saw no birds anywhere. If animals had ever crossed this valley, the crust retained no sign of their passage.

There should have been *aliantha*. Those life-giving shrubs had survived the Sunbane. Surely they could endure this winter? But Linden thought that she knew why the valley was so lifeless. Her health-sense grew steadily stronger in the absence of Kevin's Dirt; and as she trudged across the iced expanse, she began to feel that she trod on graves. The whole valley held a muffled sensation of death, as if the snow cloaked shed blood and slaughter. The ground had absorbed too much violence to nurture treasure-berries.

Perhaps Covenant or the Theomach would condescend to tell her what had happened here.

Before she could speak, however, a brief flare of energy like an after flash of lightning shredded the air near Covenant; and Jeremiah staggered to his knees as though he had been created – or re-created – from the raw stuff of emptiness and cold.

He was gasping as if he had survived a fight for his life.

She forgot everything else in her rush to reach him. Instinctively she reached for Earthpower. If Esmer or some other foe still harried her son—

At once, however, the Theomach stepped or appeared in her way. She collided with him hard; stumbled backwards.

'God *damn* it—!'

'Do not!' he commanded sharply. His cerement-clad figure confronted her across the trampled snow. 'Do not invoke the Staff. And do not attempt to place your hands upon them, neither the Halfhand nor your son. If you err in this, your losses will be greater than you are able to conceive. That I cannot prevent. My purpose lies elsewhere.'

At the same time, Covenant turned towards Jeremiah. 'There you are. I was beginning to wonder.'

Jeremiah lifted his face to the Unbeliever. The sweat of intense exertion streamed from his cheeks and forehead: his heated skin steamed in the cold. But he was grinning hugely.

'Jeez, that was hard,' he panted. 'I knew Esmer was tough, but I didn't realise—' In spite of his gasping, his voice seemed to throb with triumph. 'It's a good thing those ur-viles attacked when they did. I didn't want to have to call for help.'

Covenant nodded. 'I knew you could do it. I told you that, didn't I? He changes his mind too often. There's always a flaw somewhere.'

Biting her lip, Linden swallowed every natural impulse. 'All right,' she muttered to the Theomach. 'You've made your point. I need them as much as they need me. Now get out of my way.'

The Theomach gave her a shrouded nod and stepped aside.

With more caution, she approached her son and Covenant.

Jeremiah was gazing around; and as he did so, his manner changed. 'Jeez,' he panted again. 'What went wrong? We aren't supposed to be *here*.'

'I know,' replied Covenant sourly. 'Look behind you.'

With a boy's ungainly alacrity, Jeremiah lurched to his feet. His gaze touched Linden for only an instant. 'Oh, hi, Mom,' he said absently, as if he had already put her out of his mind. His attention was focused on the Theomach.

'*You*,' he said in surprise. He was still trying to catch his breath. 'You're one of *them*. I never met you. But I heard them talk about you. You're the Theomach.'

The concealed figure sketched a mocking bow. 'Assuredly.' Then he added more sternly, 'Be guided by the Halfhand, youth. I have set you upon a path which will unmake all of your desires if you step aside from it.'

Jeremiah glanced at Covenant, then shrugged. 'It doesn't matter to me. As long as we're together, I don't care how we do this. Covenant knows I trust him.'

His tic was barely noticeable.

Linden took another step closer. 'Jeremiah, honey. Are you all right? When I was suddenly here,' wherever here was, 'and you weren't, I thought that I'd lost you again.'

His muddy gaze avoided hers. 'I'm fine.' His respiration had almost returned to normal: he was too young – or too full of magic – to breathe hard for long. 'It's what I said, that's all. Esmer is tougher than he looks.' He flashed another grin at Covenant. 'But I beat him.'

Plainly reluctant to talk to Linden, the boy made a show of scanning the valley again. 'What do we do now?'

Her son had recovered his mind – and he did not want to talk to her. She bowed her head so that he would not see her face twist or her eyes burn.

'Your mother is being stubborn,' replied Covenant heavily. 'As usual. She wants an *explanation*. We'll go up there' – he pointed vaguely at the nearest hills – 'and take a look around. Maybe then she'll feel less contentious. Or at least less disoriented.

'After that, we'll need to make some decisions. Or she will. Thanks to the Theomach, we're in a hell of a mess. And he thinks we should let her figure out how to cope with it.

'We'll have to give that a try,' Covenant concluded in disgust. 'He hasn't left us much choice.'

With his back to Linden, Jeremiah said, 'Then let's go. I think it'll be OK. Sometimes she does exactly the right thing without even knowing it.'

Taking her torn heart with him, he led Covenant towards the slopes at the southern edge of the valley.

Eventually Covenant moved into the lead. Jeremiah followed in his footprints while the Theomach remained off to one side, accompanying himself obscurely over the brittle surface. Linden lagged behind Covenant and Jeremiah; used the path that they had trampled to make her own passage somewhat easier.

Sometimes she does exactly the right thing– Her son had given her that, although he obviously preferred Covenant's company in spite of her dedication and love. –*without even knowing it*. He may have been referring to the raceway construct which she had enabled him to build. To that extent, at least, he acknowledged her importance in his life. Yet even that oblique validation carried a message of pain.

By buying the tracks and pylons for Jeremiah's raceway, she had in some sense freed him; or had given him the means to free himself. She had made possible an escape from blankness into the wealth and wonder of the Land. And in so doing, she had lost him to Covenant. But that, she insisted to herself, was not the crucial point. The crux of what she had inadvertently achieved was this: she had supplied her son with an alternative to ordinary consciousness, ordinary responses and emotions; ordinary life. She had made it easier for him to escape than to strive for a more difficult and precious form of recovery.

It was conceivable that Linden had failed her son as entirely – and as unintentionally – as she had failed Joan.

Arguing with herself as she plodded ahead, Linden countered, Yes, that was conceivable. But it was also conceivable that Jeremiah would not have been capable of his present sentience, or his disturbing loyalties, if he had not been granted an escape from his mental prison. His mind might have died, utterly alone inside his skull, if he had not found his way to the Land.

The simple fact was that Linden was too human to know the truth. She could not assign responsibility, blame, or vindication because she was inadequate to gauge the condition of Jeremiah's soul. He was closed to her. He had always been closed.

In the years since she had travelled and suffered and loved with Thomas Covenant, she had endeavoured to become content with her inadequacy. She would have admitted with unruffled confidence that she healed none of her patients. Instead, at her best, she merely encouraged them to heal themselves. But now, in the Land, she was less able to accept her limitations.

There was too much at stake—

She understood almost nothing that had happened since Covenant and Jeremiah had ridden into Lord's Keep. And she had no reason at all to believe that she was strong enough for what lay ahead of her. But she told herself that such things were trivial. The only inadequacy that truly mattered was her inability to measure the health or illness of Jeremiah's restored mind.

How could she make choices, or defend what she loved, when she did not know whether or not he still needed her?

The ascent to Covenant's destination was as difficult as she had feared it would be. Although the snow on the northward slope had seen less sunlight and formed less ice, it was also deeper. The hillside itself was hazardously steep. And the eldritch heat which Covenant had given her faded ineluctably, leaving her with nothing except her clothes and her exertions to ward off the cold.

Nevertheless she struggled upwards. And when she finally gained the hilltop, stood panting in the comfortless sunshine of early afternoon, her doubts and confusion had settled into a grim determination. The Theomach had told Covenant that he must allow her to make her own decisions. She meant to do so. She had never used her inadequacy as an excuse, and did not intend to start now.

While Jeremiah shuffled his feet, Covenant scowled into the distance, and the Theomach hummed tunelessly to himself, Linden scanned her surroundings. Here the glare from the snow was less severe. In this cold, any wind would have cut at her eyes; but the air was almost entirely still. She was able to look around without the blur of tears or the danger of snow-blindness.

Covenant had chosen an effective vantage-point. On all sides, the unimpeded sunshine etched the shapes and edges of the terrain in sharp detail. From this crest, she saw that the hills which bordered both sides of the valley stood in rough rows that gradually lost height from west to east. And they were only two rows among many: a range of rugged slopes and crooked valleys extended farther than she could see into the northwest as well as towards the southeast. The entire landscape was tossed and crumpled, like a discarded blanket. As it tended eastward, it smoothed out in small increments.

If these were the foothills of mountains in the west, those peaks were too distant to be seen. But as she scanned the vistas, she found that their contours allowed her to see farther into the southwest as well as the southeast. In that direction also, the hilltops sank slowly lower. And beyond their ridges—

She blinked hard in an effort to clear the ache of brightness from her sight. There was something– For a moment, she closed her eyes; rested them. Then she looked again.

Now she was sure that she could see trees. At the limits of vision, deciduous trees clung to each other with their stark and naked limbs. And among them a few tall evergreens – cedars, perhaps, or redwoods – stood like sentinels, keeping watch over their winter-stricken kindred. At this distance, she could see only a sliver of woodland past the obstruction of the hills. But percipience or intuition told her that she was squinting at a forest.

We're too far from her time. Under the Sunbane, the last vestiges of the ancient woods west of Landsdrop had been utterly destroyed. Yet she remained in the Land: she was sure of that. And there were forests—?

She wanted to demand, Covenant, damn you, what have you *done?* But determination had settled into her like the cold, and it brought with it a kind of calm. She was frightened enough for rage; could have slipped easily into fury. Nevertheless she refused to be swayed by her emotions.

Until she learned the truth about her son, she intended to hold herself in check. She would do anything and everything that fear or imagination suggested; but she would do it coldly. And she would *think* about it first.

Like paralysis, panic served the Despiser.

'All right, Covenant,' she said when she was ready; when she could bear Jeremiah's reluctance to look at her, 'you promised me an explanation. It's time.'

'Well, time,' he replied. His voice was a harsh rasp. 'That's the problem, isn't it. It's all about time. Even distance is just a matter of time.'

Then he sighed. Gesturing around him, he began. 'We're a little less than two hundred leagues from Revelstone. These are the Last Hills, the last barrier. Where we are now, they separate the Center Plains from Garroting Deep.'

Two hundred *leagues*? Linden thought; but she was not truly surprised. The suddenness of her transition to this place had prepared her for imponderable dislocations.

'That piece of forest,' Covenant continued, 'is Garroting Deep. Eventually it'll be considered the most dangerous of the old forests. Of course,' he added, 'they're all places you don't want to go. In this time, anyway. Morinmoss, Grimmerdhore, hell, even Giant Woods – they're all protected by Forestals.'

Now she was taken aback, although she tried not to show it. If Forestals still defended the trees, she was deep in the Land's past; deeper than she had dared to imagine. During the time of the Sunbane, Caer-Caveral had preserved Andelain; but he had been the last of his kind. According to the tales which Covenant had told her long ago, most of the Forestals had disappeared before his first experiences in the Land. If that were true—

Oh, God.

—she was now more than seven thousand years before her proper time.

However, Covenant had not stopped speaking. She fought down her chagrin in order to concentrate on him.

'But Garroting Deep is the worst,' he was saying sourly. 'Giant Woods is practically benign, probably because Foul and the Ravers spend most of their time south of the Sarangrave. Sometimes you can get through

Morinmoss. On a good day, you can survive in Grimmerdhore for a few hours. But Caerroil Wildwood is an out-and-out butcher. He pretty much slaughters anything that doesn't have fur or feathers.'

While Linden stared at the distant trees in wonder and dismay, the Theomach put in casually, 'Perhaps it would profit her to know why the Forestal of Garroting Deep has grown so savage.'

His manner seemed to imply an oblique warning.

'There are a lot of reasons.' Covenant's tone was leaden with sarcasm. 'The Colossus of the Fall is losing its power. Too many trees are being butchered. There are too many people, and they're too greedy. All the Forestals are getting weaker.

'But Caerroil Wildwood has lost more than the other Forestals. And he knows more about Ravers. You can't see it from here, of course, but Doriendor Corishev is practically on Wildwood's doorstep. It's only sixty leagues from Cravenhaw. And Cravenhaw and Doom's Retreat are the only gaps into the Land from Doriendor Corishev.

'A long time ago, when the southern kingdoms spread north towards the Land – even before the kings set up their capital in Doriendor Corishev, and *samadhi* Sheol got involved – they hacked down a lot of trees. A *hell* of a lot of trees. Which ruined the watershed. And ruining the watershed dried out the southlands. The old domain of the kings was becoming the Southron Waste. So they kept pushing north. Naturally they liked conquest. But they also needed arable land.'

Jeremiah had placed himself so that Linden could not see his tic. He seemed to be keeping an eye on her with his peripheral vision, but he did not look at her directly. Instead he resumed playing with his racecar while Covenant described details that did not interest him – or that he already knew.

'And then *samadhi* began spreading his poison,' Covenant muttered. 'In this time, Foul still hasn't shown his face. But a century or two ago, *samadhi* came west behind the Southron Range. Eventually that brought him to Doriendor Corishev.

'When he got there, he didn't actually possess any of the kings. Not even Berek's King. He didn't want to risk getting too close to Caerroil Wildwood. But he *incited*– In fact, he did a shitload of inciting. He encouraged generations of kings to think all their problems would be solved if they could overrun the Land. Because of him, whole armies tried to slash and burn their way through Cravenhaw.

'That's where Wildwood beat them. The terrain makes a kind of bottleneck. He could concentrate his power there. And he could *smell* that Raver. He knew who was responsible for slaughtering his trees. On his own ground, with the full force of Garroting Deep behind him, nothing could stand against him. He stopped generations of kings dead in Cravenhaw – and I do mean dead. In effect, he forced them to turn towards Doom's Retreat. If they'd kept on trying to force a passage through Cravenhaw, that damn Forestal would have left none of them alive.

'By the time they gave up, he'd developed a grudge you wouldn't believe.'

The Theomach nodded as if in confirmation.

With less acid in his voice, Covenant explained, 'Berek's King is – I mean *was* – the last of their line. I know some of the old legends say the Land was one big peaceful nation, and Berek's King and Queen were happy, but it wasn't like that. People tell themselves simple stories because they're easier to live with than the truth. In fact, the Land was never a nation, and the southern kings never actually succeeded at over-running it.

'But it wasn't for lack of trying. And Berek's King was the most bloody-minded and stubborn of them all. His whole lineage was grasping and brutal, but he was something more. He didn't just take *samadhi* Sheol's advice. Indirectly that Raver *ruled* him. And when Berek's Queen de-cided she didn't like what her husband was doing, *samadhi*'s influence turned an ordinary struggle for new territory into an all-out civil war.

'Maybe you noticed the smell of death behind us? About a year and a half ago, one of the worst battles of the whole war was fought in that valley. The ground is so full of blood, even birds don't go there.' With dark satisfaction, Covenant stated, 'Under all that snow, we were walk-ing across corpses.'

The idea made Linden wince inwardly; but she kept her reactions hidden. She could no longer estimate how far into the Land's past she had been brought. Yet Covenant's revelations changed nothing. A val-ley drenched in bloodshed changed nothing. He still had not told her anything that explained his intentions, or the Theomach's – or her own plight. Holding his gaze, she waited for him to go on.

After a moment, he looked away. With renewed sarcasm, he remarked, 'But you haven't noticed what's going on east of us.' He waved one hand negligently in that direction. 'Or maybe you can't see that far. I'm sure the all-wise and all-knowing Theomach can. In fact, I'm sure that's why he brought us here.

'There's smoke on the horizon. The smoke of battle. Good old Berek is fighting for his life. Has been for the past three days.

'Hell and blood!' he snapped suddenly. 'I wish I didn't have to do this. It's so damn *gratuitous*.' Then, however, he made a visible effort to master his ire.

'When the Fire-Lions rescued Berek on Mount Thunder,' he said like a shrug, 'they won a battle for him. A turning-point. But they didn't win the war. The King's supporters took up the fight. And *samadhi* eggs them on from the safety of Doriendor Corishev, where Caerroil Wildwood can't reach him, and he doesn't have to worry about the Colossus. Berek still has a long way to go.

'Of course, it's just a mopping-up operation. He has *power* now, power no one has ever seen before. Eventually he'll win this battle. He'll win the war. But *he* doesn't know that. The people fighting and dying for him – or for the Queen – don't know it. All they know is, they think they've found something they can believe in. Something they consider more precious than new territory and fresh resources and plain greed.

'Berek was alone on Mount Thunder. His army was scattered, effectively crippled. But they weren't all dead. When the Fire-Lions answered him, it was a spectacle you could see for twenty or thirty leagues. Some of his survivors witnessed forces they couldn't even imagine. And since then the rest have seen him do things– To them, he looks like he's more than human. *Better*. They know about his vow, and they're looking at this war through his eyes.

'That's the real reason they're going to win. Even with Berek's power – which he doesn't understand yet – they don't have superior force. And they sure as hell don't have superior numbers.' Again Covenant's sarcasm mounted. 'But they *believe*. They aren't conscripts fighting because they'll be cut down if they don't. They're fighting a damn *holy war*.'

Linden listened and said nothing. Moment by moment, she became increasingly certain that Covenant was no longer the man who had changed her life. He had lost some aspect of his humanity in the Arch of Time.

'It'll all be wasted, of course,' he asserted trenchantly. 'Just about two thousand years from now, poor doomed Kevin is going to join Foul in the Ritual of Desecration, and everything Berek and his true believers are fighting for will fall apart.

'After that, it'll be a downhill battle all the way.'

Abruptly Covenant turned on the Theomach. 'Which is why I'm so God damn *pissed off* at you! You and your fucking arrogance. We aren't *supposed* to be here. We shouldn't have to go through all this. *She* shouldn't have to go through it.

'And I'm in a *hurry*. Never mind how hard I have to work just to keep us in one piece, or how long it's going to take. I can handle that. Hellfire! I'm in a hurry because I'm trying to stop Foul before he finds a way to massacre everybody who has ever cared about the Land, or the Earth, or at least bare survival.'

Before the Theomach could reply, Linden intervened. She suspected that Covenant's vehemence was a ploy, a diversion; and she had no intention of permitting it to distract her. He still had not come to the point of his explanation.

'Covenant,' she asked sharply, 'when *is* this? How far back did you bring us?'

Jeremiah gave her a quick, troubled glance, then looked away again. After studying his useless toy for a moment, he put it away in the waist-band of his ruined pyjamas.

With a shrug, Covenant seemed to dismiss his anger. He sounded almost nonchalant as he said, 'Ten thousand years. Give or take.'

Ten thousand—? Ten *thou*—?

Still Linden kept her face blank. 'And if the Theomach hadn't inter-fered?' she persisted. 'If we were where you wanted? When would *that* be?'

'Five hundred years after all this.' He indicated Berek's struggle in the east. 'Roughly. I haven't actually counted. It isn't worth the effort.'

She stared at him. Her voice rose in spite of her determination to contain herself. 'So if we were doing this the way you wanted, we would still be nine and a half thousand years away from where we belong?'

'It isn't just the time, Mom,' Jeremiah offered as though he wanted to placate her. 'It's the whole situation.'

Covenant nodded. 'That's right. Time is only part of the problem. We're also not supposed to be *here*. We're supposed to be over *there*.' He pointed past her thin glimpse of the forest. 'On the other side of Garroting Deep. Ninety leagues or so, if we could fly.

'But of course we can't,' he said acidly. 'And we can't go through the Deep. So we'll have to go around. *All* the way around. Which is more like two *hundred* leagues. *Up* through the Westron Mountains. *In* the dead of winter. *Without* food or warm clothes or horses. And we can't take any shortcuts because the bloody Theomach won't *let* us. He's afraid we might change history.'

'With good cause,' remarked the Theomach ambiguously. 'Other puissant beings occupy this age of the Land. And the forces at your command are misplaced here. Any encounter threatens a disturbance of Time which I will be unable to contain. You cannot safely attain your goal except upon the path that I have prepared for you – the path of the lady's choices and desires.

'Even you, Halfhand, with your daring and folly,' the man stated, 'even you must endeavour to avoid or mislead notice.'

'Oh, thanks.' Covenant snorted bitterly. 'I didn't realise that. I feel *so* much better now.'

'Covenant, stop,' Linden put in. 'You can complain as much as you want later. You still haven't explained anything. You haven't told me why. What can you possibly hope to accomplish this far from where we belong? You said that you know how to save the Land.' And Jeremiah. 'Why do we have to be thousands of years and hundreds of leagues away from where we're needed?'

The Unbeliever gave her a look dark with resentment, then turned his head away. 'The Theomach is right about one thing,' he muttered. 'If we can get there, we might still be able to do it.' He sighed heavily. 'But what I wanted—

'Ah, hell.' With an air of disgust, he seemed to concede defeat. 'I was aiming for the time of Damelon. High Lord Damelon Giantfriend,

Berek's son. I wanted to catch him when he reaches *Melenkurion* Skyweir. Right before he figures out how to get at what he's looking for.

'I was planning to sneak in behind him. Before he started thinking of ways to keep people out. Between the two of us, Jeremiah and I can do that, no matter how much lore he has. Then we could just hide until he left. That would leave us free to do whatever we wanted.'

With difficulty, Linden swallowed an impulse to yell at him. 'I still don't understand,' she insisted. 'What's so important about *Melenkurion* Skyweir? What's Damelon looking for? Damn it, Covenant, you told me that you know what to do, you talk and talk, but you don't *explain* anything.'

Keeping his face turned away, Covenant answered, 'The Skyweir is on the other side of Garroting Deep. It's the biggest mountain in the west. Somewhere deep inside it are the springs that form the Black River. That's another reason Caerroil Wildwood is so strong. The Black River feeds him. It carries a lot of power. Because one of its springs is the Blood of the Earth.'

While Linden's mind reeled, Covenant drawled over his shoulder, 'Drinking the EarthBlood gives the Power of Command. Hellfire, Linden, I must have told you that.'

Then he announced grimly, 'I intend to use the Power of Command to stop Foul. I'm going to do what I would have done if you hadn't created that damn Staff. I'm going to freeze time around him. And around Kastenessen while I'm at it. Encase them in temporal ice. That way, I can finally put a stop to all these atrocities without risking the Arch.'

At last, the cold found its way through Linden's clothes to her heart. *You must be the first to drink of the EarthBlood.* Esmer had known exactly what Covenant and Jeremiah had in mind.

Chapter Seven:

Taking the Risk

The cold seemed to speak directly to Linden: she saw its uncompromising beauty. Certainly it could kill her. It had no pity. And she was not dressed warmly enough to contain her body's inadequate heat. The sensation of fire that Covenant had given to her was slipping away. Already shivers began to rise through her undefended flesh. Soon she would lose control of her limbs; or she would have to implore Covenant to succour her again.

Nevertheless the austerity and precision of the cold gave it a numinous glory. The sunlit crystalline untrammelled brilliance of the snow on all sides defined the contours of the hilltop as distinctly as etch-work in purest glass. The air itself might have been glass. Every slope and crest around her seemed to burn as though it were afire with cold.

And winds had shaped and sculpted the crust as it melted and refroze repeatedly between day and night. She could see delicate, dazzling whorls everywhere; sastrugi as scalloped and articulate as hieroglyphs or runes; ridges and hollows as suggestive as the elaborate surface of the sea. With every step that she and Covenant and Jeremiah had taken, or would take, they marred instances of the most casual and frangible loveliness.

Covenant had not stopped speaking: he seemed unaware that she heeded a voice other than his. Trenchant with bitterness, he was saying, 'Of course, the *Elohim* could have done the same thing, saved us all this trouble, if they weren't so damn self-absorbed. And if they didn't *object* to messing around with time. That was Kastenessen's original crime. They Appointed him to contain the *skurj* because he shared himself with a mortal lover, gave her some of who he was. He wanted her with him, so he gave her the power to stay young. To defy time. To use magicks like his. So naturally the *Elohim* took offence.'

With her health-sense, Linden felt each probing finger of winter as it found its way through her garments to touch her skin with ice. If she had known how to interpret the speech of wind and weather, she might have been able to name every avatar of the snow and cold: every flake and crystal, every self-sufficient pattern; every broken and unbreakable rumple in the cloak that covered the hillsides. The stark and brittle branches of the distant forest might have spoken to her.

'And if you do all that,' she asked Covenant as if she were unaware of her own voice, 'what happens to Jeremiah? Will he be freed? Will he be safe?'

Would she be able to find him?

Her son was in more danger than anyone; more peril and more pain. Although he stood at Covenant's side, his tangible body remained at Lord Foul's mercy. Because he was her son, the strange bifurcation of his torment seemed too great to be borne.

Covenant sighed. In a gentler voice, he replied, 'Unfortunately, no. Oh, his suffering will end. As soon as I freeze Foul, everything he's doing will stop. But drinking the EarthBlood, using the Power of Command—Unleashing forces on that scale will pretty much overwhelm us. Jeremiah and I will disappear. We'll snap back to where we belong.' If he felt any grief at the prospect of losing his physical existence – or losing Linden – he did not show it. 'He won't hurt anymore, but he'll still be trapped wherever Foul has him. And he won't know any more about where that is than he does now. He'll still need rescuing.'

Before Linden could pull her thoughts out of the cold to protest, he added, 'That's one of the reasons you're here. In fact, I never even considered doing this without you. After Jeremiah and I vanish, it'll be your turn. Once we're gone, you can drink the EarthBlood yourself. You can Command—' His tone remained gentle. 'Hellfire, Linden, you can Command any damn thing you want. All you have to do is *want* it, and you and your kid will be reunited. In your proper time. Anywhere you choose. If it'll make you happy, you two can live in Andelain together for the rest of your natural lives.'

Trembling with relief and cold – with a hope so sudden that it seemed to shake the marrow of her bones – she asked, 'Is that true? Is that what you meant? When you said that you can't do this without me?'

At once, Covenant's manner became aggrieved. 'What, did you think I didn't *care*? Did you think I'm not trying to do what's best for you and Jeremiah as well as for the Land and the rest of the Earth? I'm *Thomas Covenant*, for God's sake. I've saved the Land *twice*. And I sure as hell didn't get myself killed because I *like* being dead.

'Yes,' he admitted sharply, 'you're why the *Elohim* won't interfere. I brought you for that. You're the Wildwielder. As long as you're here, they think they don't have anything to worry about. But I also want to save your kid.'

Abruptly the Theomach began to laugh.

'What's so funny?' demanded Covenant.

The stranger's laughter stopped. 'I find amusement in your justifications.' He did not sound at all amused.

Again Linden seemed to feel an afterflash of power as she had when Covenant had warmed her earlier. The Theomach vanished from the hilltop.

With a shudder, she dragged her attention away from the beauty which the snow and wind and sun had wrought. 'Then why didn't you transport us straight to *Melenkurion* Skyweir? Why did we have to come *here*? Into the past?'

And why so *far* into the past?

But Covenant had turned his back on her. Instead of facing her question, he was staring back down into the valley.

Jeremiah came a step or two closer. Then he met her gaze on Covenant's behalf. 'Because, Mom, the Blood of the Earth isn't accessible in the time where we belong.' Now her son's eyes reminded her of Esmer's: they seemed to blur and run, melting from the silted hue of dark loam to the pale dun of fine sand. 'There have never been more than one or two ways to approach it, and Elena's battle with Kevin wrecked those passages.'

Jeremiah's tic signalled his discomfort. 'But even before that battle, it wasn't accessible. The first thing Damelon did after he discovered the EarthBlood was put up wards. He thought the Power of Command was too dangerous for anyone to use. He left all kinds of barricades behind.

We would have to fight our way in, and you're the only one of us who can do that. Which would banish Covenant and me before we could accomplish anything. We have to get inside the mountain before Damelon seals it.'

'But' – troubled by Jeremiah's disquiet, Linden struggled to think – 'if Covenant shuts down Lord Foul now,' thousands of years before his first confrontation with the Despiser, 'won't he destroy the Arch of Time?'

Surely such an exertion of Command would unmake all of Lord Foul's actions for the next ten thousand years?

'He could,' Jeremiah conceded without hesitation. 'But he won't. What would be the point? He's trying to save the Land, not destroy it. He'll seal Foul right after we left to come here. Ten thousand years from now, in the time where you and I belong. That way, the Arch won't be in any danger.'

Tremors ran through Linden's chest and arms; through her voice. 'Then why are we still standing here?' If she did not draw on the Staff for warmth, she would not be able to remain coherent much longer. 'Why don't the two of you transport us right now? Get us to *Melenkurion Skyweir* before I freeze?'

The scraps of Jeremiah's pyjamas gave him scant protection; much less than Linden's cloak and clothes. Nevertheless he seemed unaware of the chill. His encrypted uneasiness had nothing to do with ice and snow.

He looked to Covenant as if he were loath to answer her without Covenant's support or approval; and as Jeremiah turned his head, the Theomach came lightly up the hillside. His wrapped feet made no mark on the surface of the crust. Once again, he conveyed the eerie impression that he occupied more than one time and place; that with every step he blurred the definitions of reality.

He ascended as if he meant to accost Covenant. But when he was still nearly a dozen paces away, he halted. Behind his bindings, his eyes seemed to study Covenant for some promise of violence.

'That was just a warning,' Covenant pronounced harshly. 'Next time, I'll actually hurt you.'

The Theomach shrugged. His tone implied its own threat as he said, 'Do not doubt that I remain able to frustrate your designs. I have counselled wisdom as well as caution, yet you give me cause to doubt that you will heed me.'

'Just so we understand each other,' Covenant retorted. 'I'm *on* your damn path. I'll *stay* on your damn path. But I'm tired of being taunted.'

The stranger nodded once, slowly. Then he seemed to slip sideways and was gone. Linden could not detect any evidence that he had ever been present.

Apparently unsurprised, Jeremiah moved closer to Covenant. When Covenant glanced at him, the boy said, 'Mom wants to know why we don't just transport ourselves to *Melenkurion* Skyweir. But I think there's something more important.' He seemed unsure of his ability to form an independent opinion. 'It's too cold for her. She's going to—'

'Oh, bloody hell,' muttered Covenant. 'I keep forgetting.'

His halfhand drew a brusque arc in the air. Linden only registered the gesture as a trail of phosphenes like the sweep of a comet: she hardly saw the red flicker of heat in the depths of his eyes. Then a second tide of warmth flooded through her, washing the ice from her skin in an instant, dispelling shivers from the core of her body. Between one heartbeat and the next, she felt a flush of fire, as if Covenant had ignited her blood.

Momentarily helpless with relief, she breathed, 'God in Heaven. How do you *do* that?'

Covenant frowned critically at his hand; flexed his fingers as though they did not entirely belong to him. 'It doesn't matter. Being part of the Arch isn't exactly fun. It ought to be good for at least a few tricks.'

A moment later, he looked at Linden, and his expression changed to a humourless grin. 'But as it happens, there's a perfectly good reason why we can't "just transport ourselves". I mean, aside from the fact that the Theomach won't let us. He may be right. It could be too dangerous.'

Covenant sighed. 'This is a pivotal time for the Land. New possibilities are coming to life. Old powers are changing. In the grand scheme of things, it won't be all that long before the Forestals start to fade.' Some of his earlier scorn returned. 'They'll make the mistake of thinking the Lords can take care of the forests for them. And of course people just naturally like cutting down trees.'

Then he appeared to shake off an impulse to digress. 'But that's not the problem. The problem is those "puissant beings" the Theomach mentioned. If Jeremiah and I risk using power now, we'll be noticed. And not in a good way. We could run into opposition. The kind of opposition that might damage the Arch.'

Linden wanted to ask, What beings? But she had more immediate concerns. The heat in her veins had given her a sense of urgency. And it had restored a measure of her earlier determination. Covenant and Jeremiah had answered some of her most compelling questions; but she had more.

'All right,' she said, nodding more to herself than to Covenant. 'We can't do this the easy way. So what are we going to do? You said it yourself. We have two hundred leagues to go. On foot in the dead of winter, with no food or shelter. You and Jeremiah don't look like you feel the cold, but it can kill me. And I assume that you need to eat. How do you expect us to survive?'

Covenant looked away. 'Actually,' he said as if he could taste bile, 'that's up to you.' Then he met her gaze again, glaring angrily. 'This whole mess is the Theomach's idea. He expects *you* to make the decisions.

'Right now, you sort of *are* the Arch of Time. Or you represent it. You're the only one of us who's *all* here. Or *just* here. You're the only one who isn't already a walking violation of Time. So you're the only one who might be able to do things safely. Your kid and I can keep you alive – as long as we don't attract any attention. As long as no one sees us do anything that isn't supposed to happen in this time. But you have to take charge.

'Should be simple enough,' he growled in disgust. 'All we have to do is reach *Melenkurion* Skyweir. Without going through Garroting Deep.

'I'm ready when you are.'

Linden stared at him. 'You can't be serious.'

In response, Covenant wheeled away from her. Brandishing his fists, he shouted into the air over the valley, 'Do you hear that? She thinks you aren't *serious*!'

He must have believed – or known – that the Theomach was still nearby.

'We don't really have much choice, Mom,' Jeremiah said tentatively. 'We weren't expecting to end up here. What we wanted to do was pretty easy. This is much more complicated. Right now, we're as lost as you are.'

Reflexively Linden wanted to reassure him. 'That's all right, honey. I'll think of something.' In fact, she did not need to think. Her choices were already plain to her. The shaped snow had whispered them to her; or she had seen them in the winter's irrefusable beauty. 'There's just one more thing that I want to understand.'

She had many other questions, a long list of them. But first she needed to leave this hilltop; needed an answer to the cold. And the potential for redemption in Covenant's intentions urged movement. For the first time since Roger had taken her son, she seemed to see a road which might lead to Jeremiah's rescue, and the Land's.

Covenant spun back towards her as if he meant to yell in her face. But his tone was unexpectedly mild as he said, 'Just one? Linden, you astonish me.'

'Just one for now,' she acknowledged. 'But it's important. In spite of the Theomach, you make it sound like there's hope. If I choose the right path. If we can get to *Melenkurion* Skyweir. So why did the ur-viles try to stop you?'

The implications of their attack undermined Covenant's explanations. What did they see that she did not?

'Is *that* all?' Covenant scowled sourly. 'Hell and blood! They're *Demondim-spawn*, Linden. Their makers are besieging Revelstone. Don't tell me you still imagine they want to *help* you?

'*Think*, for God's sake. They made Vain so you could create that Staff, which has effectively prevented me from stopping Foul. Then they guided you to it so you would have the power to *erase* me anytime you don't happen to like what I'm doing. Sure, they gave you what you needed to weaken the Demondim. Hell, why not? If I don't succeed, Revelstone is going to fall eventually, and in the meantime they want to stay on your good side. Every bit of trust they can squeeze out of you serves the Despiser. They're trying to turn you against me.'

Linden did not believe him: she could not. The ur-viles had done too much– And whenever he reproached her for forming and using the Staff of Law, her instinctive resistance to him stiffened. The man whom she had accompanied to his death would not have said such things.

His scorn and ire made her ache for the Thomas Covenant who had once loved and accepted her.

But she had nothing to gain by arguing. If the ur-viles had intended their manacles for Covenant, they had failed. She would have to live with the consequences of their failure.

'All right,' she said as if Covenant's vehemence had persuaded her. He had enabled her to withstand the cold – temporarily, at least. To that extent, he resembled his former self. 'I'm just trying to understand. If I have to decide what we're going to do, I need to understand as much as I can.'

She took a deep breath, let it out slowly. 'Here's an idea. Why don't we call the Ranyhyn?'

Hyn would not be born for thousands of years. Even the herd that had reared to Covenant lived millennia in the future of this present. But Linden did not know how to gauge the mysterious relationship between the Ranyhyn and Time. Her constrained linear conceptions had been proven inadequate repeatedly. Hyn's far distant ancestors might already be aware of her need for them.

But Jeremiah covered his face as if she had embarrassed him. And Covenant exploded. 'Hellfire and bloody damnation! That's another terrible idea. In fact, it's even worse than wanting to go to Andelain.'

Holding his glare, Linden made no effort to interrupt him.

'Maybe they can hear you,' he told her hotly. 'Maybe they can't. If they can, they'll probably answer. They're loyal enough for anything. That's not the point. You'll be asking them to violate the Land's history. To risk the Arch.'

'How?' she countered.

Covenant made a visible effort to recover his composure. 'Because right now there aren't any Ranyhyn in the Land. After Foul killed *Kelenbhrabanal*, he drove them away. If they hadn't left, he would have exterminated them. They won't come back for another three or four hundred years. Until they find the Ramen – or the Ramen find them. Without *Kelenbhrabanal*, they need the Ramen to lead them.

'If you summon them now – and they answer – the consequences will ripple for millennia. And they'll only get worse. One thing will lead to another. They'll cause more and more changes.'

Linden waited coldly until Covenant was done. Then she said without inflection, 'I didn't know any of that. There are too many things that you haven't told me. I don't have any way to tell the difference between good ideas and bad ones.'

'She's right,' Jeremiah put in hesitantly. 'We're asking an awful lot of her. It isn't her fault if she gets some of it wrong.'

His apparent reluctance to defend her – or to disagree with Covenant in any way – made her bite her lip. She needed that small hurt to conceal her deeper pain. She had spent much of his life caring for him with her whole heart; and during that time, Covenant had become more essential to him than she had ever been.

She remembered a Covenant who would not have blamed her—

She did not fault her son for his loyalties. She loved him enough to be grateful that he had grown capable of the kind of attachment which he felt for Covenant. But her helpless rage at what the Despiser had done mounted with every fresh sign that Jeremiah did not love her.

Covenant avoided her gaze. 'I get mad too easily,' he admitted as if he were speaking to the empty air. 'I know that. It's the frustration– What I'm trying to do is hard as hell. And it hurts. But it's nothing compared to what Jeremiah is going through. I want to help him so bad—' After a moment, he added, 'And you. And the Land. You didn't cause any of these delays and obstacles. But they're making me crazy.'

He seemed to be attempting an apology.

Linden did not care. He could have asked for her sufferance on his knees without swaying her. For Jeremiah's sake, however, she replied quietly, 'Don't worry about it. Eventually we'll learn how to talk to each other.

'We're all tired of frustration. We should go before it gets any worse.'

The relief on Jeremiah's face was so plain that she could not bear to look at it.

Covenant jerked his eyes to hers. A sudden intensity exaggerated the strictures of his face. 'Go where? You still haven't—'

Linden cut him off. 'Where else? Berek's camp. You said that he's in the middle of a battle. But he has food. He has warm clothes.' Even *true believers* could not fight on faith alone. 'And I'm willing to bet that he has horses. If we can reach him' – if she could endure the cold long enough – 'he might be persuaded to help us.'

She was serious: she did not know how else she could hope to reach

Covenant's goal. But she also wanted to hear what he would say about ripples now. If her choices and actions were somehow consonant with the Arch— The Theomach had asserted that *her deeds will do no harm. That I will ensure.*

Surely entering Berek's camp would be less dangerous than redirecting the entire past of the Ranyhyn?

'I *told* you,' Jeremiah crowed. 'Sometimes she does exactly the right thing. This is going to work. She'll *make* it work.'

For a long moment, Covenant studied her sceptically, as if he suspected a trick of some kind. Then he seemed to throw up his hands. 'It's worth a try. Berek is still in the dark about almost everything. He hardly knows what he can do, or how he can do it. He isn't likely to recognise the truth about any of us. And he definitely has horses.

'I should warn you, though,' he added grimly. 'You'll *have* to make this work because *I* sure as hell can't. He doesn't realise it yet, but he's full of Earthpower. He can erase us. If he so much as *touches* us, this whole ordeal will be wasted.'

Linden nodded to herself. She was not surprised: she was only sure. If she stepped aside from the Theomach's "path", he would correct her.

At first, she led the way, not because she knew the location of Berek's battle, but because she was in a hurry to leave the hilltop. She did not want to exhaust herself by following the difficult crests: she needed the less arduous passage of the valley bottom, in spite of its death-laden atmosphere. So she headed downwards across the slopes at the best pace that she could manage, keeping her back to the west.

Her haste caused her to slip often as her boots skidded over buried stones or bones. Sometimes she fell. But her cloak gave her a measure of protection from the snow. She did not slow her steps until she reached the floor of the valley.

There the implications of the fallen were stronger. The mere thought that she trod over abandoned corpses daunted her. But the sun was westering; and with its light behind her, she did not suffer from its flagrant glare. Now she moved more slowly for the same reason that she had hurried to reach the valley: she feared exhaustion. The laborious hesitation-and-plunge of every step drained her strength. And the cold grew sharper as the sun lost its force. If she tried to walk too quickly, she would soon defeat herself.

Before long, Covenant and Jeremiah caught up with her. For a time, they matched her burdened plod, keeping a safe distance from her. But they both seemed proof against exertion as well as cold; and gradually they began to draw ahead as if they were reluctant for her company.

'Covenant, wait,' Linden panted. 'I have another question.' She did not want to be left behind.

Covenant and Jeremiah exchanged comments too low for her to hear. Then they slowed their strides.

Hardly able to control her breathing, she asked, 'How far do we have to go?'

'Three leagues,' Covenant answered brusquely. 'Maybe more. At this rate, we won't get there until after dark.'

Until even the insufficient warmth of the sun had vanished from the Last Hills.

If she did not think about something other than her own weakness, she would lose heart altogether. 'I have no idea what we're getting into,' she admitted. 'I know that there are things the Theomach doesn't want you to say. But what *can* you tell me?'

Covenant scowled at her. 'You want me to describe the battle? What does it matter? People are hacking at each other, but they're too tired to be much good at it. From one minute to the next, most of them don't know if they're winning or losing. There's yelling and screaming, but mostly it's just hacking.'

Linden shook her head. She had already been in too many battles. 'I meant Berek. You said that he doesn't realise what he can do. Or how he can do it. But he summoned the Fire-Lions. He must have some kind of lore.'

'Oh, well.' Covenant seemed to lose interest. 'It wasn't like that. He didn't exactly *summon* the Fire-Lions. He didn't even know they existed. But he got their attention, and for that he only had to be desperate and bleeding. And he had to have a little power. The real question is, where did he get power?

'According to the legends, when Berek was desperate and bleeding and beaten on Mount Thunder, the rocks spoke to him. They offered him help against the King if he pledged to serve the Land. So he swore he would, and the rocks sent the Fire-Lions to decimate the King's forces.

'But that doesn't actually make sense. Sure, the stone of the Land is *aware*. That's especially true in Mount Thunder, where so many forces have been at work for so long. But it doesn't talk. I mean, it doesn't talk fast enough for most people to hear it.

'So how did Berek do it?' Covenant asked rhetorically. 'How did he tap into the little bit of Earthpower he needed to call down the Fire-Lions?'

Concentrating so that she would not think about her weariness, Linden waited for him to go on.

'This is the Land, remember,' Covenant said after a moment. She could not read him with her health-sense; but his manner betrayed that he was losing patience again. His tone gave off glints of scorn. 'Earthpower runs near the surface. And Berek has what you might call a natural affinity. He just didn't know it. The damn stones were more *aware* than he was.'

'Then how—?' Linden began.

Without transition, Covenant seemed to digress. 'It's easy to criticise Elena,' he drawled. 'Silly woman. Didn't she know despair is a weakness, not a strength?' He was talking about his own daughter. 'Didn't she know Kevin dead was bound to be weaker than he was alive?

'But she had precedent. She understood that better than anybody. Which is probably why they made her High Lord. No matter what you've heard, the Old Lords were all about despair. It gave them some of their greatest victories. And it's what saved Berek.

'It opened him up. Tapped into his natural affinity. Being half insane with pain and blood-loss and despair made him *raw* enough to feel what's really going on here. What the life of the Land is really like. That's all it took. When he finally felt the Earthpower in Mount Thunder, he felt it in himself as well. And the Fire-Lions felt *that*. They responded to it because that's what they do.'

As Covenant's restiveness mounted, he began to pull ahead, taking Jeremiah with him. Without turning his head, he finished, 'The rest of it, all the legends people told about him— That stuff was just a way to make what happened sound heroic.'

Because of Berek, everything in the Land had changed. It had been made new. He had given its inhabitants their heritage of Earthpower. Yet Covenant disdained Berek's achievement.

She did not ask him to wait for her: she hardly wanted his company now. But in one sense, he had not answered her question. Breathing painfully, she increased her pace for a moment.

'Just tell me one more thing,' she panted at his back. 'What's Berek like? What kind of man is he?'

If she wanted the first Halfhand's help while he fought a fierce battle that would leave many of his supporters dead, she needed to know enough about him to gain his sympathy.

Covenant quickened his strides. Keeping his face to the east, he replied harshly, 'He's charismatic as all hell. Basically a good man, or his despair wouldn't have left him so raw. And half the time he has no earthly idea what he's doing.'

Then, for no apparent reason, he added, 'When Elena summoned Kevin, he didn't fail her. She failed him.'

After that, he and Jeremiah left Linden to struggle along as well as she could.

Gradually the uneven shadows of the hills spread into the valley. As much as possible, trying to conserve her strength, Linden followed the trail that Covenant and Jeremiah broke in the crust ahead of her. But more and more often, their way took her into the shade; and then she understood that the coming night would be far more cruel than the day. The temperature of the air seemed to plummet whenever she crossed out of the light.

She did not know how much longer she could go on.

When Covenant and Jeremiah were forty or fifty paces ahead of her – far enough to fade in the shadows, so that she could only be sure of them when they returned to sunlight – she began to draw cautiously on the sustenance of the Staff, evoking a slow current of heat and fortitude from the untroubled wood. Doubtless her son and her former lover would warn her if she endangered them. They had too much to lose. And she needed the nourishment of Law and Earthpower. Without it, she would have to ask for more of Covenant's inexplicable fire; and that prospect increased her sense of helplessness.

The more time she spent with him, the less she trusted him.

She was prepared to support his purpose. But she would do so for Jeremiah's sake, and to oppose the Despiser, and so that she would not find herself stranded ten thousand years before her proper time. Covenant had been too profoundly altered: Linden no longer knew how to believe in him.

In that fashion, she continued her burdened trudge through the snow and the cold while the shadows deepened and the valley grew dim. Long after she should have fallen on her face, she kept walking because the Staff of Law nurtured her.

But then, in one of the last swaths of sunshine, she saw Jeremiah dropping back. He let Covenant forge ahead alone so that she would be able to catch up with him.

Of its own accord, Linden's heart lifted. Involuntarily she pushed herself to move faster; and as she did so, she quenched the Staff's subtle warmth. She did not intend to threaten her son.

He started talking as soon as she drew near enough to hear him. He sounded tense; uncomfortable with her. Or perhaps he had been afflicted with Covenant's frustration, Covenant's impatience. He almost babbled as he said, 'This isn't normal. We're too far south. The winters aren't usually this bad.'

Nevertheless he had elected to accompany her, at least for a while. He must have felt some concern for her, despite his devotion to Covenant. That was enough to encourage her.

'It's an after-effect of the war,' Jeremiah went on as if he could not stop, 'when Berek was losing. Nobody in this time knows Foul. They won't meet him until after Kevin becomes High Lord. But he's in the Land. He has a home where nobody can stumble on him by accident. He's waiting. Until the Lords become powerful enough, they won't have a realistic chance of breaking the Arch.'

As Linden drew level with him, Jeremiah matched his pace to hers. He kept a distance of four or five steps between them, and he stayed on her left: she could not see his tic. But he did not pull ahead again, or fall behind. And he did not stop talking.

'But earlier Foul wasn't *just* waiting. Once *samadhi* started this war, Foul did what he could to help Berek's King win it.

'Of course, if that happened, there wouldn't be any Lords. But Foul didn't want Lords then. He wanted the King to win. That whole kingdom had the right attitude. I mean the right attitude for Foul. He could manipulate them easily. If they won, he could teach them how to set him free. They could use the Earthpower in the Land to provoke the Creator until the Creator had to intervene. That would break the Arch. Or Foul could get them to rouse the Worm.

'So Foul tried to help Berek's King by sending darkness out of Ridjeck Thome. Malice so thick it blotted out the sun. It practically broke the hearts of Berek's people. And it weakened Berek himself. Almost got him killed. He's a great warrior, but when he fought the King, he'd lost a lot of his strength. That's why the King was able to beat him.

'This winter is sort of left over from losing the sun for a season or two.'

Jeremiah was watching Linden sidelong, apparently studying her, although he looked away whenever she turned towards him. 'But the air's getting warmer,' he said. 'Can you tell?' His voice had taken on a faintly pleading tone. 'This valley goes down into the Center Plains. It's still going to be cold when the sun sets. But Covenant can help you. All you have to do is ask.'

He seemed to want her to accept her dependence on Covenant.

She wanted to hear her son justify his loyalty to Covenant. He had called Covenant *the best*. How had Covenant won Jeremiah's heart? But she did not wish to risk alienating him. Instead of rejecting his implicit appeal directly, she said, 'I'm hanging in there, Jeremiah, honey. I'll make it somehow.

'But it really helps when you talk to me. Can I ask you something?'

The boy frowned at Covenant's dark shape as if he were unsure of himself. 'I guess, Mom. If it'll do any good. Depending on what it is.'

They were deep in shadow; still far from the nearest dwindling patch of sunshine. Without light, Linden could not insist on an answer to the question that mattered most to her. For the moment, she concentrated on other concerns.

'I understand that there are things you can't tell me,' she began, keeping her tone as neutral as possible. 'They'll interfere with the – I'm not sure what to call it – the continuity of what we're doing.' *In this circumstance, her mind cannot be distinguished from the Arch of Time.* 'But I'm curious. How do you know the Theomach? You said that you've never met him, but you obviously recognised him.'

'Oh, that.' Jeremiah's relief was plain in his voice. Clearly her question did not trouble him. 'I heard about him, that's all. He's one of the Insequent.

'I told you I've been here a lot. I mean, in the Land. And around the Earth. Sort of disembodied, like a ghost. Most of the time, I didn't choose where I was. Choosing is hard. And I never knew *when* I was. But once in a while, I met one of the Insequent. They talked about him. The Theomach. I guess he's their biggest hero. Or he's going to be. It's confusing. I don't know when any of them talked to me, but it seems like it must have been after where we are now. I can't see why he's supposed to be such a big deal, so maybe being a hero comes later.

'But there was one– I saw him a bunch of times. I don't think that was an accident. I think he was looking for me. He called himself the Vizard. He said he wanted us to be friends, but I thought he really just wanted me to do something. When I saw him, he almost always talked about the Theomach. I got the impression he was jealous or something.'

In the distance ahead, Covenant passed back into sunlight; and the sudden change seemed to make him flare as if he had emerged from a dimension of darkness.

Waiting for her opportunity – for the burst of light that might be her last chance – Linden asked carefully, 'What did he want you to do?'

Jeremiah shrugged. 'Build something, I guess. Like the door that let me come here. Only what he wanted was really a trap. A door into a prison.'

Simply to keep her son with her, she asked, 'Why did he want that?'

'Oh,' he replied as if the subject were inconsequential, 'it was for the *Elohim*. All of them. I guess they hate each other. The Insequent and the *Elohim*. The Vizard thought if I made the right door it would lure them in and they wouldn't be able to get out. And maybe if he just talked about it enough I would know how to make it.

'But I wasn't really listening. I didn't like him. And nothing made sense. I didn't understand why he hated the *Elohim*. He didn't seem to have a reason. I decided he just wanted to prove he's greater than the Theomach, so I stopped paying attention.'

A few steps more: only a dozen or so. Jeremiah could not conceal his disquiet. He had retrieved his racecar and was playing with it tensely, flipping it back and forth between his hands. Ahead, Covenant had vanished back into shadow. As the sun fell closer to setting, the shadows grew darker: Linden could hardly be sure that he still existed. And Jeremiah gave her the impression that he might bolt at any moment, overcome by the stress of talking to her.

'Just a little longer, honey,' she urged quietly. 'I can see that it's hard for you to be around me. But there's one thing I have to know. I'm not sure that I can keep going without it.'

'What is it?' His manner was suddenly thick with distrust.

Linden hazarded a moment or two of silence. Then through the crunching of her boots and the crisp stamp of the Staff, she said, 'You won't have to talk at all. You can just show me.'

Half a stride ahead of her, Jeremiah crossed into the light of the sun.

It was pale with constriction and approaching twilight, but it seemed bright as morning after the gloom of the shadows. As soon as she reached the sunshine herself, and her son was fully illumined, she halted. Bracing her fears on the Staff, she said, 'Jeremiah,' as if she had the right to command him, 'take off your shirt. Let me look at you. I have to know if you were shot.'

Harsh as a blow, he wheeled to face her. The mud of his gaze roiled with darkness and anger. At the corner of his left eye, the muscles beat as steadily as a war-drum; a summons to battle.

Startled and afraid, Linden flinched as if her son had threatened her.

But he complied. Vehemently, almost viciously, he undid the remaining buttons of his pajama top; tore it from his shoulders; flung it to the snow at his feet. If he felt the cold, he did not show it.

As if she had demanded a violation which he resented fiercely but could not refuse, he turned in a circle, letting her scrutinise his naked back as well as his chest. But there were too many stains on his skin, too much grime. If he had been wounded and healed, she could not find the scars.

He must have recognised her uncertainty. Abruptly he stooped, punched his fists through the icy crust, and scooped up handfuls of snow. Then he slapped the snow onto his chest and stomach, rubbing furiously until he had cleaned away the marks of struggle and torment.

In the sun's failing light, his skin looked as healthy and whole as if she had bathed him herself; as if he were the son whom she had loved and tended for so many years.

'Are you *satisfied?*' he hissed venomously. '*Mom?*'

Oh, God. Instinctively Linden hugged the Staff to her chest, covered her face with her icy hands. Sweet Jesus. The previous day – or ten thousand years in the future – she had asked Jeremiah if he had been shot. At first, he had tried to avoid an answer. Then he had replied, *I'm not sure. Something knocked me down pretty hard, I remember that. But there wasn't any pain.*

But he had *not* been shot. Somehow Barton Lytton's deputies had missed him. Instead he had merely been struck, perhaps by Roger's falling body. Therefore he remained alive in the world to which he had been born; the world where he belonged. His life, his natural birthright, could still be saved. In fact, if she understood what she had once experienced herself, and what Covenant had explained about his own visits to the Land—

She heard Jeremiah retrieve his shirt and shove his arms into the sleeves; heard him stride angrily away. But she could not uncover her eyes to watch him leave her. If she understood the rules, the Law, governing translations to the Land, Jeremiah could not be slain here while he remained alive in his proper reality. Lord Foul might torture him until his mind tore itself, but the Despiser could not kill him. Instead Jeremiah would only remain in Lord Foul's power until his summoner passed away. Then he would be released to his former life. And his body would bear no sign of what he had endured. Only his sane or shredded mind would suffer the consequences of his time in the Land.

My son– Unregarded tears froze on Linden's cheeks and fingers. Covenant had indeed offered her hope. But he had also misled her. Worse than that, he had lied to her.

If he succeeded against the Despiser, Jeremiah's summoner would die. Linden knew Joan too well to believe otherwise. Joan was too frail, too brittle, to preserve herself. Wild magic and her own agony were too destructive to be endured. Without the imposed goad and sustenance of Lord Foul's servants, she would perish quickly.

Then Jeremiah's torment would end. He would vanish from the Land.

Linden would remain because she was already dead. Even Roger might remain, *seeking such havoc that the bones of mountains tremble to contemplate it*. But Jeremiah—

If he returned to his natural world a mental cripple, she would not be there to care for him. He would be lost to her forever.

That was the lie. Covenant had said that *he'll still be trapped wherever Foul has him*, but Jeremiah would not be, he would *not*. *He'll still need rescuing*. Yet surely Covenant knew that Joan's death would release the boy?

Nonetheless Linden had been given a reason to hope. The Despiser's defeat would spare her son's life.

And she had another reason as well; an entirely different kind of reason. The Blood of the Earth. *You can Command any damn thing you want. All you have to do is want it, and you and your kid will be reunited. Anywhere you choose*. She could block Jeremiah's return to the world of her death: she could keep him in the Land. Then she would not need to fear for the condition of his mind. Here he could be truly restored, healed.

But she would still lose him. *If it'll make you happy, you two can live in Andelain–* There Covenant had misled her. Jeremiah's vehemence towards her moments ago, like his devotion to Covenant, proclaimed the truth. If she enabled him to remain in the Land, he would not choose to live with her. He did not love her. He had never loved her. For years while she had lavished her heart on him, he had been absent from himself. Dissociated and unreactive, he had been more conscious of Covenant's friendship than of anything that she had done or felt.

From his damaged perspective, he had no cause to love her—

An uncertain future in his natural world or a life of wholeness in the Land. The Power of Command would enable her to provide one or the other for her son. But that choice was not hers to make: it belonged to him. Either way, he would be lost her to her; but her bereavement was beside the point. She had already lost him. And he was not responsible for her dedication – or her sorrow.

Covenant was another matter entirely. He had *lied* to her. Deliberately he had tried to obscure the true crux of Jeremiah's straits – and of her own.

She needed to talk to him. She needed to talk to him *now*.

But when she snatched down her hands and opened her eyes to the dying light, she found the Theomach standing in front of her.

Instinctively she clasped her numb fingers around the Staff. But she did not call upon its power. She felt no threat from the Insequent. To her health-sense, he still appeared to be an ordinary man beneath his strange habiliments; devoid of any inherent theurgy. If she had not fallen so far down into her grief and anger, she would have discerned him as soon as he approached her.

Instead of fire, she drew a little heat from the ready wood, a little comfort, so that she would not collapse into shivering.

She meant to demand, Tell me. I have to know. Why did Covenant *lie* to me? But before she could form the words, the Theomach held up his hand to forestall her. His wrapped and hidden face regarded her with an attitude of grave attention.

'Lady,' he said in his light voice, 'understand that your son's plight is not a simple matter – as yours is not. Even the Halfhand is not free of pain.

'I may say nothing of his designs. You must earn the knowledge that you seek. However,' he added as she started to protest, 'I will accompany you now, if you will permit it. In recompense for your courtesy, I will answer any questions which do not undermine the integrity of Time, or of my own purposes.' Then he lowered his voice as if he did not wish to be overheard. 'Also I will ease your passage through this winter, so that you need not hazard either your own fire or the Halfhand's. Perhaps my aid will enable you to gain your destination with strength sufficient for what must be done.'

Linden stared at him. He had surprised her out of her immediate turmoil, but she did not forget it. And she was sick to death of people who sought to manipulate her by concealing the truth. However, she understood nothing about the Theomach – and he had offered to answer questions.

After a moment, she said stiffly, 'I'm not sure that I want company.' Convince me. 'Let's start with this. If Covenant stays on your path – and I do – will I get a chance to find out what he isn't telling me?'

The Theomach bowed as though her query signalled acquiescence.

'Lady, I believe that you will. You have displayed cleverness, and perhaps wisdom as well. You will contrive opportunities to wrest what veracity you may from your companions.'

What veracity you may— Linden heard disturbing implications in the words, but she was too distraught to consider them. She already knew that she did not trust Covenant.

And her son had not been shot. He would live, whatever happened.

'In that case,' she replied, 'I can't pretend that I don't need help. What can you do to make this easier?'

Her companion gestured along Covenant's and Jeremiah's trail. 'Words will not demonstrate my intent. Walk and you will witness my aid.'

Linden stared at him for a moment longer. Then she sighed to herself. Gripping the Staff tensely in one hand, she resumed her long floundering trudge through the snow.

But she did not flounder: her boots did not break through the crust. Instead she found herself striding like the Theomach over the unreliable surface, unimpeded by brittle ice or clogging snow. The iron heel of the Staff struck the crust with a muted thud like a buried echo, but did not pierce it.

The change relieved her tired muscles and worn resolve more than she would have thought possible. She felt lighter, as though a portion of her mortal dross had been lifted from her. —with strength sufficient for what must be done. She had no idea what the Theomach meant; but now she could believe that she would be able to reach her immediate goal.

'All right,' she said when she had passed back into the shadows and could see no more sunlight along her way. 'That's one promise you've kept. As long as you don't vanish again—'

'I will not.' Her companion sounded mildly offended. 'Here my path lies with yours. You serve my purpose. Therefore I must serve yours.'

'Good.' She nodded to herself several times, arranging her thoughts to the rhythm of strides and echoes. 'In that case, I'll try a few questions. I need something to think about besides the cold.' She meant, Besides Covenant's lies and my son's life.

As she walked, she continued to pull a gentle current of warmth and sustenance from the Staff. She needed more support than the Theomach could give her.

'As you wish, lady.' Now his tone suggested an admixture of satisfaction and secret relief. 'I will answer as our circumstances permit.'

'"The Theomach" seems a bit unwieldy,' Linden began. 'Do you have a name?'

'I do. But it is not for your use.'

His words were brusque, although his manner was not.

She shrugged. 'Never mind, then.' She had not expected him to reveal himself. 'Since Jeremiah has already mentioned your people, maybe you can tell me something about them.

'Why do you hate the *Elohim*? And what did the Vizard want with Jeremiah? Do your people really think that my son can build a trap,' a prison, 'to hold the *Elohim*?'

The Theomach replied with a shrug of his own. 'Lady, we loathe the *Elohim* for their arrogance, and for their ease. Every other being that strides the Earth must strive for knowledge and power sedulously, at great cost. But the *Elohim are* power. They do not strive – and seldom encounter unease. Yet they do not scruple to determine the deeds and dooms of any striving being that mischances to attract their opprobrium.

'The differences between us are various and vast, but the chiefest is this. The *Elohim* have no hearts. I am not present in the Vizard's thoughts. All of the Insequent hold their own counsel and knowledge, and some are spiteful. But where our interests oppose those of the *Elohim*, we are seldom petty. There larger concerns move us.'

For a moment, the Theomach walked beside Linden in silence, appearing to shift slightly in and out of definition with every step. Then he added, 'Does your son possess both the knowledge and the prowess to devise a snare which the *Elohim* could not evade, and from which they would not escape? Of that I will not speak. It is a matter for another time. A *distant* time, lady.'

In the setting dark, Linden was slow to realise that the hills on either side of the valley had begun to slump away. But when she extended her health-sense, she felt the changing shapes of the terrain. Gradually the Last Hills were fading towards the flatland of the Center Plains.

Vexed by all of the secrets that surrounded Jeremiah, she let a taste of acid into her voice. 'Then I don't suppose that you'll tell me how you're going to "humiliate" the *Elohim* yourself?'

'I will not.' Her tone did not ruffle the Theomach's aura. 'Were I to do so, you would feel the Arch of Time tremble to its roots. The Halfhand should not speak as he does.'

Linden took a deep breath, trying to calm herself. In an abstract sense, she understood his refusals and obfuscations. She was ten thousand years away from her own present. She could not begin to guess what the consequences of her actions might be. And inevitably her choices would be influenced by what she was told. Whatever the Theomach's motives might be, they required him to strike a complex and ambiguous balance between his impulse to aid her and his determination to preserve the security of Time.

Although the details of their situation were very different, Covenant and Jeremiah faced the same problem. With the Staff of Law and Covenant's ring, Linden had the power to alter the Land's past irrevocably. If she acted on knowledge which she should not have been able to possess—

More to herself than to her companion, she muttered, 'Are we having fun yet?' Then she resumed her questions.

'We're going to Berek's camp because we're in an impossible position. We need help, and I couldn't think of anywhere else to get it. But it's pretty obvious that this is what you had in mind for us. If all you wanted was to interfere with Covenant's plans, you could have left us anywhere. You *picked* this place. This time.

'I assume that what we're doing suits your purpose, whatever that is. But isn't it *dangerous*? For God's sake, we're about to meet the most famous of the Land's old heroes.' Covenant had warned her about ripples. 'No matter how careful we are, he'll see and hear things—'

'Lady,' the Theomach put in, 'be at peace.' His tone was gentle; meant to soothe her. 'I have said that you serve my purpose. Therefore I must serve yours.

'Here the preservation of the Arch need not trouble you. That burden is mine. At great cost, I have garnered knowledge which you lack, and my knowledge is profound. Be assured that I will watch over you. Indeed, I have already done so. I have set you at a distance which ensured that my theurgy would not be witnessed, but which will not prevent the accomplishment of your intent.

'Where my guidance is needed, I will provide it. And I will accommodate the effects of both your presence and your deeds. You need only trust in yourself – and heed my counsel. In the fullness of time, my aid will demonstrate its worth.'

To her surprise, Linden found that she believed him. He was not closed to her: she could hear his sincerity.

In dreams, Covenant had told her to trust herself. And he had sounded like himself; like the Covenant whom she remembered rather than the man who led her eastward. The man who had lied—

'And I guess,' she murmured to the cold and the waiting night, 'that I'll have to take your promises on faith.'

Her companion answered her with a silence that seemed to imply assent.

By slow degrees, stars began to prick the darkening sky as if they were manifesting themselves like Covenant and Jeremiah across an unfathomable gulf of time. Warmed by Earthpower, Linden could endure the piercing accumulation of the cold. Nevertheless the first few stars seemed as chill as absolute ice, gelid with distance and loneliness. She could have considered herself one of them, unfathomably alone in spite of the Theomach's presence.

Still she had to make use of the time which had been given to her – or imposed upon her.

'In that case,' she went on, 'can you tell me why you interfered with Covenant and Jeremiah in the first place? What was so dangerous about what they were trying to do?'

'Lady,' the Insequent answered without hesitation, 'I do not consider it plausible that you would have been able to avoid High Lord Damelon's notice. From this arises the true peril. He holds the Staff of Law. The first Staff, of which yours is but an unfinished semblance.'

Linden wanted to ask, Unfinished? But the Theomach did not pause.

'Surely it is plain that the simultaneous proximity in Damelon's presence of two such implements of Earthpower would cause a convulsion in the Arch. And your own knowledge that such an event both did not and should not occur would increase the violence of the violation. You are fully aware that your Staff was created many centuries after the destruction of the Staff which Damelon Giantfriend will hold upon his approach to *Melenkurion* Skyweir. That awareness would sever the continuity of the Land as it exists within your own experience. It would sever the essential continuity of Time.'

In this circumstance, her mind cannot be distinguished from the Arch of Time.

His explanation shocked her. 'Then why—?' She faltered in dismay, unable to complete the question. Why would Covenant want to take that kind of risk? What had he hoped to accomplish?

'Lady, nothing is certain,' her companion said as if he wanted to reassure her. 'Yet the peril cannot be doubted. In fear, I disturbed the Halfhand's designs. And also in pride,' he admitted, 'for assuredly the *Elohim* would have done so if I did not. Here both your presence and your ignorance ward the Halfhand. But neither would suffice to forestall the *Elohim* if High Lord Damelon became cognisant of your Staff.'

He paused for a moment, then added carefully, 'It is sooth that you aid my purposes. But I do not require such service. I am able to achieve what I must. I was not compelled by my own needs to thwart the Halfhand.'

His tone asked Linden to believe him. She heard an emotion in it which may have been sympathy or pleading.

The heavens held too many stars: she could not imagine them all. They seemed as profligate and irredeemable as the motes of dust in a wilderland. Directly or indirectly, Covenant had lied to her. And he had planned to chance exposing Linden and Jeremiah and the Land and Time itself to the possibility of a catastrophic encounter with Berek's son.

As she walked on across the surface of the snow and ice into the unknown dark, she clung to the Staff of Law, *her* Staff; and to Covenant's ring on its chain under her shirt; and to the warning that Esmer had given her.

You must be the first to drink of the EarthBlood.

She absolutely did not trust the man who had brought her son back to her with his mind restored and his heart shut against her.

Some time later, long after her comparatively easy progress had become a stupefied trudge of hunger and weariness, and even the Staff's given warmth had been enclosed in a cold as pitiless as the sky's bedizened infinity, she caught the first scent of smoke.

When she noticed it initially, she was not sure of it. But soon it became unmistakable: woodsmoke, the distinctive tang of a campfire. Somewhere within the range of her senses, people had lit flames against the winter's cruelty.

She lifted her head as her pulse quickened. 'Is that—?' she asked the Theomach. Studying the smells, she detected many fires. And now the smoke carried faint intimations of cooking; of meats being roasted, stews bubbling, poultices steeping over the fires.

'Berek's camp is nigh,' her companion confirmed. 'Half a league, no more. Shortly we will encounter those who scout the night for the protection of their comrades.'

As her percipience attuned itself, Linden became conscious of more than fires and food. She heard or felt muffled groans, oaths muttered in anger or pain, occasional sharp commands. They came to her through the silence, carried on the frigid air. And her nerves found an early taste of suffering; of wounds that threatened death, and hurts that were worse than dying. Among them, she perceived the sickly odours of illness, malnutrition, infection: foetid bowels, running sores, flesh in all of the crippling stages of putrefaction: the consequences of a prolonged and brutal struggle. Camped somewhere ahead of her were the remnants of two desperate armies; forces which had warred against each other season after season in a running battle across much of the Land's terrain. Berek and his warriors – and their enemies – must have been marching and fighting and dying for two years or more. Those among them who had somehow remained hale enough to give battle must be pitifully few – and growing fewer by the day.

'If I am not mistaken,' the Theomach remarked after a brief pause, 'the Halfhand and your son have marked the presence of Berek's scouts, and have concealed themselves in darkness, awaiting our accompaniment ere they venture farther.'

Linden hardly heard him. She had begun to push her pace into a shambling rush, not because Covenant and Jeremiah might be in danger, but because she was needed. She was a physician; and Berek's sick, wounded and dying numbered in the hundreds.

People are hacking at each other, but they're too tired to be much good at it. Sheer attrition should have forced them to surrender this war *seasons* ago.

'How many men has Berek got left?' she asked the Insequent.

'Men and women,' he amended. 'Perhaps thirty score.'

'And how many of them are actually fit to fight?'

'Perhaps a third.' His tone suggested a shrug. 'Others contribute as they can. They serve as wagoners and drovers, foragers and healers. Still others are able only to be conveyed in wagons and litters while they await their deaths.'

Linden swore under her breath. She had always hated wars. This one sickened her, and she had not yet encountered it.

For Jeremiah's sake, and Covenant's, she stemmed the flow of Earthpower from the Staff, although she craved its generous vitality. Then she asked the Theomach, 'What about the other army? The King's supporters?'

'Their numbers are thrice Berek's. And they have this vantage, that they abandon their wounded and infirm as well as their dead. Thus they are unencumbered, as Berek is not. And indeed his straits are more narrow than I have described, for he retrieves the living fallen among his foes and accords to them the same succour which he provides for his own, scant though that succour assuredly is.

'Yet he continues to harry his foes towards Doom's Retreat. They have lost heart and purpose, and give battle only because they fear to do otherwise. They adjudge Berek by the standard of themselves, and so they believe that to surrender is to be slaughtered.'

Linden went on swearing to herself. Now she wished that she could run; that she had the strength— Every passing moment meant more death.

When Covenant and Jeremiah appeared suddenly out of the dark, they startled her as if she had forgotten all about them. They moved without a sound. Here the snow was not as deep as it had been in the valley, and the ice did not break under them.

'Linden, slow down,' Covenant whispered urgently. 'Berek has scouts out here. One of them just missed us. And there are outriders closer to the camp. We need a way to get around them.'

Linden strode past him and her son without hesitation. Deliberately she raised her voice. 'Well, we certainly aren't going to sneak up on them. We aren't their *enemies*, for God's sake.' And she was needed. 'Maybe those outriders will let us use their horses.'

'Mom!' Jeremiah protested; but she did not pause, even for him.

The Theomach matched her stride. 'Lady,' he remarked, 'it grows ever more apparent that your folly is wisdom disguised.'

In response, she began to shout, punctuating each sentence with a stamp of the Staff. 'Listen to me! I'm a healer! The people with me are my friends! We want Berek's help, but we also want to help *him*!'

If the scouts did not hear her, they were too far gone in privation and weariness to be of any use.

Almost at once, however, they reacted. Leather slid over slick ice as they ran. Linden heard the muted jangle of armour, the scrape of drawn blades.

She continued ahead; but she stopped shouting. She had attracted enough attention.

Covenant swore as he and Jeremiah scrambled to catch up with her. Then the night in front of her seemed to solidify, and she found herself facing three warriors with their swords drawn.

Reluctantly she halted. She could not make out their features, but she felt their trepidation as well as their exhaustion: two men and a woman who had endured for seasons or years on raw courage and belief alone. The woman had a badly infected cut in one bicep. One of the men had been slashed across the side of his face recently. The other bore so many smaller wounds that Linden could not count them all.

'There are four of us,' she stated. Her voice shook with exertion. 'I'm a healer. The others are my friends. We've been walking all day. From the west,' she added because she guessed that Berek's foes were in the southeast. 'And we're too tired to have much patience. We need to talk to Berek. But first I want to help your wounded. Some of them can still be saved.'

If she distanced herself from Jeremiah and Covenant, she could use her Staff.

'Spies would say the same,' countered the woman. The arm holding her sword trembled. 'Doubtless *Lord* Berek' – she stressed the title grimly – 'will speak to you when our Warhaft has ascertained your true purpose.'

'When you see the truth,' Linden retorted, 'you'll regret that you held us back. If you want to escort us to your camp, we won't give you any trouble. But we aren't going to waste time on some useless interrogation. This is too important.' She wanted to yell, but she swallowed the impulse. 'Too many of your people are dying.'

Turning to the man with the smaller wounds, she commanded, '*You*. Go tell your outriders that we're coming. They can warn Lord Berek. And maybe they can spare some horses for us.'

When none of the scouts moved, she said between her teeth, 'Do it now. I won't tolerate delays.'

'You are mistaken,' the woman replied more harshly. Her sword-arm stiffened. 'You will tolerate this delay, and more. We have not suffered the struggles and pain of this war to be daunted by imperious strangers whose purposes are hidden. You will remain where you stand until we have gathered a force sufficient to ensure that you cause no harm. Then we will escort you to our Warhaft. Mayhap he will deign to treat gently with you.'

Linden did not hesitate: she was done with hesitation. 'Jeremiah,' she ordered quietly, holding the scouts with her glare, 'ask them to step aside, please.'

'Mom?' he protested; then, 'Covenant?'

'Do it carefully,' she insisted. 'Don't hurt anyone.'

'Hellfire,' Covenant muttered. 'You know your mother. If we don't help her, this mess is going to get worse fast.'

Linden resisted a fierce desire to thrust her way between the warriors; to force them aside with the Staff if necessary. Biting her lip, she waited for Jeremiah.

The scouts took a step backwards, prepared to swing their weapons. Their stances shouted belligerence; nerves stretched past weariness into unthinking rage. Then Linden felt a warm wave of force flow past her from Jeremiah's out-stretched hand. At once, the man with the slashed face lurched out of her way. The woman and the other man stumbled aside.

While her son's weird theurgy held, she set off quickly in the direction of the camp with the Theomach silent at her side and Covenant and Jeremiah following close behind her.

When the scouts recovered their balance, they swore in fear and anger; tried to rush an attack. But Jeremiah's unseen magic repulsed them: they rebounded from it as though they had encountered a barricade.

Walking with as much speed as she could manage, Linden asserted as if she spoke to the frigid darkness, 'I've already told you that I'm a healer. I want to help. And we don't want trouble. You're in no danger. There's no need to turn this into a fight. You've done too much fighting as it is.

'Why don't you just escort us while one of you lets Lord Berek know that we're coming? If nothing else, you have to think that we're *strange* enough to be worth his attention.'

For a long moment, the scouts held back. Then, abruptly, the woman sheathed her sword. 'Very well,' she rasped. 'It will be as you have said.'

She made a rough gesture that Linden felt rather than saw; and at once, the man with the smaller wounds sprinted away, clearly heading towards the nearest of Berek's outriders. The woman jogged to catch up with Linden at a safe distance, while her comrade took a similar position on the far side of Linden's small company.

After a brief hesitation, Jeremiah lowered his barrier. Linden sent him her silent gratitude, hoping that he would be able to read her aura. But she did not pause to thank him aloud. The woman who led the scouts was speaking again.

'Comprehend me, however,' she said in a bitten voice. 'I accede because I know not how to oppose you. But you are folk of power, hazardous in this war. If by any word or deed you threaten the Lord, or cause harm to those who stand with him, I will contrive to slay you. I have learned much of death. By some means, I will evade your eldritch force and end your haughtiness.'

Linden sighed. Without turning her head, or shifting her attention from the burgeoning and hurtful emanations of Berek's camp, she asked, 'Don't you have anyone with you who can hear truth? I would have thought that by now,' under the influence of the Land's rich Earthpower, 'some of you would start to notice changes in what you can see and feel and hear.'

'What do you know of such matters?' demanded the woman suspiciously.

She seemed unaware that Jeremiah's barrier was gone.

'This war,' Linden replied. 'It changed on the slopes of Mount Thunder. That's when Lord Berek started to show signs of power you hadn't seen before. But I find it hard to believe that he's the only one.' Surely Berek was not alone in his sensitivity to the true life around him? 'There have to be more of you who can sense things that seem impossible.'

Now the woman sounded less sure of herself. 'Krenwill avers that he has become able to distinguish truth from falsehood.' A jerk of her head indicated the scout striding opposite her. 'At first, I deemed him a fool. Yet I have beheld proofs– Commonly now, our Warhaft enlists his aid in the questioning of prisoners, for the Lord frowns upon harshness towards our foes when they cannot defend themselves.'

Linden glanced at the man, a vague shape in the night. With every step, the sensations of Berek's camp became stronger: the fear and pain bordering on madness; the frantic fatigue; the stunned, almost unreactive resolve. And now she could smell horses, already half-maimed by inadequate provender and far too much exertion. The cold carried the scents of dung and rotting straw as clearly as sounds.

'Then listen,' she told the scout Krenwill. 'I'm a healer. I want to help. Not with the war. With the wounded. And my companions don't mean you any harm.'

The man studied her in silence for a moment. Then he announced softly, 'I hear truth, Basila. If her words are false, she does not know them to be so.'

Linden felt a grudging, uncertain relief from the woman. Still suspiciously, Basila asked, 'You say that you desire Lord Berek's aid. What do you wish of him?'

The clatter of hooves on ice came faintly through the dark, growing louder. Linden counted two riders approaching cautiously. And they were alone. Presumably the man who had run to warn them had continued on towards the camp.

'Horses,' she answered, brusque with the effort of sustaining her haste. 'Food. Warm clothes. I want to get as far away from here as possible.

'That's a lot to ask, I know,' she added. 'But first I'm going to earn it.'

If the stubborn hostility of men and women who had seen too much war did not prevent her—

'Wisdom indeed,' the Theomach remarked to the forlorn multitude of the stars. Then he told Linden, 'You have been well-chosen, lady.'

'Hell and blood,' Covenant muttered at her back. 'How did the two of you become such buddies? *I'm* the one who's trying to save the damn world.'

'There is your error,' replied the Theomach over his shoulder. 'You aim too high. The Earth is too wide, and rife with mystery, to be saved or damned by such as you.'

Peering ahead, Linden studied the approach of the riders. Long ago, Covenant had told her of prophecies which the Council of Lords had preserved concerning the white gold wielder.

> *And with the one word of truth or treachery,*
> *he will save or damn the Earth*
> *because he is mad and sane,*
> *cold and passionate,*
> *lost and found.*

She did not know what she would do if the outriders blocked her path. She needed to reach Berek's camp while she still had enough stamina to be of some use. But she was reluctant to call on Jeremiah's aid again. She did not understand his power, and feared its consequences.

With a muffled clash of tack and an uneasy skitter of hooves, two mounted horses condensed from the dark. Involuntarily she slowed to a stop; leaned on the Staff while she strove to steady her breathing. The riders were both women. When they had halted, one of them asked gruffly, 'What transpires, Basila? All darkness is fraught with peril, and the coming of these strangers does not rest lightly upon us.'

Basila's manner conveyed a shrug. 'Krenwill conceives that the woman speaks sooth.'

'That she means no harm?' insisted the rider. 'That she is a healer, and intends healing? That she seeks aid of the Lord?'

'Aye,' Basila replied. And Krenwill said, 'If there is falsehood here, or peril, she has no knowledge of it.'

'And the theurgy which compelled you to let them pass?' the rider continued. 'Does it ward them still?'

Basila extended her arm towards Linden; moved closer until she was almost near enough to touch Linden. Then she let her arm drop. 'It does not.' As if she wished to be fair, she added, 'And we received no hurt from it. We were merely' – she shrugged again – 'repelled.'

'Then we will not tarry,' the rider announced. She radiated a desire for haste that had nothing to do with Linden's urgency. Rather she seemed to feel exposed on the open plain; eager for light – and for the support of Berek's army. 'Warhaft Inbull will adjudge the matter. A healer we would welcome gladly. But that the woman speaks sooth promises little for her companions.

'Resume your watch,' she told the scouts. 'This seems a night for hazards. If four strangers approach from the west, eight may follow, or a score, or—' She left the thought unfinished. 'Epemin and I will continue your escort.'

Relieved, Linden started forward again with her companions. At once, the two riders separated, turning their weary horses to take the positions that Basila and Krenwill had occupied; and the scouts drifted back into the night.

Linden forgot the scouts as soon as they were gone. Her percipience was focused on the growing emanations of Berek's camp. Her face felt frozen and all of her skin ached with cold. Nonetheless her nerves were certain. She was nearing a large body of men and women – and a much smaller number of horses. She sensed the turmoil and determination among the warriors; the prolonged strain of overexertion and blood loss and insufficient food; the instances of agony and anguish. As well as she could, she watched the east for the glow of campfires. But her eyes themselves felt frozen, and ordinary sight was of little use to her. Unable to sustain herself with Earthpower while Covenant and Jeremiah were nearby, she had nothing to rely on except her health-sense.

In her concentration, she was slow to realise that the nearer rider, the woman who had spoken earlier, was speaking again. 'I am Yellinin,' the woman said, 'third after Warhaft Inbull in the tenth Eoman of the second Eoward. He will require your names. And if indeed you come as friends, I would wish to speak of you courteously. How shall I introduce you to the Warhaft?'

Linden bit down on her numb lip. She had no time, and less strength, for questions. And she had caught her first glimpse of firelight. It dimmed the stars, diminished the depth of the night – and limned a long, low rise ahead of her, the last obstacle between her and the encampment. The sight increased her feeling of urgency. Nevertheless she tried to contain her impatience.

'I'm Linden Avery. The man beside me is the Theomach. Thomas Covenant and my son, Jeremiah, are behind us.' Then, because she was desperate in her own way, she asked, 'Can't we just skip arguing with your Warhaft? I don't mean to be rude myself. But you have an appalling number of wounded. I can feel them from here. It would be better for all of us if you took me straight to your field hospital' – she grimaced at the awkwardness of using a term which might not be familiar to Yellinin – 'or wherever you care for your wounded.

'Let me prove myself,' she urged the rider as they began to ascend the rise and the light of uncounted campfires grew brighter. 'Then your Warhaft – or Lord Berek – can decide what he thinks of me.' Suddenly an idea came to her. 'In the meantime, you can take my companions to your Warhaft. Let him ask them as many questions as he wants.' Linden wished him joy of the experience. Together, Covenant, Jeremiah and the Theomach were probably cryptic enough to confound tree trunks or plinths of basalt. But if Berek's cutters and herbalists had no other resources, she would need to draw on the Staff of Law – and for that she required as much distance from Covenant and Jeremiah as possible. 'Think of them as hostages to ensure my good faith.'

'*Mom*,' Jeremiah objected: he sounded frightened. And Covenant muttered, 'Bloody hell, Linden. Just when I think you've run out of terrible ideas.'

Her son's alarm tugged at her as Covenant's vexation did not. But she kept her back to them; hardened her heart. Her attention was fixed on the injuries of Berek's people, and her gaze focused her appeal on Yellinin. If she had not been so tightly clenched to her purpose, she might have said, Please. I beg of you.

'Wisdom, as I have proclaimed,' the Theomach announced. 'Lady, I am both pleased and gratified.'

The mounted woman leaned down from her saddle, trying to study Linden's face in the dim glow of the camp. 'You ask much, Linden

Avery,' she replied severely. 'If I judge wrongly – or if Krenwill's hearing has misled him – you may cause great woe.'

'And if I'm telling the truth,' Linden countered, 'you'll save lives.' She did not slow her strides to accommodate Yellinin's uncertainty.

After a moment, the outrider said slowly, feeling her way, 'It was the one whom you name Jeremiah – was it not? – who wielded theurgy against Basila and her comrades? If you are parted from him, he will be unable to ward you.'

Her tone added, And in your absence, he will be free to wreak any harm which he may desire.

'Yes,' Linden answered at once, 'it was. But I don't need his protection.' If she had been a different woman, she could have challenged Berek's foes for him; perhaps routed them. 'He won't use his power again unless Covenant tells him to – and Covenant won't do that.' Covenant had accepted the path which the Theomach had laid out for him. Linden was confident that he would not risk Berek's enmity: not in the Theomach's presence. 'I can't promise that your Warhaft will like their answers. But they won't fight him.'

'Assuredly I will not,' the Theomach offered lightly. 'And I will watch over your companions.'

'Linden.' Covenant's voice was harsh with warnings or threats. 'You know what can go wrong here.'

'Sure,' she replied over her shoulder. Disturbances in the integrity of Time, lethal discontinuities. And she had been warned that Berek held enough Earthpower to erase Covenant and Jeremiah— 'But *you* know what we have to gain. You'll be all right without me for a while.'

Abruptly Yellinin dismounted. Leaving her horse, she came to Linden. In spite of her obscured features, her sword and cuirass and her warrior's bearing, she radiated concern rather than suspicion as she grasped Linden's arm and pulled her away from her companions.

Softly, tensely, Yellinin said, 'Linden Avery, if you choose to part from your comrades, I must inform you that Warhaft Inbull is not known for gentleness. Lord Berek endeavours to restrain him, but he has suffered much in this war – lost much, endured much – and has become cruel. Upon occasion, he has refused Krenwill's aid because he desires to discover truth with pain.

'Is it truly your wish that your son should be delivered to the Warhaft?'

For the first time since she had become aware that she was needed, Linden faltered. Instinctively she looked at the pleading on Jeremiah's face. He, Covenant and the Theomach had stopped: they stood watching her; waiting for her. She could not read Covenant or her son; but the meaning of Covenant's scowl was obvious, and Jeremiah's open chagrin seemed as poignant as a cry.

—has become cruel.

He's full of Earthpower. If he so much as touches us, this whole ordeal will be wasted.

But the call of the wounded was too strong. She was a physician and could not refuse it.

Like Covenant and the Theomach, Jeremiah had resources which surpassed her ability to measure them.

Deliberately Linden turned back to Yellinin. 'My companions don't mean any harm.' She made no effort to conceal the pressure rising in her. 'They won't cause any trouble. I keep saying that. But they can protect themselves if they have to. Right now, people are *dying. Your* people.' She could feel them: they were as vivid to her as the ravages of the Sunbane. 'The sooner I get to work, the more of them I can help.'

The outrider remained caught in indecision for a moment longer. Then she shook it off. She was a fighter, uncomfortable with doubt and hesitation.

'Accept my mount, Linden Avery,' she said as if she were sure. Her hand released Linden's arm. 'If you are indeed able to feel the wounded and dying, you will have no difficulty discovering where they lie. Should any seek to thwart you, reply that you act by Yellinin's command. Epemin and I will escort your comrades to the Warhaft. If I have erred, I will bear his wrath, and Lord Berek's.'

'I don't believe it,' Covenant growled under his breath. 'Here she is, completely lost, with no idea what's at stake – and total strangers still do what she wants.'

'That's my mom,' Jeremiah sighed glumly. He sounded like a boy who had resigned himself to an unjust punishment.

But Linden ignored them now. As soon as Yellinin let her go, she strode to the woman's mount; grabbed at the reins. When she had found the stirrup, she heaved herself into the saddle.

'Thank you,' she said to the outrider. 'You're not going to regret this.' Then she called, 'Jeremiah! I'm counting on you!' She did not trust Covenant. 'Don't make these people sorry that they helped me.'

No one responded – and she did not wait. Digging her heels inexpertly into the horse's sides, she headed for the top of the rise as swiftly as her shambling mount could carry her.

God, she loathed war.

Chapter Eight:

The Stuff of Legends

Her mount was no Ranyhyn, and the beast was frail. It stumbled under her whenever a hoof skidded on the glazed ice. She could feel its heart strain against its gaunt ribs. But as soon as she was thirty or forty paces beyond her companions, Linden began to draw Earthpower from the Staff, using its vitality to nurture her horse as well as to warm her numb skin, her cold-stiff limbs. Surely she would not endanger Covenant and Jeremiah now, when her mount increased the distance between them with every stride?

Gradually the horse grew stronger. Its gait increased towards a gallop as she fed it with the substance of life.

Then she crossed the crest of the rise, and Berek's camp appeared like a tapestry woven of fires and tents and wagons; picket-lines and latrines; gritted pain, exhaustion and graves.

The encampment seemed huge, although she knew that it was not. The surrounding dark dwarfed it. Nevertheless it was all that the night contained. The larger host of Berek's foes lay beyond the reach of her senses. Even the stars were lessened by the human multitude of the camp's fires.

As she crossed the ridge, she was already near enough to see individual figures; dim tottering shapes that moved among the tents and campfires. Most of the tents were small, hardly big enough for two or three warriors to share their meagre warmth. But a few were larger: mess-tents, perhaps, or command posts. One of these occupied the centre of the encampment. Linden guessed that it was Berek's. However, three of the tents were the size of pavilions, and their burden of suffering drew her towards them immediately. Enclosed by thick clusters of wagons, they had been erected along the northern edge of the encampment, as far as possible from any attack; and they called out to every dimension of her health-sense, beseeching her for succour. There the most grievously wounded of Berek's army carried on their faint and fading struggle for life.

Linden was an unskilled horsewoman, but she knew enough to turn her mount's head so that the beast directed its lengthening strides towards the pavilions. At the same time, she urged more power from the Staff to protect the horse from slipping on the treacherous slope. In that way, she gathered her own strength as well as her mount's, so that she would be able to bear what lay ahead of her.

Her haste attracted attention at several points along the edge of the camp. And as she approached the light, her open cloak, red shirt and stained jeans marked her as a stranger; a likely threat. Shouts rose against her. At least half a dozen warriors ran for their horses, plainly intending to intercept her.

In response, she summoned fire like a shout from the end of the Staff and kicked awkwardly at her mount's sides, trying to compel more speed.

Her display made the men and women racing for their mounts hesitate. More shouts scattered through the camp, dragging warriors urgently away from their chores and cookfires. Doubtless Berek's forces were acquainted with theurgy. The King whom they had opposed had been counselled by a Raver. They had felt black malevolence from the east, and knew their Lord's unforeseen might. A few of them had witnessed the salvific rampage of the Fire-Lions. Nonetheless it was likely that none of them had ever seen Earthpower in thetic fire. And apparently most of them had not yet felt the first stirrings of health-sense. They could not look at Linden's emblazoned rush and recognise that she wielded the same Law which had brought the Fire-Lions to Berek's aid.

Commanders yelled orders. A few warriors flung themselves onto their mounts, followed by others – and by still others. As Linden reached level ground and sped towards the tents of the wounded, holding aloft her pennon of power, a thickening barricade of riders surged into formation across her path.

She could not fight them. Nor could she bear to be stopped. In her ears, the need of Berek's wounded and dying was as loud as a wail, and as compulsory as blood. Even the men and women who rode out to refuse her were rife with injuries.

Mustering fire, she called in a voice of flame, 'By *Yellinin's command!* I'm a *healer*! Let me pass!'

Again Berek's warriors hesitated. Some began to rein in their mounts: others veered aside. But an older veteran, hardened and glaring, yelled back, 'Yellinin's command does not suffice! Halt and answer!'

Linden swore to herself. If she could elude the riders, she suspected that her mount would be able to outdistance them. Its energy was the Staff's. But they were mere heartbeats away. And the prospect of delays and argument was intolerable.

Shouting, 'In Lord Berek's name!' she mentally stamped one heel of her Staff against the frozen ground. With Earthpower and Law, she sent a concussion like the tremor of an earthquake rolling under the hooves of the advancing horses.

Covenant and Jeremiah had withstood worse when she had closed the *caesure* of the Demondim. The Theomach might not protect them; but they had risked too much: they would not allow themselves to be banished now.

Instinctive animal terror cleared her passage. Some of the beasts stumbled, pitching their riders. Others shied; reared; wheeled away. Their panic forced the riders behind them to struggle for control.

Through the momentary turmoil, Linden's mount raced like Hyn, pounding the ice and dirt towards the tents of the wounded. Followed by shouts of rage and alarm, she ran for her destination.

She was now little more than a hundred paces from the edge of the encampment. When she dismounted, she would be within twenty or thirty steps of the nearest pavilion. But during her dash at the camp, Berek's commanders had readied a wall of swords and spears to resist her. Warriors stood clenched against their fear. *Damn* it: this was the cost of her haste. She had left behind anyone who might have spoken for her. Now she seemed to have no choice except to fight or fail.

But she had seen too much death and could not do otherwise than she had done.

She began to pull on her mount's reins, slowing the beast so that the warriors ahead of her would see that she did not mean to hurl herself onto their weapons. While riders swept towards her, she eased the horse to a canter; to a walk. Then she slipped down from the beast's back and left it.

A heartbeat later, horses clattered to a halt behind her. But she did not turn towards them. Striding directly at the wall of warriors, she let the Staff's fire die away. She wanted Berek's people to recognise that she had no wish to harm them. Then she said as calmly as she could, knowing that she was close enough to be heard, 'By Yellinin's command, and in Lord Berek's name, let me pass. Please. I would beg you, but I don't have time. Your friends are dying in those tents.'

Still the points of the spears and the edges of the swords confronted her. Berek's forces had grown accustomed to fear and death: they may not have been capable of heeding her.

'I'm a healer.' She walked straight at the barricade of warriors. 'I intend to help. Either cut me down' – she did not raise her voice – 'or let me pass.'

No one answered her. She heard no order given; felt no conscious decision reached. Yet something in her tone or her manner, her strangeness or her steady stride, must have inspired conviction. When she drew near enough to spit herself on the first of the spears, it lifted out of her path. Abruptly several men and women lowered their swords. More spears followed the example of the first. The warriors stared at her with fierce concentration: their eyes held every shade of apprehension and doubt. Nevertheless they parted so that she could walk between them.

For a moment, tears blurred her sight. 'Thank you,' she murmured unsteadily, 'thank you,' as she moved unhurt into the encampment.

Men and women formed an aisle for her, a gauntlet, all with their weapons held ready – and all motionless in spite of their uneasy tension. Here and there, firelight reflected in their eyes, or on the battered metal of their breastplates. Many of them wore hardened leather caps in lieu of helmets; leather vambraces and other protection. All were variously clad in blood and bandages. As individuals, they ached with weariness and old wounds, entrenched loss and desperation. Together they hurt Linden's senses like a festering abscess. Yet she caught only hints of hopelessness or despair. Berek's people were sustained by their deep belief in him. It kept them on their feet.

She loathed war and killing. At times, she did not know how to accept humankind's readiness for evil. But she was already starting to admire Berek, and she had not yet met him. His spirit preserved his people when every other resource failed. And he was the reason – she was sure of this – that they had refrained from slaying her. She had invoked his name. They strove to prove themselves worthy of him.

Roughly she rubbed away her tears. Without hesitation, she followed the aisle and her raw nerves towards the nearest pavilion.

As she approached the heavy canvas, torn and filthy from too much use, her perceptions of distress accumulated. The naked human suffering ahead of her was worse than any she had faced before.

She had spent years preparing for such crises. Nothing in that tent was more severe than the mangled cost of car wrecks or bad falls; the outcome of drunken brawls and domestic abuse; the vicious ruin of gunshots. Berek's people were not more severely damaged than Sahah had been, or others of the Ramen, or the Masters who had opposed the Demondim.

But there were so *many* of them– And they were being given such primitive care– During the last strides of her approach to the pavilion, she felt three of them die. More than a score of them lingered on the absolute edge of death, kept alive only by simple unbending steadfast-ness; by the strength of their desire not to fail their Lord. Before long, they would slip away, some stupefied by their wounds, others in pure agony. And this was only one tent: there were two more.

Never before had Linden faced bleeding need on this scale: not by several orders of magnitude. The grim, frantic hours that she and Julius Berenford had spent in surgery after Covenant's murder were paltry by comparison.

And her nerves were raw; too raw. She felt every severed limb and broken skull, every pierced abdomen and slashed joint, as if they had been incused on her own flesh. Nevertheless she did not falter. She *would* not. Confronted with such pain, she would allow nothing to prevent her from doing what she could.

Trust yourself.

As if she had forgotten her own mortality, she thrust the stiff fabric of the opening aside and strode into the tent.

She hardly noticed that no one entered behind her.

The tent was supported by four heavy poles, each more than twice her height. And the interior was illuminated by oil lamps, at least a score of them. Nevertheless she could scarcely descry the far wall. The whole place was full of smoke, a heavy brume so thick and pungent that her eyes watered instantly and she began to cough before she had taken two steps across the dirt floor.

God *damn* it, she might have shouted, are you trying to *suffocate* them? Almost at once, however, her senses came into focus, and she saw and smelled and felt that the rank fug arose from burning herbs. It was a febrifuge of some kind, intended to combat fever. In addition, it had a degree of virtue against infection. Beyond question, it hurt the lungs of the wounded. But most of them had grown accustomed to it, or were too weak to cough. And it kept some of them alive.

They lay on the iron ground in long rows, protected from the cold only by thin straw pallets padded with blankets. But the blankets had been fouled by months or seasons of blood and pus and sputum, urine and faeces: they were caked and crusted with disease. Still coughing, Linden discerned pneumonia and dysentery rampant around her, exacerbating the bitter throng of wounds and a host of other illnesses.

Then she understood that the true horror of this war was not that so many people were dying, but rather that so many still clung to life. Death would have been kinder– The men and women who served as Berek's physicians had wrought miracles against impossible odds.

There were three of them in the tent, two men and a woman: three to care for twenty or thirty times that many wounded and dying. As one of them came towards her, she saw that he wore a thick grey robe nearly as vile as the blankets. A length of rope cinched his waist, and from it hung several pouches of herbs – his only medicines – as well as a short heavy sword and a crude saw which he obviously, too obviously, used for amputations. He trembled with fatigue as he approached, a heavy burden of sleep deprivation. Rheum dulled his gaze, and the weak flat sound of his cough told Linden as clearly as blood work that he had contracted pneumonia.

Nevertheless he did his best to accost her. 'Begone,' he wheezed irritably. 'This is no place for you, stranger, madwoman. I will summon—'

Linden silenced him with a sharp gesture. Before he could protest, she drew flame blooming from her Staff.

She had spent ten years without percipience and Earthpower, restricted to the surface of life. During that time, she had lost much of her familiarity with the Land's gifts. But in recent days, she had made repeated use of the Staff. Unaware of what would be required of her, she had nonetheless trained her nerves and sharpened her perceptions for this crisis, this multitude of pain. To that extent, at least, she was ready.

Carefully she sent out sheets of yellow fire, immaculate as sunshine, and wrapped them like a cocoon around the physician.

She knew exactly what he needed: she felt it in her own blood and bone. Swift as instinct, she found his tiredness, his illness, his unremitting exposure to infection, and she swept them away.

She barely heard the other two physicians yell in alarm. From their perspective, their comrade must have appeared to blaze like an auto da fe. And she paid no heed to the answering shouts from outside the tent. When warriors burst past the tent-flaps behind her, she ignored them. Her concentration admitted no intrusion.

The physician's heart had time to beat twice or thrice while she worked. Then she released him from fire. The emotional and spiritual toll of his labours she could not heal, but she left him physically whole: staggering with surprise, and exalted by relief and wellness.

At once, Linden turned away and dropped to her knees beside the nearest of the wounded.

This warrior was a woman, and Linden knew that she was not yet dying. She might linger for several days, excruciated by fever and infection. The sword-cut which had split her breastplate and opened her ribs was not necessarily fatal. With cleanliness and rest, it might heal on its own. But her left foot had been amputated above the ankle, and there her real danger lay. Her shin suppurated with infection and anguish. Slivers of bone protruded from the mass of pus and maggots where one of the physicians had attempted to save her life.

She was far from being the most needy warrior here. She was simply the nearest. For that reason, Linden had chosen her.

The other physicians still called for help. Linden heard quick steps at her back; swords drawn. No one here could comprehend what she was doing. They saw only fire and were afraid. She needed to show them what her actions meant before a blade bit into her back.

Hurrying, she closed her eyes; refined her attention; swathed the wounded woman in Earthpower. With flame, she burned away infection and maggots, cleansed poisons, excised and sealed necrotic tissues, knit together shards of bone. And she caused no pain: the bright efficacy of the Staff was as soothing as Glimmermere's lacustrine roborant.

Near her, the physician yelled frantically, '*Halt!*' She felt him leap to intercept the stroke of a sword. '*Do not!*' His voice became a roar as he found his strength. 'Heaven and Earth, are you *blind*? She has *mended* me!'

There must have been whetted iron mere inches from her neck; but Linden allowed nothing to interrupt her as she assoiled the fallen woman's injuries.

When she was done, she quenched the Staff and raised her head.

The rumpled hood of her cloak touched the edge of a sword. 'What madness is this?' demanded one of the warriors behind her, a man. 'She has set flame to a woman who might have lived, and you wish her *spared*?'

'Unclose your eyes,' retorted the physician. 'Behold what she has done. It is not *harm*.

'By my life,' he added more softly, in wonder, 'I had forgotten that there was once a time when I was not ill.'

The healed woman tried to lift her head from the pallet. 'What—?' she asked weakly. 'What has become of my pain? Why am I not in pain?'

Daring Berek's people to cut at her now, Linden braced herself on the Staff and rose to her feet. She felt their astonishment; their reluctance to credit what they saw and heard. They had so little experience of the Land's true life– They could not imagine its implications.

However, the physician did not leave the warriors to reach their own conclusions. Suddenly resolute, he commanded, 'Begone!' as he had tried to command Linden. 'This lady' – he could hardly find words for his amazement – 'will do no hurt. Mayhap she will work great good, if she is not hindered. Depart, that I may beseech her aid.'

Flapping both arms, he gestured in dismissal until the men and women behind Linden complied. Then he turned to her while his fellow healers hastened among the rows towards him.

'My lady,' he began, flustered by healing and hope, 'I comprehend naught here. Such fire— It is beyond—'

'But' – he seemed to grasp himself roughly with both hands – 'I do not require comprehension, and must not delay. Will you grant us further flame? We are badly surpassed. The need is too great to be numbered. Our simples and implements redeem few. Most perish.' The rheum in his eyes had become tears. 'I will prostrate myself, if that will sway you—'

He began to sink to his knees.

Still Linden did not falter. The tent had become an emergency room, and she was a surgeon. Grabbing quickly at the man's arm, she said, 'Of course I'll help. That's why I'm here. But I need you to do triage for me.' When he frowned at the unfamiliar word, she explained, 'I should treat the worst cases first, but I don't know who they are. You'll have to tell me.' *Guide me.* The sheer scale of the suffering around her confused her perceptions. 'And get me some drinking water.'

She would need more than the Staff could provide to sustain her during the ordeal ahead.

The man's mouth formed the word 'cases' in silent confusion. Nevertheless he grasped her meaning. 'Then commence with the fifth in this row,' he replied, nodding to Linden's left. He seemed ready to obey her smallest word. 'Palla and Jevin will direct you further.' Plainly he meant his fellow physicians. 'I am Vertorn. I will command wine from the guards to refresh you.'

Good enough, Linden thought. She had to get to work. Pausing only to say, 'I'm Linden. Don't be afraid of anything you see,' she strode towards the pallet Vertorn had suggested.

When she saw how badly the man there had been slashed and pierced, she might have quailed, overwhelmed by the scale of her dilemma. He looked like he had been hung up like a dummy and used for weapons practice. His life was little more than a wisp of breath in the back of his throat. With her Staff, she had the capacity to fill the entire tent with vivifying flame. The iron-shod wood was constrained only by her own limitations. But she was too human to function in that way. She had to *see* what she strove to heal; needed to focus her attention on each individual wound and illness. In her hands, an undefined broadside of Earthpower might do more harm than good. She could only struggle to save one patient at a time, treat one need at a time, as she had always done.

And they were so many—

But during the single heartbeat when her courage might have broken, she felt a woman immediately behind her slip into death. After that, she did not hesitate. Unfurling the Staff's severe and kindly puissance like an oriflamme, she began her chosen task.

She had called herself a healer. Now she set about justifying her name.

She did not know how long she laboured; could not count the men and women whom she retrieved from the ruins of war. When smoke and strain blurred her vision, the woman, Palla, led her by the hand while the man, Jevin, called out the location of her next patient. Whenever Vertorn thrust a flagon into her grasp, she gulped down a few swallows of whatever it contained. Everything else was a nightmare succession of rent flesh, shattered bone, rampant infection and multiplied agony.

People were reduced to this by battle and pain: they became nothing more than the sum of their sufferings. And like them, she shrank. Long after she had passed the conscious borders of her endurance and had become mere scraps of awareness, fragments composed almost exclusively of health-sense and Earthpower – blinded by tears, deaf to sobbing and wails, nearly insensate – she continued from hurt to hurt and did not heed the cost. That she could not save them all, just one tent of three, meant nothing to her. Only the wound immediately in front of her held any significance: the mortifying infection; the instance of pleurisy, or pneumonia, or scabies, or inanition; the mute or whimpering protest of savaged flesh.

Dimly she felt in Palla's touch, heard in Jevin's voice, that their ailments were no less than Vertorn's had been. But she had nothing to spare for them. And she neglected to draw on the Staff for her own needs. She had grown unreal to herself; had become mere percipience and flame. A healer who collapsed from exhaustion could treat no one.

But she trusted the steady exertion of so much Earthpower to protect her from prostration.

Then, however, she finished tending a man whose abdomen had been savagely lacerated – and Jevin did not call her to a new location. Nor did Palla draw her along the rows.

Instead a voice that may have been Vertorn's addressed her.

'My lady?' he said tentatively. 'My lady Linden. You must desist. You must restore yourself. Lord Berek has come. He requires speech with you.'

When Linden did not respond, the physician reached through flame to slap her cheek lightly. 'My lady, hear me. It is Lord *Berek* who desires to speak with you.'

Linden drew a shuddering breath. Unsteadily she released the Staff's power; let it fall away. Then she found herself hanging between Palla and Jevin while they struggled to uphold her. Blinking at the smoke in her eyes, the blood, the lingering sight of wounds, she saw Vertorn offer a flagon to her lips.

'Drink,' he commanded, peremptory with trepidation. 'The wine is rank, but I have included herbs to nourish you. You must be restored. It is imperative.'

Dully she accepted a few swallows from the flagon. The wine had an acrid taste, raw and biting, but it gave a small measure of energy to her overstrained nerves and muscles.

Lord Berek—

There was something that Vertorn wanted her to understand.

Lord Berek has come.

She tried to say, Let him wait. This is more important. But she was not strong enough. And Vertorn's interruption forced her to recognise that she could not refuse him. She had only reduced the suffering in the tent; the argute throb of infection and fever; the predatory crouch of death. She would not be able to end it alone.

She needed help—

The thought that Berek wished to speak with her seemed inconsequential; unworthy of regard. But she had to speak to him.

Now she clasped the Staff hungrily, almost begging for its beneficence. Without its nourishment, she would hardly be able to walk. The plight of the wounded required more from her.

When she had imposed a degree of Earthpower on her depleted nerves, her worn heart, she murmured hoarsely, 'You'll have to lead me. I can't see very well.'

There was too much smoke in the air. And the outcome of sword-cuts and disease was more vivid to her than mere rows of rancid pallets or insignificant tent-poles.

Jevin and Palla continued to support her. While she moved – slowly, slowly, feeble as an old woman – she sent some of the Staff's sovereign healing, as much as she could muster, through herself into the physicians. Faintly she gave them a little Earthpower, a small portion of health. Like Vertorn, they were essential: they would have to care for the fallen when she was gone.

In spite of the smoke, she saw her task clearly. It was too much for her. Somehow she would have to win Berek's aid.

She must have been closer to the opening of the tent than she realised. When Vertorn stepped aside, bowing his deference, she beheld Berek Halfhand for the first time.

Involuntarily she stopped; stared. She had not expected to encounter a man who seemed more compelling, more crucial, than the injuries and deaths of his warriors.

There was Earthpower in him, that was obvious: as potent as Anele's inheritance, but closer to the surface, more readily accessible. However, his numinous energy was not what caused him to stand out from his escort of warriors as if he were somehow more real than they, more significant and substantial.

Nor did his vividness, his particular intensity, arise from his physical presence. He was little more than half a head taller than Linden: a stocky man, broad of shoulder and girth; prematurely bald, with deep eyes, a short-cropped beard the colour of old iron, and a nose that had been dented by a blow. His hands looked as heavy as truncheons, and they had seen hard use in spite of the loss of two of his fingers; the same two which had been amputated from Covenant. The slashed and battered condition of his cuirass and vambraces proclaimed that he did not remain aloof from battle. He was a powerful man, familiar with fighting for his life. Yet that also did not account for his obvious dominance, his air of unmistakable authority. Most of the men and women in his escort were muscular and injured, marked by an interminable series of fierce engagements.

No, it was his emotional aura that made him seem more distinct, more *necessary*, than the people with him. Covenant had said, *He's charismatic as all hell*, but Linden saw more. With her full senses, she discerned that he was haunted by death; that loss and despair had been carved into the bedrock of his nature. And the sheer depth of his bereavements had taught him a desperate compassion. She loathed war, but her abhorrence lacked the intimacy of his, the hideously prolonged exposure to that which rent his heart. Now he grieved for his foes as much as for his own forces. When he slew them, he did so as if he were weeping; as if his strokes were sobs. He fought – and fought endlessly, season after season, battle upon battle – only because the darkness which drove his enemies left him no choice. And because he had given his oath to the Land.

He would have questions for her. He would demand answers. And Linden could not imagine arguing with such a man, or attempting to persuade him. When Vertorn announced with a bow, 'My lord Berek, here is my lady Linden,' she did not respond. Nothing that she could say would raise her to the stature of the man who had created the first Staff of Law and founded the Council of Lords.

Yet Berek bowed to her as though her muteness were eloquence, and his gratitude enfolded her like an embrace. 'My lady,' he said in a voice made gruff by incessant shouting, 'your coming is a great benison, a boon beyond our conception. Already you have wrought miracles among us. Yet even a sightless man may behold your weariness. Will you not rest? With your consent, I will provide food and safety, and such small comforts as we possess, and will count myself glad to do so.'

Without warning, tears which were not caused by smoke and fatigue filled Linden's eyes. She had not expected gentle courtesy from a man fighting for survival. Nevertheless she stiffened slightly; drew back as if she had taken offence. *Surely*, she would have said if she had not forgotten her voice, *surely your wounded are more important? There are two more tents.*

Berek studied her, apparently gauging her silence. Then he offered in the same tone, 'If you will not rest, name any aid that you require. If it exists, and if it is possible for us, it will be granted to you.'

He seemed to understand that she could not turn away from his injured, his dying. In her place, he would have felt as she did.

Roughly Linden squeezed the tears from her eyes. Like wild magic, her voice was hidden from her; but she searched until she found it.

'Lord Berek,' she said in a thin croak. 'My lord.' That was as close as she could come to matching his courtesy. 'You've changed. You see different things now. New things.'

He nodded, frowning. 'It is strange to me, glorious but unclear.' Her question may have perplexed or disturbed him: he had reason to wonder how she knew such things. Yet he answered without hesitation. 'I cannot identify the significance of that which I now behold.'

You will, Linden would have told him. Just give it time. But too many people were dying. She could not afford to waste words. Instead she asked, 'Have you seen any mud – or fine sand – that sparkles? Gleams? Like it has bits of gold in it? Or flecks of sunlight?'

Berek's frown deepened. 'I have, my lady.' Plainly he wanted to inquire, What do you know of this? How is it that you comprehend my transformation? But he did not. 'It lies along the flow of water in streams and rivers. Sadly, I have no lore to name it.'

Her heart lifted a little. 'Is there any of it nearby?'

'There is, my lady.' Again he did not question her. 'We endeavour to place our encampments near water, as armies must. A creek lies a stone's throw distant. When we broke the ice to draw water, I glimpsed a sand such as you describe.'

To herself, Linden breathed, Thank God. 'It's called hurtloam.' Unexpected hope filled her with trembling. 'It's full of the same power that's changing you, the same power that you saw in the Fire-Lions. It heals.'

Hearing herself, she wanted to wince. *Heals* was too small a word for the mystery of hurtloam. But she continued in spite of her inadequacy. 'We need it. As much as you can find. Bring it here. And carry it in stone.' Stone would preserve its efficacy. 'I'll show your people how to use it.'

Surely now he would question her, and expect to be answered? Surely he would not comply merely because she had spoken?

But Berek turned at once to his escort. 'Hand Damelon.'

A young man stepped forward promptly. Linden would have guessed that he was no older than Liand, although he had seen as much hard combat as anyone around him. He saluted by tapping his right fist twice against his twisted and mended cuirass, then asked, 'My lord?'

Linden was too tired and numb to feel surprise. Damelon– Through the grime and blood of battle, the young man's resemblance to his father was unmistakable, although he was somewhat taller and not as broad. Also he lacked Berek's damaged nose as well as Berek's emanation of Earthpower.

She was looking at the future High Lord Damelon Giantfriend, the man who would one day discover the Blood of the Earth.

Humbled by the presence of legends, she hardly heard Berek say, 'Hand, you have gathered the names of those who report alterations to their sight and senses.'

'I have, my lord.' Presumably a *Hand* was an aide of some kind. 'Some two score remain able to wield their weapons.'

In response, Berek ordered, 'Inform each Haft and Warhaft,' although there was no command in his voice. He had no reason to doubt that he would be obeyed. 'All who are able to discern the gleaming in the sand will hasten to the creek, bearing any stone which may be used to convey the sand hither. They will search diligently for as much as may be found. Others will bear torches to light the search.'

Damelon nodded. 'At once, my lord.' With a second salute, the young man strode quickly out of the tent.

Berek returned his deep gaze to Linden. 'Surely there is more, my lady?' His voice was rough with compassion. 'You are one, and those who suffer, many. For their sake, will you not name further aid?'

Linden took a step backwards. She had felt another warrior perish, a man no more than half a dozen paces away. Everywhere in the tent, she heard wounds cry out for succour.

'Just let me work, my lord.' She doubted that Covenant, Jeremiah or the Theomach would – or could – help her. And Covenant and Jeremiah would not be able to abide Berek's presence. Assuming that they had reached the camp unhindered— 'I can't think of anything else.' She did not feel equal to the challenge of explaining *aliantha*. 'We need to talk. I know that. But first—' She gestured weakly around the wide tent.

'Yet you are weary,' Berek countered, 'nearly falling. Is there naught that you require for yourself?'

Linden paused for a moment. Almost timidly, she murmured, 'I left three companions behind. I hope that they're safe.' Then she turned her back on Berek Halfhand.

While she reached out mentally for the strength of the Staff, she whispered to Palla, 'Guide me, please. I need to rest my eyes.' She did not know another way to contain her weeping.

If Berek's people found enough hurtloam, she could allow herself—

As Palla led her away, Berek commanded gently, 'Healer Vertorn, you will interrupt the lady Linden after each healing. You will not permit her to continue until she has swallowed a little of your wine and eaten a mouthful of bread.'

'My lord, it will be done,' replied the physician. Linden felt him hurrying after her.

But she soon forgot such details. Within moments, she had immersed herself once more in the hurts of the wounded and the fire of the Staff.

This time, however, she did not neglect to draw on Earthpower for support. And she did not resist Vertorn's efforts to minister to her. The prospect of hurtloam had that effect on her: she no longer felt driven to care for every need except her own.

At some point during her endless progress back and forth around the tent, she became peripherally aware that Berek had not departed. He seemed to be standing guard, not over her, but for her; ready to give her his assistance if she required it. But she did not let his presence distract her from the next sword-cut and spear-thrust, the next trauma, the next putrefying infection. She swallowed wine and chewed bread as Palla guided her from patient to patient, and did not relax her flames.

By degrees, she grew stronger, in spite of her exertions. Vertorn's herbed wine was a mild restorative. Bits of bread gave her a little nourishment. And the Staff sustained her. It could not redeem her mortality, but it preserved her concentration so that she was able to work effectively.

Then the first of the hurtloam arrived, carried in stone urns or on brittle pieces of slate. Linden dipped her finger into the glittering sand to show Vertorn, Palla and Jevin how little was required for each wound, and how wondrously it took effect; and as she did so, she granted healing to herself. Spangles of revitalisation lit the blood in her veins, coursing through her heart until her pulse lost its febrile weakness and the trembling in her muscles receded. Gradually the illimitable gift of the Land restored her to herself.

She was dimly amazed by the abundance of the vein of hurtloam which Berek had discovered. A score of his people made several trips each to convey the sand. Perhaps this was simply another instance of the Land's largesse, undiminished because it had not been used until now. Or perhaps, like the Fire-Lions, it expressed the Land's response to Berek's oath.

When Linden could finally blink the smoke and tears from her eyes – when she was able to see as well as feel the excitement, the near ecstasy, of the three physicians – she sent Vertorn, Jevin and the irregular stream of warriors bearing hurtloam to the other tents. Those warriors, too, had been healed as they gathered the sand, and they carried their burdens with eager alacrity.

She did not think about ripples or time. She thought about lives that would have been lost, men and women who still needed care; and she was not afraid.

For a while, she and Palla laboured over the pallets alone, moving as efficiently as they could through the array of injuries and infections. But soon she realised that the worst was over. Dozens of warriors remained stricken, but none were near death. Some would cling to life for another day or two, some considerably longer. And Berek understood hurtloam now: he would search for it everywhere. In addition, Linden saw in Palla that touching the ineffable sand had awakened the physician's latent health-sense. She, and Vertorn and Jevin, and perhaps every warrior who had been healed by it, would now be able to recognise hurtloam for themselves.

If Linden rested now, she would not have so many – too many – lives on her conscience.

To spare herself, she began a more partial form of treatment, focusing on infections, pneumonia and other illnesses rather than wounds. These required her keenest percipience, but they needed subtler care; demanded less raw power.

In her concentration, she did not immediately notice the growing mutter of voices outside the tent; the occasional shouts. But then she heard Covenant rasp distinctly, 'Hellfire! Get your hands off me, you overgrown oaf!'

'Covenant!' protested Jeremiah. 'We can't— Berek—!'

Other voices protested as well. 'Warhaft!' Yellinin shouted, 'Lord Berek commanded courtesy!' And Basila added, 'Are you deaf? The tale of her healing is everywhere!'

But Krenwill, who had vouched for Linden's truthfulness, countered, 'You do not *see* them, Basila. *I* did not until we gained the light of the encampment. They are sealed against discernment. Unnaturally sealed. They may conceal vast powers. *Fatal* powers, Yellinin. If they mean harm to Lord Berek—'

'Warhaft Inbull!' roared a man who sounded like Damelon. 'You will *desist*! Lord Berek has commanded *courtesy*.'

'I will not,' a guttural voice retorted. 'Let Lord Berek chastise me if he must. I will not hazard his life on the faith of strangers merely because they journey with a woman who *heals*.'

Oh, shit. Forgetting the wounded, Linden dropped her fire and ran.

Ahead of her, the tent-flaps burst open. Both Jeremiah and Covenant were flung inwards by a huge man with rage on his face and blood on his knuckles.

An instant later, Damelon sprang in front of the Warhaft, attempting to restrain Inbull by main strength. But the big man swatted Damelon aside as though the Hand were a minor annoyance.

Linden saw him clearly, in spite of the smoke; *saw* him as if he were surrounded by torches. He looked as solid as oak, with massively gnarled limbs and a mouth full of broken teeth. The heavy slash of a sword had cut deeply into the left side of his face and head, smashing bone and cutting away flesh; chopping out a crease which had collapsed his features. The only expression left to him was a grimace as suggestive of death as a rictus.

Between one heartbeat and the next, running frantically, Linden understood that he was a traitor. His brutality was the self-loathing of a man who had turned his back on a cause in which he had once believed. She did not know how or why his loyalties had changed. Nonetheless his betrayal was as palpable as a chancre.

He had brought Covenant and Jeremiah here violently because he hoped to provoke an attack.

At the same time, almost simultaneously, she saw Jeremiah stumble to his hands and knees near Berek's feet. And she saw that he had been hit. His left eye had been struck as if with a club. Some of the bones there may have been cracked. His eye had already swollen shut, silencing the cypher of his tic.

His blood still tainted the Warhaft's knuckles. That was how Inbull had prevented Jeremiah from defending himself and Covenant. The Warhaft had taken her son by surprise, *her son*, striking him down before he recognised his peril.

And at the same time again, as though the images were superimposed, Linden saw Covenant struggling to avoid a collision with Berek. Covenant too had been struck: he staggered as if his ribs had been broken. But his efforts to recover his balance were hindered by the fact that he kept his right hand, his halfhand, thrust deep in the pocket of his jeans.

Frowning darkly at the clamour, Berek turned in time to reach out with one strong hand. While Linden strove to shout a warning and could not – the crisis came upon her too swiftly – Berek caught Covenant by the shoulder and steadied him.

Then Berek snatched back his hand as though he had been scalded. Involuntarily he gasped—

—and Covenant did not disappear.

Nor did Jeremiah. He remained on his hands and knees, staring with his good eye at Covenant and Berek in dismay.

Cursing, Covenant jerked away from Berek; into Inbull's reach.

The Warhaft cocked his fist as if he had been justified by Berek's reaction – and still Linden could not summon a shout. Although she ran desperately, she hardly seemed to move.

In a tone like the bite of a sword, Berek snapped, 'If you strike again, Warhaft, I will have your head.'

Without warning, Linden was wrenched to a halt, caught in the grasp of the Theomach. Somehow he had passed through the throng of warriors as though they did not exist; or he did not. Now he stood in front of her. Catching her arms in a grip as compulsory as manacles, he absorbed the force of her haste effortlessly.

Her heart may have had time to beat once. She heard both Covenant's voice and Berek's, Covenant swearing viciously, Berek demanding explanations. But then everything blurred as if the Theomach had lifted her partway into a different reality, shifted her slightly out of sequence with her surroundings; and all sound was cut off. She seemed to stand with the Insequent in a hiatus between moments, a place where causality and result had not yet moved on to their next incarnation.

Within their private silence, the Theomach urged her softly, 'Say nothing, lady. Do not speak here. There are intentions at work which you do not yet comprehend, and upon which the outcome of this time in large measure depends.'

She fought him briefly. When she realised that she could not break free, however, she ceased struggling. Only her Staff and Covenant's ring would aid her here; and they might prove disastrous.

Able to raise her voice at last, she shouted into the Theomach's face, '*You* did this! This is *your* path. Jeremiah can't defend himself. There's nothing Covenant can do. You haven't left them any *choice*!'

He shrugged. 'That is sooth.' His wrapped face made him appear as cryptic and careless as an oracle. 'I regret that I did not foresee the Warhaft's falseness and brutality. I desire only to aid Lord Berek. Therefore I employ your wisdom – aye, and your valour also – to appease his mistrust towards strangers. Thus I am indeed culpable for the harm which has befallen your comrades.'

Linden spat an oath. At that moment – between those moments – the Theomach's intentions meant nothing to her. Ignoring his near-apology, she demanded, 'But why didn't Covenant vanish?' And Jeremiah? 'He said that Berek's Earthpower is too strong—'

The Insequent studied her through his cerements. 'The force within Lord Berek has not yet fully awakened.' As he spoke, he eased his hard clasp on her arms. 'And he whom you name Covenant is more hardy than he has encouraged you to believe.'

Then he urged again, 'Still I must insist, lady. I must caution you. Say nothing in the presence of others. When Lord Berek speaks with you and your companions alone, as he must, be chary in your replies. If you are at any time uncertain of what may be said, permit me to answer in your stead. By my true name, which is known to you, I assure you that my first purpose is to aid Lord Berek – and to preserve the Arch of Time.'

He did not wait for her to find a response. When he released her, her surroundings – the tent and the smoke, the pallets of the wounded, the conflicted outrage facing Berek – sprang back into clarity; and she heard Covenant snarl, '—fire, Berek, this is intolerable. We don't *deserve* it.'

'You do not.' Berek's voice held its cutting edge. 'Warhaft Inbull has harmed you, and will answer for his deeds. I demand only the name of the power which has burned my hand.'

Freed from the Theomach's theurgy, Linden would have rushed to Jeremiah's side. She might have forgotten that he had forbidden her to touch him. But the Insequent arrived ahead of her. Without apparent transition or movement, he stood between Berek and Linden's companions. Yet Berek was not startled. None of the observers reacted to the Theomach's suddenness. He had cast a glamour on their senses – or on Linden's.

'My lord Berek,' he said smoothly, 'permit me to intercede. I am the Theomach. The fault of this contention is mine. This man and this boy are companions of the lady. She names them Covenant and Jeremiah, her son, as she names herself Linden. They have come by my guidance. I drew them hither because I deemed her aid a treasure beyond estimation, and because I desire to aid you also. Surely her companions may be forgiven much, despite their unruly puissance, for the sake of what she has wrought.'

At last, Linden was able to move normally. With a few quick strides, she skidded to her knees beside Jeremiah; almost within reach of his battered head. 'Jeremiah, honey,' she panted, 'are you all right? How badly did he hurt you?'

Her furious desire to lash out at Inbull, she suppressed. The Theomach had warned her. And she judged Berek to be a man who would not let the Warhaft's mendacity pass.

Inbull may have hurt Berek's own son as well.

Reflexively Linden stretched out her hand to Jeremiah.

'Don't, Mom,' he gasped. His face was full of alarm. 'Don't touch me. Don't heal me. Or Covenant. We'll be all right. The Staff—' Blood spread down his cheek, catching in his nascent stubble until the left side of his face seemed webbed with pain; snared in deceit and cruelty. 'Even hurtloam will erase us. You don't understand how *hard* this is.'

Oh, Jeremiah. Linden stopped herself. Her upper arms throbbed where the Theomach had gripped her. Swallowing a rush of grief, she asked, 'Can you heal yourself? That looks pretty bad. He must have cracked some of the bones.'

She could not determine how gravely he had been injured. He remained closed to her; unnaturally impenetrable, as Krenwill had claimed.

'Covenant will take care of it.' Jeremiah pulled himself up from his hands, kneeling beyond her reach. His attention shifted back to Covenant and Berek; dismissed Linden.

Berek continued to confront the Theomach. Doubt rasped in his voice as he asked, 'What aid do you offer, stranger?'

The Insequent tapped his bound chest with his fist twice, imitating Damelon's earlier salute. 'My lord, if it is your will, I will teach you the meaning of your new strengths.'

Berek raised his eyebrows. 'And whence comes this un-looked-for wish to aid me?'

'That, my lord,' the Theomach replied, unruffled, 'I may not bespeak openly. The lore which I offer is for you alone.'

Berek returned an unconvinced snort. But he did not press the Theomach. Instead he looked at Linden. His eyes seemed to probe her soul as he said, 'My lady Linden, you have performed such service here that no honour or guerdon can suffice to repay it. Yet the task entrusted to me exceeds these wounded. It requires also the defeat of the Queen's foes. Ultimately it demands the nurturance of the Land. Therefore I must remain wary while my heart swells with thankfulness.

'Will you claim my sufferance on behalf of your companions?'

Abruptly wary herself, and abashed in Berek's presence, Linden rose to her feet. Hugging the Staff to her chest, she met his gaze, although his penetration daunted her.

'Jeremiah is my son,' she began awkwardly. 'Covenant is—'

For a moment, she faltered. She did not need the Theomach's warnings to convince her that any reply might prove dangerous. Like Joan, if in her own way, she bore the burden of too much time. The wrong word might ripple outward for millennia.

But Covenant, Jeremiah, the Theomach and Berek Halfhand were all studying her. With an effort, she forced herself to continue. 'Where I come from,' she said carefully, 'Covenant is a great hero. There are things about both of them that I don't understand. But they're with me, and I need them.'

Then she squared her shoulders. 'I made the decision to come here. If it was a mistake, it's my doing, not theirs.' Unsteadily she finished, 'We'll leave as soon as we can.'

Berek scrutinised her for a moment longer. Then he nodded decisively. 'My lady, we will speak with less constraint in my tent, you and your companions' – he glanced at the shrouded figure of the Insequent – 'not excluding the Theomach.

'Hand Damelon?'

Berek's son stepped forward. 'My lord?' He was flushed with the effects of Inbull's blow; but Linden saw that he had not been seriously hurt. Not like Jeremiah— The breastplate of his cuirass had absorbed much of the impact.

'Has Warhaft Inbull dared to harm one of my Hands?' asked Berek. His self-command did not waver. Nonetheless Linden heard the throb of cold fury in the background of his voice.

'He has dared, my lord,' Damelon replied stiffly, 'but he has not succeeded. His affront does not merit your concern.'

Berek flashed his son a quick glance of concern and approbation. However, his tone did not relent. 'I command here. The affront is mine to gauge, and to repay.' Then he told Damelon, 'While I do so, escort the lady Linden and her companions to my tent. See that they are provided with warmth and viands, and with water for the cleansing of wounds. If their hurts require any healing that we may supply, command it in my name. I will attend upon them shortly.'

Hand Damelon saluted again. 'At once, my lord.' Like his father, he kept his anger to himself.

Turning to Linden, he gestured towards the opening behind Inbull. 'My lady, will you accompany me?'

'We will, Hand,' the Theomach answered for her. His manner suggested a smile of satisfaction. 'Accepting your courtesy, we hope to honour you in return.'

Linden let the Insequent take charge of the situation. He understood its implications better than she did. But she did not allow him to hurry her. Stooping to Jeremiah, she asked, 'Can you stand, honey? Are you able to walk?'

'Hell, Linden,' Covenant growled under his breath. 'Of course he can. This is important.'

'He's right, Mom.' Jeremiah did not look at her. 'It already hurts less.' With a teenager's graceless ease, he surged to his feet. 'I'll be fine.'

Linden nodded, too baffled to question him further. According to Covenant, Berek's touch would banish both of them. Yet they remained. She felt that she had been given hints or portents, glimpses of revelation, which she could not interpret. What did Covenant dread, if Berek's inchoate strength posed no threat? Why had she been forbidden to hug or care for her son?

Wearily she trailed behind Jeremiah as he followed Covenant, the Theomach, and Damelon out of the tent; away from needs that she could comprehend towards an unfathomable encounter with the dangers of Time.

While she and her companions passed between Berek and Inbull, the Warhaft glared hatred at them. If he feared Berek's wrath, he did not show it. Either he was too stupid to recognise his own peril, or he knew Berek better than she did.

As she had earlier, Linden walked along aisles of warriors who had gathered to catch sight of the strangers. They all had their own wounds, their own ailments; their own yearning for restoration. But they kept their wonder and pain to themselves while she and her companions were led and warded by Damelon.

Berek's tent was a frayed and soiled stretch of canvas supported by a single central pole. When Damelon ushered his charges inward, Linden found herself in a space large enough to hold twenty or thirty warriors standing.

In every respect, Berek's quarters were as rudimentary as the tents of the wounded. His pallet and blankets resembled the bedding of the fallen. Apart from a low table on which rested an old longsword in a plain scabbard and a wooden chest that – she could only guess – might hold maps, the tent had no other furnishings. Two small oil lamps hanging from the tent-pole cast a dim yellow illumination that seemed to shed no light, reveal nothing: the whole space was full of uncertainty like implied shadows. And scraps of ice still glazed the dirt floor. Her breath plumed as she looked around. She did not know how long she had laboured at healing; but midnight had surely passed, and winter had sunk its teeth into every vulnerable instance of warmth.

After ushering Berek's guests into the tent, Damelon ducked past the flaps to call for braziers, honeyed wine, cured meat, dried fruit. When he returned, he said, 'My lady, I crave your pardon. Our rude comforts are no true measure of our gratitude. The day will come when we stand again within the walls of Doriendor Corishev. Mayhap then you will permit us to celebrate your benisons in a more seemly manner.'

He may have been taught to speak so, with confidence and conviction, by his father's knowledge of despair.

Linden sighed. 'Don't worry about it, please.' Barred from using the Staff, she had no defence against the cold except her cloak. And she was so tired– Already she had begun to shiver again. 'We can only imagine what you've suffered. If you can give us heat and food, we'll be all right.'

'"All right",' Covenant muttered sourly. 'Sure. Why not?'

The Theomach turned to him as if in warning; but Damelon ignored both of them. Instead he studied Linden like a man who wanted to imprint her on his thoughts. 'You are gracious, my lady. I will not question you. That is my lord Berek's task. But warmth and viands you will have.' More softly, he said, 'Soon you will be able to rest.'

Perhaps his own percipience had begun to awaken.

Moments later, the tent-flaps were pushed aside, and a pair of warriors entered, bearing a blackened metal brazier between them. It was full of coals and fire, so hot that it had to be carried on the shafts of spears. More warriors followed until the tent held four flaming pans. Then Berek's people brought ironwood stands to support the braziers. By the time the men and women left, heat began to bless the air.

Then other warriors brought hard clay urns of warmed wine, its acidulous aroma softened with honey. A tray laden with meat and fruit arrived. Linden, Covenant and Jeremiah were given flagons: wine was poured for them. But the Theomach refused with a bow. Nor did he touch the food. Apparently he lived on some form of nourishment entirely his own.

For a long moment, Linden held the Staff in the crook of her arm and simply cupped her flagon with both hands, savouring its heat and its sweet scent. Then she sipped gently. She had felt frozen for so long, in spite of her own efforts and Covenant's to fend off the cold. If he and Jeremiah had not been somehow more than human, they would have suffered from frostbite.

Questions swirled around her, but she was too tired to sift them into any kind of order. What did the Theomach want with Berek? Why had Covenant lied about his vulnerability to Berek? How had Berek failed to discern Inbull's betrayal? And how could she and her companions hope to reach *Melenkurion* Skyweir? She had seen for herself that Berek would be able to offer them nothing except starving horses, tattered blankets and a little food.

How much power did Jeremiah have? And how in God's name could Linden try to learn the truth – *any* truth – when she had to guard against the possibility that some action or inaction of hers might threaten the integrity of the Arch?

Ripples– As far as she knew, she had not altered the essential nature of Berek's struggle, or the outcome of his war. Not yet. Otherwise the Theomach would have intervened. But even her trivial knowledge of the Land's history could be fatal. With a word, she might affect Berek's actions, or Damelon's, altering the flow of cause and effect for generations.

The Theomach was right: she had to let him speak for her as much as she could – and to pray that Covenant would do the same in spite of his resentment.

She was not conscious of hunger; but she forced herself to chew a little tough meat and dried fruit, washing them down with honey and acid. She had to be able to think clearly, and could not imagine doing so.

Lost in questions, she ignored Damelon's departure. But then he returned, bearing a bowl of hot water and some relatively clean scraps of cloth. These he offered to Linden, suggesting that she tend to Jeremiah's injury.

'I can't,' she muttered before she could catch herself. 'He doesn't want me to touch him.'

The Hand gave her a perplexed frown. While he hesitated, however, the Theomach stepped forward. 'Nonetheless, my lord Damelon,' he said smoothly, 'the cleansing of her son's wound will comfort the lady.' Turning to Jeremiah, he inquired, 'Will you permit me?'

'I don't need—' Jeremiah began, but a fierce glare from Covenant stopped him. 'You're right,' he told the Theomach with a shrug. 'It'll make Mom feel better.'

Covenant kept his right hand grimly in his pocket.

Saluting as he had to Berek, the Theomach accepted the bowl and rags from Damelon's mystified hands. His manner suggested pity as he moistened a cloth, then reached out carefully to stroke drying blood away from Jeremiah's cheek and eye.

That task should have been Linden's. For a moment, her grief became a kind of rage, and she trembled with the force of her desire to extract real answers from her companions. But she contained herself. There was too much at stake for anger. Her emotions would exact too much from those who needed her.

For a moment, the Theomach continued to wash Jeremiah's wound assiduously. Jeremiah suffered the Insequent's ministrations with glum resignation. And Covenant took long draughts of the harsh wine with an air of outrage, as if he were swallowing insults. Then Linden felt Berek approaching: his aura of Earthpower, compassion and grimness preceded him like a standard-bearer.

Damelon seemed to become aware of his father's nearness almost as soon as Linden did. Bowing to her, the Hand murmured, 'My lady,' and left the tent.

When Berek entered, he came like a man wreathed in storms. Indignant lightnings flickered in the depths of his eyes, and his expression was a thunderhead. Linden might have flinched if she had believed, even for an instant, that his ire was directed at her; or at Jeremiah and Covenant. But she grasped instinctively that he would not have been so unguarded if any of his guests had angered him.

'What have you done about Inbull, my lord?' she asked without thinking. 'He's betraying you. You must know that?'

The Theomach stiffened, but did not speak. Instead he dabbed at Jeremiah's eye as if he had heard nothing to alarm him.

Berek took a moment to compose himself. He poured wine into a flagon, drank a bit of it, grimaced ruefully. When he faced Linden's question, he had set aside his personal storm.

'The Warhaft has betrayed us. He betrays us still. Therefore he is of use.

'It is well that you did not accuse him in his presence. He believes himself unsuspected. Rather I have encouraged him to consider that he is secretly valued for his harshness. This night, I have strengthened his misapprehension.' The memory brought back Berek's anger and disgust, although he did not unleash them. 'He has contrived a means to communicate with the commander of our foes. Warmark Vettalor is a man with whom I am well familiar. We served together before my Queen broke with her King. I know his method of thought. Through Inbull, I am able to supply the Warmark with lies' – Berek snarled the words – 'which he will credit. While the Warhaft's falseness remains unexposed, I hold an advantage which Vettalor does not suspect.

'I loathe such deceit,' the first Halfhand admitted bitterly. 'But my forces do not suffice to defeat Vettalor's. And I have no source of supply apart from the battlegrounds where I prevail, and the food which I scavenge from needy villages, while Vettalor retreats ever nearer to the wealth of Doriendor Corishev. It would be false service to my Queen, and to my warriors, and to my oath, if I declined the benefits of Inbull's treachery.'

Which explained his ire and disgust, Linden mused. It explained why despair clung to him in spite of his salvation by the Fire-Lions and his subsequent victories. By his severe standards, he bartered away his self-respect to purchase victory.

The Old Lords were all about despair. It gave them some of their greatest victories. To that extent, at least, Covenant had told her the truth. *It's what saved Berek.*

With an effort, Linden said quietly, 'I see the problem.' She wanted to cry out, *He hit my son!* But larger considerations – Berek's as well as her own – restrained her.

Whatever the Theomach's motives might be, he had given her good advice.

Nevertheless she pushed Berek further. 'What did you tell Inbull about us?' She wanted some indication, however oblique, of where she and her companions stood with the future High Lord.

Drinking again, Berek replied, 'Naught. His uncertainty concerning you will serve me well. I have merely' – his voice carried a sting of repugnance – 'assured him privily that I find worth in his brutality.'

Flourishing his arm in an obvious attempt to attract Berek's attention, the Insequent finished cleaning Jeremiah's wound. With the blood and grime gone from her son's face, Linden saw to her surprise that he had already begun to heal. Despite the swelling, he could slit open his left eye. To her ordinary senses, his eye itself appeared bloodshot, but essentially undamaged.

When Berek voiced his approval of the Theomach's care, the wrapped man replied, 'My lord, it suffices that I have been of service. If I may say so without disrespect, however, greater matters than this boy's hurt or Inbull's betrayal lie between us. We would do well to speak of them while we may.'

'Perhaps.' Berek's worn sound grated against the Theomach's light assurance. 'Certainly you are strange to me. And your offer of aid is disquieting, for it appears to be given without cause. We will speak of it. If my many needs compel me to endure Inbull's betrayals, I can refuse no other assistance. But the queries which fill my heart pertain chiefly to the lady Linden.

'Of her companions, I ask nothing. She has vouched for them, and her word contents me. To them I say only' – now he turned to Linden's son and the Unbeliever – 'Jeremiah, Covenant, I regret that my use of Inbull has harmed you. If you wish any boon that I may grant in my present straits, you need merely name it.'

Jeremiah ducked his head; said nothing. Glowering with the heat of embers in his eyes, Covenant muttered, 'Just give Linden whatever she wants so we can leave. We're in a hurry. We shouldn't be here at all.'

'My lord Berek,' the Theomach put in insistently, 'you do well to accept the lady's word. And the man suggests truly that his only desire is to depart. Will you not accept my word also? The powers which this man and this boy – aye, and the lady also – command have no meaning here. Her purpose, and that of her companions, lies at a great distance from all that you do. It will in no wise affect you. For the sake of your many needs, you must speak to *me*.'

Berek folded his arms across his thick chest. In a voice as heavy as his hands, he announced, 'Stranger, I do not accept your word. Yet we will speak, since you would have it so. If you seek to be heeded, tell me what you are.'

'My lord,' the Theomach replied promptly, 'I am three things. First, I am a seeker after knowledge. My people live in a land too distant to be named, for its name would convey nothing. We have no concern for the small affrays of the Earth. Yet we wander widely – though ever alone – questing for knowledge wherever it may be gleaned. My questing has brought me to you.'

While the Insequent answered, Linden crossed the tent to align herself with Covenant and Jeremiah. They had brought her here. Although she did not trust Covenant, he and her son were her only defence against Berek's probing.

'Second,' the Theomach continued, 'I am a warrior of considerable prowess. At your leisure, you may test my claim in any form that pleases you. For the present, I will state plainly that none of your foes can stand against me in battle.'

Whispering in the hope that only Covenant and Jeremiah would hear her, Linden asked, 'Is that true?'

Perhaps Berek did not hear her. If he did, he kept his attention and his deep gaze fixed on the Theomach.

But Covenant was less discreet. 'Hell, yes,' he growled. 'You have no idea. You've seen that knowledge he's so proud of in action. Think about what he could do in a fight.'

If the Theomach were able to step between moments, he could strike as often as he wished without being seen or opposed—

Still he spoke as if he and Berek were alone. 'Third,' he continued, 'I am a teacher. Much has occurred to you and within you that remains unexplained. I comprehend such matters, and I desire to impart my understanding. Lord Berek, my instruction will increase your strength and insight. It will ensure your triumph in this war.'

'Oh, please,' Covenant put in sardonically. 'Tell him the truth.' His impulse to provoke the Insequent seemed to increase with every swallow of wine.

The Theomach shrugged. 'In truth, I do not doubt your triumph, my lord, with or without my aid. Against Warmark Vettalor and such force as he commands, yours is the feller hand. Yet I fear no contradiction when I avow that my guidance will preserve many lives among your warriors. And I state with certainty that you will never fully grasp the extent of your oath, or the import of your larger purpose, without my teaching.'

'You are facile, stranger,' said Berek gruffly. With his arms folded, he looked as immovable as a tree. He had become the centre on which his world turned, and he kept his self-doubt hidden. 'You speak of aid, but you do not reveal your purpose. Why do you offer your assistance?'

If the Theomach had any acquaintance with self-doubt, he, too, concealed it. Shrugging again, he admitted, 'My lord, I have no reply that will readily content you. The questing of those who seek for knowledge is by necessity oblique, instinctive and indefinite. They themselves cannot name their object until it is discovered. I am able to say only that I believe I will gain knowledge in your service – aye, knowledge and honour – which would otherwise remain beyond my ken.'

'He's a plausible bastard,' Covenant remarked after a long gulp of wine, 'I'll give him that.'

Slowly the Theomach turned his secreted face towards Covenant. His manner caused Linden to hold her breath in apprehension.

'He's telling the truth,' murmured Jeremiah uncomfortably.

'Oh, sure,' Covenant snorted. 'So could I. If only life were that simple.'

But Berek refused to be distracted. 'If you indeed desire to aid me,' he demanded, 'and wish to be known as the Theomach rather than as a stranger, I require some sign of truth or fealty. Display evidence of your knowledge. Demonstrate that your aid will not serve my foes.'

Again the Theomach turned his head towards Covenant and Jeremiah like a warning.

Abruptly Covenant tossed his flagon into the nearest brazier. 'Come on, Jeremiah.' The coals were dimmed, and the reek of burning wine and honey steamed into the air. Then the wooden vessel took flame, making the tent bright for a moment. 'Let's go find Damelon. Maybe he'll help us pick a fight with Inbull.' He held his left hand over his sore ribs, still keeping his halfhand in his pocket. 'I want to repay some of this pain.'

At once, Jeremiah set his flagon down beside Berek's longsword. Avoiding Linden's gaze, he accompanied Covenant obediently. They kept their distance from both Berek and her as they crossed the tent and ducked out under the flaps.

Linden appealed to Berek with her gaze, mutely asking him to call her companions back. But he answered her aloud. 'A measure of retribution at their hands will serve my purposes. And Hand Damelon will ensure that Inbull suffers no lasting harm.'

'It is well,' pronounced the Theomach. He may have been giving his approval to Berek's words – or to Covenant's and Jeremiah's departure. Then, however, he made his meaning clear. 'In their absence, I may speak more freely.'

Linden swallowed a desire to follow her son. She ached to protect him. And instinctively she wanted to avoid being alone with Berek. But she needed his help. And she could not imagine how the Theomach would convince Berek of anything.

The future High Lord searched the Insequent closely. 'Do so, then.'

'My lord Berek' – the Theomach's confidence was palpable – 'you require evidence of my fealty, and I provide it thus.

'The tale is told that in your despair upon the slopes of Mount Thunder, ancient Gravin Threndor, the Fire-Lions or the mountain or the very Earth spoke to you. Yet to avow that you indeed heard their speech is not sooth. It is merely a convenience, a means for passing over that which cannot be explained. The truth is both more simple and more profound. Inspired by despair and desperation, you called out for succour, offering your oath in recompense. This you did because your need was absolute, and because you sensed, in a fashion which defies your explication, that Mount Thunder was a place of power amid the supernal loveliness of the Land. How or why your appeal was received and answered, you cannot declare.'

Berek made a visible effort to mask his surprise; but his growing wonder was clear in spite of his self-control.

'Nonetheless,' the Theomach continued, 'a form of speech occurred. Words became known to you, Words which you did not hear, and which you could not comprehend. Because they had been given to you, their puissance was evident. Also no other course remained to you. Therefore you uttered them aloud. When the Fire-Lions replied, you were as astonished as your foes.

'Since that moment, however, the Words have gone from you. You recall them only in dreams, and when you awaken naught but sorrow remains.

'Is this not sooth, my lord?'

Berek nodded as if he were unaware of the movement. His troubled awe revealed that the Theomach was right.

'Then heed me well.' Now the Insequent's tone took on a gravitas that compelled attention. Even the light appeared to condense around him, as if the lamps and the braziers and the very air were listening. 'The Words were Seven, and they are these.

'The first is *melenkurion*, which signifies bastion or source. The second is *abatha*, suggesting endurance, or the need for endurance. Third is *duroc*, a reference to Earthpower, the substance of the fire which the lady wields. Fourth comes *minas*, which also means Earthpower, but in another sense. It indicates Earthpower as a foundation rather than as a form of theurgy.'

As he spoke, each Word seemed to resonate and expand until it strained the fabric of the tent. 'The fifth Word is *mill*, which cannot be defined in human speech, but which implies invocation. The sixth, *harad*, may be understood as a stricture against selfishness, tyranny, malice, or other forms of despair. It binds the speaker to make no use of Earthpower which does not serve or preserve the munificence of creation. And last is *khabaal*, to which many meanings may be ascribed. In your mouth, it is an affirmation or incarnation of your sworn oath to the Land.'

The Theomach paused as if to let Berek – or perhaps Linden – absorb his revelation. They were silent. Echoes filled Linden's ears: she felt the potency of the Words ramify around her, multiplied towards horizons that lay beyond her comprehension. They encompassed possibilities which were too vast for her.

She had never heard Covenant mention the Seven Words. But the

Theomach had just restored them to Berek's conscious mind. Surely they had not been lost before Covenant's first translation to the Land?

They had been given to her as well—

A moment later, the Theomach said, 'This tongue is spoken nowhere, other than by one race that I scorn to name, for it is the language of the Earth's making and substance rather than of the Earth's peoples. Yet it may be discovered, word by word, by those who seek deeply for knowledge – and who do not wish to bend or distort that knowledge for their own ends.'

Then, unexpectedly, he turned to Linden. She could not see his expression through his bindings. Nevertheless she received the clear impression that he sought to sway her as much as to convince Berek.

'Aloud,' he said distinctly, 'the Seven Words are spoken thus. *Melenkurion abatha. Duroc minas mill. Harad khabaal.*'

Before he had pronounced ten syllables, the Staff of Law burst into flame. With each Word, the fire mounted until it enclosed her in conflagration: power gentle as a caress, entirely without hurt or peril, and jubilant as a paean. Soon the whole tent was full of blazing like joy and rebirth, exuberance and restoration; the true vitality of Law.

Some part of Linden clung to it, revelling in its exaltation. It resembled the gift of *vitrim* and the benison of Glimmermere, the tang of *aliantha* and the sovereign gold of hurtloam; the Land's limitless potential for glory. However, another aspect of her was mortal and afraid. The Words were distilled puissance. She had not chosen them, and could not hope to control their implications.

Reflexively she strove to quell the flames – and as soon as she did so, they fell away. Without transition, the fire was quenched, leaving her to the truncated insight of the lamps and braziers.

Within herself, she staggered at the suddenness of the change. When she remembered to look at her companions, she saw that Berek was both stunned and eager. He seemed unable to comprehend what he had heard and seen – and yet he had been lifted up in spite of his bafflement. A long burden of bereavement had fallen from his shoulders; and for a few moments, at least, fanged loss no longer gnawed at his spirit.

The Theomach watched her and Berek with apparent satisfaction. 'Are you content, my lord?' he asked as if he were sure of the answer.

'Will you now accept my companionship, that I may aid and tutor you?'

Shuddering with effort, Berek mastered himself. When he had swallowed several times to clear his throat, he said hoarsely, 'My gratitude is certain. I will say more when my lady has assured me that she is unharmed.'

Linden could not rival his self-command; but she replied as clearly as she could, 'Look at me, my lord. You can *see*. I'm as surprised as you are.' And she wanted to weep with regret at her own weakness. 'But I'm not hurt.'

Slowly Berek nodded. 'Yes, my lady Linden. I am indeed able to discern that you are whole. Therefore I will say to the Theomach' – still slowly, he turned to the Insequent as if each small movement cost him an exertion of will – 'that my gratitude is certain, but my acceptance remains in doubt. One further glimpse of your knowledge will content me.'

The Theomach waited, motionless; but whether he intended to acquiesce or refuse, Linden could not determine.

With rigid care, Berek said, 'You spoke of the munificence of creation. Will you name that munificence? Wherein does it lie? What is its nature? What does it portend? If these Seven Words will bind me, I must know that to which I will be bound.'

'Life,' replied the Theomach simply. 'Growth. Enhancement.' Then he added in a tone like an apology, 'You will understand, my lord Berek, that neither I nor anyone may grasp the mind of this world's Creator. The needs and desires of that which is eternal surpass finite comprehension. Yet I deem that the Earth, and within it the Land, were formed as a habitation where living beings may gaze upon wonderment and terror, and seek to emulate or refuse them. The Earth and the Land are a dwelling-place where life may discover the highest in itself, or the lowest, according to its desires and choices.'

Berek frowned, not in disapproval or chagrin, but in intense consideration. For a long moment, he regarded the Theomach as though he strove to penetrate the stranger's secrets with his burgeoning health-sense. Then he asked over his shoulder, 'My lady Linden, do you conceive that the Theomach speaks sooth?'

His question startled Linden, and she answered without thinking, 'I don't care.' If she had paused for thought, the sheer weight of his query would have sealed her voice in her throat. 'I want it to be true. So do you. Isn't that what matters?' Who was she to articulate the meaning of life? 'Isn't it the only thing that matters?'

Berek growled in the back of his throat, a wordless sound fraught with both recognition and uncertainty. Still studying the Insequent, he announced formally, 'Then I will say to my lord Theomach that I accept your companionship. Both aid and guidance will I greet with welcome. A man who speaks as you have done must be heeded, whatever his intent may be.'

The Theomach responded with a bow and a salute, tapping his fist to his chest in homage. Interfering with Covenant's designs, he had gained what he wanted for himself. Inadvertently Linden had helped him win a measure of Berek's trust.

Having made his decision, however, Berek did not hesitate to move on. 'Now you will leave us,' he informed his new counsellor. 'I must speak with my lady Linden alone.'

Oh, God. Linden flinched. Abruptly the entire space of the tent seemed to become a pitfall: she felt beset by snares which she did not know how to avoid. *In this circumstance, her mind cannot be distinguished from the Arch of Time.* One wrong word—

At once, the Theomach demurred. 'My lord, this is needless. That which the lady desires of you is simple, and I do not doubt that her requests will be easily met. Nor will she and her companions endanger you in any fashion. You have accepted my aid and guidance. Do not unwisely set them aside.'

Berek drew back his shoulders, lifted his chin. His tone was mild, but its mildness veiled iron. 'My lord Theomach, I have said that my gratitude is certain, as is my welcome. Yet my wisdom is my own. If I prove unwise, as I have often done, it will be through no fault of yours.'

Linden wished that she could see the Theomach's eyes. She had the impression that his gaze shifted rapidly between Berek and her, searching for an argument that would sway the Halfhand – or for a way to warn her of perils which he could not state aloud. But then he repeated his bow and salute. Instead of stepping between moments to address Linden where Berek could not hear him, he turned to the flaps and left the tent.

A crisis was upon her, and she was not prepared for it. The Seven Words still echoed around her, baffling her with hints of hope and calamity.

But she had spoken and acted by instinct for long hours now. She was too weary to do otherwise. *Trust yourself.* If she had truly heard Covenant's voice in her dreams, not that of some malign misleading chimera—

As Berek stepped closer with gentleness on his face and resolve in his eyes, Linden shrugged off her cloak as if to rid herself of an obstruction. The braziers had warmed the air: soon she would be too warm, alarmed or shamed by her conflicted doubts. Clinging to the Staff with both hands, she braced herself to meet his probing gaze.

He approached until he was little more than an arm's length away. There he stopped. Deliberately he folded his arms across his chest: a gesture of determination. He seemed to tower over her as he said, 'My lady, you are troubled. Surely there is no need? My gratitude is boundless, and my respect with it. The aid that you have both given and brought is beyond estimation. Why, then, do you fear me?'

Linden could not answer him: any explanation would reveal too much. Instead she fell back on matters that she understood; subjects which she could broach safely. 'Lord Berek, listen,' she said with a tremor in her voice. 'There are things that you have to do. Essential things. If you don't do them, you could win this war and still lose, even with the Theomach's help.'

Speaking brusquely because she was frightened and tired, she told him, 'You're killing your own wounded. Do you know that? Those blankets and pallets – the bandages – the tents— They breed death. Your healers don't see it yet, but you will.' The restoration of the Seven Words would evoke his latent powers. 'You can't prevent your people from being cut down,' hacked at, pierced, trampled, 'but you can save some of their lives.'

Perplexed and frowning, Berek began, 'With hurtloam—'

'*No*,' Linden countered. 'I don't know when you'll be able to find more of it, or how much of it you'll find. And it starts to lose its effectiveness as soon as it's scooped out of the soil. You can't carry it very far.'

In haste because she could not bear to be interrupted, she said harshly, 'You need to take a day off from this war. A day or two. Let your enemies retreat. If you think that they might counterattack, use Inbull to scare them out of it. Instead of fighting, soak every blanket and scrap of bandage in boiling water. If you can replace the pallets, burn them. Otherwise pour boiling water over them. And tell your healers – tell all of your people – to wash every wound. Those injuries have to be kept *clean*.

'I don't care how long it takes. *Make* the time. Your people are dying in droves, and I can't stay. If you want to save any of them after I'm gone, you have to keep them clean.'

The grief in his gaze wrenched her heart. 'And if we cannot, my lady?' he asked softly. 'If the blankets fall to tatters when they are boiled, and the bandages likewise, and we glean no resupply from the encampments which our foes abandon? What must we do then?'

'Oh, God.' The extremity of his plight was unmistakable: it exceeded her courage. In his place, she would have been paralysed by dismay long ago. 'If the Theomach can't tell you what to do, you'll have to find more hurtloam. And if you can't find enough hurtloam' – she swallowed a lump of empathy and anguish – 'you'll have to pour boiling water on those infections.' The burns would be terrible, but they would slow some of the poisons. 'Anything to keep them clean.'

As she faltered, however, he grew stronger. His bravery was founded on the needs of the people around him. He had come so far and accomplished so much, not because the Fire-Lions had responded to his desperation, but simply because he could not turn away from the plight of his people and his Queen. He was full of grief and understood despair: therefore he rejected both fear and defeat.

'My lady,' he said with rough kindness, 'we will attempt your counsel. I cannot avow success, yet the gift of your lore will be treasured among us. As occasion permits, we will garner its benefits. You teach the worth of healing. It will not be forgotten. Songs will be sung of you to lift the heart, and tales will be told that surpass generations. Wherever those who serve my Queen and the Land are gathered together—'

'No!' Linden protested frantically. The thought of *ripples* appalled her. They would expand— '*No*, it's better, believe me, it's *better* if you don't talk about this. I mean about anything that's happened tonight. Don't discuss it, don't refer to it. Don't keep the story alive. I'm begging you, my lord. I'll get down on my knees if you want.' Vertorn had offered to prostrate himself: she would follow his example. 'And the Theomach will insist – I can't stay. And I don't deserve—'

A legend of Linden the Healer would alter the Land's known history. It might do enough harm to topple the Arch.

Berek raised his hands: a gesture of placation. 'My lady,' he murmured to soothe her. 'My lady. Quiet your distress. There is no need. I will honour your wish.

'All in this camp will deem it strange that I do not speak of you. But if you seek the boon of my silence, it will be granted. And in this I may command my Hands, Damelon and the others. My Hafts also may heed me. My word will not still every voice. Yet I will do all that can be done, since you desire it so.'

Linden stared at him until she was sure that she could believe him. Then she sagged. Thank God– she thought wanly. Thank God for men who kept their promises. If she had been equally confident of Covenant's word, she would not have felt fretted with dread.

'I might inquire, my lady,' Berek continued after a moment, 'what harm resides in the tale of your deeds. But I will not. My silence on that score is implicit in the boon you seek.

'Yet,' he said more sternly, 'there are queries which demand utterance. My oaths of service, to my Queen as to the Land, require this of me. Understand that I intend neither affront nor disregard. However, I must be answered.'

Wincing inwardly, Linden started to say, Don't, please. You don't understand the danger. But Berek's deep gaze held her. His will seemed greater than hers. She did not know how to refuse anyone who had suffered so much loss.

Berek's mien tightened. 'My lady Linden, it is plain that you bear powers – or instruments of power – greater than yourself. I know naught of such matters. Nonetheless I am able to discern contradiction. Though your powers exceed you, you have it within you to transcend them.'

Her mouth and throat suddenly felt too dry for speech. She should not have been surprised that he was able to perceive Covenant's ring under her shirt. Still she was not prepared. And neither the Theomach nor Covenant was here to advise her.

'My lord,' she said weakly, trying to fend him off, 'I can't talk about this. It doesn't have anything to do with you. It won't affect your war, or your Queen – or your oath,' not without destroying Time. Bitter with memories, she added, 'And you haven't earned the knowledge. You aren't ready for it. It can only hurt you.'

She could not gauge what anything that she might say – or refuse to say – would cost Berek. Similar knowledge had damaged her immeasurably. But it had also redeemed her.

He did not relent. 'Yet I wish to hear them named.'

His eyes and his tone and his vital aura compelled her. Guided only by intuition, she held the Staff in one hand. 'My Staff is about Law and Earthpower. It exerts the same force as the Seven Words, but in a different form.' With the other, she indicated Covenant's hidden ring. 'This is white gold.' She felt that she was accepting responsibility for all of the Earth's millennia as she said, 'It wields the wild magic that destroys peace. But it isn't natural here.

'If you want to know more, you'll have to ask the Theomach.'

She saw that she had baffled him; and she braced herself, fearing that he would demand more. Yet he did not. Instead he rubbed at his bald scalp as though he sought to massage coherence into his scattering thoughts.

'This is bootless, my lady,' he grumbled. 'It conveys naught.' Then he dropped his hand, and his uncertainty with it. 'However, I will not press you, for your discomfiture is evident. Instead I will pose a query of another kind.

'It has been averred that your powers and your purpose do not pertain to me. How may I be assured of this? My force is greatly outnumbered. And as I drive my foes before me, I strengthen them, for they draw ever closer to Doriendor Corishev and reinforcement. I can not ignore the prospect of a threat from another quarter.'

'The Theomach—' Linden tried to offer.

'My lady,' Berek interrupted more harshly, 'I do not ask for aid. That the Theomach may well provide, as he has avowed. Rather I ask how I may fear nothing from the needs which compel you. There is no wish for harm in your heart, of that I am certain. Your companions, however, are closed to me. I know naught of them but that they wield strange theurgies, and that their manner is ungentle.

'Answer this, my lady, and I will not disturb you further.'

Linden sighed. 'My Lord, there are only two things that I can tell you.' To describe Covenant's intentions in this time would be ruinous. 'First, we're going northwest – and we have a *long* way to go. Something like two hundred leagues. Everything that Covenant and Jeremiah and I are trying to do, everything that brought us here in the first place— It'll all be wasted if we don't cover those two hundred leagues as quickly as possible.

'Second,' she continued so that Berek would not interrupt her, 'the last thing that the Theomach wants is trouble from us. And I do mean the *last*. You have no idea how powerful he is. I don't understand it myself. But you can be sure of this. If we try anything that might threaten you, he'll stop us. We can't fight him. Not here. No matter how strong you think we are.'

The Insequent had demonstrated his ability to override Covenant's intentions. She was sure that he meant her no harm; but she did not doubt that he would banish Covenant, Jeremiah, and her in an instant if they endangered his relationship with Berek – or the security of the Arch of Time.

Berek regarded her sombrely. In his gaze, she could almost trace the contention between his visceral impulse to trust her and his necessary concerns for his people, his Queen, his oath. Then she saw his expression soften, felt the tension in his shoulders relax; and she knew before he spoke that she had gained what she needed most from him.

'My lady Linden,' he said with wry regret, 'these matters surpass me. I lack the lore to comprehend them. But a trek of two hundred leagues in this winter– That I am able to grasp. It will be cruel to you, bereft as you are of food, or horses, or adequate raiment.

'To the extent that my own impoverishment permits, I will supply all that you require' – he held up his hand to forestall any response – 'and count myself humbled because I cannot equal your largesse. The knowledge of hurtloam alone is incomparable bounty, yet you have given more, far more. If you are thus generous in all of your dealings, you will need no songs or tales of mine to honour you, for you will be fabled wherever you are known.'

Linden wanted to protest, No, my lord. You're the legend here. I'm not like that. But his unanticipated gentleness left her mute. She was too close to tears to find her voice.

If she could have believed in Covenant's honesty, her gratitude would have been more than she knew how to contain.

Chapter Nine:

Along the Last Hills

For three days, Linden, Covenant and Jeremiah rode into the northwest, hugging the Last Hills as closely as they could without venturing onto terrain that would hamper their gaunt and weary horses. Over her cloak and her old clothes, Linden wore a heavy robe lined with fur which – according to Hand Damelon – had been scavenged from one of Vettalor's abandoned camps. Her hands she kept swaddled in strips cut from the edge of a blanket: a wider strip she wrapped like a scarf around her mouth and neck. Still the cold was a galling misery, day and night. And during the day, hard sunlight glanced like blades off the crusted snow and ice, forcing her to squint. Her head throbbed mercilessly.

With Covenant and Jeremiah riding nearby, she could not draw on the Staff of Law, even to sustain her abject mount. Instead she carried it quiescent across her lap; clung to the reins and the saddle with her abused hands. Somehow Covenant had endured Berek's touch. Still she feared that he and Jeremiah would not be able to withstand close proximity to the Staff's power.

They had their own difficulties. Their mounts were restive, hard to control. The beasts shied at every shadow despite their weariness. At times, they made frail attempts to buck. Linden suspected that the horses sensed something in her companions which she could not. On a purely animal level, they were disturbed by the secretive theurgy of their riders.

But Covenant and her son scorned their mounts' uneasiness. They stayed near Linden at all times, as though they meant to ensure that she did not use her Staff. And they appeared oblivious to the cold;

preternaturally immune to the ordinary requirements of flesh and blood. They had refused cloaks and robes, did not wear blankets over their shoulders. Yet they revealed no discomfort. Only Covenant's seething impatience and Jeremiah's glum unresponsiveness betrayed their underlying discontent.

They ate the stale bread, tough meat and dried fruit that Berek had provided: they drank the water and the raw wine. Those simple human needs they retained. And at night, they built campfires which generated enough heat to encourage slumber. As far as Linden knew, however, neither of them slept. Whenever she was roused by cold or nightmares, she saw them still seated, wakeful and silent, beside the fading coals. At daybreak, they were on their feet ahead of her.

They hardly spoke to each other: they seldom addressed her. Nor did she question them, although the throng of her doubts and concerns clouded her horizons in every direction. She and her companions were constrained because they were not alone.

At Berek's command, Yellinin rode with them, leading a string of six more horses laden with supplies: food, drink, blankets and firewood, as well as provender for the mounts; as much of Berek's generosity as the horses' meagre strength could carry.

The outrider herself said little. Berek had ordered her to ask no questions; and she obeyed with hard-bitten determination, stifling her curiosity and loneliness. She could not have been sure that she would ever see her lord or her comrades again. Yet even when Linden tried practical queries – How far have we ridden today? Do you think that this weather will hold? – Yellinin answered so curtly that Linden's more personal questions seemed to freeze in her mouth.

At all times, Covenant kept his right hand hidden in his pocket. Linden supposed that he did so in order to conceal his one resemblance to Berek Halfhand. But she felt sure that his caution was wasted. With his awakened senses, Berek must have discerned the truth for himself.

Jeremiah also was a halfhand, although he had lost different fingers. Legends might grow from such small details—

By the end of the third day, Linden reached the limit of her endurance. Yellinin's emotional plight nagged at her like a bad tooth: she was acutely aware of the slow erosion which wore the outrider's determination down to bereavement. Nor could she ignore the leaden distress of the horses. And the questions that she needed to ask her companions were becoming a form of torment: as bitter as the cold, and as relentless.

In addition, she felt a grinding anxiety for Jeremiah. According to Yellinin, the riders had covered no more than twenty-five leagues when the sun set on the third day. Measured by the necessity of ascending among the Westron Mountains in order to avoid Garroting Deep, their progress was paltry. At this rate, Covenant and Jeremiah would never attain their goal. The horses would not survive: Linden was sure of that. If she could not sustain herself with Earthpower, she herself would fail long before she caught sight of *Melenkurion* Skyweir.

Her son would be Lord Foul's prisoner forever.

That night, as she faded shivering towards sleep, she realised that most of her decisions in this time had been inspired by cold; predicated on the brutality of winter. She had chosen to trek towards Berek's camp because she was freezing and could not think of an alternative. But when she had achieved her aim – horses, blankets, food – she had accomplished nothing. The journey ahead of her was still impossible, just as it had been four days ago. Yellinin and her mounts were giving as much help as their worn flesh allowed, and it was not enough.

Linden had already watched too many innocents suffer and die for her sake.

Now the cold required another decision of her. She had to accept that her choices had been proven inadequate; that the obstacles in her road were not ones which she could surmount. The time had come to admit that she was too weak to carry the burden of Jeremiah's need, and the Land's. This winter demanded more strength than she possessed.

Therefore she would have to find a way to trust Covenant.

The next morning, when she struggled out of the scant warmth of her blankets, she learned that two of the horses had died during the night: Covenant's mount, and Jeremiah's. Then she could no longer deny the truth. The cold had beaten her. If bearing her companions killed just two horses every three days – and if there were no storms – and if the terrain did not become more demanding – Yellinin's dogged aid would nonetheless cease to serve any purpose long before the Last Hills merged with the mountains.

Coughing at the bite of ice in her lungs, Linden gathered what warmth she could from the campfire while Berek's warrior cooked a breakfast of gruel laced with fruit. She took as much time as she needed to eat what she believed would be her last hot meal. For a while, she held her robe open to the flames, hoping that the fur would absorb enough heat to preserve her. Then, when Yellinin had prepared mounts for the riders and had withdrawn to ready the remaining horses, Linden quietly asked Covenant and Jeremiah to ride ahead without her.

To answer Covenant's vexation and Jeremiah's alarm, she explained, 'I need a little distance so that I can use my Staff. Don't worry, I'll catch up with you.' She could hardly miss their trail through the hard snow. 'I want Yellinin to turn back. But convincing her probably won't be easy. I'll have to show her that we don't need her, and for that—'

Linden indicated the Staff with a shrug.

'It's about time,' muttered Covenant as if he had expected her to make up her mind days ago. 'Just don't trust her. Berek didn't send her out here to help us. He wants her to warn him if we double back. Hell, he probably has scouts on our trail right now, just in case we kill her and try to take him by surprise.'

Staring at him, Linden felt a slash of yearning for the Thomas Covenant of her memories. Surely he could see that Yellinin was *dying* to return to her people? But she did not argue. Her suspicions ran too deep. If she challenged him, she would make him wary; and then she would lose any possibility that he might reveal the truth about himself.

'Just go,' she urged him stiffly. 'And brace yourself. I'll take care of Yellinin.'

Jeremiah attempted an unconvincing smile. 'Thanks, Mom. You're doing the right thing.' To Covenant, he added, 'The Theomach won't object. He trusts her now.'

'I know,' Covenant sighed as he and Jeremiah mounted their new horses. 'I'm just too bloody frustrated to be gracious about it. This is our fifth day and we're still nowhere near *Melenkurion* Skyweir. These damn delays are killing me.'

Rolling its eyes, Jeremiah's mount flinched. Covenant's emaciated mustang stumbled awkwardly. But they kept their seats. In moments, they rode out of sight around the curve of a hill.

Linden remained where she was, clinging to the last of the campfire while she waited for Yellinin.

When the other horses were ready, the outrider walked grimly towards Linden. Daylight emphasised her years as well as her weariness: she seemed old for a warrior, aged by interminable seasons of battle and injury. And her eyes betrayed her uneasiness. Clearly she had guessed why Linden had stayed behind to talk to her; and her heart was torn. Her devotion to Berek's commands vied with a vivid ache for her comrades and her cause. Studying her, Linden recognised her reluctance to die for people who refused to reveal either their loyalties or their purposes.

When Linden did not speak at once, Yellinin asked cautiously, 'What transpires, my lady? Why have your companions departed?'

In the outrider's tone, Linden heard that Covenant had named at least one aspect of the woman's dilemma. Yellinin was worried that Covenant and Jeremiah, if not Linden herself, might still pose some inexplicable threat to Berek's army.

'I need distance,' Linden replied in wisps of vapour. 'I'm going to use my Staff. That's dangerous for them.' And for herself: without Covenant and Jeremiah, she would be stranded in this time. 'If they're far enough away, they'll be safe.'

Yellinin frowned. 'My lady, you know that I have been commanded to question nothing. Yet it may be that I will fail in my duty if I do not speak. Therefore I ask what use you will make of your fire.'

'Two things.' Linden could not bring herself to say, I don't want you to throw your life away. 'With your permission, I'll do what I can to make you and your horses stronger. And I hope that I can persuade you to rejoin Lord Berek.'

Before Yellinin could object, Linden said, 'You and your horses have already suffered too much. No matter what I do, they won't last much longer. And we don't need you to guide us. Covenant knows the way.

'I want you to pack three horses with as much food as they can carry. I'll ride one and lead the others. We'll send the mounts that Covenant and Jeremiah have now back to you. Then I want you to leave. Tell Lord Berek that I sent you away because you've already done more for us than we had any right to ask.'

Yellinin set her jaw in spite of her tangible wish to comply. 'My lord Berek's command was plain.'

'I know.' Linden sighed a gust of steam. The dying embers of the campfire no longer warmed her. She closed her robe to hold in as much heat as she could. In the cold, her face felt stiff with renunciation. 'And he expects to be obeyed. But something else about him is plain as well. If he could think of a way to win his war without sacrificing any more lives, he would do it in a heartbeat. He doesn't want you to die, Yellinin.'

Earnestly Linden said, 'Once I use my Staff, you should be able to do what Krenwill does. You'll *hear* truth. Then you won't have to worry about what Covenant and Jeremiah and I have in mind. You'll believe me when I say that they don't want to turn back – and I wouldn't allow it if they did.'

Yellinin made a visible effort to stifle her yearning. 'Then I will accept the hazard of your fire, my lady. For the sake of the horses, if for no other cause, I cannot refuse.

'But I will not consent to part from you,' she added dourly. 'I have not experienced Krenwill's discernment. I cannot be certain of its worth.'

Linden studied Yellinin for a moment longer, measuring the quality of the outrider's torn desires. When she felt sure that her companions had ridden far enough to protect themselves, she closed her eyes and caused gentle Earthpower to bloom like cornflowers and forsythia from the apt wood of the Staff.

Enclosed in fire, Yellinin could not conceal her amazement at the fundamental healing and sustenance of Law. Her first taste of percipience as she watched her horses gain new vitality filled her with shock and wonder. Her own abused flesh was soothed in ways which she had never experienced before. Now she could understand the true nature of the forces which had transformed Berek Halfhand. And her heart belonged to him, in spite of her gratitude for Linden's gift. When the flames subsided, and Yellinin heard the truth of Linden's assurances, her resistance slowly faded.

Glowing with gladness, she gave Linden her consent; her eager co-operation. As soon as she had rearranged the burdens of the beasts as Linden had requested, she tapped the breastplate of her cuirass in salute.

Then she stood at attention while Linden mounted and gathered up the reins of the other horses.

Linden believed that she was doing the right thing; that she could not have justified any other choice. Nevertheless the outrider's attitude exacerbated her own sense of isolation. She seemed to be leaving behind her last ally as she rode away alone.

On a completely irrational level, she wished that Berek had come with her. She needed someone of his stature to help her face the conundrum of Covenant and Jeremiah.

The renewed vigour of her mounts allowed Linden to pursue her companions at a canter. She caught up with them within half a league.

Apparently Jeremiah had been watching for her. As she approached, he turned almost immediately to Covenant; and at once, they reined in to wait for her.

Neither of them spoke to her. They seemed to know without explanation what she had done. When she had joined them, Jeremiah said diffidently to Covenant, 'We should change horses right away. If we keep Yellinin waiting, she might change her mind. And we'll be able to travel faster' – he glanced at the mounts with Linden – 'at least for a while.'

'Sure.' Covenant sounded almost amiable, as if the outrider's absence eased his frustration. 'Let's do it.'

Together, he and Jeremiah dismounted, turned their horses back the way they had come, and slapped them into motion. The beasts trotted off promptly, relieved to escape their riders. Their energy would not last: that was obvious. But Linden had confidence that Yellinin would care for them. Berek's army could not afford to lose mounts unnecessarily.

Jeremiah reached the saddle of his fresh horse without much difficulty, although the beast's sides quivered fretfully at his touch. But Covenant's mount shied away whenever he tried to step up into the stirrup. Swearing almost cheerfully, he manoeuvred the horse against Jeremiah's so that it could not evade him. Then he swung himself into the seat with a fierce grin.

The instinctive repugnance of the beasts for Covenant and Jeremiah disturbed Linden. And releasing Yellinin did not make her feel any less helpless. She still could not imagine how any of them would survive to reach *Melenkurion* Skyweir.

For the time being, however, she kept her many questions to herself. The relentless cold numbed her thoughts; sapped her will. It was rife with implications of failure. And she did not know what had caused the change in Covenant's manner. Yellinin's absence seemed to free him from some unexplained constraint.

As Linden and her companions resumed their plod northwestward through the raw and glistening winter along the margin of the Last Hills, Jeremiah rode on her right, between her and Covenant. Since their departure from Berek's camp, his wound had healed completely: she could see the twitch at the corner of his eye signalling. However, its indecipherable message had lost some of its urgency. Like Covenant's, Jeremiah's spirits had lifted.

After a while, he asked Covenant, 'How much longer do you think we'll have to do this?' His tone suggested that he already knew the answer; that he had posed the question for Linden's sake.

'Today,' Covenant answered casually. 'Maybe tomorrow.' He did not glance at Linden. 'After that we should be safe enough.'

'Safe?' Linden inquired. The idea that any form of safety might be possible in this winter seemed inconceivable.

'From the Theomach,' explained Jeremiah. He sounded cheerful. 'So far, we're doing things his way. We aren't attracting any attention. We haven't violated what people know about this time. But we're travelling too slowly. We need to go faster. That's why we had to get away from Yellinin. So she won't see us use power.

'The Theomach still won't like it. If he senses it, he'll think he has to interfere again.' Jeremiah rolled his eyes in mockery. 'So we'll wait until we're farther away. We'll give him a chance to get caught up in Berek's war. Then we won't have to worry about him anymore.'

A reflexive tug of hope surprised Linden. She craved anything which might alleviate the impossibility of their trek.

Covenant had warned her that the dangers were real. *If Jeremiah and I risk using power now, we'll be noticed. We could run into opposition.* But the cold persuaded her that attempting to pass through the Westron Mountains would be worse.

'How are you going to do it?' she asked carefully. 'Covenant said that your magic isn't safe here.'

The kind of opposition that might damage the Arch.

The Theomach had mentioned *puissant beings.*

'It's better if we talk about this later,' Covenant replied. 'Tonight, if you can't wait any longer.' He did not so much as glance at Linden. 'Every league takes us a little closer to the Theomach's limits. And Berek is going to want more from him by the hour. More help. More knowledge. Berek is starving to understand what he can do. He's desperate for it. The more he gets from the Theomach, the more he's going to want.'

'We probably wouldn't be overheard where we are,' Covenant admitted. 'But I don't want to take the chance.'

Where we are, Linden thought with a forlorn ache. Apart from Yellinin, she had not seen an ordinary human being for more than three days of abrading cold. On her right, the Center Plains were a bitter wasteland, snow-cloaked and featureless as far as she could see: a tangible avatar of the gelid loneliness within a *caesure,* the ruin which represented the ultimate outcome of Joan's madness. And on her left, the Last Hills raised their heads in forbidding scarps and crags. Some of their lower slopes were mild; others, more rugged. But boulders and bare granite knotted their crests. And all of them were clotted with ice or caked with brittle snow.

She could not wait for the interminable shivering length of another day to pass. She felt too much alone.

When she and her companions had ridden in silence for a time, she said tentatively, 'All right. You can stop me if I ask anything dangerous. But this isn't hard only on you. It's tough for me, too. You at least have a plan.' Something to look forward to. 'I'm just lost.'

She did not want to freeze to death in the middle of nowhere for no reason which she could comprehend.

'If nothing else,' she pleaded, 'I need you to talk to me. I need to hear voices.'

Her longing for the companionship of Liand, Stave, the Ramen and even Anele was so poignant that it closed her throat.

Jeremiah seemed to consult with Covenant, although she heard nothing pass between them. Then he glanced at her sidelong. 'That's

OK, Mom,' he replied uncomfortably. 'You can ask. Just try to be careful. If the Theomach hears us, a question might cause just as much trouble as an answer.'

His willingness surprised Linden; but she did not want to miss her chance. Striving for caution, she said, 'So why does the Theomach care what we do now? Didn't he get what he wanted?' Obliquely, inadvertently, she had helped him win a place at Berek's side. 'Unless I missed something—'

He claimed that she knew his *true name*; but she had no idea what it was.

Jeremiah nodded. 'He's done with us.' Apparently he saw no danger in discussing the Insequent. 'He's where he has to be. Where he's supposed to be. He would have gotten there anyway, but you made it easier for him. He should be grateful.

'But he still wants to protect the Arch. Or he says he does, anyway. He put us here. That makes him responsible for us. If you can believe him, I mean.

'He isn't worried about *you*.' Jeremiah's tone hinted at anger. 'You he trusts. And he knows how to cover for you. But he thinks Covenant and I are capable of' – ire emphasised the muddy hue of his eyes – 'practically anything. He doesn't understand—' Swallowing convulsively, Jeremiah fell silent. Covenant rode gazing into the distance as if he had no interest in the conversation.

Cover for you? 'Understand what?' Linden asked.

Jeremiah curled his hands into fists on his mount's reins. Fiercely he retorted, 'He doesn't understand how hard we're trying to do exactly the right thing. Mom, if we deserved what he thinks of us, Covenant wouldn't have brought me to you in the first place. It isn't just insulting, it's *so* frustrating—'

Again Jeremiah stopped. This time, he made an obvious effort to master himself. When he continued, he sounded sad; pained.

'And it's a lot worse for Covenant than it is for me. We've had to endure too much Earthpower. He's holding us together. But that's not all. He's keeping what's really happening to me – what Foul is doing to my actual body—' Jeremiah shuddered. 'He's my friend. He's keeping me from going crazy.'

Then he shrugged unhappily. 'I told you I didn't like the Insequent.'

One called the Vizard had urged him to construct a snare for the *Elohim*—

His manner made Linden regret her question. 'I'm sorry, honey,' she murmured. 'I didn't mean to upset you. In a way, I can understand the Theomach's attitude. I'm your mother, and *I* forget what you're going through. You're so brave about it, you don't let it show. The truth is' – she searched their shared distress for words – 'worse than I can imagine.'

Jeremiah shrugged again. 'That's okay.' Like Covenant, he did not look at her. 'Covenant protects me pretty well.' For a moment, his tic conveyed the incongruous impression that he was winking.

Shaken by images of what the Despiser might be doing to her son, she let the hard silence of winter reclaim her. Apart from the occasional faint whisper of the breeze, the only sounds were the erratic thud and crunch of the horses' hooves, muted when they struck hard snow, sharper when they broke through crusts of ice. The plains and the hills were locked in unrelieved cold: cloudless, brilliant and punishing. Studying the sky, she found no sign of a change in the weather. Nevertheless the chill grew deeper as the terrain climbed higher. The air scraped at her throat and lungs, and the warmth that she had garnered from Yellinin's last campfire had been leeched away.

Eventually she would be forced to ask Covenant for heat. Or she would need to separate herself from her companions so that she could draw on the Staff.

Seeking distraction, she sifted her throng of questions for one to which the Theomach could not object. Finally she said, 'I was surprised that Berek found so much hurtloam.' And so close to his camp. 'I don't have much experience with it, but I've never seen that much hurtloam in one place. Is that normal?' She meant, In this time? 'It seemed too good to be true.'

Jeremiah glanced at Covenant. But Covenant rode as though he had not heard her; and after a moment, Jeremiah said, 'You don't know much about the geography of the Land,' as if he were explaining her situation to himself. 'You've never seen a map. And the Sunbane confused everything.'

Then he seemed to gather his thoughts. 'Some of it's about time.

Where we are – I mean, when – there's more of practically everything. More trees, more Forestals, more *griffins*, *quellvisks* and other monsters, more Cavewights, more powers. Between now and the time where we belong, things get used up. Or killed in Foul's wars. Or ruined by the Sunbane. Or just lost. But that's not the main reason.

'Berek found so much hurtloam, and he's going to keep finding it, because he's moving towards the Black River. The Black River comes out of *Melenkurion* Skyweir.'

Linden listened intently. Long ago, she had ridden a raft through the confluence of the Black and Mithil Rivers with Covenant and Sunder. But Covenant had told her only that the Black separated the Center Plains from the South.

'There are a lot of springs under that mountain,' Jeremiah continued. 'They come out together at the base of the cliff. Most of them are just water, but one of them is EarthBlood. It's only a trickle, but it's *intense*– When the Black River pours out into Garroting Deep, it's full of Earthpower. That's part of why the Deep is so deadly. Caerroil Wildwood draws some of his strength from the river.

'Of course, it gets diluted. The Black joins the Mithil and after that you can hardly tell it comes from *Melenkurion* Skyweir. But the Last Hills are right on the edge of Garroting Deep. From there, the power of the EarthBlood spreads into the plains.

'All that hurtloam is sort of a side-effect,' he concluded. 'Earthpower has been seeping out of the mountain practically forever. Maybe that's why the One Forest used to cover the whole Land. Back in those days – ages ago – you could have mined hurtloam along every stream and river in the Center and South Plains.'

His explanation saddened Linden. While she grieved quietly for what the Land had lost, or would lose, over the millennia, Jeremiah turned to Covenant. 'She's getting cold again,' he observed with more certitude than he usually displayed when he spoke to Covenant. 'You have to keep her warm.'

'Oh, hell,' Covenant muttered distantly, as if his thoughts were lost in Time. 'You're right. I should pay more attention.'

As before, Linden felt no invocation; discerned no rush of power. She saw only the abrupt arc of Covenant's right hand as he gestured absentmindedly, leaving a brief streak of incandescence across her vision. At once, however, heat flushed through her, banishing the cold in an instant, filling her clothes and cloak and robe with more warmth than any campfire. Her toes inside her meagre socks and thin boots seemed to burn as their numbness was swept away. When Covenant's strange theurgy faded, it left her blissfully warmed – and unaccountably frightened, as if he had given her a minuscule taste of poison; a sample of something dangerous enough to destroy her.

Presumably he protected himself – and Jeremiah – from the elements in the same fashion; but she could not *see* it.

For the rest of the day, she rode in silence, huddling into herself for courage as she huddled into her robe for protection. Covenant had suggested that he might answer her at the end of the day's ride: she needed to be ready. The nature of his power eluded her percipience. And he had already indirectly refused to explain it. Therefore his peculiar force aggravated her sense of vulnerability. She was utterly dependent upon him. If he abandoned her – or turned against her – she could keep herself warm with the Staff. She might conceivably be able to stay alive. But she would be helpless to return to her proper time.

For that reason, she contained herself while the horses trudged abjectly northwestward along the ridge of hills. At intervals, she and her companions paused to feed and water their mounts at the occasional ice-clad rill or brook, or to unwrap a little food and watered wine from one of Yellinin's bundles. But the halts were brief. Covenant seemed eager to cover as much ground as possible; and Jeremiah reflected his friend's growing anticipation or tension. Neither of them appeared to care that they were killing their animals, despite their insurmountable distance from *Melenkurion* Skyweir.

Jeremiah had implied that he and Covenant intended to use their innominate magicks for some form of translocation. And Covenant had admitted that to do so would be perilous.

Gritting her resolve, she kept her mouth shut throughout the prolonged misery of the day. Explicitly she did not ask Covenant for more heat, although Jeremiah prodded him to ease her whenever her shivering became uncontrollable. Nor did she mention that their small supply of grain and hay for the horses would not last for more than another day. Instead she fed the beasts as liberally as they needed. She could not bear to deprive them – and she had too many other worries. If necessary, she would demand more compassion from her companions later.

At last, they rode into a premature dusk as the sun sank behind the hills; and Covenant surprised her by announcing that they would soon stop for the night. She had expected him to continue onwards as long as possible, but instead he muttered, 'It's around here somewhere. We'll spot it in a few minutes.'

A short time later, Jeremiah pointed ahead. Squinting into the shadow of the hills, Covenant nodded. When Linden looked there, she saw what appeared to be a narrow ravine as sheer as a barranca between two high ice-draped shoulders of stone. Why Covenant and Jeremiah had focused their attention on this particular ravine, she could not guess. They had passed any number of similar formations since they had left Berek's camp. Nevertheless Covenant aimed his staggering mount in that direction. With Jeremiah and Linden, he rode up the ragged slope and into the deep cut of the ravine.

When the three of them had entered the defile and passed a short way along its crooked length, he halted. His voice held a note of satisfaction as he said, 'Shelter.' Then he dismounted.

Shelter? Linden wondered numbly. Here? Untouched by the sun for more than a brief time every day, the ground was frozen iron. Against one wall of the barranca lay a streambed. She could detect a faint gurgling of water under its ice. But shelter? The shape of the ravine concentrated and channelled the slight breeze of the open plains until it became a fanged wind so sharp that it seemed to draw blood. If Covenant intended to spend the night here, he would find Linden and the horses as cold and dead as the ground in the morning.

But she did not protest. Instead she slid awkwardly from her mount's back and stood shivering beside the exhausted beast, waiting for an explanation.

'Rocks,' Covenant told Jeremiah when the boy joined him. 'A big pile. Put them right by the stream. We can get water at the same time.'

Obediently Jeremiah began to gather stones, prying them out of the hard dirt as if his fingers were as strong as crowbars, and stacking them in a mound where Covenant had indicated.

Covenant looked at Linden. She could not make out his expression in the thick gloom, but he may have been grinning. 'It's these walls,' he informed her. 'All this old granite. It'll be damn near impossible for the Theomach to eavesdrop. Or anyone else, for that matter.'

Shelter, Linden thought. From being overheard. She would be able to ask as many questions as she wished – as long as Covenant kept her alive.

Apparently he did not expect a response. While she struggled to unburden and feed the horses, he went to help Jeremiah gather rocks.

When they had raised a mound the size of an infant's cairn, Covenant began to gesture at the stones, weaving a lattice of phosphenes across Linden's retinas. Almost at once, the rocks started to radiate comfort. As he sent his power deeper and deeper among them, the surface of the mound took on a dull ruddy glow. Soon the pile poured out enough heat to scald her flesh if she touched it, and some of the rocks looked like they might melt. Warmth accumulated as it reflected back and forth between the walls of the barranca until even the wind was affected: a kind of artificial thermocline deflected the frigid current upwards, away from Linden and her companions.

Gradually the ice in the streambed began to crack and evaporate. Before long, a rivulet of fresh water was exposed beside the cairn. When a wide swath of the ice had melted, the horses were able to drink their fill without standing uncomfortably near the fiery stones.

Covenant's theurgy disturbed Linden, despite her relief. Its effects lingered in her vision, but his magic itself remained hidden; closed to her senses. He could have been Anele in one of the old man's self-absorbed phases, gesturing at nothing.

When she was satisfied with the condition of the horses, she knelt beside the brook to quench her own thirst. There she noticed that the water flowed into the ravine instead of out towards the plains. She and her companions had not encountered a stream as they entered the barranca. Apparently the water was snowmelt, and the ravine's floor sloped downwards as it twisted deeper among the Last Hills.

Careful to keep his distance from Linden, Jeremiah unpacked food while she set out blankets on the softening ground. Covenant continued to gesture until he had infused the mound with so much heat that it seemed to have magma at its core. Then he lowered his halfhand. Shaking his fingers as though they had cramped, he took the last of the wine and retreated to sit against the wall of the ravine opposite the brook. There he began to drink with an air of determination, as if he wanted to insulate himself from Linden's questions. The glow of the stones seemed to light echoes in his eyes, filling them with implied flames.

She did not hurry. At a comfortable distance from the cairn, she was able to remove both her robe and her cloak, and set them near the stones to dry, without shivering. When she drew breath, her lungs did not hurt. There was no pain in her throat as she ate dried meat, stale bread and old fruit; drank more water. Under other circumstances, she might have felt soothed rather than threatened.

But she had too many questions. She needed to ask them.

Jeremiah had settled himself near Covenant against the ravine wall. Protected by blankets from the dampness of the thawing dirt, Linden sat on the floor of the barranca so that she could watch her companions' faces.

She had spent the day attempting to organise her thoughts. And she had already decided to avoid challenging Covenant directly. If she made him angry – or cautious – she might lose more than she could hope to gain. Instead of voicing her deeper concerns, she broke the silence by saying with feigned nonchalance, 'I'm just curious. What did you two do to Inbull?'

I want to repay some of this pain.

Covenant's attitude then, like his misdirections and falsehoods, violated her memories of the man he had once been.

He emptied the wineskin, tossed it aside; wiped his mouth with the back of his hand. 'Nothing much.' Obliquely Linden noticed that he was not growing a beard. His physical presence was solid, demonstrable; but it was also incomplete. 'Jeremiah held him down while I kicked him a few times. I wanted to break some of his ribs. But he's too tough. I just bruised him a bit.'

The Unbeliever snorted a laugh. 'Damelon didn't like it. For a warrior, he's still pretty squeamish. He'll have to grow out of that if he wants to make a good High Lord. But he didn't let anyone interfere.'

Linden studied him sharply, watching the alternation of embers and darkness in his gaze. Beyond question, he was not the man whom she had known. He had blamed the change on millennia of participation in the Arch of Time; but she was less and less inclined to believe him. The difference in him was too great.

She could not conceal her underlying seriousness as she changed the subject.

'I keep thinking about what happened in Berek's camp. It worries me. Is it really true that we didn't change the Land's history? How is that possible? I healed too many people,' affected too many lives. 'And too many people know about it. How can that not—?'

'Hellfire, Linden,' Covenant interrupted with apparent good humour. 'Don't waste your time on that. If you have to worry, pick something worth worrying about. It's the Theomach's problem. He brought us here. He has to clean up after us.

'I don't know how he'll do it. I could figure it out, but why should I bother? He's right where he's supposed to be. Where he would be if he hadn't interfered with me. Now it's up to him to make sure there's no damage.

'At any rate, he's serious about preserving the integrity of Time. More than anything, he doesn't want to make the *Elohim* notice him. They will if he lets history twist out of shape.'

Covenant's eyes reflected the pale crimson-orange of the cairn. 'Keeping everything on track shouldn't be hard,' he mused, 'being as how he's Berek's teacher and all. You changed some things, sure, but that can be a ripple or a thread. If he finds a way to weave what you did back into the tapestry of what's supposed to happen, there's nothing to worry about.'

'How can he do that?' Linden asked reflexively. Covenant's unconcern troubled her. He was too glib—

'Hell, Linden,' he drawled, 'you saw how effective a story can be. Mount Thunder didn't *really* talk to Berek. Or not in a way he recognised. All he did was bleed and feel desperate and mumble some nonsense he didn't understand. But he *says* the rock spoke to him, and people believe him because the Fire-Lions came to his rescue. It's how he tells the story that makes him the kind of hero his whole army is willing to die for.'

Nonsense—? She bit her lip. She was determined not to confront him; not to protest in any way. But she knew that the Seven Words were not nonsense—

'If the Theomach is clever enough when he talks about you,' Covenant continued, 'he can make it fit right in with all the old legends.

'And I won't even mention how stone-ignorant Berek is.' He snorted contemptuously. 'Eventually the Theomach is going to make him High Lord. On his own, Berek sure as hell couldn't acquire all that lore and power. He's got too far to go to be the kind of man who can find the One Tree and make a Staff of Law. He'll believe anything that damn Insequent tells him.'

As an afterthought, Covenant added, 'And I'm still part of the Arch. Did you forget that? You can't see it, but I've never stopped defending Time.'

Now Linden had to grit her teeth to stifle her protests. Covenant's scorn repulsed her. Berek did not merit his disdain.

But this was the approach which she had chosen – and this was why she had chosen it. So that Covenant would speak more openly; expose more of himself. The first words which she had heard the Theomach say were, *And do you not fear that I will reveal you?* She wanted to provoke the revelations which the Theomach had withheld.

And she did not intend to risk alienating Jeremiah any further. She had already lost too much of him, and would lose more. For his sake as well as her own, she swallowed her indignation.

Controlling herself grimly, she asked, 'What do you think, Jeremiah? Can the Theomach really protect the Land from what I've done?'

The boy shrugged without looking at her. 'Sure. It's what he's good at. He must have spent a long time learning enough about time and history to interfere with us. For him, stopping a few ripples is probably trivial.'

His reply reminded her that it was not the Theomach who had objected to the idea of summoning the Ranyhyn: it was Covenant.

'All right,' she said slowly. 'If you say so, I believe you. It's just that the Theomach confuses me.' She hesitated for a moment, then turned back to Covenant. 'You may not have heard him, but he told me that I already know his "true name". Is that even possible?'

'Of *course* it's possible,' retorted Covenant sardonically. 'It has to be. He wanted you to do things his way. If he said something like that, and you could be sure it wasn't true, he would be cutting his own throat.'

'But it can't be true,' Linden countered. 'How could it? I never even heard of the Insequent until Jeremiah mentioned them. How could I—?'

Covenant held up both hands to silence her. 'It's no good, Linden. You can't ask us that. The Theomach was right about one thing. While we're here, we can't distinguish between what you know and the Arch of Time. You've seen and heard and experienced too much about things that haven't happened yet. In fact, most of them aren't going to happen for thousands of years. If we even try to answer a question like that, the *Elohim* will erase us. They could make us disappear before we got to the second syllable.

'And since they're the fucking *Elohim*,' he sneered, 'they might not bother to put you back where you belong. They don't *approve* of messing around with Time.'

'All right.' In spite of her visceral distrust, Linden accepted his assertion. Both he and the Theomach had made the same point days ago. If they agreed with each other, she could assume that they were telling the truth – or some aspect of the truth. 'I can live with a certain amount of ignorance.

'But it would help me to know more about what we're trying to accomplish. Can you tell me why you wanted to reach the EarthBlood when Damelon first discovers it?' The Theomach had said, *The peril of your chosen path I deemed too great.* And he had explained his reasons to Linden privately. 'How would that have been better? You have so much power– Wouldn't Damelon notice us? Wouldn't that cause all kinds of trouble?'

Covenant seemed inclined to humour her. 'You should stop obsessing about the Theomach,' he said easily. 'He likes to talk, but most of what he said was bullshit. He just wanted your help.

'I could have kept Damelon from catching even a whiff of us. And Jeremiah has talents the Theomach can't grasp.' With embers for eyes,

Covenant gazed at the opposite wall. 'What we had in mind was better because we wouldn't have had to come this far back. The closer we stayed to your "present", the safer we would have been.' For a moment, his voice held a splash of acid. 'And we wouldn't have had to cope with this winter, or the distance, or Berek, or any of the other problems we have now.

'Personally, I'm going to be *delighted* when the bloody Theomach finally gets what he deserves.'

'All right,' Linden said again, sighing inwardly. 'I've been confused for so long that I'm getting used to it.' From her perspective, the difference between being nine and a half instead of ten thousand years away from her proper time was too vague to have any significance. Impelled by a growing sense of alarm, she edged closer to her more fundamental questions. 'But there's something that I really do need to know.

'Tell me if I have this right. We're trying to find the Blood of the Earth. You want to use the Power of Command to trap Lord Foul and Kastenessen. Then I can use the same Power to free Jeremiah. And get back to where I belong.'

She would never leave the Land. She was already dead in her natural reality. But Jeremiah was not: she had seen his chest unmarked by bullets.

Covenant nodded, shedding shadows and reflected fire. 'That's the general idea. But you'll have to think of a way to do everything you want with one Command. The EarthBlood is more powerful than you can imagine. No one survives tasting it twice.'

'In that case—' Linden faced her son squarely, although he still did not look at her. The emanations of the cairn felt like fever on her cheeks. 'Jeremiah, honey. I have to ask you what you want from me.

'I assume that Joan will die as soon as Lord Foul stops keeping her alive. When that happens' – her throat closed for an instant – 'you'll leave the Land.' She no longer cared that Covenant had lied about this. 'The EarthBlood might let me do something about that.

'I might be able to protect your mind. Keep it the way it is now,' although she could not be confident that any Command of Earthpower would survive the translation between realities. 'Or I can concentrate on rescuing you from wherever you're hidden. I can try to free you so that you'll be able to live the life you want here.' If she could phrase her Command to accomplish such things. 'But I can't do both. And I can't make that choice for you. It's up to you.'

She did not believe that any single act of will would affect both her and her son. She would not be able to save herself as well as him. Aiding him would doom her: she would remain where she was now. And no *caesure* would help her. Neither the Law of Death nor the Law of Life had been broken yet. If she succeeded at creating a Fall, the Arch would surely be destroyed.

When – or if – Covenant succeeded in his designs, Jeremiah would be lost to her forever.

Covenant turned his head to look at her. Slowly he rubbed his cheeks. As he did so, the echoes of heat faded from his gaze. His eyes held only darkness.

She thought that she was ready to accept her bereavement until Jeremiah said without hesitation, 'I want to stay here. With Covenant.' Then tears burst from her, as hot as the stones and as impossible to console. She was barely able to keep herself from sobbing aloud.

She had been obsessed by her desire to save Jeremiah from the Despiser, consumed by images of his torment: she had hardly considered the outcome of Covenant's designs. Now she saw what would happen.

Her desire to put her arms around her son was so acute that it cut her heart.

Stop, she told herself.

Stop.

It doesn't help.

Cold seemed to creep up her back even though the furnace of stones retained its fierce radiance.

We still have to get there.

And she did not trust Covenant.

I want to repay some of this pain.

The peril of your chosen path I deemed too great.

And I won't even mention how stone-ignorant Berek is.

This version of Thomas Covenant had lied to her about Jeremiah's circumstances as well as her own: a revealing mistake.

Deeply shaken, Linden strove to master her tears. She could not meet Covenant's scrutiny, and did not try. Instead she clung to her Staff with her head bowed until the first torrents of her dismay had passed.

She meant to ask him how he intended to reach *Melenkurion* Skyweir against *The kind of opposition that might damage the Arch.* But when she had swallowed her grief and scrubbed away her tears, she did not raise that subject immediately. Instead she asked in a raw voice, 'What about Roger?'

Glowering suddenly, Covenant turned away.

With a visible effort, Jeremiah met her gaze. The muscles at the corner of his left eye clenched and released erratically. 'What about him, Mom?'

'I don't know where he is, or what he wants, or what he's doing.' Linden was pitifully grateful to have this much of her son's attention. 'I'm pretty sure that Lytton's deputies killed him. But Anele told us that he's here. In the Land.' *Seeking such havoc that the bones of mountains tremble to contemplate it.* 'Shouldn't we be worried about him?'

Someone must have healed him during his translation, as she had healed herself with wild magic. Lord Foul? Or Kastenessen? Was the enraged *Elohim* sane enough for such a task? Joan certainly was not—

Reluctance seemed to erode Jeremiah's eyes until they slipped away from hers. 'I don't see why,' he murmured uncomfortably. 'When Covenant stops Foul, there won't be anything left for Roger to do. He's just a man. He doesn't have any power.'

He will if he can get his hands on Joan's ring, Linden thought. But she kept that fear to herself. Joan's white gold did not belong to Roger: he was not its rightful wielder. If Covenant had told her the truth about anything, Roger's ability to unleash wild magic would be limited.

But even limited wild magic—

Grimly Linden strove to appear calm. She did not want what she was thinking to show on her face.

—might be enough to release Lord Foul after Covenant snared him.

And if Roger failed or died, some other dark being might make the attempt.

Covenant's *design for the salvation of the Land* did not take Joan's ring into account. Another revealing mistake; one which might prove fatal.

Abruptly Covenant surged to his feet. Keeping his back towards Linden, he moved to stand over the small cairn as if he felt a need for heat; more heat than ordinary flesh should have been able to endure. Then he gestured along the barranca. For no apparent reason, he announced, 'This place is called Bargas Slit. Or it will be, when somebody gets around to discovering it.' He sounded strangely cheerful, despite his glower earlier. 'It has a name because it's unique. It goes all the way through. In fact, it's the only place north of the Black River where you can walk into Garroting Deep without having to climb the Last Hills.'

He may have sensed the direction of Linden's thoughts. Once again, his manner conveyed an impression of disharmony: it seemed poorly tempered, slightly off-pitch.

'We can leave the horses here. We won't need them anymore. If we get an early start, we can be at the edge of the Deep by mid-morning.'

Linden stared at his back, but he ignored her. When she looked at Jeremiah, she found him playing with his racecar, concentrating intently as the toy tumbled back and forth among his fingers.

She cleared her throat, hoping that Covenant would face her. When he did not, however, she said carefully, 'I don't understand. Didn't you say that we can't go into Garroting Deep?'

'That's right.' His tone was amiable. The heat of the rocks seemed to give him an obscure pleasure. 'And we can't go over it either. It's Caerroil Wildwood's domain. On his own turf, his power is absolute. Every bird and breeze in the whole forest needs his permission just to move from one branch to another. If we try to get past him, we'll all three of us be dead before your heart can beat twice.

'And I don't mean banished,' he said with an odd timbre of satisfaction, 'sent back where we came from. I mean stone-cold absolutely by hell *dead*. The only good part is, it'll happen so fast we won't have time to feel bad about it.'

Baffled, Linden asked, 'Then why do you want to go there? What's the point?'

'Because,' he told her without hesitation, 'there are times when it's useful to be stuck between a rock and a hard place.'

He sounded unaccountably proud of himself.

Before Linden could think of a response, he added, 'You should get some sleep. I'm serious about an early start.'

Still without looking at her, he picked up one of the blankets, returned to the place where he had been sitting and wrapped the blanket around his head and shoulders as if to conceal himself from her questions. Hidden by the dirty fabric, he seemed to blend into the wall of the ravine. The dull laval glow of the mound barely revealed his shape against the inaudible rock.

Jeremiah promptly followed his example. In moments, her son too was little more than an extrusion of the stone.

Linden had not seen either of them sleep; not once since they had entered Revelstone ten thousand years in the Land's future. Doubtless they would not slumber now. But they made it plain that they would not answer if she spoke.

Esmer had told her, *You must be the first to drink of the EarthBlood*, but she did not know what would happen to Covenant and Jeremiah if she did as Cail's son had instructed; if she tried to save her boy before Covenant could act on behalf of the Land.

Jeremiah was lost to her, no matter what she did. Nevertheless she loved him – and the Land. And she had no intention of forgetting about Roger. Or Joan's ring.

Chapter Ten:

Tactics of Confrontation

As Covenant had promised, they emerged from Bargas Slit by mid-morning; and Linden saw Garroting Deep clearly for the first time. After a long cold trudge through the constricted dusk of the barranca, she and her companions regained open sunlight no more than a stone's throw from the verge of the great forest. Behind them, the Last Hills formed a ragged, crumbling wall against the Center Plains and the rest of the Land. Ahead of them spread the vast expanse of Caerroil Wildwood's demesne, dark and forbidding as far as she could see.

Standing under the sun on the bare hillside beside the ravine's small rivulet, she felt that she was in the presence of something ancient, ineffable and threatening.

Although she stretched her health-sense, she could discern no sign of theurgy or peril; no hint of anything that resembled the numinous music which she had last heard in Andelain. She saw only trees and more trees: majestic cedars and firs interspersed with pines, occasional lambent Gilden and other evergreens clinging stubbornly to their leaves and needles; oaks, elms and sycamores, aspens and birches denuded by winter, their boughs stark and skeletal in the sunshine. A few scrub juniper, desiccated ferns and *aliantha* lived between the trunks, but for the most part uncounted centuries of fallen leaves formed a rich carpet of decay and sustenance.

Nonetheless Garroting Deep seemed irreducibly ominous. Its dark foliage and naked branches whispered warnings in the morning breeze. For millennia, the trees of the Land had suffered slaughter; and here, in their potent and baleful heart, they nurtured outrage.

Linden had hoped to catch a glimpse of the Westron Mountains, and perhaps even of *Melenkurion* Skyweir. But Garroting Deep was too wide, and too many of its trees were giants, towering monoliths as mighty as sequoias: they hid what lay beyond them.

Before dawn that morning, she had left the horses behind, as Covenant had instructed. An unavoidable decision: one of the mounts, the beast that he had ridden last, had perished during the night; and the two remaining animals could not bear three riders. Instead of using one or both of them to carry supplies, she had spilled what was left of the grain and hay to the ground and had abandoned the horses to fend for themselves. There was nothing more that she could do for them. When she had packed as much food as she could lift comfortably into a bundle which she slung over her shoulder, she had followed Covenant and Jeremiah deeper into the gloom and the scraping wind, rough as a strigil, of Bargas Slit.

Their passage along the ravine had seemed interminable and bitter; fundamentally doomed. Covenant had called Garroting Deep *the most dangerous of the old forests.* He had said that *Caerroil Wildwood is an out-and-out butcher.* Yet now he sought out that fell place and its fatal guardian. *There are times when it's useful to be stuck between a rock and a hard place.*

Standing at last in sunlight near the edge of the trees, she understood him no better than she had the previous evening. Garroting Deep was impassable. And the slopes of the Last Hills here looked even more rugged than those facing the Center Plains. Over the ages, the forest had lapped against them like a sea; had broken them into cliffs and gouges as though they had been raked by claws. Finding a route along them would be far more difficult than she had imagined.

Fortunately the atmosphere here was warmer than the winter of the Center Plains. The trees absorbed and held more of the sun's heat; or Caerroil Wildwood exerted himself to moderate the after-effects of Lord Foul's long shadow. There was no snow within the Deep itself. And the small scarps and fans of ice clinging to the hills looked porous, vaguely rotten; made frangible by evaporation and old resentment.

The journey ahead may have been impossible. Nonetheless Linden was grateful to escape the worst of the cold.

She dropped her burden so that she could rest her shoulder and arms. 'All right,' she remarked to Covenant, 'this is definitely "a rock and a hard place". How does it help us?'

'Well,' he drawled without meeting her gaze, 'that's not exactly what I meant.' He was studying the line of hills to the northwest. 'But it's a step in the right direction. For one thing, the Theomach won't be able to keep an eye on us anymore. The Last Hills have soaked up a lot of rage from the Deep. And of course,' he added sardonically, 'the stone of the Land has always sympathised with trees. All that rock and indignation will shield us pretty thoroughly.

'Which means,' he said with harsh satisfaction, 'we can finally start to travel faster.'

'But you—' Linden began, alarmed in spite of her determination to maintain a calm façade. Then she caught herself. Taking a deep breath, she asked more casually, 'Won't we be noticed? You said something about "opposition".'

'It's a risk,' he admitted. 'We'll try to minimise it. Stay below the radar.' Abruptly he glanced at Jeremiah. 'What do you think? That ridge?' He pointed. 'The one with the crescent of obsidian? Looks like about three leagues to me.'

Jeremiah considered the distance for a moment. Then he suggested, 'What about the next one? It looks like somebody took a bite out of it. I think it's a bit more than four leagues.'

'Fine.' Covenant nodded decisively. 'Your eyes are better than mine. As long as you can see it—'

At last, he turned to Linden. 'We want to do this with as little fanfare as possible.' His eyes seemed empty, devoid of embers; almost lifeless. 'The more effort we put into it, the more attention we'll attract. So we're going to move in short hops. Strictly line-of-sight. And we'll stay as close to the Deep as we can. The way the Forestal and his trees talk to each other emits a lot of background noise. Ordinary people can't hear it, but it's there. It'll make us harder to spot.'

'What are they saying?' Linden asked impulsively.

Covenant shrugged. 'How should I know? I'm not a piece of wood.'

He had claimed that he was *The keystone of the Arch of Time— I know everything. Or I can, if I make the effort.*

Jeremiah looked at her, but she could not read his expression. His soiled gaze may have held reproach or commiseration. 'Actually, Mom,' he said uneasily, 'they're talking about us.' The muscle at the corner of his left eye twitched. 'They hope we'll go into the forest. They like the taste of human blood.'

Before she could respond, he asked Covenant with his familiar diffidence, 'You're ready, aren't you?'

'Hell, yes,' muttered Covenant. 'I've been ready for days.'

Like the taste– And if they liked it so much that Caerroil Wildwood reached out past the borders of his demesne? What then?

'Just tell me one more thing,' Linden said, hurrying. 'The Theomach can't see us anymore. Having me with you is supposed to placate the *Elohim*. Whose "opposition" are you worried about?'

Covenant seemed too impatient to answer. Instead Jeremiah said, 'It's better if we don't tell you, Mom.' His tone reminded her of his anger when she had insisted on seeing whether he had been shot. 'They're more likely to notice us if we say their names.'

Ah, hell, Linden sighed. *In this circumstance, her mind cannot be distinguished from the Arch of Time.* Perhaps that made sense. In the wrong time and place, unearned knowledge could be more dangerous than ignorance. She was acutely aware of the manner in which her companions manipulated her. Nevertheless she had come too far, and had accepted too much, to infuriate Covenant and threaten her son with protests.

'All right,' she said warily. 'Just tell me what to do.'

'It's simple, really.' Jeremiah recovered his equanimity quickly. 'All you have to do is stand still. And make sure you don't touch either of us. We'll do the rest.

'We'll be using as little magic as possible, so we don't need much preparation. And we won't have to worry about wearing ourselves out. I know four leagues doesn't sound like much. But if nothing goes wrong, you'll be amazed how much progress we can make.'

Covenant kicked at the dirt with the toe of his boot, lifted his palms to the morning breeze, turned his head from side to side as if he were studying the conditions for travel. Then he said brusquely, 'Let's do it. I'm not getting any younger.'

Obeying gestures from her son, Linden retrieved her bundle, braced the severe comfort of the Staff against her chest. Reflexively she used her free hand to confirm that she still bore the unyielding circle of Covenant's ring. Then she pulled her robe more tightly around her cloak and moved to stand near Covenant.

Jeremiah positioned himself at her back: Covenant faced her. Now she seemed to see sparks or glowing coals in the deep background of Covenant's gaze. But he did not appear angry. Instead his mien suggested anticipation or fear. His strict features were distorted by a grin like a snarl.

Slowly he raised his arms until they pointed into the air above Linden's head. As he did so, he began to radiate heat as if he had eased open the door of a furnace: the conflagration of his true nature. Glancing behind her, she saw that Jeremiah had lifted his arms also. From him, she felt a mounting pressure, warm and solid; a force which would drive her to her knees if it became too strong.

In some fashion, Covenant and Jeremiah were creating a portal—

To her right, the Last Hills rose bluff and uncaring, too enwrapped in their slow contemplations to heed beings as brief as Linden and her companions. But on her left, Garroting Deep seemed to glower avidly, hungry for the taste of flesh. The cold sky and the comfortless sun covered her with their disregard.

Softly she breathed, 'I'm trusting you, Jeremiah, honey.'

She meant, Don't betray me. Don't let Covenant betray me. Please.

Then the divergent forces arching over her head combined and gathered to form a concussion as lurid as lightning, as bleak and disruptive as thunder. In that instant, everything around her ceased to exist—

—and was instantly re-created as though nothing had occurred. Covenant's arms, and Jeremiah's, held no power. The sky and the hills and the trees seemed unaltered; untouchable. The sun had not moved.

Nevertheless Linden stumbled, disoriented by the unexpected angle of the ground under her feet. Covenant and Jeremiah jumped away to avoid her as she floundered for balance. A second ago, less than a heartbeat, she had been standing on a hillside that sloped downward towards Garroting Deep. Now she found herself on a surface which tilted in the opposite direction.

She and her companions must have gained the ridge that Jeremiah had suggested: she appeared to be standing on the treeward side of a notch or gouge in one of the granite ribs of the hills. Somehow Covenant and Jeremiah had avoided arriving amid a cluster of shattered rocks nearby. Those jagged shards would surely have caused her to fall.

A sharp veering sensation unsettled her: the visceral effect of movement without transition. For a moment, she had difficulty remaining on her feet. But the hills here were distinctly themselves; beyond question not the slopes and crags which had risen above her when she had emerged from Bargas Slit. As she concentrated on their uncompromised shapes, she slowly regained her stability.

Breathing deeply, almost gasping for calm, she panted, 'Just like that.'

She felt vaguely appalled, even though she had known what would happen. As far as she could determine, no harm had been done, either to her surroundings or to any aspect of Law. The mundane physical exertion of movement had simply been replaced by an effort of theurgy. Surely she had no cause for chagrin? Yet she felt unaccountably distressed, as if she had been aided by an act of violence.

'Just like that,' agreed Covenant. Behind his apparent satisfaction, Linden heard an undercurrent of acid. 'It isn't much. But every little bit helps. And once we reach the mountains' – he gestured towards the northwest – 'we won't have to be so careful. That damn Forestal won't be able to get at us.'

His distaste for Garroting Deep was unmistakable. Yet he had chosen to come near the forest—

—*between a rock and a hard place.*

Linden remembered, aching, that Thomas Covenant had viewed the woodland beauty of Andelain with a boundless love. He had treated Caer-Caveral with respect and honour. And she herself was only frightened by the Deep's clenched anger: she understood it too well, and saw too much loveliness hidden in the heart of the forest, to be repulsed by it.

She did not comprehend the man who claimed that he was leading her to the Land's salvation.

I want to repay some of this pain.

Yet his sore ribs – like Jeremiah's battered face – had healed with remarkable celerity. And he must have known that his hurt would be brief. Under the circumstances, he might have considered it trivial. In his previous incarnation, he would certainly have done so. He had allowed Joan to hurt him repeatedly; had sacrificed himself for her—

The Thomas Covenant who had twice defeated Lord Foul would not have sought to punish Inbull.

Linden missed her former lover as sorely as she grieved for her son. Nevertheless she was forced to acknowledge that he was gone. There was no portal to that past.

Four 'short hops' later, Linden and her companions had covered fifteen more leagues – according to Jeremiah's estimates – and she found that her imbalance, her almost metaphysical sense of dislocation, was growing worse. Each succeeding rupture weakened her. More and more, the energy which Covenant and Jeremiah invoked appeared to resemble Lord Foul's iterated lightning when the Despiser had taken Joan's life. Linden had seen eyes like fangs among the savage blasts of the storm. Now she saw – or seemed to see – the Despiser's carious malice in each detonation of theurgy which bore her along the marge of Garroting Deep.

She may have been hallucinating; imagining nightmares to account for her disorientation and weakness, her loss of perceptual coherence. Nonetheless a sense of crepitation gathered in her nerves like an accumulation of static, primed for a discharge which would shred her flesh.

She had also seen Lord Foul's eyes in the bonfire which had maimed Jeremiah—

Struggling to manage her mounting paraesthesia, she begged, 'Can we take a break? Something's wrong. I need—'

'No!' snapped Covenant. 'They're aware of us now. We have to keep going.'

The strain in his voice – the strident admixture of exultation and dread – snatched at her attention.

He was sweating profusely, as if the cost of carrying his many burdens had finally begun to break down his unnatural endurance. The whites of his eyes glistened with incipient panic. His hands shook.

Wheeling to face her son, Linden saw that he too was sweating as though he had run for leagues. Alarm or concentration darkened the muddy hue of his gaze. And his mouth hung open, as slack as she remembered it: he looked like he might start to drool at any moment, lost in his personal dissociation.

The subliminal mutter of Garroting Deep's many voices had grown louder. A kind of aural brume filled the forest, ominous and inchoate, confusing Linden's percipience.

'What's happening?' she asked her son urgently. 'They're aware of us? What does that mean?'

'They're fighting us.' His chest heaved. 'Putting up barriers. We have to push our way through. If we can't outrun them—'

'Come *on*,' Covenant demanded. 'They're going to catch us.'

Immediately Jeremiah flung up his arms, casting his magic to complete the arch of Covenant's heat over Linden's head. Their blast of power blinded her; snuffed out the stubborn bulk of the hills and the crouching menace of the trees; cast her adrift.

This time, however, the wrench of movement was not instantaneous. Instead of staggering without transition, flailing to find her balance on a hillside for which her muscles were not prepared, she seemed to hang suspended in a darkness as absolute as extinction. While her heart beat frantically, she heard nothing, saw nothing; felt nothing except her own fear. The tangible world had passed away, leaving her alone in a void like the abyss between the stars.

Then, distinctly, she heard Covenant rasp, 'Hell*fire*!' Heat struck her like a hand, slapping her back into existence.

She fell. For one small instant, a tiny sliver of time, she appeared to fall interminably. Then her feet hit the slope of a steep hill, and she tumbled headlong downwards.

She lost her grip on the Staff; her bundle of food vanished in residual midnight. Instinctively she ducked her head, tucked herself into a ball. When she collided with the hard earth, the impact drove the air from her lungs, but she rolled instead of breaking.

Dirt and rock and sky whirled around her indistinguishably, too swift to be defined. There was no sunlight: she had plunged into shadow. Gloom and stones crowded around her as she rolled. Her companions and the Staff were gone. Covenant and Jeremiah were closed to her, Covenant wanted to *repay some of this pain*, but she should have been able to discern the presence of the Staff, *her* Staff, the instrument of Law which she had called into being with love and grief and wild magic.

An instant later, she felt her opportunity. Kicking out her legs, she caught herself in mid-plummet and stumbled to her feet.

Her surroundings continued to whirl, dusk and sky and bitter yearning in a vertiginous gyre. She may have splintered bones, torn open flesh: if so, her hurts brought no pain. Shock muffled everything that she might have known about herself.

Covenant and Jeremiah had disappeared, but she did not stand in shadow. As the spinning of the world slowed, she saw clear sky overhead; saw the sun. Its cold illumination should have reached her. Yet the gloom persisted. She stood near the bottom of a hollow between two outstretched ribs of the Last Hills. To her left, veiled by impossible twilight, lay the threatening wall of the forest. Through the dusk, she saw jutting plinths of stone below her, sharp spurs that strained out of the dirt like doomed fingers clutching for air and open sky; release. Among them, she thought that she recognised the shape of her bundled supplies.

A few steps farther down the slope, near the jagged stones, she saw the unmistakable length of her Staff. Its clean wood glowed softly in the eldritch twilight.

But Covenant— Her son—

'Linden!' Covenant shouted.

Jeremiah called, 'Mom!'

She barely heard them. Their voices were wrapped in dusk, muted and unattainable: they seemed to come from some other dimension of reality, a plane beyond her grasp. She would have tried to answer them, but she had no air in her lungs; had forgotten how to breathe.

Stiff-kneed and lurching, she made her way down into the hollow to reclaim the Staff.

'*Linden!*' Covenant may have howled, raging. 'Hell and *blood!*' But she could not be certain that she heard him.

As soon as her fingers closed on the immaculate surface of the wood, a taste of Law flowed into her, and she regained an aspect of herself. Gasping, she began to suck air fervently into her lungs. Between one heartbeat and the next, she discovered that she had suffered a dozen scrapes and bruises, but had broken nothing. A moment of the Staff's flame – only a moment – would be enough to ease her battered condition. If she dared to raise power in this preternatural shadow, and could be sure that Jeremiah and Covenant would not suffer for it—

She restrained herself, however. The comfort of the Staff in her hands was enough to sustain her until she could determine why her son's voice and Covenant's reached her as though they occupied some other time and place, a world beyond her grasp.

The sun shone on the Last Hills and Garroting Deep, but its light did not touch her. It could not illumine the hollow, or the straining stones, or the consequences of her fall.

'Mom!' Jeremiah called from the far side of the heavens. 'Can you hear me?'

She should have tried to respond. But her throat was full of twilight and trepidation: she seemed to have no words and no voice. Moment by moment, the Staff reawakened her health-sense. She felt *intentions* in the caliginous air. An impression of purpose and desire swirled about her as though the gloom were mist. She was in the presence of sentience, encompassed by a being or beings as impalpable as thought, and as analytic.

Puissant beings– They're going to catch us.

But her perceptions remained vague, as disquieting as a badly smeared lens: they spurned accuracy. Instead her paraesthesia intensified in spite of her grasp on the Staff. She saw the sound of her own hoarse breathing as if it emerged from her mouth in twisted blotches of distress. In the gloom, she heard shapes and precision which her senses were too blunt to identify. The cold was the distant clatter and collision of thunder. Her hurts smelled like bile, tasted like sulfur.

Confusion filled her sight, muffling her companions' shouts. Evening crept along her skin like the play of ruinous fingers: it probed her flesh to determine who and what she was. Loud forms twisted and squirmed around her, evanescent as tendrils, dangerous as tentacles; but an eerie delinition prevented her from hearing them clearly.

Somewhere beyond her, Jeremiah was saying, howling, murmuring, 'Covenant, they've got her! The Viles! They don't want us. They want *her*.'

The shadow had a voice which she could not hear. They had voices which surpassed her senses, etiolating Jeremiah's fright, forcing her to mistake the colour of her own heartbeat. At the same time, however, she felt crepuscular ropey streamers coalesce into deeper darkness: she saw them speak. They had only one voice, but they were many. They said many things. She saw one of them – or saw several of them one at a time.

Limned in condensation and grue, the voice announced, **Her,** as if it had heard Jeremiah. **Of course. How should it be otherwise?**

Distinctly she heard tentacles curl and shift; saw them pronounce, **The others are perilous. They have power. They exert themselves.** And they responded to themselves, **Yet hers is as great, and she does not. Within her she holds the devastation of the Earth,** yet she permits the others to have their will.

It is unseemly, the same voice said or answered. **It is a mystery.** And again, or differently: **Our lore does not account for this.**

With the nerves of her skin, Linden felt Covenant raging, *'Hellfire, Linden! Give me my ring! Just throw it. I'll catch it. I can't protect you without my ring!'*

Viles, she thought dimly. Sensory distortion made a writhen vapour of her mind. She could not think consecutively. Covenant wanted his ring. The beings around her were Viles, the makers of the Demondim: absent in her proper time, but present here. He had always wanted his ring, ever since he had first ridden into Revelstone with Masters and Jeremiah.

Spectres and ghouls. Tormented spirits.

Esmer had tried to warn her. Instead of answering her most necessary questions, he had described the history of the Viles and Demondim.

Her former lover hungered for wild magic: he craved it *to repay some of this pain,* although he had not said so.

Fragments of the One Forest's lost soul. Creatures of miasma, evanescent and dire.

Do you not know, Esmer had asked her, *that the Viles were once a lofty and admirable race?*

It must be extinguished. The voices spoke to themselves, wisps and tendrils of elusive, impermeable darkness, using words which Linden could see but not hear, feel but not smell or taste.

It does not concern us. In the swirl of shadow, she recognised hebetude, condescension, disdain. **It does not interest us.**

New possibilities are coming to life. Old powers are changing.

It interests us intimately, an image or sensation argued. **She is a lover of trees.**

She is. Still she does not concern us.

Deliracy possessed her, a whirl of memory and confusion as lurid as fever, gravid as nightmare. Eidolons spoke so vividly that she winced. *I can't do it without you.* At the same time, Esmer continued his remembered impatient peroration. *For an age of the Earth, they spurned the heinous evils buried among the roots of Gravin Threndor—*

'Damnation, Linden!' Covenant's fury crawled down her spine. *I can't help you unless you find me.* 'Give me my ring!'

—and even in the time of Berek Lord-Fatherer no ill was known of them.

Ravers did this, she thought disjointedly. Esmer had told her so. Sounds danced around the desperate fingers of stone. *Just be wary of me. Remember that I'm dead.* She could not escape the rampant blurring discontinuity in her nerves, the disorder of her mind. The Ravers *began cunningly to twist the hearts of the sovereign and isolate Viles.*

Still words effloresced in the hollow. **She does. She must be extinguished. Her power must be extinguished.**

With whispers and subtle blandishments, and by slow increments, the Ravers obliquely taught the Viles to loathe their own forms.

Other shapes and images agreed. **We will not survive her presence.**

Their transformation had begun with *mistrust and contempt towards the surviving mind of the One Forest, and towards the Forestals.*

Somewhere beyond or beneath perception, Jeremiah replied, 'She can't hear you. They've overwhelmed her. She's lost.'

Linden, find me.

Lost, she echoed. Oh, yes. Nothing in her life had equipped her to disentangle such chaos. If she could have lifted her fingers to the ring hanging from its chain around her neck, she might have drawn it over her head and tossed it aside, abdicating its indelible responsibility. But even that effort surpassed her. Her grasp on the Staff of Law was all that preserved her from tentacles of twilight, and she clung to it with both hands.

Survive her presence—? That made no sense. She posed no threat to such creatures. Even Covenant's plans would not affect the fate of the Viles. Heeding the Ravers, they had decided their own doom.

Is that cause for regret? multifarious voices countered in visions, pictographs, as ultimate as ebony. **It is not. We are not what we were.**

And she is a lover of trees. Another Vile – or the same Vile in another avatar. **Let her destroy them as she does us. She will reproach herself hereafter. We will be spared.**

Spared? Linden saw indignation. **Do you name extinction 'spared'?**

We do. Existence is tedium. Naught signifies. What are we, that we should seek to prolong it?

–a lover of trees. In spite of her fragmentation, the reiteration of that accusation touched something deep within her, some delitescent capacity for passion and choice. She was Linden Avery, a lover of trees in all sooth. Long ago, her health-sense had opened her to the vital loveliness of the woods and blooms and greenswards of Andelain. Their beauty had exalted her when she had taken hold of Vain and Findail with wild magic in order to fashion a new Staff of Law. Now she grasped that Staff in her mortal hands.

Because she was who she was, and did not mean to fail, she opened her mouth so that a shape could emerge into the swirling, interwoven gloom. It formed a yellow moiré, oneiric and tenuous.

'Why?'

In response, she smelled surprise. As it bled across her senses, its tang was unmistakable.

She speaks, one or all of the Viles displayed across her vision. And one or several replied, **What of it? It is not lore.** And again: **Ignorance and falsehood guide her kind.** Their boredom reeked. **It was ever so. They are a pestilence which the Earth endures solely because their lives are brief.**

Were the Viles *lofty and admirable*? Perhaps they had once been. Perhaps they remained so. In the texture and hue of their voices, however, Linden discerned the black urgings of *moksha, turiya* and *samadhi*.

They also do not concern us.

Under other circumstances, she might have been appalled. Now she was not. She had uttered a single word – and the Viles had heard her.

'Why?' she repeated. Her voice was fulvous in the imposed twilight; tinged with brimstone. 'Why are you here? Why do you care? This doesn't have anything to do with you.'

Another scend of surprise stung her nose, her eyes. Tears ran like stridulation down her cheeks.

She does not merely speak. She speaks to us. She desires to be heard.

What of it? they answered themselves in knots and coils of darkness. **She holds great powers without lore. No word of hers has meaning here.**

Have done with this, several Viles urged at once. **Extinguish her. Her life does not profit us.**

Others disagreed. She saw their severity as they answered, **When power speaks, it is wisdom to give heed.**

And still others: **When have we ever done otherwise?** And others, contemptuously: **In what fashion does unexercised power imply wisdom?**

Their debate made her stronger. She held the Staff of Law. And they were divided in their desires. They were Viles, on the cusp of learning to despise themselves.

The *Elohim* considered her the Wildwielder. If they were right, the Viles should have feared her. She might bring Time and all existence to an end.

'You can hear me,' she pronounced, speaking now in lambent chrysoprase and jacinth rather than saffron blots. 'I deserve an answer. If you think that you have the right to destroy me, you owe me an explanation. I haven't done anything to you. I wouldn't harm you if I could.

'Why are you here?'

Semiprecious gems winked and hinted among the streaming tendrils. Then they were gone.

We will not heed her. Disdain and scruples crept over her skin. **We must.**

Before she could insist on a reply, all or several or one of the Viles stated in stark obsidian, **Lover of trees, we are here because the others exert hazardous theurgies – and you permit them, holding powers which have no need of theirs. Your folly compels us. The wood that you claim must defy them, yet it does not.**

Simultaneously other avatars proclaimed, **You strive towards Melenkurion Skyweir and the Power of Command. But the master of white gold has no use for the EarthBlood, and its Power cannot Command wild magic.**

You serve a purpose not your own, and have no purpose.

The voices daunted her. Her commingled senses confounded her. The Viles knew too much – and yet they did not know enough to recognise their true peril. Nor could they comprehend her love for her son. They were not mortal.

We will not survive—

The wood that you claim must defy them—

They had answered her. Yet they had not told her what she wanted to know.

Shaping her bafflement into a form of persistence, she said, 'No. Not that.' Now the words emerged as emerald and malachite; reified consternation. 'I've already told you. That doesn't have anything to do with you.

'Why are you *here*? In this part of the Land? You live in the Lost Deep.' *—in caverns as ornate and majestic as castles.* 'If you weren't so far from where you belong, you wouldn't know or care about us.'

There they devoted their vast power and knowledge to the making of beauty and wonder, and all of their works were filled with loveliness.

Covenant and Jeremiah may have continued calling to her, but she could not feel their voices.

This time, the surprise of the Viles smelled of decay and old rot; mouldering. **She has lore. To assume ignorance misleads us.**

She does not, they declared scornfully. **No mere human knows of our demesne.**

Separately and in unison, one at a time, together, they announced, **She has been taught. Advised. Therefore she hazards devastation.**

Therefore, they concluded, **she must be answered.**

Therefore, they also decided, **she must not.**

Their darkness gathered until it threatened to blot out the sun. **Are we not Viles? Do we fear her?** If they chose to extinguish her, they would be able to do so. The bewilderment of her senses left her vulnerable.

When she fell, they might claim Covenant's ring—

Yet she saw them pronounce clearly, **We do not.**

We do not, they agreed. **We also have been advised.**

Their ire and assent as they answered her smelled as mephitic as a charnel. **Lover of trees,** they flared like a plunge into a chasm, lightless and unfathomable, **we have learned that this remnant of forest despises us. Its master considers us with disdain. We have come to discover the cause of his contumely. We have done naught to merit opprobrium among the woodlands.**

Linden might have been horrified; incapable of argument. But Esmer had prepared her for this. *That which appears evil need not have been so from the beginning, and need not remain so until the end.* Hidden among his betrayals were gifts as precious as friendship.

In shapes as ready as knives, colours as obdurate as travertine, she countered, 'That's a lie. You were "advised". You said so. By the Ravers. But they didn't tell you the truth. These trees don't despise you. They're too busy grieving. It's humans they hate. My kind. Not yours.'

'Damnation,' said Covenant in a visceral mutter, a sensation of squirming across Linden's defenceless skin. 'She's trying to *reason* with them.'

'I told you.' Jeremiah's voice made no sound, but she could see it. It was crimson, the precise hue of blood; bright with disgust and grudging admiration. 'I remember her. She doesn't give up.'

'Then we'll have to do it.' Covenant's reply itched like swarming ants. 'Get ready.'

Linden's heart yearned for her companions. But she ignored them. She could not reach them now. Surrounded by Viles and implicit death, she had brought herself to a precipice, and could only keep her balance or die.

The makers of the Demondim might resolve their hermetic debate by snuffing out her life. But the risks if she swayed them were no less extreme. Contradicting the seductions of the Ravers, she might irretrievably alter the Land's history. A cascade of consequences might spread throughout time. If the Viles did not learn to loathe themselves, they would not create the Demondim – who would in turn not create—

With every word, she risked the Arch of Time.

Nevertheless she did not allow herself to hesitate or falter. Here, at least, she believed that calamity was not inevitable. The Law of Time opposed its own disintegration. And the effects of what she did might well prove temporary. Her arguments might do nothing more than delay the gradual corruption of the Viles.

The wood that you claim must defy them, yet it does not.

'Sure,' she continued as though her companions had not spoken, 'the Forestal is angry. His trees have been slaughtered. But his rage isn't aimed at you. If you don't threaten Garroting Deep, he won't even acknowledge that you're here.'

Risking everything, uttering sulfur and incarnadine to the gloom, she averred, 'You've been lied to. You're being manipulated. The Ravers hate trees. They want you to do the same. Not because they care about you. Not because you're in any danger. They just want you to start *hating*.' Extinguishing. 'If you do that enough, you'll end up just like them.'

All contempt turns upon the contemptuous, as it must.

For an immeasurable time, the Viles were silent. Linden felt serpentine darkness coil and twist around her, a nest of snakes and self-dissent; smelled subterranean stone and dust, caves so old and deeply buried that they may have been airless. *Get ready.* Jeremiah and Covenant had reached a decision, but it lay beyond her discernment. Sensory confusion cut her off from everything except the hollow and the dusk.

Then all or some of the black tendrils repeated, **She has lore.** And others insisted, **It is not lore. It is given knowledge. She has been taught. She merely holds powers which surpass her.**

They debated among themselves, gathering vehemence with every assertion. **Then the others must concern us.**

They do not. They are no mystery to us.

This contention is foolish. The fierceness of the voices blinded Linden. She no longer saw sounds: she felt them. They scraped along her skin like the teeth of a rasp. **We cannot accuse her. She has spoken sooth. We also are moved by given knowledge. Have we not heeded those who report that we are despised?**

We have. What of that? We seek only comprehension. The intent of her companions is far otherwise. And she consents by withholding her strength. For that reason, we confront her.

Unrestrained anger. **For that reason, she must be extinguished.**

Stern contradiction. **For that reason, she must be understood. Her inaction requires justification.**

As one, the voices turned against Linden. **Give answer, lover of trees. Why do you permit the purposes of the others, when you have no need of it?**

There her determination stumbled. The Viles' question was more fatal than their ire. *In this circumstance, her mind cannot be distinguished from the Arch of Time.* How could she explain herself without violating the strictures of history? Her choices could only be justified by events which had not yet occurred; events which would not occur for thousands of years. If she answered, the repercussions would exceed any hope of containment.

Desperately she countered the challenge of the Viles with one of her own.

'You aren't thinking clearly. You've got it backwards. Before you question me, you have to question yourselves. Why do you listen to *Ravers?* Don't you realise that they're lying? Beings like you?' –*lofty and admirable*– 'I can't answer you if you aren't able to recognise the difference between truth and lies.'

Instantly the twilight grew darker. She saw only stark ebony as if it were the benighted hearts of the Viles. The scents of offal and new blood and repudiation were flung into her face. The ground under her boots thrummed as though the bones of the Last Hills had begun to vibrate. The taste of dead branches and twigs filled her mouth, as bright as brass.

Voices clawed at her skin. **She dares to speak so. To us.** When they replied to themselves, they spoke in fangs. **Yet she speaks sooth. We have heeded that which desires only slaughter.**

We seek comprehension.

We seek meaning. Our lives are sterile.

Nonetheless their vehemence no longer threatened Linden. Their conflict did not include her. If she felt savaged by it, that was a side-effect of their black theurgy.

They uttered falsehood. What of that? they countered. **They also spoke sooth.**

Truth may mask lies. It may mislead.

Yet it was indeed sooth. Was it not? Have we not acknowledged that it was?

We have. We were informed without chicane that we are self-absorbed spectres, affectless and wasted. The loveliness which we devise and adore is without meaning or purpose. Our lore is great, and our strength dire, yet we are but playthings for ourselves. This is sooth. We have acknowledged it.

Linden groaned. She flinched at the touch of every claw and tooth. There could be no question about it: the Ravers had been at work. She recognised their malignancy, their acid gall.

And have we not also acknowledged that therefore we may be deemed paltry by the wider world? Have we not come to this place seeking truth? Is not our first purpose to determine if the Forestal indeed views us with scorn? Only when that is known can we consider the cause of his scorn.

Yet is not our reasoning flawed, as the lover of trees has proclaimed?

She is specious. Unjustified. Her own reasoning is flawed.

No, she wanted to protest. *No.* Everything that you heard from those Ravers was a lie. Even if it sounded like the truth. You can't *listen*—

But she had no voice and no will: she hardly seemed to think. The mounting debate left her mute as well as blind; nearly insensate. She had come to the end of words as though it were the end of worlds.

Agreed, the Viles continued, scoring her flesh, rending her courage. Yet our reasoning is also flawed. We acknowledge that we are self-absorbed and affectless. But we mislead ourselves if we conclude that therefore we are deemed paltry. The attitude of the wider world cannot be inferred from the disdain of those whom she names Ravers.

No. We have not erred in that fashion. We have come to this woodland that we might distinguish truth from falsehood.

We have erred in precisely that fashion. We have come to this woodland expecting to discover that we are scorned. We have been taught scorn for ourselves. Is this wisdom? Is it just? Do we merit disdain because we have clung to loveliness, ignoring the concerns of the Earth?

That's it! Linden fought to say; to confirm. That's what the Ravers want. —scorn for ourselves. But still she could not speak. Somehow the Viles had silenced her. They would not permit her to intrude on their dissension.

When she felt Covenant's voice roar through her clothes, 'Now, Linden! *Run!*' she did not hesitate, although she could not tell where she was and had no idea where she was going.

She feared a collision with the upthrust stones; feared falling; feared the outrage of the Viles. She could hardly be certain that she still held the Staff of Law. Every step carried her from nothing to nothing. Under her feet, the packed dirt sounded as unsteady as water: it felt as suffocating as a cave-in. Nevertheless she attempted to flee, seeking the tone or scent of higher ground.

For an instant, she thought that she heard the Viles muster black madness against her. But then a gap opened in her writhing paraesthesia. Through it, she felt Covenant hurl a torrent of heat and fire down into the hollow, power as liquid as magma, and as destructive. At the same time, Jeremiah's unexplained magic gathered until it seemed to tower over the forest. Then it crashed like a shattered wall down onto the trees of the Deep.

Chaos erupted among the Viles; rage and force virulent enough to strip flesh from bones. Simultaneously, however, the disruption faded from Linden's senses, swept aside by Covenant's fire, or by the horrendous response of the Demondim-makers. In that swift rush of clarification, time and her frantic breathing and even the urgent throb of her heart: all seemed to stop at once.

In tiny increments, miniscule fragments of infinity, she saw the hillside under her feet; saw herself striving to run diagonally up the slope towards Covenant and Jeremiah; saw the Staff clenched in her urgent fist. Above her, Covenant faced the Viles with heat spouting viciously from his halfhand. While she watched, the creatures parted like mist to evade his attack, then swirled together to concentrate their corrosive theurgy.

A mere shard of an instant later, she saw Jeremiah standing near Covenant with his back to the Viles, flinging repulsion like frenetic blows into Garroting Deep. Exposed. Defenceless—

The sides of the hollow blocked Linden's view of the Deep. Nevertheless she felt as well as heard an abrupt cavalcade of music among the trees.

It shocked her; held her nearly immobile in mid-stride while slivers of time accumulated to create a single moment. The leaves sang a myriad-throated melody of ineffable loveliness while the twigs and boughs contributed chords of aching harmony and the trunks added a chaconne as poignant as a lament. Each note seemed as pristine and new as the first dew of springtime, dulcet as daisies, thorny as briars. Together the thousands upon thousands of notes fashioned a song of such heartbreaking beauty that Linden would have wept to hear it if she had not been trying feverishly to run – and if her companions had not stood in the path of havoc.

Within the profound glory of the music lay a savage power. Her nerves were stunned by the sheer magnitude of the magic which the singing summoned. It was not merely beauty and grief: it was also a tsunami of rage. Somewhere beyond the hillside, Caerroil Wildwood must have come to the verge of the Deep; and there he sang devastation for every living being that opposed him.

Separately the Viles and the Forestal were potent enough to banish Covenant and her son, *her son*. Together their energies would rend both of her loves. Jeremiah and Covenant would not simply disappear: they would perish utterly.

Without Covenant's support, the Arch of Time itself might be undone.

Then we'll have to do it. Get ready.

She could not reach them; could do nothing to protect them.

She had scarcely finished one stride and begun the next, however, when Covenant and Jeremiah turned away from their peril. Running headlong, they sprinted down the slope towards her. Again Covenant yelled, '*Now*, Linden!'

Behind them, a tremendous explosion shook the hills as focused serpentine vitriol struck lucent melody. The impact seemed to jolt the sky, jarring the sun, spilling winter brightness back into the hollow: it made the ground under Linden's boots pitch and heave. At once, time began to race like Covenant and Jeremiah, like Linden herself, as if opposing forces had knocked the interrupted moments loose to bleed and blur. The Viles released an unremitting gush of black unnatural puissance. Caerroil Wildwood sang in response, using the given lore of the *Elohim* and the sentient Earthpower of trees by the millions. Suddenly Linden and her companions were able to close the gap between them.

'Now!' Covenant panted yet again. 'While they're fighting each other!'

She stopped as if he had commanded her; as if she understood him.

Scrambling to a halt, he and Jeremiah positioned themselves on either side of her, front and back. They flung up their arms. Against a background of incompatible magicks as flagrant as an avalanche, she felt their powers rise. She had time to think, They *did* this, they tricked—

There are times when it's useful to be stuck between a rock and a hard place.

Then thunder or lightning arched over her head, and everything vanished as though her existence had been severed with an axe. During the immeasurable interval between instants, she and her companions fled.

Without transition, the acrid midnight of the Viles and the angry music of the Forestal sprang into the distance. Unbalanced by the shifting ground, Linden stumbled; flung out her arms to catch herself. Then, still reeling, she looked wildly around her.

Covenant and Jeremiah had brought her to the ridge of another twisted rib among the Last Hills. On one side, the slopes rose into intransigent bluffs and crags: with each translocation, their resemblance to nascent mountains increased. On the other, Garroting Deep lapped against the hills as though the trees had been caught by winter and cold in the act of encroaching on their boundaries. With her first unsteady glance, Linden saw no significant change in the forest. Slight variations in the textures of the woodland: trees differently arranged. Nothing more. Yet she sensed that the intentions of the Deep had been altered at their roots.

The forest no longer hungered for human flesh. Instead Garroting Deep's mood had become outrage, and its appetite was focused elsewhere.

In the southeast, at least two or three leagues away, the Viles and Caerroil Wildwood made war on each other. Their might was so intense that Linden could descry each scourging strike of scorn and blackness – and each extravagant note, each instance of pure fury, in the Forestal's vast song. Rampant obsidian and glory were plainly visible, hectic and unappeased, against the horizon of the hills. Even here, the ground trembled at the forces which the combatants hurled at each other.

Both Covenant and Jeremiah had dropped to their knees to avoid Linden's floundering. But Jeremiah still held his arms high. From them, energies poured upwards as if he sought to ward away or channel the collapse of the sky. The muscles at the corner of his eye sent out messages which she could not interpret.

A heartbeat later, wood began to rain from the empty air. Deadwood, twisted and knaggy: leafless twigs and branches of every size and shape, all broken by weather or theurgy from what must once have been a majestic oak. Linden and her companions could have been beaten bloody or killed by the sudden downpour. But Jeremiah's power covered them. Twigs as slender as her fingers and boughs as thick as a Giant's leg rebounded in mid-plunge and toppled to the dirt in a crude circle around the rim of Jeremiah's protection.

Unbalanced by shock and surprise, Linden braced herself on the Staff. Too much had happened too quickly: her nerves could not accommodate it. She still seemed to see the speech of the Viles blooming darkly in her vision, clawing at her skin. All of that wood had fallen from the featureless sky, and she had done her utmost to sway the makers of the Demondim from their doom.

But she had failed. *—a rock and a hard place.* The Viles would never forgive the forests of the Land now. They had *learned the loathing of trees—*

Almost at once, Covenant jumped to his feet. 'Get to it,' he snapped at Jeremiah. 'We don't have much time.' Then he faced Linden. 'Do what I tell you,' he demanded harshly. 'Don't ask questions. Don't even think. We're still in danger. We need you.'

She did not think. When she said, 'You tricked them,' she was surprised to hear herself speak aloud. 'The Viles and the Forestal.' Like Covenant, Jeremiah had leapt upright. In a rush, he gathered the deadwood, tossing or tugging the heavier branches into a pile, throwing twigs by the handful among them. 'You made them think that they were attacking each other.'

And she had helped him. Her attempts to reason with the Viles had distracted them—

'Damnation, Linden!' yelled Covenant. 'I told you—!' But then he made an obvious effort to control himself. Lowering his voice, he rasped, 'We don't have time for this. I know you feel overwhelmed. But we can't afford a *discussion* right now.

'The Viles aren't stupid. They're going to figure out what happened. They'll know who to blame. If that damn Forestal stops *singing* at them, they'll come after us. And even *he* can't hold them. Any minute now, they'll find a way to evade him.

'Linden, we *need* you.'

Tense with purpose, Jeremiah hurried around the circle of wood, collecting branches of all sizes.

Linden was not sure that she could move. If she tried to take a step, she might collapse. Covenant had told her not to think. She seemed to have no thoughts at all.

'Can't you outrun them?'

'Hellfire!' Blood or embers flared in his eyes. 'Of *course* we can outrun them. *If we have time*. But they can move pretty damn fast. We need *time*.'

As soon as they broke off their engagement with Caerroil Wildwood—

'You planned all of this,' she responded dully. 'Or you planned for it.'

'Snap out of it!' Covenant retorted, yelling again. 'Do what I tell you!'

Already Jeremiah had gathered half of the torn and splintered wood. In the distance, combat blazed and volleyed, wreckage against song, burgeoning disdain against ancient wrath.

'Where did all this wood come from?' she asked. 'What's it for?'

'*Linden!*' Covenant protested: a howl of frustration.

But Jeremiah paused, sweating despite the cold. 'There was a dead oak at the edge of the trees,' he said without looking at her. 'Or almost dead. Anyway, it had a lot of dead branches. I hit it. We picked up the wood when we escaped. We're going to need it when we get to *Melenkurion Skyweir*.'

Abruptly he resumed his task.

Trying to think, Linden wondered, Torches? Campfires?

But Jeremiah had broken enough boughs for a full bonfire – and most of them were too large to be carried as torches.

She gave it up: it was beyond her comprehension. The after-effects of synaesthesia left her in disarray. Her synapses seemed to misfire randomly, afflicting her with instants of distortion and bafflement. Sighing, she made an effort to stand without the support of the Staff.

'All right,' she murmured to Covenant. 'We don't have time. This makes me sick. What do you want me to do?'

She could not imagine how she might impede the pursuit of the Viles.

'Finally!' Covenant growled.

'Go down there,' he told her at once, indicating the southeastward slope of the ridge. 'Twenty or thirty paces. That should give us enough room. Use the Staff. Make a Forbidding. As big as you can. That won't stop them, but it'll slow them down. They'll want to understand it.'

Linden peered at him, blinking vaguely. 'What's a Forbidding?'

'Hell and blood!' Now his anger was not directed at her. 'I keep forgetting how ignorant—' Grimly he stopped himself. For a moment, he appeared to study the air: he may have been searching through his memories of time. Then his gaze returned, smouldering, to hers. 'Don't worry about that. What we need is a wall of power. *Any* kind of power. It just has to be dangerous. And it has to cover that whole hillside.

'Go,' he insisted, gesturing her away. 'Do it *now*.'

Linden watched her son piling wood. In some sense, Covenant was telling her the truth. She felt the garish battle in the distance shift as the Viles adjusted their tactics to counter Caerroil Wildwood's clinquant melodious onslaught. The creatures might soon break free. She took a step or two, still gazing at Jeremiah with supplication in her eyes. *Please*, she had tried to urge him earlier. *Don't betray me*.

She did not understand why he needed so much wood.

And she could not conceive of any barrier except fire.

Fire on the verge of Garroting Deep.

Hardly aware of what she did, she trudged downwards. Her mind was full of flames. Flames at the edge of the forest. Flames which might leap in an instant to dried twigs and boughs. If she did not tend them constantly, keep them under control, any small gust of wind might—

Lover of trees.

Still she descended the hillside, trying to find her way through memories of twisted blackness, solid irruptions of sound, music that should have been as bright and beautiful as dew. What choice did she have? They're going to figure out what happened. They'll know who to blame. She had baited a trap by trying to reason with the Viles. They would attempt to kill Covenant. They would certainly kill her son. Moment by moment, Caerroil Wildwood was teaching them to share his taste for slaughter.

But *fire*—? So close to Garroting Deep? The Forestal would turn his enmity against her. If any hint of flame touched the trees, she would deserve his wrath.

As she moved, however, she grew stronger. That simple exertion reaffirmed the interconnections of muscles and nerves and choice: with each pace, she sloughed away her confusion. And when she had taken a dozen steps, she began to sip sustenance from the Staff, risking the effect of Law on Covenant and Jeremiah. That strengthened her as well.

By degrees, she became herself again. She began to think.

What would happen if she raised a wall of fire *here*?

Caerroil Wildwood would see it. Of course he would. And he would respond— For the sake of his trees, he would forego his struggle with the Viles in an instant.

Then the Viles would be released to pursue the people who had tricked them. Linden and her companions would be assailed by both forces. It was even conceivable that the Forestal and the Viles would form an alliance—

If that happened, what she knew and understood of the Land's history would be shattered. The ramifications would expand until they became too fundamental to be contained.

Covenant was urging her to hazard the Arch of Time.

You serve a purpose not your own, and have no purpose.

He and Jeremiah had decided to set Caerroil Wildwood and the Viles against each other before they had entered Bargas Slit. They may have decided it days ago. And they had kept it from her.

In the distance, the battle raged on. The Viles may have been trying to disengage, but they had not succeeded.

'No.' Linden did not shout. She did not care whether or not Covenant heard her. 'I won't do it. I won't. It's too dangerous.' Turning sharply, she began to stride back up the slope. 'You'll have to think of something else.'

Quenching the Staff so that it would not imperil her companions, she approached them with her refusal plainly written on her face.

'Linden, God *damn* it!' Covenant raged down at her. Wailing like a child, Jeremiah protested, '*Mom!*'

She ignored them until she was near enough to meet Jeremiah's stricken stare, Covenant's hot ire. Then she stopped.

'It's too dangerous,' she repeated as if she were as resolute as Stave, as certain as Mahrtiir. 'Fire is the only barrier that I know how to make. I won't risk the trees.

'If you can't outrun the Viles, you'll have to come up with another plan,' another trick.

God, she missed Thomas Covenant: the man he had once been. Her disappointment in her companions was too profound for indignation.

They froze, poised on the brink of eruptions. Briefly their disparate faces mirrored each other. In them, Linden saw, not alarm or dismay, but naked anger and frustration. Jeremiah's eyes were as dark as blood. Ruddy heat shone from Covenant's gaze. She had time to think, They don't care about the Deep. Or Caerroil Wildwood. Or me. Maybe they don't even care about the Arch. They just want to do what they've been planning all along.

Then together Covenant and Jeremiah wheeled and ran, rushing to collect the last twigs and branches.

A moment later, they were done: their pile of deadwood was complete. In the distance, music and vitriol vied for harm. Quickly Covenant and Jeremiah moved to stand facing each other, leaving space between them for Linden and the Staff.

Grieving, she entered the ready arch of their arms.

According to Jeremiah, their next dislocation took them four leagues farther along the Last Hills. Another burst of power crossed five. Then three. Then five again. Indirectly they violated time rather than space: they excised the hours and effort necessary to travel such distances.

Their mound of broken wood accompanied them through every

imponderable leap. Somehow they drew it with them without enclosing it in their arc of power.

Eventually they stopped. While Linden stumbled to her knees, utterly disoriented by the shifting ground and the veering horizons, the unsteady stagger of the world, Covenant and Jeremiah retreated from her. 'This should be far enough.' Covenant seemed to struggle for breath. 'We can rest here. At least for a few minutes.'

The anger in his voice was as raw as his respiration.

Linden's head reeled: her entire sensorium foundered. She could not discern any sign of the distant battle.

'Covenant,' Jeremiah gasped. He sounded more tired than irate. 'This isn't a surprise.' He may have been warning his only friend. 'She is who she is. She's never going to trust us. Not until we prove ourselves.'

Breathing deeply, Linden lifted her head; focused her eyes on the Staff of Law and refused to blink until it no longer yawed from side to side. Through her teeth, she insisted, 'It was too dangerous.'

'Dangerous how?' asked Covenant. His tone had become level despite his hard breathing. Apparently he had decided to curb his anger. 'All you had to do was give me my ring.'

When she was sure of the ground under her, she climbed to her feet. 'Not that,' she said, trembling. 'Fire. The only barrier that I know how to make. I might have broken the Arch.'

Jeremiah did not look at her. His face was slick with sweat, flushed with intense exertion. His tic signalled feverishly. But Covenant faced her. Apart from his ragged respiration, he now seemed completely blank, sealed off; as severe as one of the Masters. The sporadic embers in his eyes were gone, extinguished or shrouded. In spite of her resolve to avoid challenging him, she had made him wary.

'I don't see how.'

She forced herself to hold his gaze. 'Flames would have spread to the trees. I couldn't prevent that unless I stayed behind.' Surely she was still Covenant's and Jeremiah's only protection against the *Elohim*? 'But even if they didn't,' even if she had remained to control her conflagration, 'the Forestal would have forgotten about the Viles as soon as I raised fire that close to the Deep. Or he would have joined them. They had a common enemy.' That was Covenant's doing, and Jeremiah's. 'They might have come after us together.' Cold seeped through her cloak, her robe. It oozed into her clothes. 'Then—'

Covenant cut her off. 'Oh, *that*. That was never going to happen.'

In a tone of enforced patience, he said, 'I know I haven't given you all the explanations you want. And you obviously don't like it. But we didn't have *time*. I couldn't afford to spend a few hours teaching you other ways to use the Staff. And I didn't know I needed to tell you why the Arch wasn't in danger.

'The Viles aren't stupid. They're capable of alliances. But Wildwood isn't. I don't mean he's stupid. He just doesn't think that way.

'He's a Forestal. He doesn't think like people – or even Viles. He thinks like trees. And for them, life is pretty simple. Soil and roots. Wind and sun and leaves. Birds and seeds. Sap. Growth. Decay.' Just for an instant, Covenant's deliberate restraint cracked. '*Vengeance*.' Then he flattened the emotion in his voice. 'As far as they're concerned, there's no distinction between sentience and fire or axes. Anything that's mobile and has a mind can kill them. The Viles are just like us. We're already Wildwood's enemies. By definition.

'Trust me,' he concluded heavily. 'There was never any chance he would join the Viles.'

Never any chance that the logic of the Land's past might be severed—

'He's right, Mom,' Jeremiah offered. His gaze had paled to the hue of sand. 'We couldn't make Wildwood team up with the Viles even if we wanted to. Which of course we don't. All we want is to get to *Melenkurion Skyweir*. So Covenant can save the Land – and you can save me.'

Linden could not argue; not with her boy. But she was not appeased. She had been used. *–a rock and a hard place*. Covenant and Jeremiah had deliberately exposed her to the Viles – and for what? So that she would surrender Covenant's ring? And when she ignored him in order to argue with the Viles, he and Jeremiah had created a conflict between them and Caerroil Wildwood.

What would he have done if she had complied? Would he have abandoned her to the debate of the Demondim-makers?

His *design for the salvation of the Land* made no provision for his ex-wife's wedding band – or for their fatal son.

'What about the battle?' she asked in anger and misery. 'Doesn't that affect history?'

'Hell, no,' Covenant snorted as if he had come to the end of his forbearance. 'It confirms what was going to happen anyway. Now the Viles despise Wildwood. They despise Garroting Deep. They're ready to listen to the Ravers. And nobody else knows they ever fought. We didn't change anything.'

He made the statement sound like an accusation.

A moment later, he and Jeremiah prepared their next arch so that they could move on. As she stepped between them, Linden felt like weeping. But she refused her tears; her intensifying bereavement. They had become useless to her.

Chapter Eleven:

Melenkurion Skyweir

Sickened by disorientation and doubt, Linden Avery arrived with her companions on the broad plateau of *Melenkurion* Skyweir high above Garroting Deep early in the afternoon of that same day.

Safe from the Viles, Covenant and Jeremiah moved in longer and longer jumps, carrying their jumble of wood with them. But they continued to respect the threat of Caerroil Wildwood's power. Instead of crossing over the forest, they followed the line of the Last Hills until they gained the packed snow and ice of the Westron Mountains at the northwestern limit of the Deep. Then they turned towards the south among the crags, devouring distance in instantaneous bursts of twenty or thirty leagues.

The intervening crests and tors blocked Linden's first sight of *Melenkurion* Skyweir until Covenant and Jeremiah paused to rest before opening their final portal. While they recovered from their exertions, however, she was given a brief opportunity to study the mighty peak; see it for what it was.

The effects of dislocation and the hard cold of the mountains, the air as sharp and pointed as augury, had already left her gasping. Otherwise *Melenkurion* Skyweir might have taken her breath away.

Made brilliant by sunshine, it dominated the south. Indeed, it seemed to command the entire range. Although the neighbouring peaks and spires – mottled by endless ice and snow, defined by raw granite against the pale cold depth of the sky – were gigantic in themselves, they resembled children beside the towering head of the Skyweir, with its crown and chin raised to the heavens as if in defiance. As it presented its nearly sheer front to the east, it created the impression that it had been frozen in the act of striding massively towards Landsdrop and the Sunbirth Sea, drawing with it like acolytes or escorts all of the other mountains.

But while its eastern face fell precipitously for fifteen or twenty thousand feet, its other slopes were more gradual. On the north and west, they blended with the lower peaks in scalloped cols and coombs, or in ragged moraines. Those sides held centuries or millennia of impacted ice like glacial fragments; scraps and swaths of ice so old and deep that in sunlight they were more blue than the winter sky.

Backed by rugged grandeur, the single titan of *Melenkurion* Skyweir confronted the east and Garroting Deep as though here, at least, if nowhere else in the Land, the Earth's fundamental rock had risen up to watch over the dark trees.

Somehow the mountain appeared impervious to doubt or reproach; immune to time.

The thin, sharp air held no taint, and the angle of the sun had not yet cast the Skyweir's eastern face into shadow. As a result, Linden could discern the precise contours of the plateau which girdled the tremendous stone. It began among *Melenkurion* Skyweir's northern slopes, spread out below the stark eastward cliffs, and disappeared behind the mountain's bulk towards the south. From her vantage, the plateau resembled a wide altar, a gathering place for humility and worship. The whole mountain and its surrounding rock might have been a fane erected for and sanctified to the august beauty of the world.

And somewhere deep within that temple lay hidden the spring of EarthBlood, the source of the Power of Command: the Power with which Covenant had promised to end Lord Foul's malice, and Kastenessen's: the Power that would enable Linden to redeem her son.

She would be left behind; alone and lost in this time. Jeremiah would be free at last. But there would be no one to prevent Roger from seeking out his mother's ring.

Shivering in the cold – at this elevation, the chill resembled shards of glass – she gazed through her steaming breath towards *Melenkurion* Skyweir and tried to imagine how she might navigate the complex ramifications of her suspicion and grief.

The coming crisis would end her life. If other outcomes were possible, she could not see them.

Her companions were too eager to pause for long. 'We should go,' Jeremiah murmured to Covenant. 'She lost her supplies back there.' Among the Viles. 'She's hungry and thirsty, and it's going to get worse. We should try to do this quickly.'

Covenant nodded at once. 'Linden,' he said, peremptory with antici-pation, 'come on. You can pull yourself together later. We'll have time to talk soon enough.'

Neither he nor Jeremiah felt the cold. They were oblivious to the weaknesses which defined her. Yet she seemed to hear real concern in her son's voice, and so she did not hesitate. After all, he was right. Covenant's strange powers could warm her, but they did not spare her from hunger and thirst and weariness. She was already shivering. Soon she would lose more of her frayed strength. And searching for the Blood of the Earth might require hours or days.

Obediently she moved to stand between her companions while Jeremiah and Covenant summoned their eldritch doorway.

Afterward, as she staggered to regain her balance, she found that her son and her former lover had brought her to the centre of *Melenkurion* Skyweir's plateau. They were halfway between the towering plunge of the cliffs and the jagged rim of the plateau; at the mid-point of the wide altar. Jeremiah's collection of torn branches and twigs had landed with a clatter nearby. As always, he and Covenant had stepped away so that she would not touch them inadvertently, either with her hand or with the Staff.

Starving for stability, Linden lowered herself to her knees, then placed the Staff beside her and braced her hands on the bare stone. The granite here was free of ice and snow: the entire plateau appeared to have been swept clean. She thought that if she extended her health-sense towards the mountain's depths, she might draw some of its knowledge and per-manence into herself. Perhaps she would find a form of courage among *Melenkurion* Skyweir's fundamental truths.

For a moment, she felt only cold through her palms and fingers, through the knees of her stained jeans; cold as irrefragable as the stone, and as unyielding. But then her percipience grew sharper, and she realised that the chill, the reified frost, was not as severe as she had expected it to be. Somewhere far beneath her, beyond the range of her senses, ran a source of warmth.

The Blood of the Earth: Earthpower in its purest and most absolute incarnation. Its implied presence seemed to throb like a pulse in the veins among the mountain's roots.

As she attuned her perceptions to the rock, however, she realised that she was wrong, not about the stone's comparative warmth, but about its pulse. The beating deep under her hands and knees was not the rhythm of *Melenkurion* Skyweir's heart. It was a tremor of strain, the slow tectonic grinding of imponderable pressures so distant that they were barely palpable. Somewhere far beneath the plateau and the immense peak, irresistible forces were rising. Her nerves caught the first dim elusive hints of a mounting cataclysm, a convulsion which would alter everything.

The sensation reminded her of the damage which she had felt in Kevin's Watch when she had first arrived in the Land. But the subcutaneous tremors here were not the result of imposed harm or unnatural powers. Rather they were an expression of the Earth's internal necessities, as natural as the world's slow respiration, and as potentially destructive as a hurricane, an avalanche, the calving of icebergs.

Clutching at the Staff, Linden struggled to her feet. When Covenant and Jeremiah turned to look at her, she announced unsteadily, 'There's going to be an earthquake.'

Covenant nodded. 'I know.' His unconcern was plain. 'And it'll be massive. It'll split the Skyweir from top to bottom. Right where we're standing, there'll be a crevice all the way down to the Black River. Something like four thousand feet. When he gets here, Damelon is going to call this place Rivenrock. And the mountain will have two crests. The quake will crack it along a seam in the stone. It'll look like two mountains shoved together.

'No one in the Land will even know it happened. Except Wildwood, of course – and he won't care. Once Earthroot fills up, the flow of water will return to normal. He won't be affected.' Covenant shrugged. 'Oh, sure, people are going to feel the quake. Even as far away as Doriendor Corishev. But this place is so remote– No one will know the quake hit here, or what it did to the mountain. When Damelon shows up, he'll think *Melenkurion* Skyweir was always split like that.

'But it won't happen for years and years. A decade at least. We don't need to worry about it.'

'All right.' Linden tested her perceptions and found that she believed him. The almost subliminal vibration in the stone disturbed her health-sense as if the surface under her had become subtly unreliable; but the peak's heavy intransigence held. It might hold for a long time– 'That's a relief,' she admitted. 'It makes me nervous.'

According to the Theomach, *Melenkurion* Skyweir could be approached safely in this time – or more safely than while High Lord Damelon searched for the mountain's secrets.

'But Jeremiah is right,' she went on. 'Without supplies,' or the use of the Staff, 'I'll be in real trouble.' She would need Covenant's aid – or a bonfire – to survive a night exposed to the mountain winds. She was weary; deeply aggrieved. And she had no idea how long a fumbling trek into the bowels of the Skyweir might take. 'Can I assume that you know the way to the EarthBlood?'

Covenant bared his teeth. 'I do.' He sounded pleased with himself. 'There are two of them. But we won't use them.'

Before she could react, he explained, 'One is way the hell on the other side of the mountain. The other involves getting down into Garroting Deep and then following the Black River upstream. Which naturally Wildwood won't let us do. But in any case, both routes are bloody difficult. We could be clambering in the dark for days. And you still wouldn't have any food' – he shrugged again – 'although I'm sure we'll find water easily enough.'

Linden held his gaze warily. 'So you're going to transport us?'

If Jeremiah did not need his wood for campfires and torches, what purpose did it serve?

Covenant's grin widened. 'Unfortunately, no. That won't work. The Blood of the Earth is just too damn powerful. It puts out too much interference. Once we get close to it, I'm going to need every ounce of power I can muster just to keep the two of us' – he nodded towards Jeremiah – 'from evaporating like steam.

'And we still have the *Elohim* to worry about. They don't approve of what we're trying to do. You haven't stopped us yet, and they don't know why. If they can tell we're going in, they might lose patience with you. I don't want to take the chance.'

Linden studied him. With an effort, she kept her voice low. 'Then what *are* we going to do?'

Still grinning, Covenant looked at her son. 'Tell her, Jeremiah. Why should *I* have all the fun?'

Jeremiah ducked his head as if he were embarrassed; but he, too, was grinning. The fever of his tic contradicted his obvious excitement.

'That's what this wood is for. It's one of the main reasons we had to make the Viles and Wildwood fight each other. So I could get enough branches.

'I'm going to build a door.' Eagerness seemed to crackle and spatter in his voice. 'Like the one in my bedroom that let me visit the Land. Like that one, it won't look like a door. It'll be more like a big box. Once we climb inside, and I put the last pieces in place, we'll disappear *here*' – his gaze touched Linden's briefly, then dropped away – 'and reappear *there*. Where we're going.'

The muddy hue of his eyes had turned the colour of dark loam.

'And the best part is, the *Elohim* won't know what we're doing. We'll be invisible. They'll think we're just *gone*.'

Linden stared at her son as though she had never seen him before.

'I know what you're going to say,' Covenant put in. Now his smile looked false; feigned and strangely vulnerable. 'If he can do all that, why didn't he do it days ago? Why didn't we come straight here from Revelstone? We could have avoided the Theomach completely. And why can't the *Elohim* see us? Don't they know everything? They sure as hell *think* they do.'

Linden shook her head, effectively dumbfounded. In one sense, she understood what she heard. The words were simple; within her grasp. But in another, she was completely baffled. Jeremiah might as well have spoken in an alien tongue. He was going to build a *door*? When he had talked earlier about using his raceway construct as an entrance to the Land, his explanation had had the same effect: it conveyed nothing that she knew how to comprehend.

Jeremiah? she wanted to ask. Jeremiah—? But she had no language for her question. Her son had remained cruelly unreactive during all of their time together; and yet for years he had been capable—?

One of the Insequent, the Vizard, had tried to persuade him to build a prison for the *Elohim*.

She was so cold—

'Come on, Linden.' Covenant's voice seemed to reach her from a great distance; across a gulf of millennia and ambiguous intentions. 'It's going to take him a while to do this. It has to be done exactly right. Let's leave him to it. We can go for a walk.' He missed a beat, then said, 'We need to talk.'

She hardly heard him. 'I would rather stay here,' she murmured. 'I want to watch. I could watch him all day.'

She had spent innumerable hours absorbed in her son's inexplicable abilities.

'Actually, I could too,' Covenant said without conviction. 'But this is important. We're only an hour or two away from saving the world. We need to be clear.'

His tone rather than his statement caught Linden's attention. His eyes were dull, almost lifeless. The embers which smouldered sporadically in his gaze had been banked with ash; hidden away. His grin had become a coerced grimace.

Apparently he had chosen to suppress his anger and frustration; his disappointment in her.

'All right.' She, too, needed to be clear. The time had come for decisions which surpassed her. Tightening her grip on the Staff, she checked to be sure that his ring still hung from its chain around her neck. 'Let's walk.'

Movement might hold her shivering at bay.

Covenant gestured towards the rim of the plateau. Keeping a safe distance between them, he accompanied her as she started in that direction.

But he did not speak. When he had been silent for a few moments, her thoughts reverted to her son, drawn there by the mystery that Jeremiah had become.

'How does he do it?' she asked; almost pleaded. 'Is this more "leakage"? Power he gets from being in two places at once? Because Time is bleeding?'

'No, no.' Covenant flapped one hand dismissively. 'Making a door like this one – or the one in his bedroom– That's natural talent. The right shapes can change worlds. They're like words. He does it all himself. *Leakage* is when he puts up a barrier. Or when we move from one place or time to another. Then he's using what spills out while I fold Time.'

Linden nodded as though she understood. Jeremiah's ability to prevent her from touching him was an acquired magic. He had not been born with it. She wanted to believe that it was not inevitable or necessary; that she would be able to hug him before the end.

'This talent—' She remembered faery castles, unexplained monuments, wooden toys. Revelstone and Gravin Threndor. 'How big is it? How far does it reach? What can he do?'

Ever since she had first discovered his gift for building, she had prayed that he might construct his own escape from his mental prison.

Again Covenant grimaced. 'I'll get to that. None of this is as simple as you want it to be.'

Instead of continuing, however, he fell silent again.

Gradually they neared the edge of the plateau. Covenant seemed to be waiting for that. He wanted to show her something that could only be seen from the precipice above Garroting Deep. Or he wanted to be sure that he was entirely out of Jeremiah's earshot. Or he—

He did not slow as he approached the rim; but Linden held back. Kevin's Watch had been shattered under her, and she still did not know how she had saved herself and Anele. She feared another fall.

Nonetheless Caerroil Wildwood's demesne opened before her with every step: an unfurling tapestry of trees, dark with winter and old hate. Hills lay under the forest like the waves of a sea, seething too slowly for her limited senses to descry. Soon she could see the crooked line of the Black River through the woods. True to its name, its waters did not reflect the cold sky or the comfortless sunlight. Rather the river seemed thick with Earthpower and slaughter.

Covenant had called the Forestal *an out-and-out butcher.*

At last, he stopped with his boots on the jagged verge of the plateau. Now it was Linden who kept her distance, from him as well as from the cliff. For a while, he waited for her to join him. Then he turned to face her, sighing quietly.

'When the water comes out down there' – he indicated the base of the sheer drop behind him – 'it's sort of red. In the right light, it looks like blood. The ichor of the Earth. But Wildwood uses it to wash the death out of Gallows Howe. That's what turns the river black.'

Without pausing, he said, 'Your kid makes doors. All kinds of doors. Doors from one place to another. Doors through time. Doors between realities. And doors that don't go anywhere. Prisons. When you walk into them, you never come out. Ever again.'

Linden gripped the Staff of Law until her knuckles ached; bit down sharply on her numb lip until she felt the pain; said nothing. Her son had such power—

'I can't explain how he does it. Talent is always a mystery. But I can tell you a couple of things.

'First, he has to have the right materials for the door he wants to make. Exactly the right wood or stone or metal or bone or cloth – or racetracks. And they have to be in exactly the right shapes. In theory, he could have made a box or portal to take us straight here from Revelstone just after Damelon arrived.

'Incidentally,' Covenant remarked, 'that's how we were going to make sure Damelon didn't know we were there. Jeremiah would have built a door to hide us.' Then he continued.

'But in practice, he didn't have the right materials. There wasn't enough' – Covenant spread his hands – 'of whatever he needed in Revelstone. And putting one of his doors together takes too long. The ur-viles were always going to try to stop us. Plus no one ever knows what Esmer might do.

'No,' he asserted, 'we had to travel the way we did. And we had to use you and the Viles to distract Wildwood so we could get the wood your kid needs for *this* door. Without it, the *Elohim* are definitely going to interfere.

'That's the other thing. The *Elohim*. They're– I don't know how to put it.' His mouth twisted in disgust. 'They're *vulnerable* to certain kinds of structures. Like Vain. Maybe because they're so fluid. Specific constructs attract them. Exactly the right materials in exactly the right shape. Other structures repel them. Or blind them.

'That's one reason Findail haunted you the way he did. As hard as he tried, he couldn't get away from Vain.

'With the right materials, Jeremiah could make a door to lure the *Elohim* in and never let them out. Which is what the Vizard wanted. They wouldn't be able to stop themselves. But *this* door they just won't look at. It'll take us where we want to go, and they won't know we're doing it.' Covenant gave another stiff shrug. 'Hell, they won't even know they don't know.'

Linden stared in awe. Her *son* could do such things. The idea filled her with wonder and reverence; potential joy. Jeremiah had always been precious to her, but now he seemed priceless in ways which she could not have imagined.

Yet the mystery of his abilities was also fraught with anguish. She had not known: she had never known. Now he was going to be taken from her. Again. Just when she had finally been granted a glimpse of his true nature—

We're only an hour or two away—

Beyond question, she needed to be clear.

Abruptly Covenant changed directions. 'Of course, we don't have to do this. It's not too late. You can still give me my ring.'

She met his lightless gaze without faltering. 'Then what?'

He failed to hold her stare. Something within him appeared to cringe or hide. Glancing aside, he frowned at the uneven rock of the plateau.

'Then we go back where you and your kid belong,' he said flatly. 'I stop Foul. And put Kastenessen out of his misery. With that kind of power, I can find where Foul's been keeping Jeremiah. When Joan dies, the *caesures* stop. Everybody lives happily ever after.'

'And what if—?' Linden began. Then she halted. For Jeremiah's sake, she did not wish to provoke Covenant.

'Go on, say it,' he urged without rancour. 'What if I'm not telling the truth? Isn't that what scares you? Isn't that why you're afraid to trust me?'

Instead of answering directly, she countered, 'Covenant, what's happened to you?' Encouraged by his restraint, she risked saying, 'You talk about how much strain you're under, but it was always like that. Ever since I've known you, everything has always mattered too much, there were always too many lives at stake, the Land was always in too much peril.' And he had judged himself harshly, accepting his own hurts while he struggled to spare the people around him. 'But you didn't react the way you do now.' He had tended her when she had been most frail; wounded and broken. Even when she had opposed him, possessed him, he had covered her with forgiveness. 'Now you don't seem to care about anything except making me do what you want.'

For a moment, he looked at her, still frowning. His eyes were empty, unreadable; devoid of depth. Then he bowed his head. His fingers tapped against his thighs as if he required an outlet for a tension which he was determined to conceal.

'I miss my life, Linden.' He seemed to address the grass stains on her jeans. 'I miss living. When you made that Staff, you trapped me. I know it's not what you intended, but it's what you did. I've been stuck for millennia. It's made me bitter.

'I yell because I *hurt*. And I don't tell you everything because you don't trust me. I don't know what you're going to *do*. I'm sure you won't hurt your kid, but I don't know what you might do to *me*. If you won't give me my ring—' His tone suggested that she might destroy him out of spite.

Slowly he raised his eyes until he appeared to be studying the band hidden under her shirt. 'That's why I need to be sure we're clear. I'm stretched too thin for any more surprises. I have to know what you're going to do.'

There Linden reached her decision.

Jeremiah had made his choice. He wanted her to prevent Joan's death from banishing him. He wanted to stay in the Land, conscious and whole. With Covenant. The EarthBlood would enable her to grant his desire.

Then she would lose him forever. For his sake, she could bear that. In addition, she would be lost herself, trapped ten thousand years before her proper present. And in this time, she and her Staff and Covenant's ring would pose a profound threat to the Arch of Time; a living affront to the Land's history. But she could worry about that later, after Jeremiah and the Land had been spared. She could even set aside the conundrum of Roger, the peril of Joan's white gold. Such things were problems for a future in which she would play no part.

Nevertheless Covenant's underlying falseness surpassed her. She could not suffer it.

He feared the Staff of Law. He insisted that any contact with her would unmake the distortion of Time which allowed him – and Jeremiah – to exist in her presence. Yet Berek's touch, Berek's awakening strength, had not harmed him. And he showed no fear when he proposed to approach the Land's purest and most potent source of Earthpower.

He wanted her to believe that she was more fatal to him than Berek Halfhand or the Blood of the Earth.

When he had said to her in dreams, *Trust yourself*, and, *You need the Staff of Law*, and, *Linden, find me*, he had sounded more true to himself, more like the man who had twice redeemed the Land, than he ever did when he spoke in person.

More than once long ago, she had believed that he was wrong; that his actions would lead to loss and doom. More than once, she had tried to prevent him. And he had shown her that he had made the right choice. By the simple force of his courage and love and will, he had forged salvation from the raw materials of disaster.

But he had done so without imposing his desires on her. Nor had he ever – not once – suggested that she was responsible for his dilemmas.

Do you not fear that I will reveal you?

Therefore she did not hesitate. Carefully neutral, and deliberately dishonest, she replied, 'We're clear. Jeremiah will take us to the EarthBlood.' She was astonished that her voice did not tremble. Yet it remained steady, as if she were stronger than the stone of Rivenrock. 'You'll drink it and use the Power of Command. After that, you'll disappear,' undone by the scale of the powers which he had released, 'and I'll take my turn so that I can save Jeremiah.'

She had made her choice. Nevertheless she prayed that she was wrong; that she would be given a reason to change her mind; that Covenant would do or say something to account for his lies – or perhaps merely to show that he cared about her fate. The man whom she remembered would not have been content to abandon her in the depths of *Melenkurion Skyweir*.

But this Covenant seemed to have no room in his heart for her. Lifting his head, he let her see the flicker of embers in his eyes as he said, 'Good.'

With that one word, he sealed her decision.

Beware the halfhand.

*

When they returned to the centre of the plateau, Linden found her son constructing what appeared to be a crude cage. Around a clear space large enough for at least three people to stand without touching each other, he stacked crooked branches to form walls. Some of the limbs looked so heavy that he must have had difficulty lifting them: others seemed too slight and brittle to support the weight above them. And they gave the impression that they were precariously balanced, almost haphazardly poised on top of each other. Yet he worked steadily, without faltering or hesitation. Guided by an instinct beyond her comprehension, he used his stolen boughs and twigs as if they were Tinkertoys or pieces of an Erector set, and all of his movements were certain. Even his maimed hand never fumbled.

With unconvincing nonchalance, Covenant asked, 'How's it going, Jeremiah?' but the boy did not answer. His concentration was as complete as it had ever been in Linden's living room. His eyes had resumed the muddy hue with which she was familiar – the colour that she had learned to love – and he seemed lost in his task; reclaimed by dissociation.

Already he had raised the walls of his construct to the height of Linden's chest. When she walked around it in a vain attempt to understand it, she saw that he had left a gap in the side towards *Melenkurion* Skyweir's cliffs. *Once we climb inside–* For a moment, she wondered whether the opening would be too small for her. But he knew what he was doing. If she turned sideways, and handled the Staff carefully—

Without apparent effort, Jeremiah picked up a log which he should have needed help to lift and put it in position, propping its ends atop branches that were obviously too unstable to hold its weight. Yet the structure did not topple: it hardly wobbled. Then it seemed to become visibly sturdier.

As he began to devise a roof for his edifice, Linden felt faint emanations of power from the construct. And they grew stronger with every added branch. Somehow the shapes and positions and intersections of his materials evoked a form of theurgy from the dead wood.

His magic did not smell or taste familiar. Certainly it did not resemble any manifestation of the Earth's essential vitality that she had encountered before. Nor did it remind her of the darkness of the Viles, or the malign vitriol of the Demondim. It did not imitate the illimitable liquid possibilities of the *Elohim*, or Esmer's storm-charged potency, or the dangerous eagerness of wild magic. Yet she discerned no *wrongness* in the energies of the construct; no violation of Law.

Linden's son had brought into the Land a form of puissance entirely his own.

When he had finished bracing and balancing dead limbs to fashion a roof, the entire construct seemed to thrum with constrained readiness. At the same time, it looked as solid and irrefusable as the rock of its floor. And on a level too visceral for language, it *called* to Linden. Although the wood was dead, it possessed – or Jeremiah had given it – a palpable intention, a will to be used. In spite of her rapt surprise and her many fears, she wanted to enter the portal immediately.

But this was Jeremiah's magic, not hers. She needed his instructions or permission: she owed him that. Out of respect for his talent, his accomplishment, she waited until he stepped back from his task and looked around, first at Covenant, then at her.

'Good,' Covenant pronounced with obvious approval. 'That should do it. Looks like we're ready.'

Linden's reaction was stronger. When Jeremiah met her gaze, blinking as though he had been asleep, she allowed herself a moment of simple humanity. 'Oh, Jeremiah, honey,' she breathed. 'My God. You said that you could do this, but I had no idea– I didn't really understand. This is the most wonderful—'

Her throat closed. Under other circumstances, her eyes would have filled with tears. But there was no room for weeping or grief in what she meant to do.

His tic intensified, signalling until he could hardly open his left eye. 'I'm glad you like it,' he said bashfully. 'I could do a lot more, if I had the right things to work with.'

Then he faced Covenant again. 'We should go. You've been under too much strain for a long time.'

Covenant grinned fiercely. 'I'm ready. If I get any readier, I'm going to rupture something.'

He must have believed that he had persuaded Linden—

'Then, Mom—' Jeremiah kept his face turned away from her. 'You go first. Be careful with the Staff. It won't fit. You'll have to poke it through a gap. Once you're inside, get down on your hands and knees at the back. Brace yourself. We'll be in there with you. When the ground shifts, you might touch one of us. Or the Staff might. We won't have room to dodge.'

'All right,' she murmured. 'I understand.'

She approached the opening slowly, searching for the best way to enter. She did not fear treachery here. It would serve no purpose. But she had to be sure that she did not dislodge any detail of Jeremiah's design.

At last, reluctantly, she placed her Staff near the opening. Without it, she turned sideways, trusting percipience to guide her as she hunched down and stepped warily into the structure.

Inside the cage, she grasped the Staff by one end and pulled it after her. Near a corner of the back wall, Jeremiah had left a space between the branches and Rivenrock's granite. As she drew the Staff inwards, she slid one of its heels through that space. With elaborate care, she positioned the Staff so that it lay on stone near the wall without touching any of the deadwood. Then she knelt over it, planting her hands and knees so that she could simply crumple and lie flat if she lost her balance – and so that she could grab the Staff quickly if she needed it.

At once, the cold of the rock began to soak into her like water. Aching spread from her palms and fingers towards her wrists: shivers accumulated in her chest like the mountain's impending earthquake.

The precise emanations of the construct did not waver or change. Although they had called to her, they did not react to her presence. The thoughtless intention humming in the wood was not yet satisfied. Or it had not been completed—

As soon as she was in position, Covenant followed, moving brusquely as if he were confident that he would not disturb Jeremiah's theurgy. Unlike Linden, however, he did not kneel or sit down. Instead he stood crouching with his hands braced on his thighs for support.

He had placed himself as far from Linden as he could without obstructing Jeremiah. His eyes watched the boy: she could not see them.

I yell because I hurt. Perhaps he understood Kastenessen. *Everything he does is just another way of screaming.*

And when that doesn't work—

Yet Covenant did not give the impression that he was in pain. He was closed to her health-sense; but her ordinary perceptions had been whetted by years of training. She saw nothing to confirm his claims of distress and exertion.

For a moment after Covenant had entered the crooked box, Jeremiah remained outside to gather up the last twigs and small branches. Then he too slipped through the opening without hesitation, sure of his relationship with his construct.

'Get ready, Linden.' Covenant's voice was husky with anticipation. He sounded like a man on the verge of a defining triumph. 'It won't be long now.'

And when that doesn't work, he maims—

Carefully Jeremiah fitted his larger pieces of deadwood across the gap, set them in position to complete his portal. As he did so, the power constrained within the construct increased again. Its vibrations grew more urgent. The cage still seemed stable, inert; petrified in place. It made no audible sound. Nonetheless its thrumming affected Linden's nerves as if it might shake itself apart at any moment.

When he had adjusted the final branches, he began to balance his twigs among them apparently at random. The mute call of the construct became a cavernous growl. She felt it in the base of her throat, the centre of her chest.

'Fuck the Theomach,' Covenant muttered through his teeth. 'Fuck the *Elohim*. Fuck them all.'

Then Jeremiah was finished. Instantly *Melenkurion* Skyweir and Rivenrock, the sunlight and the wide sky, disappeared as though they had been wiped from the face of the world. Linden and all of her choices were plunged into absolute darkness.

She felt the stone under her slip and tilt. She started to drop down, lie flat: then she caught herself. The tilt was slight; so slight that the Staff did not move. Braced, she was able to keep her balance while her senses reeled, scrambling to accommodate realities which had been profoundly altered.

The rock under her fingers was wet. Dampness filled the air: already a spray as fine as mist moistened her cheeks, her hands. She felt inestimable masses crowding around her, basalt and obsidian, schist and granite on all sides; league after league of the Land's most ancient stone.

Jeremiah had transported her into the depths of the mountain.

The surface on which she knelt had been worn smooth by eons of water. Yet it was warm rather than cold; palpably heated by the energies within the Skyweir. The droplets on her face felt like sweat.

The imminent tremors which had disturbed her on the plateau were stronger here. Underground, she was closer to the pressures which would one day split *Melenkurion* Skyweir to its foundations. But that upheaval would not happen now. More force would be required to bring about the inevitable crisis.

Those sensations were small things, however; effectively trivial. The unexplained moisture in the air and the nearly audible groaning among the mountain's roots were dwarfed as soon as she recognised them, swept away like the plateau and the open heavens by raw power.

She was surrounded by Earthpower, immersed in it. Its primaeval might seemed as immense as the Skyweir itself, and as unanswerable. By comparison, the healing potency of Glimmermere and the mind-blending waters of the horserite tarn were minor instances of the Earth's true life, and everything that Linden had done since she had returned to the Land paled into insignificance. *Here* was the uncompromised fount of the Land's vitality and loveliness. If it had not been natural and clean, as necessary as sunlight to every aspect of the living world, its simple proximity would have undone her.

And yet—

As soon as she recognised the concentrated presence of Earthpower, she realised that she had not yet reached its source. The vast strength flowing around her had been attenuated by other waters. The spray that beaded on her forehead, trickled into her eyes, ran down her cheeks, arose from less eldritch springs. They were rich with minerals, squeezed from the mountain gutrock to nourish the world. If she had submerged herself in them, they might have washed the weariness from her abused flesh. But they were not the Blood of the Earth.

Now she shivered, not because she was cold, but because she was afraid. The crux of her intentions was near, and she might fail.

'Jeremiah?' she croaked. 'Honey? Covenant?' But no sound answered her. Silence entombed the space around her. Earthpower stilled the spray and the stone and the damp air.

Panic clutched at her chest. She jerked up her head, closed her fingers around the Staff. Then she stopped.

The wood of the construct had begun to shine. Or perhaps it had been shining all along, and her senses had failed to register the truth. Every bit of deadwood from the smallest twig to the heaviest bough emitted a murky phosphorescence. Each detail of the cage was limned in nacre, defined by moonlight. Yet the glow shed no illumination. She could not see the stone on which she knelt, or the Staff clutched in her hand. The portal's luminescence referred only to itself.

Nevertheless the white outlines enabled her to discern the black silhouettes of her companions. Covenant still crouched in one corner of the box. Jeremiah remained near the place where he had sealed his construct.

Linden's pulse drummed in her ears. Around her, the lightless phosphorescence of the wood intensified. Covenant and Jeremiah sank deeper into darkness as the nacre mounted. Briefly the cage resembled a contorted meshwork woven of sterile wild magic, affectless, its purpose exhausted.

A heartbeat later, the entire construct flared soundlessly and vanished as every scrap and splinter of deadwood was consumed by the after-effects of Jeremiah's theurgy.

She expected unilluminable midnight. Instead, however, a warm reddish glow opened around her as if the last deflagration of Jeremiah's door had set fire to her surroundings.

The light was not bright enough to hurt her eyes. She blinked rapidly, not because she had been dazzled, but because the sudden disappearance of the box exposed her to the full impact of Earthpower. Ineffable puissance stung her eyes and nose: tears joined the spray on her cheeks as if she were weeping. Through the blur, she saw Covenant stand upright, arch his back as if he had been crouching for hours. She saw her son look at Covenant and grin like the blade of a scimitar.

Then her nerves began to adjust. Slowly her vision cleared.

She and her companions were on a stone shelf at the edge of a stream nearly broad enough to be called a river. Jeremiah's construct had brought them to a cavern as high and wide as the forehall of Revelstone. The arching rock was crude, unfashioned: clearly the cavern was a natural formation. But all of its facets had been worn smooth by millennia of spray and Earthpower.

And they radiated a ruddy illumination that filled the cave. The particular hue of the glow – soft crimson with a fulvous undertone – made the rushing current look black and dangerous, more like ichor than water. The stone seemed to contemplate lava, imagine magma. It remained gently warm, stubbornly solid. Nevertheless it implied the possibility that it might one day flow and burn.

Linden had seen illumination like this before, in the Wightwarrens under Mount Thunder. Covenant had called it 'rocklight', and it was inherent to certain combinations of stone and Earthpower. It had not been caused by Jeremiah's theurgy. Instead his portal had temporarily blinded her to the lambent stone, the tumbling stream. Spray and warmth and Earthpower had entered through the gaps among the branches: light had not.

In spite of the water's speed and turbulence, it was utterly silent. It raced along its course without the slightest gurgle or slap. She might have believed that she had been stricken deaf; that the concentration of Earthpower was too acute for her ears. But then she heard Covenant speak.

'Good,' he announced for the third time. 'We're almost there.'

Only the water had been silenced by the weight of Earthpower.

Involuntarily Linden's gaze followed the current as it spilled into a crevice at the end of the cavern. But when she turned her head in the other direction, she felt a rush of astonishment. The source of the stream – and the fine spray – was a high waterfall that spewed from the cave's ceiling and pounded in turmoil down onto a pile of slick stones and boulders at the head of the watercourse. Every plume and spatter of the torrent caught the fiery light in a profuse scattering of reflections: the waterfall resembled a downpour of rubies and carbuncles, incarnadine gemstones; profligate instances of Earthpower. Yet the towering spectacle was entirely soundless. The bedizened tumult of spume and collision had no voice.

'How—?' Linden breathed the question aloud simply to confirm that she could still hear. 'How is it possible?'

She did not expect an answer. But Covenant muttered, 'Beats the hell out of me. I've never understood it. There's probably just too much Earthpower here for our senses to handle.'

Like the waterfall, the spray on his face sparkled redly. His features were webbed with droplets of light and eagerness.

'That's just water,' he said, dismissing the lit implications of the falls. 'When it finds its way out of the mountain, it'll be the Black River. But the Blood of the Earth comes in here. It leaks out through those rocks.' He indicated the foot of the waterfall. 'That's what causes all this rocklight. Earthpower has soaked into the stone. But it's too thin for what we need. We have to get to the source.'

Linden could see no obvious way in or out of the cavern. But Covenant pointed at the waterfall. 'Through there.'

'There's a tunnel on the other side,' added Jeremiah. His muddy gaze had assumed the colour of hunger; avarice. The corner of his eye beat frenetically. In his right hand, his halfhand, he clutched his racecar as though it were a talisman. 'It leads to the place where the EarthBlood oozes out of the rock. That's where we have to go. Covenant has to drink right from the source. Otherwise there's no Power of Command.'

'But how?' Linden asked weakly. 'That much water– We'll be washed away.'

For a moment, Covenant looked at her directly; let her see rocklight like coals in his eyes. In the presence of more Earthpower than she had exerted since the time when she first formed her Staff of Law and unmade the Sunbane, he showed no sign of strain; gave no hint that he could be effaced.

Grinning avidly, he replied, 'No, we won't. *I* wasn't when Elena brought me here. You'll probably have to crawl. But you can do it. All this Earthpower– It's making you stronger. You just don't feel the difference because there's so much more of it.'

Then he turned back to the falls as though he had no more attention to spare for her. Motioning for Jeremiah to join him, he moved towards the gemmed cascade.

Jeremiah complied at once. Side by side, he and Covenant headed through the spray to essay the wet jumble of rocks.

As she watched them stride away, panic tugged at Linden again. She had to blink constantly at the sting of puissance; could hardly breathe against the might and dampness of the mist. Reflections of rocklight confused her, threatening her balance. Covenant was wrong. She could not withstand that torrential mass of water.

But she had already made her decision. She had to try—

For a moment longer, she watched Covenant and Jeremiah take their first steps into the waterfall. As they ascended the clutter of stone, she saw forces which should have crushed them crash onto their heads and shoulders, and splash away swathed in jewels. At erratic intervals, the mountain's epitonic bones trembled.

Then, fiercely, she set down the Staff so that she could fling off both her robe and her cloak: protections which she had been given by people who wanted to help her. She did not need them in the warm cavern. And she feared that their weight when they became soaked would drag her to her death.

Clad only in her red flannel shirt, her jeans, and her boots, as she had been when she had first left her home to pursue Roger Covenant and his victims, Linden Avery took up the Staff and set herself to bear the brunt of the waterfall.

Spray drenched her before she reached the falls itself. Her face streamed: her shirt and jeans clung to her skin. She felt a fright akin to the alarm which had afflicted her at the Mithil's Plunge. Ahead of her lay a fatal passage in which everything that she had known and understood might be transmogrified into the stuff of nightmares.

As soon as she felt the first impact of the falls, she knew that she would not be able to climb the rocks standing. The worn granite and obsidian were as slick as glazed ice, and the water had the weight of an avalanche. Helpless to do otherwise, she dropped to her hands and knees. Then she wedged one end of the Staff into a crack between the stones and pulled herself up the shaft as if it were a lifeline.

The wood was smooth and wet: perhaps it should have been as slippery as the rocks and boulders; as unreliable. But she had fashioned it out of love and grief and her passion for healing. Her hands did not lose their grip as she crept slowly deeper into the full force of the waterfall.

It threatened to smash her; carry her away. She could not draw breath. Nevertheless she dragged herself along the Staff until she found a place where she could jam one arm securely among the stones. Anchored there, she used her free hand to haul the Staff after her and brace its iron heel against a boulder. Then she worked her way up its length again while the falls bludgeoned her, filled her eyes and nose and mouth, tore at her clothes.

Once more she anchored herself, raised the Staff higher, gripped it desperately so that she could climb the rocks. And before she reached the end of the shaft, her head emerged from the pitiless cascade into complete darkness.

Gasping, she scrambled out of the waterfall onto flat stone. Her arms and legs quivered as though she had ascended a precipice: she felt too weak to shake the water out of her eyes. No glint or suggestion of rock-light penetrated the falls. She crouched over the Staff in untrammelled midnight. If her companions made any sound – if they waited for her instead of hastening towards their destination – she did not hear it. She only knew that she *could* hear because her gasping seemed to spread out ahead of her, adumbrated by the constriction of granite.

The rock under her was as slick as the stones of the waterfall. It was not wet; had not been worn to treachery by ages of water. Rather it resisted contact. The scent and taste of Earthpower was far more concentrated here, so thick and poignant that it made her weep: too potent to condone the touch of ordinary flesh. Stone which had become half metaphysical spurned her hands, her knees, her boots.

And the smell– The odour of distilled strength swamped all of her senses. She foundered in it. It transcended her as profoundly as any *caesure*, although it held no *wrongness*. In its own way, it was as immense and fraught with mass as *Melenkurion* Skyweir. Her mere brief mortality could not encompass it.

Instinctively she pressed her forehead to the stone, performing an act of obeisance to the sovereign vitality of Earthpower.

The wood of the Staff had become hot. It radiated heat as if it had been forged of molten iron. It should have burned her unbearably; scalded the skin from her fingers; set fire to her drenched clothing. But it did not. It was *hers*. Her relationship with it enabled her to hold it, unharmed, in spite of its inherent response to the EarthBlood's extravagance.

A tunnel, Jeremiah had said. On the other side.

Still she heard nothing. Covenant and Jeremiah must have gone on ahead of her. Covenant had told her that if she did not drink the Blood of the Earth immediately after he and Jeremiah disappeared, she might be too late to save her son from the consequences of Joan's death. Yet they had left her behind.

She needed light. And she needed to be able to stand on stone which repulsed every touch. If she could not catch up with her companions—

'She made it,' Covenant remarked abruptly. Linden thought that she heard satisfaction in his voice.

I can't do it without you.

He bore the flagrant hazard of the tunnel easily, as though it had no power to affect him. He had lied about his reasons for seeking to avoid Berek Halfhand's touch. And hers.

'I told you she would.' Jeremiah sounded like the darkness. 'You did, when you were with Elena. And you weren't half as strong as she is.'

Just be wary of me. Remember that I'm dead.

Tears coursed from Linden's eyes. She could not stop them.

'Jeremiah, honey,' she panted, still braced on her hands and knees as if in supplication, 'where are you? I can't see.'

The peril of your chosen path I deemed too great. Therefore I have set you upon another.

But if Jeremiah possessed the ability to construct portals which would foil the perceptions of even the *Elohim*, surely he could evade High Lord Damelon's discernment? Where was the peril? What had the Theomach meant? Had he simply been ignorant of Jeremiah's talent? Or had he foreseen some more oblique danger?

I do not desire the destruction of the Earth. If you are wise – if wisdom is possible for one such as you – you also will not desire it.

Fuck them all.

Without warning, a sulphurous illumination blossomed in the darkness. Light with the hue and reek of brimstone shone from the clenched fist of Covenant's halfhand. Through her reflexive weeping, Linden saw him and Jeremiah. They were no more than two or three strides away.

Both of them seemed taut with impatience or excitement.

Beyond them, a tunnel as straight as a tightened string led away from the waterfall into fathomless night. Its ceiling was little more than an arm's span above Covenant's head; but the passage was wide enough for two or three people to walk abreast beside a small rill running towards the falls.

In the red and charlock glow, the fluid of the rivulet had the rich deep colour of arterial blood. And it shouted, yelled, positively *howled* of Earthpower.

It was the living Blood of the Earth. It had seemed pure in the cavern of the waterfall, but it was more so here; far more. Nothing that Linden had ever done with her Staff could match the absolute cleanliness and vitality of the liquid flowing past her.

Somewhere beyond Covenant and Jeremiah lay their destination.

'Come on, Linden,' Covenant said harshly. 'You don't have to grovel here. It's undignified. And I'm sick to *death* of waiting.'

He wanted her to stand. She needed to stand. He may have recognised the lie when she had said, *We're clear*. That was possible. He may have remembered her well enough—

Why had he and Jeremiah waited for her? Was Covenant honest after all? More honest than she had been? Or did he simply want her to witness what he did, for good or ill?

'All right,' she muttered through her teeth. 'Give me a minute.'

Perhaps he feared that she would attack him from behind if he did not wait; that she would dare– If she had made her suspicions too obvious—

Wherever she placed her hands, they tried to skid out from under her. She could not trust her weight to them. And her boots might have been coated with oil. Every shift of her balance threatened her with slippage.

But the Staff had been formed for Earthpower. When she braced one of its heels on the rock, it held; gave her an anchor.

Carefully, by small increments, she rose to her feet. Still she felt her boots trying to slide away. One slip would pitch her onto her face. But the Staff gripped the stone, and she clung to the Staff.

'Are you *ready*?' demanded Covenant. 'Hellfire, Linden, it's not that hard. *I* did it, and I didn't have your damn Staff.'

She ignored the embers glaring in his eyes; did not risk gazing directly at his fiery halfhand. Instead she looked at her son. Facing the hunger which distorted the colour of his irises, the fervid clutch of his halfhand around his racecar, the frantic cypher of his tic, she tried to accept them, and found that she could not.

Silently, hardly moving her lips, she said, If I'm wrong, I'm sorry. Try to forgive me.

Then she threw herself headlong towards her companions; stretched out into a dive along the glazed surface of the stone.

In a flare of brimstone surprise and fury, both Covenant and Jeremiah leapt aside. Cursing viciously, Covenant hugged the tunnel wall opposite the rill of EarthBlood. Tense with shock, Jeremiah did the same. Neither of them lost their footing.

Linden landed heavily; skidded past them. As she hit the stone, she slid, and went on sliding, as if she would never stop. She felt only the impact: no friction, no abrasion; nothing that would slow her. She wanted that. She counted on it. Otherwise Covenant and Jeremiah might get ahead of her again.

But her slide took her closer to the rivulet. She did not know what would happen if she plunged into the Blood of the Earth, but she doubted that she would survive an immersion. More by instinct than intention, she dragged one heel of the Staff along the stone.

The iron seemed to meet no resistance. Nevertheless she began to lose momentum. Within half a dozen paces – and mere inches from the rill – she coasted to a halt.

Covenant's curses followed her down the tunnel. They drew closer as he and Jeremiah rushed to catch up with her.

Shedding incessant tears, Linden called yellow flame like sunshine out of the Staff; a sheet of fire from the entire length of the wood. For an instant, her fire guttered as if it were humbled in the EarthBlood's presence. Then it shone forth strongly. And while her blaze lit the tunnel, she used that exertion of Earthpower to secure her footing so that she could stand. Then she wheeled to confront her companions as though they had become her foes.

Covenant stamped to a halt a few paces away from her. The fire had fallen out of his hand: he stood glaring at her with no light on his visage except hers. Jeremiah came a step closer, then stopped as well. His precious face was bright with dismay.

'Hellfire and bloody damnation, Linden!' raged Covenant. 'What the *fuck* do you think you're doing?'

'Mom, what's wrong?' panted Jeremiah. 'Did you fall? Are you hurt? *Are you trying to banish us?*'

The wood that you claim must defy them– Linden gripped her Staff grimly and did not falter. *You must be the first to drink of the EarthBlood.* She stood between her companions and their goal.

Indirectly Esmer had prepared her for her encounter with the Viles. Had he also betrayed her?

'Oh, stop,' she breathed heavily, feigning anger to disguise her sorrow and resolve. 'I'm obviously not going to "banish" you. You've never been in any danger. There's more power here than I could ever muster. It doesn't bother you. And when Berek touched you—'

She left the rest of her protest unsaid. Covenant and Jeremiah had some other reason for rejecting contact with her. But she did not waste her scant strength on recriminations. When Covenant started to swear again, she took a step backwards. And another.

'You said that you want to be clear,' she reminded him. Her voice was husky with effort and Earthpower. 'So do I. I don't' – she grimaced – 'trust this situation.'

'Linden.' Covenant suddenly became calm. He kept his gaze away from hers; did not let her see his eyes. But he sounded almost gentle. 'You don't have to make a fight out of this. Talk to us. Tell us what you want. We'll figure it out together.'

She continued moving slowly backwards. She could not see either him or Jeremiah clearly. Her vision was an irredeemable smear of tears. But her tears were not weeping, and her nose ran only because it was stung by Earthpower.

'So you say.' Even now she lied without hesitation. 'Here's the problem. I can't debate with you anymore.' If Covenant carried out his stated intentions – and if she succeeded at saving her son – she would be abandoned *here*, ten thousand years away from where she belonged. 'You'll come up with too many arguments, and I won't be able to think.' Her mere presence and power in this time might suffice to alter the Land's history; unmake the Arch. The Thomas Covenant whom she had known would not have asked or expected that of her. 'So I'm just going to drink the EarthBlood first. I'm going to get Jeremiah away from Lord Foul with his mind whole. I'll make sure that he can stay in the Land after Joan dies. Then I'll get out of your way and let you do whatever you want.'

'Mom!' Jeremiah protested urgently. 'If you do that, I *will* vanish. I won't be with you anymore!'

Still retreating along the tunnel, Linden gazed at him through her tears. 'I believe you.' A surge of grief slipped past her self-command. Then she forced it down. 'I'll never see you again. But at least I'll know that you're safe.'

Another faint shudder undermined the stone, but she did not lose her balance.

If she severed the bond between her son and Covenant, Covenant might become honest. But she did not intend to rely on that slim possibility.

If you err in this, your losses will be greater than you are able to conceive.

'Damnation, Linden.' Covenant still spoke calmly, although he crowded after her with an air of desperation. 'It isn't that simple. What makes you think I can stand by while you use the Power of Command? You're the only one of us who's *real* enough to survive forces on that scale.'

He and Jeremiah pushed towards her. Yet they did not risk coming near enough to be touched by her fire. Upheld by the Staff, she took one step after another.

She could feel the crushing mass of the mountain lean over her. It seemed to hold its breath as though it awaited her decision; her actions. *You serve a purpose not your own, and have no purpose.* That may have been true earlier. It was not true now.

The intensity in the air increased. It exceeded Linden's ability to measure its increments – and went on increasing. The untrammelled might of the EarthBlood accumulated at her back.

'I'm not so sure,' she retorted, still pretending ire which she did not feel. 'You're part of the Arch of Time. There's nothing you can't do.'

She had seen Thomas Covenant become a being of incarnate wild magic. Even the imponderable capabilities of the *Elohim* would be too weak to contain him. He could have brushed aside their interference. If he feared them, he had some other reason.

'Hellfire!' he countered more hotly. 'That isn't how it works. Right now, I'm as mortal as you are. You've got my ring. You've even got your damn Staff. I've got nothing. And your kid has less than that.

'When I was here before' – he lowered his voice again – 'I had my ring. That's the only reason I wasn't wiped off the face of the Earth when Elena summoned Kevin. Without it, I'm *vulnerable*. Why do you think I had to let the Theomach push me around? Why do you think I've been worried about the *Elohim*? While I'm in two places at once, two different kinds of reality, I'm practically crippled.'

Linden took another step backwards, and another, holding the Staff of Law alight. She could not gain what she needed by any form of argument or persuasion. Through Anele, Covenant had told her, *I can't help you unless you find me*. Then he had ridden into Revelstone with her son on the strength of his own will? No. Either the being who had spoken to her days ago had deliberately misled her, or the man who stood before her now was false in ways that exceeded her imagination.

'Maybe that's true,' she muttered through her teeth. 'Maybe it isn't. I really don't care.' If her son had let her touch him, she might not have been able to go on lying. But he and Covenant gave her nothing which would have compelled her to tell the truth. 'I only care about Jeremiah. I'm going to save him. The Land is your problem.'

He should have known that she was lying. He and Jeremiah both should have known.

Then the tunnel expanded into a widening like a cul-de-sac; and at once, every nerve in her body recognised that she had reached the source of the EarthBlood. Covenant and Jeremiah might not attempt to rush her through the flame of the Staff, but she could not be sure. She trusted nothing. Facing the rill, she turned sideways so that she could glance into the end of the passage without losing sight of her companions.

At the back of the cave, a rude plane of stone as black as obsidian or ebony protruded like the exposed face of a lode from the surrounding granite. Peering at it, Linden blinked furiously, strove to clear her sight. The dark wet rock appeared to shimmer: its sharpness and stark purity overwhelmed her eyes. Through the blur, she seemed to see a facet of weakness in the substance of reality, a place of distortion where the tangible rock and the possibilities of Earthpower merged.

From the whole surface of the plane seeped the gravid liquid of the EarthBlood. Trickling down the face of the lode, it gathered in a shallow trough before it flowed thickly away down the length of the tunnel.

There, Linden thought in wonder and terror: there was the source of the Power of Command. In that trough, the concentration of Earthpower was so extreme that it seemed to fray the fabric of her existence, pulling her apart strand by strand.

She would have to drink—

'Mom!' Jeremiah cried, pleading with her. '*I don't want that. I don't want you to rescue me if the Land is still at Foul's mercy! My life isn't worth it.*'

'Hell and blood, Linden!' Covenant shouted. 'You don't have to do this! Weren't you listening to the Viles? The Power of Command can't touch wild magic, and whoever holds my ring doesn't need the Power!

'For God's sake! If you can't do anything else, at least give me back my ring! Give me a chance to save the Land!'

For a moment, Linden hesitated; questioned herself. Could she carry out her intent without the EarthBlood, using only the Staff? Both Covenant and Jeremiah feared the fire of Law, that was obvious. But she did not believe that she possessed enough sheer power. No flame of hers would be more potent than the air of the tunnel – and her companions breathed it without wavering. She could not gain what she needed with the Staff alone. And she could not wield the Staff and Covenant's ring together. She had done so once, when she had unmade the Sunbane. But then she had been insubstantial, already half translated away from the Land. She had occupied a transitional dimension, a place of pure spirit; supernal rather than human. And Lord Foul's frantic exertion of wild magic had opened the way for her; attuned her to a power which was not hers by right. Here the contradictory theurgies of white gold and the Staff would destroy her.

Either alone will transcend your strength, as they would that of any mortal. Together they will wreak only madness, for wild magic defies all Law.

She had made her decision. The time had come act on it.

Trust yourself.

I want to repay some of this pain.

In the end, she placed more faith in her dreams than in Covenant or her son.

Be cautious of love. It misleads. There is a glamour upon it which binds the heart to destruction.

'Jeremiah, honey,' she said through her determination and woe, 'I love you. Try to forgive me.'

Before her companions – or her own fears – could intervene, Linden Avery the Chosen stooped to the trough and drank the Blood of the Earth.

Then she jerked erect, stood rigid as stone, while utter Earthpower reified in liquid transformed her mouth and throat and heart – her entire body – to exquisite unendurable fire.

Now it was not only the Staff of Law that shed flame: her whole being had become a conflagration. She burned like an auto da fe, as if she had been ignited by the sun's inferno. Yet her flesh was not consumed, and her only pain was the agony of an intolerable exaltation. The EarthBlood raised her so far above her limitations and alarms that the discrepancy threatened to incinerate her, not because it was *wrong* or hurtful, but because she was inadequate to bear it.

If she did not express her incandescence at once, utter her Command, the puissance which she had swallowed would sear her to the marrow of her bones.

All you have to do is want it—

Enfolded from head to foot in unanswerable fire, she turned to her companions.

She could see them clearly now. Flames had burned away her tears; her weakness. Covenant stared at her with his mouth open as if he were enraptured by eagerness and dread; and the red embers which filled his eyes shone so hotly that they fumed in the viscid air. Jeremiah had thrown his head back as if he were howling. In his halfhand, he clutched his racecar; held it out towards her as though it might ward off an attack.

When Linden spoke, her words were a shout of fire. With the full force of the Power of Command, she demanded of her companions, '*Show me the truth!*'

Then she watched in horror as her loves flew apart like leaves in a high wind.

Chapter Twelve:

Transformations

While her Command compelled obedience to her will, Linden remained clad in fire. Briefly she had become Earthpower, and could not be refused. She saw every detail with lucent precision while her desires were imposed on her companions.

Covenant's jeans and T-shirt slumped away as the truth was revealed. They became an indeterminate grey shirt and khaki slacks. Three bullet holes formed an arc across the centre of his shirt. They had been healed; but their edges were still crusted with blood.

His features blurred as though she had begun to weep again, although she had not; could not. His face became rounder, softer. Lines of severity melted from around his mouth, leaving his cheeks unmarked. The corners of his eyes no longer expressed any intimacy with pain. And he shrank slightly, grew shorter. At the same time, his torso swelled with self-indulgence. Even his posture changed. He stood with a familiar combination of looseness and tension: the looseness of weak muscles; the tension of poor balance.

A glamour upon it—

It was not Thomas Covenant who stood before her, exposed by fire and Command. It was Covenant's son, Roger, *seeking such havoc that the bones of mountains tremble to contemplate it.* Linden could not fail to recognise him now.

Do you not fear that I will reveal you? The Theomach must have known—

The embers were gone from Roger's eyes: his gaze had regained the exact hue of his father's, the troubled colour of suffering and ruin and unalloyed love. Nevertheless he had been altered; terribly transformed. His right hand was whole, but it had lost its humanity. Instead it was composed of magma and theurgy, living lava and anguish. Its fiery brutality reminded her of the devouring serpents which she had seen during her translation to the Land, the malefic creatures of lava and hunger that Anele had called the *skurj*.

Roger Covenant's right hand had been cut off. It had been replaced by *that*—

And when that doesn't work, he maims—

Somewhere in the background of Linden's mind, a voice gibbered, Oh God. OhGodohGodohGod. But she hardly recognised her own fear.

Kastenessen had merged part of himself with the *skurj*. Roger himself in his father's guise had told her that. The deranged and doomed *Elohim*'s escape from his Durance had been *more painful than you can imagine*.

Kastenessen is all *pain. It's made him completely insane.*

She had been given hints. And she blazed with Earthpower: her perceptions were preternaturally acute. She jumped to conclusions instinctively, instantaneously – and trusted them completely.

Being part skurj *isn't excruciating enough, so he surrounds himself with them, he makes them carry out his rage. And when that doesn't work*—

Sweet Jesus. Kastenessen had severed his own right hand and given it to Roger Covenant. He had granted Roger the magic to conceal himself from her percipience; had turned Roger into an entirely new kind of halfhand—

The truth of the man who had brought her here appalled her; shocked her to the core. Roger's presence in his father's place exceeded her sharpest fears. Nevertheless the sight of her son was worse.

Jeremiah also had been concealed. Now his plight was unmasked. He stood gazing vacantly at her or through her; unaware of her. The stain in his eyes seemed to blind him. His mouth hung open, the lower lip slack. Drool ran down his chin. His twitch was gone, erased from his empty features. Linden saw at a glance that he had relapsed to his former unreactive dissociation.

But there was more—

Despite his overt passivity, his arms did not dangle at his sides. Instead his fists were raised in front of him. In his right, his halfhand, he clutched his racecar; gripped it so hard that he had crumpled the metal. In his left, he held a piece of wood as slim and pointed as a stiletto, a splinter of the deadwood which he had gathered from Garroting Deep.

From his shoulders, his blue pyjama shirt hung in tatters. Horses reared from scrap to scrap, torn apart by blows and falling. Bruises covered his arms and chest. Yet the unassoiled discoloration of his contusions did not mask the violence of the bullets which had pierced his flesh. His rank wounds, one in his stomach, the other directly over his heart, oozed dark blood that formed a web of crust and fluid on his torso, trickling at last into the waistband of his pyjama bottoms.

He had died in his natural world. Like Linden: like Joan. He would never be freed from the Land.

Yet even that was not the worst.

A small hairless creature like a deformed child clung to his back. Its clawed fingers dug into his shoulders: its sharp toes gouged his ribs. Its malign yellow eyes regarded Linden while its teeth chewed ceaselessly at the side of Jeremiah's neck and its mouth drank his life.

And from the creature came waves of eldritch force so cruel and bitter that they turned the air in Linden's lungs to ash. In its own way, the creature was as mighty as Roger. Its power matched the potential for sav-agery and devastation of Kastenessen's severed hand. But the creature's strength had more in common with the black lore of the Viles than with the laval hunger of the *skurj* – or with the covert transformations of the *Elohim*. It was an altogether different threat; a danger comparable to the Illearth Stone in its violation of Law.

Nonetheless Linden recognised it instantly. Twice before, she had met a similar magic, a comparable ferocity.

The creature was one of the *croyel*: a parasite or demon which throve by giving power and time to more natural men or women or beasts as it mastered them. Long ago, Findail the Appointed had described the *croyel* as *beings of hunger and sustenance which demnify the dark places of the Earth. Those who bargain thus for life or might with the* croyel *are damned beyond redemption.*

But Jeremiah was not damned, she insisted to herself. He *was not.* He was not like Kasreyn of the Gyre: he had made no bargain. He could not have made one. Lost within himself, he more closely resembled the *arghuleh* of the Northron Climbs, mindless ice-beasts which had simply been enslaved by the *croyel*. The bargain here was Lord Foul's, not Jeremiah's.

Still her son was effectively possessed. The Ranyhyn had done what they could to forewarn her. But her fears had tended towards Ravers – or towards the Despiser himself. She had not come close to imagining Jeremiah's true peril.

Empowered by the Blood of the Earth, Linden screamed raw fire down the stone throat of the tunnel.

Her flame was met by a blast of heat like the opening of a furnace. Roger's given hand flung its own brimstone conflagration against her, vicious as scoria. If she had not been enclosed in Earthpower, and warded by the Staff of Law, she would have died before her heart could beat again. Instead, however, she was only quenched. The flame which the EarthBlood had given her was snuffed out: the illuminating fire of the Staff vanished as though it had been doused.

The sudden vehemence of the attack staggered her. For a brief moment, a small sliver of time, she tottered on the brink of the trough. Then, reflexively, she dropped to her knees, snatching herself back from a second contact with the Blood.

Reclaimed by mortality, her vision blurred again. Only Roger's crimson virulence remained to light his malice and Jeremiah's emptiness and the insatiable eyes of the *croyel*. But she saw them as nothing more than shapes and points of light; instances of bereavement.

'Actually, Dr Avery,' Roger drawled, 'I like this better. If you weren't so damn determined to interfere, Foul and Kastenessen and I would already have everything we ever wanted. I suppose that ought to piss me off. But it doesn't. Ever since I first met you, I've wanted to crush you. Now I can.'

If he had struck at her then, he might have slain her. She was lost and aghast, overwhelmed with rue: she could not have defended herself. White gold was a mystery to her, too complex and hidden to be approached in the EarthBlood's presence. The resources of the Staff seemed to have passed beyond her reach.

But Roger held back. His desire to crush her entailed something more than mere death.

For her son's sake, and the Land's, Linden used that moment of life and breath to regain as much of herself as she could.

Vestiges of utter Earthpower lingered in her yet. They left incandescent suggestions in her veins. Her heart throbbed with remembered might. She could still think, and had already begun to tremble with fury.

Leaning her weight on the Staff, gripping it with both hands while she knelt, she panted as though she were nearly prostrate, 'That's why you didn't want me to touch you. You weren't afraid of my power. You knew that if I touched you, I would feel the truth.' Roger and the *croyel* had feared her health-sense. 'Your disguise wouldn't hold.'

Roger glanced at Jeremiah's master; gave a harsh burst of laughter. Then he faced Linden again with flame frothing from his fist. 'Of course,' he jeered. 'I'm just astonished it took you so long to figure it out.'

She ignored his scorn: it could not hurt her now. 'And it's why you didn't want me to summon the Ranyhyn. They would have recognised you right away.'

'Of course,' he repeated, mocking her. 'Go on. You can't stop there.'

Jeremiah did not speak. He did not react in any way. He could not. The *croyel* ruled him, and the creature no longer needed either words or gestures. It had stolen into her son's mind in order to find the memories and knowledge which would give substance to its charade, and to Roger Covenant's. Now it was done with pretence.

Linden trembled, scrambling inwardly, and grew stronger. 'It's also why you didn't want me to go to Andelain. You couldn't fool the Dead. They would have exposed you.'

'Well, sure.' Roger shrugged. 'If that's the best you can do. But I have to admit, I'm disappointed. You're supposed to be a *doctor*. Keen mind. Trained intellect. I expected more.'

Think, Linden commanded herself. If she could understand her straits, she might find her way through them.

Clearly Esmer had advised her well. And then he had counterbalanced his aid by opposing the ur-viles when they had tried to prevent Roger and the *croyel* from snatching her out of her natural present.

'Tell me,' she demanded hoarsely. 'You like to gloat.' He coveted her dismay. 'What am I missing?'

Roger snorted another laugh. 'For one thing, you brought this on yourself. All of it. If you hadn't gone to get that damn Staff – and if you hadn't told Esmer you wanted to visit Andelain – nothing that's happened since would have been necessary. You forced us to intervene. Once you had the Staff, we had to keep you out of Andelain.'

Linden sensed as much as thought that he was attempting to mislead her again. He was not closed to her now. Her senses discerned subtleties of truth and falsehood. He – or Lord Foul – had wished to preclude her from Andelain: she believed that. But her Staff was not his real concern. If he and Jeremiah had not ridden into Revelstone, they would have been in no danger from her.

Roger and his masters or guides – the Despiser and Kastenessen – had a deeper reason for seeking to ensure that she did not approach the Andelainian Hills.

Trying to probe further, Linden asked, 'You said "for one thing". What else have I missed?'

Again Roger appeared to consult his companion. Then he replied in a voice full of scorn, 'Why not? You obviously think I'm stupid. You want to keep me talking so you'll have time to recover. But you really don't understand. You don't understand *anything*. I can't lose here.'

'I'm going to answer your questions for a while because I want you to know what *despair* feels like.'

Long ago, Thomas Covenant had said to her, *There's only one way to hurt a man who's lost everything. Give him back something broken.* Roger and Lord Foul had done that to her now. But Roger's father had not allowed his pain to rule him.

'Go on,' she said more firmly. 'I'm listening.'

Roger flicked his lurid hand; sent an arc of fire like a streak of molten stone across the ceiling of the cave. But he did not direct his force at her. A grin of grim delight showed his teeth as he replied, 'For another, there was always the chance you might actually give me my ring. That would have saved all of us no end of trouble.

'I tried to talk you into it. The *croyel* thinks I should have tried harder. But I knew you wouldn't do it. You love power too much.'

Linden heard him clearly. He meant that in her place he would not have surrendered his father's ring. He did not comprehend her at all.

'That's not an answer,' she retorted. As the transcendence of her

Command faded, she recovered more and more of herself. 'Why did you care if I went to Andelain? Tell the truth for once. You're part *Elohim*. And the *croyel*—' The creature had raped her son's trapped mind in order to manipulate her. 'They seem like they're capable of anything. If the two of you aren't strong enough to destroy the Arch of Time on your own, why didn't you just come here? What did you need me for? What was so important about keeping me away from Andelain?'

Jeremiah himself, the ensnared boy whom Linden had adopted and loved, did not react. He could not. He wandered a chartless wilderness of loneliness and abandonment while the *croyel* clung like a tumour to his back. His disfocused gaze and his damp mouth promised only sorrow.

Nevertheless he struck without warning. Dropping his ruined racecar, he sprang at Linden. A reflection of ruddy fire flashed on his oaken dagger as he raised it high. Guided and compelled by the fulvous glare and sharp teeth of the *croyel*, he hammered his splinter of deadwood into the back of her right hand where it gripped the Staff.

He may have wanted to nail her hand to the long shaft; cripple her somehow. If so, he failed. The clean wood of the Staff was impervious to his stiletto. When it had pierced her hand, his sharp scrap of Garroting Deep was turned aside.

For a moment, however, the pain of her wound nearly unmade her. It bit into her nerves like fangs and acid. She scarcely felt the warm spurting of her blood as it streamed over her left hand and down the Staff; yet she might as well have been crucified. She would have lapsed into shock at once if the air of the cave had not filled her lungs with distilled Earthpower. But instead she cried out as though Jeremiah's blow had ripped through the centre of her chest. A brief rush of tears joined the pulsing flow of her blood.

Then, as suddenly as a crisis of the heart, she detached herself from the pain; distanced it as though it belonged to someone else. Dispassionately she surveyed the shard jutting through her hand. The confusion of her health-sense was gone: in chagrin and desperation, she had at last tuned her perceptions to the precise pitch and timbre of the EarthBlood's atmosphere, and her eyes no longer required the protection of tears. She could see her injury distinctly. Apart from the pain, it was not serious: that was plain. Her son's – no, the *croyel*'s – dagger had skidded between the bones. It had missed the larger arteries and veins. She would not lose dangerous amounts of blood. If she survived Roger's and the *croyel's* intentions, any untainted application of Earthpower would heal her.

But she could not unclose her fingers from the Staff. The wound paralysed them: their nerves had shut down. And she had no attention to spare for them. Other exigencies consumed her.

She could see clearly; might never weep again. Nevertheless she made no attempt to stand. Instead she remained on her knees as though the *croyel's* attack had accomplished its purpose.

Roger waited until Jeremiah had stepped back; resumed his pose of slack passivity. Then Covenant's son jeered, 'Shame on you, Dr Avery. You should know this. The Theomach is a meddling asshole, but he doesn't lie. And I told you the truth.

'Why did we need you? Because otherwise the *Elohim* would have stopped us. They're terrified *somebody* is going to wake up the Worm of the World's End. As long as we had the *Sun-Sage*, the *Wildwielder*' – he pronounced her titles contemptuously, scathing her – 'they could convince themselves they didn't need to do anything. They believe you're going to protect the Arch and deal with Kastenessen, so why should they bother?

'No, Doctor. The question you should be asking is, why did we have to take you out of your own time to get what we wanted?'

He paused, apparently expecting her to respond – or enjoying her helplessness. But she was not beaten: not yet. Her detachment defended her from the excruciation of Jeremiah's dagger in her hand. And her son's enslavement galvanised her. While Roger mocked her, she gathered herself.

He still had not explained why he – or his masters – considered it vital to keep her away from Andelain. The creature had attacked to distract her.

Apart from the claiming of your vacant son, I have merely whispered a word of counsel here and there, and awaited events.

Goaded by her son's suffering, Linden wanted to rage at Roger, This is all *your* doing. Kastenessen is in too much pain to think. Lord Foul isn't willing to risk himself. And Esmer can't pick a side. It's on *your* head. Even your own mother– You're responsible for *all* of it.

He had kidnapped her son; had dragged Jeremiah into the path of death.

But she remained where she knelt as if she were transfixed between her own agony and Jeremiah's. She did not choose to waste the remnants of her will and courage on empty recrimination.

It was clear that Roger would not explain his fear of Andelain. She set that issue aside.

'All right.' She did not raise her voice above a lorn whisper. She had no strength to spare. 'Tell me, since that's obviously what you want. Why did you take me out of my own time?'

'It's complicated,' he said at once, gleefully. 'Of course, we told you the truth. The EarthBlood really isn't accessible where you belong. Elena's battle with Kevin is going to tear this whole place apart. There won't be anything left of this tunnel and that nice convenient trough.

'But Foul still wants to break the Arch of Time. He wants to escape. He wants *revenge*. And he's tired of being defeated by my shit of a father. This way—' Roger cast another swath of fire and eagerness around the cave. 'Dr Avery, this way he can't fail.

'First,' he explained as if he were proud of himself, 'there was always the chance you might do something to violate Time. We gave you plenty of opportunities. If you did, good. We'd be spared the trouble of coming here. But if you didn't, you still might trust us enough to let one of us drink first. Then we could Command the Worm to *wake up*.'

He grinned ferociously. 'Since you haven't done either of those things, we can just kill you and drink anyway.

'But even if *that* doesn't work – if we can't kill you, which doesn't seem very plausible under the circumstances – you're still stuck *here*.' His half-hand blazed, casting familiar embers into his eyes. 'Ten thousand years in your own past. *With* a Staff of Law. *And* my ring. Every breath you take is going to violate Time. And you can't escape without a *caesure*.' He snarled a laugh. 'I almost hope you survive so you can *try* that. *Please*. The Laws of Death and Life haven't been damaged yet. You'll shatter the world. But if you don't, you're still going to change *everything*.

'There's more, of course, but I won't bother you with it. Here's the point. Frankly, Dr Avery, ever since we got you away from your present, there haven't been any possible outcomes that don't give us exactly what we want. Plus, of course, we get to watch you *cower*. We get to watch you suffer for your poor kid. That alone makes all this trouble worthwhile.'

Linden should have quailed. His certainty was as bitter as the touch of a Raver: it should have defeated her. But it did not. How often had she heard Lord Foul or his servants prophesy destruction, attempting to impose despair? And how often had Thomas Covenant shown her that it was possible to stand upright under the weight of utter hopelessness?

Still kneeling, feigning weakness, she protested, 'You aren't making sense.' Deliberately she let the pain in her hand leak into her voice. 'You want to rouse the Worm. You want to break the Arch. But then *you'll* be destroyed. Lord Foul can escape. *You* can't. Why are you so eager to die?'

'Well, it's true,' Roger drawled happily. 'Kastenessen hasn't thought it through. All he cares about is wreaking havoc on the *Elohim*. If he's killed in the carnage, at least he won't *hurt* anymore.

'The *croyel* and I have other plans. Foul has promised to take us with him. And he'll keep that promise. He needs your kid. Hell, he *owns* him. How else do you suppose the *croyel* got access to everything your kid knows, everything he can do? He's *belonged* to Foul for years.

'But even if Foul tries to cheat us, we'll still get what we want. The *croyel* can use your kid's talent. You've seen that. He'll make us a door. A portal to eternity.' He glanced around at the tunnel. 'All the materials he needs are right here. While the Worm tears this world apart, we'll open our door and go through it.

'Face it, Dr Avery.' Passion and brimstone condemned Roger's gaze. 'You've done everything conceivable to help us become *gods*.'

Inadvertently Roger aided her. He hurt her more severely than any mere physical wound. The thought that the Despiser had claimed her son long ago – that Jeremiah may have participated in his own subservience to the *croyel* – was worse than any threat of absolute ruin, any image of apocalypse. Roger may have been lying in an attempt to break her. Instead he transfigured her.

They have done this to my son.

While Roger talked, she anchored herself on the muddy void of Jeremiah's gaze, the slackness of Jeremiah's cheeks and jaw, the useless dexterity of his dangling hands. Her pain and blood and repudiation she focused on the cruel parasite feeding from his neck.

'I'm sure that's fascinating,' she said through her teeth. 'You'll enjoy it. But there are a few things *you* don't understand.'

His eyes widened in amusement; false surprise. 'Like what?'

Linden bowed her head as though she intended to prostrate herself. Past the concealment of her hair, she muttered, 'Like who I am.'

Then she drew lightning as pure as charged sunlight from the upraised iron heel of the Staff and hurled it simultaneously at both Roger and the *croyel*.

While her blast flared and echoed in the constriction of the tunnel, she surged to her feet. Unable still to uncramp her pierced hand from the Staff, she used her left to shift the shaft so that she could brace its length under her left arm, hold it like a lance.

Her attack was abrupt and brief; yet it should have damaged her foes. But it did not. It failed to reach them. Reeling backwards, Roger flung out an eruption of magma to intercept the Staff's blaze. Swift as prescience, the *croyel* emitted a vehement wall which blocked and dispersed Linden's blow.

Roger caught himself; roared with fury. Aiming his fist at her, he unleashed a scend of fire and lava. At the same time, the creature sent waves of force towards her like crashing breakers in a storm. Together he and the *croyel* strove to drive her back against the lode-face of the EarthBlood.

If she fell there, the Blood itself would incinerate her.

She responded with untarnished Earthpower and Law; threw pure flame against the corrupted theurgy of Kastenessen's hand and the savage unnatural coercion of the *croyel*. Shouting her son's name as though it were a warcry, she met the ferocity of her enemies with power that filled the depths of the mountain like daylight.

Yet Roger and his companion were not damaged or daunted: they hardly seemed to feel her assault. Grinning as if he could taste triumph and delight, Roger poured out magic to cast down her fire; tried to melt her flesh. And the creature raised Jeremiah's arms to invoke invisible forces. Pressures grated in the air like grinding teeth as they mounted against her; against the lash of flame which was her only defence.

The Staff bucked in Linden's grasp. It seemed to burn. Its limitations were hers: it could not channel more force than her human blood and bone could summon or contain. She stumbled half a step towards the trough. Her flame no longer flooded the cave. The *croyel*'s barricade held it back. Crimson and sulphur tainted her sunfire as Roger's eagerness probed into it; reached through it.

Abruptly the deadwood piercing her hand caught fire and burned away, searing the inside of her wound; sealing it. She was scourged backwards again.

For an instant, she seemed to see herself falter and fail, see her flesh scorched like charcoal, see the Staff turn black as Roger's heat devoured it. Then she rallied.

They have done this to my son.

With a wordless shout, she thrust the Staff behind her so that its end plunged into the trough of EarthBlood.

At once, fresh strength galvanised her. A torrent of Earthpower rushed through the Staff and became incandescence. Her conflagration spurned the stain of brimstone: it pounded heavily against the repulsion of the *croyel*. Light that should have blinded her and could not washed through the cave and along the tunnel as the brilliance of Law scaled higher; expanded until it appeared to transcend *Melenkurion* Skyweir's constricting rock.

The wall emanating from Jeremiah's enslaver receded. Eldritch dazzling effaced the *croyel*'s eyes: she could no longer see them, or they had been liquefied in the creature's skull. Briefly Roger's flail of scoria lost a portion of its virulence. Kastenessen's might and pain contracted around Roger's quivering fist.

But he seemed able to draw on limitless power as though he siphoned it from the magma of the Earth's core. Even as Linden's fire grew and grew, claiming more and more puissance from the mountain's ichor, his ruddy heat swelled again. A furnace spilled from his hand. Heat like liquid granite drove back her bright flame.

Again the creature pressed its strength against hers. Its eyes emerged from the flood of sunfire. The Staff thrummed and twisted in her hands, against her ribs. Concussions ran unsteadily along its shaft: she felt the wood's desperation pulse like a stricken heart. Every iota of force that she could summon spouted and flared from the iron which bound her Staff – and it was not enough.

Yet even then she was not defeated. *They have done this to my* son! Instead of recognising that she was lost, she remembered.

I do not desire the destruction of the Earth.

She did not believe that the Theomach had aided her entirely for his own ends. He had given her as many hints as he could without violating the integrity of the Land's history.

In this circumstance—

And he had risked revealing secrets to Berek Halfhand in her presence; secrets which she would never have known otherwise.

—her mind cannot be distinguished from the Arch of Time.

She accepted the danger. She was Linden Avery, and did not choose to be defeated.

Bracing her Staff in the trough of EarthBlood, she shouted in her son's name, 'Melenkurion abatha! Duroc minas mill! Harad khabaal!'

Instantly her fire was multiplied. It seemed to increase a hundredfold; a thousand— She herself became stronger, as if she had received a transfusion of vitality. The fear – even the possibility – that she might fall and perish dropped from her. The Staff steadied itself in her clasp. The whole mountain sang in her veins.

They have done this *to my son!*

She shouted and shouted, and did not stop. 'Melenkurion abatha!' And as she pronounced the Seven Words, both Roger's pyrotic fury and the *croyel*'s invisible repulsion were driven back. '*Duroc minas mill!*' Roger gaped in sudden fright. The abominable gaze of the creature wavered, considering retreat. '*Harad khabaal!*' Flames like a volcanic convulsion staggered her foes.

And the Skyweir's deepest roots answered her.

From Rivenrock, she had felt the imminence of an earthquake. Roger had confirmed it. *It'll be massive.* Irrefusable pressures were accumulating in the gutrock; natural forces so cataclysmic that they would split the tremendous peak. *But it won't happen for years and years.*

He had not expected her to fight so fiercely. Their battle must have triggered a premature tectonic shift; loosed a rupture before its time.

She did not care. The granite's visceral groan meant nothing to her.

She fought for her son, and went on shouting; invoking Earthpower on a scale that staggered her foes. When the floor of the cave lurched as though the whole of *Melenkurion* Skyweir had shrugged, she gave no heed.

But Roger and the *croyel* cared. Consternation twisted his blunt features: he feared the mountain's violence. And the creature turned away from her, apparently seeking escape. They assailed her for a moment longer. Then the stone lurched again, and abruptly they fled.

'*Melenkurion abatha!*'

Pausing only to retrieve Jeremiah's crumpled racecar, Linden followed them; harried them with fire. As she pursued them along the tunnel, she continued to shout with all of her strength. And she trailed the end of her Staff in the rivulet so that she would not lose the EarthBlood's imponderable might.

'*Duroc minas mill!*'

Roger and the *croyel* did not strike at her now: they fought to preserve themselves. He sent gouts and gobbets of laval ire to hinder the impact of her sunflame. His companion filled the tunnel with a yammer of force, striving to slow her onslaught.

'*Harad khabaal!*'

Her power was constrained by the tunnel; concentrated by it. But theirs was also. Although she strode after them wreathed in fury, unleashing a continuous barrage of magic and Law, she could not break through their brimstone and repulsion swiftly enough to outpace their retreat. In spite of the EarthBlood and the Seven Words and the Staff of Law – in spite of the extravagance of her betrayed heart – they reached the subterranean waterfall unscathed.

The falls erupted in steam as Roger passed through it; but the *croyel*'s barrier warded off the scalding detonation. For a moment, no more than a heartbeat or two, Linden lost sight of them as they rushed down the piled rocks. Then the stone shuddered again, harder this time. She lost her footing, fell against the wall of the tunnel. At once, she sprang up again, borne by fire. With Earthpower, she parted the crushing waters and began to hasten perilously over the slick stones. But her foes were already halfway down the length of the cavern, limned in rocklight.

The mountain's tremors repeated themselves more frequently. Their ferocity mounted. Soon they became an almost constant seizure. As

Linden skidded to the cavern floor and tried to race after Roger and her helpless son, slabs of granite and schist the size of houses sheared off from the ceiling and collapsed on all sides.

Thunder filled the air with catastrophe. It seemed as loud as the ruin of worlds.

Now she had to fight for Jeremiah's life as well as her own. She knew what Roger and the *croyel* would do. Given any respite from her assault, any relief at all, they would combine their lore to transport themselves out of the mountain. They might fail in the presence of so much Earthpower, but they would certainly make the attempt. She had to do more than compel them to defend themselves. She had to drive them apart, fill the space between them with a ravage of flame. Otherwise her son would be snatched away. She was ten millennia from her proper time, and would never find him again.

But the ceiling was falling. Even the sides of the cavern were falling. Massive stone columns and monoliths toppled as the roots of *Melenkurion Skyweir* shook. The river danced in its course; overran its rims amid the hail of shattered menhirs and rubble. Orogenic thunder detonated through the cavern.

The *croyel* repelled the rock. Despite the magnitude of the quake, the creature protected Jeremiah and Roger. But Linden had no defence except Earthpower; no lore except the Seven Words.

The rocklight grew pale and faltered as the damage to the cavern increased.

Screaming, '*Melenkurion abatha!*' she tuned her fire to the pitch of granite and made powder of every crashing stone that came near her. '*Duroc minas mill!*' Hardly conscious of what she did, she shaped the mountain's collapse to her needs; formed pillars to support the Skyweir's inconceivable mass; dashed debris from her path so that she could strike at Roger and the *croyel*. '*Harad khabaal!*' Striding through havoc, she pursued her son's doom amid the earthquake.

But the titanic convulsion took too much of her strength. More and more, she was forced to ward off her own ruin. And she had lost the direct use of the EarthBlood. She could not reach Roger and Jeremiah; could not strike hard enough, swiftly enough, to penetrate her betrayers' defences.

In the Staff's flame and the last of the rocklight, she saw lightning arch between Roger's arms and Jeremiah's. She saw them vanish.

Then the earthquake took her; the river took her; and she was swept from the cavern.

PART II

'victims and enactors of Despite'

Chapter One:

From the Depths

When Linden Avery emerged from the base of Rivenrock into Garroting Deep, the sun was setting behind *Melenkurion* Skyweir and the Westron Mountains. The trees here had fallen into shadow, and with the loss of the sun, the air had grown cold enough to bite into her bereaved throat and lungs. Winter held sway over the Deep in spite of Caerroil Wildwood's stewardship. And she had been soaked by frigid springs as well as by diluted EarthBlood during her long struggle through the guts of the mountain. She was chilled to the marrow of her bones, weak with hunger, exhausted beyond bearing.

But she did not care.

Her son was dead, as doomed as she was, shot down when she and Roger had been slain. He belonged to Lord Foul and the *croyel*: they would never let him go. And she had no hope of reaching him. Too much time separated her arms and his; her love and his torment.

She had become a stillatory of pain, and her heart was stone.

She did not know how she was still alive, or why. After Roger's and Jeremiah's escape, she had somehow preserved herself with Earthpower and instinct, shaping the stone to her will: knocking aside thunderous slabs of granite; plunging in and out of the lashed river; following water and fire as the earthquake shook *Melenkurion* Skyweir. The upheaval had split the plateau as well as the vast mountain, buried the edges of the forest under a torrent of rubble, sent a vehement fume of dust skywards, but she was aware of none of it. Nor did she notice how much time passed before the roots of the Skyweir no longer trembled. The watercourse was nearly empty now. Deep springs slowly filled the spaces which she had formed under the peak. But she could not tell how long she scrambled and stumbled through the wreckage until she found her way out of the world of ruin.

When she clambered at last over the new detritus along the south bank of the Black River, and saw the fading sky above her, she knew only that she had lost her son – and that some essential part of her had been extinguished, burned away by battles which surpassed her strength. She was no longer the woman who had endured Roger's cruelties for Jeremiah's sake.

She had suffered enough; had earned the right to simply lie down and die. Yet she did not surrender. Instead she trudged on into Garroting Deep. Here the Forestal would surely end her travails, if sorrow and privation did not. Nevertheless she continued to plod among the darkening trees. Her right hand remained cramped to the Staff, unhealed and unheeded. In her left, she held Jeremiah's crumpled racecar. At the core, she had been annealed like granite. The dross of restraint and inadequacy and acceptance had been consumed in flame. Like granite, she did not yield.

The Staff no longer lit her way. She had lost its fire when she left the mountain. In the evening gloom and the first glimmer of stars, she hardly recognised that the extravagant energies which had enabled her to fight and survive had remade the shaft. Its smooth wood had become a blackness as deep as ebony or fuligin. With the Seven Words and the EarthBlood, she had gone beyond herself; and so she had transformed her Staff as well.

Like her son, the natural cleanliness of the wood was lost.

But she did not concern herself with such things. Nor did she fear the cold night, or the prospect of prostration, or the Forestal's coming. Her own frailty and the likelihood of death had lost their meaning. Her stone heart still beat: the tears were gone from her eyes. Therefore she walked on with her doom wrapped around her.

She travelled beside the Black River because she had no other guide. In the deeper twilight of the riverbed, a slow trickle of water remained. She caught glimpses of it when it rippled over rocks or twisted in hollows and caught the burgeoning starlight. It looked as unilluminable as blood.

The Ranyhyn had tried to caution her. At the horserite which she had shared with Hyn and Hynyn, and with Stave, she had been warned. Hyn and Hynyn had shown her Jeremiah possessed, in torment; made vile. They had revealed what would happen if she tried to rescue him, heal him, as she had once redeemed Thomas Covenant from his imprisonment by the *Elohim*. And they had compelled her to remember the depth to which she herself had been damaged. They had caused her to relive the maiming heritage of her parents as well as the eager brutality of *moksha* Raver.

It was possible that she should have known—

If your son serves me, he will do so in your presence.

But her fears had been fixed on Ravers and the Despiser. She had failed to imagine the true implications of Hyn and Hynyn's warning. Or she had been distracted by Roger's glamour and manipulations; by the *croyel's* intolerable use of Jeremiah. Ever since they had forbidden her to touch them – ever since they had turned her love and woe against her – she had foundered in confusion; and so she had been made to serve Despite.

You've done everything conceivable to help us become gods.

She did not surrender. She would not. But she could not think beyond doggedly placing one foot in front of the other, walking lightless and unassoiled into Garroting Deep.

She did not imagine that she might reach her proper time by creating a *caesure*. *You'll shatter the world.* And even if she did not, she would still be lost. Without the Ranyhyn, she could not navigate the chaos of a Fall.

Nor could she save herself with the Staff of Law. No power available to her would transcend the intervening centuries.

The Theomach had recognised Roger and the *croyel*, and had said nothing. While they abided by the restrictions which he had placed upon them, he had left her to meet her fate in ignorance.

—her mind cannot be distinguished from the Arch of Time.

In her own way, she chose to keep faith with the Land's past.

Therefore she stumbled on into Caerroil Wildwood's angry demesne, guiding herself by the darkness of the watercourse on her left and the star-limned branches of trees on her right. When she tripped, she caught herself with the Staff, although the jolt caused the scabbing of her wounded hand to break open and bleed. She had nowhere else to go.

Roger had called the Forestal *an out-and-out butcher*.

On his own ground, with the full force of Garroting Deep behind him, nothing could stand against him.

Why had he not already slain her?

Perhaps he had discerned her weakness and knew that there was no need for haste. If a badger took umbrage at her encroachment, she would be unable to defend herself. A single note of Caerroil Wildwood's multifarious song would overwhelm her.

Some things she knew, however. They did not require thought. She could be sure that Roger and the *croyel* – and Kastenessen and Joan – had not yet accomplished the Despiser's desires. The Arch of Time endured. Her boots still scuffed and tripped one after the other along the riverbank. Her heart still beat. Her lungs still sucked, wincing, at the edged air. And above her the cold stars became multitudinous glistening swaths as the last daylight faded behind the western peaks. Even her exhaustion confirmed that the strictures of sequence and causality remained intact.

Therefore the Land's tale was not done.

Her confrontation with Roger had rubbed the truth like salt into a wound: for her, everything came back to Thomas Covenant. He was her hope when she had failed all of her loves. —*help us become* gods. In his own way, and for his own reasons, he himself had become a kind of god. While his spirit endured, she could refuse to believe that the Despiser would achieve victory.

The Earth held mysteries which she could not begin to comprehend. Even Jeremiah might someday be released. As long as Thomas Covenant remained— He might guide her friends to rouse the *Elohim* from their hermetic self-contemplation; or to thwart Roger and Lord Foul in some other fashion.

For that reason, she continued walking when she should not have been able to stay on her feet. She had failed utterly, and been filled with despair; but she no longer knew how to break.

Around her, full night gathered until the ancient ire of the trees seemed to form a palpable barrier. Aside from the soft liquid chatter of water in the riverbed, the whisper of wind among the wrathful boughs, and the unsteady plod of her boots, she heard only her own respiration, ragged and faltering. She might have been alone in the wide forest. Still her heart sustained its dark labour. Intransigent as the Masters, she let neither weakness nor the approach of death stop her.

Some time later, she saw a small blink of light ahead of her. It was too vague to be real: she could more easily believe that she had fallen into dreams. But gradually it gained substance; definition. Soon it resembled the caper of flames, yellow and flickering.

A will-o'-the-wisp, she thought. Or a hallucination induced by fatigue and loss. Yet it did not vanish and reappear, or shift from place to place. In spite of its allusive dance, it remained stationary, casting a faint illumination on the nearby tree trunks, the arched bare branches.

A fire, she realised dully. Someone had set a fire in this protected forest.

She did not hasten towards it. She could not. Her pulse did not quicken. But her uneven trudge took on a more concrete purpose. She was not alone in Garroting Deep. And whoever had lit that fire was in imminent peril: more so than Linden herself, who could not have raised any hint of flame from her black Staff.

The distance defied her estimation. By slow increments, however, she began to discern details. A small cookfire burned within a ring of stones. A pot that may have been iron rested among the flames. And beside the fire squatted an obscure figure with its back to the river. At intervals, the figure reached out with a spoon or ladle to stir the contents of the pot.

Linden seemed to draw no closer. Nonetheless she saw that the figure wore a tatterdemalion cloak against the winter. She saw a disregarded tangle of old hair, a plump shape. To her depleted senses, the figure appeared female.

Then she entered the fringes of the light; and the figure turned to gaze at her; and she stopped. But she was unaware of her own surprise. She still swayed from side to side, precariously balanced, as if she were walking. Her muscles conveyed the sensations of steps. In her dreams, her legs and the Staff carried her forward.

The fire was small, and the pot shrouded its light. Linden blinked and stared for several moments before she recognised the woman's blunt and skewed features, her patchwork robe under her open cloak, her mismatched eyes. Briefly those eyes spilled shifting reflections. Then Linden saw that the left was a dark and luminous blue, the right a disconcerting, unmistakable orange.

The woman's air of comfortable solicitude identified her as readily as her appearance. She was the Mahdoubt. Linden had last seen her in Revelstone ten thousand years from now, when the older woman had warned her to *Be cautious of love.*

The Mahdoubt was here.

That was impossible.

But Linden did not care about impossibilities. She had left every endurable aspect of her existence behind. At that moment, the only fact which held any significance for her was the Mahdoubt's cookfire.

The kindly woman had dared to ignite flames in Caerroil Wildwood's demesne.

Staring, Linden meant to say, You've got to put that out. The fire. This is Garroting Deep. She thought that she would speak aloud. She ought to speak urgently. But those words failed her. Her mouth and tongue seemed incapable of them. Instead she asked, faint as a whisper, 'Why didn't they just kill me?'

At any other time in her life, under any other circumstances, there would have been tears in her eyes and weeping in her voice. But all of her emotions had been melted down, fused into a lump of obsidian. She possessed only anger for which she had no strength.

'Across the years,' the woman replied, 'the Mahdoubt has awaited the lady.' She sounded complacent, untroubled. 'Oh, assuredly. And once again she offers naught but meagre fare. The lady will think her improvident. Yet here are shallots in a goodly broth' – she waved her ladle at the pot – 'with winter greens and some few *aliantha*. And she has provided as well a flask of springwine. Will the lady not sup with her, and take comfort?'

Linden smelled the savour of the stew. She had eaten nothing, drunk nothing, for a long time. But she did not care. Wanly she tried again.

That fire— The Forestal—

'Why didn't they just kill me?'

Useless screaming had left her hoarse. She hardly heard her own voice.

The Mahdoubt sighed. For a moment, her orange eye searched Linden while her right regarded the flames. Then she turned her head away. With a hint of sadness, she said, 'The Mahdoubt may answer none of the lady's sorrows. Time has been made fragile. It must not be challenged further. Of that she gives assurance. Yet she is grieved to behold the lady thus, weary, unfed and full of woe. Will she not accept these small comforts?' Again she indicated her pot; her fire. 'Here are aliment, and warmth to nurture sleep, and the solace of the Mahdoubt's goodwill. Refusal will augment her grief.'

Sleep? A dim anger at herself made Linden frown. At one time, she had ached to speak with the Mahdoubt. *There is a glamour upon it which binds the heart to destruction.* That, at least, had been the truth.

She made another effort to say what the woman's kindness required of her. 'Please—' she began weakly, still swaying; still unsure that she had stopped moving. 'Your fire. The Forestal. He'll see it.' Surely he had already done so? 'We'll both die.

'Why didn't they kill me?'

Roger and the *croyel* could have slain her whenever she slept.

'Pssht, lady,' responded the Mahdoubt. 'Is the Mahdoubt disquieted? She is not. In her youth, such concerns may perchance have vexed her, but her old bones have felt their full measure of years, and naught troubles her now.'

Calmly she added, 'Hear her, lady. The Mahdoubt implores this. Be seated within her warmth. Accept the sustenance which she has prepared. Her courtesy merits that recompense.'

Again the Mahdoubt lifted her strange gaze to Linden's face. 'There is much in all sooth of which she must not speak. Yet the Mahdoubt may speculate without hazard – yes, assuredly – if she speaks only of that which the lady has properly heard, or which she might comprehend unaided, were she whole in spirit.'

Linden blinked vacantly. She had heard or tasted Caerroil Wildwood's song: she knew its power. Surely she should have protested? She would have owed that much to a total stranger. The Mahdoubt deserved more—

But the balm of the Mahdoubt's voice overcame her. She could not refuse that blue eye, or the orange one. As if she were helpless, she took one step towards the fire, then sank to the ground.

It was thickly matted with fallen leaves. They must once have been frozen to the dirt, but they had thawed to a soggy carpet in the heat of the cookfire. Gripping the Staff with her scabbed and seared fist, Linden struggled to sit cross-legged near the ring of stones.

Abruptly the Mahdoubt's orange eye appeared to flare. 'The lady must release the Staff. How otherwise will she sup?'

Linden could not let go. Her cramped grasp would not unclose. And she would need the Staff. She had no other defence.

Nevertheless it slipped from her fingers and dropped soundlessly to the damp leaves.

Nodding with apparent satisfaction, the Mahdoubt produced a wooden bowl from a pocket or satchel under her cloak. As she ladled stew from the pot, she spoke to the cookfire and the louring night as though she had forgotten Linden's presence.

'Assuredly the lady's treachers required her absence from her condign time, lest she be succoured by such powers as they could not lightly oppose – by ur-viles and Waynhim, and perchance by others as well. Also they feared – and rightly – that which lies hidden within the old man whom the lady has befriended.'

Without glancing at Linden, she reached into her cloak for a spoon. When she had placed the spoon in the stew, she handed the bowl to Linden.

Like a bidden child, Linden began to eat. On some inchoate level, she must have understood that the older woman was saving her life – at least temporarily – but she was not conscious of it. Her attention was fixed on the Mahdoubt's voice. Nothing existed for her while she ate except the woman's words, and the looming threat of melody.

'Yet when she had been removed from all aid,' the Mahdoubt informed the trees placidly, 'the lady's death would serve no purpose. Indeed, her foes have never desired her death. They wish her to bear the burden of the Land's doom. And the virtue of white gold is lessened when it is not freely ceded.

'Nor could she be engaged willingly in such combat as would endanger

Time. With the Staff of Law, she might perchance have healed any harm. And she might have slain her betrayers with wild magic. That they assuredly did not desire. Nor could they assail the Arch directly, for the lady would then have surely destroyed them. Such errant evil craves its own preservation more than it desires the ruin of Life and Time.'

Linden nodded to herself as she slowly lifted stew into her mouth. She did not truly grasp what the woman was saying: her fatigue ran too deep. But she understood that Roger's and the *croyel's* actions could be explained. The Mahdoubt's unthreatened tranquillity gave her that anodyne.

'Nor could the lady be merely forsaken in this time,' continued the Mahdoubt, 'while her treachers sought the Power of Command. She might contrive means or acquire companions to assail them ere their ends were accomplished. Nor could they be assured that any use of that Power would accomplish their ends, for the Blood of the Earth is perilous. Any Command may return against its wielder, bringing calamity to those who fear no death except their own.'

By degrees, Linden began to detect strands of melody among the woman's words; or she thought that she did. But they had the same quality of hallucination or dream that she had felt earlier. She could not be sure of anything except the Mahdoubt's voice.

Without realising it, she had emptied the bowl. The Mahdoubt glanced at her, then retrieved the bowl, filled it again, and returned it to her. But the older woman continued to speak as she did so.

'The Mahdoubt merely speculates. Of that she assures herself. Therefore she does not fear to suggest that the chief desire of the lady's betrayers was the lady's pain.'

Facing the trees and the blind night, she reached once more into her cloak and withdrew a narrow-necked flask closed with a wooden plug. Its glassy sides shed reflections of viridian and tourmaline as she removed the plug and passed the vessel to Linden.

When Linden drank, she tasted springwine; and her senses lost some of their dullness. Now she was almost sure that she heard notes and words, fragments of song, behind the Mahdoubt's voice. They may have been *dusty waste* and *hate of hands*; or perhaps *rain and heat and snow.*

Nevertheless the Mahdoubt went on speaking as though the forest's anger held nothing to alarm her.

'By that hurt, they sought to gain the surrender of white gold. And if they could not obtain its surrender, they desired the lady to exert the ring's force in the name of her suffering under *Melenkurion* Skyweir, either for their aid or against their purpose. In such an outcome, the Staff of Law and the EarthBlood and wild magic would exceed the lady's flesh, and Time would be truly endangered. Her foes could not have believed that she would find within herself force and lore sufficient to oppose them without recourse to white gold.'

At last, Linden raised her head. She had become certain that she heard pieces of music, the scattered notes of an unresolved threnody. They came skirling among the trees, taking shape as they approached, implying words which they did not utter. *I know the hate of hands grown bold.* She flung a look at the Mahdoubt and saw that both of the woman's eyes were alight, vivid blue and stark orange. The Mahdoubt had fallen silent; or the song had stilled her voice. Yet she appeared to face the Forestal's advance with comfortable unconcern.

> *Since days before the Earth was old*
> *And Time began its walk to doom,*
> *The Forests world's bare rock anneal,*
> *Forbidding dusty waste and death.*

As if in response, the Mahdoubt murmured,

> 'Though wide world's winds untimely blow,
> And earthquakes rock and cliff unseal,
> My leaves grow green and seedlings bloom.'

A wind rose through the woods, adding the dry harmony of barren boughs and brittle evergreen needles to the mournful ire of the music. Stern snatches of melody seemed to gather around the campfire like stars, underscored by the almost subterranean mutter of trunks and roots. Linden had seen and felt and tasted that song before, but in an angrier and less laden key. Now the woodland dirge held notes like questions, brief arcs and broad spans tuned to the pitch of uncertainty. Caerroil Wildwood may have intended to quash those who had raised flames here, but he had other desires as well, purposes which were not those of *an out-and-out butcher*.

A shimmer of melody rippled the surface of the night like a breeze passing over a still pool. The presence and power of the song was palpable, although Linden beheld it only with her health-sense. Nevertheless each note and chime and lift of music swirling from the branches like autumn leaves implied an imminent light which gradually coalesced into the form of a man.

Instinctively she reached for the Staff. But the Mahdoubt halted her by grasping her arm.

'Withhold, lady.' The older woman did not glance at Linden. Instead she studied the Forestal's coming with her lit gaze. 'The Great One's knowledge of such power suffices. He has no wish to witness it now.'

Linden understood in spite of her bottomless fatigue. The Mahdoubt did not want her to do anything which might be interpreted as a threat.

Linden obeyed. Resting her hands on her thighs, she simply watched the stately figure, lambent as a monarch, walking among the dark trees.

The Forestal was tall, and his long hair and beard flowed whitely about him like water. From his eyes shone a piercing and severe silver which showed neither iris nor pupil; light so acute that she wanted to duck her head when his gaze touched her. In the bend of one arm, he carried a short, twisted branch as though it were a sceptre. Flowers she could not identify ornamented his neck in a garland of rich purple and purest white; and his samite robe was white as well, austere and free of taint from collar to hem. As he passed among the trees gravely, they appeared to do him homage, lowering their boughs in obeisance. His steps were wreathed in song as if he were melody incarnate.

The Mahdoubt's eyes gleamed in appreciation. Their weird colours conveyed a placid warmth untrammelled by fear or doubt. When the Forestal stopped, regal and ominous, at the edge of the cookfire's glow, she inclined her head in a grave bow.

'The Mahdoubt greets you, Great One,' she said with no trace of apprehension. 'Be welcome at our fireside. Will you sup with us? Our fare is homely – oh, assuredly – but it is proffered with gladness, and the offer is kindly meant.'

'Presumptuous woman.' Caerroil Wildwood's voice was the music of a rippling stream, delicate and clear. It seemed to chuckle to itself, although the silver flash of his eyes under his thick white brows denied mirth. Rather his glances demanded awe at his withheld wrath. 'I do not require such sustenance.'

Linden bit her lip anxiously; but the older woman's smile was unconcerned. 'Then why have you come? The Mahdoubt asks with respect. Has this revered forest no need of your might elsewhere?'

'I am throughout the trees,' sang the Forestal, 'elsewhere as well as here. Seek not to mislead me. You have intruded fire into Garroting Deep, where flames are met with loathing and fear. I have come to determine your purpose.'

'Ah.' Linden's companion nodded. 'This the Mahdoubt questions, Great One.' She raised both hands in deprecation. 'With respect, with respect.' Then she rested her arms on her plump belly. 'Do you not crave our extermination? Is it not your intent to slay all who encroach upon the ancient Deep?'

The guardian of the trees appeared to assent. 'From border to border, my demesne thirsts for the recompense of blood.'

The Mahdoubt nodded again. 'Assuredly. And that thirst is justified, the Mahdoubt avers. Millennia of inconsolable loss provide its vindication.'

'Yet I refrain,' Caerroil Wildwood replied.

'Assuredly,' repeated the Mahdoubt. 'Therefore the Mahdoubt's heart is rich with gratitude. Nonetheless the purpose which the Great One desires to determine is his, not ours.

'Gazing upon us, he has observed that he has no cause for ire. And he has discerned as well that he must not harm the lady. He has heard all that the Mahdoubt has said of her. He perceives her service to that which is held dear. He has come seeking the name of his own intent, not that of the Mahdoubt, or of the lady.'

When the Forestal fixed his burning stare on Linden, she felt an almost physical impact. Fighting herself, she met his eyes; let him search her with silver. She heard a kind of recognition in his music, a wrath more personal than his appetite for the blood of those who slaughtered trees. Slowly his gaze sank to consider her apparel, study Covenant's ring through her shirt, acknowledge the bullet hole over her heart, regard the Staff of Law. He noted her grass stained jeans – and did not sing of her death.

Instead he returned his attention to the Mahdoubt.

'I am the Land's Creator's hold,' he pronounced in melody. 'She wears the mark of fecundity and long grass. Also she has paid the price of woe. And the sigil of the Land's need has been placed upon her.' He may have been referring to her stabbed hand. 'Therefore she will not perish within this maimed remnant of the One Forest. Nor will any Forestal sing against her while she keeps faith with grass and tree.

'Come,' he commanded in a brusque fall of notes. 'My path is chosen. She must stand upon Gallows Howe.'

Turning his back, he strode away.

At once, but without haste, the Mahdoubt rose to her feet. 'Come, lady,' she echoed when Linden hesitated. 'And now the lady must bring the Staff. Assuredly so.' She nodded. 'The Great One will grant a boon which she has not asked of him, and he will require that in return which she does not expect. Yet his aid must not be refused. His desired recompense will not exceed her.'

Linden blinked at the woman. She understood nothing, and her heart was granite: beneath her fear of the Forestal, she held only Jeremiah and anger – and Thomas Covenant. For food and drink and warmth, she might have been thankful; but she had lost her son. Caerroil Wildwood had already promised that he would not slay her. What need did she have for an ambiguous gift which she would not know how to repay?

Caerroil Wildwood could not return her to her proper time. No Forestal had that power.

Carefully she set the Mahdoubt's flask against a stone; but she did not stand. Instead she looked into the strange discrepancy of the Mahdoubt's eyes.

'You told me to "Be cautious of love".' *There is a glamour upon it—* 'You knew who they were.' Roger and the *croyel*. 'Why didn't you just say so?'

If the Mahdoubt had spoken plainly—

For the first time, the older woman's mien hinted at disquiet; perhaps even at unhappiness. 'It is not permitted—' she began, then stopped herself. When she had closed her eyes for a moment, she opened them again and faced Linden with chagrin in her gaze.

'Nay, the Mahdoubt will speak sooth. She does not permit it of herself, though her heart is wrung in her old breast by what has ensued, as it is by what may yet transpire. Her intent is kind, lady. Be assured that it is. But she has acquired neither wisdom nor knowledge adequate to contest that which appears needful. Others do so, to their cost. The Mahdoubt does not. If she craves to be kind in deed as well as intent, she has learned that she must betimes forbear. Yet she has won gratitude from other people in other times, if not from the lady.

'The Great One bids us,' she finished softly. 'We must follow.'

Linden wanted to refuse. She wanted to demand, Needful? *Needful?* The Forestal and even the Mahdoubt surpassed her. But what choice did she have? Ever since she had returned to the Land, she had been guided by other people's desires and demands, other people's manipulations, and all of her actions had been fraught with peril. She could not afford to reject aid in any form.

Sighing, she clasped the Staff of Law and pushed herself to her feet.

As she did so, she found that the Mahdoubt's providence had done her more good than she had realised. Her muscles protested, but they did not fail. Indeed, they hardly trembled. Food and springwine and soothing warmth had eased her weakness, although they could not relieve her exhaustion, or soften her heart.

When the Mahdoubt gestured towards the trees, Linden accompanied her into the forest, led by the majesty and restraint of Caerroil Wildwood's music.

The way was not far – or it did not seem far in the thrall of the Forestal's singing. Briefly Linden and the Mahdoubt walked among trees and darkness; and on all sides sycamores and oaks, birches and Gilden, cedars and firs proclaimed their unappeased recriminations. But then they found themselves on barren ground that rose up to form a high hill like a burial mound. Even through her boots, Linden felt death in the soil. Here centuries or millennia of bloodshed had soaked into the dirt until it would never again support life. This, then, was Gallows

Howe: the place where Caerroil Wildwood slew the butchers of his trees.

At first, she winced in recognition at every step. Until her betrayal under *Melenkurion* Skyweir, she had not understood people or beings or powers that feasted on death. She had been a physician, opposed to such hungers. Evil she knew, in herself as well as in her foes: she was intimately acquainted with the desire to inflict pain on those who had not caused it. But this unalloyed and unforgiving compulsion towards revenge; this righteous rage– She had not known that she contained such possibilities until she had beheld her son's suffering.

Here, however, she found that she welcomed the taste of retribution. It made her stronger.

She knew what it meant.

Bringing her to this place sanctified by slaughter, Caerroil Wildwood had already given her a gift.

In starlight and the lucent allusions of the Forestal's music, she saw two dead black trees standing beyond the lifeless hillcrest. They were ten or more paces apart, as strait and unanswerable as denunciations. All of their branches had been stripped away except for one heavy bough in each trunk high above the ground. Long ages ago, these limbs had grown together to form a crossbar between the trees: Caerroil Wildwood's gibbet. Here he had hanged the most fatal of those adversaries that came within his reach.

Linden's reluctance beside the Mahdoubt's gentle cookfire was gone. Gaining strength with every step, she ascended the Howe. She could think now, and begin to strive. On this denuded hill, beneath those pitiless trees, she might accept any boon – and pay any price.

At the crest, she and her companion stopped. For a moment, they appeared to be alone: then Caerroil Wildwood stood before them with song streaming from his robe and bright silver in his eyes. The Mahdoubt lowered her gaze as though she felt a measure of diffidence. But Linden held up her head, gripped her Staff and waited for the Forestal to reveal his intentions.

For a time, he did not regard either woman. Instead he sang to himself. His song conveyed impressions of Ravers and loss; of a fading Interdict as the Colossus of the Fall waned; of Viles and rapacious kings and disdain.

And it implied the era of the One Forest, when the Land had flourished as its Creator had intended, and there was no need of Forestals to defend the ravaged paean of the world. He may have been probing his own intentions, testing his decision to withhold Linden's death, and the Mahdoubt's.

Linden suspected that if she listened long enough she might hear extraordinary revelations about the Land's ancient past. She might be told how the Ravers had been born and nurtured, or how they had come under Lord Foul's dominion. She might learn how even the great puissance of the Forestals had failed to sustain the forests. But she had lost her patience for long tales which would not aid her. Without conscious forethought, she interrupted the sumptuous reverie of Caerroil Wildwood's music.

'You can't stop the Ravers,' she said as though she had forgotten that the Forestal could sing the flesh from her bones. 'You know that. When you kill their bodies, their spirits just move on.'

He turned the piercing silver of his gaze on her as if she had offended him. But apparently she had not. In spite of his old anger, he did not strike out.

'Nevertheless,' he countered, 'I have a particular hunger— '

Again Linden interrupted him. 'But there's going to come a time when one of them does die.' *Samadhi* Sheol would be *rent* by Grimmand Honninscrave and the Sandgorgon Nom. 'It can happen. You can hope for that.'

She hazarded Time, and knew it. Speaking of the Land's future might alter Caerroil Wildwood's actions at some point during his long existence. But the Mahdoubt did nothing to forestall or caution her. And Linden had already taken greater risks. She was done with hesitation. If she could do or say anything that might encourage the Forestal to side with her, she would not hold back.

However, his response was sorrow rather than grim anticipation. His music became a fugue of mourning, interminable bereavement sung to a counterpoint of forlorn self-knowledge.

'While humans and monsters remain to murder trees, there can be no hope for any Forestal. Each death lessens me. The ages of the Earth are brief, and already I am not as I began.'

Then his melody sharpened. 'But you have said that the death of a Raver will come to pass. How do you know of this?'

Linden held his gaze. 'I was there.'

Her past was the Land's future. She hardly dared to imagine that Caerroil Wildwood would understand her, or believe. But her statement did not appear to confound him. Her displacement in time may have been as obvious to him as the stains on her jeans.

'And you played a part?' he asked while the wide forest echoed his words avidly.

'I saw it happen,' she replied steadily. 'That's all.' To explain herself, she added, 'I wasn't what I am now.'

When Thomas Covenant and his companions had faced the na-Mhoram in the Hall of Gifts, Linden had contributed nothing except her fears and her health-sense. But she had borne witness.

The Forestal withdrew his scrutiny. For a long moment, he appeared to muse to himself, harmonising with the trees. Now the Mahdoubt regarded him complacently. Under her breath, she made a humming sound as if she wished to contribute in some small way to the myriad-throated contemplations of Garroting Deep. When he sang in words again, he seemed to address the farthest reaches of his woods, or the black gibbet towering above him, rather than either Linden or her companion.

'I have granted boons, and may do so again. For each, I demand such payment as I deem meet. But you have not requested that which you most require. Therefore I will exact no recompense. Rather I ask only that you accept the burden of a question for which you have no answer.'

The Mahdoubt smiled with satisfaction; and Linden said, 'Just tell me what it is. If I can find an answer, I will.'

Caerroil Wildwood continued singing to the trees rather than to her. 'It is this. How may life endure in the Land, if the Forestals fail and perish, as they must, and naught remains to ward its most vulnerable treasures? We were formed to stand as guardians in the Creator's stead. Must it transpire that beauty and truth shall pass utterly when we are gone?'

Surprised, Linden murmured, 'I don't know.' She had seen Caer-Caveral sacrifice himself, and he was the last. The Sunbane had destroyed every remnant of the ancient forests west of Landsdrop.

Still smiling, the Mahdoubt said, 'The Great One is aware of this.

Assuredly so. He does not require that which the lady cannot possess. He asks only that she seek out knowledge, for its lack torments him. The fear that no answer exists multiplies his long sorrow.'

'I will,' repeated Linden, although she could not guess what her promise might cost her, and had no idea how she would keep it. Caerroil Wildwood was too extreme to be refused.

'Then I will grant that which you require.' The Forestal sang as though he spoke for every living thing throughout the Deep.

At once, music gathered around Linden's grasp on the Staff. Involuntarily she flinched. Unbidden, her fingers opened. But the Staff did not fall to the ground. Instead it floated away from her, wafted by song towards the Forestal. When it was near, he reached out to claim it with his free hand; and his clasp shone with the same silver that illumined his eyes.

'This blackness is lamentable' – his tone itself was elegiac – 'but I will not alter it. Its import lies beyond my ken. However, other flaws may be amended. The theurgy of the wood's fashioning is unfinished. It was formed in ignorance, and could not be otherwise than it is. Yet its wholeness is needful. Willingly I complete the task of its creation.'

Then he sang a command that would have been *Behold!* if it had been expressed in words rather than melody. At the same time, he lifted his gnarled sceptre. It, too, radiated silver, telic and irrefusable, as he directed its singing at the Staff.

Slowly a nacre fire began to burn along the dark surface of the shaft from heel to heel; and as it did so, it incised shapes like a jagged script into the wood. Radiance lingered in them after the Forestal's magic had passed: then it faded, line by line in dying streaks of argent, until the Staff had once again lapsed to ebony.

Runes, Linden thought in wonder. Caerroil Wildwood had carved runes—

A moment later, he released the Staff. Midnight between its bands of iron, it drifted through the air to Linden. When she closed her fingers around it, the shapes flared briefly once more, and she saw that they were indeed runes: inexplicable to her, but sequacious and acute. Their implications seemed to glow for an instant through the wound in her right hand. And as they fell away, she felt a renewed severity in the wood, a greater and more exacting commitment, as though the necessary commandments of Law had been fortified.

When the last of the luminance was gone from the symbols, she found that her hand had been healed. Pale against the black shaft, her human flesh too had become whole.

She had entered Garroting Deep bereft of every resource; exhausted beyond bearing; upheld by nothing except clenched intransigence – and thoughts of Thomas Covenant. But the Mahdoubt had fed and warmed her. Comforted her. And now Caerroil Wildwood had given her new power. Gallows Howe itself had made her stronger. All of her burdens except the pressing weight of millennia and incomprehension had been eased.

Finally she roused herself from her astonishment so that she could thank the Forestal. But he had already turned to walk away with his threnody and his silver eyes. And as he passed between the stark up-rights of his gibbet, he seemed to shimmer into music and disappear, leaving her alone with the Mahdoubt and the starlight and the ceaseless sorrowing wrath of the trees.

For a long moment, Linden and the older woman listened to Caerroil Wildwood's departure, hearing it fade like the future of Garroting Deep. Then the Mahdoubt spoke softly, in cadences that echoed the Forestal's lorn song.

'The words of the Great One are sooth. His passing cannot be averted, though he will cling to his purpose for many centuries. These trees have forgotten the knowledge which enables him, and which also binds the Colossus of the Fall. The dark delight of the Ravers will have its freedom. Alas for the Earth, lady. The tale of the days to come will be one of rue and woe.'

With an effort, Linden shook off the Forestal's ensorcellment. She had been given a gift which seemed to hold more meaning than she knew how to contain. Yet it changed nothing. The task of returning to her proper time still transcended her.

Standing on wrath and death, she confronted her companion.

'I just made a promise.' Her voice was hoarse with the memory of her promises. She had made so many of them— 'But I can't keep it. Not here. I have to go back where I belong.'

Darkness concealed the strange discrepancy of the Mahdoubt's eyes, giving her a secretive air in spite of her comfortable demeanour. 'Lady,' she replied, 'your need for nourishment and rest is not yet sated. Return with the Mahdoubt to warmth and stew and springwine. She urges you, seeing you unsolaced.'

Linden shook her head. In this time, the Mahdoubt had not referred to her as *you* until now. 'You can help me. That's obvious. You wouldn't be here if you couldn't move through time.' Her urgency increased as she persisted. 'You can take me back.'

The Mahdoubt seemed tranquil, but her tone hinted at sadness as she said, 'Lady, the Mahdoubt may answer none of your queries. Nor may she lightly set aside the strictures of your plight. Nor may she transgress the constraints of her own knowledge. Assuredly not.' She touched the bare skin of Linden's wrist near the Staff, allowing Linden's nerves to feel her sincerity. 'Will you not accompany her? The Great One cannot grant your desire, and this place' – she inclined her head to indicate Gallows Howe – 'augurs only death.

'Will sustenance and companionship harm the lady? The Mahdoubt inquires respectfully, intending only kindness.'

Linden could not think of a reason to refuse. She felt a disquieting kinship with the Howe. And its blood-soaked earth held lessons which she had not yet understood. She was loath to leave it. But the Mahdoubt's touch evoked a need that she had tried to suppress; a hunger for simple human contact. Jeremiah had refused her for so long– She could plead for her companion's help beside the cookfire as well as here.

With a stiff shrug, she allowed the Mahdoubt to lead her back down the dead slope in the direction of food and the Black River.

The distance seemed greater than it had earlier. But once Linden and her guide had left Gallows Howe behind and had spent a while moving like starlight through the bitter woodland, she began to catch glimpses of a soft yellow glow past the trees. Soon they reached the riverbank and the Mahdoubt's cookfire.

To every dimension of Linden's senses, the flames looked entirely mundane, as plain as air and cold – and as ordinary as the Mahdoubt's plump flesh. However, they had not died down while they went untended. The pot still bubbled soothingly. And its contents were undiminished.

Sighing complacently, the older woman returned to her place with her back to the thin trickle of the river. Squatting as she had earlier, she stirred at her pot for a moment, smelled it with contentment, then retrieved Linden's bowl and filled it. When she had set the bowl down near the warming flask of springwine, she looked up at Linden. Her blue eye regarded Linden directly, but the orange one appeared to focus past or through her, contemplating a vista that Linden could not discern.

'Be seated, lady,' she advised mildly. 'Eat that which the Mahdoubt has prepared. And rest also. Sleep if you are able. Will your dreams be troubled, or your slumber disturbed? No, assuredly. The Mahdoubt provides peace as she does food and drink. That gift she may bestow freely, though her infirmities be many and the years weigh unkindly upon her bones. The Great One will suffer our intrusion.'

Linden considered remaining on her feet. She felt restless, charged with new tensions: she could not imagine sleep. And an impossible journey lay ahead of her. More than food or rest, she needed some reason to believe that it could be accomplished.

The Mahdoubt had not come here merely to feed and comfort her, or to provide for her encounter with the Forestal: Linden was certain of that. While she remained in this time, she could not keep her promise to Caerroil Wildwood, or act on what she had learned from Gallows Howe, or try to rescue her son, or search for Thomas Covenant and hope—

But the aromas arising from the pot insisted that she was still hungry. And the Mahdoubt's intent was palpably charitable, whatever its limitations. Abruptly Linden sat down within reach of the cookfire's heat and set the Staff beside her.

Lifting the flask, she found it full. At once, she swallowed several long draughts, then turned the surface of her attention to the stew while her deeper mind tried to probe the conundrum of her companion. Doubtless food and drink and the balm of the cookfire did her good; but those benefits were trivial. In her present straits, even Caerroil Wildwood's gifts were trivial. What she needed most, required absolutely, was some way to return to her friends and Revelstone.

That she would never find without the Mahdoubt's help.

When she was ready – as ready as she would ever be – she arose and took her bowl to the edge of the watercourse. There she searched by the dim glitter of the stars until she located a manageable descent. Moving cautiously through mud that reached the ankles of her boots, she approached the small stream. There she rinsed out the bowl; and as she did so, the Earthpower pulsing along the current restored her further. Then, heedless of the damp and dirt that besmirched her clothes, she clambered back up the bank and returned to the Mahdoubt.

Handing the bowl to the older woman, she bowed with as much grace as she could muster. 'I should thank you,' she said awkwardly. 'I can't imagine how you came here, or why you care. None of this makes sense to me.' Obliquely the Mahdoubt had already refused Linden's desire for a passage through time. 'But you've saved my life when I thought that I was completely alone.' Alone and doomed. 'Even if there's nothing more that you can do to help me, you deserve all the thanks I have.'

The woman inclined her head. 'You are gracious, lady. Gratitude is always welcome – oh, assuredly – and more so when the years have become long and wearisome. The Mahdoubt has lived beyond her time, and now finds gladness only in service. Aye, and in such gratitude as you are able to provide.'

For a moment longer, Linden remained standing. Gazing down on her companion might give her an advantage. But then, deliberately, she set such ploys aside. They were unworthy of the Mahdoubt's kindness. When she had resumed her seat beside the fire and had picked up the Staff to rest it across her lap, she faced the challenge of finding answers.

Carefully, keeping her voice low and her tone neutral, she said, 'You're one of the Insequent.'

The Mahdoubt appeared to consider the night. 'May the Mahdoubt reply to such a query? Indeed she may, for she relies on naught which the lady has not gleaned from her own pain. For that reason, no harm will ensue.'

Then she gave Linden a bright glimpse of her orange eye. 'It is sooth, lady. The Mahdoubt is of the Insequent.'

Linden nodded. 'So you know the Theomach. And—' She paused momentarily, unsure whether to trust what the *croyel* had told her through Jeremiah. 'And the Vizard?'

The Mahdoubt returned her gaze to the shrouded darkness of Garroting Deep. 'Lady, it is not so among us.' She spoke with apparent ease, but her manner hinted at caution, as if she were feeling her way through a throng of possible calamities. 'When the Insequent are young, they join and breed and make merry. But as their years accumulate, they are overtaken by an insatiable craving for knowledge. It compels them. Therefore they turn to questings which consume the remainder of their days.

'However, these questings demand solitude. They must be pursued privately or not at all. Each of the Insequent desires understanding and power which the others do not possess. For that reason, they become misers of knowledge. They move apart from each other, and their dealings are both infrequent and cryptic.'

The older woman sighed, and her tone took on an uncharacteristic bleakness. 'The name of the Theomach is known to the Mahdoubt, as is that of the Vizard. Their separate paths are unlike hers, as hers is unlike theirs. But the Insequent have this loyalty to their own kind, that they neither oppose nor betray one another. Those who transgress in such matters – and they are few, assuredly so – descend to a darkness of spirit from which they do not return. They are lost to name and knowledge and purpose, and until death claims them naught remains but madness. Therefore of the Theomach's quests and purposes, or of the Vizard's, the Mahdoubt may not speak in this time.

'All greed is perilous,' concluded the woman more mildly. 'Hence is the Mahdoubt wary of her words. She has no wish for darkness.'

Linden heard a more profound refusal in the Mahdoubt's reply. The older woman seemed to know where Linden's questions would lead – and to warn Linden away. Nevertheless Linden persevered, although she approached her underlying query indirectly.

'Still,' she remarked, 'it seems strange that I've never heard of your people before. Covenant—' She stumbled briefly, tripped by grief and rage. 'I mean Thomas Covenant, not his sick son—' Then she squared her shoulders. 'He told me a lot, but he didn't say anything about the Insequent. Even the Giants didn't, and they love to explore.' As for the *Elohim*, she would not have expected them to reveal anything that did not suit their self-absorbed machinations. 'Where have you all been?'

The Mahdoubt smiled. The divergent colours of her eyes expressed a fond appreciation for Linden's efforts. 'It does not surpass conception,' she said easily, 'that the lady – aye, and others as well, even those who will come to be named Lords – know naught of the Insequent because apt questions at the proper time have not been asked of those who might have given answer.'

Linden could not repress a frown of frustration. The woman's response revealed nothing. Floundering, she faced the Mahdoubt with her dirt-smeared clothes and her black Staff and her desolation. 'All right. You said that you can't answer my questions. I think I understand why. But there must be some other way that you can help me.' Why else had the older woman awaited her here?

Abruptly she gave up on indirection. She had recovered some of her strength, and was growing frantic. 'The Theomach told me that I already know his "true name".' Therefore she assumed that *true names* had power among the Insequent. 'How is that possible?'

If you won't rescue me, tell me how to make him do it.

Slowly the older woman's features sagged, adding years to her visage and sadness to her mien. Linden's insistence seemed to pain her.

'Lady, it is not the Mahdoubt's place to inform you of that which is known to you. Assuredly not. She may confirm your knowledge, but she may neither augment nor explain it. Also she has spoken of the loyalty of the Insequent, to neither oppose nor betray. Long and long has she spurned such darkness.' She shook her head with an air of weary determination. 'Nay, that which you seek may be found only within yourself.

'The Mahdoubt has urged rest. Again she does so. Perchance with sleep will come comprehension or recall, and with them hope.'

Linden swallowed a sarcastic retort. She was confident that she had never heard the Theomach's true name. And she was certain that she had not forgotten some means to bypass centuries safely. But she also recognised that no bitterness or supplication would sway the Mahdoubt. After her fashion, the woman adhered to an ethic as strict as the rectitude of the *Haruchai*. It gave meaning to the Mahdoubt's life. Without it, she might have left Linden to face Garroting Deep and Caerroil Wildwood and despair alone.

For that reason, Linden stifled her rising desperation. As steadily as she could, she said, 'I'm sorry. I don't believe it. You didn't go to all of this trouble just to feed and comfort me. If you can't tell me what I need

to know, there must be some other way that you can help. But I don't
know what it is.'

Now her companion avoided her gaze. Concealing her eyes behind
the hood of her cloak, the Mahdoubt studied the night as if the darkened trees might offer her wisdom. 'The lady holds all knowledge that is
necessary to her,' she murmured. 'Of this no more may be said. Yet is the
Mahdoubt saddened by the lady's plight? Assuredly she is. And does her
desire to provide succour remain? It does, again assuredly. Perchance by
her own quest for knowledge she may assist the lady.'

Without shifting her contemplation of the forest, the older woman
addressed Linden.

'Understand, lady, that the Mahdoubt inquires with respect, seeking
only kindness. What is your purpose? If you obtain that which you covet
here, what will be your path?'

Linden scowled. 'You mean if I can get back to the time where I belong? I'm going to rescue my son.'

'Oh, assuredly,' assented the Mahdoubt. 'As would others in your
place. The Mahdoubt herself might do so. But do you grasp that your
son has known the power of a-Jeroth? He that is imprisoned, a-Jeroth of
the Seven Hells?'

Linden winced. Long ago, the Clave had spoken of a-Jeroth. Both
she and Covenant had taken that as another name for Lord Foul: an
assumption which Roger had confirmed.

'He's Lord Foul's prisoner,' she replied through her teeth. *Tell her that
I have her son.* 'I've known that since I first arrived. One of the *croyel* has
him now, but that doesn't change anything.'

The older woman sighed. 'The Mahdoubt does not speak of this.
Rather she observes that a-Jeroth's mark was placed upon the boy when
he was yet a small child, as the lady recalls.'

Her statement struck Linden's heart like iron on stone; struck and
shed sparks. The bonfire, she thought in sudden anguish. Jeremiah's
hand. He had been in Lord Foul's power then, hypnotised by eyes like
fangs in the savage flames; betrayed by his natural mother. He had
borne the cost ever since. And when his raceway construct freed him
to visit the Land, he may have felt the Despiser's influence, directly or
indirectly.

The Mahdoubt seemed to suggest that Jeremiah had formed a willing partnership with the *croyel*. That his sufferings had distorted and corrupted him within the secrecy of his dissociation.

If Linden's heart had not been fused—

The older woman seemed unaware of Linden's shock; or she chose to ignore it. 'Respectfully the Mahdoubt inquires again. What is your purpose?'

Anchoring herself on stone, Linden answered, 'That doesn't change anything. Even if you're right. I have to get him back.' Somehow. 'If he's been marked' – claimed? – 'I'll deal with that when he's safe.'

'Assuredly,' countered the woman. 'This the Mahdoubt comprehends. Yet her query remains unmet. What will be your path to the accomplishment of your purpose?'

If her questions and assertions were kindly meant, their benignance had become obscure.

'All right.' Linden gripped the Staff with both hands as if she intended to lash out at the Mahdoubt. But she did not; would not: she clenched the Staff only because she could not close her fingers around the hardness that filled her chest. 'Assuming that I'm not stuck in this time, I'll go to Andelain. Maybe the Dead are still there.' Maybe Covenant himself would be there: the real Thomas Covenant rather than his son's malign simulacrum. Her need for him increased with every beat of her heart. 'They might help me.' Even the spectre of Kevin Landwaster had once counselled her according to the dictates of his torment. 'But even if they aren't—'

When Linden fell silent, holding back ideas that she had kept to herself for days, the Mahdoubt prompted her, 'Lady?'

Oh, hell, Linden muttered to herself. What did she have left to lose? An idea that she had concealed from Roger and the *croyel* could not hurt her now.

Harshly she told her companion, 'Maybe I can find Loric's *krill*.' She had heard that there were no limits to the amount of force which could be expressed through the eldritch dagger. 'Covenant and I left it in Andelain.' Millennia hence, it would enable the breaking of the Law of Life. And the clear gem around which it had been forged had always responded to white gold. She was counting on that. 'If it's still there,

I'll have a weapon that might let me use wild magic and my Staff at the same time.'

Had the Mahdoubt asked her why she wanted to wield power on that scale, she would have had difficulty answering. Certainly she needed all the puissance she could muster against foes like Roger, Kastenessen and the Despiser. But she had begun to consider other possibilities as well; choices which she hardly knew how to articulate. She had already demonstrated that she was inadequate to the Land's plight. Now every effort to envision some kind of hope brought her back to Covenant.

But the older woman did not pursue her questions. Wrapping her cloak more tightly about her, she shrank into herself.

'Then the Mahdoubt may say no more.' Her voice emerged, muffled and saddened, from her shrouded shape. 'The lady is in possession of all that she requires. And her purpose exceeds the Mahdoubt's infirm contemplation. It is fearsome and terrible. The lady embraces devastation.'

A moment later, she spoke to Linden more directly. 'Nonetheless her years have taught the Mahdoubt that there is hope in contradiction. Upon occasion, ruin and redemption defy distinction. Assuredly they do. She will trust to that when every future has become cruel.

'Lady, if you will permit the Mahdoubt to guide you, you will set such thoughts aside until you have rested. Sleep comforts the wracked spirit. Behold.' The woman's hand emerged from her cloak to indicate her flask. 'Springwine has the virtue to compel slumber. Allow ease to soften your thoughts. This she implores of you. If you make haste towards the Earth's doom, it will hasten to meet you.'

When her hand withdrew, she became motionless beside her steady cookfire as though she herself had fallen asleep.

Like her advice, her statements conveyed nothing. —in possession of all that she requires. Such assertions left Linden unillumined; or she could not hear them. As far as she was concerned, her own ignorance and helplessness were all that gave meaning to words like *doom*.

Nevertheless she did not protest or beg. She made no demands. The Mahdoubt had come to this time to rescue her: she was certain of that. The Mahdoubt's desire to accomplish something good here was unmistakable, in spite of the obfuscation imposed by her peculiar morality. She had travelled an inconceivable distance in order to meet Linden's simpler needs. She had spoken for Linden when Caerroil Wildwood might have slain her. The woman's human aura, her presence, her manner – everything about her that was accessible to Linden's percipience – elicited conviction.

And she had insisted that Linden was *not* ignorant. The lady is in possession of all that she requires.

When Linden could no longer contain the pressure of her caged passions, she rose to her feet. Taking the Staff with her, she began to pace out her futility on the cold-hardened ground of the riverbank.

She did not walk away into the trees, although the gall and ire of Gallows Howe seemed to whisper a summons. There, at least, she would not be urged to sleep. The Forestal's gibbet would recognise her rage, and approve. Nevertheless she did not intrude on the Deep. She had no desire to test the extent of Caerroil Wildwood's forbearance. And the glowering resentment of the forest would not encourage her to think more clearly.

Instead she strode along the narrow strip of open ground at the edge of the Black River. And when she had walked far enough to reduce the Mahdoubt's cookfire to a small glimmer, she turned back, passing the older woman and continuing on until she was once more in danger of losing sight of her companion. Then she turned again as if she were drawn by the innominate and undiminished promise implicit in the gentle flames.

Repeatedly tracing the same circuit from verge to verge of the cookfire's light, with the runed black wood of the Staff gripped in her healed hand, she tried to solve the conundrum of the Mahdoubt's presence.

The older woman had suggested that sleep might bring *comprehension or recall*. Comprehension was beyond Linden; as unattainable as sleep. But recall was not. For long years, she had sustained herself with remembrance. Pacing back and forth within the boundaries of the fire's frail illumination, she tried to recollect and examine everything that the Mahdoubt had said since Linden had come upon her beside the river.

Unfortunately her battle under *Melenkurion* Skyweir, and her brutal struggle out of the mountain, had left her so frayed and fraught that she could remember only hazy fragments of what had been said and done before the Forestal's arrival.

—answer none of the lady's sorrows. The Mahdoubt had tried to explain something. *Time has been made fragile. It must not be challenged further.* But in Linden's mind the words had become a blur of earthquake and cruelty and desperate bereavement.

Stymied by her earlier weakness, she had to begin with food and forbearance and Gallows Howe; with runes and assurances.

Must it transpire that beauty and truth shall pass utterly when we are gone?

If I can find an answer, I will.

After that, the Staff of Law had been restored to her, written with knowledge and power. It had made her stronger. The Howe itself had made her stronger. Her memories were as distinct as keening.

This blackness is lamentable—

But nothing in her encounter with Caerroil Wildwood relieved her own lament.

Again and again, however, the Mahdoubt had avowed that her wishes for Linden were kindly. Apart from her obscure answers to Linden's questions, the Mahdoubt had treated Linden with untainted gentleness and consideration.

And when Linden had tried to thank her, the Mahdoubt had replied, *Gratitude is always welcome— The Mahdoubt has lived beyond her time, and now finds gladness only in service. Aye, and in such gratitude as you are able to provide.*

Gratitude.

Linden could have gone on, remembering word for word. But something stopped her there: a nagging sensation in the back of her mind. Earlier, days ago, or millennia from now, the Mahdoubt had spoken of gratitude. Not when the woman had accosted Linden immediately before Roger's arrival in Revelstone with Jeremiah and the *croyel*: not when she had warned Linden to *Be cautious of love.* Before that. Before Linden's confrontation with the Masters. The day before. In her rooms. When she and the Mahdoubt had first met.

Linden's heart quickened its beat.

Then also the older woman had offered food and urged rest. She had explained that she served Lord's Keep, not the Masters. And she had asked—

Linden's strides became more urgent as she searched her memories.

She had asked, *Does the wonder of my gown please you? Are you gladdened to behold it? Every scrap and patch was given to the Mahdoubt in gratitude and woven together in love.*

My gown. That was the only occasion when Linden had heard the Insequent refer to herself in the first person.

Full of other concerns, Linden had missed her opportunity to learn more about the patchwork motley of the Mahdoubt's garb. But Liand had supplied what Linden lacked, as he had done so often.

That it is woven in love cannot be mistaken. If I may say so without offence, however, the gratitude is less plain to me.

In response, the Mahdoubt had chided him playfully. *Matters of apparel are the province of women, beyond your blandishment.* And then she had said—

Oh, God. Linden was so surprised that she stumbled. When she had recovered her balance, she stood still and braced herself on the Staff while she remembered.

The Mahdoubt had said, *The lady grasps the presence of gratitude. And if she does not, yet she will. It is as certain as the rising and setting of the sun.*

Gratitude. In the gown, *my* gown: in the disconcerting unsuitability of the parti-coloured scraps and tatters which had been stitched together to form the garment. Other people in other times had given thanks to the Mahdoubt – or had earned her aid – by adding pieces of cloth to her raiment.

The lady is in possession of all that she requires.

The Mahdoubt had already given Linden an answer.

—such gratitude as you are able to provide.

Shaken, Linden entered a state of dissociation that resembled Jeremiah's; a condition in which ordinary explicable logic no longer applied. She leapt to demented assumptions and did not question them. Suddenly the only problem which held any significance for her was that she had no cloth.

For that matter, she had neither a needle nor thread. But those lacks did not daunt her. They hardly slowed her steps as she hurried to stand across the campfire from the Mahdoubt.

Hidden within her cloak, the woman still squatted motionless. She did not react to Linden's presence. If she felt the blaze of confusion and hope in Linden's gaze, she gave no sign.

Linden opened her mouth to blurt out the first words that occurred to her. But they would have been too demanding and she swallowed them unuttered. If she could, she wanted to match the Mahdoubt's courtesy. Intuitively she believed that politeness was essential to the older woman's ethos.

She took a deep breath to steady herself. Then she began softly, 'I don't know how to address you. "The Mahdoubt" seems too impersonal. It's like calling you "the stone" or "the tree". But I haven't earned the right to know your name,' her true name. 'And you don't use mine. You call me "lady" or "the lady" to show your respect.

'Would it be all right if I called you "my friend"?'

Slowly the Mahdoubt lifted her head. With her hands, she pulled back the hood of her cloak. The jarring and comfortable contradiction of her eyes regarded Linden warmly.

'The Mahdoubt,' she said, smiling, 'would name it an honour to be considered the lady's friend.'

'Thank you.' Linden bowed, trying to honour the older woman in return. 'I appreciate that.

'My friend, I have a request.'

Still smiling, the woman waited for Linden to continue.

Linden did not hesitate. The pressure building within her did not permit it. As if she were sure of herself, she said, 'You once asked if looking at your gown made me glad. I didn't understand. I still don't. All I know is that it has something to do with the requirements of your knowledge. Your beliefs. But I would be glad to look at it again now. I'll be grateful for a second chance.'

For an instant, a burst of light appeared in the Mahdoubt's eyes; a brief reflection from the flames, perhaps, or an intensification of her unpredictable solidity and evanescence. Then she climbed slowly to her feet, unbending one joint at a time: an old woman grown frail, too plump for her strength, and unable to stand without effort. While she laboured upright, however, she seemed to blush with pleasure.

Facing Linden over the heat of her cookfire, she shrugged off her cloak so that Linden could behold the full ugliness of her piecemeal gown.

It had been made haphazardly, with a startling lack of concern for harmonious colours, similar fabrics or even careful stitches. Some scraps were the size of Linden's hand, or of both hands: others, as long and narrow as her arm. Some were brilliant greens and purples, as bright as when they were newly dyed. Others had the duller hues of ochre and dun, and showed long years of wear. The threads sewing the patches together varied from hair-fine silk to crude leather thongs.

If the garment had been worn by anyone other than the Mahdoubt, no one who saw it would have discerned *love* or *gratitude*.

Considering her task, Linden murmured with an indefinable mixture of bafflement and certainty, 'My friend, I hope that you don't mind standing. This is going to take a while.'

'The Mahdoubt is patient,' the woman replied. 'Oh, assuredly. Has she not awaited the lady for many of her long years? And is she not pleased – aye, both pleased and gratified – by the lady's offer of thanks? How then should she grow weary?'

Half to herself, Linden promised, 'I'll be as quick as I can.' Then she went to work.

She could not think about what she meant to do. It made no sense, and might paralyse her. Instead she concentrated on the practical details, the small things: matters as simple as the Mahdoubt's gifts of food and drink and warmth and company.

So: cloth first. Then a needle of some sort. After that, she would confront the conundrum of thread.

She had no knife; no sharp edge of any kind. That was a problem. Yet she did not pause to doubt herself, or consider that she might fail. Nor did she waste her attention on embarrassment. Putting down the Staff, she unbuttoned her shirt and removed it.

The shirttail seemed the best place to tear the fabric. But the red flannel had been tightly hemmed: she would not be able to rend it with her fingers. And she lacked any implement to pick the stitches.

Lifting the edge of the material to her mouth, she began trying to chew through the hem.

The flannel proved tougher than she had expected. She gnawed and plucked at it until her jaws ached and her teeth hurt, but it refused to rip.

For a moment, she studied the area around the cookfire, hoping to find a rock with a jagged edge. However, every stone in sight was old and weathered; water-rounded.

Oh, hell, she thought; but again she did not pause. Instead she took up a dead twig and poked it at the bitten fabric. Then she used the twig to thrust that small section of hem into the fire.

When the flannel began to blacken and char, she withdrew it from the flames; blew on the material to extinguish it. Knotting her fists in her shirt, she pulled against the weakened hem.

The cloth was sturdy: it did not tear easily. But when she dropped her shirt over a stone, stood on it and heaved at the shirttail with both hands, she was able to make a rent longer than a hand span.

The Mahdoubt watched her avidly, nodding as if in encouragement. But Linden paid no heed. Her task consumed her. Her palms and fingers were sore, her arms throbbed, she was breathing hard – and she had to rip another part of the hem.

This time, she did not expend effort chewing: she turned immediately to the fire. With her twig, she held the hem in the flames until the cloth and even the twig began to burn. Then she stamped on her shirt to quench the charred fibres.

Now the material tore more easily. One fierce tug sufficed to rip a sizable scrap from the shirttail.

More out of habit than self-consciousness, Linden donned her shirt and buttoned it, although it was filthy, caked with mud and dead leaves. For a moment while she caught her breath, she reminded herself, One step at a time. Just one. That's all. She had procured a patch. Next she needed a needle.

Trusting that Caerroil Wildwood would not take offence, she went to the nearest evergreen – a scrub fir – and broke off one straight living twig. She wanted wood that still held sap; wood that would not be brittle.

Beside the cookfire, she rubbed her twig on the stones until it was as smooth as possible. Then she held one end in the small blaze, hoping to harden it. Before it could catch fire, she pulled it out to rub it again.

When she had repeated the process several times, her rubbing began to produce a point at the end of the twig.

'The lady is resourceful,' remarked the Mahdoubt in a voice rich with pride. 'Must the Mahdoubt dismiss her fears? Assuredly she must. The lady has foiled her foes under great *Melenkurion* Skyweir. How then may it be contemplated that the Earth's doom will exceed her cunning?'

Briefly Linden stopped to massage her tired face, stroke her parched eyes. All right, she told herself. Cloth. A needle. Now thread.

As far as she knew, the forest offered nothing suitable. Its thinnest vines and most supple fibres would eventually rot away, invalidating her gratitude.

Sighing, she spread out her scrap of flannel and began trying to pick threads from its torn edge with the point of her twig.

This was difficult work, close and meticulous. It brought back her weariness in waves until she could hardly keep her eyes open. Her world seemed to contract until it contained nothing except her hands and needle and a stubborn scrap of red. The weave of the flannel resisted her efforts. She had to be as careful and precise as her son when he worked on one of his constructs. She had watched him on occasions too numerous to count. His raceway in his bedroom may have enabled him to enter the Land, for good or ill. And she had seen him build a cage of deadwood to reach the depths of *Melenkurion* Skyweir. She knew his exactitude intimately; his assurance. Time and again, her needle separated stubby threads too short to serve any purpose. Nevertheless she persevered. Now or never, she repeated to herself like a mantra. Now or never.

In her exhaustion, she believed that if she put her task down to rest or sleep, she might give her enemies the time they needed to achieve the Earth's end.

Finally she had obtained five red threads nearly as long as her hand. That, she decided, would have to suffice. Cloth. A needle. Thread. Now she lacked only a method of attaching thread to her twig.

While she groped for possibilities, she picked up the flask of springwine and drank. For a moment, she blinked rapidly, trying to moisten eyes that felt as barren as Gallows Howe. Then she took her sharpened twig and broke it in half.

The wood snapped unevenly, leaving small splits in the blunt end of her needle.

On her knees, she approached the Mahdoubt.

'Be at peace, lady,' the Insequent said softly. 'There is no need for haste.'

Linden hardly heard her. The world had become cloth and thread, a wooden needle and the hanging edge of the Mahdoubt's robe. When she was near enough to work, Linden laid her few threads out on a stone and examined the woman's gown until she located a place where her patch could be made to fit. Still kneeling, and guided only by her memories of Jeremiah, she took one fragile thread, wedged it gently into a split at the end of her needle, and began sewing.

As she worked, she held her breath in an effort to steady her weariness.

Her needle did not pierce the fabric easily. And when it passed through her scrap of flannel and the edge of the gown, it made a hole much too large for her thread. But she knotted the thread as well as she could with her sore fingers, then forced her twig through the material a second time.

While she laboured, she felt the Mahdoubt touch her head. The older woman stroked Linden's hair, comforting her with caresses. Then, softly, the Mahdoubt began to chant.

Her voice was low, as if she were reciting a litany to herself. Nevertheless her tone – or the words of her chant – or Linden's flagrant fatigue – cast a trance like an enchantment, causing the world to shrink further. Garroting Deep ceased to impinge on Linden's senses: the raw teeth of winter and the kindly flames of the cookfire lost their significance: darkness and stars were reduced to a vague brume that condensed and swirled, empty of meaning. Only Linden's hands and the Mahdoubt's gown held any light, any purpose. And only the Mahdoubt's chant enabled Linden to continue sewing.

'A simple charm will master time,
   A cantrip clean and cold as snow.
It melts upon the brow of thought,
As plain as death, and so as fraught,
   Leaving its implications' rime,
For understanding makes it so.

'The secret of its spell is trust.
    It does not change or undergo
The transformations which it wreaks—
The end in silence which it seeks—
    But stands forever as it must,
For cause and sequence make it so.

'Such knowing is the sap of life
    And death, the rich, ripe joy and woe
Ascending in vitality
To feed the wealth of life's wide tree
    Regardless of its own long strife,
For plain acceptance makes it so.

'This simple truth must order time:
    It simply is, and all minds know
The way of it, the how, the why:
They must forever live and die
    In rhythm, for the metered rhyme
Of growth and passing makes it so.

'The silent mind does not protest
    The ending of its days, or go
To loss in grief and futile pain,
But rather knows the healing gain
    Of time's eternity at rest.
    The cause of sequence makes it so.'

Linden did not understand – and neither knew nor cared that she did not. While she worked, she set all other considerations aside. With her abused fingers and her blurring vision, she concentrated solely and entirely on completing her gratitude; her homage.

But when she came to the end of her thread, and the scrap of her shirt was loosely stitched to the Mahdoubt's robe – when the older woman removed her hand, ceasing her chant – Linden thought that she heard a familiar voice shout with relief and gladness, 'Ringthane! The Ringthane has returned!'

At the same time, she seemed to feel sunrise on her back and smell spring in the air. She appeared to kneel on dewy grass at the Mahdoubt's feet with the sound of rushing water in her ears and the Staff of Law as black as a raven's wing beside her.

And she heard other voices as well. They, too, were known to her, and dear. They may have been nickering.

As she toppled to the grass, she fell out of her ensorcelled trance. She had a chance to think, Revelstone. The plateau.

The Mahdoubt had restored her to her proper time and place.

Then exhaustion claimed her, and she was gone.

Chapter Two

In the Care of the Mahdoubt

Linden awoke slowly, climbing with effort and reluctance through the exhaustion of millennia. The years that she had bypassed or slipped between seemed to multiply her natural age; and her attempts to open her eyes, confirm the substance of her surroundings, felt hampered by caducity. She did not know where she was. She had told herself that she had reached the plateau above Revelstone in her proper time. She had believed that, trusted it; and slept. But the surface on which she lay was not fresh grass in springtime. Linen rather than soiled garments covered her nakedness, and her feet were bare. The light beyond her eyelids was too dim to be morning.

And she was diminished, truncated, in some fashion that she could not identify.

Yet she was warm, comfortably nestled. The unremitting clench of winter had released her. Her bed supported her softly. Like her eyes, her mouth and throat were too dry for ease, but those small discomforts were the normal consequences of unconsciousness. They did not hamper her.

For a moment like an instant of panic in a dream, quickly forgotten, she imagined that she had been taken to a hospital; that paramedics had rushed her, sirens wailing, to a place of urgent care. Had the bullet missed her heart? But the deeper levels of her mind knew the truth.

Gradually she recognised how she had been reduced.

Her skin felt nothing except the tactile solace of linen and softness and warm weight. She smelled nothing except the faint tang of woodsmoke and the precious scent of cleanliness; heard nothing except the subtle effort of her own breathing. None of her senses extended beyond the confines of her body.

She did not know where she was, or how, or why – she hardly knew who – because her health-sense was gone. She had grown accustomed to its insights. Its absence diminished her.

Nonetheless she was paradoxically comforted by the realisation that Kevin's Dirt had regained its hold. Now she could be certain that the Mahdoubt had brought her near to her rightful time.

In any case, her benevolent rescuer would not have stranded her earlier than she belonged. Then she would still have posed a threat to the integrity of the Arch. Nor had the Mahdoubt greatly overshot the day of Linden's disappearance in rain from the upland plateau. She seemed to recall that she had heard Bhapa's voice announcing her presence. If that were true, then she had also heard Manethrall Mahrtiir and Cord Pahni answer Bhapa's call.

Surely they would not have awaited her return indefinitely? Not while their choices were constrained by the Masters – and the Demondim. At some point, they would have left Revelstone to rejoin their people, or to seek out a defence against the Land's foes.

Linden had not been absent long enough to exhaust her friends' hopes. And she had felt spring in the air—

When she was sure that the Mahdoubt had delivered her to the proper season in the proper year, a few of her numberless fears faded. At last, she allowed herself to remember why she was here.

Jeremiah. The *croyel*. Roger Covenant. Purpose and urgency.

Heavy with sleep, she raised her hands to confirm that Covenant's ring still hung from its chain around her neck. Then she lifted them higher to rub her face. But she was not yet ready to sit up. She needed a moment to acknowledge that she had done Thomas Covenant the shameful injustice of permitting herself to be misled by his son.

She should have known better. Her dead love had earned more than her loyalty: he had earned her faith. Recalling the long tally of her mistakes, she was grieved that she let Roger tarnish her memories of the man who had twice defeated Lord Foul for the Land's sake.

Grieved and angered.

Jeremiah's presence had accomplished Roger's intentions perfectly: it had distorted her judgment, leaving her vulnerable.

No more, she vowed. Not again. She had fallen in with the Despiser's machinations once. She would not repeat that mistake.

Instead she meant to exact a price for Jeremiah's torment.

But she was getting ahead of herself. Her night with the Mahdoubt in Garroting Deep had taught her – or retaught her – an important lesson. One step at a time. Just one. First she needed to absorb the details of her present situation. And she had to retrieve her Staff so that she could cast off the pall of Kevin's Dirt. She would determine other actions later, after her true strength was restored.

Blinking against the smear of nightmares and regret, she looked around.

Strange, she thought. She was in a small room which she knew well enough, although it seemed vaguely unreal, dislocated by the passage of too much time; too much cold and desperation, battle and loss. She lay under blankets in a narrow bed. A pillow cradled her head. A shuttered window in the smooth stone wall above her admitted a dull grey light that could have been dawn or dusk. A doorway in the opposite wall past the foot of the bed held a soft illumination, yellow and flickering, which suggested lamps or a fire. Near her head, a second doorway led to a bathroom.

The chamber appeared to be the same one in which she had spent two nights before Roger and the *croyel* had translated her out of her time. She remembered it as though she had visited it in dreams rather than in life.

Yet she was here. As if to demonstrate the continuity of her existence, the Staff of Law leaned like a shaft of midnight against the wall at the head of the bed. And in a chair at its foot sat the Mahdoubt, watching Linden with a smile on her lips and gloaming in her mismatched eyes.

When Linden raised her head, the Mahdoubt left her chair, moved into the next room, and returned with an oil lamp and a clay goblet. The little flame, soothing in spite of its unsteadiness, accentuated her orange eye while it dimmed her blue one. The lurid patchwork of her robe blurred into a more harmonious mélange.

'Forbear speech, lady,' she murmured as she approached the bed. 'Your slumber has been long and long, and you awaken to confusion and diminishment. Here is water fresh from the eldritch wealth of Glimmermere.' She offered the goblet to Linden. 'Has its virtue declined somewhat? Assuredly. Yet much of its healing lingers.

'Drink, lady,' the Mahdoubt urged. 'Then you may speak, and be restored.'

But Linden needed no encouragement. As soon as she caught sight of the goblet, she became conscious of an acute thirst. Propping herself up on one elbow, she accepted the goblet and drained it eagerly.

In the absence of any health-sense, she could not gauge how much of the water's potency had been lost. Nevertheless it was bliss to her mouth and throat, balm to her thirst. And it awakened her more fully. A numinous tingling sharpened her senses, reminding her of a more fundamental discernment.

At once, she dropped the goblet on the bed, sat up and reached for the Staff.

As soon as she closed her hands on the necessary warmth of the wood and read with her fingers the deft precision of the Forestal's runes, she felt the return of a more complete life. In the space between her heart-beats, the stone of the chamber ceased to be blind granite, inert and unresponsive: it became a vital and breathing aspect of Lord's Keep. She recognised warmth and fire in the hearth of the larger room beyond her bedroom; smelled water poised to flow in the bathroom. Every inch of her skin and scalp became aware of its cleanliness. And the comfortable ease of the Mahdoubt's aura washed over her like a baptism.

Hugging the Staff to her bare breasts, Linden retrieved the goblet and handed it back to the older woman, mutely asking for more of Glimmermere's benison.

With a nod of approval, the Mahdoubt complied. When she returned from the sitting room this time, however, she brought a large wooden pitcher as well as the replenished goblet. The goblet she gave to Linden: the pitcher she placed on the floor beside the bed, where Linden could reach it easily. Then she retreated to her chair.

Until Linden had emptied the goblet again, she did not remember that she was naked.

Instinctively self-conscious, although she knew that she had no reason to be, she pulled up the sheet to cover herself. With a grimace of embarrassment, she found her voice at last.

'Who bathed me?'

Now the Mahdoubt grinned broadly. 'The lady's questions are endless. And some may be answered. Aye, assuredly, for there can be no peril in them.

'Lady, you and the Mahdoubt were chanced upon by Ramen beside the falls of Glimmermere. Their Manethrall himself bore you hither, and here – with pleasure the Mahdoubt proclaims it – you have slumbered for two days and a night. Was such rest needful? Beyond all doubt it was. But when she discerned the depth of your slumbers, she saw that other care was needful as well.

'It was the wish of all who have claimed your friendship, the flattering Stonedownor youth among them, and also he who was once a Master, to stand in vigil at your side. Assuredly. Are you not worthy of their attendance? Yet the Mahdoubt dismissed them, permitting only the Ramen girl to remain. Together she and the girl bathed you. Your raiment as well they cleansed, and in part mended, though the marks of fecundity and long grass remain – as they must. Oh, assuredly.

'When these small services had been accomplished, the Mahdoubt dismissed the girl also. The Mahdoubt is aged,' she explained lugubriously, in apparent playfulness, 'and finds only brief ease in the accompaniment of the young. They remind her of much that she has left behind.' She sighed, but her tone held no regret. 'Therefore the Mahdoubt has watched over you alone, taking satisfaction in your rest.'

The older woman's gentle voice filled the room with a more ordinary and humane solace than the relief of urgent thirst, the Earthpower in Glimmermere's waters, the recovery of percipience, the stubborn protectiveness of Revelstone, or the confirmed strictures of the Staff. Listening, Linden found that she could accept the sound and relax somewhat, despite the hard clench of her heart.

She wanted to see her friends. But the Mahdoubt's reply implied that Liand, Stave, Anele and the three Ramen were well. Indeed, it seemed to indicate that they had not been harmed by the violence surrounding Linden's disappearance, or threatened by the siege of the Demondim. And if Linden's resolve remained as unmistakable as a fist, her utter extremity had passed, sloughed off by sleep and the Mahdoubt's astonishing succour. She could afford to take her steps one at a time – and to take them slowly.

'When you washed my clothes,' she asked, holding images of Jeremiah's plight at bay, 'did you find a piece of red metal?' She could not recall what she had done with her son's ruined racecar; his only reminder of her love. 'It would have looked unfamiliar, but you could tell that it was twisted out of shape.'

The older woman nodded. 'Aye, lady.' Her expression became unexpectedly grave, as though she grasped the significance of the racecar. 'It lies beneath your pillow.'

Reaching under her pillow, Linden drew out the crumpled toy. Her fingers recognised it before she looked at it. It had been warmed while she slept, yet the *croyel's* touch lingered in it, palpable and malign; and for an instant, she could not understand why she did not weep. But of course she knew why: all of her tears had been fused into the igneous rock of her purpose.

Closing the car in her fingers, she met the Mahdoubt's sympathetic gaze. 'My friend,' she said, trying to soften her voice so that she would not sound angry, 'I don't know how to thank you. I can't even imagine how to begin. I don't understand how you helped me, or how you even knew that I needed help. And I certainly don't understand why you went to all of that trouble. But you saved me when everything that I could have hoped for was gone.' *Ever since we got you away from your present, there haven't been any possible outcomes that don't give us exactly what we want.* 'Now I hope that someday I'll be worthy of you.'

She was not one of the Land's great heroes. Her many inadequacies had almost given Lord Foul his ultimate victory. But the Mahdoubt had done more than restore her to her proper time: the Insequent had given her a new opportunity to fight for her son.

Linden did not mean to waste it.

'Pssht, lady,' replied the Mahdoubt. 'Are your thanks pleasing to the Mahdoubt? Assuredly. Yet they are sufficient – nay, more than sufficient. Already you have surpassed her own hopes. And you have enabled her to gaze more deeply into the peril of these times. That which she has seen teaches her that she is not yet done with service.

'Lady,' she went on briskly, 'one of those who is named the Humbled has discerned your awakening. Summons have been sent to your companions. Assuredly they will gather in haste, clamouring to attend upon you.' The woman smiled with evident affection. 'Ere their coming, the Mahdoubt must depart, for she will not submit to their queries. Yet she is cognisant of your need for knowledge which none here possess. Perchance some few of your questions may now be sated. If there is aught that the Mahdoubt may reveal to you, she urges you to speak of it without qualm.'

Linden sat up straighter. She had not expected the Mahdoubt's offer. And her mind was still clogged by long sleep as well as by the *croyel's* cruel spoor on Jeremiah's toy. Half reflexively, she called up a small tongue of flame from the Staff to lick away the disturbing residue in the metal. Then she scrambled to catch up with her circumstances.

She wanted details about the condition of her friends and the state of the siege. But Liand and the others would soon arrive to answer such questions in person. And the Mahdoubt was one of the Insequent. She had rescued Linden – but she had also permitted Roger's and the *croyel's* treachery.

While Linden tried to assemble her thoughts into some kind of order, she asked the first question that occurred to her.

'Before I left—' At first, words came awkwardly to her, as though she had to drag them across a vast gulf of years. 'When the ur-viles tried to stop Roger and the *croyel* from taking me. There weren't any Waynhim.' According to Esmer, he had imposed peace between the ur-viles and the Waynhim. Together they had helped her weaken the Demondim so that Revelstone might survive. 'Why didn't they join the ur-viles? Did they *want* me to get lost in the past?'

Her companion looked away. Apparently speaking to the rock of the Keep, she mused, 'Does the Mahdoubt comprehend the lady's concern in this? Oh, assuredly. The lady cannot grasp the speech of the Waynhim. Therefore she cannot inquire of them directly. And the sole interpreter known to her is betimes unworthy of credence. Do these reasons suffice to prompt a reply? They do.'

Then the woman faced Linden again. 'Lady, the Waynhim absented themselves because they foresaw peril to those who now deem themselves Masters. The esteem between the Waynhim and the mountain race of the *Haruchai* is both old and earned. The Waynhim do not desire your loss. They would do much to preserve you. Yet they declined to share in deeds which hazarded their olden allies.'

Not for the first time, Linden felt that she had wasted a question. Nevertheless she was glad to have an answer. It relieved a nagging doubt. And it gave her time to decide what she most needed to know.

'All right,' she murmured. 'That makes sense.'

Clenching Jeremiah's racecar, she asked, 'Can you tell me how to save my son? Is he already lost?'

A-Jeroth's mark was placed upon the boy when he was yet a small child—

The Insequent regarded Linden with one eye and then the other. 'Sadly,' she said, 'the Mahdoubt has no knowledge of this. It transcends her. In some measure, she has made of herself an adept of Time – as did the Theomach as well, assuredly, though in another form. But she beholds only the time in which she manifests herself, neither its past nor its future. Thus she is unable to witness her own future. Her present is here. Beyond this moment, she may estimate intentions and perils, but she cannot observe deeds and outcomes which lie ahead.

'The Theomach's powers were greater than the Mahdoubt's.'

Linden winced involuntarily; but she did not protest. She trusted the Mahdoubt. And Lord Foul had promised her through Anele, *In time you will behold the fruit of my endeavours. If your son serves me, he will do so in your presence. If I slaughter him, I will do so before you. If you discover him, you will only hasten his doom.* Roger had assured her that he and the Despiser still had plans for Jeremiah.

I do not reveal my aims to such as you.

For that reason, she chose to believe that her son was not beyond redemption. While Lord Foul still had a use for him, he would not be irreparably damaged – and she could hope to reach him.

Steadying herself on the stone of her heart, Linden said, 'In that case, tell me why you didn't expose Roger and the *croyel* when they first arrived. In Garroting Deep, you said that you aren't wise enough to interfere with what you considered "needful". But that was ten thousand years ago. You had to be careful. This is now. How could what Roger and that monster did to me be *needful*?'

The Mahdoubt could have spared her—

In response, chagrin and sorrow closed the woman's features. She lowered the contradiction of her eyes: for a moment, she seemed to fumble within herself. When she replied, her voice was thick with sadness.

'Lady, the Mahdoubt comprehends your pain. Assuredly she herself must appear to be your treacher, for she stood aside while betrayal was wrought against you. If you choose condemnation, she cannot gainsay you.'

The Insequent knotted her fingers together. Her hands twisted at each other. 'But if in aught the Mahdoubt has won your regard, then she observes – with respect, aye, and mourning also – that you have gained knowledge which you did not formerly possess. And had you not suffered and striven as you did, you would not have become who you are. The Mahdoubt could not foresee such an outcome when you were taken by your foes. She was able only to perceive that you were not then equal to the Land's plight.

'Lady, you have become greater. That the Mahdoubt deemed needful.'

Linden scowled at her companion; but her anger was for herself, not the Mahdoubt. 'Forgive me. I didn't mean that to sound like an accusation.' It was certainly true that she knew more now. 'I'm proud to call you my friend. I'm just trying to understand as much as I can.'

She had not become greater. She had simply been made harder and more certain.

Slowly the Mahdoubt raised her head. Her blue eye was damp with relief or gratitude, but the orange one glared like a promise of ferocity. 'Pssht, my lady,' she said again. 'You have no need of the Mahdoubt's forgiveness. It is given before it is asked. Assuredly so. Your gratitude' – she indicated her robe – 'has claimed her old heart.'

'Inquire what you will. The Mahdoubt will attempt better answers.'

Now it was Linden who looked away. While she prepared herself, she muttered, 'My real problem with what you did is that I feel so damn *stupid*. I should have seen the truth for myself. About Roger, anyway.' Jeremiah's presence had confounded her utterly. 'But he did things—

'How could he drink springwine?' she blurted. 'How could either of them? It has *aliantha* in it.'

That was only one of the many means by which Covenant's son had confused her. The Ramen believed that *No servant of Fangthane craves or will consume* aliantha.

'Ah.' The Mahdoubt nodded in recognition. 'Assuredly. That chicane arose from the halfhand's portion of the nature of the *Elohim*. The *Elohim* are not hampered by mortal distastes. With the cursed gift of such a hand, your betrayer received both the power of glamour, of seeming, and the capacity to set aside his revulsion for the goodly health of the Land. These given strengths he also employed to veil and ward the cruel beast which rules your son. Thus his loathing, and your son's, for *aliantha* in springwine was hidden.

'Your wits did not fail you, my lady,' she added kindly. 'Think no ill of yourself. Your foes' deeds and appearances were prepared one and all for your consternation. You were hastened from event to event to assure that you found no occasion to imagine their concealment.' The woman nodded again. 'There was no fault in you.'

'Then—' With an effort, Linden dragged her attention away from Roger's and the *croyel*'s manipulations. If she considered them too closely, she might founder in outrage. *They have done this to my son.* For a moment, she closed her eyes, gathered herself. When she opened them again, she faced her companion squarely.

'The Theomach told me that he would protect history from what I did, but I don't know whether I can trust him. I don't know how that's even possible.'

How had she not set in motion ripples which would change everything?

The Mahdoubt shook her head, turning it from side to side so that first her orange eye and then her blue one regarded Linden brightly. 'My lady,' she said with an air of intention, urging Linden to believe her, 'you may be assured that the Theomach did not neglect such matters. Does your heart not beat? Do your words not convey their meaning? And do these simple truths not proclaim that the Law of Time endures? It is manifest that you have not broken faith with the past.

'Yet the Mahdoubt may observe,' she added as if Linden had expressed doubt, 'that Law seeks its own path. Diverted, it strives to return. Your exertion of Earthpower among Berek Heartthew's warriors was easily transmuted to serve the Theomach's purpose. You have not forgotten – assuredly not – that the Theomach found a place as the Lord-Fatherer's tutor. Thus he was able to account for your presence and deeds in any manner which conformed to his own intentions – and to his knowledge of Time.

'My lady, he made of you the first of the Unfettered, those who in the time of the Lords sought lore and wisdom solitarily, as do the Insequent, according to their private natures. At the Theomach's word, a tradition and a legend began from the wonderment of your aid, and all that has since transpired in the Land has confirmed it.'

Linden listened in surprise and gradual comprehension. She had heard of the Unfettered– Covenant had told her a little about them after Sunder's half-mad father had called himself a descendant of the Unfettered One.

'Understand, my lady,' the Mahdoubt continued, 'that the Theomach did not require your presence or your aid. He merely made use of you. Had you not appeared, he would have contrived to win the Heartthew's trust by other means. And he would have proposed the legend of the Unfettered to justify his own knowledge and power. Such ploys were needful to preserve the Arch.

'Nor did the visitation of your betrayers challenge the Theomach's cleverness.' The older woman sighed heavily. 'Among the Lords of later ages, there endured a belief that the Halfhand, the Lord-Fatherer, would one day return to meet the Land's need. As events befell, the Theomach was not greatly troubled to bring forth such a tale from the form of those who accompanied you.'

For a moment, her voice held an edge of disapproval. 'His purposes were his own, and selfish. All that he did conduced to his own aggrandisement. Therefore he did not scruple upon occasion to offer the Lord-Fatherer instruction which was either flawed or incomplete. Assuredly, however, he would have drawn upon the full depth of his knowledge to preserve the wholeness of that which ensued from his desires.

'The Insequent and the *Elohim* share only this, my lady, that we do not desire the destruction of the Earth.'

The Theomach had said virtually the same thing. Even Roger had said it.

And Linden had seen for herself how little Berek had known or understood in the aftermath of his encounter with the Fire-Lions. The Theomach could have told him anything and he would have had no choice except to credit it.

As she drank more of Glimmermere's waters, her mind grew sharper.

There were so many things that she wanted to know. Because the Mahdoubt had said that she would depart soon, Linden began to hurry.

'All right,' she said. 'I don't really understand how the Theomach knew what his own future required. But if you explained it, I probably still wouldn't understand.

'What can you tell me about that box? The way the *croyel* transported us into the mountain?' She winced at the memory. 'Or used my son to do it. Is Jeremiah really capable of making portals? Doors through time and distance? And if he is, what does that have to do with the *Elohim*?'

Had Roger told her the truth about Jeremiah's deadwood construct?

The Mahdoubt spread her hands to suggest a warning. 'Is the lady's query condign?' she asked herself. 'The Mahdoubt deems it so. Yet there is peril here. She must display great care.

'My lady,' she said to Linden, 'your son's gifts are certain. The Mahdoubt can estimate neither their extent nor their uses. However, their worth is beyond question. Both the Vizard's interest and a-Jeroth's machinations proclaim that there is power concealed within your chosen child.'

According to Jeremiah – or the *croyel* – the Vizard had coveted a gaol for the *Elohim*.

'The Mahdoubt,' she continued, 'has averred that neither Insequent nor *Elohim* desire the destruction of the Earth. Assuredly such havoc was the intent of your treachers. But they outdistanced the Theomach's perception, as he selfishly permitted them to do, relying upon your strength to oppose them. Therefore your companions saw no further threat in him. And they conceived that your defeat was certain. For that reason, they feared only the *Elohim*.

'The purpose of the "box", as you name it, was to blind the eyes of the *Elohim*. They are' – she searched visibly for a cautious description – 'susceptible to such structures. Its nature interacted with their fluidity, enabling your companions to elude detection. Thus were you compelled to meet the crisis of the EarthBlood alone.'

Susceptible to such structures? Linden wondered. Roger had said essentially the same thing. And she had seen how the *Elohim* had reacted to Vain, who had been a construct of the ur-viles.

If Jeremiah's talent could 'blind' the *Elohim*, what else might it accomplish?

But there again Linden hit a barrier of comprehension. Her thoughts were too sequential: she could not gauge the implications of ideas or abilities which appeared to defy linear cause and effect. And she sensed that she was running out of time. Her other friends were coming—

Swallowing bafflement, she said carefully, 'That's something else I may never understand. Can you answer one more question?'

The older woman appeared to consult the evening air through the shutters of the window. Then she gave Linden a comfortable smile. 'Assuredly. If the Mahdoubt may reply briefly.'

'We keep coming back to the Theomach and the *Elohim*,' Linden said at once. An *Elohim* had given warning of the *croyel* as well as *the halfhand*. 'Is it true that your people are the shadow on the heart of the *Elohim*?' The *Elohim* had called themselves *the heart of the Earth*. And they had admitted that within the Earth's heart, or their own, lay darkness. To account for her query, she added, 'I've heard other explanations.'

Esmer had told her, *The* Elohim *believe that they are equal to all things. This is false. Were it true, the Earth entire would exist in their image, and they would have no need to fear the rousing of the Worm of the World's End. That is shadow enough to darken the heart of any being.*

The Mahdoubt's smile sagged, and she sighed. 'My lady, the Theomach has given the *Elohim* cause to doubt their surquedry. Oh, assuredly. For that reason, many among the Mahdoubt's race name him the greatest of all Insequent. Yet she deems that her kind are not a shadow cast by the unspoken Würd of the *Elohim*. Nor do the Insequent themselves cast such shadows. They are merely men and women who crave knowledge as diligently as the *Elohim* desire the sopor of self-contentment.

'In its fashion, my lady, your comprehension of these matters is as great as the Mahdoubt's – or the Theomach's. Assuredly so. Have you not grown familiar with shadows?' Her mismatched eyes searched Linden deeply. 'And is your heart not filled with darkness still? You require no guidance to interpret the evils of the Earth, for you have encountered them within you.'

Involuntarily Linden squirmed. She had known Ravers: she recognised the nature of the passions which had driven her ever since she had coerced Roger Covenant and the *croyel* to reveal themselves. Her own shadow had responded to Gallows Howe. But she had gone beyond doubt, and did not question herself. Instead she chose to ignore the warning implicit in her companion's reply.

'That's probably true,' she said, dismissing the subject. She had confronted Lord Foul's snares now. She would not fall into them again. 'But I'm still confused about the details.

'How do I know the Theomach's true name? Where did I hear it?'

The Insequent had made themselves important to her. She wanted to know their weaknesses.

But the Mahdoubt did not react as Linden expected – or hoped. Leaning forward intently, the woman braced her plump arms on her knees. In a voice that seemed to resonate strangely, although it was as soft as a whisper, she answered, 'My lady, you have not inquired of the Mahdoubt's true name.'

Instinctively Linden pressed her back against the stone at the head of the bed. The Staff of Law lay across her lap: white gold hung against her sternum: one hand gripped her son's toy while the other held a sheet over her breasts. Yet she felt unexpectedly exposed and vulnerable, as if all of her inadequacies had been laid bare.

Whispering herself, she said, 'I'm not convinced that I deserve to know. And I'm sure that I don't have the right to ask. Your people don't use titles instead of names by accident. When the Theomach does it, he's hiding something. That makes me suspicious. But you're my friend. You didn't just save my life. You saved my reasons for living. Obviously you know all kinds of things that you've decided not to tell me. And I don't care. I respect whatever you do. Or don't do.'

The Mahdoubt's orange eye burned at Linden; but her blue one seemed to plead, asking for sufferance – or for discretion. 'Then the Mahdoubt will reveal that her true name is *Quern Ehstrel*. Thus she grants the power to compel her. And in return she requests both wisdom and restraint.'

No, Linden wanted to protest. Please. Don't you understand that I'll *use* you? I need every weapon I can get. But she had already missed her chance to forestall the older woman's gift.

Suddenly hoarse with chagrin, she asked, 'Is that why the Insequent hide their true names? Because they can be compelled?'

If so, she understood their loyalty to each other. The Insequent had too much power over their own people. Without loyalty, none of them would survive.

But the Mahdoubt did not respond directly. Instead she rose to her feet, pushing herself upwards with her hands on her knees. Her gaze she turned away, although she was smiling fondly.

'My lady, those who have claimed your friendship draw nigh. The Mahdoubt must now depart. Her time of service to Revelstone is ended, for she awaited only the lady.

'Your raiment has been prepared.' She nodded towards the bathroom. 'And she has placed a tray before the hearth, for she does not doubt that you are hungry.

'If you will permit the Mahdoubt a last word of counsel' – she gave Linden a teasing sidelong glance – 'you will clothe yourself ere your companions attend upon you. Oh, assuredly. If you do not, you will disturb their wits.'

Without thinking, Linden surged up from her bed; dropped the Staff as well as her sheet so that she could fling her arms around the Mahdoubt. Her heart was not too hard to be touched. She had spent years starving for some embrace— She did not want power over her friend; yet it had been given to her freely. She knew no other language for her gratitude.

The Mahdoubt returned Linden's hug briefly. Then she stepped back. 'Pssht, my lady.' Her voice was redolent with affection. 'The Mahdoubt merely departs. She does not pass away. Will you encounter her again? Be assured of it. It is as certain—'

'—as the rising and setting of the sun,' finished Linden. She wanted to smile, but could not. Even when her other friends arrived, she would be effectively alone without the Mahdoubt. Liand, Stave, Anele and the Ramen: none of them would understand what had happened to her as the Mahdoubt did. 'And by then I'll probably have even more reasons to be grateful.'

The Mahdoubt bowed over her girth. 'Then all is well,' she murmured, 'while the sun continues in its course.'

With her head still lowered, she left the bedroom.

Dry-eyed and aching, Linden turned away so that she would not witness the Insequent's departure. She did not hear the outer door of her rooms open or close. Nevertheless she felt the older woman's sudden absence as if the Mahdoubt had stepped into a gap between instants and slipped out of time.

Shaken, Linden went into the bathroom. While she washed and dried her face, donned her well-scrubbed clothes, and tucked Jeremiah's toy deep into one pocket, she willed herself to shed at least a few tears of thanks and sadness. But she could not. Under *Melenkurion* Skyweir, her capacity for weeping had been burned away.

Chapter Three:

Tales Among Friends

Linden was eating cheese, grapes and cold mutton, and washing them down with draughts of Glimmermere's roborant, when she heard Liand knock at her door. She recognised his touch through the heavy granite by its mingled eagerness and anxiety; and she stood up at once to answer, although the door was not latched. She was eager and anxious herself. Among a host of other things, she did not know how long she had been gone from Revelstone, or how Lord's Keep had fared against the Demondim; and she needed confirmation that her friends were unharmed.

As she opened the door, Liand burst unceremoniously into the room. He may have assumed that he would be met – and thwarted – by the Mahdoubt. When he caught sight of Linden, however, his open face seemed to catch light. His eyes shone with pleasure and his black brows soared. At once, he wrapped her in a fierce, brief hug. Then he stepped back, simultaneously abashed and glowing.

'Linden,' he breathed as if his throat were too crowded with emotion for any other words. 'Oh, Linden.'

Behind him, Manethrall Mahrtiir swept in, avid as a hawk. Standing before Linden, he gave her a deep Ramen bow, with his arms extended towards her on either side of his head, and his palms outward. His garrote bound his hair and a garland of fresh *amanibhavam* hung about his neck. The sharp scent of the flowers emphasised his edged tone as he said, 'Ringthane, you are well returned – and well restored. When first you appeared, we feared for you, though the Mahdoubt and our own discernment gave assurance that you required only rest. Our troubled hearts are now made glad.'

Mahrtiir's accustomed sternness made his greeting seem almost effusive; but Linden had no time to reply. Bhapa and Pahni followed their Manethrall, bowing as well. The older Cord's eyes were moist and grateful: an unwonted display of emotion for a Raman. But Pahni's plain joy was more complex. She appeared to feel more than one kind of happiness, as if her delight at Linden's recovery subsumed a deeper and more private gladness. And Linden detected a secret undercurrent of concern.

Leading Anele by the arm, Stave entered behind the Ramen. The old man suffered Stave's touch without discomfort: apparently even he understood that the *Haruchai* was no longer a Master. His moonstone gaze passed over Linden as if he were unaware of her. Instead of acknowledging her, he shook off Stave's hand, strode over to the tray of food, sat down and began to eat as if his decades of privation had left him perpetually hungry.

Stave responded to Anele's behaviour with a delicate shrug. Then he faced Linden and bowed. His flat features and impassive mien revealed nothing: she still could not read him. But his remaining eye held an unfamiliar brightness; and she guessed that her absence had been uniquely harsh for him. No doubt he judged himself severely for failing to protect her. In addition, however, he had sacrificed more in her name than any of her other friends. Liand had turned his back on his home, and the Ramen had left behind their lives among their people; but Stave had been effectively excommunicated by his kinsmen.

All of his wounds were long healed. In the place of his torn and soiled garment, he wore a clean tunic. Only his missing eye betrayed the scale of his losses.

Linden gazed at all of her companions with affection and relief. Often in her life, she had felt that she wept too easily. Now she regretted that she had no tears to show her friends how she felt about them. She could see that none of them had been harmed while she was away.

But she did not return Stave's bow, or those of the Ramen. She did not reply to Liand or Mahrtiir. They had not come into her rooms alone: two of the Humbled had followed them. Galt and Clyme stood poised on either side of the open door as if they suspected her of some insidious betrayal.

Many of the Masters had been slaughtered by the Demondim. More may have suffered in the battle between Esmer and the ur-viles. And they had not interfered with Linden's attack on the horde's *caesure*. But she had not forgotten what they had done to the people of the Land, or how they had refused her own pleading. And she would not forgive their repudiation of Stave. She remembered their blows as though her own body had been struck.

'Stave,' she asked as though she stood on Gallows Howe and desired bloodshed, 'what's going on?'

'Chosen,' he relied flatly, 'they are chary of me.'

Surprised, she demanded, 'You mean that they don't think they've punished you enough?'

Stave shook his head. 'As you know, my people will no longer address their thoughts to me, or respond to mine. When I had experienced their rejection for a time, I found that I wished to foil it. Though I comprehend their denunciation, I became loath to countenance it. Therefore I have learned to mute my inward voice. I hear the silent speech of the Masters, but they do not hear mine.'

While Linden stared at him, he continued, 'Formerly the Humbled might remain in the passage with the door sealed and yet would know all that I heard and said and thought. But now my mind is hidden from them. If they do not stand in your presence, they will learn nothing of your tale or your purposes, for they judge rightly that I will not reveal you to them.'

'Stave—' His explanation filled her with such wonder that she could hardly find words. 'Anyone who makes the mistake of underestimating you deserves what happens.' Then she fought down her awe and ire. 'The Land has had some great heroes. I've known a few myself,' too many to bear. 'But you – all of you' – she looked around at Liand, Anele and the Ramen – 'could hold your heads up in any company.'

Then she faced Stave again. Articulating each word precisely, she said, 'But I can't talk in front of these halfhands.' What had happened to her was too personal. 'I need them to wait outside. I know this is a lot to ask. And I'll understand if you don't want to do it. But I hope that you'll agree to answer their questions after we're done here. Assure them that you'll tell them whatever they need to know.'

The *Haruchai* raised an eyebrow; but he did not object. Instead he glanced at Clyme and Galt. Without inflection, he said, 'The Chosen has spoken. I will comply. You may depart.'

As he spoke, Linden folded her arms across her chest to conceal her fists. Glaring, she dared the Humbled to believe that Stave would not abide by his word.

They considered her for a moment. Then Galt countered, 'And if his judgment differs from ours, concealing that which we would deem necessary? What then?'

Linden did not hesitate. 'You're forgetting something.' She had beaten back Roger Covenant and the *croyel* and Lord Foul's manipulations. She had met Berek Halfhand and Damelon Giantfriend and the Theomach, *the greatest of all Insequent.* Caerroil Wildwood had given runes to her Staff. The Mahdoubt had crossed ten millennia to rescue her. She felt no impulse to doubt herself, or falter. 'The Land needs you. Even I need you. I'm still hoping that something will persuade you to help me. And Stave knows how you think. He won't withhold anything that matters to you.'

Still neither of the Humbled moved. 'You speak of us as "halfhands",' observed Clyme. 'That name we accept, for we have claimed it in long combat, and our purpose among the Masters is honourable. But is it your belief that we are "the halfhand" of whom the *Elohim* sought to forewarn the people of the Land?'

She sighed, gripping herself tightly. 'No. I know better.'

Galt, Branl and Clyme represented that aspect of the Masters which might cause them to stand stubbornly aside when they were most needed. But she had seen the truth of Roger and the *croyel*. And Kastenessen himself might now be considered a halfhand. She was sure that the *Elohim* did not fear the Humbled.

For a moment longer, Clyme and Galt appeared to consult the air of the chamber, or perhaps the larger atmosphere of Revelstone. Then they left the room without further argument, closing the door behind them.

At last, Linden bowed to Stave. 'Thank you.' When the Humbled were gone, some of her tension eased. She was finally able to look at her friends and smile.

Because Liand was the least reserved among them, and his

apprehensions darkened his eyes, she faced him, although she spoke to the Ramen and Stave as well. 'Please don't misunderstand,' she urged with as much warmth as she could muster. 'I probably don't look happy to be back. But I am. It's just that I've been through things that I don't even know how to describe. For a while there, I didn't think that I would ever see any of you again.' Her voice held steady when it should have quivered. 'If the Mahdoubt hadn't saved me, I would be as good as dead.'

The young Stonedownor's face brimmed with questions. Linden held up her hand to forestall them.

'But now I know what I have to do. That's what you see in me,' instead of gladness. 'I was betrayed, and I've gone so far beyond anger that I might not come back. I want to hear what's happened to all of you. I need to know how long I've been gone, and what the Demondim are doing. Then I have to find a way to leave Revelstone.' Trying to be clear, she finished, 'I've been too passive. I'm tired of it. I want to start doing things that our enemies don't expect.'

She was not surprised by Stave's blunt nod, or by the sudden ferocity of Mahrtiir's grin. And she took for granted that the Cords would follow their Manethrall in spite of their reasons for alarm, the ominous prophecies which they had heard from Anele. But Linden had expected doubt and worry from Liand: she was not prepared for the immediate excitement that brightened his gentle eyes. And Anele's reaction actively startled her.

Swallowing a lump of mutton, he jumped to his feet. In a loud voice, he announced, 'Anele no longer fears the creatures, the lost ones.' His head jerked from side to side as if he were searching for something. 'He fears to remember. Oh, that he fears.' With one hand, he beckoned sharply to Liand, although he seemed unaware of the gesture. 'And the Masters must be fled. So he proclaims to all who will heed him.

'But the others—' Abruptly his voice sank to a whisper. 'They speak in Anele's dreams. Their voices he fears more than horror and recrimination.'

His madness was visible in every line of his emaciated form. To some extent, however, it was vitiated by the fact that he stood on wrought stone. Here as on Kevin's Watch, or in his gaol in Mithil Stonedown, he referred to himself as if he were someone else; but shaped or worn rock occasionally enabled him to respond with oblique poignancy to what was said and done around him.

Still he beckoned for Liand.

The others—?

'Linden—' said Liand awkwardly. The insistence of Anele's gestures appeared to disturb him. He must have understood them. 'I lack words to convey—'

'Then,' Mahrtiir instructed, 'permit the Ringthane to witness his plight, as he desires. When she has beheld it, words will follow.'

The young man cast a look like an appeal at Linden; but he obeyed the Manethrall. Sighing unhappily, he reached to a sash at his waist, a pale blue strip of cloth which Linden had not seen before, and from which hung a leather pouch the size of his cupped hand. Untying the pouch, he slipped an object into his hand, took a deep breath to steady himself, then pressed the object into Anele's grasp.

It was a smooth piece of stone, vaguely translucent – and distinctly familiar. Linden's health-sense received an impression of compacted possibilities.

Anele's fingers clenched immediately around the stone. At once, he flung back his head and wailed as though his heart were being torn from him.

Instinctively Linden moved towards the old man. But Liand reached out to stop her; and Mahrtiir barked, 'Withhold, Ringthane! Anele wishes this.'

An instant later, a rush of power from Anele's closed fist washed away every hint of his lunacy.

Linden jerked to a halt and stared. That was Earthpower, but it was not Anele's inborn strength. Rather his latent force catalysed or evoked a different form of magic; a particular eldritch energy which she had known long ago.

Then the flood of puissance passed, and Anele fell silent. Slowly he lowered his head. When he looked at Linden, his blind gaze focused on her as if he could see.

'Linden Avery,' he said hoarsely. 'Chosen and Sun-Sage. White gold wielder. You are known to me.'

'Anele,' she breathed. 'You're sane.'

None of her companions showed any surprise, although their distress was plain. They had recognised the old man's gestures; must have seen this transformation before—

'I am,' he acknowledged, 'and do not wish it. It torments me, for it is clarity without succour. I cannot heal the harm that I have wrought. But I must speak and be understood. They ask it of me.'

'"They"?' urged Linden. Anele had endured Lord Foul's brutal presence, and Kastenessen's. He had felt Esmer's coercion. And Thomas Covenant had spoken through him as well: a more benign possession, but a violation nonetheless. If even sleep had become fear and anguish, how could he retain any vestige of himself?

'They do not possess me,' he replied with fragile dignity, as though he understood her alarm. 'Rather they speak in my dreams, imploring this of me. They are Sunder my father and Hollian my mother, whom my weakness has betrayed. And behind them stands Thomas Covenant, who craves only that I assure you of his love. But the intent of Sunder Graveler and Hollian eh-Brand is more urgent.'

Sunder? Linden thought dumbly. *Hollian?* She gaped at the son of her long-dead friends as he continued, 'They sojourn among the Dead in Andelain, and they beg of you that you do not seek them out. They know not how the peril of Kastenessen and the *skurj* and white gold may be answered. They cannot guide or counsel you. They are certain only that doom awaits you in the company of the Dead.'

His love. 'Anele—' Linden's voice was a croak of chagrin. 'Can you talk to them?' They beg of you– 'In your dreams? Can you tell them that I know what I'm doing?'

All of her hopes were founded in Andelain. If she were forbidden to approach the Dead, she was truly lost; and Jeremiah would suffer until the Arch of Time crumbled.

The old man shook his head. 'Sleeping, I am mute.' His moonstone eyes regarded her in supplication. 'In my remorse, I would cry out to them, but they cannot hear. No power of dream or comprehension will shrive me until I have discovered and fulfilled my *geas*.'

Then he turned away. 'Liand,' he panted, faltering, 'I beseech you. Relieve me of this burden. I cannot bear the knowledge of myself.'

Doom awaits you in the company of the Dead.

When he extended his hand and opened his fingers, he revealed a piece of *orcrest*, Sunstone. To Linden's senses, it appeared identical to the smooth, unevenly shaped rock with which Sunder had warded the folk of Mithil Stonedown from the Sunbane. Its potency made it seem transparent, but it was not. Instead it resembled a void in the substance of Anele's palm; an opening into some other dimension of reality or Earthpower.

Its touch had restored his mind.

'No.' As Liand reached for the stone, Linden grabbed Anele; forced him to face her again. She wanted to demand, *Why? You're sane now. Tell me why.* She had heard too many prophecies of disaster. Even Liand had warned her, *You have it within you to perform horrors.* She needed to know what Sunder and Hollian feared from her.

But when her hands closed on his gaunt frame, her nerves felt his excruciation like a jolt of lightning. He was sane: oh, he was sane. And for that reason, he was defenceless. Even his heritage of Earthpower could not rebuff the self-denunciation and grief which had broken his mind; blinded him; condemned him to decades of starvation and loneliness while he searched for the implications of his fractured past.

Linden's heart may have grown as ungiving and dark as obsidian; but she could ask nothing of this frail old man. Even to save her son, she could not. She had already extorted too much pain from Anele. She was done with it.

And behind them stands Thomas Covenant, who craves only that I assure you of his love.

Swallowing grief as acute as rage, Linden said softly, 'I want you to understand something. While you still can. I used you. When I was trying to convince the Masters to help me.' And she had contemplated causing him more hurt. 'But I won't do that again. I'm finished.'

She had learned at least this much from her betrayal by Roger and the *croyel*. They had wanted her to achieve their ends for them. And their manipulations had nearly destroyed her. But what the *croyel* was doing to Jeremiah was worse.

'I'll keep you with me,' she promised. 'I'll protect you as much as I can.' She had no other hope to offer him. 'But I won't ask you to pay the price for what I want. Not again.'

Anele breathed heavily for a moment. He shuddered in her grasp: his eyes were closed. When he had mastered himself, he replied, 'Linden Avery, you are the Chosen, and will determine much.' His low growl echoed Mahrtiir's severity. 'But that choice is not vouchsafed to you. All who live share the Land's plight. Its cost will be borne by all who live. This you cannot alter. In the attempt, you may achieve only ruin.'

Then he pulled away from her easily, as if her strength had failed. Leaving her confounded, he handed the *orcrest* to Liand.

As soon as the stone left his fingers, he appeared to faint.

Too late, Linden snatched at his slumping form. But Bhapa was quicker. He caught the old man and lowered him gently to the rug.

Obviously the Cord had known what to expect. All of Linden's friends had known.

'Liand?' she asked in chagrin. 'Is he—?'

Liand continued to cradle the *orcrest* in his palm as though its touch gave him pleasure. 'We have spoken of this,' he answered quietly, gazing at Anele. 'We discern no lasting hurt. He will slumber briefly. When he wakes, he will be as he was. In some form, his madness is kindly. It shields him. In its absence, his bereavements would compel despair.' When the young man looked up at Linden, his compassion for Anele filled his eyes. 'This we have concluded among ourselves, for we know not how otherwise to comprehend either his pain or his endurance of it.'

Mahrtiir nodded; and Pahni rested her hand on Liand's shoulder, sharing his sympathy.

Linden's knees felt suddenly weak. 'God,' she breathed, 'I need to sit down.' Unsteadily she moved to the nearest chair and dropped into it. Then she covered her face with her hands, trying to absorb what had just happened.

Oh, Anele. How much more of this will you have to suffer?

—that doom awaits you—

Sunder and Hollian feared intentions which Linden had not revealed, even to the Mahdoubt. She had hardly named them to herself.

And behind them stands Thomas Covenant—

Now she believed absolutely that it was her Covenant who had spoken in her dreams; who had warned her through Anele in the Verge of Wandering; who had addressed her friends on the rich grass of the plateau. No one else would have spoken as he did.

—who craves only that I assure you of his love.

For a while, her friends waited for her in silence. Then Stave said firmly, 'Chosen, we must speak. We recognise that you have suffered much. But you propose to combat the Land's foes. You speak of betrayal. And it appears that both the Unbeliever and your son have been lost, when their proclaimed intent was the Land's redemption. Such matters require comprehension.'

'Also we are bewildered by the Mahdoubt,' added Mahrtiir, 'who has shown herself able to pass through stone. She is absent from these chambers, though she was not seen to depart. Her role in your return pleads for explanation.'

Linden did not lower her hands. When her friends had come to her door, she had believed herself ready for them. Now she knew that she was not.

'Manethrall,' Stave countered, 'if you will heed my counsel, we will not consider the Mahdoubt until other concerns have been addressed. I do not desire concealment, either from you or from the Chosen. But I deem that the Mahdoubt's strangeness is less than urgent. The ur-Lord's fate, and our own straits, hold greater import.'

'As you will.' Linden felt Mahrtiir's nod. The mistrust which he had once displayed towards Stave was entirely gone. 'I am content to speak of her when you find it condign to do so.'

Promptly Stave continued, 'Then I will say to you, Linden Avery, Chosen, that you have been absent from Revelstone for half a moon—'

'Thirteen days, Linden,' put in Liand.

'—and have slept for two days more,' the *Haruchai* went on. 'In that time, we have feared for your life. And now that you have returned, we fear for the life of Land. Your words give us reason to conceive that the Unbeliever has failed.'

Still Linden covered her face; hid from her companions. The spectres of Sunder and Hollian distrusted her. How could she tell her friends that she had come within a few heartbeats of giving the Despiser exactly what he desired?

Gallows Howe demanded a greater champion than Linden Avery.

'Linden,' said Liand, prodding her gently, 'we did not know how to hope. When you had disappeared, Esmer likewise vanished. The ur-viles then dispersed, leaving no sign of themselves – or of the Waynhim. And the Ranyhyn had departed among the mountains, suggesting that you had no more need of them—' His voice tightened momentarily. 'That you would not return. Yet the Demondim besieged Revelstone furiously. The loss of you filled our hearts with dread.'

'It was Thomas Covenant who took you from us,' Pahni added as if she feared that Linden might doubt Liand, 'the first Ringthane. Now he is gone. Through Anele, we have been promised travails rather than relief. How then should we hope?'

Linden sighed. They were right, of course, all of them. She had to tell them what had happened. Still she was reluctant to answer them. She did not want to reveal what she had become.

Anele's warning scared her because she already knew that she would ignore it.

Soon, she commanded herself. Soon she would face the risk of her story. But she would postpone it a little longer.

Slowly she lowered her hands.

Her friends stood clustered in front of her. Pahni's hand remained on Liand's shoulder, gripping him for support or comfort. Bhapa waited near Anele, ready to help the old man when he woke. The older Cord kept his gaze averted from Linden's as if to show that he asked nothing of her; that her mere presence was enough for him. But both Mahrtiir and Stave studied her, the Manethrall avidly, the *Haruchai* without expression.

Clearing her throat, Linden asked carefully, 'How often has Anele been sane?'

'Once only,' Liand answered. 'And he retained himself only so that he might command us to grant him the *orcrest* stone when he beckoned. For ten days and more, he has not touched the stone, or spoken clearly.'

The Stonedownor's gaze encouraged her not to worry about Anele – or any of her friends. But his tone held a muffled eagerness, a whetted admixture of relief, uncertainty, and excitement. He appeared to feel elevated by the Sunstone, raised to a stature which surpassed his expectations for himself.

'And what about the *orcrest?*' Linden asked him. 'The Sunstone? How did you find it?'

In a general sense, she knew the answer. *What you need is in the Aumbrie. You'll know what you're looking for when you touch it.* But she wanted Liand's confirmation. She could not imagine why Covenant had urged him to go in search of power.

And she had never seen the Aumbrie of the Clave. She only knew that Vain had found the iron heels of Berek's Staff there while she was a prisoner in Revelstone.

But Stave intervened before Liand could reply. 'Chosen, I belittle neither Liand nor *orcrest* in saying that they do not outweigh our need for your tale. In the name of all that we have dreaded, I ask this of you. Speak to us, that we may know the truth of our peril.'

Linden did not glance away from Liand. 'Just this one, Stave.' To her own ears, she sounded as inflexible as the *Haruchai.* 'Please. I'm still trying to pull myself together. Hearing you talk – all of you – helps me.'

Their voices, and her concern, reminded her of the woman she had once been.

Stave glanced at Mahrtiir. When the Manethrall assented, Stave said stiffly, 'Be brief, Stonedownor.'

Pahni continued to hold Liand's shoulder; but she lowered her eyes as though she sought to mask the fact that where he felt excitement she knew only trepidation.

Abruptly Liand seated himself near Linden. Bracing his elbows on his knees, he leaned towards her; held his piece of *orcrest* like an offering or demonstration between them. His concern for her crowded against the surface of his attention. But his desire to speak of the Sunstone temporarily took precedence.

'In this matter, Linden, I am not formed for brevity. At your side, I have been mazed by marvels which surpassed all conception. But until I placed my hand upon this stone, and felt my spirit answer to its astonishment, I had not imagined that I, too, might find myself exalted.'

In life, Sunder had wielded his piece of Sunstone skilfully. But he had been educated by the Clave's Rede. Liand had no such instruction; no lore of any kind. Only the inborn resources of his Stonedownor blood might enable him to make use of *orcrest.*

'You must comprehend,' he explained earnestly, 'that we were distraught to the depths of our hearts. The Unbeliever and your son had rent you from us, promising salvation. Yet the ur-viles opposed them – and were in turn opposed by Esmer, whose disturbed loyalties appear to shift at every occasion. Also a voice had spoken to us through Anele, foretelling obscure needs and burdens. And the Demondim battered Revelstone heinously. The Masters responded with valour, but their losses were grave, and none knew how long they might deny the horde.

'It is your word that you have endured events which defy description. Our consternation also exceeded telling.'

Pahni's fingers dug into Liand's shoulder; but she would not meet Linden's gaze.

Liand continued to search Linden's face for an answer to his underlying apprehension. 'Galled by helplessness, we endeavoured to busy ourselves. Daily we bathed in Glimmermere to banish the bale of Kevin's Dirt. The Ramen tended the mounts of the Masters. And Stave – as he later informed us – laboured to acquire the secret of silencing his thoughts. But Anele and I were without purpose or relief.

'He remained as he was, compliant and mumbling incoherently. Of him I knew only that he misliked the nearness of the Masters. I, however—' Liand shrugged at the memory. 'I had no place in the defence of Lord's Keep. My presence merely hindered the Masters. The Ramen sought a use for my aid, but their skills eluded me, though I have cared for horses since boyhood. I could discover no trace or trail of the Demondim-spawn. And Stave declined to guide me to the Aumbrie, declaring that the Masters would permit no approach to implements of Earthpower.

'Linden, the thought that I was barred from that which I had been advised to seek became anguish. In your company, I have encountered the greatness and import of the Land. But in your absence, I was no more than a foolish Stonedownor, superfluous and ignorant. Even the benison of Glimmermere gave me no solace. Were it not for Pahni's attentiveness and generosity' – he smiled quickly at the young Cord – 'I might have flung myself against the Demondim merely to relieve my futility.'

With an aborted snore, Anele raised his head, peered blindly around the room. Then he appeared to catch the scent of food. Muttering, 'Anele is hungry,' he braced himself on Bhapa's prompt support, climbed to his feet and went at once to sit near the tray so that he could resume his interrupted meal.

If his temporary lucidity had left any after-effects, they lay beyond the reach of Linden's senses.

'Briefly, Liand,' muttered Mahrtiir in a low voice. 'The Ringthane's heart is sufficiently fraught. Do not dwell upon griefs which have passed.'

At once, Pahni turned to the Manethrall, apparently intending to defend Liand. But Mahrtiir silenced her with a frown and she ducked her head again.

'I crave your pardon,' Liand said to Linden. 'The Manethrall speaks sooth. Your sorrows indeed defy utterance, for the fate of the Land rests with you. It is plain that the Unbeliever's purpose has failed and your son is lost to you. I speak of my plight only so that you may comprehend my transformation' – again he looked at the Ramen girl – 'and Pahni's dread.'

'Don't worry about it.' Linden's tone resembled Stave's stoicism. 'It's going to be a long night, and there isn't much that we can do until morning.' She might not be able to leave Revelstone until she found a way to help the Masters defeat the Demondim. 'We don't need to hurry.'

Liand's countenance revealed his gratitude – as well as his alarm at her manner – as he resumed his explanation.

'On the fourth day from your disappearance, Stave approached me to announce that the time had come. He had learned to conceal his thoughts from the Masters. And the Masters themselves were heavily engaged by the Demondim. He conceived that we might therefore approach the Aumbrie without opposition. His kinsmen were too few to guard us closely.

'I accepted at once, though Pahni protested. I required some task or deed which might offer meaning to my days.

'Leaving Anele with the Ramen, we descended into the depths of Revelstone, where no lamps burned except that which Stave bore and the neglected dust of many and many years had gathered heavily. There we entered a passage which appeared to serve no purpose, for it ended in blank stone. Glimmermere had refreshed my discernment, however, and when I had studied the wall for a time, I perceived a faint residue of glamour or theurgy.

'Though it was veiled from simple sight, a tracing of red outlined the shape of a portal. I have no knowledge of such matters, as you are aware. Yet to my senses, the tracing flowed towards a place of accentuation in the centre of the lintel. Testing me, perhaps, Stave offered no counsel. Nonetheless I dared to set my hand upon that accentuation. And when I had done so, a door became evident within the pattern of the lines.'

Linden listened closely, trying to prepare herself; bracing her resolve on Liand's story. Some of its details begged for examination. Surely the Masters knew that he now held a piece of Sunstone? And they must have sensed Liand's entrance into the Aumbrie. Why had they not taken the *orcrest* from him as soon as he found it?

His tone intensified as he continued. 'Moved by an ancient magic beyond my ken, the door opened of its own accord, admitting us to corridors thick with dust and dank air. Thereafter Stave resumed his guidance, for the passages gave no hint of their design or intent. Soon the air grew nigh too foul to breathe and Stave's lamp faltered. Ere it failed, however, we came upon an iron door, heavy and dark, lying discarded upon the floor. And from the chamber which the door had once sealed shone the lumination of the moon at its full. Also I discerned an aura of eldritch vitality as poignant as Glimmermere's, but immeasurably more complex. Indeed, I recognised nothing except that the atmosphere was compounded of Earthpower in a multitude of forms.

'To my inquiries,' Liand said, 'Stave replied only that the chamber was the Aumbrie of the Clave, that the door had been wrested from its mounts by the ur-vile-made man or creature named Vain, and that none had seen a need to repair the door, guarded as it was by its outer theurgy. Then he did not speak for a time. Rather he appeared to listen for the inward speech of the Masters so that we might be forewarned if we were threatened. In silence, we entered the Aumbrie together.'

His effort to contain the wonder of what he had seen was plain: it showed in his grasp on the *orcrest*. As his fingers tightened, the stone began to glow softly, white as washed cotton and clean as his heart.

'The chamber was large, perhaps twice the size of your quarters taken together, and clearly a storehouse for implements and talismans of aged puissance. Indeed, I was hardly able to advance against the radiance of Earthpower on every side.

'Tables crowded the floor as shelves covered the walls, their surfaces laden. Everywhere I saw scrolls and casks, amulets and torcs, periapts beyond my naming of them, swords of many shapes and fashions, staffs which compelled me to imagine that they had once been clasped by Lords. The light itself was emitted by three munificent caskets upon the shelves, as well as by some few objects upon the tables. Yet wherever I turned my senses, I beheld potencies of such transcendence that my spirit was dazzled by them.'

Suddenly Liand stopped. Easing his grip on the Sunstone, he let its light fade. Then he sat up straight, tucked the *orcrest* away in its pouch and faced Linden with his hands braced on his thighs. An unexpected anger sharpened his tone.

'Linden, the proscriptions of the Masters no longer appear arrogant to me. Now I name them madness. I comprehend that the *Haruchai* eschew weapons, trusting solely to strength and skill. This they deem necessary to their vision of themselves. And the Ramen are the servants of the Ranyhyn. They find no use in the exercise of theurgy, for the great horses do not require it of them. Yet the sheer waste of that which the Aumbrie contains staggers me. I discern no conscience in the denial—'

Linden interrupted him. Defending herself as much as Stave and the Masters, she stated heavily, 'It isn't that simple. You don't just need the instrument. You have to know how to use it.'

'Yet—' the Stonedownor tried to protest.

She did not let him go on. 'Liand, what happened to you in that room? How many of those things did you have to examine before you found what you were looking for?'

'Many,' he admitted uncomfortably. 'Some felt inert to my touch, though their power was visible. Others refused my hand entirely. The markings upon the scrolls conveyed no meaning, and the radiance of the caskets forbade me to open them. For a time, I craved a sword or a staff, but they proffered no response.'

'You see?' said Linden more gently. 'Maybe the Masters were wrong. I think they were. But it doesn't matter now. All of the old knowledge, the lore of the Lords, even the Rede of the Clave. It's gone. It's been lost.

And without it—' She lifted her shoulders in a stiff shrug. 'I can use the Staff of Law because I made it. But I can only call up wild magic because Covenant left me his ring.' In a sense, she had inherited it from him. 'I'm surprised you found even one thing that felt right to you.'

Although he seemed unconvinced, Liand nodded. 'And all that the Aumbrie contained bewildered me. The *orcrest* I would have ignored without Stave's counsel. When I beseeched his aid, however, he observed that I am a Stonedownor, and that therefore some object of stone might serve me.'

Glancing around at her friends, Linden saw that Mahrtiir's impatience was growing, and even Bhapa appeared restless. Pahni held herself motionless with her hand on Liand's shoulder and her body stiff. Only Stave remained impassive, studying Linden with his single eye. And only Anele ignored the tension in the room.

Linden sighed. She could not postpone her own explanations much longer.

'But you found it,' she said to hasten Liand. 'As soon as you touched it, you were sure. It makes you feel like you've come to life. We can all see what it means to you.' His heritage glowed within him as though the blood in his veins had taken light. 'Now I need you to skip ahead.

'Tell me why the Masters didn't stop you. From their point of view, it was a major concession when they let me keep my Staff and Covenant's ring. And they remember *orcrest*. They remember everything. Why didn't they take it away from you?'

Liand glanced at Stave. 'When we returned to the door of theurgy,' the Stonedownor told Linden, 'Branl of the Humbled awaited us, barring our passage. He demanded of me that I must replace the *orcrest* in the Aumbrie.' Then the young man's grave eyes met hers again. 'Stave dissuaded him.'

Linden caught her breath. Staring at Stave, she asked softly, 'Did you *fight* him?'

The *Haruchai* shook his head. 'There was no need. To some small extent, the indulgence which the Masters have granted to you, and to Anele also, wards the Stonedownor as well. But that alone—' Stave shrugged.

'However, an uncertainty has been sown in the hearts of the Masters. They have not forgotten your words when you argued for their aid. In addition, the ur-Lord Thomas Covenant urged the Voice of the Masters to persuade you from your purpose against the Demondim. Yet it is apparent even to the least tractable of my kinsmen that only your quenching of the Fall, and thus of the Illearth Stone, has enabled Revelstone to withstand the horde.

'Afterward' – again Stave shrugged – 'the Unbeliever took you from among us in a manner which encouraged doubt. And when the Unbeliever and your son had removed you, the siege remained. The unremitting attacks of the Demondim demonstrated that the ur-Lord had not accomplished his purpose – or that his purpose was not as he had avowed.

'Therefore the Masters have become uncertain. They do not yet question their own service. But they inquire now if they have justly gauged your worth. For that reason, Branl was reluctant to strike down even the least esteemed of your companions.'

Between her teeth, but quietly, Pahni exclaimed, 'He is not the least. He is the first of the Ringthane's friends, and the foremost.'

Involuntarily Liand blushed; but Linden kept her attention on Stave. 'Are you telling me,' she asked, 'that Branl let him keep something as Earthpowerful as *orcrest* because the Masters are *uncertain*?'

'No, Chosen,' replied Stave. 'I have said only that Branl felt reluctance because the Masters have become uncertain. He did not reclaim the *orcrest* from Liand because I challenged him to the *rhadhamaerl* test of truth.'

Linden's mien must have exposed her incomprehension. Without pausing, Stave explained, 'In your sojourn with the ur-Lord, you knew only the Clave and the Sunbane. Your knowledge of the Land does not extend to the time of the Lords, when the stone-lore of the *rhadhamaerl* was the life and blood of every Stonedown, just as the *lillianrill* lore enriched and preserved every Woodhelven. You are unacquainted with the test of truth.

'It was performed with *orcrest*, or with *lomillialor*, to distinguish honesty from falsehood, fealty from Corruption. Such testing was known to be imperfect. At one time, Corruption himself accepted the challenge, and was not exposed. Among such lesser beings as the Ravers, however, or those who are mortal, the test of truth did not fail.

'I observed to Branl that Liand himself had met the test, though the lore of the *rhadhamaerl* has been lost for millennia. He held *orcrest* in his hand and suffered no hurt. And I proposed to endure the test as well, if Branl would do likewise.'

Liand nodded. In his face, Linden could see that Stave had surprised him then. He was not accustomed to thinking of any *Haruchai* as a friend.

'That challenge he refused,' Stave continued. 'He did not doubt its outcome for himself. But such matters have too much import to be decided by a single Master when the Masters together have become uncertain. They have spurned me. In their sight, I have betrayed their chosen service. If I failed the test of truth, I would confirm their judgment. But if I did not, much would be altered. Therefore Branl permitted us to pass unopposed.

'Now Liand is suffered to hold the *orcrest* just as Anele is suffered to move freely and your own actions have not been hindered. We are warded by the uncertainty of the Masters.'

Linden shook her head. 'I'm sorry, Stave. I don't understand. What would be altered?'

'Chosen,' Stave answered without impatience, 'the *Haruchai* have not forgotten their ancient esteem for those dedicated to the *rhadhamaerl* and *lillianrill* lore. My kinsmen recall that the Bloodguard honoured the test of truth. If the *orcrest* did not reject me, the Masters would be compelled to consider that mayhap they had erred when I was made outcast. Thereafter other doubts would necessarily ensue. Then would their uncertainty burgeon rather than decline.

'The Masters in conclave might perchance have accepted the hazard. Branl alone could not. And the extremity of Revelstone's defence precluded careful evaluation.'

'All right,' Linden said slowly. 'Now I get it. I think.' She could never be certain that she grasped the full stringency of the Masters. But her own circumstances demanded all of her conviction. And she had already made her companions wait too long. 'Thank you.'

She suspected that the doubts of the Masters would eventually make them more intransigent rather than less. And she did not know how to tell her friends that she had become as rigid and unyielding as Stave's kindred.

Instead of standing to meet her own test, she allowed herself one last distraction. With as much gentleness as she could summon, she said, 'Pahni.'

Quickly the young Cord lifted her troubled gaze to meet Linden's, then dropped her eyes again. 'Ringthane?'

With that one brief look, Pahni seemed to bare her soul.

Linden caught her breath; held it for a moment. Then she murmured like a sigh, 'Liand has what Covenant told him to find,' Thomas Covenant himself, not some malign imitation. 'Now you're afraid of what's going to happen to him.'

Pahni nodded without raising her head. Her grip on Liand's shoulder looked tight enough to hurt; but he only reached up to rest one of his hands on hers, and did not flinch.

At last, Linden rose to her feet. For her own sake as much as for Pahni's, she said, 'What you'll have to face is going to be harder.' Covenant had said so through Anele. 'I don't know what it is. I don't know what's going to happen to any of us. But I know that you and Liand need each other.' She was intimately familiar with the cruelty of being forced to face her doom unloved. 'Try to understand his excitement. For the first time in his life, he has something that you've never lacked,' something comparable to the way in which the Ramen served the Ranyhyn. 'A reason to believe that what he does matters.' The Masters had taken that away from all of the Land's people. 'A reason to believe in himself.'

Covenant had given Linden's friends a message for her. *She can do this. Tell her I said that.* She did not believe him – or disbelieve. She could only promise that she would let nothing stop her.

She had also made a promise to Caerroil Wildwood which she meant to keep.

Standing, Linden looked around at her companions: at Mahrtiir's champing frustration and Stave's impassivity, Bhapa's conflicted desire to hear and not hear her tale, Anele's inattentiveness, Liand's growing concern; at Pahni's surprise and appreciation. Then, for the first time since the Humbled had left the room, she let her underlying wrath rise to the surface.

'As it turns out,' she said like iron, 'the *Elohim* told the truth.' He or she had given warning of *croyel* as well as *skurj*. And both the Ramen and the people of the Land had been urged to *Beware the halfhand.* 'If they hadn't been so damn cryptic about it, they might have actually done us some good.'

Had you not suffered and striven as you did, you would not have become who you are.

'Liand, would you put more wood on the fire? It's going to get colder in here.'

Before anyone could react, she walked away into her bedroom.

Temporarily, at least, she had moved past her reluctance. First she opened the shutters over the window so that the comparative chill of the spring night could flow in unhindered. She wanted that small reminder of grim winter and desperation. For a moment, she breathed the air as if she were filling her lungs with darkness. Then she retrieved her Staff and carried its rune-carved ebony back to her waiting friends.

As they caught sight of it, Liand and the Cords winced. They were not surprised: they had seen the Staff when they had brought her here from the plateau. But they did not understand its transformation.

'What has transpired?' Bhapa's voice was husky with alarm. 'Is this some new Staff?'

'Gaze more closely, Cord,' growled the Manethrall. 'This is alteration, not replacement. Some lorewise being has constrained the Ringthane's Staff, or exalted it. And she has wielded her power in battle greater and more terrible than any we have witnessed. She has met such foes—'

Abruptly he turned to Stave. 'Perhaps now we must speak of the Mahdoubt, who has retrieved the Ringthane from the most dire peril.'

Stave studied Linden closely. 'The Chosen will speak as she wills. However, I am loath to address such matters. We may consider them with greater assurance when more is known.'

'Anele sees this,' Anele remarked, peering blindly past or through the Staff. 'He cannot name it. Yet he sees that it is fitting.'

Linden shook her head. 'The Mahdoubt is beside the point.' She had no idea why Stave wanted to avoid the subject; but she did not wish to discuss the Insequent without the older woman's permission. For reasons of her own – perhaps to evade questions like Mahrtiir's – the

Mahdoubt had avoided encountering Linden's companions a short time ago. Whatever those reasons were, Linden intended to respect them. Lightly she tapped one shod end of her Staff on the floor. 'Even this isn't the point. I just wanted you to look at it. I don't know how to describe everything that happened, but I wanted to give you some idea of the *scale*.'

Now everyone except Anele regarded her intently. While the old man mumbled a disjointed counterpoint, she tried to put what she had experienced into words.

She could not do it. The stone in the centre of her chest left no room for sorrow or regret, or for the urgent bafflement and need which had compelled her actions. She still felt those things, but she could not articulate them. They had melted and joined to form the igneous amalgam of her purpose. Any language except deeds would have falsified her to herself.

Instead of the truth, she told her friends the bare skeleton of her story; bones stripped of passion and necessity. While the night air from her bedroom blew softly on the back of her neck, she recited the facts of her time with Roger and the *croyel* as if she had heard them from someone else. Although she glossed over a number of details, she skipped nothing essential – until she came to her time with the Mahdoubt in Garroting Deep. Then she spoke only of Caerroil Wildwood and runes, leaving unexplained her rescue from the Land's past.

If her companions had asked about her return to Revelstone, she would have deflected their inquiries until she understood Stave's disinclination to discuss the Mahdoubt – or until she could seek the Mahdoubt's consent. But they did not. Various aspects of her narrative snagged their attention, and they had too many other questions.

Stave and the Ramen understood more than Liand did. In their separate fashions, their people had preserved their knowledge of the Land's history. Perhaps for that reason, Mahrtiir was caught and held by everything that Linden chose to say about the Insequent: it was entirely new to him. Bhapa stumbled over her description of the Viles and seemed unable to recover his balance. Pahni listened wide-eyed until Linden related how she had entered *Melenkurion* Skyweir in Jeremiah's deadwood cage. Then confusion dulled her expression as if she had reached the limit of what she could hear and absorb. And Stave attended with a slight frown that slowly deepened into a scowl as Linden talked about Roger Covenant and the *croyel*. But he only evinced surprise when she spoke of Caerroil Wildwood. Apparently he found more wonder in the Forestal's forbearance and aid than in anything else.

In contrast, Liand concentrated on Linden herself rather than on the substance of her story. As she talked, he radiated a mounting and entirely personal distress; a concern for her which outweighed everything that he could not grasp. And when she had put in place the last bones of her denatured tale, his alarm swept him to his feet.

'Linden—' he began, groping for words that would not come until he clenched his fists and punched them against each other to break the logjam of his emotions. 'Chosen. Wildwielder. He was your *son*. And the man whom you have loved. Yet you say nothing of yourself. How do you bear it? How are you able—?'

'*No.*' Linden silenced him with sudden vehemence. His caring cut her too deeply. 'We don't talk about me. We aren't going to talk about me at all.' How could she hope to explain her essential transformation? 'I can try to answer practical questions. And I know what I have to do.' *Within her she holds the devastation of the Earth*— 'But Lord Foul took my son and gave him to the *croyel*. That I do not forgive. *I do not forgive.*'

The Ranyhyn had tried to warn her, but she had failed to heed them. She had not understood—

Liand fell back a step, shocked by her ferocity. All of her friends stared at her, their eyes wide. Even Stave seemed to wince. Anele's head flinched from side to side as if he sought to shake her words from his ears.

Thomas Covenant had urged her to find him. He had told her to trust herself.

For a long moment, no one moved. Linden heard no breathing but her own. The logs that Liand had tossed into the hearth seemed to burn without a sound. But then Bhapa shuddered as if he were chilled by the cool air from the bedroom. Raising his head, he looked directly into the mute fury of Linden's gaze.

'Ringthane,' he said unsteadily, 'you have spoken of your son's plight, but you have said little else of him. How does it chance that he, too, is a halfhand?'

A-Jeroth's mark was placed upon the boy when he was yet a small child.

She might have taken offence if she had not recognised what lay behind his question. It was a form of misdirection which she had used often herself. He did not mean to imply that Jeremiah was a danger to the Land. Instead Bhapa was trying to slip past her defences. He thought that if she began to talk about Jeremiah, she might be able to release some of her grief, and so find a measure of relief.

He did not know that she was stone and could not bend: she could only shatter.

But the Manethrall intervened at once. 'Be still, Cord,' he snapped harshly. 'Where is your sight? Are you blind to the fetters which bind her heart? We are Ramen, familiar with treachery and loss. We do not reply thus to suffering. The Ringthane will reveal more when more is needed. Sufficient here is the knowledge which we have gained – and the depth to which both she and the Land have been betrayed.'

Bhapa gave a bow of compliance to his Manethrall. Then he lowered his head and remained silent.

Liand made no protest. He may have been stricken dumb by the sight of Linden's pain. An ache of misery filled his eyes, but he accepted her refusal.

No one spoke until Stave said stolidly, 'You do not forgive.' He had recovered his flat composure. 'This we comprehend. The Masters also do not. And they bear the cost of it, as you do.'

Then he added in a more formal tone, 'Linden Avery, Chosen and Wildwielder. Tell us of your intent, that we may make ready. If you would seek out and confront the Land's foes, we mean to accompany you. Doubtless, however, some preparation is needful.'

He sounded like a man who saw the necessity of risk and death, and was not afraid.

Privately Linden had feared that her friends would flinch away when they heard her story. She had given them a host of reasons to question her judgment – and would give them more. But Stave's assertion affirmed their fidelity. They had given her no cause to believe that they would ever spurn her.

Whether she went to salvation or doom, she would not be alone; not as she had been in Roger's company, and the *croyel*'s.

'All right,' she replied when she meant, Thank you. Simple gratitude was beyond her: telling her tale had expended too much of her self-possession. 'This is what I have in mind.'

The Mahdoubt had called Linden's intentions *fearsome and terrible*. The Viles had spoken of *the devastation of the Earth*– Liand himself had said, *You have it within you to perform horrors*. But Linden did not pause to doubt herself.

'First,' she began, 'I'll have to end the siege somehow.' She could not leave Revelstone to the depredations of the Demondim. 'But then I'm going to Andelain. If I can, I want to find Loric's *krill*. It's supposed to be able to channel any amount of power. It might let me use white gold and my Staff at the same time.'

Stave nodded as if to himself; but she did not stop.

'And I want to meet the Dead.' Before anyone could object, she continued grimly, 'I know what Anele said. I heard him as well as you did. But I need answers, and there's no one else that I can ask.'

She was done with Esmer: his attempts to aid her were too expensive. And she was sure that Sunder and Hollian were not the only shades who walked among the Andelainian Hills. Others of the Land's lost heroes would be there as well, and might view her desires differently.

Mahrtiir and Stave exchanged a glance. Then the Manethrall faced Linden with a Ramen bow. 'As you will, Ringthane. We will make such preparations as the Masters permit. And,' he added, 'Cord Pahni will share with Liand any comprehension of your tale which the Ramen possess. Some portion of his ignorance she will relieve.

'However,' he continued more harshly, 'you are unaware of one event which has occurred in your absence.'

His manner claimed Linden's full attention. Studying him, she saw predatory approval – although behind it lay a degree of apprehension.

'The siege,' she breathed.

Mahrtiir nodded. 'It is gone.'

She stared. 'How?' She could not believe that the Masters had defeated their enemies. The Demondim had too much power—

'Understand, Ringthane,' he replied, 'that the battle to preserve Revelstone raged furiously, and for many days the eventual defeat of the Masters appeared certain. But then, ere sunset on the day before your return, a lone figure in the semblance of a man arrived on the plain. None beheld his approach. He merely appeared, just as you later appeared with the Mahdoubt. Alone, he advanced against the horde.'

Now Linden understood his desire to speak of the older woman earlier.

'The Demondim turned upon him in rage,' Mahrtiir went on, 'and their power was extreme. Yet he defeated them to the last of their numbers. In the space of five score heartbeats, or perhaps ten, all of the Render's Teeth ceased to exist.'

Linden made no effort to conceal her astonishment. Again she asked, 'How?'

For a moment, no one responded. Then Liand cleared his throat. 'Linden,' he said uncomfortably, 'to our sight, it appeared that he devoured them.'

In that instant, the chill of the night air overtook the warmth of the fire. A shiver of hope or foreboding ran down Linden's spine and her limbs ached suddenly, as though she had fallen back into the cruel winter where she had been betrayed.

Chapter Four:

Old Conflicts

Linden tightened her grip on the Staff. —*devoured them*. All of those monsters: the entire horde. Hardly aware of what she did, she drew a subtle current of Earthpower from among the runes to counteract the cold touch of dread and desire. A man who could do that— Then she forced herself to look around at her friends.

It was plain that Liand understood what he had told her no better than she did.

Stave and the Ramen met her gaze. Anele had turned his head away; shifted sideways in his chair so that he could lean his cheek against the wall as if for comfort. His only reaction was a fractured muttering.

'Who is he?' Linden asked.

With a shake of his head, Mahrtiir deferred to Stave.

'None have inquired of him,' Stave replied stolidly. 'The Masters permit no one to pass Revelstone's gates.'

His response surprised Linden further. However, she held the obvious question in abeyance. 'But he's still there?'

'Aye, Chosen,' answered Stave. 'He remains at no great distance, warming his hands by a small fire which he does not replenish, yet which continues to burn. He appears to neither eat nor sleep. Rather it would seem that he merely waits.'

Linden caught her breath; held it briefly. She had seen a fire that did not need to be fed, and beside it a figure patiently motionless. Her mind raced as ideas reeled into new alignments. The Earth was vast, and inhabited by beings and powers which she had never encountered. The Land's present as well as its past held mysteries. She could not be sure that she knew what a waiting figure beside a steady fire signified.

'Why haven't the Masters talked to him? Why won't they let anyone go out there?'

Stave lifted his shoulders in a *Haruchai* shrug. 'They are uncertain. His puissance is manifest. They question the wisdom of accosting him. In addition' – he hesitated slightly – 'there are other matters which I would prefer to name when more is known.'

Other matters, Linden thought. Like the Mahdoubt. Stave and the Masters knew something which they did not wish to reveal.

She wanted to pursue her instinctive assumptions immediately. She had slept for a long time. She had eaten well. And the unexpected doom of the Demondim distracted her from loss and rage. She was eager to act on her decisions.

But her companions had preparations to make. In addition, she had promised the Humbled that they would be told whatever they needed to know. She could not justify concealing the truth about Roger Covenant and the *croyel* from Stave's kinsmen.

'All right,' she said while her thoughts ran in several directions at once. 'We'll let that go for now.' She had to resist an impulse to pace as she said, 'We should start getting ready. Manethrall, I hope you'll take care of that for me, you and your Cords. And Liand.'

When she felt the Stonedownor's protest, she faced him squarely. 'Pahni will explain some things while you're finding supplies. Tomorrow I'll answer your questions.' With her eyes, she added mutely, If they aren't about me. 'In the meantime, please take Anele with you. I need a chance to think.'

Then she said to Stave, 'You should talk to the Humbled. Tell them' – she opened her free hand in a small gesture of surrender – 'everything.' More sharply, she went on, 'But when you're done with that, I want to see you again. You can tell me how they take the news.'

That was only a portion of what she had in mind. However, she felt sure that Stave understood the rest.

She saw in the concentration of Mahrtiir's mien that he understood as well, or guessed it. Yet he made no objection. He was a Raman, bred from childhood to unquestioning service. Without hesitation, he turned to the door, drawing Bhapa and Pahni in the wake of his authority.

For a moment, Liand continued to study Linden with a perplexed frown. But he was capable of dignity. And he had shown repeatedly that he could set his own desires and confusion aside whenever she asked that of him. Drawing himself up, he inclined his head in acquiescence. Then he approached Anele, urged the old man gently to his feet and led him after the Ramen.

Stave bowed before he withdrew. Linden could only guess what sharing her story with Galt and Clyme might cost him; but he did not flinch from it.

As soon as he closed the door behind him, she began to stride back and forth in front of the hearth, stamping the Staff of Law lightly on the floor with each step. She had told the truth: she needed to think. But she was also restless for action. She had let too much time pass. Surely her foes had already formed new plans and started to carry them out? Roger and the *croyel* had escaped the convulsion under *Melenkurion* Skyweir. *Moksha* Jehannum's role remained hidden. If they and the *skurj* and Kastenessen and Esmer and Kevin's Dirt and Joan's *caesures* did not suffice to achieve Lord Foul's desires, he would devise new threats. The stranger outside Revelstone's gates might be one such peril. Or he might be an ally as unexpected as the Mahdoubt.

Yet Linden could not leave her rooms without Stave. She did not know her way through Lord's Keep. And she needed him for other reasons as well. Therefore she had to wait.

While she paced, she tried to imagine what she would have done if she had been free to exact answers from the Theomach.

Slowly the flames in the hearth dwindled, allowing a chill to fill Linden's rooms. But she did not close the shutters, or put more wood on the fire. The darkness outside Revelstone would be colder.

When she heard a knock at her door, she called out immediately, 'Come in!'

As the door opened to admit Stave, she saw all three of the Humbled behind him. But they did not follow him inside, or prevent him from closing the door. Apparently they were content to ensure that she could not leave her quarters without their consent.

'Chosen.' Perhaps to reassure her, Stave bowed yet again. 'I have fulfilled your word. All that you have elected to relate, I have conveyed to the Masters.'

Poised and impatient on the verge of attempting to take charge of her fate, Linden found that her mouth and throat had gone dry. She could feel her heart's labour in her chest. Her voice was unnaturally husky as she asked, 'How did they react?'

He gave a small shrug. 'They are the Masters of the Land.'

She tried to grin, but succeeded only at grimacing. 'In other words, they didn't react at all.'

Stave faced her with his one eye and his flat countenance. 'They chafe at my ability to silence my thoughts. For that reason, they seek to mute their own. But they cannot. Their communion precludes them from acquiring my skill.

'They conclude that you propose to confront the stranger who has brought an end to the Demondim. This they conceive in part because it is your way to leave no obstacle unchallenged, and in part because you have declined to speak of the Mahdoubt.'

'And that's why,' muttered Linden harshly, 'there are now three of them outside my door.' Then she forced herself to soften her tone. 'But do they believe me?'

'That you have spoken sooth,' he replied without inflection, 'is plain to me. Therefore I have made it plain to them.'

'Good.' A small relief lessened her tension briefly. 'Thank you.'

While she could still bear to remain passive, she drank the last of Glimmermere's water. Anele had not touched it, presumably for the same reason that he refused to bathe in the lake, or suffer the touch of hurtloam.

'Tell me,' she said, striving to sound conversational; undemanding. 'Why don't you want to talk about that stranger? Or about the Mahdoubt?'

He did not look away. 'Like the Masters, I am uncertain. Therefore I prefer to await the resolution of my doubts.'

Linden scrutinised him. 'Uncertain?'

'The Mahdoubt and the stranger are entwined in my thoughts. I speculate concerning them, but my imaginings are unconfirmed. If I am mistaken, I do not wish to compound my error by speaking prematurely.'

She nodded. 'I understand. I don't know why the Mahdoubt disappeared when she did, but she's my friend. She saved my life. That's
why I didn't say anything. As far as I'm concerned, she should be allowed
to keep her secrets.' Then Linden added, 'But I don't feel that way about
our stranger. He's a bit too fortuitous for my taste.' His defeat of the
horde resembled Roger's and the *croyel*'s arrival in glamour. 'I think that
we should go relieve some of our ignorance.'

Stave appeared to hesitate. 'Do you conceive that the Masters will
permit it?'

Linden tightened her grip on the Staff. 'Oh, they'll permit it, all right.
You told them my story. Right now, they need answers as badly as we
do.

'I'm sure that they still don't trust me. And the fact that they were so
wrong about Roger and my son might make them even more suspicious.
Now they really don't know who to trust.

'But you told them about the Theomach. And they know that the
Mahdoubt isn't just a servant of Revelstone. If they want to go on calling
themselves the Masters of the Land, they need to know who that stranger
is. They need to know how he disposed of the Demondim.' And why. 'If
I'm willing to risk talking to him, I don't see how they can object.'

After a slight pause, Stave nodded. 'As you say, Chosen. If they reason
otherwise, they will reconsider.'

Then he turned to open the door.

In the hall outside, the Humbled stood arrayed like a blockade; and
for an instant, Linden's steps faltered. But Branl, Clyme and Galt parted
smoothly, permitting Stave to walk between them. At the former Master's
back, she left her rooms unopposed. As she followed Stave, the Humbled
formed an escort behind her.

So far, at least, they tolerated her actions.

Her boots struck echoes from the smooth stone, but the *Haruchai*
moved soundlessly. Obliquely she regretted that she had sent the rest of
her friends away. Their company might have comforted her. *You hold great
powers. Yet if we determine that we must wrest them from you, do you truly
doubt that we will prevail?* She had heard too many forecasts of disaster.
On some deep level, she feared herself in spite of her granite resolve; or
because of it.

Nevertheless she kept pace with Stave as he guided her through the intricate passages of Lord's Keep. She could acknowledge doubts and distrust, but they did not sway her.

Stairways descended at unexpected intervals. Corridors seemed to branch randomly, running in all directions. At every juncture, however, the way had been prepared. Lamps and torches illumined Stave's route. And he walked ahead of her with unerring confidence. Apparently the Masters condoned her intentions.

The passages seemed long to her. Yet eventually Stave led her down a short hall that ended in the high cavern inside Revelstone's inner gates. There, too, lamps and torches had been set out for her; and when she looked past Stave's shoulder, she saw that the Keep's heavy interlocking doors stood slightly open.

That they remained poised to close swiftly did not trouble her. The Masters were understandably chary. One man, alone, had defeated the entire horde of the Demondim – had eaten them, according to Liand – in spite of their prodigious theurgies and their apparently limitless power to resurrect themselves. Naturally the defenders of Revelstone wanted to be ready for the possibility – the likelihood? – of calamity.

Now her steps no longer echoed. The vast forehall swallowed the clap of her boots, diminishing her until she seemed laughable in the face of the dangers which crowded the Land's deep night. Still she followed Stave. Occasionally she touched the cold circle of Covenant's ring. If at intervals she wished for Liand's presence, or for Mahrtiir's, she did not show it.

As she trod the length of the forehall, she hoped that Galt, Clyme and Branl would remain in Revelstone. She did not want to hold herself responsible for either their actions or their safety. And she was in no mood to argue with them if they disapproved of her choices. But when they accompanied her through the narrow gap between the gates into the walled courtyard that separated the main Keep from the watchtower, she shrugged off her wish to be free of them. She could not pretend, even to herself, that she might not need defenders.

Apparently she was doomed to pursue her fate in the company of halfhands.

While she walked along the passage under the watchtower, the warded throat of Revelstone, she heard her boot heels echoing again. The sound seemed to measure her progress like a form of mockery, a rhythmic iteration of Lord Foul's distant scorn. And the air became distinctly colder. Involuntarily she shivered. She felt Masters watching her, wary and unreadable, through slits in the ceiling of the tunnel; but she could not discern what they expected from her.

During her previous time in the Land, she had been able to rely on the *Haruchai* even when they distrusted her. For a moment, the fact that she could not do so now filled her with bitterness. But then she passed between the teeth of the outer gates, and had no more attention to spare for the intransigence of the Masters.

Night held the slowly sloping plain beyond the watchtower and the massive prow of Revelstone. High in the eastern sky, a gibbous moon cast its silver sheen over the ground where the Demondim had raged, seething with frustration and corrosive lore. The after-effects of their ancient hatred lingered in the bare dirt. But overhead a profusion of stars filled the heavens, glittering gems in swaths and multitudes untouched by the small concerns of suffering and death. They formed no constellations that she knew, but she found solace in them nonetheless.

Following Stave through the darkness, she was glad to be reminded that her fears and powers were little things, too evanescent and human to impinge upon the immeasurable cycles of the stars. Her life depended on what she did. It was possible that Stave and the Humbled and all of Revelstone's people were at risk. In ways which she could not yet imagine, Jeremiah's survival – and perhaps that of the Land as well – might hang in the balance. Yet the stars took no notice: they would not. She was too small to determine their doom.

As was the man who had destroyed the Demondim. He might well surpass her. But while the heavens endured, she could afford to push her limits until they broke – or she did. Like her, the stranger lacked the power to decide the destinies of stars.

In faint silver, Stave led Linden forward; and when she lowered her gaze from the sky, she saw the flickering of a campfire. Its lively flames cast the stranger into shadow, but he appeared to be seated with his back to her and his head bowed. If he heard her steps, or sensed the advancing *Haruchai*, he gave no sign. His limned shape remained motionless.

Within a dozen paces of the stranger, Linden halted Stave with a touch on his shoulder. He glanced at her, a quick flash of reflected firelight in his eye. Drawing him with her, she began to circle around the campfire so that she could approach the stranger in plain sight, unthreateningly – and so that she could watch his reactions.

She expected the Humbled to accompany her, but they did not. Instead they stopped where she and Stave had paused, no more than a few running strides from the stranger's back. Swearing to herself, she considered gesturing – or calling aloud – for them to join her. But she felt sure that they would ignore her.

Grateful for Stave's presence at her side, she continued to circle towards the far side of the fire.

As she entered the stranger's range of vision, he lifted his head slowly. But he did not react in any other way until she and Stave stood near the flames. Then, as lithe and easy as if he had not been sitting still for days, he rose to his feet.

'Lady,' he said in a voice as deep and rich as the loam of a river delta. '*Haruchai*. You are well come. I feared that I would be compelled to await you for seasons rather than mere days. Such is the obduracy of those who rule yon delved dwelling.'

Linden stared at him, unable to mask her surprise. She had heard that voice somewhere before—

He was clad all in leather, and all in subtle shades of brown. Nevertheless his garb was unexpectedly elaborate: if its hues had been less harmonious, it would have seemed foppish. Boots incused with arcane symbols extended up his calves almost to his knees, then folded down over themselves and ended in dangling tassels. Leggings that looked as supple as water clung to his thighs, emphasising their contours. Above them, he wore a frocked doublet ornately worked with umber beads, the sleeves deeply cuffed. It was snug at the waist, unbelted, and hemmed with a long, flowing fringe. From his shoulders hung a short dun chlamys secured by a bronze clasp: the only piece of metal in his costume. The clasp resembled a ploughshare.

If he bore any weapons, they were concealed under his chlamys or inside his doublet.

He had a lean, muscular figure with strong hands, a neatly trimmed beard, and close-cropped hair. And every shade of his features, from his weathered cheeks and mouth to his hair and whiskers, blended subtly with the browns of his raiment. The combined effect suggested that his garments were not mere clothing: they expressed his identity.

But his eyes were a startling black, so stark and lustreless that they might have been holes or caves leading into subterranean depths.

Disturbed in spite of her efforts to prepare herself, Linden instinctively avoided meeting his gaze. Instead of looking directly into his face, she let her eyes wander over his broad shoulders, down the fluid folds of the chlamys. As far as she could discern with her health-sense, he was simply a man, devoid of magic or force. But at one time, she had mistaken the Mahdoubt for an ordinary woman. Even the Masters had done so. And Linden had failed to detect the Theomach's secret puissance—

She held her runed Staff and Covenant's ring. Alone, she had beaten Roger and the *croyel* back from the brink of the Land's doom – and she had done it without drawing on wild magic. Yet she felt oddly abashed in the stranger's presence; unsure of herself; exposed and frail.

His voice was familiar. Where had she heard it before?

She wanted to speak confidently, but her voice was an unsteady whisper. 'You *ate* them? You ate the *Demondim*?'

The stranger laughed briefly, a comfortable sound with a slight trace of ridicule. 'Alas, lady, that is imprecise. Were I able to consume them, I would have taken their power into myself and become stronger. Belike I would then have no need of you.

'No, the truth is merely that I have made a considerable study of such beings. Their lore is both potent and unnatural. It holds a great fascination for me. For many and many a long year, I have devoted myself to the comprehension of their theurgy. And I have learned the trick of unbinding them.'

Linden's eyes flicked close to his. '"Unbinding"?'

He inclined his head. 'Indeed, lady. Having no tangible forms, they would be lost to will and deed without some containing ensorcellment to preserve them from dissolution. Imagine,' he explained, 'that they are bound to themselves by threads of lore and purpose. The threads are many, but if one alone is plucked and severed, all unravel.

'Thus I disposed of the Demondim, for their presence in this time endangered my desires.'

Again she felt her gaze drawn towards his. With an effort, she forced herself to concentrate on the centre of his forehead. At her side, Stave stood without movement or speech, as if he saw no threat in the stranger and had lost interest.

Yet he, too, had heard that voice before. It had addressed Linden through Anele after she had quenched the horde's *caesure*. She remembered it clearly now.

Such power becomes you. But it will not suffice.

Abruptly she stood straighter, holding her Staff like an asseveration. This stranger had imposed himself on Anele; had taken advantage of the old man's vulnerability. As far as she knew, he had only done so once. But once was enough to win her animosity. He was not Thomas Covenant, striving to help her in spite of the boundaries of life and death. He was simply careless of Anele's suffering.

In the end, you must succumb. If you do not, you will nonetheless be compelled to accept my aid, for which I will demand recompense.

Ignoring the seduction of the stranger's eyes, Linden said like the first soft touch of a flail, before it began to swing in earnest, 'You're one of the Insequent.'

Stave must have guessed that the stranger belonged to the same race as the Mahdoubt and the Theomach—

Now the stranger's laugh was ripe with pleasure. 'Lady, I am. You are known to me, together with all of your acts and powers, and your great peril. Permit me the honour of presenting myself. I am the Harrow.'

He bowed with courtesy as elaborate as his apparel; but Linden did not. Already she was starting to loathe the sound of his voice. He was not the first to foretell failure for her. But he had hurt Anele—

Before she could retort, however, a rush of movement behind the Harrow caught her attention. She looked past him in time to see the Humbled emerge from the darkness, flinging themselves as one at his undefended back.

Instinctively she cried out, '*No!*' but the Masters ignored her. Galt leaped high to punch at the Harrow's head. Clyme drove a kick at the centre of his spine while Branl dove for his knees.

Even a Giant might have been felled by their assault. But the Harrow was not. All three of the Humbled struck him – and all three rebounded to the dirt as if they had been slapped away. The Harrow remained standing, apparently untouched. Neither his posture nor his amiable smile suggested that he had noticed his attackers.

'Lady,' he observed with easy nonchalance, 'you have not inquired into the nature of my desires.'

Shocked, Linden realised too late that she was looking directly into the black caves of his eyes. They caught her and held as if they were sucking at her mind.

None of the Humbled hesitated. The force which had repulsed them must have hurt; yet they sprang up instantly to attack again. This time, however, they did not leave their feet. Planting themselves around the Harrow, they hammered him with blows too swift and heavy to be distinguished from each other. A plinth of sandstone might have been pulverised by their onslaught.

Still he ignored them. Instead he gazed at Linden, drawing her deeper and deeper into the fathomless abysm of his eyes. She could not think or move; could not look away. The frenzy of the Humbled and the cheerful dance of the campfire became imprecise, meaningless: they had slipped sideways somehow, into a slightly different dimension of existence. The Harrow himself had slipped. Only his eyes remained fully real, his eyes and the rich loam of his voice; only the darkness—

Vaguely she tried to summon the power of her Staff. But she was already lost. The hands of her volition hung, useless, at her sides. She could not lift them.

'First,' he said pleasantly, 'I desire this curious stick to which you cling as though it possessed the virtue to ward you. Second, I crave the circle of white gold which lies hidden by your raiment. And last, I covet the unfettered wrath at the centre of your heart. It will nourish me as the Demondim did not. Though the husk of yourself is comely, I will discard it, for it does not interest me.'

He laughed as he added, 'Did I not forewarn you that you must succumb?'

Stave may have shouted Linden's name. She was almost sure that he had joined Galt, Branl and Clyme, assailing the Harrow with all of his prodigious strength. But she knew that none of them would prevail. Knowledge is power, she thought absently. The Harrow had destroyed the entire horde of the Demondim. He could certainly withstand the *Haruchai* while he consumed her soul.

Long ago, she had succumbed. More than once. She was familiar with self-abandonment. Now she resisted. Desperately she tried to say the Seven Words. Any of them. She remembered them all: she could form them in her mind. But they required utterance. They had no efficacy without breath and effort. The Harrow cocked an eyebrow as if he were aware of her attempt, and mildly surprised by it. Nevertheless he went on laughing with the ease of complete certitude.

There was no pain; no falling; no sensation at all. She was not possessed and tortured as she had once been by a Raver. Nor did she feel the illimitable excruciation of a *caesure*. Her own capacity for evil held no horror. The voids of the Harrow's eyes had simply grown as infinite as the heavens. But no stars sanctified them. No glimmering articulated their emptiness. Absolute loss unredeemed by choice or possibility claimed her. She could do nothing except observe her ruin until every particle of her being was devoured.

She wanted to plead with him somehow; beseech him to let her go. He did not care about Jeremiah. Her son would never be freed if she could not convince the Harrow to release her.

But she did not know his true name. She lacked the means to make him heed her.

There was another name, one which had been given to her for a reason, and which she had not forgotten. She was no longer substantial or significant enough to speak it.

Stave and the Humbled beat themselves raw on the Harrow's impervious form. They hit and kicked so hard that any bones except theirs would have shattered. The skin of their fists and feet became pulp. With every blow, they splashed blood that did not touch the Insequent.

They could not save Linden.

Still they were *Haruchai*, deaf and blind to defeat. With a suddenness which would have startled her if all of her reactions had not been sucked away, Stave gouged at the Harrow's eyes.

Stave was imponderably swift. Nevertheless the Harrow snatched

Stave's hand aside before it reached his face. To prevent another strike, he kept his grip on Stave's wrist.

Surprised by the Harrow's quickness, Stave may have faltered for a small fraction of a heartbeat. Then he attacked the Insequent's eyes with his other hand.

That blow the Harrow caught and held easily as well; so easily that even Stave's boundless courage must have known dismay.

But the Humbled followed the former Master's example. Branl and Clyme grasped the Harrow's arms in an attempt to prevent him from moving: Galt leaped onto the Harrow's back. With both hands, Galt clawed at the Insequent's eyes.

Within herself, Linden continued to struggle.

The Harrow did not try to defend himself physically. Instead he released Stave and let out a roar of force which flung all of the *Haruchai* from him. They were tossed through the air like dolls to land in darkness beyond the reach of the firelight.

But while he scattered his attackers, his will or his attention wavered for an instant. And in that instant, Linden gasped softly, '*Quern Ehstrel.*'

At once, the Harrow staggered as though an avalanche had fallen on his shoulders. He stumbled into his campfire. Flames flared hungrily over his boots and onto his leggings.

And the grasp of his gaze snapped.

As his blackness vanished from Linden's mind, she recoiled; pitched headlong to the ground with her hands clamped over her eyes. She had dropped her Staff and did not care. Released, she returned to herself with a shock as violent as a seizure. Her muscles spasmed as she lay in the dirt, unable to move or think. At that moment, she only knew that she had to protect her eyes.

'Fool.' The Harrow's voice was velvet with rage. 'You are doomed, damned, ended. If you do not extinguish yourself, the entire race of the Insequent will rise up to excoriate your intrusion. Every commandment of what we are requires—'

'Oh, assuredly,' put in the Mahdoubt complacently. 'By this deed, the Mahdoubt completes her long years of service. Yet her doom is not immediate. Even your animal fury cannot demand madness of her until her interference is beyond denial.'

Linden's appeal had been answered.

Squeezing her eyes shut, she moved her hands. Although her arms trembled in reaction and her heart shook, she fumbled around her for the Staff. But she found only bare ground and the residual loathing of the Demondim, bitter as gall.

The Mahdoubt had come. But surely she had no power to compare with the Harrow's? She could cross time. And she could pass unseen to appear where she was needed. She was provident and considerate. But she had evinced no magic like that with which the Harrow had repulsed Stave and the Humbled.

'You prevaricate, old woman' – the largesse of the Harrow's anger filled the night – 'as has ever been your wont. You have intervened in my triumph, which no Insequent may attempt without cost. If you deny this, you are false to yourself as to me.'

Linden's head reeled. Her whole sense of herself seemed to stagger drunkenly. Nevertheless she could not remain sprawling, blind and helpless, while the Mahdoubt confronted the Harrow on her behalf. Fearfully she slitted her eyes; confirmed that she was facing away from the campfire. Then she pushed herself up onto her knees and glanced around rapidly, looking for the Staff.

It was out of reach behind her and to the left. Even if she dove towards it while the Harrow was distracted, he might be too quick for her. She was still too dazed to summon Earthpower and Law without touching the black wood.

'Rage as you wish,' answered the Mahdoubt, unperturbed. 'Assuredly the Mahdoubt seeks to defy the commandments of our kind. This she acknowledges. And in so doing, she hazards her life. Yet even your arrogance cannot proclaim that she has prevented your designs. Her intrusion has merely delayed them. She cannot be named inexculpate until she has coerced you to forswear your purpose against the lady's person.'

Linden braced herself to lunge for the Staff. As she did so, however, Stave came to stand between her and the campfire. Blood dripped from his hands: it trickled down his shins, oozed from his feet. But he disdained his hurts.

Stooping, he retrieved the Staff and passed it to Linden. 'Rise, Chosen,' he said quietly. 'It appears that the Mahdoubt will have need of you.'

At once, she surged to her feet. For a moment longer, she kept her back to the flames and the Insequent while she assured herself of Earthpower. Then, abruptly, she turned to see what the Mahdoubt and the Harrow were doing.

The Harrow laughed with renewed confidence. 'Forswear my purpose?' he countered in a tone of abundant mirth. 'I? As the years pass, you have become an object of ridicule. At one time, you were remembered respectfully among the Insequent, but now you are viewed with scorn.

'This, however, I will grant,' he added more dangerously. 'I have merely been delayed, and will yet triumph. If you depart now, you may perchance retain some portion of your mind.'

Keeping her eyes lowered, Linden scanned the vicinity of the camp-fire. The Harrow stood on the far side of the flames with his arms folded across his chest, defiant and dire. Although he had staggered into the blaze, his boots and leggings were undamaged. Like their wearer, they seemed impervious to ordinary harm. The bottomless holes of his gaze tugged at Linden. But she did not allow herself to glance above the level of his waist.

While she looked around, she readied her own fire.

Opposite the Harrow – directly between him and Linden – the Mahdoubt squatted as she had beside her gentle flames in Garroting Deep. She faced her fellow Insequent steadily. The curve of her back suggested poised stillness rather than relaxation. Shining through the unkempt tangle of her hair, the firelight seemed to crown her head with an oblique glory, subtle and ineffable. Stark against the campfire, she wore a nimbus of determination.

Stave stood at Linden's side a little ahead of her. Perhaps he thought that if the Harrow snared her again he would be able to save her by stepping in front of her; blocking the Harrow's gaze.

The Humbled also had emerged from the night. They had positioned themselves behind the Harrow, waiting to see what would transpire. They had fought longer than Stave: their bruises and abrasions were worse. Nevertheless Linden did not doubt that they would attack again without hesitation if they saw a need to do so.

The random flare and gutter of the flames effaced the stars overhead. But around the horizons of the plain, and along the rims of Revelstone, faint gleams still defined the dark like sprinkled flecks of ice. And behind her, Linden felt the moon arc placidly across the heavens, undismayed by earthbound conflicts.

'On other matters,' the woman was saying as if the Harrow had not spoken, 'the Mahdoubt does not intrude. Assuredly she does not. You will act according to your desires. But she will see your threat to the lady's mind and spirit and flesh abandoned. If you accede, no evil has occurred. And if she fails, there is again no evil. But if you seek to measure yourself against her, and are outmatched, she will require your bound oath.

'Then will your paths be altered in all sooth, and there will be no gainsaying the Mahdoubt's culpability. She herself will not question it.'

The campfire dwindled, and night crowded closer, as the Mahdoubt said distinctly, 'Choose, then, proud one. Accede or give battle. The Mahdoubt has grown weary in the service of that which she deems precious. She does not fear to fail.'

The Harrow's voice was full of amusement as he replied, 'Do you dare this challenge?' Yet behind his mirth, Linden thought that she heard the gnashing of boulders. 'Have you fallen prematurely into madness?'

'Pssht,' retorted the woman dismissively. 'Words. The Mahdoubt will have deeds or naught.'

Linden wanted to protest, No, don't do this! I can fight for myself! The Mahdoubt had nothing to gain here: she could only lose. And she was Linden's friend. But Linden's voice was locked in her throat.

Urgent fire curled around her fingers and ran along the Staff as she prepared to defend the older woman.

'Then ready yourself, relic of foolishness,' the Harrow pronounced with plush confidence. 'You cannot rule me.'

Stave shifted closer to the direct line between Linden and the Harrow's eyes.

Linden saw nothing to indicate that a contest had commenced. Her health-sense discerned nothing. To all appearances, the Harrow simply stood with his arms folded over his chest, a figure of irrefragable self-possession and surety. Opposite him, the Mahdoubt squatted motionless, seemingly devoid of power or purpose; as mundane as the gradual slope of the plain.

But the campfire continued to shrink as though moisture from some cryptic source were soaking imperceptibly into the wood. Around the battle, darkness thickened like a wall.

If she could have spoken, Linden would have asked Stave, What are they doing? She might have asked, Have they started yet? But she had no voice. As the flames died, they seemed to draw sound as well as light with them. Nothing punctuated the night except her own taut breathing and the muffled thud of her heart.

But then, subtly, by increments too small to be defined, the Harrow began to fade as if his physical substance were being diluted or stretched thin. Some undetectable magic siphoned away his tangible existence.

For long moments, Linden watched the change, transfixed, until she was able to catch glimpses of the Humbled through the Harrow's form.

With a palpable jolt, the Mahdoubt's opponent snapped back into solidity. The flames of his fire flared higher, driving back the encroachment of the night.

Without risking the hunger of his eyes, Linden could not see his expression. But his chest heaved, and his strained breathing was louder than hers.

A heartbeat later, he started to fade again, leaking out of himself into some other dimension of reality. Or of time.

This change was more rapid. He seemed to dissolve in front of her as the fire died towards embers. Clyme, Branl and Galt were clearly visible through the veil of the Harrow's substance.

The impact when he forced himself back into definition was as visceral as a blow. Linden felt the intensity of his exertion. It touched her percipience on a pitch that scraped along her nerves, vibrated in the marrow of her bones. His flames guttered higher as he gasped hoarsely. Hazarding a glance upwards, she saw that his cheeks were slick with sweat. Fine droplets caught a skein of ruddy reflections in his beard.

The Mahdoubt was beating him—

His arms remained clasped across his chest. Yet Linden could see that they trembled. All of his muscles were trembling.

The Mahdoubt still had not moved. But now her plump form and rounded shoulders no longer suggested quiet readiness. Instead they were implacable; vivid with innominate strength. She had made herself as unyielding as the bedrock of mountains.

Earthpower and protests itched for expression in Linden's hands as the Mahdoubt renewed the Harrow's failure.

Now he did not fade slowly towards evanescence; dissolution. Instead he appeared to flicker. For an instant, he was nearly solid: then he came so close to transparency that only his outlines remained: then he struggled back into substance. Linden felt every throb and falter of his efforts to find some fingerhold or flaw in the Mahdoubt's obdurate expulsion.

If Stave and the Humbled had struck at him, they might have broken his bones; or they might have passed through him as if he were no more than mist. But they merely witnessed the eerie conflict, as unmoving as the Mahdoubt, and as unmoved.

Linden did not realise that she was holding her breath until a sound-less implosion snatched the air from her lungs. The sudden inrush of force swallowed the Harrow's power, and the Mahdoubt's. As Linden panted in surprise, the Harrow's campfire burned normally again. He stood across the flames from the Mahdoubt as if nothing had occurred. Only the heaviness of his respiration and the sweat on his face and the wincing hunch of his shoulders betrayed the truth.

'That is difficult knowledge,' he remarked when he was able to speak evenly. 'It emulates the Theomach's. Yet I am not displaced.'

'Assuredly.' The Mahdoubt shook her head as if she were casting sparks from her hair. 'The Mahdoubt acknowledges that choices remain to you, flight among them. But you will not flee. Greed will not permit you to surrender your intent. Nor are you able to withstand the Mahdoubt's resolve.'

'You know me, then,' he admitted. 'Yet you are thereby doomed. While I endure, your long service comes to naught.'

Again the woman shook her head. 'Perchance it is so. Perchance it is not.' Her tone was as implacable as her strength. 'No conclusion is reached until you have given your bound oath.'

Grimly Linden hoped that the Harrow would refuse. If he continued to fight, or chose to retreat, she could argue that the Mahdoubt had not prevented his designs. And if she cast her own force into the fray, surely the Mahdoubt could not be held accountable for the outcome? Damn it, the woman was her *friend*.

But the Harrow accepted defeat. 'It is given.' Resentment pulsed in his voice. 'If it must be spoken, I will speak it.

'My purpose against your lady's person I forswear.' As he uttered them, the words took on resonance. They expanded outwards as if they were addressed to the night and the uncaring stars. 'From this moment, I will accept from her only that which she chooses to grant. No other aspect of my desires will I relinquish. But my efforts against her mind and spirit and flesh I hereby abandon. In herself, she will have no cause to fear me. And I adjure all of the Insequent to heed me. If I do not abide by this oath, I pray that their vengeance upon me will be both cruel and prolonged.'

When he was finished, his voice relapsed to its normal depth and richness. 'Does this content you, old woman?'

'It does.' The Mahdoubt's reply was soft and faintly forlorn, as if she rather than the Harrow had been humbled. She slumped beside the fire as though her bones had begun to crack. 'Assuredly. The Mahdoubt acknowledges your oath and is content.'

'Then,' responded the Harrow with fertile malice, 'I bid you joy in your coming madness. It will be brief, for it brings death swiftly in its wake.'

Offering his opponent an elaborate and mocking bow, he turned away.

At last, Linden found her voice. 'Just a minute!' she snapped. 'I'm not done with you.'

Cocking an eyebrow in a show of surprise, the Harrow faced her. 'Lady?'

As he had sworn, his eyes exerted no compulsion. Nevertheless Linden avoided them. Instead she moved to crouch beside the Mahdoubt. Resting a hand on the older woman's shoulder, she murmured, 'Are you all right?'

She meant, Why did you do that? I needed you at first. But then I could have fought for myself.

With an effort that made her old muscles quake, the woman straightened her back and raised her head to look at Linden. 'My lady,' she said in a voice that quavered, 'there is no need for haste. The Mahdoubt's doom is assured, yet it will not overtake her instantly. You and she will speak together, friend to friend.' Her mismatched eyes searched Linden's face. 'The Mahdoubt prays that you will not prolong the Harrow's departure on her behalf.'

'Are you sure?' Linden insisted. 'There must be something that I can do for you.'

'Assuredly,' replied the old woman; a dying fall of sound. 'Permit the Mahdoubt a moment's respite.' Her chin sagged back down to her breast. 'Then she will speak.'

Her words were sparks in the ready tinder of Linden's outrage.

'In that case—'

Abruptly Linden surged upright to confront the Harrow.

He had recovered his air of undisturbed certitude. The night had cooled his cheeks and brow, and his strong arms rested casually on his chest as if his struggles had already lost their meaning. His eyes probed Linden, daring her to look directly into them; but she refused. If she could, she intended to scald the danger out of them. For the moment, however, she fixed her gaze on the hollow at the base of his throat.

'I think that I understand this,' she said between her teeth. 'But I don't have much experience with you Insequent, and I want to be sure that I've got it straight.

'I'm safe from you now? Is that right?'

Stave had joined her beside the Mahdoubt. He looked at her intently. He may have wished to warn her; to explain something. But what he saw in her silenced him.

The Humbled remained poised, apparently passionless, behind the Harrow. They paid no attention to their hurts.

'Indeed.' The Harrow's defeat left a caustic edge in his voice. 'Until you are minded to grant my desires, I will not attempt to wrest them from you.'

'And your desires are—?' Linden demanded. 'I want to hear you say it again.'

'What I seek, lady,' he answered without hesitation, 'is to possess your instruments of power.' Then he shrugged. 'What I will have, however, is your companionship.'

Linden glared at his throat as though she meant to rip it open. 'What in God's name makes you think that I'm going to let you follow me around?'

The Harrow laughed mordantly. 'Apart from the mere detail that you cannot prevent me? There is a service which I am able to perform for you, and which you will not obtain from any other living being.'

Oh really? 'In that case,' she repeated, 'there's something that you should know about me.'

Again he laughed. 'Elucidate, lady. If there can be aught that I do not know of you, I will—'

Softly, almost whispering, Linden pronounced, 'The Mahdoubt is my friend.'

As swift as anger, she summoned a howl of power from her Staff and hurled it straight into the Harrow's eyes.

Her vehemence was hot enough to resemble the fire which had fused her heart. It should have burned its way deep into his brain. If it had left him blind and useless, as doomed as the Mahdoubt, she would not have permitted herself one small stumble of regret. This was what she had become, and she did not mean to step back from herself.

But she was not as quick as the Harrow. Before her blast struck him, he slapped a hand over his eyes. Her fire splashed away like water.

For a long moment, she poured Earthpower at him, dispersing the dark; trying to overwhelm his defences. However, he was proof against her: he appeared to withstand her assault easily, almost negligently. When she had tested him until she was sure that she could not daunt or damage him with the Staff alone, she released her flame and let night wash back around the campfire.

As the Harrow lowered his hand to gaze at her, unconcerned, she said harshly, 'You're tough,' loathing the tremor in her voice. 'I'll give you that. But don't think for a second that I can't hurt you. If you know as much about me as you claim, you know that I can do a hell of a lot more than this.'

Masked by his beard, the Harrow's mouth twisted. 'As your "friend" has said, perchance it is so. Perchance it is not. For your part, know that my oath does not preclude me from causing you such pain that you will regret your unseemly defiance.'

Before she could retort, he added, 'I bid you farewell. Rail against me at your pleasure. I will claim your companionship when you attempt aught which interests me.'

Brusquely he bowed. Then he turned and strode away in the direction of Revelstone. The Humbled did not step aside for him. Nevertheless he passed through them, leaving them untouched – and visibly startled in spite of their stoicism. Then he seemed to evaporate into the darkness. In an instant, he was gone.

The Humbled stared after him. Their stances suggested that they expected to be assailed. After a moment, however, they appeared to accept his disappearance. Shrugging, they dismissed him and approached the campfire.

The Mahdoubt made a vague plucking gesture. When Linden saw it, she moved at once to the woman's side and extended her arm. The Mahdoubt grasped it feebly, tried to heave herself to her feet. At first, she failed: her strength had left her. But then Stave added his support and she was able to rise.

Clinging to both Linden and the former Master, the Mahdoubt panted thinly, 'My lady. In one matter. You have erred.' She took a moment to calm her breathing, then said, 'Your challenge was unseemly. He has given his oath. Assuredly so. And the choice to demand it of him was freely made. It is through no act of his that the Mahdoubt must now pass away.'

'I don't care.' Linden hunched close to the woman, trying vainly to transmit some her own health into the Mahdoubt's sudden frailty. 'I care about you.'

'And you do not forgive,' Stave put in sternly. His tone held a hint of reproach. 'This you have demonstrated. You are altered, Chosen and Sun-Sage. The woman who accompanied the ur-Lord Thomas Covenant to the redemption of the Land would not have struck thus.'

'What do you want from me?' Linden countered. She could not bear sorrow or shame: they would unmake her. Under *Melenkurion* Skyweir, such emotions had been clad in granite. 'Am I supposed to call him back and *apologise*? God damn it, Stave, she's going to *die*, and she did it for me.' More softly, she repeated, 'She did it for me.'

Stave held Linden's glare without blinking; but the Mahdoubt intervened. 'Oh, assuredly,' she said with more firmness. 'Of a certainty, the Mahdoubt will perish. But first she will fall into madness.'

Swallowing anger, Linden asked, 'Does that have to happen? Isn't there something we can do about it?'

The woman sighed. 'It is the way of the Insequent, inherent in us. It is required of the Mahdoubt by birth rather than by choice or scruple. The Insequent exert no demands upon each other, for the cost of such conflict would be extinction. Some centuries past, the Vizard sought to thwart the Harrow's desires, for he deemed them contrary to his own purpose. Thus was the Vizard lost to use and name and life. The outcome of what the Mahdoubt has done will not be otherwise.'

The eyes of the Humbled widened momentarily, and Stave cocked an eyebrow; but Linden paid no attention to them.

'Ere that end, however,' the Mahdoubt continued, 'there is much that must be said.' She glanced at Stave. 'You also must speak, *Haruchai*. The Mahdoubt falters, for her years come upon her swiftly. She is too weary to relate the tale of your people. Yet that tale must be told.'

'It must not,' countered Clyme promptly. 'There is no need. And the will of the Masters has not been consulted.'

The Mahdoubt squinted at Clyme with her orange eye. In spite of her weakness, she retained enough force to silence him. 'Were you efficacious against the Harrow, Master? Did he not dismiss your efforts, as did the Vizard in a distant age and place? Then do not speak to the Mahdoubt of "need". While she retains any portion of herself, she will determine what is needful.'

To Linden's surprise, all three of the Humbled bowed, and said nothing more.

While she scrambled to grasp why any Master would show the Mahdoubt such respect when earlier the Humbled had attacked the Harrow without provocation, Stave said, 'If there is much that must be said, perhaps it would be well to speak first of this "service" which the Harrow may elect to perform for the Chosen.'

The Mahdoubt shook her head. 'Nay. Doing so will alter my lady's path – and the Mahdoubt has given her life in the belief that my lady must be trusted, though her deeds engender horrors. The Mahdoubt will not disturb a future which eludes her sight.'

'Then tell me why you did it,' Linden asked; pleaded. 'I needed you at first. You saved me. But then I could have defended myself,' while the Harrow's intentions had only been delayed. 'You didn't have to sacrifice yourself.'

The woman sighed. 'Has the Mahdoubt not said – assuredly, and often – that she is weary?' Linden could feel the Mahdoubt's vitality slowly seeping from her limbs. 'She prefers her own passing to a life in which she may behold the end of days.'

Then she turned her blue eye on Linden. 'Yet if she is craven, persuaded to madness and death by apprehension, she is not merely so.

'My lady, you have become the Mahdoubt's friend, as she is yours. You are sorely transformed. That is sooth. You have become fearsome. Yet in Garroting Deep, you found within yourself the means to warm the Mahdoubt's heart. There she learned that the mystery of your needs and desires is unfathomable. It resembles the mystery of life, rich in malice and wonder. That good may be accomplished by evil means defies explication. Yet the Mahdoubt has assured herself that you are equal to such contradictions. Therefore she believes that you must not be turned aside.'

Slowly the Mahdoubt lowered her head to rest her tired neck. At the same time, however, her tone became sharper, whetted by indignation.

'My lady, the Harrow's purpose lies athwart your path. His blandishments you may withstand. But if he failed here to consume your choices and your love, he would attempt the same wrong at another time. Oh, assuredly. Again and again he would attempt it, relentlessly, until your strength faltered. Then would you be altogether lost.

'This the Mahdoubt could not suffer, trusting you as she does. Therefore has she spent her mind and life to obtain the Harrow's oath of forbearance.'

Aching at the scale of the Mahdoubt's sacrifice, Linden said in a small voice, 'Then tell me how. How did you beat him?'

'My lady,' the Mahdoubt sighed, 'knowledge precludes knowledge. Our mortality cannot master one thing, and then another, and then yet another. The Harrow unmade the Demondim. The Mahdoubt could not have done so. But she has given centuries to the contemplation of Time. He has not. He passes from place to place as he wills – oh, assuredly – but he cannot journey among the years.

'The Mahdoubt gained his oath by revealing that her knowledge might displace him to another age of the Earth, a time in which the objects of his greed would not exist. There he would remain, abandoned, useless to himself, until his spirit was broken.

'For that reason, he acknowledged defeat.'

Her muscles trembled as she shifted her attention to Stave.

'Now, *Haruchai*,' she commanded softly, 'you must speak. You have ascertained that the Mahdoubt is of the Insequent. You have been informed of the Vizard's passing. And you have heard my lady's mention of the Theomach. Share with her the tale of your people. It is the last boon which the Mahdoubt may grant.'

In the Harrow's absence, his campfire died slowly, and with it the yellow elucidation of the flames. Shadows passed like small gusts of night over the older woman's sagging frame and Stave's unread countenance. More stars became visible overhead, throngs poised to hear or ignore what was unveiled in the dark.

Unsteady reflections in the former Master's eye suggested conflicting emotions, obscure reluctance and rue, as he gazed past the Mahdoubt at Linden. 'Chosen,' he said in a voice that sounded as removed as Revelstone and the Westron Mountains, 'in the distant past, some centuries before the coming of the *Haruchai* to the Land, our ancestors encountered the Insequent.'

While Linden studied him in surprise, he continued, 'We have ever been a combative race, glorying in struggle, for by such contests we demonstrate our worth – and it is by our worth that we survive the harsh ardour of the peaks. We have eschewed weapons because they detract from the purity of our battles, and because we did not desire our own destruction. Yet for many a century we were content to battle among ourselves, striving for wives, and for supremacy of skill, and for pride.

'There came a time, however, when we were no longer content. Ourselves we knew too well, speaking mind to mind. We desired to measure our worth against other peoples in less arduous climes, for we conceived that the rigours of the mountains had made us great. Therefore twenty-five score *Haruchai* journeyed together westwards, seeking some race whom we might best in battle.'

Stave's tone took on a defended formality as he explained, 'Understand, Chosen, that we did not crave dominion. We sought only to express the heat of our pride.'

Peripherally Linden was aware that the Humbled had turned away as if to disavow Stave's tale – or his telling of it. Galt, Clyme and Branl withdrew to the edges of the light, standing guard. But she paid no real attention to them. She was immersed in the sound of Stave's voice.

He spoke of *we* as though he had been one of those five hundred *Haruchai* thousands of years ago.

This, she knew, was an effect of their mental communion. They had shared their thoughts and passions and memories so completely, and for so long, that each of them embodied the long history of their race. Stave remembered his distant ancestors as if he had been present with them.

'After a trek of many days,' he said, 'we at last left behind our high peaks and biting snows, and found a fertile lowland lush with crops and waters, a region in which we deemed that even a slothful and unstriving people would flourish. For a time, we encountered none of the region's inhabitants. At last, however, we came upon a lone hut with a single occupant.

'The hut was a rude structure of wattle and thatch, and the man who emerged from it was clad in rags which scarcely covered his limbs. Furthermore both his flesh and his hair were clotted with filth, for he seemed unconscious of his person.

'Yet he addressed us courteously, offering both shelter and sustenance, though we were twenty-five score and his hut was small. In response, we declined, also courteously. Then he inquired, still courteously, of our purpose in the land of the Insequent. Intending no offence to one who plainly could not oppose us, we replied that we knew nothing of the Insequent, but that we had come in search of combat, seeking confirmation that our prowess knew no equal.'

The effect of what she heard on Linden was both immediate and detached. She seemed to experience Stave's tale through a veil of imposed dispassion. She saw everything that he described, but it did not touch her. Her sensitivity to the Mahdoubt's sinking vitality muffled her reactions.

'Hearing us,' Stave went on, 'the man became haughty. He informed us that the Insequent were far too mighty and glorious to heed such trivialities. Sneering, he proclaimed that if we did not immediately depart, he would punish our arrogance with his own hands, driving us defeated back to our mountains.

'We had no wish to harm him, for he appeared frail to us, beneath our strength. Yet we were also loath to turn aside from any challenge. Therefore one among us, Zaynor, whom we deemed the least of our company, stepped forward. He inquired if the Insequent would consent to display his skill for our edification.

'The man laughed scornfully. To our sight, he became briefly indistinct. Then Zaynor lay senseless at his feet. Upon Zaynor's face and limbs were the marks of many blows.'

While Stave spoke, the fire continued to shrink, contracting its light until the Mahdoubt clung in gloom to Linden's and Stave's support, and only coals reflected like memories in the former Master's gaze.

'Though we vaunted ourselves for our readiness in all things, we were surprised. Yet we were not daunted, for we conceived that the lone man's prowess lay in supernal swiftness, and we believed ourselves able to counter it, having been forewarned. Three of our number advanced to request a second demonstration of the man's worth.

'His response was mockery. Rather than suffer the continued affront of our presence, he avowed that he would defeat all of us together, thereby teaching us a condign humility.'

Stave paused as though he had to search for words. When he resumed, his tone suggested a remembered disbelief.

'Chosen, we were twenty-five score, and we credited our might. We did not scoff in reply, for we consider scorn the refuge of the weak. Also our opponent appeared to be a madman. Yet he had felled Zaynor. For that reason, we contemplated the means by which a supernal swiftness may be defeated and we stood prepared.

'Nevertheless he passed among us as wheat is scythed. Before the last of us recognised astonishment, twenty-five score *Haruchai* lay unconscious upon the ground, all pummelled insensate during the space of perhaps three heartbeats.'

The Mahdoubt sighed in sadness or disapproval, but she did not interrupt. Linden wanted to protest, Wait a minute. *All* of you? Five *hundred*—?' If anyone else had told her this, she would not have believed it. However, she swallowed her shock for the Mahdoubt's sake as much as for Stave's.

Inflexibly he said, 'When we began to regain our wits and rise from the ground, the man stood before us still, showing no sign of exertion. Only our battered flesh, and the blood of many blows upon his hands and feet, verified that he had struck us down bodily rather than causing us to slumber by theurgy.

'Then we conceived that we had been humbled. Therefore we made obeisance, declaring our opponent *ak-Haru*, the greatest warrior known to the *Haruchai*. But his reply taught us that we had not yet discovered humility within ourselves.'

Ak-Haru? Linden thought in sudden recognition. Stave had reached the cusp of his story, the point on which everything else turned. She wanted to interrupt him with questions simply so that she would have time to brace herself for what was coming. Only her concern for the Mahdoubt restrained her.

'Courteous once more, he bowed, saying that he had foreseen neither doughtiness nor fair speech from such small folk. Then he informed us that among the Insequent he was known as the Vizard.'

Linden swore inwardly at that name; but she forced herself to remain silent.

'The Insequent, he explained, did not reveal their true names. Rather they claimed obscure and gratifying titles for their own amusement. Yet he bid us welcome, both to his dwelling and to the land of the Insequent, cautioning us only that to every man or woman of his kind we must make obeisance. The Insequent – so he averred – wielded skills as diverse as their numbers, and few shared his indulgent nature.

'Lastly he proclaimed in a manner which forbade contradiction that he was unworthy to be named *ak-Haru*, for he was not the greatest of his people. There we found that humility had a deeper meaning than we had recognised. The Vizard did not merely refuse the honour which we ceded to him. He named the Theomach as the only Insequent who would be deemed deserving by his own kind.'

Linden stared at Stave through the encroaching night, shaken in ways which she could not have articulated. Briefly she forgot the Mahdoubt's plight. Roger had made cryptic comments about the Theomach's role in the Land's history. And the Theomach had assured her that she knew his true name—

Stave faced her like a man who had determined to spare himself nothing. 'It was the Vizard's word that the Theomach had joined himself to a great Lord in a land beyond our mountains to the east. In the Lord's company, he had quested far across the Earth, risking *Nicor* and the Soulbiter and many other perils to discover the hiding place of the One Tree. That alone, said the Vizard, was knowledge of surpassing difficulty, deserving accolade. The One Tree may be found only by those who do not seek the thing they seek, yet the Theomach resolved the conundrum by seeking the One Tree on the Lord's behalf rather than his own. For himself, he desired not the One Tree, but rather its Guardian.

'Therein lay his greatest feat. In single combat, he defeated the hated *Elohim* who stood as the Tree's Appointed Guardian. Thus the Theomach became the Guardian in the *Elohim*'s stead. Alone among the Insequent – so said the Vizard – the Theomach passed beyond self and craving to join the rare company of those who do not heed death. And therefore the Vizard did not scruple to reveal the Theomach's true name, for he could no longer be harmed by it.'

'*Kenaustin Ardenol*,' Linden breathed. 'Oh my God.'

She had known the Theomach's true name for ten years. But she could not have recognised it until now.

He had become more than Berek Halfhand's companion and teacher: far more.

She heard hints of mourning in Stave's voice as he said, 'To the Vizard, we granted that we would name the Guardian of the One Tree *ak-Haru*. But we could not further swallow our crippled pride. That we had been bested by a single opponent who then refused our acknowledgment did not teach us humility. It taught us humiliation.'

The Mahdoubt raised her head, although the effort made her shudder. 'Such was the Vizard's intent.' Anger throbbed in her voice. 'Assuredly. His peculiar greed ruled him, and no word or ploy of his was kindly. Even his courtesy was scorn. Had he lived to achieve his purpose, he would have undone the entire race of the *Elohim* to sate his hungers.'

Stave nodded. The night made him appear carved in stone.

'Being humiliated, we did not accept the welcome of the Vizard. Nor did we sojourn among the Insequent. Rather we returned in pain to our snow-clad peaks. When at a later time, we again elected to measure our worth, we did so in pain. In pain, we turned our trek to the east, for that was the direction named by the Vizard. In pain, we challenged High Lord Kevin Landwaster and all of his great Council. And when our challenge was met, not with combat, but with open-hearted respect and generosity, our pain was multiplied, for we were accorded a worth which we had not won. Therefore we swore the Vow of the Bloodguard, setting aside homes and wives and sleep and death that we might once again merit our own esteem.'

Now Linden could not remain silent. Impelled by her own ire, she said unsteadily, 'It's also why you abandoned your Vow.' She was learning to understand what the Vizard's whims had cost Stave's people. 'When Korik, Sill and Doar failed, you decided that you didn't *deserve* to help the Lords fight Lord Foul.'

Again Stave nodded; but she did not stop. Her indignation rose into the night as if it were directed at every *Haruchai* who had ever lived, although it was not. For Stave's people, she felt only a sorrow which she could not afford.

'And it's why you never actually got together to fight the Clave, even though your people were being slaughtered,' shed to feed the Sunbane. 'Even after Covenant saved you, only a few of you joined us. You knew that we were going to search for the One Tree and you didn't consider yourselves worthy to face your *ak-Haru*. You couldn't commit yourselves to defend the Land until Brinn proved that he could take the Guardian's place. Until he became the *ak-Haru* himself.

'That's when you finally started to believe in yourselves again.'

The Masters had carried their perception of *worth* too far. Now she knew why. After millennia of loss, they had regained their self-respect, but they had never learned how to grieve. Liand was right about them. They could only find healing in the attempt to match Brinn's example. Their humiliation had made them too rigid for any other release.

'So of course,' Linden continued, 'the Humbled attacked the Harrow before he did anything to threaten us. They had to. He's one of the Insequent. That's all the provocation they needed.'

'Indeed.' Stave stood in darkness, as unrevealing as the stars. 'Aspiring to Brinn's triumph, they now desire to prove themselves against any of the Insequent. For that reason, among others, I did not wish to speak of the Mahdoubt, or of the stranger, until we were certain of their nature.'

'But you didn't tell anyone about all this?' That, too, might have healed them. If nothing else, it might have eased their loneliness. 'Anyone at all? Didn't you think that someone might need to know your story?'

Her protest was addressed to the Mahdoubt as well.

The Humbled had moved closer, following the light as it shrank and faltered. They stood around Linden, Stave and the Mahdoubt like sentinels or accusers, stiff with wariness or reproach.

'Until this moment,' Stave acknowledged, 'no *Haruchai* has spoken of these matters aloud, saving only Brinn during your approach to the One Tree. In the time of the Lords, the Bloodguard would have answered if any Lord or Giant had inquired. But none knew of the Insequent. There were no queries. Even in the approach to the One Tree, neither you nor the Unbeliever nor any Giant questioned Brinn and Cail concerning *ak-Haru Kenaustin Ardenol*, though you were informed that our knowledge was older than the time of the Bloodguard.

'As you have confirmed, Berek Halfhand knew of the Theomach, as did Damelon Giantfriend. Yet that tale was transformed at its birth. It was told to suit the Theomach's purpose. This also you have confirmed. No mention was made of the Insequent in Berek Heartthew's presence, or in his son's. Rather the first Halfhand's thoughts were guided along other paths.

'Nor have we deemed it needful to reveal our ancient shame. Though it remains fresh from generation to generation among us, the Insequent played no part in the stratagems of Corruption or the perils of the Land. We could not state with certainty that the Vizard's kind had not ceased to exist. Why then should we speak of our humiliation?'

Little more than embers remained in Stave's eye as he said to Linden, 'Perhaps now you will grasp the import of Brinn's victory over the Guardian of the One Tree. It inspired the *Haruchai* to believe themselves equal to the Mastery of the Land, for it redeemed us to ourselves.'

Linden grasped too much: she could not absorb it all. The acquiescence of the Humbled when the Mahdoubt had contradicted their wishes made sense to her now. But she did not know why the Mahdoubt had insisted on Stave's tale. How was it *needful*, except as a farewell?

When Stave was done, the Insequent seemed to call up old reserves of fortitude or determination. Straightening her shoulders arduously, she raised her chin to the advancing night.

'Accept the Mahdoubt's thanks,' she said to Stave, quavering. 'She desires to end her days with kindness. On her behalf, you have granted my lady a precious boon.'

In an instant, the woman's utter frailty snatched away Linden's other concerns. 'My friend,' she murmured, bending close to the Mahdoubt. 'Please. Isn't there anything I can do? I've been trained to heal people. And I have the Staff of *Law*, for God's sake. Surely I can—?'

'My lady, no.' The old woman sounded sure in spite of her weakness. 'The Mahdoubt's knowledge does not partake of Law. It has preserved her far beyond her mortality. Assuredly. Now her end cannot be undone.

'Her last boon,' she went on before Linden could protest, 'is meant as solace. It is her wish to lessen your fears and sorrows. She desires you to be assured that you may trust this spurned Master. He has named his pain. By it he may be invoked.'

Stave lifted his eyebrow, but did not respond.

Damn it! Linden tried to protest. I know I can trust him. You don't have to do this. But her grief remained trapped in her chest. She did not have the heart to plead, Please don't leave me.

Instead she said, 'Thank you.' She was able to summon that much grace. 'You've been my friend in more ways than I can count. I can't honestly say that I understand you, but I know your kindness. And you've saved me—' For a moment, her throat closed. 'If I ever manage to do something good,' by evil means or otherwise, 'it will be because you believed in me.'

The Mahdoubt lowered her head. 'Then *Quern Ehstrel* is content.'

There Linden nearly lost the clenched wrath that defended her. Trembling with imminent bereavement, she whispered, 'Now please. Let me at least try to stop what's happening to you. There are a lot of things that I can do, if you'll let me.' Stave and Anele had refused her healing. They had that right. 'I might find something—'

'Forbear, my lady.' The Insequent's voice held a desperate severity. 'Permit to the Mahdoubt the dignity of departure.'

'I know your true name,' countered Linden hoarsely. 'Can't I compel you?'

The woman nodded. 'Assuredly. The Mahdoubt begs that you do not.'

With a tremulous effort, she detached one arm from Stave's support. Tears blurred the discrepancy of her eyes, urging Linden to release her.

When Linden let go at last, the Mahdoubt turned slowly from the dying embers of the campfire and began to walk away, tottering into the night. The Humbled bowed as they watched her pass. And Stave also bowed, according her the stern respect of the *Haruchai*.

Linden could not match their example. Instead she hugged her Staff and bore witness.

As the Mahdoubt reached the failing edge of the light, she tried to chant, 'A simple charm will master time.' But her voice broke after a few words; shattered into giggling. And with every step, she lost substance, macerated by darkness. Dissolving from sight, she left a mad mirth behind her, laughter pinched with hysteria.

But Linden closed her heart to the sound. As if in defiance, she concentrated instead on the salvific unction of the verses which had retrieved her from the Land's past.

> *The silent mind does not protest*
> *The ending of its days, or go*
> *To grief in loss and futile pain,*
> *But rather knows the healing gain*
> *Of time's eternity at rest.*
> *The cause of sequence makes it so.*

No, she thought. I do not forgive. I will not.
She knew no other way to say goodbye.

Chapter Five:

Departure from Revelstone

The walk back to Lord's Keep seemed unnaturally long to Linden. She had gone farther from herself than she realised. Neither Stave nor the escorting Humbled spoke: she did not speak herself. The night was mute except for the sound of her boots on the hard ground. Yet the Mahdoubt's broken giggling seemed to follow every step. In retrospect, Linden felt that she had wasted her friend's life.

Behind her, the Harrow's campfire died at last. And the lamps and torches in Revelstone had been extinguished. The Masters may have been reluctant to proclaim the fact that the Keep's gates remained open. Only the cold stars and the moon remained to light her way; but now she found no comfort in them.

Stave would have directed her, of course, but she did not need that kind of help. She required an altogether different guidance. First she found her way by the limned silhouette of Revelstone. Then she headed towards the notched black slit where the gates under the watchtower stood partway open.

When she entered the echoing passage beneath the tower – when she heard the massive granite thud as the gates were sealed behind her – and still the Masters offered her no illumination, she brought up flame from the end of the Staff, a small fire too gentle and dim to dazzle her. Earthpower could not teach her to accept the Mahdoubt's passing, but it allowed her to see.

Growing brighter and more needy with every stride, she paced the tunnel to the courtyard between the tower and the main Keep. Memories of giggling harried her as she approached the gap of the inner gates and the fraught space within them.

There also the lamps and torches had been quenched. And they were not relit as the gates were sealed behind her. The darkness told her as clearly as words that the Masters had reached a decision about her.

Defiantly she drew more strength from her Staff until its yellow warmth reached the ceiling of the forehall. With fire, she seemed to render incarnate the few Masters who awaited her. Then she turned to consider Stave and the Humbled.

She could not read the passions that moved like the eidolons of their ancient past behind their unyielding eyes; but she saw clearly that their injuries were not severe. Doubtless their bruises and abrasions were painful. In places, blood continued to seep from their battered flesh. Stave's wrists had been scraped raw by the Harrow's grasp, and the bones were cracked. But he and the Humbled were *Haruchai*: their wounds would soon heal.

After a brief scrutiny, Linden ignored Galt, Clyme and Branl. Speaking only to Stave, she tried to emulate his unswayed demeanour.

'I know that you'll mend. I know that you don't mind the pain.' His tale had taught her that the *Haruchai* were defined by their hurts. 'And I know that you haven't asked for help. But we'll be in danger as soon as we leave here.' She was confident that Kastenessen and Roger – and perhaps Esmer as well – would attempt to prevent her from her goal. 'It might be a good idea to let me heal you.' Stiffly she added, 'I'll feel better.'

She had lost the Mahdoubt. She wanted to be able to succour at least one of her friends.

Stave glanced from the Humbled to the other Masters. He may have been listening to their thoughts; their judgments. Or perhaps he was simply consulting his pride, asking himself whether he was willing to appear less intractable than his kinsmen. Cracked bones broke easily: they might hinder his ability to defend her.

'Chosen,' he remarked, 'the days that I have spent as your companion have been an unremitting exercise in humility.' He spoke without inflection; but his expression hinted that he had made the *Haruchai* equivalent of a joke.

He extended his hands to her as if he were surrendering them.

His decision – his acceptance – touched her too deeply to be acknowledged. She could not afford her own emotions, and had no reply except
fire.

With Law and Earthpower and percipience, she worked swiftly. While
the men who had spurned Stave watched, rigid in their disdain, she
honoured his sacrifice; his abandoned pride. Her flame restored his flesh,
sealed his bones. His gift to her was also a bereavement: it diminished
him in front of his people. Thousands of years of *Haruchai* history would
denounce him. Still she received his affirmation gladly. It helped her
bear the loss of the Mahdoubt.

When she was done, she turned her senses elsewhere, searching
Revelstone's ambience for some indication of how much of the night
remained. She was not ready for dawn – or for whatever decision the
Masters had reached. She needed a chance to think; to absorb what she
had seen and heard, and to ward away her grief.

After a moment, Stave asked as though nothing profound had occurred,
'Will you return to your rooms, Chosen? There is yet time for rest.'

Linden shook her head. The Keep's vast bulk muffled her discernment, but she felt that sunrise was still a few hours away. She might have
enough time to prepare herself—

'If you don't mind,' she said quietly, 'I want to go to the Hall of
Gifts.'

She wished to visit Grimmand Honninscrave's cairn. Old wounds
were safer company: she had learned how to endure them. And remembering them might enable her to forget the Mahdoubt's fading, shattered
laughter. She had failed the older woman. Now she sought a reminder
that great deeds could sometimes be accomplished by those who lacked
Thomas Covenant's instinct for impossible victories.

Fortunately Stave did not demur. And the Masters made no objection.
If they had ignored the Aumbrie since the fall of the Clave, they had
probably given even less attention to the Hall of Gifts. Indeed, Linden
doubted that any of them had entered the Hall for centuries, except
perhaps to retrieve the arras which she had seen hanging in Roger's and
Jeremiah's quarters. Her desire would not threaten them: they had made
up their minds about her.

At Stave's side, she left the forehall, escaping from new sorrows to old and lighting her steps with the ripe corn and sunshine comfort of Staff-fire.

Her destination was deep in Revelstone's gutrock: she remembered that. But she had not been there for ten years. And Revelstone's size and complexity still surprised her. She and Stave descended long stairways and followed unpredictable passages until the air, chilled by the tremendous mass of impending granite, grew too cool for comfort; cold enough to remind her of winter and bitterness. She warmed herself with the Staff, however, and did not falter.

Like the cave of the EarthBlood, the Hall of Gifts was a place where Lord Foul's servants had suffered defeat.

At last, Stave brought her to a set of wide doors standing open on darkness. From beyond them came an impression of broad space and old dust. As far as she knew, they had not been closed for three and a half thousand years.

Lifting her flame higher, Linden entered with her companion into the Hall.

It was a cavern wider than Revelstone's forehall, and its ceiling rested far above her on the shoulders of massive columns. Here the Giants who had fashioned Lord's Keep had worked with uncharacteristic crudeness, smoothing only the expanses of the floor, leaving raw stone for the columns and walls. Nevertheless the rough rock and the distant ceiling with its mighty and misshapen supports held a reverent air, clean in spite of the dust; an atmosphere as hushed and humbling as that of a cathedral.

She had never beheld this place as its makers had intended. It had been meant as a kind of sanctuary to display and cherish works of beauty or prophecy fashioned by the folk of the Land. Long ago, paintings and tapestries hung on the walls. Sculptures large and small were placed around the floor or affixed to the columns on ledges and shelves. Stoneware urns and bowls, some plain, others elaborately decorated, were interspersed with works of delicate wooden filigree. And a large mosaic entranced the floor near the centre of the space. In colours of viridian and anguish, glossy stones depicted High Lord Kevin's despair at the Ritual of Desecration.

Until the time of the Clave, the Hall of Gifts had been an expression of hope for the future of the Land. That was the mosaic's import: Revelstone had survived the Ritual with its promise intact.

For Linden, however, the cavern was a place of sacrifice and death.

When she had followed Covenant here to challenge Gibbon Raver, she had been full of battle and terror. Instead of looking around, she had watched the Giant Grimmand Honninscrave and the Sandgorgon Nom defeat Gibbon. Honninscrave's death had enabled Nom to destroy *samadhi* Sheol. For the first time since their birth in a distant age, one of the three Ravers had been effectively slain, *rent*; removed from Lord Foul's service. Yet *samadhi* had not entirely perished. Rather Nom had consumed the fragments of the Raver, achieving a manner of thought and speech which the Sandgorgons had never before possessed.

In gratitude, it seemed, Nom had raised a cairn over Honninscrave's corpse, using the rubble of battle to honour the Master of Starfare's Gem.

Linden had come here now to remember her loves.

The mound of broken stone which dominated the centre of the cavern was Honninscrave's threnody. It betokened more than his own sacrifice: it expressed his brother's death as well. And it implied other Giants, other friends. The First of the Search. Her husband, Pitchwife. Ready laughter. Open hearts. Life catenulated to life.

Link by link, Nom's homage to Honninscrave brought Linden to Sunder and Hollian, whom she had loved dearly – and whom she did not intend to heed.

They beg of you that you do not seek them out. Doom awaits you in the company of the Dead. But where could she turn for insight or understanding, if not to the people who had enabled her to become who she was?

Everything came back to Thomas Covenant.

As she began to move slowly around the cairn, studying old losses and valour by the light of Law, brave souls accompanied her, silent as reverie, and generous as they had been in life. And Stave, too, walked with her. If he wondered at her purpose here – at the strangeness of her response to the Mahdoubt's fate – he kept his thoughts to himself.

He could not know what she sought among the legacies of those who had died.

When she had completed two circuits of the mound and begun a third, she murmured, musing, 'You and the Masters talked about the Mahdoubt. "She serves Revelstone", you told me. "Naught else is certain of her".' And Galt had said, *She is a servant of Revelstone. The name is her own. More than that we do not know.* 'Looking back, it's hard to imagine that none of you even guessed who she was.'

Her mind was full of slippage and indirect connections. She was hardly aware that she had spoken aloud until Stave stiffened slightly at her side. 'Chosen? I do not comprehend.' Subtle undercurrents perplexed his tone. 'Are you troubled that you were not forewarned?'

'Oh, that.' Linden's attention was elsewhere. 'No. The Mahdoubt could have warned me herself. You all had your reasons for what you did.'

Honninscrave had died in an agony of violation far worse than mere physical pain. Like him, she had once been possessed by a Raver: she knew that horror. But the Giant had gone further. Much further. He had *held* Sheol; had contained the Raver while Nom killed him. In its own way, Honninscrave's end daunted her as profoundly as Covenant's surrender to Lord Foul.

She would not hesitate to trade her life for Jeremiah's. Of course. He was her son: she had adopted him freely. But for that very reason, her willingness to die for him seemed trivial compared to Honninscrave's self-expenditure, and to Covenant's.

'What then is your query?' asked Stave.

She groped for a reply as if she were searching through the rubble of the cairn. 'Everything seems to depend on me, but I'm fighting blind. I don't know enough. There are too many secrets.' Too many conflicted intentions. Too much malice. 'Your people don't trust me. I'm trying to guess how deep their uncertainty runs.'

How badly did it paralyse the Masters? How vehemently would they react against it?

Stave studied her for a long moment. 'I have no answer,' he said finally. 'Your words suggest an inquiry, but your manner does not. If you wish it, I will speak of the Masters. Yet it appears that your desire lies elsewhere. What is it that you seek in this place?'

Linden heard him. She meant to answer. But her thoughts slipped again, seeking links and meaning which she could not have named.

Distracted, she veered away towards the pillars near one end of the Hall, where the Gifts had not suffered from Gibbon Raver's struggles. Bearing her light with her, she walked between the columns until an odd statue caught her eye. It stood alone, thickly layered with dust, on an open stretch of the floor.

At first glance, it appeared to be a random assortment of rough rocks balanced on top of each other to form a distorted shape nearly as tall as she was. Because it was riddled with gaps, it resembled the framework for a sculpture more than a finished piece. Puzzled, she looked at it from all sides, but could not make sense of it. But then she took several steps backwards and saw that the stones outlined a large head. After a moment, she realised that the statue was the bust of a Giant.

The stones had been cunningly set so that the gaps between them suggested an expression. There was the mouth in a wide grin: there, the heavy bulge of the nose. And there, the holes of the eyes seemed to have crinkles of laughter at their corners.

Linden could almost have believed that the rocks had been selected and placed to convey an impression of Pitchwife's visage. But clearly the bust had been fashioned long before Pitchwife's sojourn in the Land.

'Who do you suppose this is?' she asked.

Stave appeared to consider his memories. 'The *Haruchai* do not recall the Stonedownor who crafted this countenance, or the name of the Giant here revealed, or indeed the name given to this Gift. The craft itself, however, is *suru-pa-maerl*. In the ages of the Lords, artisans among the Stonedowns sought long and patiently to discover unwrought stones which might be combined and balanced to form such depictions.'

'When you stand back,' Linden murmured, 'it's pretty impressive.' If Jeremiah had been free, he might have constructed works like this one. Distantly she added, 'I'm trying to put the pieces together myself. There's one thing that I'm sure of now.

'I know why Roger didn't want me to go to Andelain. Or Esmer either, for that matter.' After she had spoken of her intentions, Cail's son had left the cave of the Waynhim in apparent vexation or distress. 'It's not just that they don't want me to meet the Dead. They don't want me to find the *krill*. They're afraid of what I might be able to do with it.'

She had seen how its gem answered to the presence of white gold.

According to Thomas Covenant, High Lord Loric had formed the *krill* so that it would be *strong enough to bear any might.*

Stave considered her flatly. 'Then what is it that you seek to comprehend? You have not yet named your true query.'

Linden turned from the *suru-pa-maerl* Giant as if she were shying away. Aimlessly she carried the flame of her Staff among the columns, describing in fire slippages and connections which she did not want to put into words. She should have obtained an answer from the Mahdoubt – and had missed her only opportunity.

After a few steps, she asked, still indirectly, 'How many times was Covenant summoned to the Land? I mean, before he and I came here together?'

'Four of which the Bloodguard had knowledge,' answered Stave.

'Who summoned him?'

Her companion had apparently accepted her fragmented state. He replied without hesitation, 'The first summoning was performed by the Cavewight Drool Rockworm at Corruption's bidding. The second, by High Lord Elena. The third, by High Lord Mhoram. In each such call, the necessary power was drawn from the Staff of Law. But the fourth was accomplished by the Giant Saltheart Foamfollower and the Stonedownor Triock, enabled only by their own desperation, and by a rod of *lomillialor,* of High Wood, gifted to Triock by High Lord Mhoram.'

Momentarily distracted, Linden asked, '"*Lomillialor*"?' Stave had mentioned that name once before.

He shrugged. 'These are matters of lore, beyond the devoir of the *Haruchai*. I know only that *lomillialor* was to the wood-lore of the *lillianrill* as *orcrest* was to the stone-lore of the *rhadhamaerl*. With it, Hirebrands and Lords invoked the test of truth, spoke across great distances, and wrought other acts of theurgy.'

She nodded as though she understood. Wandering, she recovered the thread of what she had been saying.

'But when Covenant and I came here together, we were summoned by Lord Foul. Back then, I didn't wonder about that. But now I think he made a mistake. It may have been his biggest mistake.' Like Covenant before her, Linden had been freed when her summoner was defeated. 'He tied our lives to his.

'That's why he used Joan this time. Roger's mother.'

Roger had made that possible. And he had kidnapped Jeremiah. Directly or indirectly, he had delivered Jeremiah to Lord Foul – and to the *croyel*.

'Was it not Corruption who summoned the ur-Lord's former wife?' Stave may have been trying to help Linden think.

'Oh, sure.' She shook her head to dismiss the implications. 'But she was already lost. What I'm trying to understand is "the necessity of freedom". I don't know what that *means*.'

'Chosen?'

She turned at a column, headed in a different direction. But she clung to her musing. It protected her from a deeper fear.

'Before I came here the first time,' she said, 'Lord Foul went after Covenant by attacking Joan. He pushed Covenant to sacrifice himself by threatening her. And Covenant did it. He traded his life for hers.'

'The part that I don't understand—' Linden searched for words. What she sought was only related by inference to what she asked. 'When he saved her, did he give up his freedom? Was that why he could only defeat Lord Foul by surrendering? Because in effect he had already surrendered? Did saving Joan cost him his ability to fight?'

Would Linden doom the Land if she sold herself for Jeremiah?

Stave appeared to study the question. 'This also is a matter of lore, beyond my ken. Yet I deem that it is not so. The Unbeliever's surrender was his own, coerced by love and his own nature, not by Corruption's might. Sacrificing himself, he did not sacrifice his freedom. Rather his submission was an expression of strength freely wielded. Had he been fettered by his surrender in your world, Corruption's many efforts to mislead and compel him would have been needless.'

Honninscrave also had spent himself to win a precious victory.

Linden sighed as if she were baffled, although she was not. The Mahdoubt's giggling had receded into the background of her thoughts, but she had not forgotten what she had lost. She understood the importance of choice.

Veering again, she found her attention fixed on a statuette poised on a ledge in one of the columns. It caught her notice because it represented a horse, clearly a Ranyhyn – and because it reared like the beasts ramping across Jeremiah's pyjamas. It was perhaps as tall as her arm, and charged with an air of majesty, mane and tail flowing, muscles bunched. When she blew away its coat of dust, she saw that it was fashioned of bone. Over the millennia, it had aged to the hue of ivory.

Like all of the Land's knowledge and secrets, the statuette had become an emblem of antiquity and neglect.

Unlike the *suru-pa-maerl* bust, however, the Ranyhyn did not appear to be something that Jeremiah could have made. Although it had been formed from many pieces, its components had been fused in some way, melded to create an integral whole.

'Can you tell me anything about this, Stave?' she asked in a tone of reverie. 'Who worked with bone?'

Who among all of the people that had perished from the Land?

Watching her, he said, 'It is perhaps the most ancient of the Gifts in the Hall. It exemplifies a Ramen art, called by them marrowmeld, bone-sculpting and *anundivian yajña*. I know naught of its history, for the Ramen do not speak of it. In the ages of the Lords, they said only that the art had been lost. Mayhap the loss occurred during their flight with the Ranyhyn to escape the Ritual of Desecration, for much that was treasured did not survive the Landwaster's despair. Or mayhap the truth lies hidden in some other tale.

'The Manethrall may give answer, if you inquire. He may refuse. Yet still you have not named your true query.'

Linden could not face him. The image of the Ranyhyn, in old and dusty bone before her, and in dyed threads on Jeremiah's ruined pyjamas, seemed to demand more of her than Stave did. But the sculpted horse could not look into her eyes and see her fear.

God, she needed Covenant! His unflinching acceptance might have enabled her to envision a path which was not laid out by wrath and bitterness. Honninscrave's cairn counselled sacrifice – but it was not enough. Gallows Howe made more sense to her.

By degrees, she reduced the flame of the Staff to a small flicker that scarcely illuminated Stave's visage. Isolated by darkness, Linden tried to name the search which had brought her to this place of bloodshed and remembrance.

'She said—' she began, faltering. 'The Mahdoubt. She reminded me—'

For a moment, pain closed her throat. The Harrow had shown her that she could still be made helpless, in spite of everything which she had learned and endured. Because of her paralysis ten years ago, Covenant had been slain – and Jeremiah had been compelled to maim himself in the Despiser's bonfire. 'Roger said that Lord Foul has owned my son for a long time. Ever since Covenant and I first came to the Land. That Jeremiah belongs to the Despiser,' and all of Linden's love and devotion meant nothing. 'The Mahdoubt seemed to think that might be true.'

Every word hurt, but she articulated them without weeping. In her eyes burned fires which she withheld from the Staff.

Stave appeared to examine her for a moment. Then he said as if he could not be moved, 'I know naught of these matters. I do not know your son. Nor do I know all that he has suffered. But it is not so among the children of the *Haruchai*. They are born to strength, and it is their birthright to remain who they are.

'Are you certain that the same may not be said of your son?'

Linden took a deep breath; released it, shuddering. No, she was not certain. She had always believed Jeremiah's dissociation to be a defence as much as a prison, a barricade against hurt. That it walled him off from her was almost incidental. And the Mahdoubt had not averred that Jeremiah belonged to the Despiser. She had only observed *that a-Jeroth's mark was placed upon the boy when he was yet a small child—*

Lord Foul *had* marked Jeremiah: that was true enough. In their separate ways, both Linden and Covenant had been marked. And perhaps the Despiser conceived that his mark constituted ownership. He had acted on similar convictions in the past – and had been proven wrong.

If her son had not willingly joined himself to the *croyel—*

Slowly she turned to meet Stave's gaze; and as she did so, she restored the brightness of the Staff. She could not read his spirit: no doubt she would never be able to see past his physical presence. Nonetheless she suspected that his passions ran to depths which she could hardly fathom. Like Jeremiah's dissociation, his stoicism might be a defence – and a prison.

'Thank you,' she said softly. 'That helps. He isn't my son because I gave him birth. He's my son because I *chose* him. I don't know what the truth is. I may never know. But I can still choose. I'm going to believe that he has the right,' every child's right, 'to be himself.'

To her surprise, Stave responded with a deep *Haruchai* bow. 'Chosen,' he replied, unexpectedly formal, 'thus would I speak of my own sons, though they remain among the Masters, and with the Masters have spurned me.'

Linden stared at him in chagrin. His sons—? She had known in the abstract that his people had wives and children. How could they not? But she had never considered the possibility that he might have sons who had turned their backs on him.

His determination to stand with her had cost him more than she had ever imagined.

You didn't— She wanted to say, You didn't tell me. You never even hinted– According to the Mahdoubt, *He has named his pain.* But he had not truly done so until now.

Before she could find her voice, however, he went on more sternly, 'Now I comprehend your query. And you have answered it. Here the Giant Grimmand Honninscrave accepted possession by *samadhi* Sheol and remained himself. You will not think less of your son than of any Giant whom you have known.'

His manner forbade questions. He would not think less of his own sons—

Trust yourself.

At last, the Mahdoubt's voice fell to silence in Linden's mind.

With an effort, she swallowed her protests. When she felt ready to respect his privacy – and his loneliness – she said, 'All right. I don't know how long we've been here, but it must be time to go. Mahrtiir will wonder where we are. And if he doesn't, Liand will.' For Stave's sake, she attempted a smile. 'In any case, they're probably as ready as they'll ever be.' Glancing around to locate the doors, she added uncomfortably, 'There's just one more thing.'

The rejected Master faced her as though nothing had passed between them. 'Chosen?'

'I don't know how much of your story you want to tell. It's your story. I won't say anything. But the others,' Liand and the Ramen, 'should at least know that the Mahdoubt and the Harrow are Insequent,' linked to the Theomach. 'It might help them understand what we're up against.'

Stave shrugged slightly. 'As you say.'

With that she had to be content.

Sighing, she started towards the doors. Walking together in spite of his acute separation, she and Stave left the Hall of Gifts.

There may have been thousands of stairs. It was conceivable. The Hall lay a considerable distance below the level of Revelstone's gates, and her rooms were high in the Keep's south-facing wall. By the time she and Stave gained the corridor outside her quarters, her legs were trembling with strain, and she had to pant for breath. Only the coolness of the air spared her from sweating through her shirt.

Outside her door, Liand, the Ramen and Anele awaited her. With the exception of Anele, they radiated varying degrees of anxiety and frustration. On the floor around their feet lay a number of bedrolls, bundles, and sacks: supplies for an unpredictable journey. Whatever the Masters may have decided, the servants of Revelstone had been generous.

In spite of his scrapes and bruises, Galt guarded her door. Clearly he had refused admittance to Linden's companions. His stance may have been intended as courtesy towards her. Or it may have been a foretaste of the Masters' attitude.

Liand greeted her with a gust of relief. 'Linden!'

'Ringthane.' Mahrtiir was less easily reassured. 'This Master,' he snorted, slapping a gesture at Galt, 'grants nothing. He has refused to reveal your whereabouts. He will say only that in your absence we may not enter your chambers. Yet it is manifest that he has seen combat. Events of import have transpired while we are kept in ignorance, confined by stone.

'Does some new threat confront this harsh Keep?'

Bhapa shared the Manethrall's ire. Pahni stood beside Liand, holding his arm as if she were determined not to let him go. Under his breath, Anele mumbled his distrust of the Masters and imprisonment.

Linden held up her hands to quiet Mahrtiir's vexation. Still panting, she said, 'I'm sorry. We're all right. You can see that. There were a couple of things that I needed to do while you were getting ready. Stave will tell you about them when he gets a chance. Right now' – she tasted the air and found that daybreak was near – 'we should head down to the gates. We have a long way to go, and I don't think that any of it will be easy.'

She had left nothing of hers in her rooms.

'Linden Avery,' Galt began firmly, 'the Masters—'

She cut him off. 'Don't say it. I already know.' And she was not yet sure what form her response might take. 'If I'm wrong, Handir won't hesitate to set me straight.'

The Humbled raised an eyebrow in apparent disapproval. But he did not insist on speaking.

Mahrtiir flashed a fierce grin at Galt; at Linden. Linden did not know what the Manethrall saw in her – or in the Humbled – but he was eager for its outcome.

Bhapa and Pahni said nothing: they would not when their Manethrall was silent. But Linden expected a flood of questions from Liand. She braced herself to fend them off.

He surprised her, however. With unfamiliar ease, he dammed his baffled concerns. Studying him, she guessed that Pahni had relieved much of his ignorance. But the change in him had another source as well: she could see it. On a visceral and perhaps unconscious level, the focus of his attention had shifted. It was now concentrated on Pahni. He was Linden's friend: he would always be her friend. He would stand by her with the same steadfastness that she had known in Sunder. But she no longer consumed his thoughts, or his heart.

His alteration gave her a touch of relief, which she attempted to conceal for his sake. It freed her to focus more closely on her own intentions.

Even when her thoughts were elsewhere, everything that she felt and did revolved around Jeremiah.

Stave faced her with inquiry in his eye. He may have wanted to know how she would reply to the Masters. When she said nothing, however, he gave another small shrug and went to help the Ramen and Liand carry their burdens.

As soon as her companions had shouldered their bedrolls and supplies, Mahrtiir nodded sharply. With Stave beside her to lead the way, Linden headed back down the many stairs and passages towards the forehall. Her companions came after her; and Galt followed behind them as if to ensure that they did not change their minds.

After a short distance, Linden asked Liand to walk with her. In spite of her relief, she needed to talk to him. Through Anele, Covenant had promised the Stonedownor an obscure and difficult burden. And Liand had given her more generosity and consideration than she could measure. She wanted to contribute to his sense of discovered purpose. She owed him that much.

He left Pahni and Anele to join her. For a moment, she studied him sidelong, observing the ease with which his sturdy frame bore two bedrolls and a bulging sack; measuring the extent of his new anticipation. Then, trying to sound casual, she said, 'I promised you some answers. Pahni has told you what she can. Stave will fill in a few of the gaps. But you and I—' She paused briefly to consider what she could offer him. Not for the first time, she regretted that he was not safe in Mithil Stonedown. *I wish I could spare you.* But there was no safety anywhere: not now. 'We should talk about *orcrest.*'

His eyes widened. 'Linden?' He could not mask his excitement.

'It suits you,' she said. 'That kind of Earthpower– It feels right.' He had inherited it across scores of generations. 'But I wonder if you've had time to explore what it can do.'

'I have seen that it gives light at need,' Liand replied with a mixture of awe, appreciation and doubt. 'It is puissant to reunite the fragments of Anele's thoughts. And Stave has spoken of the test of truth. But I have gained no other knowledge.'

Carefully Linden probed with her health-sense at the pouch hanging from his belt, studying the strange textures of the Sunstone; tasting its unique savour. The impression of absence which it conveyed to ordinary sight was belied on other planes of perception.

'I think that there's more.' Wonder as gentle as a breeze curled through Linden. 'If I'm not mistaken, it can counter the effects of Kevin's Dirt. And not just for you. You should be able to help the rest of us. You won't need me,' or Glimmermere, 'to fend off that kind of blindness.

'In fact, you might be able to go further. I get the impression that *orcrest* can do some healing. Not physical. Spiritual.' With the Sunstone,

Liand might be able to redress afflictions of *wrongness*. 'And that's not all.'

Then she snatched herself back, startled by what she felt. 'My God, Liand,' she breathed; but she should not have been surprised. Over and over again, the Land had demonstrated its provident richness. 'I think that you can affect the *weather*.'

With enough practise – and enough courage—

Liand stared at her. 'Surely that cannot be done.'

Linden tried to meet his disbelief; but before she found a reply, Stave said impassively, 'The *Haruchai* remember it. During the ages of the Bloodguard and the Lords, masters of the *rhadhamaerl* lore betimes performed such deeds with *orcrest*. In that use, however, the stone was destroyed. Therefore *orcrest* was seldom thus expended, for all Stonedownors loved the Land's rock.'

He may have been cautioning Liand.

Watching the young man's gaze grow lambent with excitement, while behind him shadows filled Pahni's eyes, Linden murmured, 'I can't be sure. And I don't know how much lore is involved. I'm not even sure that I know what "lore" means. But it's obvious that you have your own power now.'

She intended what she said as an affirmation, and in that she succeeded. Light and promises seemed to illumine Liand like a sunrise. But for Linden his reaction was eclipsed by Pahni's troubled pride and dread. Power imperilled its wielder, as Linden had learned repeatedly. The young Cord was afraid for him.

Sighing to herself, Linden walked towards her confrontation with the Masters. *Hell, I wish any of us could spare you.* She could afford to spare none of her companions. Not now: not after everything that she had learned and endured under *Melenkurion* Skyweir. And the Mahdoubt's fate had demonstrated that Linden did not suffice to make their choices for them.

Her friends would live longer if they did not rely on her to protect them.

Eventually they reached the forehall, followed by Galt; and still Linden did not know how she would respond to the decision of the Masters. But when she found Handir waiting for her among a score of other Masters, including Clyme and Branl, with the gates of Revelstone sealed at his back, she knew that she had gauged their resolution accurately.

The Masters knew that she meant to leave Revelstone. They knew why. Stave had told them at her request. And they knew that she had heard the tale of their ancient encounter with the Insequent.

The closing of the gates was their answer.

For reasons of their own, they had provided lamps and torches aplenty. The forehall was bright with their rejection. In spite of their characteristic dispassion, the Voice of the Masters and Stave's other kinsmen conveyed the impression that they were poised for battle.

Linden did not hesitate. Striding directly to Handir, she stopped in front of him; inclined her head in acknowledgment. 'Handir. Please open the gates. My friends and I need to go.'

She could imagine no circumstances under which the Land might be saved by people who remained in Revelstone. And the *croyel* would not bring Jeremiah to her again. She could only rescue her son by going in search of him.

Handir replied to her bow with a nod. Formally he announced, 'Linden Avery, the Masters will not permit your departure.'

Behind Linden, the Manethrall muttered sour objurgations. Protests thronged in Liand. But they did not intrude between her and the Voice of the Masters.

Although she had known what to expect, Linden had to stifle a flare of anger. 'Would you mind telling me why?'

She hugged the Staff against her chest to steady herself on its refined and blackened strength – and to show Handir that she did not mean to challenge him with Law and Earthpower.

The inflexibility of his response seemed to give his words the force of a decree. 'We recognise that you are Linden Avery, Chosen and Sun-Sage, who accompanied ur-Lord Thomas Covenant to the redemption of the Land. Nonetheless we have not been swayed.

'At your word, we have not imprisoned the old man. Yet we are not persuaded that he may safely roam the Land. For reasons which Stave has doubtless described, we have not opposed the Stonedownor's possession of *orcrest*. But our acquiescence does not suggest that we see no hazard in his ignorance. We deem that he, also, may not safely roam the Land.'

The Voice of the Masters paused momentarily. Then he conceded, 'These are small matters, however. In your name, we might set them aside. But we have greater concerns.'

Tension mounted among Linden's companions. Anele shook his head anxiously from side to side while the Ramen tried to contain their indignation. With one hand, Liand gripped the pouch containing his piece of Sunstone. Only Stave appeared untouched by the attitude of the Masters.

Doubtless he knew precisely how and why they had reached their decision.

Holding her breath, Linden waited for Handir to continue.

'Linden Avery,' he pronounced, 'you have grown in power, and may therefore wreak more harm. We must reason more stringently concerning your deeds and purposes.

'It appears that we erred gravely in granting credence to the semblance of the ur-Lord. His glamour defied our discernment. For that reason, however, we must consider that you also may be masked in glamour. Indeed, we must consider that perhaps there has been no other glamour than yours. Thus it becomes conceivable that you removed the ur-Lord and his companion in order to prevent the salvation of the Land, and that you now seek darker hurts.'

Grimly Linden contained herself: she felt sure that Handir was not done. But Mahrtiir did not emulate her restraint.

'Then you are indeed fools,' he snapped. 'From the first, the distinction between the Ringthane and the seeming Unbeliever has been vivid to the Ramen. Her spirit is open to both love and injury. In all things, his purposes were concealed.

'And if our judgment may be questioned, that of the Ranyhyn may not. She has partaken of the horserite.' The Manethrall's voice throbbed with anger. 'The Ranyhyn have bowed their heads to her – aye, and to Stave as well. If you assert that she is false, you have forgotten the faith of the Bloodguard and are unworthy to name yourselves their descendants.'

Linden saw Masters on both sides of Handir clench their fists. Both

Branl and Clyme stepped forward; and Galt left the rear of Linden's small group to stand with the other Humbled.

'Protect,' urged Anele, whispering as if he feared to speak more loudly. 'Protect Anele. He is the Land's hope. *They* will doom him.'

If Handir took umbrage, however, he did not show it. His countenance revealed nothing as he gazed past Linden at Mahrtiir.

'I do not say, Manethrall, that Linden Avery is false,' he answered flatly. 'I say only that we must consider it.'

Then he faced her again. 'Yet the state in which you have returned to us is beyond question. You now resemble the transformed Staff of Law. Darkness fills your heart. Indeed, you are as tinder, awaiting only a spark to achieve destruction. According to your tale, this alteration has been wrought by the Blood of the Earth and your son's plight. Mayhap you have spoken truly. Yet the threat remains, regardless of its cause.

'More than any of your companions, you may not safely roam the Land. You have become an avatar of woe and ire, and all of your deeds will conduce to evil.'

Gritting her teeth, Linden swallowed an impulse to say, If any of that is true, you might want to ask yourself why I'm not threatening *you*. When she had first entered Revelstone, Handir had assured her that the Masters could wrest her powers from her. She had believed him then: now she was not convinced. But she did not mean to respond with defiance. She simply wanted Handir to understand that she was not afraid. She had become a kind of *Haruchai* herself: like them, she could not be swayed.

Stiffly she asked, 'Is there more?'

'There is,' he acknowledged. 'A man who has shown himself greater than the Demondim is now among us. He is of the Insequent, as you have found to your cost. Yet in the spanning memory of the *Haruchai*, no Insequent has intruded upon the Land. In this, they resemble the *Elohim*. Heretofore both *Elohim* and Insequent have held themselves apart, except at the birth of Berek Halfhand's High Lordship, and during the slow decline of the One Forest.

'Linden Avery, these are bleak auguries. And we have seen that the Harrow's prowess exceeds you. If your own desires do not breed ruin, his craving for white gold and the Staff of Law will surely do so. To permit your departure will be to invoke calamity.'

There the Voice of the Masters stopped. He had said enough: Linden did not need to hear more in order to grasp the uncertainty of Stave's kindred.

She felt surprise and confusion among Liand and the Ramen. They had not yet been told of her meeting with the Harrow, or of Stave's tale, or of the Mahdoubt's passing. Nevertheless Handir compelled her full attention. Because she needed some outlet for her bitterness, she asked, 'I don't suppose this has anything to do with the fact that Stave defied you by telling me about the Vizard and the Theomach?'

Handir regarded her without expression. 'Stave has been adjudged. No further repudiation is seemly.'

After a moment, Linden nodded. In some ways, the worst part of Stave's punishment was that the Masters no longer considered his actions to be of any consequence.

She was tempted to turn her back on them and their support. Let them continue to serve Lord Foul, in effect if not in intent, by clinging to their doubts in isolation. She would find some other way to leave the Keep. For the Land's sake, however, more than for Jeremiah's, she tried one last argument. She did not doubt that the Masters would be needed—

'All right,' she said harshly. 'I think I understand why you don't trust me. But there's one thing that you haven't explained.

'You weren't able to beat the Demondim. If I hadn't closed their *caesure*, you wouldn't have been able to hold Revelstone. So what changed while I was away? What makes you think that *now* you can handle Esmer and Kastenessen and the *skurj* and Kevin's Dirt and Falls and Roger Covenant and the Insequent, never mind Ravers and the *Elohim* and Joan's ring and Corruption himself?

'Hasn't it occurred to you yet that you need me? That you need all of us, and any other allies you can find?'

The Voice of the Masters shook his head. His countenance revealed nothing. Nonetheless some subtle shift in the quality of his intransigence gave his reply a faint patina of sadness.

'Still you do not comprehend our Mastery. We do not seek to prove ourselves equal to every peril which besets the Land. We seek only to forestall Desecration. Such evils may be performed only by those who wield power and love the Land and know despair.

'The true Thomas Covenant, ur-Lord and Unbeliever, charged us to preserve Revelstone. We will willingly spend our lives in the attempt. But our larger purpose does not require us to redeem the Land. It requires us to ensure that a new Landwaster does not commit a second Ritual of Desecration.'

In spite of her determination, Linden sagged. He was right: she had misapprehended the Masters. She had fixed her attention on the effects of what they had done; on their arrogance— As a result, she had missed the real point of Stave's patient explanations. All of her attempts to persuade Handir and his kinsmen had been predicated on a misconception, an oblique error. She had faulted the application and results of their Mastery instead of addressing their fundamental concerns; and so her efforts to move them had failed.

Now it was too late. She could not promise Handir that his concerns were groundless; that she would never become another Landwaster. Too many people had seen darkness in her: she had seen it herself. Too many people feared that her intentions would lead to ruin rather than hope.

You have it within you to perform horrors.

Within her she holds the devastation of the Earth—

Doom awaits you in the company of the Dead.

All right, she tried to tell herself. She had failed here. She needed an entirely different approach. But for a few moments, she was caught and held by her regret for what her inadequacies had cost her. Standing before Handir, she bowed her head like an admission of defeat.

Her heart was stone: she was not beaten. But she needed a little time to recover her concentration.

While she tried to think of an alternative, Stave stepped forward unexpectedly. 'It boots nothing to bandy words,' he said to Handir. 'I propose a test of truth.'

A slight lift of Handir's chin betrayed that Stave had surprised him.

While Liand fumbled in consternation at his pouch, Stave explained, 'I do not suggest the use of *orcrest*. A challenge by Earthpower will not suffice among *Haruchai*. Rather I offer a test of truth by combat.'

'Stave, no,' Linden protested. She had not forgotten the blows which he had already received from his kinsmen.

'I have no wish to cause harm,' he said, holding Handir's gaze. 'And it is certain that the Chosen does not, for she comprehends that the Land requires the *Haruchai*. Therefore I will confront any three of the Masters. Let each in turn assail me. If I drive each from his feet and do not fall, you will permit the Chosen to depart. If I am thrown and any of the three remains standing, she will withdraw to the plateau and seek her son's salvation by some other means.'

Before the Voice of the Masters could speak, Galt replied with unwonted eagerness, 'The Humbled accept this contest.' Apparently he, Clyme and Branl had seen a personal affront in Stave's actions or attitude.

'*Damn* it, Stave,' Linden muttered; but she knew of no argument that he would heed. His offer did not commit her to anything which would block her search for another egress. And after all that he had done for her, she could not say aloud that she believed he would fall.

Liand began to object hotly; but Mahrtiir's voice rode over his. Clarion as a trumpet, the Manethrall announced, 'I also propose a test of truth.'

Linden wheeled towards him as he proclaimed, 'Permit the Ringthane to enter the courtyard beyond this dark stone. Enclosed by the outer gates, she will summon the Ranyhyn. Their approach will be witnessed by those Masters who watch from the tower.

'Heretofore the Ranyhyn that have answered her need are seven, Hynyn, Hyn, Narunal, Hrama, Rhohm, Whrany and Naharahn. If she is answered now by more than those seven, you will acknowledge that the great horses approve both her desires and your caution. They have determined that she must depart – and that some among you must accompany her. If she is answered by no more than seven, you will recognise that the Ranyhyn do not share your fear of Desecration. You will honour their wisdom. And if she is not answered, we will accept your refusal.'

Shaken, Linden strove to compose herself. Like Stave's, Mahrtiir's challenge did not undermine her. The Ranyhyn would answer: she was sure of that. Still the Manethrall's audacity staggered her. Surely in their entire history no Ramen had ever suggested making commitments on behalf of the great horses?

Yet Stave's test was no less bold. He had been healed: the Humbled had not. But he had lost an eye. He was subtly crippled by the truncation of his sight.

Nevertheless Linden could not refuse either Stave's aid or Mahrtiir's. She *needed* to leave Revelstone – and had no clear idea how to do so.

Liand brimmed with protests; but Pahni drew him aside, whispering urgently. She appeared to be asking him to accept the Manethrall's authority.

When Handir responded, Linden faced him again.

To Stave, the Voice of the Masters said, 'It is Linden Avery who threatens Desecration. You do not. How will the success or failure of your strength measure the Land's peril?'

'It will not,' Stave replied stolidly. 'It will measure your worthiness to adjudge her as you have adjudged me.'

Linden groaned to herself. If Stave failed, he would validate the repudiation of his people.

'The Humbled have spoken,' Galt put in sharply. 'We will accept the contest.'

'But *I* have not spoken,' Handir returned with a tinge of asperity. 'By right of years and attainment, I am the Voice of the Masters. I must be heeded.'

'As the Humbled also must be heeded,' Galt reminded him.

For a long moment, the Humbled and Handir regarded each other. Then all four of them nodded; and the Voice of the Masters shifted his attention to Mahrtiir.

'Manethrall, we have heard you. Though your ire is unseemly, you are a Manethrall of the Ramen, and we hear you with respect. But we do not perceive how the will of the Ranyhyn pertains to the nature of our service.'

Keen as a raptor, Mahrtiir answered, 'The Ranyhyn are inherent to the Land as the *Haruchai* and even the Ramen are not. The great horses partake of the Land's essence and grandeur, for they are expressions of Earthpower, wholly and purely themselves, unflawed by either lore or aggrandisement. They stand high among the wonders which have caused you to choose the nature of your service. Also their foresight is both well known and inestimable.

'Inform me, then, how any Master may disdain the choices of the Ranyhyn and yet claim that he serves the Land.'

Although several of the other Masters emanated indignation, Handir did not appear offended. Instead he nodded as if to acknowledge that the Manethrall had made a valid point. Linden gnawed her lip while Handir remained silent, presumably communing with the *Haruchai* in the forehall.

For no apparent reason, Anele stated, 'Anele does not fear horses. He does not fear the dark ones. He fears *them*.'

Then the Voice of the Masters spoke. 'Linden Avery,' he said as if words uttered aloud had become awkward for him, 'you have healed Stave. The Humbled remain hindered by injury.'

He may have been asking her to disavow Stave's test of truth.

If so, he had misjudged her. Stave had sacrificed his bond with his own sons for her sake. In spite of her apprehension, she replied, 'And he only has one eye. I call that even.'

In any case, the hurts of the Humbled were superficial. And Stave had blows to repay—

'Linden,' breathed Liand, warning her. *You have it within you*—

For a few heartbeats, Handir resumed his silence. Then he shifted his stance to address everyone around him.

'It is decided,' he said rigidly. 'Both tests have merit. Neither suffices.

'However, we do not desire Linden Avery's enmity. Nor do we intend any slight to the Ramen, or to the majesty of the Ranyhyn. And the Humbled must be heeded. Therefore both tests will be essayed in turn. If Stave withstands each of the Humbled, Linden Avery will then summon the Ranyhyn, as the Manethrall has urged. If Stave falls, no summons will be countenanced.'

After a brief pause, he continued, 'It is in my heart, however, that such trials resolve naught.' Again his manner or his tone seemed to imply a veiled sorrow. 'Conceding them, we accept only the hazard of greater uncertainty, for the strictures of our service will not be set aside. If Linden Avery's release is won, we will be compelled to consider whether we have damned the Land. Yet if Stave or the Ranyhyn fail her, she will not thereby be persuaded to accept our Mastery. Rather the darkness within her will deepen. And Desecration may be wrought as readily in Revelstone as in Kiril Threndor. Thus will we again be compelled to consider whether we have damned the Land.

'I am Handir, by right of years and attainment the Voice of the Masters.

I have spoken. But my words will bear no sweet fruit. Rather they will ripen to gall and rue.'

When he was finished, he and the other Masters immediately withdrew, leaving only Galt, Clyme and Branl between Linden's company and the clenched gates. Clearly Handir intended the tests to begin at once.

Hugging the Staff harder, Linden tried to breathe as if she were calm. She was not sure that she could bear to see Stave beaten again.

While Stave advanced to confront the Humbled, Mahrtiir and Liand stood with Linden. 'Gall and rue are the inescapable outcome of your Mastery,' the Manethrall said to Handir. 'Do not complain of them here, where those who seek to preserve the Land wish only to do so without opposition.'

Then he whispered privately to Linden, 'I proposed a test of the Ranyhyn hoping to spare Stave. He has been harmed in both body and spirit, and I feared for him. It was not my intent to hamper you, Ringthane.'

'I know,' she murmured tensely. 'I'm scared, too. If they hurt him again, I don't know how I'm going to forgive myself. But I just don't have any better ideas.'

'Ah, Stave,' sighed Liand. 'Now I am truly shamed that I have thought and spoken ill of you.'

As one, Stave and the Humbled bowed to each other with ritual formality. Then Branl and Clyme retreated to clear a space for Galt and Stave.

Involuntarily Linden remembered another battle in this place. When Nom had broken the inner gates, she and Covenant had entered the forehall with Sunder and Hollian, a few Giants, and a small company of *Haruchai*. Here they had fought desperately against the Clave, Coursers, and the na-Mhoram's *Grim*. Old frenzy, terror, and bloodshed seemed to harry her now, as bleak as Handir's omens.

So suddenly that she nearly gasped, Galt struck. Blood still crusted his hands and feet. Nonetheless he launched a blow swift and hard enough to crush the blinded side of Stave's face.

Stave had said that he did not wish to cause harm. Plainly Galt's intentions were more extreme. He seemed to want to eradicate Stave from his sight.

The lamps and torches provided light in abundance. Yet Linden could not distinguish the vicious blur of Galt's punch from the details of Stave's response. She saw only that Stave remained poised in front of Galt's fist – and then he stood behind the Humbled with his hands on Galt's shoulders. With delicate precision, he kicked away one of Galt's feet and jerked the Humbled backwards.

Galt fell: he could not prevent it. But as he fell, he twisted in the air; caught hold of Stave's tunic; tried to wrench Stave down with him.

Stave countered by letting himself drop so that his knees landed heavily on Galt's ribs. With his arms braced against Galt's grasp, Stave kept his balance so that no part of him except his feet touched the floor.

A wince of shock or chagrin flashed over Galt's features and vanished. For an instant, Linden feared that the Humbled would refuse to cede defeat; that he would attempt to roll Stave into a fall. Instead, however, Galt released Stave and relaxed. His *Haruchai* rectitude did not permit him to violate the conditions of the test.

Nodding, Stave rose smoothly to his feet and turned towards Branl and Clyme.

Handir and the observing Masters concealed whatever they may have felt. Linden found that Liand had placed his hand on her shoulder. He gripped her tightly to contain his suspense.

Clyme was the next to approach Stave. While they gazed at each other, motionless, the concentration – or perhaps the firelight – in the Humbled's eyes conveyed the impression that he was probing Stave's defences.

Linden knew that she would receive no forewarning; that even her health-sense could not anticipate the instant when either of the *Haruchai* would move. That in itself was a kind of presage. Nevertheless she was not ready. She flinched instinctively as Clyme attacked.

Smooth as oil and swift as light, the Humbled lashed a kick at Stave's abdomen.

Once again, Stave did not appear to react until he had already done so. Stepping aside, he swung an arm like a bar of iron across Clyme's chest. Stave's arm stopped Clyme's momentum while Clyme's kick carried him forward. Opposing forces swept the Humbled's supporting leg out from under him.

Like Galt, Clyme clutched at Stave as he fell. Clasping Stave's arm, the Humbled attempted to yank Stave from his feet. But Stave responded by crouching quickly, using Clyme's hold to drive the Humbled downwards.

Clyme landed hard. His shoulder blades could have been cracked. Certainly the breath should have been knocked from his lungs. But he was *Haruchai*: he did not react to the impact. Instead he let go of Stave's arm, acknowledging defeat.

Again Stave stood upright. While Clyme rose and walked away to join his kinsmen, Stave waited for the last of the Humbled.

'My God,' Linden breathed to Liand and Mahrtiir. 'They can't hear his thoughts, but he still hears theirs. He knows exactly what they're going to do.'

Even if he had lost both eyes, he might have been able to defend himself against his own people. Over the millennia, the *Haruchai* had become dependent on their mental communion. Linked to each other, they could not adjust their tactics to accommodate his unfamiliar blend of isolation and awareness.

But Branl appeared to understand the reasons for Stave's success. The pace of his approach – or perhaps merely its tone – implied caution. And Handir studied the Humbled in a way that seemed to suggest inward counsel. All of the Masters may have been reminding Branl to fight as though Stave were not *Haruchai*.

Instead of striking, Branl circled Stave slowly. He may have wanted Stave to make the first move; to commit himself.

Yet even then Stave had the advantage. He had heard Handir's advice – and Branl's response. He understood Branl's preparations. When Stave jabbed suddenly at Branl's head, the blow was a feint.

The Humbled replied with a block which flowed seamlessly into a wheeling kick powerful enough to crumple Stave. But Stave had already stepped inside the kick and slapped down the block. While Branl snatched back his leg, Stave clipped him across the forehead with one elbow.

To Linden's slower perceptions, the touch of Stave's elbow looked harmless: a glancing blow, nothing more. The collision of bone with bone sounded too soft to have any force. Yet the Humbled sprawled backwards.

In the fraction of a heartbeat remaining to him, Branl endeavoured to execute a flip which would land him on his feet. But he did not have enough time. His knees and then his hands hit the floor.

When he stood again, he gave Stave a small bow and withdrew to join the rest of the Masters.

For a moment or two, a silence as gravid as an aftershock held the forehall. Linden imagined that she could hear the preconceptions of Stave's kinsmen crumbling. Then Liand crowed, '*Stave!*' and pumped jubilation into the air with both fists. 'Heaven and *Earth*, Stave!'

Grinning fiercely, Mahrtiir growled, 'Well done, *Haruchai*. Well done in all sooth. Here is a tale to gladden the hearts of the Ramen. At last blows have been struck which may humble the sleepless ones. And we have witnessed it, a Manethrall and his Cords. No longer may these Masters feign that their worth exceeds yours.'

Linden felt suddenly weak; drained by relief. She wanted to sit down. Stave had already suffered too many hurts in her name. Now he was safe – at least for the moment. But she clung to her resolve and hid her frailty. Holding herself upright, she gave thanks with her eyes.

Impassively Stave turned to Mahrtiir. 'Manethrall, it was not done to demonstrate my worth. In their place, I would conduct myself as the Masters do. Rather it was done in the Chosen's service – and to teach my people that they also may exceed themselves, if they elect to make the attempt.'

Mahrtiir replied with a deep Ramen bow as if he were accepting a reprimand; but his whetted grin remained.

'Worth is not at issue,' Handir said sternly. 'One fall does not define merit or prowess. Yet we honour Stave's wish to cause no harm, as we must. And we acknowledge the outcome of his trial.

'Behold.'

He nodded towards the gates; and as he did so, the massive stone began to open, turning soundlessly on its Giantish pivots or hinges. The savour of the air, chilled to crispness and redolent with springtime, told Linden that the sun was rising. Its light was blocked by the bulk of the watchtower; but a grey illumination washed inward, softening the flames of the lamps and torches.

'Linden Avery,' the Voice of the Masters announced, 'you may summon the Ranyhyn.'

His words seemed to dismiss some of the trepidation from the forehall.

She resisted an impulse to head immediately for the walled courtyard. The taste of the air, and the prospect of leaving Revelstone, restored her eagerness. She was confident now. She had shared a horserite with Hyn and Hynyn: she knew that they would answer.

But she had other concerns—

First she faced Handir and bowed, although he had never bowed to her. 'Even when I believe that you're wrong,' she said quietly, 'I don't question your integrity. If I've ever said anything to make you think otherwise, I regret it. I hope that someday we'll be allies again,' as they had been in the time of the Sunbane. 'But for now, I just hope that you'll try to withhold judgment.'

She did not expect a reply, and Handir did not proffer one. She felt a tinge of sadness like an echo of his as she gestured for her friends to gather around her.

'The Ranyhyn won't fail us,' she told them. 'You all know that. And Handir is going to let us leave.' She had sensed it in his hidden sorrow. 'He doesn't like the fact that Roger and the *croyel* tricked him. None of the Masters do. And we're a constant reminder that they can make mistakes. Once we're gone, they can debate their definition of service in peace.'

If any peace remained to the Land—

Stave nodded his confirmation.

'But when we go,' Linden continued, 'we have to remember that Anele is vulnerable when he stands on anything except stone.' Beyond the watchtower lay bare dirt. 'Kastenessen can reach him. Lord Foul can reach him. Even Esmer can interfere with him. And there's Covenant,' the real one, 'who seems to suffer in the process as much as Anele does.

'Whenever he isn't riding, we have to be sure that he's on stone. If we can't find stone, maybe we can convince him to climb a tree. And if there aren't any trees, a bedroll might be enough to protect him.

'Or—' She held Liand's gaze steadily. 'If we don't have any other options, you'll have to let him hold your *orcrest*. I know that he hates being sane. But anything is better than allowing Kastenessen or Lord Foul to hurt him again.'

Certainly the mad *Elohim* or the Despiser would be able to locate Linden if they were allowed to enter Anele. They would know where to send their forces.

'As you say, Ringthane,' Mahrtiir promised. 'The Ramen will not neglect the old man's straits.'

Liand ducked his head. When he looked at Linden again, she saw shadows and pain in his eyes. Carefully he said, 'I cannot unremember the fire of violence and rage which has twice claimed Anele. His anguish as he holds the *orcrest* is fearsome. Yet in my sight it is a lesser torment than that which is inflicted upon him by possession. I will do what must be done to ward him.'

Pahni gripped the Stonedownor's hand as he spoke; and Stave nodded again.

'Good.' At last, Linden unfolded her arms from the Staff. Taking it in her right hand, she stamped one heel on the stone. With her left, she reminded herself that Covenant's ring still hung under her shirt; that one of her pockets held Jeremiah's twisted toy. Then she turned towards the courtyard. 'In that case, I'm as ready as I'll ever be. Let's do this.'

Flanked by her companions, she strode through the inner gates to the open air between the watchtower and the main Keep. Behind her walked Handir and his phalanx of Masters as if they had become spectators at an event which no longer held their interest.

In the centre of the courtyard, she stopped. Here, she told herself. Now. But she had never summoned the Ranyhyn: Stave had done so for her. And she did not know how to whistle as he did, shrilly, and as poignant as keening.

In a low voice, she asked Stave, 'Would you mind?'

He complied at once. Raising his fingers to his mouth, he gave a sharp whistle like a flung shaft of sound. It resounded from the smooth granite of Revelstone, echoing off the Keep's buttresses, repeating itself darkly from the passage under the watchtower; and Linden's heart lifted with it. He had surpassed himself for her sake. Both Liand and Mahrtiir had given more than she could have asked of them. Even poor Anele— The Ranyhyn would do no less.

Then Stave whistled again, and the echoes multiplied until they beat like wings around the courtyard. When he whistled a third time,

Linden seemed to hear the pinions of an imminent and ominous bird: a great raven, perhaps, just out of sight beyond the tower, and poised for augury.

Slowly the echoes died away, emptying the sky. The heavy stone of the outer gates hampered her percipience. But she was not afraid. At that moment, she feared nothing except that her foes might prevent her from reaching Andelain.

Instead of holding her breath or fretting, she counted her heartbeats until she heard the Voice of the Masters say her name. Then she met his flat gaze like a woman who had already departed, leaving her doubts and even her capacity for uncertainty with him.

'It is as the Manethrall proposed,' Handir announced. 'This test of truth also has been satisfied. The Ranyhyn have answered. They await your will beyond the gates.'

For an instant, he appeared to hesitate. Then he admitted, 'Their number is ten.'

Ten. Oh, God, *ten*. Seven for Linden and her friends: three for the Masters.

'Thus,' Handir continued, 'the great horses acknowledge both your intent and your capacity for Desecration.'

In effect, he had given his permission.

Linden meant to offer him a parting bow. In her relief, she might have thanked him. The Masters were *Haruchai* and deserved as much. But she could not stop herself: she was already running towards the tunnel under the watchtower as if the sheer force of her yearning would compel the gates at the end of the lightless passage to set her free.

Chapter Six:

Sons

In sunrise, the Ramen and the *Haruchai* – the Humbled and their gathered kinsmen as well as Stave – gave homage to the Ranyhyn while Linden greeted Hyn gladly. Although she was impatient to be on her way, she did not chafe at the delay as Manethrall Mahrtiir named each of the great horses to the Masters: the seven who had borne Linden's company as well as Mhornym, Bhanoryl and Naybahn, who would be ridden by the Humbled. And she was not surprised that Handir had selected Branl, Galt and Clyme to accompany her. Doubtless the Humbled had insisted on assuming that duty. They may have wanted another opportunity to prove themselves.

Still she mounted Hyn quickly when the Ramen and the *Haruchai* had completed their ceremonies of respect. As soon as Stave and Mahrtiir indicated that her companions were ready, she turned her back on Revelstone and rode away as if her path towards Andelain held fewer perils than the defended Keep.

Foes like Kastenessen and Roger, the Harrow and Lord Foul, merely wished to break her so that she might surrender or misuse her powers. The Masters believed that she could not be trusted.

Mahrtiir sent his Cords scouting ahead. The Manethrall and Stave rode on either side of Linden. Liand accompanied Anele behind her. The Humbled ranged around the company. In that formation, the Ranyhyn cantered easily into the southeast, angling across the light of the new sun.

From the vicinity of the fields that fed Lord's Keep, the riders travelled down the bare plain which had been the battlefield for the Despiser's final war against the Lords; his last attempt to achieve his ends through sheer force. But the swift gait of the Ranyhyn soon carried the company past the plain into a region of tumbled hills that stretched for leagues.

The hills permitted easy passage. Their slopes were gentle, worn down by ages of time and weather. Still they constricted the horizons on all sides. For safety's sake, Mahrtiir joined his Cords searching the terrain while the *Haruchai* rode closely around Linden, Liand and Anele. And the ground was clad in the tough, raw-edged grass that Linden feared for the old man's sake. Throughout the first day of their journey, whenever the riders paused for food and water, or to scavenge a few treasure-berries, they remained on horseback.

As she rode, Linden watched for villages – for any habitations – but she saw none. Surely the Land's people did not avoid living in the vicinity of Revelstone? She assumed, therefore, that the Ramen chose a path which would allow them to pass unseen. Perhaps Mahrtiir's keenness to leave Lord's Keep behind urged him to avoid encounters that might slow the company. Or perhaps he understood that the Humbled would oppose exposing villagers to the dangerous knowledge and magicks of Linden and her friends.

She also scanned the hillsides for some sign of the Harrow. But the Insequent did not appear. If he travelled somewhere nearby, neither the Ramen nor the *Haruchai* could discern him.

After Linden's first rush of excitement, the day seemed to pass slowly. Yet Hyn's comfortable strength supported her. And she was encouraged by the sensation that she had finally begun to take charge of her own fate; that she had wrested the initiative away from her enemies. For too long, she had simply reacted to their various gambits. Now they would be compelled to react to hers.

With luck and courage, and the inestimable aid of her friends, she might be able to surprise the Despiser's allies.

That night, however, she and her companions made their camp on a swath of rubble which had spilled down over centuries or millennia from a rugged escarpment among the hills. A bed of tumbled and weathered stones protected Anele, but granted her no more than a little fitful sleep. As the night wore on, her anticipation became a restless anxiety.

An attack was likely. Kastenessen and Roger would surely try to stop her. Other foes – less predictable ones – would do the same. She had been warned away from Andelain by friends as well as enemies. And while she lay awake, she felt the constant bale of Kevin's Dirt etiolating her resolve. *Beyond question the Falls are a great evil*, Liand had once said to her. *Yet I deem them a little wrong beside the deprivation imposed by Kevin's Dirt.* In darkness, the impending weight of imminent blindness had the power to erode her judgment and conviction as well as her senses.

Under the circumstances, she was both comforted and disturbed by the fact that the *Haruchai* did not appear to sleep. Perhaps Stave, Galt, Branl and Clyme dozed with their eyes open while they rode, or snatched naps when they were certain that their companions were safe.

In addition, they appeared to eat little, although they did not refuse treasure-berries. It was instinctive with them, Linden supposed, to keep private anything that resembled ordinary mortal needs and vulnerabilities. Thousands of years after the Vow of the Bloodguard had been broken, Stave and the Masters continued to emulate the *Haruchai* who had once served the Lords.

She could rely on their stringent inflexibility. But it was also their gravest weakness.

Fortunately Liand had spent a considerable time during the day's ride, and in the evening, poring over his *orcrest*. The next morning, he demonstrated that Sunstone could indeed counteract Kevin's Dirt. With quiet exultation, he restored health-sense to the Ramen, Linden, and himself, sparing her the exertion of her Staff. After that, she felt less alone; reassured to know that hers were no longer the company's only instruments of power.

During the day, she was soothed by Hyn's steady gait, as secure as a throne. And the hills opened into a billowing grassland that seemed to expand the possibilities of the world. Like the relief provided by Liand's *orcrest*, being able to see farther eased some of her trepidation.

Near sunset, the company stopped for the night in an arroyo with a brisk stream rushing down its centre and a bed composed primarily of broken shingle and slate: enough stone to protect Anele from possession, but free of the deep rock which would expose him to his worst memories. The water was runoff from seasonal showers and mountain snows. Among its liquid secrets, it carried the faint flavours of rainfall and blizzards, new warmth and older ice. In summer, the watercourse would be turbulent to its rims, a small river hastening generally southward. Now, however, the littered bottom of the arroyo was the safest place that the scouting Ramen had found for Anele to spend the night.

For herself, Linden planned to lay out her bedroll on the softer ground above the stream. Her companions could watch over her wherever she made her bed. And she did not doubt that the Ranyhyn also would guard the company. After the discomforts of the previous night, she wanted a chance for better rest.

But first she sat with her back against the dry wall of the gully while twilight deepened into evening overhead, and Liand and Pahni readied a meal over a cheery cookfire. There she was able to relax and think.

When the company had eaten – when the Ramen had returned from tending the Ranyhyn, and the Humbled had taken places above Linden and her friends along the edges of the watercourse – Stave finally broached the subject of the Harrow and the Mahdoubt. He described their eerie contest and its outcome. And he repeated what Linden had already heard about the Vizard and the Theomach, although he did not explain how the *Haruchai* knew of the Insequent. The ancient defeat of his people he kept to himself, perhaps to protect his own hidden emotions, or perhaps to appease the Humbled.

Watching Liand and the Cords, Linden saw that they had questions which they would have liked to ask. But Stave's uninflected severity forbade inquiry. However, the sharpness of Mahrtiir's concentration suggested that he would ask his questions in spite of Stave's reticence. For the former Master's sake, Linden forestalled the Manethrall.

'Stave,' she asked quietly, 'what can you tell us about where we are and where we're going? You and the Humbled know this area. We don't.' When she and Covenant had begun their search for the One Tree long ago, she had been in no condition to attend to her surroundings. She remembered only that they had left Revelstone eastward against the lethal permutations of the Sunbane. 'I want some idea of what we have ahead of us.'

Once again, she encouraged him to violate the prohibitions of the Masters – and to do so in their presence. However, she doubted that the Humbled would object. Having committed themselves to this endeavour, they could not very well claim that she and her friends had no need of their knowledge.

Stave's manner remained stiff, but he did not hesitate. 'The distance from Revelstone to the northwestmost verge of the Andelainian Hills is ninety leagues. Riding as we have, without urging the Ranyhyn excessively, thirty now lie behind us.'

'So four more days,' murmured Linden.

The *Haruchai* shook his head. 'Chosen, your count presupposes that we will encounter neither delay nor opposition. Opposition I am unable to foretell, though we have been warned of the *skurj*, and the chance of Falls must not be forgotten. But some delays may be desirable, while others cannot be avoided.

'On the morrow, we will pass nigh unto First Woodhelven, so named because it was the first, and indeed the most viable, of the attempts by Sunder Graveler and Hollian eh-Brand to create anew the tree-dwellings which were among the Land's wonders during the ages of the Lords. You may wish to pause there, for the *Haruchai* remember that you have never beheld a true Woodhelven. Also it would perhaps be wise to refresh our supplies, if the Humbled will permit it.'

Linden felt sure that the Humbled would reject any meeting with the villagers. But if they reacted to Stave's suggestions, they did so in silence, and he did not share what he heard.

She tightened her grip on herself. Roger Covenant in his father's guise had told her that Kastenessen now occupied Andelain, that he commanded the *skurj*, and that he could send those devouring monsters to meet her because he was able to locate her through Anele. But Roger had lied about so many things– She was not convinced that Kastenessen could detect the old man unless Anele touched bare dirt.

Also she considered the idea that the enraged *Elohim* occupied Andelain implausible. Surely such a being would shun the quintessential health and beauty of the Land? He might well loathe the austere strictures of the Dead. And an attack on Andelain would only waste his strength: it would not threaten his people, and so it would not relieve his fury.

No, on this subject she believed none of Roger's assertions except that Kastenessen ruled the *skurj* – and that the Land's enemies would try to thwart her purpose. If Kastenessen sought to acquire Loric's *krill* for himself – if the *krill* were not inherently inimical to him – she suspected that he would do so indirectly.

'Go on,' she urged Stave softly. 'What else can you tell us?'

His expression remained stubbornly neutral. But if the Humbled urged him to say no more, he did not heed them.

'Of the many wounds inflicted by the Clave and the Sunbane, the most grievous was the loss of the great forests. On the Upper Land, they were three. Dark Grimmerdhore lay to the east of Revelstone, but it extended southward towards Andelain. Our path lies across a portion of the region where Grimmerdhore once flourished, and where it perished.

'Southeast of Andelain between the Black River and the Roamsedge stood brooding Morinmoss. There the Unbeliever was once retrieved from death by an Unfettered healer. And southwest of the Center Plains and the Last Hills rose Garroting Deep, mighty and bitter.

'But there was also a fourth forest, Giant Woods, which survived the Sunbane, and which still remains, lying as it does on the Lower Land north of the fouled waters of Sarangrave Flat.'

The Sarangrave Linden remembered. There she and Covenant, with Sunder, Hollian and a small band of *Haruchai*, had nearly fallen to the lurker, and to the lurker's corrosive minions, the *skest*. And there they had encountered the Giants of the Search, who had made possible the Despiser's defeat and the Land's healing. But she did not let memories of friends whom she had loved and lost interrupt Stave.

'Some measure,' he said, 'of what transpired after Corruption's overthrow and the Sunbane's unmaking was first told to the *Haruchai* by the Giants of the Search, though the tale was later repeated by Sunder Graveler and Hollian eh-Brand.

'For a time, Sunder and Hollian were confined to Andelain. She was newly reborn, he had expended much of himself to restore her, and the Sunbane's ill lingered in the Land. The First of the Search and Pitchwife had given the Staff of Law into their care, but they had not yet learned its uses. They required Andelain's wealth of Earthpower. Therefore they remained among the Hills, and studied the Staff, and grew stronger.'

Linden leaned forward, listening closely as Stave's flat voice defined the darkness around the small campfire. Like Anele's tale of the One

Forest, her encounter with Caerroil Wildwood had left her hungry to know more about forests. And she treasured the *Haruchai*'s recollections of her friends. Her last deed before she was dismissed from the Land had been to reach out to Sunder and Hollian. She had wished them to know that they were loved – and had reason for hope.

Liand and the Ramen also listened, rapt, to Stave's explanation. Millennia ago, the Ramen had led the Ranyhyn away from the Plains of Ra to escape the Sunbane. And none of them had returned, except to scout along the Land's borders at long intervals, until Hyn and Hynyn had declared their devotion to Linden. As a result, Mahrtiir and his Cords knew little of events in the Land during their people's self-imposed exile.

'However,' Stave continued, 'Sunder and Hollian remembered well the majesty of Giant Woods. And she was an eh-Brand, born to the love of wood. Among the great and vital tasks which they had accepted with their acceptance of the Staff, they desired first to begin the restoration of forests to the Land.

'Yet they had no knowledge of Grimmerdhore, or of Morinmoss, or of Garroting Deep. Nor did the Giants of the Search. And no *Haruchai* sought for Sunder and Hollian. Until the Giants returned to Revelstone, the *Haruchai* did not know that Sunder and Hollian remained living. Thus the Graveler and the eh-Brand were not guided by the history of forests in the Land.

'Rather they devised their own purpose. When their comprehension of the Staff had grown sufficiently to heal the last of the Sunbane's ravages within Andelain, they turned their attention outward. Around all of the boundaries of Andelain, from Landsdrop north of Mount Thunder westward, then into the southeast towards the Mithil River, thence across the Mithil east to the region where Morinmoss once endured, and finally northward along the Mithil to the southmost slopes of Gravin Threndor, Sunder and Hollian inspired and nurtured one encompassing forest which they named Salva Gildenbourne to honour the Gilden trees of Andelain.'

Again Stave considered the Humbled, perhaps offering them an opportunity to advise him. But he did not query them aloud, and so they did not answer. After a moment, he gave a small shrug and went on.

'Had they been able to do so, the Graveler and the eh-Brand would have extended the largesse of woodlands over all the war-ravaged earth between Andelain and Landsdrop. There, however, they were baffled. Their comprehension of the Staff – or perhaps the Staff itself, being incomplete – could not entirely overcome the harm wrought by Corruption's ancient armies and battles.'

Facing Linden directly, Stave concluded, 'Salva Gildenbourne stands across our approach to Andelain. After its fashion, it is a wondrous region, precious to the Land. But it was formed without the benefit of lore, and has grown both vast and unruly. If we are not opposed or delayed, we will gain its marge in three days. However, Salva Gildenbourne itself hinders passage. And there the Ranyhyn cannot quicken our way. For that reason, I gauge that the forest must add two days and more to our journey.'

Linden nodded to herself. Six days, then – and only if the Land's foes did not strike. She wanted to travel with more haste; to ride harder and longer. She could not truly begin to search for Jeremiah until she accomplished her purpose in Andelain. But when she thought back, she could still hear the rabid howling of the *kresh*. An *Elohim* had warned the Land of Sandgorgons as well as *croyel* and *skurj*. She did not know what had become of *moksha* Jehannum, the Raver who had once possessed her. Doubtless he was at work somewhere, serving Lord Foul. And she had not forgotten *turiya* Herem's possession of Joan. It was conceivable that *turiya* might be able to impose a degree of focus on Joan's madness. If he did so, her blasts of wild magic might achieve a measure of direction and intent–

Haste would almost certainly increase the danger to Linden and all of her companions. The Ramen and even the Ranyhyn would be more easily ambushed.

Musing, Liand said, 'I have never beheld a forest. Pahni urges me to imagine the trees of the upland plateau multiplied a thousand fold, or a thousand thousand. But it lies beyond my conception.'

The Manethrall nodded sharply. 'The Ramen love openness and long hills. Nevertheless our ancestors held the forests of the Land in reverence. Their many-splendoured grandeur surpassed description. I am eager now to cast my gaze upon Salva Gildenbourne, and to pass among its uncounted majesties.

'You are a Stonedownor,' he added to Liand, 'born to rock and permanence. Yet I do not doubt that you also will be moved to worship by the glories of wood. And we have not yet spoken of Andelain, where the Land's loveliness thrives in abundance.'

The Ramen and Liand continued to talk while Anele snored fitfully beside the fire and the Humbled stood guard; but Linden hardly heard them. Isolated by her apprehensions, she wrapped a blanket around her shoulders to ward off the chill of the spring night, and tried to think.

According to Covenant's son, Kastenessen had only summoned a few *skurj* to the Land. On that point, Roger may have been telling the truth. Surely a throng of those creatures could not have evaded the notice of the Masters? Nevertheless the monsters which Linden had seen during her translation to the Land were capable of tremendous devastation. Already she had succeeded twice at extinguishing Falls – and she was stronger now. The Staff itself was stronger. But she could not guess whether Law and Earthpower would be enough to hold back the *skurj*. The *Elohim* might not have Appointed Kastenessen to his Durance if any other theurgy could contain those horrific creatures.

Yet when she slept at last, her dreams were not haunted by the jaws of kraken, or by cruel yellow fangs, or by the excruciation of *caesures*. Instead she seemed to fall endlessly into the numb black abysm of the Harrow's eyes, where there was no sound except her son's anguished weeping.

She awoke in a mood of fretful urgency. Over and over again, the pressures and dilemmas of her immediate circumstances pushed thoughts of Jeremiah into the background; but whenever the extremity of his plight reclaimed her, it did so with redoubled force. She still had a long way to go to reach Andelain, Loric's *krill*, and the Dead. But those were only the first stages of her quest to find her son. Ultimately such things were necessary simply because she did not know how else to begin looking for Jeremiah.

While she ate a tense breakfast with her friends, Liand observed gently, 'You did not rest well, Linden.'

She nodded; but she was not listening. Instead she harkened to the sound of whistling and formal salutations. At her request, Stave and

Mahrtiir had joined the Humbled beyond the eastern rim of the arroyo to summon the Ranyhyn: she was waiting for Stave's return. As soon as he dropped back down into the watercourse, she handed the remains of her meal to Bhapa and rose to her feet.

'First Woodhelven?' she asked. 'How far is it?'

Stave cocked his eyebrow at her abrupt manner. 'If our way is not contested, we will near the Woodhelven before midday.'

Linden bit her lip. 'Are you sure that we should stop there? Don't we have enough supplies?'

If the Woodhelvennin needed to be warned of impending hazards, one of the Humbled could perform that task without violating their commitment to preserve the villagers' ignorance.

Stave shrugged, studying her. 'The future is uncertain, Chosen. Soon we may be driven far from our direct road. It would be improvident to neglect an opportunity to replenish our viands.'

'All right,' she muttered unhappily. 'But let's be as quick as we can. Jeremiah needs me.'

'Also you do not forgive,' Stave remarked. 'This all *Haruchai* comprehend. The Ranyhyn await you. And among themselves the Humbled acknowledge that your desire for haste is justified. We will journey as swiftly as we may without sacrificing caution.'

As if his words were a command, Liand and Pahni hurried to wash their pots, bowls and utensils while Bhapa repacked the company's bedrolls. At the same time, Branl and Galt surprised Linden by leaping down into the gully. Without a word, they searched the shale and shingle of the riverbed until they found a large pane of slate perhaps two fingers thick on which one or two people could have stood. Lifting it together, Branl and Galt tossed it up to Clyme at the rim of the watercourse. When Clyme had secured his grip on the slate, he carried it out of sight.

To Linden's perplexed stare, Stave explained, 'Though a fertile lowland girdles First Woodhelven, the surrounding hills are barren, as is much of the region which we must traverse this day. While he can, Clyme will bear his stone upon Mhornym's back. At need, it may ward the old man from Kastenessen's touch.'

Linden made a whistling sound through her teeth. 'That's good.' She was familiar with the preternatural strength of the *Haruchai*, but she often forgot just how strong they were. 'I'm glad one of you thought of it.'

Repeatedly she had promised Anele her protection – and repeatedly she concentrated on other concerns instead.

Grinning, Liand clapped Stave appreciatively on the back. Then he offered to help Linden clamber out of the arroyo.

When she gained the rim, she found Mahrtiir there with the gathered Ranyhyn. Hyn approached Linden with a look of affection in her soft eyes: Hynyn stamped his hooves imperiously. Clyme had already made a harness of thongs for the slate, set it on his back, and mounted Mhornym. Linden saw now that Mhornym was nearly a hand taller than the other horses, with heavily muscled thighs and a deep chest. Clearly the stallion would be able to bear the added weight of Clyme's burden.

The chief purpose of the Humbled may have been to guard against Linden, but they also took the task of aiding her and her friends seriously. In this, they resembled the *Haruchai* whom she had known with Thomas Covenant. For a long time, Brinn, Cail, Ceer and Hergrom had distrusted her profoundly, but their doubts had not prevented them from warding her with their lives.

When they had become the Masters of the Land, the *Haruchai* had not ceased to be themselves.

Reassured by that recognition, and comforted by Hyn's steady acceptance, Linden grew calmer for a while. But when she and her companions were mounted at last, and the Ranyhyn had turned towards the southeast across the sunrise, she had to resist an impulse to urge Hyn into a gallop.

As long as Lord Foul and the *croyel* held Jeremiah, he might never see the sun again. The Despiser preferred the dark places of the world. And under *Melenkurion* Skyweir, he had nearly lost Jeremiah. She felt sure that Lord Foul would not take that risk a second time.

Whatever happened, Andelain and Loric's *krill* would be the beginning of her search rather than the end.

With the sun like a barrier in her eyes, she felt time drag, leaden with worry. For her sake, however, the Ranyhyn quickened their fluid canter. Mahrtiir sent Bhapa scouting far ahead of the company: Galt and Branl travelled as outriders nearly out of sight on both sides. And gradually the flow of Hyn's gait settled Linden's nerves. The mare's undisturbed rhythm seemed to impose a subliminal equipoise, soothing Linden as though she were being rocked in protective arms. She stopped watching the sun, and so her perception of progress was altered.

Stave and Mahrtiir rode with her. Behind them came Liand and Pahni flanking Anele. And Clyme kept Mhornym close to the heels of the old man's mount. Pausing only for occasional sips of water, or for a few treasure-berries, the riders made their way around the slopes of low hills, over incremental ridges, and through swales and small valleys punctuated by copses and lone trees like eyots in the slow surge of a grass-foamed sea.

As the sun passed the middle of the morning sky, Linden's tuned senses caught the first whiff of *wrongness*.

At first, it was too evanescent to be defined: as elusive as will-o'-the-wisps; scarcely distinguishable from the overarching fug of Kevin's Dirt. She had no idea what it might represent. But when she glanced around her, she saw Mahrtiir scenting the air. Anele had become restive on Hrama's back, jerking his head awkwardly from side to side. And both Branl and Galt had drawn closer to the company as if they were tightening a cordon.

Liand turned a puzzled look towards Pahni. But he did not call out to her over the constant rumble of hooves, and she did not answer his gaze.

There: Linden felt the sensation again. It was less an odour than a form of stridulation, as if something cruel had scraped briefly against her percipience, making her nerves vibrate. She was about to shout a question at the Manethrall or Stave when she saw Bhapa ahead of her, racing to rejoin the company as though *kresh* harried him.

But it was not the musky foetor of wolves that Linden had sensed. It was something darker; something without hunger or intention – and far more fatal.

By touch, or perhaps merely by thought, Stave and Mahrtiir slowed Hynyn and Narunal; and the rest of the Ranyhyn followed their example. The horses were barely trotting when Bhapa rode near enough to report without yelling.

'Manethrall, Ringthane, it is a *caesure*.' Ramen rigour vied with urgency in his tone. 'I have not beheld it, for it lay at the limit of my discernment. Yet I am certain of it. Such evils cannot be mistaken.'

Turning Whrany to pace at Mahrtiir's side, the Cord continued, 'At first, it stood directly before us. But it moves, as do all *caesures*. For the present, it drifts southward as if borne by the wind, though the wind is from the west. If some caprice does not alter its course, it will not endanger us. Indeed, it may pass a league or more beyond our path.'

'How close did it get to First Woodhelven?' Linden asked. 'Can you tell?'

She had stood on Kevin's Watch when it fell; she and Anele. She groaned as she imagined what a *caesure* might do to any substance less stubborn than granite.

Bhapa looked helplessly at Mahrtiir. 'Alas, I know not. The auras of human habitations are little things on the scale of Falls. I was able to descry the *caesure*, and to be certain of it, because it is an immense ill. I felt nothing of the Woodhelven.'

'In that case,' said Linden grimly, 'I think it's time to ride hard. The Woodhelvennin might need us. And if they don't, I want to get past that thing before it can change directions.'

Automatically she dismissed the idea of pursuing the *caesure* in order to quench it. Doing so would delay her. Each of Joan's temporal violations was short-lived: she knew that. Otherwise the Arch would already have fallen. If no one – no other force – sustained the Fall, it would soon expend itself and vanish.

The Manethrall and Stave shared a nod. Then all of the Ranyhyn stretched their strides in unison, accelerating smoothly until they raced like coursers into the southeast.

Under other circumstances, Hyn's vitality and swiftness might have exhilarated Linden. But now her attention was focused ahead. With the Staff, she sharpened her senses and cast her percipience farther, seeking the *caesure*.

Initially she felt it in small suggestions, innominate flickers of distortion. But soon she was sure of it. She had learned to distinguish between the queasiness that afflicted her in Esmer's presence and the more visceral sick squirming caused by the proximity of Falls. Esmer made her ill by disturbing her connection with aspects of herself: the impact of *caesures* ran deeper. On an almost cellular level, they threatened her dependence upon tangible reality.

And a *caesure* was *there*, where Bhapa had indicated: ahead of her and to the right, slipping erratically southward. If its heading did not shift, it would not endanger her company. Rather it would carry Joan's unreasoning violence into the distance until it dissipated itself. And while it lasted, its destructiveness would depend less on the amount of wild magic that Joan had unleashed than on what lay along its mindless road.

With an effort, Linden swallowed her fear of what the Fall might do. The silent acquiescence of Stave and the Humbled assured her that there were no villages or habitations near the *caesure*'s present course. The *Haruchai* would certainly have warned her if lives were at stake.

Only one concern remained: First Woodhelven.

Gripping the Staff of Law until her knuckles ached, Linden leaned along Hyn's neck, silently urging the mare and all of the Ranyhyn to run faster.

A long rising slope blocked the view ahead. It fell away to lower ground on the south: to the north, it mounted towards a rocky tor, rugged with old stone. But along the company's path the ascent was too gradual to slow the pounding horses. They sped upwards over earth that lost its scruff of grass to become an ungiving admixture of flint, crumbled shale, and bare dirt. The hooves of the Ranyhyn pelted debris behind them with every stride. The horses following Linden were forced to space themselves so that they did not run in the spray of jagged pebbles and grit kicked up by Hyn and Hynyn, Whrany and Narunal.

Along the lower terrain, she saw evidence of the *caesure*'s passage. The ground there was as barren as the slope, but it had a churned look, as though it had been raked by thousands of claws. A stretch of disturbed soil nearly a stone's throw across led like a crooked road into the south.

God, the Fall was *big*—

Now Linden spotted what appeared to be a storm around the *caesure*'s seething column. The sky was free of clouds, uncluttered from horizon to horizon. Nevertheless lightning flared in the distance, crackling around the *caesure* like a nimbus. The air thickened as if it were crowded with thunderheads; full of theurgy rather than moisture and wind.

She stifled a gasp of chagrin. The Fall was not the only peril. Some power as lorewise and puissant as the Demondim was striving urgently to interrupt or influence the *caesure*.

Biting her lip, she turned her head away. Stave had said that First Woodhelven occupied a fertile lowland surrounded by bare hills. If it lay beyond this rise, it may have been directly in the path of the Fall.

The crest was near. Already she could see past it to more hills perhaps half a league distant; slopes as barren as the dirt over which the Ranyhyn galloped.

Oh, God, she groaned as Hyn bore her to the top of the rise. Please. No.

Then the Ranyhyn swept over the crest, poured like a torrent down the far side; and Linden saw that First Woodhelven had not been spared.

It occupied a wide, low valley which stretched beyond the tor in the northwest and curved away to the east; a slow crescent of soil made arable by a bright brook and seasonal flooding. As Stave had suggested, the lowland was contained by hills like mounds of shale, dirt and marl. But centuries of water and overflow had made the bottom of the valley as hospitable as pasturage.

At one time – perhaps as long as half an hour ago – the tree-village must have been extraordinary: a magnificent banyan straddling the stream, sending down tendrils in thick clusters to become new roots and secondary trunks until the single tree formed an extensive grove. Massive boughs by the thousands must have offered their leaves to the heavens, growing between and among each other until they provided abundant opportunities for homes as well as for paths from trunk to trunk. And the homes themselves must have been extraordinary as well, for they would have been fashioned not of planks and timbers, but of interwoven limbs and branches, and sheltered by a dense thatch-work of twigs and leaves. All along the brook, the crops of the Woodhelvennin would have flourished.

If Linden had seen First Woodhelven before the *caesure* hit, the sight might have gladdened her sore heart. She would have been so proud of Sunder and Hollian– But she and her companions had not reached the tree-village in time to save it.

Now it looked like a cyclone had torn through it. Ancient trunks as thick as five or six Giants standing together had been shattered; split apart and scattered like kindling. Their oozing stumps were jagged as fractured bones. Broken boughs made a trail of wreckage in the wake of the Fall: rent wood in jumbled clusters resembled the piles of pyres: leaves littered the ground like bloodshed.

After millennia of growth and health, generation following generation, a thriving community had become a catastrophe.

Yet for Linden that was not the worst of it, although the damage cried out to her senses. The tree was only wood. Precious beyond measure, its ruin nonetheless did not communicate the full cost of the *caesure*. More poignant to her was the condition of the fields – and of the Wood-helvennin themselves.

On either side of the Fall's path, the fields remained untouched. They had been recently ploughed and tended, and wore the fresh vulnerable green of new crops. But where the *caesure* had passed, it had dragged carnage through the soil, maiming First Woodhelven's hopes for food; for a future. Raw dirt ached in the sunlight like a weeping gall in the body of the Land.

And all around the calamity of their homes stood the banyan-dwellers, hundreds of men, women and children milling in shock and dismay, utterly lost.

Among them moved two Masters. No doubt that explained why the Woodhelvennin were still alive: the unblinded senses of the Masters had warned the villagers to gather their families and flee before the Fall struck. And a few horses had been saved as well. But the *Haruchai* could do nothing to ease the effects, the force and impact, of the disaster. The Woodhelvennin gazed dumbly upon the devastation of their lives, too appalled to think or take action. They did not know how to bear the sheer casualness, the complete lack of purpose or desire, with which their homes and possessions and tasks had been reduced to debris.

Lacking any knowledge of the Land's history, they had no context for atrocity.

In Berek Halfhand's camp, Linden had gone without hesitation to do what she could for the victims of his war. This was different. The Woodhelvennin were not wounded: their hearts rather than their bodies had been pierced. With all of her power, she could not make their spirits whole again.

And she had shared no responsibility for the sufferings of Berek's warriors. First Woodhelven's razing she could have prevented, if she had insisted on haste hours earlier, when her company had broken camp—

If she had not restored Joan's wedding band—

She hardly noticed that the Ranyhyn, the whole company, had slowed to a halt on the rise above the shattered grove. A deep rage held her attention.

Roger had said of Falls, *Wherever they are at a particular moment, every bit of time in that precise spot happens at once.* He had tried to explain why the fabric of reality had not already been irreparably shredded. *Since they're moving, they give those bits of time back as fast as they pick up new ones.* In addition, the Law of Time strove to preserve itself. Presumably Thomas Covenant himself fought to defend it. And Joan's inability to concentrate prevented the *caesures* from expanding to consume everything. Thus the larger integrity of causality and sequence endured despite the severity of the Falls.

Nevertheless the restoration of Law as the *caesure* passed contributed to its destructiveness. Every instant of First Woodhelven's life had been superimposed – and then those instants had been flung back into their natural order. The result was a doubled violation. In effect, the Fall's departure did as much harm as its arrival.

Linden concentrated on such things in an effort to control the wild scramble of guilt and sorrow that made her want to rage at the heavens rather than seek some means to ease the villagers. In another moment, she might turn her back on them. She hungered to ride like vengeance after the Fall and *rip* it out of existence. The eldritch storm surrounding it she would sweep aside. She had stood on Gallows Howe: she yearned to repay savagery with destruction.

'Chosen.' Stave put his hand on her arm as if to pull her back from a kind of insanity. 'The fault is mine. I urged caution when you craved haste.'

In response, Mahrtiir made a fierce spitting sound. 'Do not speak of *fault* here, *Haruchai*. Neither you nor the Ringthane is gifted with foreknowledge. There *is* no fault. There is only the need of these stricken Woodhelvennin.'

Fault, Linden thought, biting her lip until it bled. Oh, there was *fault*, and plenty of it. The Manethrall was right: she could not have known. Even Joan, abused and broken, did not deserve blame. But Lord Foul was another matter. Kastenessen and Roger, the Ravers and the *skurj* and the *croyel*: the Despiser had aimed them like a barrage at the Land.

'All right,' she said with her mouth full of blood. 'I understand. Let's go see what we can do for those poor people.'

But she did not move. Instead she struggled to suppress her outrage. She needed a moment of clarity, of containment, in which she might regain some aspect of the Linden Avery who healed. That woman had never fully emerged from the depths of *Melenkurion* Skyweir.

There must be *something*—

Rubbing the blood from her lip with the back of her hand, she tightened the grip of her heels on Hyn's flanks; mutely asked the mare to approach the remains of First Woodhelven. But as Hyn began to walk, Galt called sharply, 'Linden Avery!'

He rode a short way off to her right, guarding the company from the south. When she jerked a look at him, he announced, 'The Fall's course has been altered. It turns towards us, compelled by some power which we do not recognise. And it moves swiftly. If it does not veer aside, it will soon be upon us.'

Flinching, Linden snatched her percipience towards the south and saw that he was right. The *caesure* was retracing its ruin, harried by a palpable cloudless storm. And it was coming fast—

Some silent part of her snarled curses, but she paid no attention to them. The Fall's advance evoked a different clarity than the one that she had tried to impose on herself.

'Go!' she shouted at Galt and his comrades as though she had the right to command them. 'Get those people out of there,' away from their riven homes, their lost lives. 'Take them west. I'll try to snuff that thing. But I don't know what I'm up against. If something goes wrong, they'll be right in front of it.'

If the *skurj* came, they would approach from the east.

Because he was a Master, she expected him to refuse. Yet he did not. Wheeling his Ranyhyn, he headed at a gallop into the lowland.

Immediately Branl joined him. Clyme took a moment to unsling the slate from his back and pass it in its harness to Stave, transferring responsibility for Anele. Then he sped after the other Humbled.

In their minds, all three of them may have been calling to the Masters among the Woodhelvennin.

So many people— It would take time to rally them. They were too stunned to think for themselves.

'Mahrtiir!' Linden flung a gesture after the Humbled. 'Help those people. What's coming isn't just a Fall. Somebody is *pushing* that thing.' Someone nearby: someone who wanted the *caesure* to devour the Woodhelvennin – or to assail her. 'Get as many of them on horses as you can. Make them *move*.'

When the Manethrall hesitated, she urged him, 'Go! Leave Liand and Anele with me.' She could not ask Liand to watch over Anele and aid the villagers at the same time; and the old man was close to panic, filled by the old dread which had driven him to climb Kevin's Watch. If he left Hrama's back and tried to fend for himself – if his feet touched barren ground— 'Stave will take care of them.'

'Ringthane.' Mahrtiir nodded an acknowledgment, then turned Narunal to follow the Humbled. As the Ranyhyn gathered speed, the Manethrall shouted, 'Cords!'

Bhapa was already in motion, racing to catch up with Mahrtiir. Pahni gave Liand a quick desperate look before she sent Naharahn after Whrany.

Liand had already taken out his *orcrest*. He gripped it tightly while he murmured to Hrama and Rhohm, imploring them to stay together.

The sight of Liand's Sunstone made Anele cower as if he feared it – feared sanity – more than the *caesure*.

On all sides of Linden and her remaining companions were flint, shale, eroded sandstone, dirt. Hardly a hundred paces away lay the torn path of the Fall. If Anele dismounted, even for a moment, Kastenessen would find him. The pain-maddened *Elohim* would know where to send the *skurj*. And if he gained full possession of the old man, he might attack Linden directly while she fought the *caesure* and its unseen drover.

Kastenessen might already be somewhere nearby. Surely he was capable of herding a Fall wherever he wished?

'How long—?' Abruptly she found that she could not speak: her throat was too dry. She had to swallow several times before she could ask Stave, 'How much time do we have?'

The *Haruchai* gazed into the south for a moment, then glanced behind him to consider the tree-dwellers. 'If the Woodhelvennin comprehend their peril, and do not refuse to be commanded, they will be spared.'

If the Fall did not change directions to pursue them—

'In that case' – Linden took a deep breath, held it, let it out – 'let's go down there.' She indicated the furrowed ground where the Fall had passed. 'We'll be able to see farther.'

On this terrain, one place would not be more dangerous than another for Anele.

Stave nodded. Beckoning for Liand and Anele to follow, he nudged Hynyn into a trot, angling across the slope to keep his distance from the blasted village while he sought an unobstructed view to the south.

Fighting her urgent anger, Linden dropped back briefly to ride beside Liand. 'You know what you have to do?'

His black eyebrows accentuated the apprehension in his eyes. 'Linden?'

'Remember what I told you,' she ordered brusquely. 'Protect Anele. Whatever happens. Get Stave to help you if you need him. I'll stop the *caesure*.' Somehow. 'But you have to keep Anele away from Kastenessen. We can't face another attack right now.'

Of any kind.

When the Stonedownor said, 'I will,' biting off the words as though they caused him pain, she left him, riding faster to catch up with Stave.

'Did you hear me?' she asked as she reached Stave's side. On his back, he bore the pane of slate. 'I know how you feel about protecting me. But you can't fight a Fall. You can't fight that storm. Helping Liand keep Anele safe is the best thing that you can do for me.'

For a moment, Stave appeared to contemplate what she requested of him. Then he replied evenly, 'Your fate is mine, Chosen. I will have no other. Yet while I may, I will do as you desire.' Without expression, he met her gaze. 'Have I not shown that I am able to abandon you for the old man's sake?'

He had left her to retrieve Anele from the horde of the Demon-dim—

Trying to smile, Linden bared her teeth. 'You have. I should know better than to tell you what to do.'

As soon as she reached the centre of the *caesure*'s raked path, she turned to face the south. For a few heartbeats, Hyn's muscles quivered as if she were afraid; as if she longed to carry Linden out of danger. Then Hynyn snorted assertively, and the mare seemed to calm herself.

The Fall was moving faster than Linden had anticipated. It was already clear to her ordinary sight: a swirling miasma of *wrongness* in the shape of a tornado. Its emanations burrowed along her nerves as though hornets hived in her belly. And it was growing— The storm driving it seemed to increase its virulence and size as well as its speed. It would strike like the bludgeon of a titan.

Now she could discern the storm itself distinctly, although it had no clouds to account for the lurid punch of its thunder or the bright flare and sizzle of its lightning. Her health-sense perceived the turmoil in etched detail: it resembled a squall at sea. But its forces were too great for a mere squall. Its vehemence suggested the fury of a hurricane.

She had never seen theurgy like that before. More than once, however, she had felt a similar puissance: when Esmer had attacked Stave; and again when he had blocked the ur-viles from assailing Roger and the *croyel*. Before she and her companions had risked the Land's past to search for the Staff of Law, the Ramen had informed her that *he wields a storm among the mountains*—

With it, he had summoned a *caesure* for her.

'*Damn* it,' she breathed more to herself than to Stave. 'That's Esmer.'

'So I deem,' replied Stave as though he had not been almost beaten to death by Cail's son.

For the first time, Linden wondered whether Esmer himself might be the *havoc* for which he had blamed Stave and the *Haruchai*.

Yet she could not believe that Esmer intended to threaten her like this. His conflicting inheritances precluded a direct assault. And a desire to ravage the Woodhelvennin seemed out of character. He had never shown the kind of omnivorous malice that delighted Lord Foul, or that Kastenessen and Roger might have enjoyed.

But *why*, then—?

An instant later, she saw an explanation. Ahead of the *caesure*, a rider fled desperately. He flogged his horse straight towards her. The Fall and the storm seemed to be chasing him.

She recognised him before Stave stated flatly, 'It is the Harrow.'

He was mounted on a brown destrier as large and strongly made as Mhornym, although the beast was not a Ranyhyn: it lacked the characteristic star-shaped blaze on its forehead; the unmistakable tang of Earthpower. Froth splashed from the horse's mouth and nostrils, and its eyes glared with dumb terror, as its rider lashed its hindquarters with a short quirt. Hunched low over his mount's neck, with his chlamys flapping, the Harrow rode for his life just ahead of the *caesure*.

He had promised Linden his companionship. Now he raced towards her as though he hoped that she would save him.

He was her enemy: she believed that. Oh, he had unmade the threat of the Demondim. But he had also tried to swallow her mind. He had cost her the Mahdoubt's friendship and support; the Mahdoubt's life.

And he coveted Covenant's ring. He wanted the Staff of Law. To tempt her, he had said, *There is a service which I am able to perform for you, and which you will not obtain from any other living being.*

Nevertheless she did not hesitate. Unfurling plumes of fire from her Staff, she began to tune her percipience to the exact pitch and timbre of the Fall. Her private rages and bereavements had no significance now. The Woodhelvennin were still in peril, and they had already lost too much.

If Esmer sought to destroy the Harrow, he did not do so for Linden's benefit, or for the Land's. In him, aid and betrayal were indistinguishable. Perhaps he saw some threat to one of his ruling compulsions in the Harrow's proposed *service*. If so, she needed to know more about the Insequent.

With the back of her neck, she felt the villagers stumbling slowly westward. They did not resist the shepherding of the Masters and the Ramen. But there were too many of them – and too many were still in shock. Their progress was sluggish, hampered by grief.

The *caesure* was no more than a stone's throw for a Giant away: it towered over her, feral and deadly. The Harrow raced less than ten strides ahead of it, and the gap was narrowing– If she ran out of time, she would be devoured by the conflagration of instants.

She could do this, she told herself. She had done it before. And Esmer's storm did not camouflage the *caesure*, or confuse her health-sense. If anything, his efforts to flail the Fall only emphasised its specific ferocity.

Muttering, '*Melenkurion abatha*,' she raised Law and Earthpower in sunlight flames to meet the impending chaos. '*Duroc minas mill.*' In one sense, every Fall was different: it occurred in a different place; shattered different fragments of time. But in another, they were all the same, and she knew them well. '*Harad* khabaal!'

Fervid as a bonfire, her power geysered into the heavens.

The Harrow gestured at her frantically, urging her to rescue him. Lightning in fatal bursts blasted the dirt between her and the destrier. Concussions of thunder shook the ground. Each searing bolt liquefied the shale and flint, leaving molten pools where it struck.

'*Anele!*'

Liand's yell nearly broke Linden's concentration. She felt the old man fling himself headlong from Hrama's back; felt him hit the stony soil rolling, wild to escape the *caesure* or the storm, she did not know which. With every nerve, she sensed the eruption of bitter magma that took hold of him.

Instantly Stave wheeled Hynyn away from Linden. At the same time, Liand sprang after Anele, still shouting.

She had no choice: she could not stop Kastenessen now. If she did not quench the Fall, she would do nothing ever again.

Fear for Anele hampered her – and for Stave and Liand as well. Kastenessen would savage the old man; but he would not kill a vessel that could still serve him. Stave and Liand were another matter. The insane *Elohim* might incinerate them.

Nevertheless Linden had grown stronger, annealed under *Melenkurion* Skyweir. And Caerroil Wildwood's runes defined her Staff; sharpened its black possibilities. Hindrances of which she had been unaware had been carved away. Between one heartbeat and the next, she gathered Law and flame into a detonation as great as any that Esmer had unleashed. Shouting the Seven Words, she hurled Earthpower into the core of the *caesure*.

Time seemed to have no meaning. For an instant or an eternity, she threw her fire at the Fall; and the Harrow raced towards her in a fever of dread; and dire lava gathered at her back. Lightning coruscated near Hyn's hooves. The *caesure* appeared to swell as though it feasted on flame.

Then she felt the sudden brilliance of *orcrest* behind her.

Through Liand's glaring light, the storm thundered in a voice like a convulsion of despair, 'Wildwielder, *do not!*'

Abruptly Kastenessen's lava imploded, sucked back into itself.

As if fetters had been struck from her limbs, Linden felt freedom and energy surge through her. Almost calmly, she thought, No, Esmer. Not until I know what's at stake. Not until one of you bastards tells me the truth.

With Law and Earthpower and repudiation, she lit a deflagration in the Fall's heart and watched while the tumult of sundered instants swallowed itself whole. Like the scoria of Kastenessen's rage, the migraine tornado appeared to consume its own substance. Moments before the *caesure* caught the heels of the Harrow's mount, the fabric of time was rewoven; restored where it had been rent.

Briefly Esmer's storm became a stentorian wail of frustration and dismay. Then it started to fray as though intangible winds were pulling it apart. Swirling like the Fall, lightning and thunder dissipated, drifting away towards all of the horizons simultaneously.

The Harrow hauled at his horse's reins; stopped short of a collision with Linden. At the same time, Esmer stepped out of the air behind the Insequent. Gales seething in his eyes, Cail's son strode forward as if he meant to assail the Harrow as he had once attacked Stave.

In Esmer's presence, Linden's viscera squirmed with an almost metaphysical nausea. But she ignored the sensation. Turning her back on both men, she looked for her friends.

Fifteen or twenty paces away, in the middle of the *caesure's* wide gall, Stave stood on the pane of slate, holding Anele upright and unconscious against his chest. On his knees near them, Liand cupped his quenched Sunstone in one hand and gazed at it in wonder, studying it as if he were amazed that the flesh had not been scalded from his fingers.

In the distance beyond them, the Masters and the Ramen continued herding the villagers into motion, a pitiful few on horseback, the rest walking. Frightened and distraught, men, women and children trudged away from the wreckage of First Woodhelven in the general direction of Lord's Keep. As a group, they radiated numbness and misery that ran too deep for utterance.

She could not help them: not with Esmer advancing on the Harrow behind her. In another moment, they might begin to lash at each other – or at her – with forces as lethal as the Fall's.

Gritting her teeth, she returned her attention to Liand, Stave and Anele.

When she had assured herself that Liand and Stave were unharmed, and that Anele was only asleep, apparently exhausted by mere moments of possession and imposed sanity, she asked unsteadily, 'How did you do that? Why aren't you hurt?'

Liand still stared at his hand and the Sunstone as though they astonished him. 'I would not have credited it,' he breathed. 'In my heart, I believed that my hand would be destroyed, and perhaps the *orcrest* with it. But when I touched the stone to Anele's forehead, the conflagration within him ended. In some fashion that I do not comprehend, Kastenessen has been expelled.'

'I can't explain it.' Liand's success confounded Linden. She had hoped only that an imposed sanity might forestall Kastenessen's violation. She had not expected Liand to exorcise the *Elohim* once Kastenessen had established his possession. Perhaps contact with *orcrest* enabled Anele to draw upon his inborn magic. 'I'm just glad that you're all right. All of you.'

'Chosen,' Stave said distinctly, warning her, 'attend.'

Instinctively she looked to the Woodhelvennin again. They had stopped moving; stood crowded together on the near side of the brook. Most of them now faced in her direction.

Both the Humbled and the Ramen were galloping swiftly towards her.

Cursing, Linden wheeled Hyn to meet the threat of the Harrow and Esmer – and saw that a multitude of ur-viles had appeared as if they had risen suddenly out of the gouged dirt, accompanied by a much smaller number of Waynhim. Sunshine on the obsidian skin of the ur-viles made them look like avatars of midnight, stark as fuligin. The greyer flesh of the Waynhim had the colour of ash and exhaustion.

They were the last of their kind—

Shit, she thought. Of course. Ur-viles, Waynhim – and Esmer. *It is their intent to serve you.* They had come for her sake. *They watch against me*—

In spite of their distrust for each other, Cail's son had brought several score of them out of the distant past. And they had earned her faith. Now she did not know whom Esmer was trying to betray.

United as if they had forgotten their long enmity, the ur-viles and Waynhim had formed themselves into two fighting wedges, one led by their only loremaster, the other by a small knot of Waynhim. Barking raucously to each other, the creatures in one wedge faced Esmer. The other formation confronted the Harrow.

The loremaster held an iron sceptre or jerrid that fumed with vitriol. The Waynhim brandished short curved daggers that looked like they had been forged of lucent blood.

Both men had stopped. Esmer stood with his fists clenched. His cymar billowed around him as if it were being tugged by winds which Linden could not feel. Spume rose like vapour from the dangerous seas of his eyes. His limbs seemed to quiver with suppressed outrage and alarm.

'Wildwielder,' he said in a voice like a blare of trumpets, 'you do not know the harm that this Insequent desires. In another moment, the *caesure* would have taken him, and you would have been spared much. It was madness to redeem him.'

Closer to Linden, the Harrow sat his destrier with an air of deliberate nonchalance, although he was breathing heavily and sweat stood on his forehead. From the symbols on his boots to the beads in his leathern doublet, he was a figure of sculpted muscle and casual elegance. The ploughshare clasp which secured his chlamys emphasised the neatness of his hair and beard. And the hues of his raiment harmonised with the moisture-darkened shades of his destrier's coat. Only the lightless depths of his eyes suggested that he had not accidentally wandered into the Land from some more courtly realm where a munificent king or queen presided sumptuously over lordlings and damsels bright with meretricious grace.

'Lady,' he said, inclining his head. 'Your intervention was indeed timely.' His voice had not lost its loamy richness, in spite of his exertions.

'I see with pleasure that you have elected to accept my companionship.'

His quirt had disappeared. He must have concealed it somewhere under his short cloak.

Tightening her grasp on the Staff, Linden forced herself to look away again. 'Stave,' she said over her shoulder, 'the Woodhelvennin need to keep moving. They have to get out of here.'

Kastenessen had touched Anele. He knew where to send the *skurj*.

Stave glanced towards the approaching riders, then met her gaze. Through the tumult of hooves, he replied, 'The Masters comprehend this. They will not neglect their care for the folk of the Land. The villagers will be urged away. If any remain living when this peril has passed, they will be escorted to Revelstone.'

The ur-viles and Waynhim continued their rasping growls and coughs, cautioning Linden or threatening Esmer and the Harrow in a tongue as indecipherable to her as the language of crows.

'All right.' Slowly Linden faced Esmer and the Harrow once more. With both hands, she gripped the Staff, anchoring herself on Law and Earthpower, blackness and runes. 'You've had your fun. Now it's my turn. You both want something from me, but you aren't going to get it this way.

'No,' she said to the Insequent, 'I *don't* accept your companionship. But you don't care about that. If you did, you wouldn't have led Esmer *here*,' where so many innocent and helpless people might have lost their lives – and might yet die if she did not find a way to defuse the danger. 'In a minute, you can justify yourself by telling me why Esmer wants you dead.' As if she were fearless, she glared into the dark tunnels of his eyes. 'Right now, you can keep your mouth shut.

'As for you,' she flung at Esmer, 'if you think that you absolutely *need* to destroy the Harrow, you could have found some other way to do it. You didn't have to drive him straight towards those poor Woodhelvennin. I don't care how much he scares you. This is just another betrayal.'

Esmer's face held a torrent of protests and indignation. But when she said the word 'betrayal' he flinched visibly, and his anger collapsed into consternation, as if she had touched a hidden vulnerability; a concealed self-abhorrence.

'So tell me—' Linden was about to say, Tell me about this *service* that he claims he can perform. But then she changed her mind. Esmer feared the Harrow's intentions; therefore he would refuse to explain them. Instead she finished, 'Tell me what the ur-viles and Waynhim are saying.'

Amid a clatter of hooves, the Humbled and the Ramen drew near. Immediately Mahrtiir rode to her side, and Bhapa joined her opposite the Manethrall. Mahrtiir's gaze was fierce, eager to repay First Woodhelven's ruin, but the plight of the villagers lined Bhapa's visage.

In a flash of brown limbs and grace, Pahni jumped down to help Liand and Stave boost Anele onto Hrama's back. Then the three of them remounted their Ranyhyn; and Stave brought Hynyn forward to guard Linden with Mahrtiir and Bhapa.

The ur-viles and Waynhim may have been asking Linden what she wanted them to do.

'I am able to interpret their speech as well as the *mere*-son,' said the Harrow with a suggestion of smugness. 'Though they recognise that you do not comprehend them, they strive to inform you that I possess the knowledge to unmake them. Also they fear my purpose, just as they fear my attacker's. In the name of their Weird, however, they will give of their utmost to preserve you, ignoring the certainty of failure and doom.'

Linden stared at him. 'Wait a minute. You understand them?'

She had made a promise to the Waynhim and the ur-viles. If the Harrow could kill them all—

'Lady,' he replied, 'I repeat that I have made a considerable study of such beings. I have pored over the Demondim, as you know, but also over both their makers and their makings. These spawn are corporeal. Therefore they are not as readily unbound as the Demondim. Yet they may be erased from life by one who has gleaned the secrets of their creation.

'Behold.'

With one hand, the Harrow performed a florid gesture as if he were drawing mystic symbols in the air. With the other, he stroked the umber beads of his doublet.

Suddenly one of the ur-viles at the edge of the wedge near him slumped. As he gestured, the creature appeared to sag into itself as if it were being corroded by its own acrid blood. In moments, it had become a frothing puddle of blackness in the ploughed dirt and shale.

From Esmer came a sound like the sighing of water over jagged rocks. A blast seemed to gather around him as if he were mustering seas.

'They will wield dark theurgies against me,' said the Harrow like a shrug. 'However, I am not troubled. I have expended much to garner difficult knowledge. It will suffice to ward me.'

What I seek, lady, is to possess your instruments of power.

Far too late, Linden shouted, '*Stop* that! God damn you, I *promised* them!' The liquid remains of the ur-vile bubbled and steamed, denaturing quickly. Soon it had evaporated. 'Do it again, and I'll *make a caesure* for Esmer to use against you!'

She was bluffing: she could not draw on Covenant's ring while Esmer stood nearby. Cail's son knew it. She gambled that the Insequent did not.

In response, he laughed. 'A dire threat, lady, but empty. You are known to me. Your desire for the service which I am able to perform will outweigh other avowals.'

'Then,' Linden snapped hotly, 'you had better explain yourself. And make it fast. If you know me even half as well as you think, you know that I'm *sick* of being manipulated. *I am not going to put up with it.*'

He had already cost her the Mahdoubt. He had put the villagers in danger to obtain her aid against the Fall; to coerce her. Now he had slain an ur-vile. And by summoning the Demondim, Esmer had caused the deaths of dozens of Masters, ur-viles and Waynhim. He had helped Roger and the *croyel* snatch her out of her proper time. Clearly he had been willing to cause the deaths of the Woodhelvennin in order to snare the Harrow.

Moving slowly, Liand brought Rhohm to Mahrtiir's side. In his hand, he still cupped the *orcrest*. The Sunstone shone again: it burned like a clean star in his palm, brilliant and ineffable. Its white light seemed to exalt him, limning both his youth and his resolve.

'Perhaps a test of truth, Linden?' he suggested. His voice shook, but his hand held steady.

Behind Linden, Pahni radiated apprehension. Yet she stayed with Anele, watching over the old man while he slept on Hrama's back.

'*No!*' Esmer shouted in a voice that resounded as though it echoed back to him from tall cliffs. 'Uncaring Insequent, your purpose is an abomination!' Energy accumulated around him, imminent and potent. If he released it, it would hit like a cyclone. 'You *will not* speak.'

The Harrow cocked a scornful eyebrow. 'How will I be prevented? Your power is great, *mere*-son. You have inherited much. Doubtless I might be slain, were I unable to step aside. Yet here there is no *caesure* to constrain me. Undisturbed by such forces, I may pass where and how I will. Strike as you choose. I will not remain to receive your blow.'

'Flee if you dare,' countered Esmer. 'I am the descendant of *Elohim*. I will harry you to the outermost verge of the Earth.'

'You will not,' the Harrow snorted. 'You are bound to the lady. Also you are no true *Elohim*. Your mortal blood cannot withstand her Staff. She will defend me because she must. She greatly desires my service. And when her fire is raised against you, it will scour you to the marrow of your bones. If you do not perish, you will be made helpless, for good or ill.'

Esmer's and the Harrow's threats were loud. Linden spoke softly. 'A test of truth. I like it.' *I wish I could spare you. Hell, I wish any of us could spare you.* The thought that she might be risking Liand's life made her heart quail, but she betrayed no hesitation. 'Does one of you want to volunteer? Should I choose for you?'

She had no idea what would happen. As far as she knew, both Liand and the *orcrest* would crumble. But she needed to counter the animosity between Esmer and the Harrow. She had to understand their fear or loathing of each other. And she wanted at least one of them to give her an honest explanation.

She thought that she saw a flicker of uncertainty in the shrouded emerald of Esmer's gaze. His incipient storm wavered. And the Harrow seemed troubled by her proposal.

Or by something else—

Unexpectedly Galt announced, 'It is needless to hazard the Stonedownor, or the *orcrest*.' He and the other Humbled had joined Linden's defenders. He spoke to her, although his gaze was fixed on the Harrow. 'This Insequent has defeated us once. But he has forgotten that Brinn of the *Haruchai* surpassed *ak-Haru Kenaustin Ardenol* in single combat. Knowing the Harrow, we will not again fail against him.'

Linden expected Esmer and the Harrow to react with scorn; but she was wrong. Suddenly vindicated or alarmed, Esmer took a few steps backwards. Ignoring Galt, the Harrow turned the caves of his eyes to the east, past Linden and her companions.

With an air of insouciance, the Insequent informed the empty air, 'This is a petty chicane. You are indeed reduced without the aid and knowledge of the *croyel*. I concede that your glamour is potent, extending as it does to conceal so many. But such ploys do not become you. If you claim the stature to stand among this company, more valour will be required of you.'

'Talk's cheap, asshole,' retorted Roger.

Twenty or thirty paces in the direction of the Harrow's gaze, Covenant's son appeared as if he had stepped through an imperceptible portal.

'Run while you can,' he continued. As he unveiled himself to her senses, Linden felt the seething rage of his right hand, Kastenessen's hand; magma and fury free of dross, distilled down to their essential savagery. 'If you don't, I'm going to fry your bones. Then I think we'll all *eat* that silly horse of yours.'

He did not have Jeremiah with him. Still Linden's heart ached as if she had been spurned.

'Indeed?' The Harrow's tone was a snarl of mockery. 'The lady will not permit it. And I will aid her against you, as will these many Demondim-spawn.'

'I *know*,' Roger spat. 'That's why I didn't come alone.'

With a gesture that left a reeking wail across Linden's sight, he unwrapped his glamour from an army of Cavewights.

Instinctively she cried out for power; and the Staff answered with a clarion spout of flame.

She had seen such creatures before, in the Wightwarrens under Mount Thunder. They were formed for delving, with huge spatulate hands like mattocks and heads that resembled battering rams; disproportionately long scrawny limbs; hunched torsos and protruding ribs. Standing erect, they were nearly as tall as Giants. Because their arms and legs were so thin, she might have expected them to be weak; but she already knew their strength. Although they could crawl in improbable spaces, they were mighty diggers, able to gouge and crush rocks in their fingers. Their heavy jaws may have been capable of chewing stone. The ruddy heat of the Earth's depths filled their eyes like molten granite.

Roger Covenant had brought at least two hundred Cavewights with him, ready for battle. They wore crude armour fashioned from thick plates of stone lashed together. And they were all armed. Some bore spears and bludgeons: others hefted hacking broadswords as brutal as claymores.

Linden had expected the *skurj*, not Roger and Cavewights. But she had told him that she planned to head for Andelain. He could assume that she would essay the most direct route from Revelstone. Certainly he had had plenty of time to position his forces. And Kastenessen had touched Anele: the *Elohim* knew precisely where she was.

Like Esmer, Roger meant to block the Harrow's intentions. If Covenant's son – and therefore Kastenessen – had wished only to prevent her from reaching Andelain, he would not have come when other powers might defend her.

The *skurj* might not be far behind—

Linden's flame rose higher, leaping into the heavens.

As if on command, Hrama and Naharahn brought Anele and Pahni close to Linden. Liand was pushed towards her as Stave and the Humbled quickly formed a cordon around the most vulnerable members of their company. At the same time, Mahrtiir and Bhapa charged at Roger and the Cavewights, two against two hundred—

In the distance, the Woodhelvennin watched the onset of battle. The Masters among them may have urged them to flee. If so, they paid no heed.

Desperately Linden prepared a scourge of fire. But she could not choose a target: she was torn between her rage at Roger and her frantic desire to protect the Ramen.

Narunal and Whrany pounded towards the army. The Cavewights responded with a cacophonous shriek. From Roger's right hand came a spew of hot theurgy like a bolt of fluid stone. It would have slain the two Ranyhyn and their riders instantly; *should* have slain them. Yet Narunal and Whrany veered aside, supernally swift, as if they had foreseen Roger's attack. His blast hit the ground, sending an eruption of flint and shale into the air, charring the dirt as if the soil were leaves and twigs. It did not touch flesh.

A heartbeat later, the Manethrall and his Cord sprang from their

mounts with their garrotes ready. They leapt past two of the leading
Cavewights; wrapped their weapons around the Cavewights' necks as
they passed. Their momentum jerked the cords taut. Then they stood
on the backs of the creatures, using the strength of their legs to strangle
the Cavewights.

Mahrtiir's opponent reached up with both hands to snatch the
Manethrall from its back. But before the long fingers found Mahrtiir,
Narunal reared, slamming his hooves into the creature's chest. As the
Cavewight toppled backwards, its neck snapped. Mahrtiir dropped to the
ground, unscathed amid an enraged throng of creatures.

Whrany endeavoured to give Bhapa similar aid, but the vicious thrust
of another Cavewight's spear forced the Ranyhyn to dance aside. Then
Whrany whinnied sharply: a warning. As the creature that Bhapa was
trying to throttle grabbed for him, the Cord released his grip and jumped
towards his mount – and a bludgeon which would have crushed him
struck the Cavewight's skull instead.

Now Linden burned to defend the Ramen. Mahrtiir was about to be
trampled: a spear would spit Bhapa if a swinging broadsword did not
catch Whrany first. But Roger had already mustered another quarrel of
magma. If she did not strike at him—

'Linden!' Liand yelled.

Instantly she was surrounded by flaring powers and combat.

Behind her, the ur-viles and Waynhim had rearranged themselves into
three wedges. One hurled a lurid splash of vitriol at the Harrow. Another
struck Esmer with concussions like the spasms of an earthquake. And
from the third, a volley of blackness roared over Linden's head to fall,
howling, towards Roger. He was compelled to redirect his blast so that
he would not be incinerated.

The Harrow seemed momentarily surprised by his danger. Wherever
he was struck, his chlamys, doublet and leggings caught fire. But with
one hand he swept the flames away: with the other he rubbed his beads
in an intricate pattern. Then he began to gesture urgently, muttering
incantations.

No more acid touched him, although the loremaster's wedge assailed
him furiously, barking like maddened dogs. Instead the corrosive fluid
evaporated before it could bite into him.

Behind the loremaster, ur-viles began to drop one by one, sagging into themselves as though they were being eaten alive by their own lore.

Esmer stood upright to meet the concussive assault, and his eyes gleamed like the glare of lightning on the waves of a bitter sea. He made no effort to defend himself. Rather he accepted each crash and detonation, although they shook him as if they struck his bones. In spite of his obvious pain, he ignored the wedge attacking him.

As he had in the Verge of Wandering, and again on Revelstone's plateau, he caused the ground to erupt like water into spouts and squalls. Dirt and broken stone became little hurricanes which swirled upwards as if they had been spewed forth by the earth. Waving his arms, he sent towering geysers, not against his assailants, but towards the Harrow.

The Harrow had said that he could *step aside* from Esmer's power; yet he did not. He may have been snared by the force of the ur-viles – or by the imminent threat of Roger's might.

Linden felt the Cavewights rushing at her. Instinctively she turned Earthpower on them, whirling the Staff around her head to flail the creatures with flame. The Cavewights wielded no magic except their own strength and weapons: alone, they were no match for the ur-viles and Waynhim. But the Demondim-spawn were fighting three other antagonists at once. They had no theurgy to spare for the Cavewights.

In one place, the charge of the Cavewights was occluded by the Ramen and their Ranyhyn. From the ground, Mahrtiir dodged blows and kicks, avoided stamping feet. At the same time, he contrived to trip creatures with his garrote. In the confusion, Cavewights trying to slash or gut him often hit each other instead. And Narunal reared to his full height, lashing out powerfully with his hooves. Meanwhile Bhapa had urged Whrany among the creatures around Mahrtiir. Whrany delivered kicks with uncanny accuracy as Bhapa sprang away. The Raman wrapped his cord around a broadsword-wielding Cavewight's arm and used his own weight and the creature's fury to redirect the blade so that it cut at other attackers.

The efforts of the Ramen and their mounts slowed one small section of the charge, leaving Linden free to fling fire and desperation at nearer foes. She could strike there without endangering her friends.

Yet a dissociated reluctance hampered her. Surely she was still a healer?

Surely she still loathed war and killing? But she had found new aspects of herself on Gallows Howe; had become a woman whom she hardly knew: she yearned to repay with death the affront of her foes. Images of the *croyel* feasting on her son's neck demanded recompense.

Her own eagerness for bloodshed dismayed her. Apart from their sheer numbers, the Cavewights had no defence against the power of her Staff. She could slaughter them too easily. In spite of her companions' peril, she unleashed only a portion of her full strength. She ached to fling it at Roger rather than at the brute rampage of the creatures.

Nevertheless she fought. Mahrtiir and Bhapa might be slain in moments. Already the Ranyhyn bled from several wounds, and both Ramen had been hurt. They needed her; needed more violence from her than she knew how to countenance. She could not save the Ramen unless she overcame her chagrin.

If Roger struck at her now—

Liand might be able to defend himself with the *orcrest*, perhaps by blinding a few assailants. Pahni might find some way to keep Anele alive briefly. But they would not survive for long.

'Stave!' Linden panted. '*Stave.*' But it was Branl and Galt who answered her.

Leaving their Ranyhyn behind to aid in the last defence, the two Humbled sprinted on foot towards the chaos clustered around Mahrtiir and Bhapa. They seemed as mighty as Giants as they hammered into the fray. With heavy punches and iron kicks and slashing elbows, they attacked the knees of the Cavewights. And when the creatures fell, squealing in pain, Galt and Branl battered their throats.

Igniting creatures until they burned like torches, Linden tried to see what happened to the Humbled and the Ramen. But the rest of Roger's army continued to surge towards her, and she could not afford to let her concentration slip.

Roger ignored the damage to his army. Now he seemed to counter the roaring blackness of the Demondim-spawn with dismissive ease. The power blazing from his right fist increased moment by moment as if Kastenessen fed it; as if the *Elohim* channelled more and more of his scoria and anguish through Roger. And as Roger drove back the assault of the ur-viles and Waynhim, he also sent shafts of rage at the Harrow.

A spear arched through the air, plummeting towards Linden. Stave knocked it aside without apparent effort. Frantically she struggled against her consternation to pour more and still more passion into the Staff's yellow fire.

Embattled, the Harrow began to give ground. When she risked a glance behind her, however, Linden saw that the Insequent fought only Roger and Esmer. The acid of the ur-viles no longer reached him. He gestured furiously with one hand and shouted commands to ward off Roger's blasts. With the other, he sketched arcane symbols in an attempt to quash earthen geysers. Frenzy filled the emptiness of his eyes. Yet the black theurgy of the ur-viles did not endanger him, although their loremaster still flung gouts of vitriol. Esmer's efforts to hurt the Harrow disrupted the attack of the Demondim-spawn.

Esmer—?

He could have attacked the Harrow from any direction. At first, Linden thought that Cail's son chose an angle of assault which blocked the magicks of the ur-viles because he did not wish to share the Harrow's death with them: he craved it for himself – or for Kastenessen. But then she saw the truth. While he assailed the Harrow, Esmer continued to leave himself exposed to the shattering concussions of the third wedge; and they were weakening him. Blood haemorrhaged from his mouth with every breath. His arms and legs were livid with detonations and bruises. His cymar hung in tatters. As a result, his force was simply not great enough to overwhelm the Insequent. Yet he accepted his own hurts in order to concentrate his waning puissance on the Harrow.

In fact, he appeared to be *protecting* the Demondim-spawn. The Harrow needed too much of his mystic knowledge to survive Roger's magma: the added threat of Esmer's swirling bombardment prevented him from unmaking any more of the ur-viles.

Aid and betrayal. Even here, the son of Cail and the Dancers of the Sea could not pick a side.

In spite of Linden's fire, the leading Cavewights drew nearer. Now Clyme charged to meet them, crashing into them with all of Mhornym's mass and might. A barrage of spears seemed to plummet as one towards Linden. Impossibly swift, Stave used one to strike the others down. The incessant clash of eldritch powers shook the ground. Hyn's hooves danced as she strove to provide Linden with a steady seat.

'*No!*' Linden howled, although she could hardly hear herself through the mad clangor and tumult of weapons, blows, screams. Nevertheless the ur-viles and Waynhim must have understood her; or understood what was happening better than she did. In unison, they stopped attacking Esmer. Turning their wedge, they began to hurl corrosion among the Cavewights.

The impact slowed the creatures' on-rush. And Linden set fires among them as if they were dried and brittle, primed for conflagration. Sickening herself, she wielded her flail of Earthpower. As long as Roger only defended himself from the Demondim-spawn while he tried to destroy the Harrow — as long as he did not strike at her and her mortal allies — she forced herself to fight his army instead of renewing the battle that had begun under *Melenkurion* Skyweir; instead of repaying him for his part in Jeremiah's pain.

In glimpses, she saw Mahrtiir and Bhapa; Galt and Branl; Clyme. The Ramen had neither the strength nor the speed of *Haruchai*: they certainly could not stand against the size and muscle of the Cavewights. Nonetheless they were experienced fighters, trained to protect the Ranyhyn with quickness and cunning. And their mounts fought for them. Gradually Galt and Branl on foot and Clyme on Mhornym lunged and dodged their way through the melee towards Bhapa and Mahrtiir.

They were all covered in blood, their own as well as the Cavewights'. The carnage among the creatures was terrible. Yet the Cavewights surged closer to Linden and her remaining defenders with every step and heartbeat.

At a word from Stave, Bhanoryl and Naybahn joined the battle for the sake of their riders, leaving only the former Master to protect Linden while Liand and Pahni guarded Anele.

Roger appeared to laugh, exulting in power. If he had turned his vehemence against the Waynhim and ur-viles, he might have butchered them all. But he was content to ward off their black lore while he strove to burn down the Harrow.

Again and again, the Insequent was driven back. If he had the ability to *step aside*, he could not use it: he was too hard-pressed by Roger's gleeful fury and Esmer's wounded assault.

Linden had no idea what a being as dangerous and greedy as the Harrow had done – or could do – to earn such enmity from Lord Foul's minions.

Still the wedge challenging the Harrow could not reach him through Esmer's ragged eruptions. Abruptly those ur-viles changed their objectives. In small groups of five or six, they began to peel away. Scampering on all fours, they sped to join the formation which fought the Cavewights.

They were too late – and the Cavewights were too many. Even Linden's desperation was not enough. In spite of the dark efforts of the Demondim-spawn, she and her last companions would soon be inundated. If Esmer and perhaps even the Harrow did not turn to aid her, she might not be able to keep herself alive. She would certainly not be able to preserve Stave and Liand, Pahni and Anele.

As far as she knew, the other Ramen and the Humbled were already dead.

While she transformed creatures into living, screaming firewood, a Cavewight hurled a bludgeon at her from a distance of no more than six or seven paces. She barely saw it before Hynyn sprang in front of Hyn, and Stave snatched the massive club out of the air. Using the weapon's velocity, he swung his arm to fling the bludgeon back at the Cavewight.

This time when Liand shouted her name, Linden looked at him; saw him pointing towards the Woodhelvennin.

They had been standing at some distance, watching in comparative safety. Now they were running towards the battle. They appeared to be yelling, although she could not hear them through the din. For an instant, she thought that they meant to join the fight; that the destruction of First Woodhelven had inspired them to strike back.

But then she saw a huge pack of *kresh* sweeping down on the villagers from the north. Easily the great yellow wolves leapt over or splashed through the brook. Men, women and children fled slaughter in the only direction open to them. The wolves would have run them down in moments if they had turned to either side.

Nevertheless they were caught between the battle and the *kresh*. Soon all of them would die.

The two Masters – the only defenders of the Woodhelvennin – had already thrown themselves at the pack. But they were only two. And their mounts were merely horses, not Ranyhyn. They would be engulfed almost immediately.

Despite the turmoil and frenzy around her, Linden felt the presence of a Raver among the *kresh*.

She knew that malign spirit well: it had once possessed her, seeking to desecrate her love for Covenant. It was *moksha* Jehannum, and it ruled the wolves, goading them until they were rabid for bloodshed.

She did not pause for thought. She had no time. An *Elohim* had warned the Land of *merewives* and *skurj* and *croyel*. He had spoken of a shadow upon the hearts of his people. He had foretold the threat of *the halfhand.*

And he had mentioned Sandgorgons—

Linden had seen his other prophecies fulfilled. Why not this one?

Distance has no meaning to such power.

Hardly aware of her own actions, she cried, '*Nom! We need you!*' Then she sent Hyn hurtling into the collision of theurgies, pounding through cataclysm towards the panicked villagers.

Instantly Stave and Liand joined her, and Pahni and Anele followed at her back, as if they – or their mounts – had known what she would do.

When Thomas Covenant had summoned Nom against the Clave, the Sandgorgon had taken some time to respond. The creature had been compelled to cross nameless oceans and uncounted leagues from *Bhrathairealm* and the Great Desert. If the same delay occurred now – assuming that Nom answered Linden at all – every human and horse in the valley, and perhaps every Demondim-spawn as well, would be dead before the creature appeared. Nevertheless she did not turn aside or look back. The straits of the Woodhelvennin drove her. For their sake, and to confront *moksha*, she could resolve the contradictions within her. With Law and Earthpower, she opened a passage through the battle. At Hyn's best speed, she raced northward.

She did not see the Harrow blanch as if he were appalled at what she had done. She only heard him call wildly, 'I am able to convey you to your son!'

He may have intended to break her heart.

Still she did not falter. She could not: at that moment, the need of the villagers outweighed every other consideration. Even her friends—Concentrating on the *kresh*, she felt rather than saw the Insequent allow his defences to collapse. Only her nerves recognised what was happening as he wrapped himself and his destrier in a different kind of knowledge and vanished.

Deprived of his immediate target, Roger gave a howl of rage. But he had other prey: he, too, did not pause. Whirling, he aimed lava and loathing at Linden's back.

She did not care. He had become incidental to her; a mere annoyance. At that moment, Gallows Howe and Caerroil Wildwood were incarnate in her. Like the Forestal, she had precious lives to defend. She only needed the Woodhelvennin to make way for her. If they did not – if they impeded her charge—

The *kresh* and the Raver were almost upon them.

Roger's first blast fell short, intercepted by roiling blackness: the ur-viles and Waynhim had adjusted swiftly to counter him. A heartbeat later, he was attacked by half or more of the surviving Demondim-spawn. The rest threw their lore against the Cavewights in an attempt to prevent Roger's army from following Linden.

But he was ecstatic with Kastenessen's power. In this time, his given hand could draw directly on its source: Kastenessen's savagery exalted him. The concussions and vitriol of his attackers he slammed aside with scornful ease. And his efforts to strike at Linden coerced them to spend their force in her defence rather than against him.

Then the Demondim-spawn themselves were assailed. In spite of his injuries and weakness, Esmer sent shocks through the ground to disrupt the formations of the Waynhim and ur-viles. He slew none of them; but his interference exposed them to the cruder force of the Cavewights. While Roger aimed his viciousness at Linden, his creatures hacked brutally at her defenders.

Almost screaming, Linden shouted the Seven Words until her Staff shone like an avatar of the sun's fire. Frantic men and women dashed out of her path, snatching their children after them. Pahni's young voice in a Ramen war-cry echoed the brilliance of Liand's *orcrest*. Stave's implacable mien promised death. Anele had awakened; but with the *caesure* gone, he clung to Hrama's neck and did not hinder the Ranyhyn or his friends.

The huge fierce wolves had already begun to tear down and rend the slowest of the villagers when Linden and her last companions crashed into the pack.

The Cavewights were thinking creatures: the *kresh* were not. The Raver was worse than any beast or creature. And the Woodhelvennin were as helpless as trees. They had children with them, *children*, and could not defend themselves. As if she had become mindless herself, she sent great waves and breakers of flame at the wolves, burning them by the score to misshapen lumps of flesh, charred and reeking.

But she barely saw individual *kresh*: she paid no attention to what became of them. She sought *moksha* Jehannum. If she could do it, she meant to light a conflagration that would end the Raver's cruelty forever.

Roger might have killed her then. She had no desire to defend herself – and no power to spare. In addition, Esmer had broken apart the wedges of the Demondim-spawn. Most of the ur-viles and Waynhim were fighting for their lives in small clusters: only a few remained to oppose Roger's scoria. While she rampaged among the *kresh*, she left herself as vulnerable as the villagers.

But Roger did not send his puissance against her. He could not. Before he could hurl another blast, half a dozen Sandgorgons smashed into the rear of his army.

Crushing Cavewights with ease, three of the Sandgorgons wrought havoc among Roger's forces while the rest attacked him directly.

Their strength dwarfed that of the Cavewights. Alone, Nom had once shattered Revelstone's inner gates; had gouged out a passage for Glimmermere's waters to quench the last of the Banefire. With Grimmand Honninscrave's help, Nom had shredded *samadhi* Sheol's spirit. Given time, half a dozen Sandgorgons could have levelled Lord's Keep entirely.

The weapons and desperation of the Cavewights could not wound them. The ur-viles and Waynhim scattered before them. And Esmer did not turn his power against them. Instead he quelled his spouts of dirt and stone, his tremors in the ground, as if he had acknowledged defeat – or achieved victory. Panting blood, he seemed to fold the air around him as he disappeared.

Roger would have been beaten to pulp if he had not turned all of his scoria and wrath against the Sandgorgons. Their blunt arms and pulverising might would have left no recognisable remains of his ordinary flesh.

Moksha Jehannum lashed the *kresh* to frothing madness; but the Raver eluded Linden. It was here and there throughout the pack, mastering the wolves, transmuting their natural fear of fire into ferocity. She feared that *moksha* would attempt to escape her by possessing one of the Woodhelvennin, forcing her to slay an innocent victim if she wished to harm the Raver. Therefore she wielded her fire like devastation, taking care only that she did not harm any human or *Haruchai* or Ranyhyn.

On one side of her, the brightness of Liand's Sunstone dazzled the *kresh* so that they gnashed and tore at each other blindly. On the other, Stave rode Hynyn and let the roan stallion fight for him while he watched over Linden. Behind them, Pahni clung to Anele with one hand, supporting him, keeping him close to her, while she used her garrote to whip away any wolf that sprang for Hrama or Naharahn.

Suddenly Stave reached down to snatch a Master out of a raging mass of wolves. Hynyn hammered with his hooves at the skulls and spines of *kresh* as Stave swung the *Haruchai* up behind him. The Master was badly rent, bleeding from many grim bites and gouges; but as soon as he settled himself against Stave's back, he kicked at every wolf that came within reach.

Of the other Master, Linden saw no sign. She did not know if Mahrtiir, Bhapa, the Humbled, or any of their mounts remained alive. But the villagers were behind her now, and she did not permit any kind of fear to inhibit her scouring flame.

Nevertheless, on some subcutaneous level of perception, she recognised that the Cavewights were being decimated. She felt them break as they died, shattered by the tremendous force of the Sandgorgons. And she sensed the precise instant when Roger's rage and frustration turned to terror. He burned the Sandgorgons until their hides bubbled and the bubbles burst, spilling viscid blood that stank of dire vitality; but he could not stop them.

He was about to meet the same doom which had fallen on his army: Linden knew that. But she did not pause to watch him fight for his life.

She was too busy killing. Too busy searching for the Raver so that she could at least try to unmake Lord Foul's ancient servant.

And she was nearing the outermost limits of her own endurance.

Gradually she began to flicker and fail. Consumed by the struggle to keep going – to seek *moksha* Jehannum with percipience and fire – she did not see Roger call the few remaining Cavewights to him, leap onto one of their backs and send them racing eastward away from the Sandgorgons.

With their long legs and their peculiar strength, the Cavewights ran as if they were as fleet as Ranyhyn. Perhaps the Sandgorgons could have caught them: the denizens of the Great Desert were also swift. But Roger had hurt all of the Sandgorgons to some extent. And he flung a terrible heat behind him as the Cavewights fled. The Sandgorgons did not give chase. Instead they began stamping to death any of their foes which they had merely crippled.

After Esmer's disappearance, the ur-viles and Waynhim had slipped away, vanishing as imperceptibly as they had appeared.

When finally the last two or three dozen wolves turned to flee, *moksha* Raver escaped among them, untouched by her flagging vehemence. Within moments, they had crossed the brook northward.

She wanted to pursue them; to go on raining down fire until she reached the Raver itself. But she could not. As the *kresh* fled, something within her broke, and she lost her grasp on Earthpower. Her flames guttered and faded in the dust of battle; the dust and the tarnished sunlight.

She had already gone too far beyond herself. She did not know how to go farther.

Chapter Seven:

An Aftertaste of Victory

In spite of her exhaustion and dismay, Linden tried to keep moving. But she was numb with killing; too profoundly weary to consider what she did. She did not go in search of her friends. She did not ask what had become of them. Instead, trembling, she fell back on years of training and experience: triage, trauma, emergency care. Her depleted spirit she focused on the needs directly in front of her.

Mutely she asked Hyn to bear her among the nearest of the fallen Woodhelvennin.

Some were dead. She ignored them. And some were so close to death that no power of hers would save them. She ignored them as well. But when she found a toddler clutched in his mother's arms, both savagely mauled, and both still clinging to life, she dropped down from Hyn's back, knelt beside them, and reached far inside herself to uncover a few faint embers of resolve.

As much as she could, Linden gave herself to the woman and her child.

I am able to convey you to your son.

After a few moments of Earthpower, the woman opened her eyes, gazed about her with dumb incomprehension. The toddler recovered enough to wail.

Linden looked to Hyn again.

The mare stood over a man whose right leg had been nearly severed. Terrible chunks had been ripped from his sides. But he, too, clung to life. Staggering towards him, Linden blessed or cursed him with frail flames until he began to feel his own agony, and she believed that he might live. Then she let Hyn guide her to another breathing victim of the *kresh*.

As she moved, stumbling, she passed the body of a Master. His flesh was a killing field, torn and bitten almost beyond recognition. Dead wolves were piled around him, blood seeping from their corpses to mingle with his and stain the churned soil. They were his legacy of service to the Land.

Hyn indicated an old couple who had fled holding hands. After they had fallen, they had continued to clasp each other as though that touch might keep them alive. Linden heard blood in their breathing, saw long gashes in their limbs and torsos. She would have passed them by, convinced that they could not be saved; but Hyn seemed to insist. Obediently Linden braced the Staff between them and dripped fire into them like a transfusion. The world tilted around her while she waited for some sign that she had not failed.

She was not the woman she had once been, the healer who had rushed headlong into Berek Halfhand's camp. Her battle under *Melenkurion Skyweir* had changed her. And here she had expended herself in bloodshed; drenched herself in it. She no longer knew what she meant when she called herself a physician.

Nevertheless the old man eventually lifted his head, coughing blood as he looked towards his companion. His wife? Linden did not know. But the woman stirred; tightened her grip on the old man's hand. Seeing her move, feeling her grasp, he smiled as if he no longer feared the consequences of his wounds.

—to convey you—

Weakly Linden reached into her pocket for the twisted remains of Jeremiah's red racecar. She closed her fingers on it, drew it out to look at it. Then she let the tilting earth lower her to the ground. Hardly conscious that she sat on a dying wolf, she peered at Jeremiah's ruined toy. It was all that she had left of him; and her heart had become stone.

—to your son.

The Harrow had destroyed ur-viles and Waynhim. More had been killed by the Cavewights. The Sandgorgons may have slain still more as they rampaged among Roger's army. She had made a promise to the Demondim-spawn. Now many of them were dead.

And the Harrow was gone.

The bullet hole in her shirt seemed a little thing, as trivial as the grass stains written on her jeans; but that small catastrophe had cost her both her life and her son. Around her, the price continued to mount.

There was movement nearby. The villagers wandered among the slain, haunted by death. Some of them searched for friends or families; lovers or elders or children. Others stumbled aimlessly, as though they had lost the meaning of their lives. Doubtless they had seen *caesures* before. They were acquainted with the depredations of *kresh*. But they knew nothing of calamities on this scale. The Masters had not prepared them—

Hyn nudged Linden, urging her to rise. There was work to be done. No one else could do it. But she had come to the end of herself. She stared at Jeremiah's toy and made no attempt to stand.

Liand and Pahni found her there. Inspired by some impulse of sanity and simple care beyond her conception, they had gone to pick through the wreckage of First Woodhelven. Now they returned, bearing waterskins, some broken bread and a small bundle of dried fruit. One of the waterskins held springwine.

While her friends watched, she drank both water and springwine greedily; ate bread until she felt strong enough to chew small bits of apple and fig. Such things could not relieve her deepest prostration, but they reduced her trembling and restored a measure of awareness.

I am able to convey you to your son.

When she regained her feet at last, she put away the racecar and resumed the labour that she had chosen for herself long ago.

Linden, find me.

She knew what Thomas Covenant and Jeremiah and the Land's plight required of her; but those burdens would have to wait. Guided by Hyn, she walked between the fallen, weaving kind fire into their wounds and gently burning away their agony. And Liand and Pahni went with her, supporting her efforts with *orcrest* and powdered flakes of *amanibhavam*, or with springwine and water.

Anele still rested along Hrama's neck, although he remained alert. His blind gaze regarded the Sandgorgons with apprehension. Yet he did not try to flee. Apparently he found the creatures less terrifying than a Fall.

Linden estimated that thirty or forty of the Woodhelvennin had been

ripped down before she struck the *kresh*. A third of them were already
dead: five or six more had passed beyond any succour except the solace
of the last sleep. With Liand's aid, and Pahni's, she retrieved the rest
from their worst wounds. Sepsis would be a serious problem later: the
fangs and claws of the wolves had left filth in every hurt. But she spent
her scant energies on only the most immediate damage. As she worked,
she slowly recovered her concern for Mahrtiir, Bhapa, the Humbled and
their Ranyhyn. When she had done what she could for the villagers
in a short time, with little strength, she asked Hyn to lead her to the
companions whom she had abandoned.

Even Galt, Clyme and Branl deserved more than she had done for
them.

Along the way, she came upon the other Master who had warded First
Woodhelven. His mangled left leg was only the most cruel of his many
injuries. Nonetheless Linden found him limping among his charges,
urging them to set aside their shock and attend to their fallen. Unable
to stand or walk without support, he had improvised a crutch from a
branch of the shattered banyan-grove. His pain was as vivid as the blood
pulsing from his leg.

His name, he informed Linden, was Vernigil. Stolidly he acknowledged
her intervention on behalf of the tree-dwellers. But when she offered to
treat his hurts, he declined. His wounds were honourable. He meant to
bear them honourably.

She was far too weary to protest. And she saw a certain logic in his
refusal. Those Woodhelvennin who were able to understand what he
had endured for them responded to the authority of his torn flesh.

Leaving the Master to live or die, Linden followed Hyn back towards the
battlefield where she had last seen Bhapa, Mahrtiir and the Humbled.

Vaguely she noticed that the Sandgorgons stood together on the far
side of the carnage. Stave was with them: he faced them as if he could
communicate with them. But she had no fortitude to spare for what
passed between them.

Her vision was a blur of fatigue. Yet she needed to watch where she
walked. The ground was littered with the corpses of Cavewights, their
long limbs jutting at odd angles where the bones had been twisted or
split. They baffled her senses: she might trip over them. And if she could

not *see*, she would be unable to find those whom she sought.

Fortunately Pahni's sight was keener; less bewildered by the ramifica-tions of slaughter. Abruptly she cried out in anguish. Racing ahead, she dropped to her knees amid the stench and confusion of the dead.

Liand hurried after her; but Linden could not hasten. She could only blink and stare, and try to find her way.

The Humbled waited near Pahni: they appeared to stand in attend-ance. Like Vernigil, they were all severely injured; cut and battered from scalp to shin. Runnels of blood flowed down their arms and legs. Yet they retained their wonted upright intransigence, as if neither pain nor death could touch them.

Now Linden saw four Ranyhyn there. She recognised Narunal. Bhanoryl, Mhornym and Naybahn were less familiar to her, but she squinted at them until she was sure. They, too, were gravely wounded; almost staggering with blood loss. But they, too, seemed to stand in attendance, as though they had come to pay homage.

They would let Linden treat them, if the Humbled would not. But it was possible that neither the great horses nor the *Haruchai* absolutely required her aid. In their separate fashions, the Ranyhyn and the Masters were preternaturally hardy. They might survive as they were.

Then Linden reached the place where Pahni and Liand knelt over Mahrtiir, Bhapa and Whrany. Pahni fought tears as she fumbled at her pouch of *amanibhavam*. Beside her, Liand's face was pale with dismay. The *orcrest* rested, inert and forgotten, in his fist. He could find no use for its magic here.

Bhapa huddled on his knees between the Manethrall and Whrany, beating his forehead on the blood-raddled ground. He did not permit himself to howl or weep, and so he had no other outlet for his pain. Peering at him, Linden discerned that he had suffered less physical dam-age than the Humbled or the Ranyhyn. He had a few broken ribs, a few slashes and contusions. Infection would kill him eventually: his injuries themselves would not. And a poultice of *amanibhavam* might suffice to save him, if Linden's stamina failed.

But Whrany was dead. The Ranyhyn's head had been almost severed from his body. His blood drenched Bhapa. The Cord wore it as if it were a winding-sheet.

Mahrtiir still breathed. That was unfortunate. Death would have been a kinder fate.

He lay on his back, gasping at the dusty reek of bloodshed. In spite of his Ramen toughness, he writhed as though he knew that he should not move – and could not restrain himself. He had been cut and pierced as severely as the Humbled; as often as the Ranyhyn. But some weapon, possibly a spear, had struck him near his left temple and carried straight through the front of his skull, ripping away both of his eyes.

Only countless hours in County Hospital's emergency room enabled Linden to study the Manethrall's face until she was sure that the bones behind his eyes remained essentially intact; that this wound had not reached his brain.

Unable to efface her weakness, she strove to ignore it. With desperation and willpower, a kind of grieving rage, she fanned embers of Earthpower into unsteady flames and spilled them over Mahrtiir until he was laved in fire.

In some sense, Linden was still a physician. She could not behold his suffering and remain passive.

Please, she prayed, although there was no one who might have heeded her. Please.

Please don't die.

Don't hate me for not letting you die.

The Manethrall had chosen to accompany her because he chafed against the predictable and unambitious lives of his people. He had craved a tale which would deserve to be remembered among the Ramen. And he had supported her with complete fidelity.

This was the result. He might live, but he would never see again.

Exhaustion left her defenceless: she could not control the intensity of her health-sense. It was empathy transmogrified into excruciation. She saw every detail of his torn tissues – flesh and muscle, nerve and bone – as if it were replicated in her own body. She could have counted every ripped blood vessel, numbered every delicate channel of lymph and mucus. And she descried precisely how each tiny increment of damage could be repaired by Earthpower and Law.

She did not have the strength for the task. Even if she had been fresh and ready – even if she had not done so much killing – she could not have restored his eyes. There was nothing left of them. But everything that was possible for her, she did, and more. When she began to falter, she reached out to Liand, mutely asking for his aid. Instinctively he gave her what she needed. Summoning light from the *orcrest*, he gripped her hand so that the Sunstone was pressed between his palm and hers.

With that influx of power, she brought Mahrtiir back from agony and the borderlands of death.

His breathing grew quieter in spite of his pain. Now Linden was the one who gasped. As she released Liand's hand, her surroundings seemed to turn themselves inside out, and she felt herself begin to fall.

But Bhapa surged to his feet and caught her in a fierce hug, ignoring his damaged ribs; staining her with Whrany's blood as well as his own. 'Ringthane,' he whispered, calling her away from collapse. 'Mane and Tail, Ringthane! My life is yours. It was so before. Now it is yours utterly.' She heard weeping in his voice. 'If the Manethrall and the Ranyhyn do not forbid it, I will accompany you into the depths of Gravin Threndor, or the inferno of Hotash Slay, or the bitter heart of the Sarangrave, and name myself blessed.'

She had no answer. She could bear neither his gratitude nor his sorrow. Mahrtiir would never see again. She had given the Manethrall a life of irredeemable darkness.

When Bhapa eased his embrace, she pulled away. '*Amanibhavam*,' she replied, panting raggedly. 'Poultices. Bandages. Stop the bleeding.' Mahrtiir had too many other wounds, and she had tended none of them. 'Then help the Ranyhyn.'

'Yes, Ringthane.' At once, Bhapa turned to obey.

Pahni had already set to work. Together the Cords mixed water with the crushed, dried blades of their potent grass to make a salve.

Helplessly Linden looked to Liand. Again he gave her what she needed. Supporting her with one arm, he lifted springwine to her lips. At the same time, he kept his *orcrest* alight. He may have hoped that the Sunstone's eldritch possibilities would lend vitality to the springwine.

His instincts had not misled him. As she drank, Linden tasted something akin to Glimmermere's lacustrine potency. If she could have bathed in the tarn, she might have been able to wash away the charnel stench of what she had done: the Cavewights burning like brittle sticks, the wolves scoured by sheets of flame– But Revelstone was too far away. She would find no healing there.

Nevertheless springwine and Liand's considerate exertion brought her back from the brink of herself once more. Soon she was able to leave Mahrtiir and the Ranyhyn to the ministrations of Bhapa and Pahni. The Humbled she consigned to their stubbornness. First Woodhelven's people needed more than she had done for them; far more.

There was a breeze blowing, some vagary of the undisturbed sunlight. Gently it carried the dust of battle and butchery away. But it could not shift the raw choleric stink of bloodshed, or the implications of Linden's inadequacy.

Liand offered to accompany her. She told him to find clean cloth for bandages instead. She felt as laden with death as the dirt of Gallows Howe. If she were alone, she might finally find tears for everything that had been lost.

But before she could move past Galt, Branl and Clyme towards the Woodhelvennin, Stave stopped her. Somehow she had failed to notice his approach.

'Chosen,' he said quietly, 'you must accompany me.' Like Liand, Pahni and Anele, he was unharmed. 'The Sandgorgons require your attendance.'

Linden gestured vaguely. 'I'm needed here.'

How was it possible that only those who had ridden with her against the *kresh* were whole?

Stave's gaze held her. 'Linden.'

His flat tone hinted at compassion. If he had ever used her given name before, she could not remember it.

'I'm not Linden.' She was dimly surprised to hear herself say those words aloud. 'I'm not her anymore. Somebody else took my place under *Melenkurion* Skyweir.'

The Harrow wanted to trade Jeremiah for the Staff of Law and Covenant's ring. Esmer and Roger would ensure that she had no opportunity to accept the Insequent's offer.

'Nonetheless,' Stave stated inflexibly, 'the Sandgorgons are insistent.' He was her only friend among the *Haruchai*. 'They will accept no reply except yours. If you do not comply, they will turn against the Wood-helvennin.'

Of course, she thought. Perfect. Just what we need.

She was still expected to choose who would live and who would not.

'All right.' Abruptly she addressed the Humbled. 'Before you bleed to death, you might as well make yourselves useful.' Her ire was not for them, but she made no attempt to stifle it. 'Liand is looking for bandages. We need hot water. Lots of it.' Surely cookpots and fabric could be found among the ruins of First Woodhelven? 'And get some hurtloam if you can. These poor people don't know what it is. They can't see it.'

Kevin's Dirt had deprived them of health-sense. The Masters had deprived them of knowledge.

Clyme nodded. At once, he, Galt and Branl limped away towards the shredded village. They looked like incarnations of pain: each step exacerbated their injuries. Yet they moved stolidly, undeterred by the cost of their actions.

Soon they were joined by a number of Woodhelvennin, sent by Vernigil to assist the Humbled.

For reasons of their own, Hyn, Rhohm and Naharahn galloped off in the direction of the brook. They may have been thirsty.

Shaking her head, Linden let Stave take her to face the Sand-gorgons.

They stood in a united cluster as if the six of them shared one mind. Apart from the wounds which Roger had inflicted on them – rank burns and boils that had already begun to heal – they matched her memories of Nom. Interminable ages of the Great Desert's iron sun had leached them of colour, leaving their hides the distressed whiteness of albinos. They were shorter than Cavewights, but much more powerfully formed, bred to withstand the harshest extremes of sand and heat and gales. Their knees flexed backwards, supported by the wide pads of their feet: they could traverse dunes and hardpan alike with tremendous speed.

However, their knees and hides were not their strangest features. Their arms did not include hands. Instead their forearms grew into flexible stumps like elastic truncheons, able to plough through sand or batter down stone. And they had no faces; no features of any kind apart from the subtle ridges of their skulls and two almost hidden slits that resembled gills where humankind and even Cavewights had ears. Like their forearms, their heads were made to crash against obstacles.

Linden remembered Nom well. But she had forgotten how much raw *force* a Sandgorgon contained. Alone, each of the creatures looked as irrefusable as a tornado. Together they seemed to reify the worst storms of the world. They were cyclones distilled to unmitigated havoc.

Long ago, Thomas Covenant had mastered Nom with wild magic and delirant resolve. At his command, Nom had crossed lands and oceans to aid him against Revelstone and the Clave. With Honninscrave's help, Nom had torn apart *samadhi* Sheol. Then, somehow, the Sandgorgon had consumed the scraps of the Raver's existence – and had thereby gained a form of sentience unknown to Sandgorgons: the ability to communicate as the *Haruchai* did, mind to mind. Millennia ago, Nom had exchanged understandings with the *Haruchai* who had fought at Covenant's side. Now, apparently, these creatures had been speaking to Stave.

'Much has transpired during the millennia of your absence, Chosen,' he said. 'I am informed that Nom returned to the Great Desert and Sandgorgons Doom bearing the rent fragments of *samadhi* Sheol's spirit. These had been forever torn from coherence, but they were not deprived of intention and malice. Nom distributed them among the Sandgorgons, giving to his kind faint remnants of the Raver's memories and lore and cruelty. Thus in small tatters the brutish minds of the Sandgorgons acquired knowledge.

'Across a great span of years, they learned to unmake the Doom in which Kasreyn of the Gyre had imprisoned them. And across a far greater span, they discovered purpose. A host of them, all those who share *samadhi* Sheol's spirit, have now come to the Land. For that reason, they were able to answer your call without delay.

'Of their host, these are but a few. The rest await the outcome of your summons.'

Linden frowned in confusion. 'I'm needed, Stave.' Bhapa had marked her with Whrany's blood, and his own. 'Get to the point.'

The former Master studied the Sandgorgons for a moment. Then he told Linden, 'They seek your acknowledgment that they have fulfilled your desire.'

As if so many deaths were not acknowledgment enough.

'Oh, hell.' Bitterly she looked around at the battlefield, the crushed and splattered bodies of the Cavewights. 'Sure. Of course.' This, too, was her doing. 'There's nothing left for them here. We can always get more corpses.'

They had threatened to attack the Woodhelvennin—

Her spirit also had been torn. But she resembled Esmer more than *samadhi* Sheol: she was appalled by what she had become.

She needed Thomas Covenant to make her whole.

In response, Stave's manner became more formal. 'Then they are done with you. You are not the ur-Lord. You did not defeat or compel Nom. But you are the last of his companions. In gratitude for the quality of mind which they now possess, they answered your summons. They will not do so again.'

Linden nodded, too weary and aghast to find words. She hardly understood what Stave was saying.

He lowered his voice. 'There is darkness in them, Chosen. Rent, *samadhi* Sheol's spirit yet clings to Corruption. They have beheld majesty in the Raver's visions of Doriendor Corishev, of kings and queens and rule. They have learned a hunger for suzerainty. In the Land, *samadhi's* thoughts assure them, they will know what it means to hold sway.

'They avow that if you oppose them, they will crush you as ferociously as they slew these Cavewights, and with the same joy.'

'I don't care.' Linden started to turn away. 'I just want them to do their crushing somewhere else.'

But then she stopped. Impulsively she suggested, 'Try telling them where Doriendor Corishev is.' Let them follow Doom's Retreat to the Southron Waste; away from the Land. She trembled to imagine what would happen if a host of Sandgorgons struck at Revelstone. 'If they want to "hold sway", they can start there. No one has held that region for thousands of years.'

Doriendor Corishev's rulers had made a wilderland of their kingdom. But the Sandgorgons were born to deserts, formed for harsh landscapes. They might like the Southron Waste.

Perhaps the fragmentation of *samadhi* Sheol's memories would prevent the Raver from directing the Sandgorgons elsewhere.

'Or if that doesn't work,' she added, 'tell them about the *skurj*. Tell them that those monsters are more powerful than they can imagine.' Perhaps the Sandgorgons could be taunted into defending the Land. 'If they want to rule *here*, they'll have to deal with Kastenessen's creatures.'

For a moment, Stave regarded her as if her advice surprised him. Then he turned back to the Sandgorgons.

Leaving him to be as persuasive as he could, Linden headed towards the tree-dwellers again.

While she stumbled among the bodies, however, the Ramen caught her attention. Unfortunately Mahrtiir was conscious. Linden wished him a respite from the enormity of his hurts. With the Staff, she might have imposed a little sleep on his wracked body and mind. But his life was in no immediate danger. Bhapa tended him diligently while Pahni did what she could for the Ranyhyn. And some of the Woodhelvennin had worse injuries. Simple triage required her to conserve her scant resources.

Liand, the Humbled, and a few villagers had emerged from the wreckage of the banyan-grove bearing bundles of garments for bandages. Three or four of them carried cookpots which could be used to heat water. In a moment, Liand rejoined the Ramen.

Although she ached for Mahrtiir, Linden pushed herself back into motion.

The Manethrall stopped her with a ragged croak. 'Ringthane.'

In spite of his agony, his health-sense enabled him to discern her presence.

'I'm here.' Linden's voice resembled his. 'You shouldn't try to talk. You've lost a lot of blood. And there isn't much that I can do about your pain right now.'

He shook his head as if he were wincing. 'My hurts are naught.' The shattered mess of his eye sockets wept slow drops of blood. 'I rue only that I am made useless to you.'

She tried to say, Mahrtiir, stop. But she could not force her mouth and throat to form words.

'Many needs press upon you,' he continued, wrenching speech past his wounds. 'I ask but one boon. There is no other Manethrall here, and a witness is required. I ask you to stand in the stead of those who lead the Ramen.'

A moment passed before Linden realised that Bhapa was whispering as if he were horrified, 'No. No. No.'

With an effort that felt like anguish, she managed to repeat, 'I'm here.' She may have been making another promise that she would be unable to keep.

Hoarsely Mahrtiir said, 'I am no longer able to bear the burdens of a Manethrall. Among the Ramen, those who have been blinded do not command the deeds of those who see. Cord Bhapa must assume my place. We cannot now perform the full ceremony of Maneing, but your witness will suffice.

'I ask Liand of Mithil Stonedown to remove the garland from my neck and set it upon Bhapa's.' His woven necklace of yellow flowers, *amanibhavam* in faded bloom, was splashed with blood. It hung in tatters, but had not been severed. 'Then he will take his long delayed place among the Manethralls, and I will serve him and you as I do the Ranyhyn, until my last breath.'

In dismay, Liand flung a look of appeal at Linden. He did not move to touch Mahrtiir's garland.

Mahrtiir, no. Linden could not find her voice. Please. I can't do this right now. I can't let you do it. If she had been able to speak, she might have said, This can wait. Then she might have turned away.

But Bhapa rushed to his feet. Softly, as if he were in tears, he cried, 'No, Manethrall. No. I will not. I am not fit for Maneing. And I cannot abide—'

Abruptly he wheeled towards Linden. His eyes were dry, but every line of his face resembled sobbing.

'Ringthane,' he said, pleading with her, 'do not permit this. It was not my tarnished sight – the sight which you have healed – that caused me to remain a Cord when others of my years had become Manethralls. It was my hesitancy. I bear uncertainties and doubts which consort ill with decision and command. I follow willingly. I am not suited to lead.'

Linden stared at him. She herself had uncertainties and doubts enough to cripple a legion. But she did not mean to let Jeremiah's suffering continue unopposed – or unpunished.

However, Bhapa seemed to need no answer from her. At once, he turned back to Mahrtiir.

'And you cannot so lightly set aside your tasks,' he told the Manethrall, 'or your yearning to be worthy of tales. You are merely hurt and blinded. You are not unmade. You are a Manethrall blood and bone. It determines you.

'Nor may you set aside the *geas* that was placed upon you.' The Cord's passion mounted. 'You were informed that you must go far, seeking "your heart's desire". And you were urged to return when you had found it, for the Land has need of you. Those words were not granted to me. They were for you alone.'

Anele had spoken to Mahrtiir on the rich grass of Revelstone's plateau. Linden believed that her friends had heard Thomas Covenant's voice through the old man.

Bhapa and Pahni had been given a different message. *In some way, you two have the hardest job. You'll have to survive. And you'll have to make them listen to you.*

'Manethrall Mahrtiir,' Bhapa concluded, 'I have obeyed you in all things. In this I will not.'

Mahrtiir bared his bloodied teeth. For a moment, he appeared to struggle with imprecations. An involuntary groan wrenched his chest. When he spoke, his voice was taut and raw.

'Then be Ramen, if you will not be Manethrall. Aid Pahni among the Ranyhyn. The needs of the great horses come foremost.'

Briefly he coughed, splashing his chest with arterial droplets. But Liand called up light from the *orcrest* and touched it to Mahrtiir's sternum. By degrees, Mahrtiir relaxed.

'And Liand tends me well,' he said: a brittle rustling like the sound of dried leaves in a breeze. 'I will not impose my garland upon you by perishing.'

Shamed in spite of her exhaustion, Linden found somewhere enough gentle fire to stop the Manethrall's bleeding and grant him sleep. For years, she had wept too easily. She wanted to weep now. But she could not. Her stone heart held no tears.

The Sandgorgons departed a short time later; pelted avidly into the east as if they were eager for more destruction. Presumably they were returning to their host. And when they were gone, Esmer reappeared.

He still wore his wounds and his shredded raiment. Perhaps his many powers did not include the ability to heal himself.

He did not approach Linden. He spoke to no one. Indeed, he seemed unaware that anyone watched him as he sent waves of force through the ground to gather up corpses: Cavewights and *kresh*; slain villagers. Intimidated by powers beyond their comprehension, the Woodhelvennin did not object.

Whrany's body he took as well: he made no distinctions among the fallen. Linden expected protests from the Ramen, but they said nothing. Even the Ranyhyn did not interfere. Instead the great horses called a kind of farewell, at once haunting and brazen, to their lost herd-mate; and Bhapa and Pahni bowed their foreheads to the ground.

When Esmer had pulled all of the dead together into a bitter mound, he called down lightning to set the pile ablaze. Then he wrapped the acrid reek of burning flesh and blood around him and vanished again. However, he left enough of his eerie force behind to keep the flames of the pyre roaring. Linden guessed that the fire would not burn down until it had consumed every scrap of slaughtered flesh.

Black smoke, viscid as oil, and sour as the fumes of a midden, rolled skyward. Fortunately the breeze tugged it away from the survivors. That, too, may have been Esmer's doing.

As soon as Cail's son removed himself, Stave returned to Linden. He said nothing about Esmer or the Sandgorgons. And she asked him nothing. Perhaps Esmer was grieved by the cost of the battle. Perhaps the Sandgorgons had gone to lead their host to Doriendor Corishev. It made no difference.

Taking Stave with her, she let him care for her with water, springwine and a little food while she exerted frail flames of Earthpower and Law among the Woodhelvennin.

She still had done nothing for the Ranyhyn. But Liand had added his efforts to Pahni's and Bhapa's. And the horses absorbed the white brilliance of his Sunstone gratefully. Earthpower in that form did not heal them; but they appeared to draw a different sustenance from it, as they did from *amanibhavam*, so that they became stronger in spite of their hurts.

Somewhere in the distance, Linden heard insistent whinnying. But she ignored it, and after a while it stopped. She did not grasp what it signified until Vernigil and a few villagers approached her bearing fired clay bowls redolent with the salvific savour of hurtloam. Apparently Hyn, Rhohm and Naharahn had galloped away to search along the brook for the healing sand. They had found a small vein in the washed streambed.

Vernigil's condition had improved visibly. Already some of the damage to his mangled leg had begun to repair itself. Yet Linden did not imagine that the Master had availed himself of the hurtloam's benison. Rather he had benefited from the humble act of carrying it.

The Woodhelvennin accompanying him were full of astonishment. They must have used their hands to scoop up the spangled sand; and Earthpower had come to life within them, banishing the pall of Kevin's Dirt. Now for the first time in their lives – the first time in unnumbered generations – they were able to *see*. They could not yet understand what had happened to them. Nevertheless they had been transformed.

Finally Linden allowed herself to rest. She touched the tip of one finger to the hurtloam, let its sovereign potency spread through her. Then she sank to the dirt and covered her face, leaving Stave and Vernigil to instruct the tree-dwellers in the use of the Land's largesse.

Later, she recovered enough to wonder why the Masters had permitted the Woodhelvennin to experience Earthpower; to discover health-sense and know what they had been denied.

In addition to the unremitting stench of the pyre, she smelled cooking. When she sat up and looked around, she saw that many of the villagers were busy at fires, using boughs and branches from their homes for fuel. Inspired, perhaps, by the miraculous recovery of their maimed and dying friends and families, they had emerged from their dismay to perform the necessary tasks of staying alive.

When she had observed them for a while, Linden saw that they were being organised by an old couple, the same man and woman whom she had aided at Hyn's insistence. She had not truly healed them: she had merely postponed their deaths. But they must have shared in the unequivocal efficacy of hurtloam. Although they were fragile and hurt, they walked among their neighbours, still holding hands as they sorted the Woodhelvennin into cooperating teams.

Hyn stood near Linden, watching over her rider. And soon after Linden sat up, Liand came to join her. Squatting comfortably on the shale and grit, he studied her for a moment to assure himself that she was physically unharmed. Then he, too, turned his attention to the villagers.

'I am told,' he remarked quietly, 'that the elders who lead them are named Heers. The customs of Woodhelvennin are strange to me.' He gave Linden a wry smile. 'I had not known that such folk inhabited the Land. But "by right of years and attainment"' – he quoted Handir good-naturedly – 'Karnis and his mate, Quilla, are the Heers of First Woodhelven. You did well to redeem their lives, Linden. They command respect among their people which the Masters do not. Vernigil nearly perished in their defence. His companion was slain. Nonetheless here the Masters appear to lack some increment of their stature in Mithil Stonedown. It was Karnis and Quilla rather than Vernigil who truly roused these folk from their bereavement.'

Linden sighed. 'The tree must have been wonderful. I wish I could have seen it. Maybe it affected them. Maybe they knew in their bones that the Land isn't as' – she grimaced reflexively – 'as superficial as the Masters wanted them to believe.'

The Masters had spent many centuries teaching the villagers to be unprepared for the peril and loss which had befallen them.

Yet now Stave's kinsmen had recanted? She did not believe it. Decades of *caesures* had not swayed the Masters: the terrible magicks of the Demondim and the Illearth Stone had not moved them. So why had Vernigil and the Humbled allowed the Woodhelvennin to touch hurtloam?

To some extent, she understood the Harrow. *I am able to convey you to your son.* The actions of Esmer, Roger and *moksha* Jehannum seemed explicable. But the Masters baffled her.

As the villagers prepared food, or searched through the grove's debris for the supplies that they would need in order to reach Revelstone, the sun sank towards late afternoon, drawing stark shadows across the stained ground. With Liand's help, Linden climbed wearily to her feet and went to check on the condition of her friends.

She was relieved to see that the Ranyhyn also had been given the benefit of hurtloam. The worst of their injuries were mending with remarkable celerity. Soon they would be able to bear their riders again.

And Mahrtiir and Bhapa had been treated with the gold-flecked sand as well. Although the Cord moved stiffly, and would no doubt feel the ache of his saft ribs for days, he was free of infection; no longer bleeding. Since the Ranyhyn no longer needed care, he and Pahni watched over their Manethrall.

Blessed by hurtloam, Mahrtiir slept deeply, and all of his wounds showed signs of swift healing. With strips of clean wool, the Cords had bandaged his gouged forehead and nose, as well as several deep slashes in his limbs and along his ribs. But first they had washed his eye sockets and cuts, removing dirt and chipped bone. Linden's health-sense assured her that he would live.

How his blindness would affect him was a different question.

Sighing again, she scanned the area for Anele. At first, she failed to spot him. But then Liand pointed at one of the cooking fires, and Linden saw the old man there amid a busy cluster of Woodhelvennin. He had dismounted beside the flames: apparently he was eager to eat. She felt a moment of trepidation on his behalf until she realised that Stave was with him. Gently but firmly, Stave kept Anele on the sheet of slate which protected him from Kastenessen.

Thank God, Linden thought wanly. Thank God for friends. Without Liand, Stave and the Ramen – without Anele and the Ranyhyn and the Mahdoubt – she would have been lost a long time ago. And all of her choices seemed to attract new enemies.

She must be doing something right.

Stave seemed to feel her gaze. When he had spoken to the villagers, presumably asking them to guard Anele, he left the fire to approach Linden and Liand.

The pyre was gradually burning itself out. But its grim smoke still tarnished the air, and Linden gauged that it would not sink down to coals until after nightfall.

As Stave drew near, she looked around for the Humbled. They stood like sentinels at separate points around the fringe of the lowland where the tree-dwellers were preparing to spend the night. They were too far away for her to see their faces, but even at this distance she could feel the concentrated harm of their untended wounds. It made them appear as forlorn as outcasts in spite of their unrelenting stoicism.

Stave greeted her with a deep bow which she accepted because she was too weary to refuse it. Still studying the Humbled, she said, 'I've seen Vernigil. He got a little healing, whether he wanted it or not. But what about them? Will they be all right?'

Stave did not glance at his former comrades. 'They are *Haruchai*. None of their hurts are mortal. And we are not prone to the corruption which devours flesh and life. They will not regain their full prowess for some days. But if we are spared a renewed assault—' With a shrug, he fell silent.

If Roger did not return with more Cavewights. If the Sandgorgons marched on Doriendor Corishev or the *skurj* instead of preferring easier victims, more immediate slaughter. If the Harrow did not appear again, drawing Esmer's storms with him. If *moksha* Raver could not gather more *kresh*.

If Kastenessen did not send his monsters—

Damn it. Linden would have to learn how to wield Covenant's ring. The Staff of Law was not enough.

Grimly she muttered, 'Then I guess we should hope that driving the Harrow away will be enough to satisfy Kastenessen and Roger,' Jehannum and Lord Foul. 'At least for the time being.'

Liand winced. 'Since the fall of Kevin's Watch,' he admitted, 'we have known incessant peril – and still I am not accustomed to it. I had not considered the likelihood of further battles' – he glanced around him – 'or the vulnerability of these Woodhelvennin when we are parted from them.'

Linden rested a hand on his shoulder, as much to steady herself as to reassure him; but she did not reply. Instead she asked Stave, 'Can you tell me why they haven't interfered?' With a nod, she indicated Clyme, Galt and Branl. 'Your people have worked long and hard to keep anyone from knowing about Earthpower. But now dozens of ordinary villagers have felt hurtloam. Temporarily, at least, they're free of Kevin's Dirt. And they won't forget what it feels like. Why didn't the Masters try to prevent that? What made them change their minds?'

Was it possible that events had forced a chink in the intransigence of Stave's kinsmen?

But Stave shook his head. 'Other matters aside, no *Haruchai* would willingly oppose the clear wishes of the Ranyhyn. Yet the Masters have altered neither their thoughts nor their commitments. They merely acknowledge that this disturbance of their service surpassed prevention. They could not have forestalled the battle, or the unveiling of powers unknown to the Woodhelvennin. By the measure of those forces, any experience of hurtloam and health-sense is a slight consideration.

'Also they acknowledge that they have failed.' Stave's tone seemed to harden. 'To prevent the misuse of Earthpower is but one aspect of their stewardship. Another is to preserve the Land's peoples. The Masters do not fault themselves for their inability to defeat the forces arrayed against them. But when they have failed, their Mastery does not require that others must suffer. They accept no ease for their wounds because they have chosen the path of their service. They do not regret its cost. But the Woodhelvennin did not choose. Therefore they are not asked to share the cost.'

After a moment, he added, 'When they have entered Revelstone, they will not be permitted to depart.'

Linden swore under her breath. But she did not protest. She had done so often enough, to no avail. Instead she said, 'I still don't understand, but that doesn't mean I'm not grateful. These people have a long way to go. They're going to need all the compassion that they can get.'

'Indeed,' assented Liand fervently.

'So tell me that I'm doing the right thing,' she continued. 'Tell me that we don't have to help them reach Revelstone. I *need* to get to Andelain. We've already lost a day here. But these poor people—'

'They will not be assailed,' Stave stated without hesitation. 'There is no gain in their deaths for the Land's foes. Neither Esmer nor the Harrow appears inclined to harm those who wield no power. And the Unbeliever's son, his Cavewights, the *skurj* and the Sandgorgons, all remain in the east. As we journey towards Andelain, we will ride between them and the Woodhelvennin, and will pose a far greater threat. Thus only the hazard of the *kresh* remains. But the carnage among them was extreme. If *moksha* Raver does not compel them, they will not soon crave human flesh.

'At another time, any Raver might revel in the slaughter of the helpless. But we seek Corruption's doom. And you bear powers sufficient to endanger him. As we distance ourselves from the Woodhelvennin, we will draw *moksha* Jehannum after us.'

'And should Stave be mistaken,' Liand put in, 'which I do not believe, there is another matter. After what has transpired here, no one among these folk will desire to delay your purpose. In this I am certain, for their hearts are open, and I have heard them speak among themselves. They are homeless and bereft, and their needs are many. But they have beheld the puissance of those who loathe the Land – and have seen you wreathed in a glory of fire and salvation. Also you have preserved the lives of their Heers. If you offered to accompany them, they would implore you not to turn aside from your intent.'

Linden did not look at either Liand or Stave: she did not want them to see that their assurances shamed her. If they had told her that every one of the villagers would die without her protection, she would have continued her journey nonetheless. She believed that she would never be able to rescue Jeremiah if she did not first reach Andelain; and so she would have abandoned the Woodhelvennin.

Linden, find me.

Everything came back to Thomas Covenant.

In spite of her shame – or because of it – she thanked the Stonedownor and the former Master. Then, as a kind of penance, she took the long walk away from the tree-dwellers and the battlefield in order to speak to each of the Humbled individually. She wanted to tell them that she valued what they had done.

That night, Linden's company and the Woodhelvennin ate a communal meal organised by Quilla and Karnis. The Heers were still too weak to haul supplies, firewood and cookpots themselves, or to prepare viands. Nonetheless they worked doggedly to ensure that none of the needs of their people were neglected.

Earlier, Linden and Bhapa had washed as thoroughly as they could in the brook. With Pahni's help, and Liand's, they had bathed Mahrtiir. And when the Ranyhyn had moved out into the gathering twilight to stand watch, Branl, Galt and Clyme had taken turns at the stream, cleansing their injuries and their tunics with equal impassivity.

Now Linden, Anele, Liand and the Ramen shared food with the

villagers, sitting around several large fires. Linden was regarded with wonder – and attended diligently. Liand and the Ramen were given care as though it were a form of obeisance. And Anele was gently prevented from leaving his plate of stone: a restriction which he accepted without protest.

Mahrtiir sat cross-legged between Bhapa and Linden, feeding himself by touch. Apart from the ruin of his eyes, he had made an extraordinary recovery, healed by *amanibhavam*, hurtloam and the Staff's flame. In the firelight, his scars seemed almost metaphysical. He sat as straight as a spear, fiercely refusing any assistance that was not absolutely necessary.

Beside him, Bhapa slumped uncharacteristically, shoulders bowed in dejection; but Linden could not tell whether he grieved for his Manethrall or for Whrany.

Later, the Heers spoke briefly. In quavering voices, they described their sorrow over their lost homes, their relief that they could seek sanctuary in Revelstone, and their astonished gratitude for all that Linden's company had done. Then, almost timidly, they asked her to explain what had befallen them.

She had no heart for the task; but Liand took it from her unasked. Standing among the fires, he emanated dignity and openness as he told the hushed Woodhelvennin what he knew. His version of the causes of the battle, and of the nature of the Land's foes, was not what Linden might have said in his place. It was simpler and more direct; unconflicted by inadequacy or bitterness. But it was also better suited to the limited comprehension of his audience, and the villagers received it as if it were an act of grace.

With every word, he violated the long prohibitions of the Masters. Yet neither Vernigil nor the Humbled interrupted him. In this, as in the use of hurtloam, the Masters seemed to take pity on the Woodhelvennin.

Linden knew better. When the tree-dwellers entered Lord's Keep, they would never leave. If that were pity, she wanted no part of it.

At last, the villagers prepared to sleep on beds of gathered leaves and retrieved blankets. In spite of Bhapa's urging, Mahrtiir refused rest. Harshly he proclaimed that he had lost only his eyes, not his ears and nose, or the use of his limbs. Alone, he walked away from the fires, clearly intending to help the Ranyhyn and the Masters keep watch. For a moment, the ruddy light of the flames seemed to cling to the pale swath of his bandaged head. Then the night took him, and he was gone.

With anguish in his eyes, Bhapa followed the Manethrall.

When Linden was offered a bed, she paused only to confirm that Stave warded Anele. Then she sank into the blankets, tucked the Staff of Law under her arm, and fell instantly asleep.

During the night, she was tormented by nightmares, not of fire and killing, but of violation. She lay like carrion, unable to move, while centipedes and venomous spiders crawled over her face, emerging from her mouth and nose. Molten worms circled her eyes: noisome things crept unhindered through the privacy of her clothes: pincers and fouled teeth gnawed her flesh. The knowledge that they had been hatched in the dank cesspit of her heart filled her with horror.

Whimpering weakly, she ached to awaken, and could not. Her dreams held her until Stave roused her with the dawn.

A sense of moral sickness clung to her as she arose, shivering, from her bed. A heavy dew had fallen, and its dampness had soaked through the blankets to her flannel shirt and jeans. Hoping to dispel her nightmares as well as the chill, she drew delicate tendrils of Earthpower from the Staff to meet the sunrise. Then she scanned the area to see how her friends and the Woodhelvennin fared.

Most of the camp was stirring. Stave had left Anele to the care of the Heers, and the old man seemed compliant in their company. Joined by Liand and Pahni, one group of villagers brought more wood from the banyans to build up the fires. Other people had begun to prepare a fresh meal. The Ranyhyn were nowhere in sight: they must have ranged far to find more grass, and to search for intimations of danger. Lit by the dawn, the Humbled and Vernigil kept a closer watch. But Mahrtiir and Bhapa had returned during the night. Now they stood at one of the fires, apparently arguing – if the Cord's diffident replies to his Manethrall's assertions could be called argument.

Bhapa urged Mahrtiir to remove the bandage from his eyes. The Cord suggested that open air and sunlight would speed Mahrtiir's healing. But the Manethrall refused to expose his ravaged face. With suppressed fury, he insisted that doing so would encourage pity. Also he averred that he required the binding around his head to remind him that he could not see. If his other senses caused him to forget his blindness, he might make some hazardous mistake.

When Linden had absorbed enough of the Staff's strength to collect her thoughts, she nodded towards the two Ramen. 'Bhapa is taking this personally.'

To her ears, she sounded callous. Her tone falsified what she felt. But remnants of dreams clung to her like revenants. Vile scurrying seemed to lurk beneath the surface of her attention. When she had restored Joan's wedding band, she had made possible atrocities like the destruction of First Woodhelven.

'The Ramen are prideful,' Stave observed with implied compassion. 'I have learned to see that this is both strength and weakness. The Cord and the Manethrall have lost much. Uncertain of himself, the Cord fears to acknowledge that he is no longer certain of the Manethrall. Dreading the outcome of his blindness, the Manethrall is guided by anger.

'For such reasons, the *Haruchai* strive to set aside passion. Yet it rules us. I am no less its servant than are the Masters.'

Nightmares had left Linden ripe for shame. She, too, had lost much, and was ruled by fears and passions which she did not know how to bear. Frowning uselessly, she went to break her fast.

With her friends, she joined the villagers around cookpots of steaming cereal sweetened with fruit.

The new sun leaned past the higher ground to the east, blunting the chill of night and dew. The air should have tasted as clean as the light, full of spring and the scents of cooking. But the ground had been ploughed to chaos by the *caesure*, charred with power and malice, steeped in blood. And the ashen reek of Esmer's pyre lingered over the slopes, irreparable as Kevin's Dirt.

Fretting at the residue of her dreams, Linden wanted to hurry. She had abundant reasons for haste, among them the chance that her presence might endanger the villagers further. Their shy greetings and thanks she brushed aside. She ate quickly; quenched her thirst at the bourn, grateful that the current had washed itself clear of killing; prepared herself to ride.

The Ramen followed her example. And Stave was always ready. Even the Humbled seemed determined to resume their journey in spite of their long, stiff scabs and damaged bones.

But Anele sat with Karnis and Quilla, devouring his meal voraciously, and making incoherent remarks which the Heers kindly elected to interpret as jests. And Liand ate with slow gravity, as if he were mustering his strength for a severe task.

Linden was tempted to prod him, but his air of purpose silenced her. She could see that he had reached a decision of some kind – and that some aspect of his intent troubled him. However, her percipience showed her only the nature of his emotions: she could not discern his thoughts.

While the Stonedownor took his time, Linden looked to Pahni and asked uncomfortably, 'Do you know what's going on? He has something in mind, but I can't tell what it is.'

The young Cord shook her head. Her soft brown eyes were dark with worry. 'I have felt his resolve. It swelled within him throughout the night, and he slept little. But he has not spoken of it. And I—' Pahni faltered. Almost whispering, she said, 'I feared to inquire. I fear for him.'

Through Anele, Thomas Covenant had told Liand, *I wish I could spare you.* Surely the Stonedownor had not decided to sacrifice himself in some extreme fashion, responding to a need which Linden as well as the Ramen and Stave had failed to perceive?

Before long, however, Liand appeared to resolve an internal debate. Nodding to himself, he gathered his bundles of supplies. Then he signalled his readiness to Linden and Stave.

Finally. 'All right,' Linden muttered. 'Let's get going.'

At once, Stave raised his fingers to his mouth and began the series of whistles which summoned the Ranyhyn.

When they heard the sound, Mahrtiir and Bhapa came towards Linden, Pahni and Stave. Vernigil and the Humbled left their posts. Even Anele jerked up his head, scanning the area with his moonstone eyes as if he were eager.

Soon the Ranyhyn swept into sight from the southeast. As they drew near, Linden counted ten of the star-browed horses.

Ten, she thought, distracted by wonder. Of course. She had been told that the fidelity of the Ranyhyn did not end in death. Whrany had fallen: therefore another of the great horses had come to bear Bhapa.

With glad homage, the Ramen greeted the Ranyhyn. Stave and the Humbled bowed gravely, honouring their mounts as the Bloodguard had done millennia ago; and Vernigil did the same, although he had not been chosen. Hrama trotted among the villagers towards Anele while Narunal offered his muzzle to Mahrtiir's uncertain hands. And Bhapa had tears of gratitude and rue in his eyes as he knelt before the tall bayard that had answered in Whrany's place.

When he stood again, he proclaimed as steadily as he could, 'This mighty stallion is Rohnhyn. I pray of all the Ranyhyn, and of revered *Kelenbhrabanal*, Father of Horses, that I may prove worthy to serve such a sovereign.'

Hyn nudged Linden affectionately. Hynyn flared his nostrils, snorting his impatience. Relieved by the prospect of departure, Linden mounted without delay, as did Stave and Mahrtiir. After a moment, Bhapa joined them. Flinging an anxious glance at Liand, Pahni followed the older Cord's example.

To Linden, the Humbled did not look hale enough to ride. Nevertheless they contrived to leap astride their horses. There they sat, rigid as stone, although the exertion had torn open some of their wounds and fresh blood seeped into their tunics.

When two of the tree-dwellers had helped Anele onto Hrama, only Liand remained unmounted.

Briefly Liand hugged Rhohm's neck. Setting his bundles on Rhohm's back, he vaulted onto the Ranyhyn. But he did not move towards Linden and the rest of her companions. Instead he rode into the centre of the encampment.

Most of the villagers were engaged in a confusion of tasks: cooking and eating; tending their children and their injured; searching their stricken homes for blankets, food, and raiment. But Liand was limned in sunlight. His high seat on his mount, and the youthful gravity of his demeanour, gradually drew the attention of the tree-dwellers. Silence spread across the camp as more and more people stopped what they were doing to gaze at him.

When he began to speak, he did not shout. In that way, he gathered his audience around him. Linden herself rode closer, accompanied by the Ramen and Stave. She needed Liand. Until she knew what he intended, she wanted to be near enough to intervene.

'Woodhelvennin, hear me,' he called quietly. 'We are scantly acquainted, yet you know me well. You have beheld me in the nature of my deeds, as you have in the valour of my companions. And you have heard me speak of the reasons for our presence among you. We must now part. The needs which compel Linden Avery the Chosen are many and urgent. But I am loath to ride from you without sharing the greatest of the benisons which I have gained in her company.'

Sighing, Linden let herself relax. When she touched Pahni's shoulder, she found that the young Cord also felt relieved. Liand did not mean to offer up his life. He was simply too sensitive and generous to leave the villagers as they were.

'It has been given to me,' he explained, 'to discern a Land which lies unseen within the lives that we have known.' To Linden, his voice sounded like the rising of the sun. His sincerity was as nourishing as sunshine. 'In its unshrouded form, the Land is a place of marvels beyond imagining, and I have been enabled to partake in its mysteries. This gift, which Linden Avery names "health-sense", I would grant to you, as it has been granted to me, if you will honour me with its acceptance.

'But it is not a gentle gift,' he warned the villagers, 'and its cost is pain and loss, anger and sorrow. Some of you have felt the healing of hurtloam and know the gift of which I speak. Others know it because you have been brought back from death by fire. When you touched the eldritch sand, or were laved in flames, your eyes were opened. All of your senses were opened as they have not been opened before. You became able to *see* truly, and all that you beheld was transformed.'

Karnis, Quilla and a number of the Woodhelvennin nodded. The rest regarded Liand with perplexed frowns.

'For a time,' he said in sunlight, 'you recognised the transcendence of that which you had deemed commonplace. Yet now your awareness of transcendence is gone. The Land has become what it was. You have become what you were. And you are no longer content.

'Others among you know nothing of this. If you inquire of those who comprehend my words, you will find them bewildered, unable to convey what they have witnessed, or what they have lost. They cannot name the cause of their sadness and ire.'

Again the healed, the Heers and those who had carried hurtloam nodded, grateful to hear their innominate grief described.

Now Liand raised his voice. Still he did not shout; but he spoke in bright tones that sent a shiver through Linden's heart. Pahni's eyes shone, and Mahrtiir heard the Stonedownor with his chin raised as though Liand had made him proud.

'Nevertheless I say to you that what they have tasted and lost is your birthright. It is the essential spirit of the Land, inherent to all that lives, and you have been made blind to it. For many generations, you have been deprived of the deepest truth of who and what and where you are.

'It is my wish to grant unto you, all of you, the gift that I have been given. I wish to share my vision of your birthright.'

There the Humbled or Vernigil might have interrupted him. But none of them betrayed any reaction. Perhaps their silence acknowledged an irreducible truth: whether Linden succeeded or failed, nothing in the Land would remain unchanged.

She had accomplished that much, at least, Linden thought grimly. Liand could speak without fear. For the present, at least, the service of the Masters had ceased to be a general prohibition. Now it was focused almost exclusively on her.

You hold great powers. Yet if we determine that we must wrest them from you, do you truly doubt that we will prevail?

If the day ever came when the Humbled decided to oppose her, every Master in the Land would become her enemy.

'But in all sooth,' the Stonedownor continued, 'it is not a gentle gift, and you will not bless me for it. In itself, it is wondrous beyond telling. While it remains to you, you will be exalted. But it will be fleeting. And when it drains away, you will be left in sorrow. Nor will you be able to regain any portion of what you have lost.

'Why, then, do I offer this increase of woe? Your destination is Revelstone, the seat and habitation of the Masters. There you will find some small safety in a world which has become perilous beyond your knowledge. And there, if you desire it, you may reclaim my gift. Above

Revelstone lies a plateau, and the plateau holds Glimmermere, a lake munificent to restore your birthright. It is a theriac for the bane which has made both you and the Land appear to be less than you are.

'Yet Revelstone is distant,' he said as if he were arguing against himself, 'and your path will be arduous. You will not soon know my gift again.

'It is here.' Reaching into the pouch at his waist, Liand drew out the *orcrest* and held it high. In his grasp, it shone like a beacon, as white as refined daylight, and as clear as the purest gem. 'If you desire to know the savour and bereavement of your birthright, approach me. If you do not, withdraw.

'Yet hear me nonetheless. Your losses have been cruel. They may worsen in your journey, or within Revelstone. Still I believe that you will not regret my gift. To know your birthright is precious, even when that birthright is denied. And if Linden Avery the Chosen does not fail in her quest, your birthright will one day be restored to all the folk of the Land.'

Linden was not surprised when most of the Woodhelvennin surged forward, crowding into the brightness around Rhohm and Liand as though the Sunstone's radiance offered meaning to their lives. She would have done the same in their place, if Liand's generosity could have eased her irreconciled heart.

With tears in her eyes, Pahni murmured, 'For this, he has become my love.'

Nodding, Mahrtiir announced, 'He reveals a greater heritage than he comprehends. In the tales of the Ramen, the ancient Lords had such stature, humble in their glory, and openhearted to every need. Yet he is more. He has touched the lore of the *rhadhamaerl*. After uncounted generations of diminishment, he is the first true Stonedownor among his kind.'

'Aye,' assented Bhapa gruffly. 'I am Ramen, and do not lightly avow that he has surpassed me.'

But Stave said without inflection, 'That is his peril. Corruption delights in the ruin of such innocence.'

Linden turned away. She could feel health-sense and excitement effloresce among the Woodhelvennin as the hindering brume of Kevin's Dirt was swept aside by Earthpower and Liand's courage. Like Pahni and the Manethrall, she was proud of him. Like Stave, she feared for him. But she was also ashamed.

If Linden Avery the Chosen does not fail in her quest—

Her mere presence among the villagers was a promise which she did not know how to keep.

Chapter Eight:

Salva Gildenbourne

I am able to convey you to your son.

The Harrow's parting words were a knell in Linden's heart. While the glory of Liand's *orcrest* washed over the villagers, she rode away from the crowd and the shattered remnants of First Woodhelven; from her friends. Doubt-ridden, and haunted by her dreams, she wanted to be alone with Hyn.

She did not understand how the Ramen seemed to know what the Ranyhyn wanted or intended: she could not even guess how the Ramen knew the names of the great horses. Nevertheless a form of communion existed between the Ramen and the Ranyhyn. She had tasted that bond herself during the horserite which she had shared with Hyn, Hynyn, and Stave. At need, Hyn never failed to grasp what Linden desired of her – and to obey.

Impelled by fears and yearning, Linden guided the mare a short distance away from her companions. There, bending low over Hyn's neck and whispering so that she would not be overheard, she asked the Ranyhyn to take her to Jeremiah.

She felt the mare's muscles quiver in willingness or trepidation. Hyn shifted her hooves restively, tossed her head, then shook it from side to side. She stood where she was.

Trying to be clear, Linden took Jeremiah's toy from her pocket and clenched it in her fist. Then she closed her eyes and visualised her son, not as she had known and loved him in their former life together, but as she had last seen him under *Melenkurion* Skyweir, with the *croyel* cling-ing savagely to his back; debased by the creature's bitter theurgy. She formed his image in precise detail and offered it to Hyn, silently pleading with the Ranyhyn.

Still the mare did not move.

Then Mahrtiir came to Linden's side, and to Hyn's, drawn by his sensitivity to Linden, or by his instinctive rapport with the Ranyhyn. Murmuring, he gentled the mare until she no longer trembled.

'Do not misunderstand, Ringthane,' he urged Linden gruffly. 'Hyn is valorous in all things. She would bear you into any of the Seven Hells, as she has into the horror of *caesures*. But she does not know where your son may be found. Mayhap she is able to discern the nature of his hiding place or prison, but she cannot determine its location. Therefore she shies from your desire.

'The son of the former Ringthane is present in this time. For that reason, I deem that your son is likewise present. As you have described them, the powers of both the halfhand and the *croyel* were required to elude the Law of Time. Therefore the halfhand's evil assures us that your son has not been secreted in some other age. He does not lie beyond your reach. But Hyn cannot pierce his concealment.'

Linden sighed. 'I didn't really expect it to work.' If she could have found her son simply by asking the Ranyhyn to aid her, the Harrow would have no leverage with her – and Roger and Esmer would have no reason to fear that she might strike a bargain with the Insequent. 'I just had to try.'

The Manethrall seemed to study her through his bandage. 'Indeed, Ringthane. Who would comprehend, if I do not? Against the Cavewights, I did not expect to retain my life. Yet I could not decline to give battle. It is ever thus. Attempts must be made, even when there can be no hope. The alternative is despair. And betimes some wonder is wrought to redeem us. Expecting death, I have sacrificed only my sight.

'Therein lay Kevin Landwaster's error – aye, and great *Kelenbhrabanal's* also. When all hope was gone, they heeded the counsels of despair. Had they continued to strive, defying their doom, some unforeseen wonder might have occurred. And if it did not, still their glory would have surpassed their failure.'

'I know,' Linden murmured: a dying fall of sound. 'The world is full of Kastenessens and Rogers.' Esmers and Joans, *croyel* and Cavewights.

'Lord Foul is everywhere. But there are still people like Liand.' And the Mahdoubt. 'Stave is on our side. The ur-viles have changed. Even the Sandgorgons—' In spite of *samadhi* Raver's shredded malignance, they had retained enough gratitude to answer her. 'I'll try anything to save Jeremiah.'

She meant her assertion as a warning, but she lacked the courage to speak more clearly. She was afraid that Mahrtiir – that all of her friends – would attempt to stop her.

As matters stood, she did not know the difference between the Manethrall's advice and the counsels of despair.

To her relief, Liand did not take long to cleanse the senses of those Woodhelvennin who desired his gift. Although his efforts left his skin pale with weariness, and he wavered on Rhohm's back, breathing raggedly, he was still able to ride. When he swayed too far, Pahni steadied him.

Now none of Linden's companions urged caution. The time had come for haste. She needed it; and the villagers would be safer when she was far from them. Her friends delayed only to consider the pane of slate which had protected Anele.

Clyme asserted his willingness to carry it – or to make the attempt – regardless of his hurts and renewed bleeding. But Linden shook her head. 'It's too heavy,' she stated as though she had the authority to command the Humbled. 'It'll get in your way if we're attacked again. We'll try blankets. Five or six of them might be enough to block Kastenessen.'

For a moment, the Masters appeared to debate their responsibilities. Then Clyme abandoned the slate.

At a word from the Heers, grateful villagers hurried to gather blankets, which they tied into a roll and handed to Pahni.

With difficulty, Linden held back her impatience as Karnis and Quilla endeavoured to express their thanks for all that she and her companions had done. But the Heers were among those who had been blessed or afflicted with percipience: they could see how she felt. Seeming flustered by her frustration, they cut short what they wished to say.

On Linden's behalf, and Liand's, Manethrall Mahrtiir responded to the Heers; but he spoke curtly. 'It is sooth that Liand of Mithil Stonedown has granted no gentle gift. Also it is sooth that neither *kresh* nor Cavewights would have assailed you in our absence. Our aid is small recompense for the harm which we have brought among you.

'The Master Vernigil will guide you. While it endures, your new sight will serve you well. May you fare in safety. Beyond question, you will fare more safely for our departure.'

At last, Linden and her companions turned away, leaving silence and uncertainty behind them. With Mahrtiir beside her, Pahni, Liand and Anele following, and Stave in the rear, she rode after Bhapa and the Humbled at a brisk canter which Hyn and the other Ranyhyn soon stretched into a rolling gallop.

For a time, they traversed rough hills of flint and shale. But then stones and scant dirt gave way to better soil as more streams traced their crooked paths across the landscape; and the riders began to encounter occasional clusters of *aliantha*. Linden called a halt at the first of these so that Liand could restore his depleted strength.

When she dismounted to join him, she noticed the marks of other hooves. To her questioning glance, Pahni replied that the Humbled and Bhapa had paused here as well.

Privately Linden hoped that the Masters were not too proud to avail themselves of treasure-berries. They were in no condition to face another conflict. They needed as much sustenance as their stubbornness could accept.

'To this place,' Pahni added, studying the ground, 'they rode together. Now, however, they have separated. Mhornym and Rohnhyn continue southeastward, but Bhanoryl's path lies to the east, and Naybahn has turned to the south. Doubtless they will guard our passage at the farthest extent of their senses.'

Linden nodded. Remembering Cail and Brinn, Ceer and Hergrom, she trusted the Humbled to protect her company as well as they could.

When Liand had eaten a handful of *aliantha*, and had recovered enough to whisper something playful that made Pahni smile and duck her head, Linden and her friends remounted. Together the Ranyhyn resumed their run, devouring the distance at a long gallop.

Before noon, the hills faded into a wide plain like a steppe lambent with grasses and bright wildflowers. Birds scattered in waves before the rush of the riders, the muffled rumble of hooves. At intervals, Linden and her companions passed a small stand of wattle or scrub oak; splashed through a rambling stream or sprang over a sun-spangled rill; swept down into a shallow swale and flowed up the far side. But such features were few. Between them, the plain unfurled itself to the horizons as if the earth had opened its heart to the sun. There the Ranyhyn seemed to run effortlessly, buoyed by the grass and the vast sky as if they were born to revel in grasslands and illimitable vistas.

For a while, Linden caught no glimpse of the Humbled and Bhapa. Under the midday sun, however, she eventually saw Clyme waiting ahead of her. Apparently he had decided that the time had come to rest the Ranyhyn while their riders ate a quick meal.

His bleeding had stopped. Aided, perhaps, by treasure-berries, his native toughness had reasserted itself. Even while he rode, his wounds healed slowly.

Before Pahni and Liand allowed Anele to dismount, Linden took a moment to study the grass. All around her, many varieties grew together. Some resembled the lush wealth of the Verge of Wandering. But among more luxuriant greens were streaks and swaths of the raw-edged scrub grass which covered the hills and slopes of the Mithil valley: the grass on which the old man was vulnerable to Lord Foul.

Here Anele needed protection.

Instead of insisting that he remain on Hrama, she decided to test the effectiveness of the blankets. At her request, Pahni unrolled the thick pad and guided Anele onto it from Hrama's back.

Warded by wool, the old man showed no sign of possession. His fractured muttering was disturbed only by his discomfort at Clyme's nearness.

The horizons remained clear. When Linden questioned Clyme, he reported no indication of danger. He and Bhapa had found evidence of Roger's army's trek towards First Woodhelven. For a time, Galt had been able to track Roger and his remaining Cavewights eastward. But nothing stirred to threaten the riders – unless it was concealed by the glamour which had enabled Roger's forces to take Linden's company by surprise.

She might have felt relief. Perhaps she should have. Apparently Roger was *indeed reduced without the aid and knowledge of the* croyel. Alone, he could not simply bypass time or space: he was forced to travel by more ordinary means.

But his limitations confirmed that he had set out to intercept her several days before Kastenessen had touched Anele. Conceivably Roger had begun to lead his army westward as soon as he and Jeremiah had returned to their proper time. Kastenessen may have precipitated Roger's attack; but Roger and his forces must have already been poised to strike. Hidden by glamour – *extending as it does to conceal so many* – he must have been waiting for her along her most direct route towards Andelain.

She had told him what her intentions were; forewarned him—

Nevertheless he had lost too many Cavewights to challenge her again soon. He knew her power. He knew that scores of ur-viles and Waynhim remained willing to serve her. And he no longer had the support of the *croyel*. He would need time to rally more of Kastenessen's – or Lord Foul's – allies.

Therefore— Linden swore under her breath. Therefore the next attack would probably come from the *skurj*.

In spite of everything that she had learned and suffered, she was inadequate to her task. If she were wiser, or stronger, or calmer– When the battle ended yesterday, she should have tried to catch Roger while he was still within reach, and vulnerable. That might have forced Kastenessen to hesitate. But she had been consumed by desperation and killing; exhaustion and remorse. She had missed her chance. Now she could only hope to outrun the maddened *Elohim*'s malice.

When she and her companions were mounted, ready to ride, she described her concerns. Then she told Clyme, 'We'll need as much warning as possible. You and Bhapa have to be able to ride as far and as fast as you can. We need you at your best.'

With difficulty, she restrained an impulse to demand, So *heal*, damn it. Or let me help you. You aren't much good like this.

His hurts were as unmistakable as groans.

Clyme faced her without expression. For a moment, he appeared to be waiting for her to say more; to speak her wishes aloud so that he could refuse her. Then he gave a slight nod. Urging Mhornym to greater speed with every stride, he rode away.

Abruptly Mahrtiir growled, 'The Ringthane speaks sooth. Yet needful tasks in which the Ramen have no equal I cannot now perform. Cord Pahni, you also must watch over this company, that no sign or hint which may elude the sleepless ones will be missed. The Stonedownor and Stave will care for Anele.'

Pahni flung a look like pleading at Liand, urging him to be safe, before she sent Naharahn into a gallop after Clyme. Behind her, the remaining Ranyhyn began to run, carrying their riders with the swift ease of birds towards Andelain and the Land's threatened heart.

While the great horses pounded the steppe, Linden prayed that she would be able to reach the Hills and Loric's *krill* in time; and that she would find Thomas Covenant and hope among the Dead.

Eventually the steppe modulated into a region of rugged, stony hills like glacial moraines. Although the horses found passage along the valleys, the littered ground forced them to slow their pace. When they finally emerged from the hills towards gentler terrain, the sun was setting.

Linden did not doubt that the Ranyhyn could travel confidently in darkness. Nevertheless she called a halt on the last of the granite debris. Temporarily, at least, her concern for Anele outweighed her desire for haste. She did not yet entirely trust his pad of blankets. Loose stone would guard him from possession as well as restore a measure of his sanity.

Mumbling to himself, he began to pick through the igneous refuse as if he were seeking a particular kind of rock; specific memories. But whenever he found a bit of granite, or schist, or obsidian that seemed to interest him, he studied it briefly, then cast it aside and resumed his search.

As Liand and Stave unpacked supplies and set out bedding, Bhapa and Pahni emerged from the dusk. They had found no cause for concern within a league of the company, and the Humbled had instructed them to rejoin their companions for food and rest. If the Manethrall approved, Bhapa and Pahni proposed to take turns standing watch atop the nearest of the hills. The Humbled and the Ranyhyn would form a more distant cordon around the company.

Mahrtiir nodded. 'It is well. Let it be so.' He sounded vexed, as though the Cords had disappointed him. But Linden understood that his ire was not directed at them. Rather he was galled by his comparative helpless-ness. As long as Linden or Liand renewed his health-sense regularly, he would remain capable of much. Still his abilities were irretrievably compromised.

Seeking to distract him while Pahni helped Liand prepare a meal, Linden said, 'I'm worried, Mahrtiir. We're pushing the Ranyhyn pretty hard. How much longer can they keep this up?'

Mahrtiir squatted among the stones until she sat down facing him. Then he said, 'Do not mistake them, Ringthane. They are far from the bounds of their endurance. Many are the great deeds that they have performed at need. I will speak of one, though it is a tale which no Ramen witnessed. We heard of it from those few *Haruchai* who chose to serve the Ranyhyn during Fangthane's unnatural winter, when the Vow of the Bloodguard had been broken.'

Linden settled herself to listen. Liand and Pahni did not pause in their tasks, but their attention was turned towards the Manethrall. Liand was always eager for tales of the Land's past; and all Ramen loved to speak and hear of the great horses.

'In the years preceding the last siege of Revelstone,' Mahrtiir told the evening and his own darkness, 'a silence had fallen over Seareach, and all who loved the Land were troubled by it. No Giants walked the Upper Land to gladden the heart with their friendship and their ready laughter. Nor did the Unhomed send word of their plight in The Grieve. Therefore two Lords and a party of Bloodguard set out for Seareach, to discover what had befallen the Giants.'

'This the *Haruchai* remember,' Stave put in. 'Lord Mhoram, seer and oracle to the Council of Lords, had discerned the peril of the Giants. Therefore Hyrim son of Hoole and Shetra Verement-mate were dis-patched to Seareach, accompanied by fifteen Bloodguard. Among that number were Runnik and Tull, who returned to tell the tale.'

Mahrtiir accepted Stave's confirmation with a nod. Then the Manethrall continued.

'The passage of the Lords and Bloodguard eastward was opposed, but their gravest hazard found them upon the Giantway within Sarangrave Flat, for that was their most direct path to Seareach. There they were beset by the lurker of the Sarangrave. So dire was the lurker's power that even the great horses could not endure it. In their fear, they endangered the Lords, and Ahnryn of the Ranyhyn was slain.

'Therefore the choice was made to abandon the Giantway – to return westward to Landsdrop and thence into the southeast towards the Defiles Course, that poisoned river which emerges from among the banes deep within Mount Thunder to corrupt Lifeswallower, the Great Swamp. The Lords had determined to fashion a raft to bear them along the Defiles Course and through the Sarangrave until they had passed beyond the reach of the lurker.

'But first it was necessary to cross many arduous leagues to approach the bitter river. The hills which foot the cliff of Landsdrop are raw and twisted, forbidding haste. Also, night had fallen, obscuring the treachery of the terrain. Yet the company's need for haste had grown extreme. And the Ranyhyn were shamed by their fear. Therefore they performed a prodigious feat. In the course of one night and a portion of the subsequent morning, they emerged from the Sarangrave and bore their riders to the Defiles Course, a distance of more than three score leagues.'

God, Linden thought. Three score– Her company had begun its journey by covering fifteen leagues a day.

'By the measure of that accomplishment, Ringthane,' Mahrtiir concluded, 'the labours which the Ranyhyn have undertaken on our behalf may be deemed paltry.' His voice was full of pride in the great horses. 'If you ask it of them, they will teach you the true meaning of astonishment.'

'Ha!' snorted Anele unexpectedly. He had given no indication that he was listening to the Manethrall; but now he held out a rough pebble as though he expected his companions to marvel at it. 'Here is astonishment. Within this stone is written the convulsion which formed Landsdrop when the Illearth Stone and other banes were buried among the roots of Gravin Threndor. Such knowledge is ancient beyond reckoning, yet it is remembered here.'

With a dismissive shrug, he tossed the pebble aside and resumed his search, apparently heedless of his friends. Indeed, he seemed unaware that he had spoken.

Linden watched his innominate quest while Liand and Pahni finished readying a meal. After the collapse of Kevin's Watch, he had told her, *I am the Land's last hope*, but she understood him no better now than she had then. Certainly he had made possible the recovery of the Staff of Law. Yet she did not see herself bringing hope to the Land: she could scarcely believe that she might eventually bring hope to Jeremiah. And if Anele had already achieved his life's purpose, she could not imagine why he still clung to his madness. Perhaps he refused lucidity only because he feared it. Or perhaps he had not yet discovered or revealed the real purpose of his derangement.

In either case, the ramifications of his condition were too vague to be trusted. As far as she was concerned, the Land's last – and best – hope lay in Thomas Covenant.

When she and her friends had eaten, they settled themselves as comfortably as the rocky ground allowed while Stave stood guard over the camp, and Bhapa kept watch from the crest of a nearby hill. Rather than allowing herself to dread Roger and attack, Linden concentrated on Roger's father as she tried to sleep. She wanted to fill herself with images and desires which might enable Covenant to visit her dreams.

But the night did not bring dreams. Instead it brought the first in a tumbled series of spring showers that followed the company for much of the next day: prolonged sprinkles and quick downpours that soaked the riders in spite of the cloaks which they had brought from Revelstone for Linden, Liand and Anele. At intervals, rain streaked the horizons, constricting the landscape to sodden grass and vleis, and to occasional copses shrouded with moisture. Then, between the showers and clouds, sunshine burst over the region, sketching bright transitory reflected jewels among the water drops until the earth and the trees were anademed in light.

Responding to the weather, the Ranyhyn slowed their fleet gallop somewhat, careful not to outrun the protection of the Humbled and the two Cords as they scouted ahead in a wide arc beyond the range of Linden's senses. Still the horses went swiftly, crossing slopes and lowlands until the contours of the Land appeared to open before them like a scroll.

Once in the distance, through a gap between showers, she glimpsed a *caesure*. But it was far against the northern horizon, seething erratically away from the riders. When Stave assured her that there were no villages or smaller habitations in the vicinity of the Fall, she decided to let it go. Deliberately she closed her mind to its migraine nausea, and by degrees it receded from her awareness.

Late in the day, the sky finally cleared, leaving the air full of sunlight as if the Land had been washed clean. Whenever Pahni or Bhapa rejoined the company to describe what lay ahead, they reported only that neither they nor the Humbled had found any evidence of danger. And the Ranyhyn quickened their strides to the pace that they had set the day before. Linden began to think that perhaps they were indeed travelling too swiftly to be caught by Kastenessen's servants, or Lord Foul's.

As for the Harrow, she could not begin to guess what he would do, or when he would do it. If she had known how to bargain with him – or been willing to do so – she still had no idea how to invoke his presence. Apparently his promise of companionship had been an empty threat.

While the company made camp that night on a broad swath of gravel and stones at the edge of a watercourse, Linden asked Stave how far they were from Salva Gildenbourne. He replied that they would catch sight of the sprawling forest before mid-morning, if they were not delayed. Then she asked Bhapa about the condition of the Humbled. She had not seen them since they had ridden away the previous morning.

The Cord considered her question for a moment, then shrugged. 'Their hardiness is remarkable,' he admitted as if he begrudged them any admiration. 'No Raman heals as they do. Yet they are not what they were. The rigours of our journey hamper them. With rest, I do not doubt that their full strength would soon return. Without it—'

Facing Mahrtiir rather than Linden, the Cord fell silent.

'Then, Cord,' replied the Manethrall gruffly, 'it falls to you, and to Cord Pahni, to increase your vigilance.

'Ringthane.' He turned the hollows of his bandage towards Linden. 'If you will accept my counsel, it is this. Request of the sleepless ones that they ride with you on the morrow. Permit my Cords to assume all the tasks of scouting. If the Masters are not yet whole, their skills will provide better service nearby than at a distance.

'Warded by Narunal's discernment where mine does not suffice, I will ride ahead of you. Thus any sudden threat will strike first against him who has the least worth in your defence.'

Surprised by Mahrtiir's suggestion, Linden faltered. Too many people had already sacrificed themselves in her name – and now the Manethrall proposed to offer himself as bait. She could not bear to think of him as having the least worth; or to consider losing him.

Hesitating, she looked to Stave.

'The Manethrall's counsel is apt,' he said at once. 'I do not fear for the Humbled. But the Land's foes must oppose you. They cannot suffer you to obtain High Lord Loric's *krill*. When they appear, you must have every aid nigh about you.'

In response, Linden made a stern effort to shake off her reluctance. In a moment of imposed coherence, Anele had informed her severely, *All who live share the Land's plight. Its cost will be borne by all who live.*

'All right,' she said through her teeth. 'We'll do that.' *This you cannot alter. In the attempt, you may achieve only ruin.* 'Bhapa, I need you to find the Humbled for me.' She had no means to contact them herself, except by a dangerous display of her powers; and the Masters would not heed Stave's mental voice. 'Make sure that they understand what we want, and why. I don't think that they'll object.' They would reason as Stave did. 'But if they do, tell them that they'll have to argue with me in person. You're just the messenger.'

When the Manethrall nodded his approval, Bhapa replied, 'As you wish, Ringthane.' Whistling for Rohnhyn, he strode out into the last of the gloaming and passed from sight. Briefly Linden heard the crunch of hooves on the stones. Then Bhapa and his mount were gone.

He did not return until after moonrise. But when he reentered the watercourse, he reported that the Humbled would rejoin Linden as she approached Salva Gildenbourne in the morning. 'They, too, deem the Manethrall's counsel apt.'

That night, Linden did not expect to sleep. The rocks on which she lay seemed full of memories and fears; as legible to her flesh as they were to Anele's peculiar sight. They jutted against her like tangible reminders of all that she had gained and lost since she had first approached the Hills of Andelain with Covenant, Sunder, and Hollian. But she called a faint current of Earthpower from the Staff to soothe her taut nerves. Then she closed her eyes to rest them – and when she opened them again a moment later, dawn had come upon her, as stealthy and unforeseen as the results of every choice that she had ever made.

Her companions roused quickly, at once eager and apprehensive. Anele scented the air fretfully, as if he could smell trouble; but the fragmentation of his mind prevented him from describing what he sensed. Perhaps anticipating another battle, Liand frowned darkly. However, he could not conceal the growing excitement behind his concern. Salva Gildenbourne promised to be unlike anything that he had ever seen.

Pahni also may have wished to gaze upon the vast woodland: her only knowledge of the Land's olden forests came from Ramen tales. Yet her anxiety for Liand dominated her. And Bhapa's emotions were similar, although he worried for the Manethrall rather than Liand. As for Mahrtiir, his belief that he had lost much of his usefulness dulled his characteristic hunger for peril and striving. The role which he had chosen for himself resembled that of a sacrificial lamb.

Only Stave faced the new day as if it were like any other. His single eye and his flat mien suggested neither hope nor trepidation.

As soon as the companions had eaten, Pahni kissed Liand quickly. Then the Cords summoned their Ranyhyn and rode away to assume the responsibilities of the Humbled.

In moments, Stave and Liand had repacked the bedding and supplies. Hyn and Hynyn, Rhohm, Hrama and Narunal answered Stave's whistle almost immediately, as if they had their own reasons for excitement or alarm. With Anele between them, Liand and Linden followed Mahrtiir and Stave to meet the horses.

The early sky looked too pristine to hold any omens. As the sun mounted, it spread light and azure across the heavens, immaculate and unfathomable; absolved from taint. If Anele were indeed able to detect an ominous scent, Linden could not. She smelled only the freshness of a bright day after rain; the gentle pleasure of grasses and wildflowers and loam in springtime.

First at a canter, then a liquid run, the Ranyhyn bore their riders into the southeast, towards the last obstacle or opportunity between Linden's company and Andelain.

Here the ground rose into a sequence of low ridges like striations across the landscape. Where the slopes were gradual, the horses confronted them directly, pounding upwards without hesitation, and descending in a rush as smooth and secure as the surface of Glimmermere. But where the ridges jutted more steeply, Narunal angled across their sides; and the other Ranyhyn followed seamlessly, letting Mahrtiir's mount lead them by a stone's throw.

In the vale between the second and third ridge, Branl awaited Linden and her companions. At the same time, Galt approached them from the south. Although he rode at a full gallop, he conveyed no impression of haste or urgency. And Stave said nothing: apparently he heard no warning in the thoughts of the Humbled. While Hynyn and Narunal nickered a greeting to Bhanoryl, all of the Ranyhyn ran at the next rise as if it were level ground.

As Hyn kept pace with the other horses, still following Mahrtiir and Narunal, Linden looked around for Clyme. Presumably Bhapa and Pahni were far ahead, searching the air and the grass and the rumpled slopes for hints of ambush. But Linden wanted to see Clyme. He would come from the east, the most likely direction of attack.

Soon he appeared against the sky on the crest of the fourth ridge. Like Galt, he rode at speed, but without indicating the proximity of foes.

In the vale beyond that ridge – low ground as narrow as a barranca, but not as sheer, with a freshet from the previous day's rain running through it – Clyme met Linden and her companions. At once, she asked the Manethrall for a halt. The morning was still early, and the stream between the ridges lay in shadow. But she did not need broad daylight in order to study the condition of the Humbled.

They were closer to wholeness than she had imagined; closer than she would have believed possible. Some of their cuts and gashes had already become scars. The rest were healing cleanly. And their cracked or broken bones were almost entirely mended.

Like their strength, the native resilience of the *Haruchai* was more than human. Hard riding had not harmed them. It had only slowed their recuperation.

Satisfied, Linden said quietly, 'All right.' Doubtless the Humbled remained uncertain of her. Perhaps their suspicions had increased. 'Let's get going.' Nevertheless she trusted them with her life – and with the lives of her friends as well. 'I've been waiting to see Andelain again for years.'

Without hesitation, the Manethrall headed along the vale until he reached a place where the Ranyhyn could surge up the sides of the next ridge. Slowly he increased his lead – or the other horses held back – until he rode a dozen strides or more ahead of Linden and her defenders.

Passing the crest, the riders ran out of shadow and down a gentle expanse of sunlit grass towards another rise. But it was little more than a line of low hillocks, and did not slow the Ranyhyn. Perhaps half a league beyond it stood a much higher ridge with more difficult slopes. Here and there, lichen-mottled fists and foreheads of bedrock jutted from the hillsides like buttresses. The horses were forced to pick a crooked and cautious way upwards.

At the end of that ascent, however, Linden and her companions saw Salva Gildenbourne for the first time. As if involuntarily, they stopped to gaze at the forest's immanent majesty.

It lay on the far side of a last ridge, a small interruption like a ripple in the earth. From the vantage of higher ground, Linden could see that Salva Gildenbourne was indeed vast. It stretched from the eastern horizon across her path and into the west, where it began to curve by slight degrees towards the south: a rich variegated green panoply bedecked at intervals with the ineffable gold of Gilden trees, and prodigal with the new growth of spring and rain; profligate with life and subtle Earthpower.

By her estimation, she was roughly fifteen leagues from Andelain. At this elevation, she might have been able to hope for a glimpse of the Hills which held the Land's defining glory. But Sunder and Hollian had wrought well when they had brought forth Salva Gildenbourne. In addition, the forest had flourished for millennia on the overflow of Andelain's fecundity. The woodland was too deep, dense, and tall to permit any faint emanation of the Hills to reach Linden's senses.

Still she searched the southeast so avidly that moments passed before she felt the tension thick around her; the growing apprehension of her companions. Then she heard Liand say anxiously, 'Linden,' and she saw him point towards the east.

The four *Haruchai* were gazing in that direction. Anele did the same in spite of his blindness. Mahrtiir had already ridden past the crest; but Narunal had halted when the other Ranyhyn did, and the Manethrall's face also was turned to the east.

As soon as Linden saw the smoke seething out of the trees at the farthest limit of her sight, she wondered how she had failed to notice it immediately.

The smoke itself was black and fatal, but it was only smoke: it did not cry out to her health-sense. Natural fires were possible. Yet the season was spring. Showers had soaked the woods. Nonetheless Salva Gildenbourne was burning.

And there was more.

At that distance, she did not expect to see flames; but she discerned something worse. Rather than fire, she descried a kind of diseased Earthpower, an organic mystical energy distilled and polluted until it had become as fiery as a furnace, as hot as lava, and incandescent with hunger.

Instantly, instinctively, Linden knew the cause of the blaze. *You'll recognise them when you see them. Foul showed you what they're like.* In imposed visions during her translation to the Land, she had seen spots of *wrongness* bloom like chancres in the body of the Land, eruptions of ruin among the grass and beauty of the landscape. And from those vile pustulent boils, buboes, infections, had squirmed forth devouring monsters which seemed to emerge from the depths of volcanoes. Serpentlike and massive, with kraken jaws formed to rip and swallow earth and grass and trees, those beasts had feasted on the Land as if it were flesh. Ravenously they had consumed the vista of her vision.

Since then, she had learned to name the monsters. They were *skurj*, and they served Kastenessen because he had released them when he won free of his Durance.

They were a distortion rather than a shattering of Law, but they had one quality in common with *caesures*: they were discrete, localised; individually small compared to Salva Gildenbourne, or to the wider Land. However, enough of them together could wreak enormous devastation. Their combined hungers might prove to be as ruinous as the Sunbane.

Linden did not say their name aloud. None of her companions uttered it. Instead she asked softly so that she would not gasp or groan, 'How far—? Stave, can you tell how far away they are?'

'A score of leagues,' the former Master replied as if he were unacquainted with dread or horror. 'Perhaps somewhat more.'

'More,' stated Galt flatly.

'Are you able to determine their number?' asked Liand. 'I cannot.'

Roger had told Linden that Kastenessen had not *brought very many of them down from the north yet*, but she had no confidence that Covenant's son had given her the truth.

'The distance precludes certainty,' answered Stave, 'but they do not appear to be as many as ten. Salva Gildenbourne has endured substantial harm. The source of this smoke is not the only region where the trees have suffered. Other portions also have been devoured, some at the verge, some in the depths, and some nigh unto Andelain itself. Yet the savaging of the forest is fresh only at the site of the smoke. Earlier flames were extinguished by rain.' He looked to the Humbled for confirmation. 'Therefore we judge that this smoke reveals where Kastenessen's beasts feed, and that the *skurj* are few in number.'

At the sound of that name, Anele groaned.

'It is conceivable,' Stave continued implacably, 'that they feed for a time, then burrow beneath the trees to emerge in another place. But this is by no means certain. It is also conceivable that other *skurj* lurk within the earth. Indeed, it is conceivable that beasts in far greater numbers are masked by trees and distance, and that the razing of Andelain has already begun.

'Nor are we able to estimate the swiftness of the *skurj*. We can be certain only that Kastenessen is aware of your journey, and of your purpose. He will not find it difficult to gauge the point at which you will enter Salva Gildenbourne.'

Linden swallowed at the dread beating in her throat. 'Then we need to move fast. And we need to go *now*,' before the distant monsters could cross twenty leagues of forest.

She had to hope that Roger and a new army of Cavewights or other forces did not await her among the trees.

Mahrtiir must have heard her – or Narunal did. At once, the Manethrall's Ranyhyn sprang into a hard gallop down the slope.

In formation, with the Humbled surrounding Stave and Linden, Liand and Anele, the company plunged after Mahrtiir.

As Hyn rushed towards the last ridge before the descent to Salva Gildenbourne, Linden confirmed that Covenant's ring still hung under her shirt; that Jeremiah's racecar remained in her pocket. Then she tightened her grasp on the Staff of Law and tried to ready herself. At her back, she felt Liand take the *orcrest* from its pouch and close it in his fist; but he did not invoke its radiance.

Clutching Hrama's mane, Anele continued to face the smoke in the east. His fixation there gave Linden reason to hope that no *skurj* were concealed closer to her small company.

In moments, the Ranyhyn were pounding up the shallow sides of the final rise; and she began to worry about Pahni and Bhapa. But as she and her companions followed Mahrtiir over the crest and downwards again, she spotted the two Cords at the edge of the forest. Their apprehension as they waved told her that they had seen the smoke and drawn their own conclusions; but their manner did not suggest any immediate peril.

Now Linden could see why Stave had described Salva Gildenbourne as *unruly. –formed without the benefit of lore.* She would not have called it a forest: it was a jungle. With no Forestal, or any other benign power, to shepherd the trees, they had thronged so close to each other over the centuries and were crowded by such a multitude of brush, fallen branches and massive moss-thick deadwood trunks, that they seemed to forbid intrusion. Indeed, they almost forbade light.

They would restrict the percipience of anyone who walked among them.

Fifteen leagues of this woodland stood between her and Andelain. Within Salva Gildenbourne, she and her companions might be taken by surprise; and she did not know how quickly the *skurj* moved.

By the time that Hyn and the other horses had slowed to join the Ramen, Mahrtiir had already spoken to Bhapa and Pahni. 'There is no present peril apart from the distant *skurj*,' he announced. 'The Cords are certain of this.

'We are Ramen. Only theurgy may baffle our skills. But there is another matter which must be decided here.'

Linden hugged the Staff to her chest. 'Go on. I don't know how much time we have.'

'Ringthane,' said Mahrtiir as if he were glowering beneath his bandage, 'we cannot ask the Ranyhyn to enter this forest. They would bear us, forcing passage among the brush and saplings. But if we were assailed, by the *skurj* or any other foe, they could neither defend themselves nor flee. Salva Gildenbourne is too densely obstructed. Such monsters as we have cause to fear would devour the Ranyhyn whole.'

Linden winced. 'You're saying that we'll have to make it on foot.' Fifteen leagues through the heaviest jungle that she had seen since the rampant dire fertility of the Sunbane. 'That doesn't even sound possible.'

'Yet the Manethrall speaks sooth,' said Stave. 'In this, the Humbled and I concur.'

Damn it, she thought. 'And there aren't any roads? Any paths? No, of course not.' The Masters had discouraged travel for centuries. They certainly had not wanted anyone to visit Andelain, where the numinous manifestation of Earthpower would undermine everything that Stave's kinsmen had striven to accomplish. 'So where is the nearest river?'

'In this region,' Bhapa offered hesitantly, 'are streams aplenty. The nearest lies no more than half a league to the east. Doubtless it provides a path into Salva Gildenbourne. Yet—'

'Yet,' rasped Mahrtiir, 'it would serve neither us nor the Ranyhyn if we are assailed. Such path would be too easily blocked against us.'

'No true river enters Salva Gildenbourne from the north,' Stave added. 'Only the nearer streams flow southward. Others gather towards Landsdrop in the east. If you seek to approach Andelain by water, we must ride west and south to the Soulsease. Even mounted as we are, that journey must delay us further. And there we will be no less distant from our goal.'

Bitter with frustration, Linden faced Stave. 'Why didn't you tell me? You *knew* all this. We could have headed straight for the Soulsease from Revelstone. We could have saved—'

'Chosen.' Stave's eye flashed. 'I did not speak of the Soulsease because I had no certain knowledge of the *skurj*. Also I deem our present course to be the safer road. Any passage into Salva Gildenbourne by river will be fraught with hazard. Doubtless the Ranyhyn would be able to bear us, swimming. But doing so, they could not guard themselves.' He indicated her other companions. 'Nor could we give battle on their behalf – or on our own. Only your powers might preserve us.'

Mahrtiir and the Cords nodded their agreement.

'A raft—?' Liand offered tentatively.

Stave held Linden's gaze. 'Grant that we may devise a raft adequate to convey us. Still we would be required to part from the Ranyhyn. And still would we be defenceless, apart from your powers. Do you relish the prospect of spears, arrows, flung stones and nameless theurgies while we stand exposed upon the unsteady support of a raft?

'If you did not ward us all, we could do naught but perish.'

From the forest's edge, Linden could not see the place where the *skurj* consumed Salva Gildenbourne. She sensed nothing of the monsters. For that very reason, she seemed to feel them rush closer by the moment.

Bracing herself on the hard stone of her purpose, she said, 'All right. I'm sorry. I didn't mean to blame you.

'I'm sure that you're right. And I really can't face the delay of riding around this forest.' She did not want to give Kastenessen or Roger that much time— 'Let's go to that stream Bhapa mentioned. We'll do what we can on foot.'

Surely any watercourse would be less occluded with brush and dead-wood than the rest of the forest?

Mahrtiir nodded his assent. Without waiting for a reply from Stave or any of the Humbled, he and his Cords sent their mounts racing eastward along the fringe of Salva Gildenbourne.

Linden ground her teeth as she and the rest of her companions fol-lowed. She was galloping straight towards the most deadly of her many foes, but she could not imagine a better alternative. She had to locate Loric's *krill*; needed to find Thomas Covenant among the Dead. She would never rescue Jeremiah without them.

The Harrow's claim that he could take her to her son meant nothing while he stayed away. He may have feared Kastenessen and the *skurj* as badly as she did—

The swift run of the Ranyhyn startled birds from the nearby trees. Grasshoppers leapt away and butterflies scattered. Linden's company ploughed a furrow of small frights, quickly forgotten in the immaculate sunlight, as the riders shortened the distance between themselves and their peril.

Soon they reached the stream. It came tumbling through a notch in the nearest ridge and down a series of flat stones like shelves or stairs, then slowed as the ground tilted more gradually towards the forest. Where it disappeared under the crowded canopy, it was little more than a rill which Linden could have crossed with a step. However, the watercourse was wider than the stream. More water often flowed there, chuckling over its rocks as it was fed by spring and summer rains. If trees and brush did not throng too closely to the stream, or spill over its banks, Linden and her companions would not be forced to walk in single file into Salva Gildenbourne.

Linden could not guess how Anele's mind would be affected by the jungle, but the stones and sand of the streambed might suffice to keep him safe.

Mahrtiir and the Cords had already dismounted when the rest of the riders arrived in muted thunder. Carrying bundles of supplies, Bhapa and Pahni entered the trees at once to scout ahead. At the same time, Stave and the Humbled sprang down from their Ranyhyn to survey the forest and take defensive positions.

For a moment, Linden, Liand and Anele remained on their horses. Now that she had decided to part from Hyn, Linden found that she was acutely reluctant to do so. She had learned to feel safe on Hyn's back – And the trees seemed to brood ominously among their shadows, in spite of the distant calling of birds and the glad rippling of the stream.

Liand was uncharacteristically anxious: he had heard the *Elohim* give warning and had spent enough time in Anele's company to absorb the old man's horror of the *skurj*. And Anele himself was obviously alarmed. He tested the air repeatedly, jerking his head from side to side as if his blindness galled him. His knuckles were white as he clung to Hrama's mane.

I could have preserved the Durance! Stopped the skurj. *With the Staff!*

Somewhere underneath his madness, he blamed himself for Kastenessen's freedom. My *fault!* Behind the Mithil's Plunge, he had begged Linden to let him die. If the *skurj* closed on him, he would be trapped between terror and culpability.

Oh, hell, Linden growled to herself. She could not heal the old man's mind: he had made that clear. She had no hope for him, or for any of her companions, if she did not reach Andelain and Loric's *krill.*

Angry at her own fear, she dropped abruptly from Hyn's back and strode over to the stream. Standing in the watercourse beside the rill, she muttered, 'Let's do this. I'm not getting any younger.

'Clyme,' she ordered as Liand dismounted and began urging Anele to join him, 'you're in the lead with Mahrtiir.' She could not bear to send the Manethrall ahead alone. 'Stave, you're with Liand, Anele and me. Galt and Branl can take the rear.' The Cords would watch over the company from among the trees. If they were fortunate, they might avoid being caught. 'We should spread out a bit. I don't want anything' – or anyone – 'to hit all of us at once.'

Facing the Humbled, she added stiffly, 'I know what Handir said. No Master will answer Stave unless he speaks aloud. This is the exception. Sound won't carry far through these trees.' And she and her companions might easily lose sight of each other along the twisted stream. 'If you refuse to communicate with Stave, you might get us killed.'

Galt, Clyme and Branl gazed at her without expression. She thought that they would take offence – or simply ignore her. But then Clyme joined Mahrtiir, and Branl gestured for Linden to precede him.

Apparently they had decided to obey her.

The Manethrall met Clyme with a keen-edged grin. He bid farewell to Narunal with a deep bow and a whinnying shout of gratitude. Then he headed into the gloom of Salva Gildenbourne, compensating for his lack of sight with percipience.

Linden did not doubt that he could sense the shape of the sand and stones ahead of his feet, feel the weight of the boughs overhead, hear the quick scurrying of beetles and small animals, smell the tangled growth of the jungle. And she trusted Clyme to protect Mahrtiir from the more insidious ramifications of his blindness. The Bloodguard had esteemed the Ramen as much as the Ramen had distrusted them.

While Liand extricated Anele from Hrama, Linden hugged Hyn's neck. She felt that she should say something to thank the great horses, all of them. But words were inadequate – and she was too full of trepidation. Instead she promised softly, 'I'll see you again. I'll need you. The Land needs you.'

When Liand brought Anele to her, she linked her free arm with his, hugging his emaciated limb. She walked in the stream so that he could remain on drier ground. The water would soon soak through her boots, but that would be a minor discomfort. She wanted the old man to feel as much tactile reassurance as possible. Sand that was not damp and stones that were not slick might soothe his distress.

With Liand and Stave a few paces behind her, each bearing two or three bundles and bedrolls, she approached the sun-dappled obscurity of Salva Gildenbourne.

She did not understand why Kastenessen was wasting his time on an undefended forest when he could have torn out the Land's heart by attacking Andelain. Surely that would have been the most effective way to counter her opposition and ruin her hopes? Under *Melenkurion* Skyweir, Roger had spoken of A *portal to eternity*. He had told her, *You've done everything conceivable to help us become* gods. Yet now he and Kastenessen appeared to have no larger objective than her death.

She looked over her shoulder to confirm that Branl and Galt were ready to follow Stave and Liand. Then she secured her grip on the Staff and took Anele into the thick veil of the trees.

As her eyes adjusted to Salva Gildenbourne's crepuscular atmosphere, she found that Mahrtiir and Clyme had already passed beyond a curve in the rill. But even if the watercourse had run straight, the Manethrall and the Humbled might have been veiled by the tangle of brush and saplings that arched over the stream. Here and there, small instances of sunshine filtered through the leaves; and in those etched rays – narrow shafts of light made precise and precious by shadows – gnats and other insects danced like motes of dust. At first, the plash of her boots in the risible current seemed loud. But gradually the jungle swallowed the implications of her passage. She could not hear Anele's breathing: she could hardly recognise her own. She moved through a louring silence as if she had inadvertently crossed the borders of deafness or substance.

When she looked back now, she could not see Galt and Branl, or the place where they had entered Salva Gildenbourne. Liand's features, and Stave's, were only distinct when a moment of light touched them.

For a time, she and Anele walked down the watercourse with comparative ease. At intervals, they had to duck under hanging branches or sidestep fallen logs, but they did not encounter any significant obstructions. As they followed their gnarled path, however, they began to meet trees that had toppled across the stream. The roots of the trees had been undermined by changes in the watercourse, perhaps, or the trunks had been struck by lightning, or they had collapsed and died under the burden of too much time. Some had failed so long ago that they had sunk into the streambed, feeding moss and mushrooms with their decay. Others were more recent victims of the forest's unchecked growth, and they bristled with branches as rampant as thickets. Linden and Anele could not pass without scrambling over or crawling under the trunks, forcing their way through the boughs.

More and more, Salva Gildenbourne resembled a maze. Linden could not tell how much time had passed, or in which direction she was moving. In spite of the woodland's naturalness, its fundamental untamed health, she seemed to wander a fatal wilderland, trackless and involuted, where she was doomed to trudge in circles until her courage drained away. She only knew that she was making progress when Bhapa or Pahni appeared suddenly to relate that they had found no hazards: no lurking Cavewights or other predators; no scent or impression of the *skurj*; no sign that any other sentient beings had joined the chary animals and birds among the trees.

Whenever Bhapa paused to speak with Linden, he assured her that Mahrtiir was unharmed and fearless in the distance ahead. But Pahni lingered for Liand rather than for Linden. She whispered to him privately, confirming that he was well; promising him her utmost care.

The brief visits of the Cords comforted Linden. When they disappeared back into the jungle, she felt an unreasoning fear that she would not see them again. They were Ramen, highly skilled: she did not doubt that they understood caution better than she did. Nonetheless her apprehension grew as she advanced into the dusk and misdirection of Salva Gildenbourne.

She was not worried about Cavewights now: not here, amid the massed impediments of the forest. They would not be able to fight effectively. In addition, she suspected that Roger was too craven to assail her alone. He would insist on allies, support; overwhelming force. Nor was she concerned about wolves or other natural predators. If they were not mastered and compelled, they would instinctively keep their distance from unfamiliar prey.

And she could discern no other dangers. Riotous growth and decay surrounded her: old monolithic cedars, contorted cypresses behung with moss, broad-boughed Gilden vivid and golden where flecks of sunlight touched them, lush ferns and creepers, occasional *aliantha* and other stubborn shrubs. Such things filled her senses; walled her away from everything except the stream and her immediate companions. Even time faded: she was no longer sure of it. Whenever Liand passed her a bit of cheese or fruit or bread, she was surprised to find that she was hungry.

Still her trepidation deepened like the imposed dusk of the jungle. And Anele felt as she did – or his nerves were attuned to other dimensions of hazard and knowledge. He became increasingly agitated. He flung his head from side to side, and his hands trembled. For no apparent reason, he slapped his face as if he sought to rouse himself from a stupor. Linden heard or tasted small fluctuations in his mental state; but she could not interpret them.

Then, in a crook of the stream, she and the old man began to cross a wide sandbar littered with the mouldering remains of a scrub oak or a stunted sycamore. Abruptly he clutched at her shoulder. Grimaces and flinching passed like darker shadows over his obscured features: his arms shook with the force of an intention which he seemed unable to express.

'Anele? What is it?'

At once, Liand moved closer. Stave stepped back to study the jungle.

Bhapa and Pahni had given no warning. Linden could not remember when she had last seen them.

Anele shuddered. He dug his toes deeper into the sand, or into the decayed and crumbling deadwood, Linden did not know which.

'Linden Avery,' he whispered. His voice was hoarse with strain. 'Chosen. Hear me.'

'I'm listening.' She feared that he had been possessed again. But if some potent being had slipped through the cracks in his mind, she could not feel its presence. He may have been speaking for the sand, or the rotting wood; or for Salva Gildenbourne.

Urgently he hissed, 'Only rock and wood know the truth of the Earth. The truth of life. But wood is too brief. Morinmoss redeemed the covenant, the white gold wielder. The Forestal sang, and Morinmoss answered. Now those days are lost. All vastness is forgotten. Unsustained, wood cannot remember the lore of the Colossus, the necessary forbidding of evils—'

Anele broke off; wrenched himself away from Linden. With one hand and then the other, he slapped his face. Then he scrubbed at his seamed forehead, his milky eyes, his weathered cheeks, as if he were struggling to wipe away his derangement.

'Linden,' Liand murmured, 'Linden,' but he did not seem to want her attention. Rather he gave the impression that he was trying to remind her of who she was.

'I'm here, Anele.' Linden stifled an impulse to summon fire from the Staff, cast away shadows. The light of Law might enable him to speak more clearly. But she did not want to announce her location. 'Go on. I'm listening.'

Morinmoss redeemed the covenant—?

The old man threw out his arms as if he were opening his heart to the forest. 'There is too much. Power and peril. Malevolence. Ruin. And too little time. The last days of the Land are counted.' His voice became a growl of distress. 'Without forbidding, there is too little time.'

He wedged his feet deeper into the damp sand and rot.

'Anele.' Linden reached out to take hold of his arm. She did not know how else to steady him, anchor him, except by repeating his name. 'Are we in danger? Are the *skurj* coming?'

Anele, make *sense*.

Flatly Stave announced, 'I descry no threat. The Manethrall and the Humbled report nothing. The Cords are distant, but they do not convey alarm.'

As if in response, Anele urged Linden, 'Seek deep rock. The oldest stone. You must. Only there the memory remains.'

She stared at him. Memory—? Did he mean the ancient lore which had been lost when the sentience of the One Forest failed, and the last Forestal was gone? Did he believe that the bones of the Earth remembered what the trees had forgotten?

Did the sand into which he had pushed his feet believe it?

'I don't understand,' she protested. 'The *Elohim* taught that lore to the One Forest.' Anele had told her so himself. 'They remember it even if the trees don't. And they obviously care,' although she could not explain their actions – or their inaction. 'Otherwise they wouldn't have tried to warn the Land. Why can't we just ask them?'

Anele gnashed his teeth. 'Forget understanding,' he snapped. 'Forget purpose.' His eyes were hints, nacre and frenetic, in his shadowed face. 'Forget the *Elohim*. They, too, are imperilled. Become as trees, the roots of trees. Seek deep rock.'

'Anele, please.' Linden wanted to swear at him. 'I'm not the one who can read stone. You are. Even if I could reach deep enough,' even if she had not lost her only opportunity under *Melenkurion* Skyweir, 'I can't *hear* rock.

'I have to go to Andelain. I have to believe in what I'm doing. Covenant told me to find him. I don't know where else to look.'

Briefly the old man pulled at his bedraggled hair. Then he appeared to make a supreme effort, as if he were clasping at lucidity that leaked through his fingers like water; and his voice changed. For a moment, a handful of words, he sounded like Sunder; like his own father, eerie and sorrowing.

'He did not know of your intent.'

Then he jerked his feet out of the sand and stamped into the stream to wash them clean of perceptions which he could not articulate. In a small voice that reminded Linden of Hollian's, he murmured, 'We are not alone. Others also are lost.'

After that, he lapsed into aimless babbling, as inchoate as the secrets of the rill.

Damn it, Linden breathed to herself. Damn it. She already knew that Sunder and Hollian did not wish her to enter Andelain. Anele had been completely sane when he had spoken for his long-dead parents. He had held the *orcrest*, and could not have been mistaken. But everything else—

Forget the *Elohim*. They, too, are imperilled.

The *Elohim*—? The people who had called themselves *the heart of the Earth*? The people who had said, *We stand at the centre of all that lives and moves and is*?

Others also are lost.

Only rock and wood know the truth—

'Linden,' Liand suggested quietly, 'perhaps it would be well to offer him the *orcrest*? Without it, he cannot speak plainly.'

She shook her head. 'I wish. But we can't risk calling attention to ourselves. We don't know what the *skurj* can sense.'

Or Kastenessen—

Studying the old man, Liand nodded sadly.

When Stave urged her to continue, Linden took Anele's arm and drew him with her along the watercourse.

Darker shadows merged into each other. The flickers of light between the leaves grew more evanescent and rare, implying that the sun had fallen far down the western sky. Still her sense of time remained vague, obscured by shade and the stream's writhen path. She could have believed that she had spent an hour or days in Salva Gildenbourne, and had drawn no nearer to the boundaries of Andelain. Eventually she might find that time had no meaning at all; that Roger and Kastenessen and the Despiser had nothing to fear because she had snared herself in a place from which she could not escape.

For a while, she continued walking only because she knew that she had no choice. Her steps became an apparently endless trudge over slick stones and damp sand. The mounting gloom seemed to swallow her mind as the trees swallowed sound. She was beginning to think that she was too tired to go on much farther when Stave announced suddenly, 'Cord Bhapa approaches in haste.'

Anele tugged against her grasp on his arm, but she did not let him go.

'Has he found some sign of the *skurj*?' asked Liand tensely.

'I do not know.' Stave's voice seemed to fade behind Linden. He had stopped to scrutinise the jungle. 'He is not *Haruchai*. I discern only his alarm.'

They, too, are imperilled, Linden repeated to herself for no particular reason. Others also are lost. Someday she would be tired enough to forgive herself. She hoped that that day would come soon.

Then Anele broke free of her, and she felt a belated pang of anxiety. She heard him splash through the stream, but she was no longer able to see him: the shadows were too thick. Instead she felt him scramble westward out of the watercourse, fleeing into darkness.

'Liand!' she called softly. 'Go after him. Find Pahni.' Intentionally or not, Anele was heading towards the young Cord. 'Keep him safe.'

The *skurj* terrified the old man. After his fashion, he had good reason. And Linden could not think of any other danger – apart from a *caesure* – that might frighten him into abandoning his protectors.

Liand paused only long enough to drop his burdens beside the rill. Then he sped after Anele.

Wheeling, Linden located Stave more by his impassive aura than by his vague shape. She was about to ask him where Bhapa was when she felt the Cord's approach through the undergrowth—

—his approach and his fear. He was close to panic; closer than he had been three and a half thousand years ago, when he had returned, seriously injured, to describe the advance of the Demondim. He had never seen such monsters before. Among them, they had wielded the emerald bane of the Illearth Stone. Yet they had not scared him this badly.

'Clyme returns,' Stave told her, 'responding to the Cord's alarm. The Manethrall cannot move as swiftly. He has elected to scout eastward alone, seeking to discover more of this peril.' A moment later, the *Haruchai* added, 'Branl also draws nigh. Like the Manethrall, Galt searches to the east.'

Linden hoped that the Humbled would keep their distance until she knew what she was up against. And she did not want Mahrtiir left alone. But she doubted that Clyme, Branl and Galt would heed her wishes.

Her fingers itched on the written surface of the Staff. Its shaft was visible only because it was darker, blacker, than the masked dusk.

Bhapa seemed to rush towards her headlong. In his place, she would have tripped and fallen; crashed into tree trunks; blinded herself on whipping branches. But he was Ramen, and his craft did not desert him. Sprinting, he slipped through the jungle and sprang down into the watercourse.

Linden could not see his expression, but she smelled his sweat and desperation. His aura was as loud as a shout.

'Ringthane.' With a fierce effort, he controlled his breathing. 'I have felt the *skurj*.'

She had expected this; assumed it. Nevertheless Bhapa's words inspired an atavistic dread. On some irrational level, she must have hoped—

Gritting her teeth, she asked, 'How many? Can you tell?'

'I felt one. But—' Frustration sharpened the edges of Bhapa's fear. 'Ringthane, I cannot be certain. Such ravening and rage are altogether beyond my knowledge. Its seeming is of a multitude. And it does not advance through the forest. Rather it flows beneath the roots of the trees. I was forewarned of its presence when I beheld leaves withering for no clear cause, and with unnatural speed, as though years of blight had passed within moments. When I then pressed my fingers to the earth, I felt—'

The Cord shuddered. Hoarsely he concluded, 'I believe that I have outrun it. But its passage is swift, and it does not turn aside. I fear that it is aware of us' – he faltered – 'of you. Of your powers, Ringthane.'

'The *skurj* draws nigh.' Stave's voice held no inflection. 'It is but one, as the Cord has discerned. And it does not rise. If it does not alter its course, it will pass below us.'

Aware—? Linden thought, scrambling to understand. Below us? The fires which she and her company had seen earlier had been at least twenty leagues away. If one of the *skurj* had crossed that distance unerringly, it must have been guided somehow.

It had been directed by its master. Or Bhapa was right: the monster could sense—

But she had not made any use of the Staff.

Below us?

Anele! Instinctively she whirled towards the west. She was merely human. Perceptions attuned to theurgy would not detect her unless she exerted her Staff or Covenant's ring. The *Haruchai* would be more noticeable than she was; easier to spot. But Anele was full of Earthpower, rife with it: he had been born to it. Although his heritage was deeply submerged, he might be a beacon for any extraordinary percipience. And if he had stepped on bare dirt, even for an instant—

As she searched the evening for some hint of the old man, she saw a glimmer of white brilliance through the dark trunks and brush; and her heart seemed to stop.

Orcrest. Liand was using the *orcrest*.

Oh, God!

Below *us*. Below Stave and her. Liand's Sunstone would attract

Kastenessen's creature. Trying to calm Anele – or perhaps simply to light their way – Liand had inadvertently exposed himself to the *skurj*.

Yelling, '*Watch out!*' she snatched power from the runes of the Staff; sent cornflower fire gusting out along the watercourse. 'I'm going to try to stop that thing!' For an instant, the stream blazed as if the current had become incandescent. Then she concentrated her flame and drove it into the ground, down through sand and soil and stone, to intercept the *skurj* before it passed.

Stunned, Bhapa stared at her. But Stave appeared to understand. Grabbing the Cord's arm, he drew Bhapa away from her; out to the fringes of her fire.

At first, she could not feel the monstrous creature. Her boots muffled the sensitivity of her feet, and her nerves had not found the pitch of ravening and rage which had appalled Bhapa. Urgently she sent Earthpower and Law deeper and deeper into the earth, deeper than the oldest roots of the most thirsty trees, and still no hunger responded to her flames.

Then Stave shouted, 'Ware, Chosen! The *skurj* rises!'

In front of her, the watercourse spat filth in a spray of water, rocks, sand. The soil of its banks began to seethe as if the trees and brush were suppurating. Leaves overhead withered and charred. At the same time, she smelled gangrene; a miasma of sickness and rot; necrosis. Disease boiled upwards as though dirt and stone and wood were dying flesh.

When her power touched the surging creature, she staggered. The sheer vehemence of the *skurj* struck her like a physical blow. God, it was strong—

Putrefaction clogged her throat: she could hardly breathe. She tasted similarities to Roger's bitter scoria. But the forces which confronted her now were worse; purer. They resembled the ruddy extravagance of volcanoes: tremendous energies barely contained by the world's friable shell.

As it came, she read the nature of the *skurj*. Mindless as cyclones and earthquakes, the monster was a product of organic magic. It had been born in magma: it throve in infernos and molten stone. And it ate the living earth. The earth's flesh sustained its savagery. Yet it was not an inherent evil comparable to the Illearth Stone. Nor did it exist outside the bounds of Law, as did the Viles and their descendants. And it did not intend ruin: it had no intention except appetite.

Over the course of millennia, however, all of the *skurj* had received the legacy of Kastenessen's rage. During his Appointed Durance, they had been transmogrified; harnessed to his service. From him, they had inherited perversion. Goaded by his hate, they had become havoc and insatiable sickness.

The creature rising to devour trees and dirt and Linden did not reason, and knew no fear. Therefore it could not be turned aside. It would *eat* and *eat*, afflicting everything in its vicinity with rot, until the very Earth was torn open at last.

Gasping at the stench, Linden felt her courage fail. She could not move or think. Around her, a wide span of the watercourse and the forest boiled and frothed, immedicably diseased. The Staff was useless to her. The *skurj* consumed her flames; swallowed or ignored her power.

Covenant had told her to find him. Lord Foul and the *croyel* held Jeremiah. She and all of her companions were here because she had decided to take the Land's fate into her own hands. Now she was helpless. Before she saw Kastenessen's beast for the first time, it had already defeated her.

For an instant, the fabric of reality seemed to rip like a fouled tapestry. The ground pitched and heaved; dropped her to her knees. The pustulent reek of mortification filled her lungs, her nerves, her wailing mind.

Then the *skurj* erupted from the earth, and she gaped into its avid mouth.

It rose as tall as a Giant above her, and as thick as a cedar. Its hide was as heavy and hot as slag: the entire length of the creature emitted a terrible heat. Yet the hide shed no light. Even the tremendous kraken maw and gullet gave no illumination. Only the teeth, the fearsome fangs, long as stakes, curved and keen as scimitars, row after row of them filling the jaws: only the teeth shone. They burned with a sick red slashing radiance like lamps along the passage into hell.

Linden did not move. She believed that she could not. Her weakness was her birthright: her parents had spent their lives so that she would receive and accept their last gifts.

Nevertheless she was not the woman she had once been; the emotional cripple who had watched, frozen, while Jeremiah had surrendered his hand to Lord Foul, and Covenant had sacrificed himself for Joan. Her heart had become stone – and the stone held.

She did not move, but she could whisper. Gazing into the fanged throat of slaughter, she murmured, '*Melenkurion abatha. Duroc minas mill. Harad khabaal.*'

The *skurj* arched over her, mindless and savage. Its lambent teeth strained towards her. It could have swallowed her in a heartbeat. Yet it did not strike. Hearing her, it hesitated, caught by the potency of the Seven Words.

Then Clyme appeared on the poisoned ground beyond the *skurj*; and the suddenness of his arrival wrenched Linden from her paralysis. He was a Master, a potential antagonist. But he was also *Haruchai*: he would not hold back. Already she saw him gather himself to spring at the monster.

One touch of that fierce hide would burn the flesh from his bones. One flash of those wicked fangs would sever his limbs.

She was on her feet before she heard herself howl, 'Clyme, *no!*' Screaming the Seven Words, she flung the full strength of the Staff at the *skurj*. Every scrap of her desperation and weakness and Earthpower she transmuted to fire and hurled against the creature.

Frantically she unleashed strength enough to set Salva Gildenbourne ablaze. But the focus of her terror and resolve was so single-minded that none of her flames touched the trees.

The *skurj* reared above her. Its jaws stretched to devour her inadequacy. For a moment or two, however, a handful of heartbeats, her coruscating incendiary repulsion sufficed to stop the beast. Although it *ate* her power, she lashed it with more force than it could consume.

Hampered by fire and the invocation of Law, the *skurj* reached towards her with its bright fangs – and failed to strike.

'Clyme!' Stave shouted: a stentorian roar which Linden scarcely heard. 'Humbled! *Preserve the Stonedownor! His orcrest may serve to distract this abomination!*'

The *skurj* forced Linden backwards step after step. Its brute force, prodigious and incapable of dismay, threatened to overwhelm her. Among the roots of *Melenkurion Skyweir*, she had outfought the combined theurgies of Roger and the *croyel*. But there she had drawn directly upon the EarthBlood: Earthpower unconstrained by mortality and fragile flesh. Here she had only herself.

Then Clyme turned from the creature and ran westward into the trees, followed by Bhapa and then Branl. When she saw that only Stave remained with her, in instant danger, Linden felt a touch of relief. Retreating, she grew stronger.

Grimly she poured torrential fire into the creature's jaws; down its gullet. She was Linden Avery the Chosen. With no resources except the Staff of Law, the Seven Words, and her own granite, she had survived *Melenkurion* Skyweir's convulsion. And Caerroil Wildwood had completed her Staff. Nothing limited the puissance available to her except her own abilities; her circumscribed humanity.

Still she retreated. She had no choice. The creature was too strong: she could not hold it back entirely. But her moment of defeat had passed. As the jaws of the *skurj* blazed towards her, she reached deeper and deeper into herself for power.

Half of the beast's serpentine length remained buried beneath it. Balancing as if it were coiled, the creature thrust itself forward. With every violent movement, the fangs burned closer to Linden, and the ground boiled and rotted.

Stave stood directly behind her; supported her with his hands on her shoulders. In part, he gave her his intransigence, his unyielding *Haruchai* valour. But he also steadied her as she stumbled backwards over sand and rocks. Unable to fight the creature himself, he preserved her from falling.

In gratitude and extreme fever, Linden howled the Seven Words, and hurled conflagration as intense as a solar flare at the *skurj* – and learned the real purpose of Kevin's Dirt.

Within its definitions – within the bounds of Earthpower and Law – the Staff had no limits except those of its wielder. And Linden's doubt and terror had passed. She had been annealed in her battle with Roger and the *croyel*: she was prepared to unleash any amount of flame against the *skurj*. It was not alone. Doubtless more of its kind rushed to assail her. She would have to slay them all. The Land's life as well as Jeremiah's depended on her. She did not mean to fail.

She should have been able to ask the Staff for as much Earthpower as she needed.

But she had forgotten the cloying pall of Kevin's Dirt. The blindness, the truncation of percipience, which it imposed was only one of its effects. Fighting for her life, she discovered that Kevin's Dirt hampered other forms of Earthpower as well.

It restricted her fire.

During her battle with Roger and the *croyel*, Kevin's Dirt had not constrained her. It had not existed in that time. And it had not prevented her from extinguishing *caesures*, or from slaying Cavewights and *kresh*, because those exertions had not required as much raw force as she sought here. *Caesures* violated all Law: all Law aided her against them. And Cavewights and *kresh* were perishable, as prone to immolation as any man or woman or child.

But now– God!

Kevin's Dirt had been created for this: to inhibit the uttermost use of Earthpower. Linden was not being driven backwards because she was human and weak, but rather because her attempts to summon the full resources of the Staff were clogged by a ubiquitous fug of *wrongness*.

And this *skurj* was only one. There would be more.

Stave was right: Linden needed a distraction. She needed to risk Liand and the *orcrest* and perhaps all of her companions. She could not stop even one of these monsters with Earthpower. She would die in moments if she did not cast the Staff aside and oppose the *skurj* with wild magic.

But that would take time. She had not begun to master Covenant's ring. And white gold defied Law. By its very nature, the Staff would hamper her. It might block her altogether. Even if she surrendered it to Stave, she might not be able to invoke *the wild magic that destroys peace* swiftly enough to prevent the *skurj* from crushing her.

Stave! she cried in silence because she could not stop howling the Seven Words. Get Liand!

Stave could not hear her thoughts. She had to rely on his instinctive comprehension of her peril. She would falter and die if Liand did not distract the creature.

Just for a moment. *Please.*

I am *not going to lose my son!*

Her task should have been impossible. Without Stave's support, she would have fallen. Nevertheless she continued to block the monster's jaws, opposing its fury with fire and utter dismay.

Dimly she heard a voice that was not hers. Somewhere in the distance, Mahrtiir yelled, '*Ringthane!*' as if the word were a battle cry.

Another roar answered his, as loud as the crushing of boulders.

Then the Manethrall crashed into her from the side; drove her staggering through the stream to collide heavily with the bank of the watercourse.

At once, her power collapsed. The breath and stench were driven from her lungs: she nearly lost her grasp on the Staff. In the sudden cessation of flame, night closed like a tomb over the forest. Only the fangs of the *skurj* still shone, gaping for prey.

Linden twisted to the side. She clutched for Covenant's ring.

Between her and the monster's maw, she saw in silhouette the mighty form of a Giant. Limned by rows of ravenous burning, he advanced on her with his arms raised over his head. In his hands, he gripped a long-sword taller than she was, a wave-bladed flamberge.

We are not alone. Others also are lost.

The Giant's features were a contorted yammer of rage and insanity as he swung his sword, trying to hack Linden in half.

Chapter Nine

The Long Journey of the Lost

Stunned by her impact with the bank of the watercourse, Linden could not breathe. She had no capacity for power. Every Giant whom she had ever known had been her friend: bluff, kindly, humorous, extravagant of heart. Some of them she had loved. She would have felt a rush of joy if she had heard that those sea- and stone-loving people had returned to the Land.

The figure looming over her with butchery in his hands was unmistakably a Giant. He was at least twice her height, twice as broad, and muscled like an oak. His weathered features looked like they had been chiselled from brown marble. Even the cropped cut of his beard might have been shaped stone.

Yet he could not have belonged to the race that had called the people of the Land 'Rockbrother' and 'Rocksister' in friendship and mirth. She had seen Giants in every extreme of desperation and agony, outrage and sorrow, yearning and fear, as well as in affection and laughter and comradeship; but she had never seen one raving with madness, or frantic for bloodshed.

She could not save herself. The wave-lined blade of his longsword plunged towards her: it would hit with the force of a guillotine. Her shocked heart would not have time to beat again.

When Mahrtiir had knocked her aside, he had fallen with her. But he had rebounded to his feet in the same motion. More swift than she would ever be, he confronted the Giant, gripping his garrote between his fists. Eyeless and human, he may nonetheless have hoped to loop his cord over the flamberge, alter its arc.

The sword was sharp iron: it would sever the garrote as though the Manethrall and his weapon did not exist.

But Stave was faster than the Manethrall – and far stronger. Cartwheeling past Mahrtiir, he intercepted the Giant's blow with his feet; slammed his heels against the vicious plummet of the Giant's hands.

Deflected, the longsword hammered into the earth a handspan from Linden's shoulder.

The Giant's might buried his blade halfway to its hilt. Raging, he snatched it back to strike again.

Stave landed on his feet. At once, he leapt at the Giant's arms, trying to pin them together; hamper the Giant's next blow.

The Giant jerked him into the air as if he were a trivial encumbrance.

In that instant, the *skurj* surged forward. It sank its fangs into the Giant's shoulder.

All light vanished as the terrible jaws closed. Linden sensed rather than saw the beast heave the Giant upwards and shake him, driving its bite deeper.

She felt Stave spring clear; felt Mahrtiir search eyelessly for an opening in which he could use his garrote.

She heard the Giant howl—

—in fury: not in pain.

Now she discerned that he was armoured in stone. He wore a cataphract of granite slabs which had been fused together by some Giantish lore. Briefly the stone protected him.

But the *skurj* fed on earth and rock: it chewed through the armour. Cruel curved fiery teeth searched for flesh and muscle and bone. In spite of the Giant's tremendous strength, his entire arm would be torn away.

Still his screams were rage rather than excruciation.

He had just tried to kill Linden. But he was a Giant, a *Giant*. Instinctively she scrambled upright to defend him. Wielding the Staff with both hands, she hurled a frantic yell of flame at the creature.

In the sudden blaze of Earthpower, its multiplied fire reflecting from the stream's turmoil, she saw the jungle along the eastern edge of the watercourse erupt with Giants.

They arrived too abruptly to be counted. Linden recognised only that they were all women; that they, too, wore stone armour and brandished longswords; and that Galt was among them.

They attacked like an explosion.

One of them hacked with a massive stone glaive at the monster's jaws. Some act of cunning or magic had hardened the sword. A single blow cut the mad Giant free. Ruddy horror splashed from the exposed fangs.

Another woman slashed iron through the thick hide of the *skurj*, spilling viscid blood that reeked of rot and disease. Then she plunged her fist into the wound – into the living magma – as if she sought to rip out the creature's heart. The monster's heat tore a shout of pain from her throat; but she did not withdraw.

A third Giant chopped at the beast's body where it emerged from the ground as if she were trying to fell a tree.

Dumbfounded, Linden remembered that Giants could endure fire, even lava – at least for a short time. In their *caamora*, their ritual of grief, they purged sorrow by immersing their flesh in flames and anguish.

By that means, Covenant had released the Dead of The Grieve. Saltheart Foamfollower had enabled him to cross over Hotash Slay.

Nevertheless she snatched back her own blaze so that it would not interfere with the creature's assailants.

When the *skurj* dropped the raving Giant, he rolled to his feet. Swinging his flamberge, he charged at Linden again.

Only Mahrtiir stood between her and the shaped blade.

By the light of the Staff, she saw the Giant clearly. Flagrant lunacy gripped his features like a rictus: his desire for her death burned in his eyes. And some time ago – a year or more – his face had suffered an edged wound. A deep, scarred dent crossed his visage from above his left eye and over the bridge of his nose into his right cheek. It gave him a crumpled look, as though the bones of his skull had tried to fold in on themselves.

He was no more than two quick strides from her, near enough to have slain Mahrtiir if he had noticed the Manethrall, when one of the women clubbed at his temple with the pommel of her longsword. At the same time, Stave kicked a leg out from under him. He fell so heavily that the ground lurched.

He tried to rise, still gripping his flamberge. But the Giant who had struck him stamped her foot down on his blade; and another woman pounced at him, landing with her knees on his back.

A heartbeat later, the Giant who had freed him from the *skurj* joined her companions. Like him – like all of the Giants – she wore armour of stone. Dropping her glaive, she reached under her cataphract and drew out two sets of iron shackles. With the help of the other women, she forced his arms behind him and secured his wrists together. Then she fettered his ankles.

As soon as he was bound, his captors jumped back. He hauled his knees under him, heaved himself upright, surged to his feet. Without hesitation, he charged at Linden again as if he meant to kill her with his teeth; bite open her throat.

Grimly the Giant who had shackled him punched him in the centre of his forehead.

Her blow stopped him; may have stunned him: it seemed to alter his rage. His roar became urgent gasping. 'Slay her!' he pleaded hugely. 'Are you blind? Are you fools? *Slay* her!'

He did not appear to be aware of his damaged shoulder.

Muttering bitterly, one of the other women jammed a rock into his mouth to gag him. Then she pulled back his head and pushed down on his shoulders, forcing him to his knees.

The Giant hacking at the creature's trunk had nearly cut through it; but still the *skurj* fought, flinging foetid gouts of blood in all directions. Its fangs flared murderously despite its maimed jaw. Where its blood struck armour, the sick fluid frothed and fumed, but did not corrode the stone.

Other Giants slashed at the monster. However, they did not press their attacks. Instead they distracted the beast so that it did not turn its teeth against the woman who had thrust her arm into its viscera. Her shout had thickened to a strangled snarl of pain, but she continued to grope inside the *skurj*, trying to grasp some unimaginable vital organ.

Then she pulled away. For an instant, Linden thought that the Giant had suffered more fire and hurt than she could endure. But in her fist, she clutched a rancid pulsing mass.

With a hideous shriek that nearly split Linden's eardrums, the *skurj* collapsed. At first, the conflagration of its fangs continued to throb and flicker. Slowly, however, darkness filled the creature's maw, and she knew that it was dead.

Growling Giantish obscenities, the woman flung the monster's organ far out over the trees.

The woman who had produced the shackles retrieved her stone longsword. When she had wiped it on the bank of the watercourse, she slipped it into a sheath at her back.

Fumbling as if he were disoriented, Mahrtiir felt his way to Linden; touched her face and arms to assure himself that she was unharmed. 'Mane and Tail, Ringthane,' he murmured. 'Are they Giants? Truly?'

She seemed to hear weeping in the background of his voice. But he was too proud to surrender to his astonishment and relief.

When she tried to answer, her throat closed on the words.

How many Giants were there? She counted ten women and the madman. Two stood guard over him, ensuring that he did not regain his feet. Seven quickly formed a protective perimeter around Linden, Stave, Mahrtiir and Galt. And one – the Giant with the shackles and the stone glaive – turned towards Linden.

She was a bit shorter and less muscular than her prisoner, but she emanated great strength. Streaks of grey marked her short hair, which appeared to sweep back from her forehead of its own accord. The lined toughness of her skin suggested age – whatever that word might mean among people who lived as long as Giants – but there was no hint of diminished vigour in her demeanour or her movements. Combat and hardship smouldered in her eyes. The precise symmetry of her features was marred by a deep bruise on her right cheekbone. Rerebraces of hardened leather protected her upper arms: old scars latticed her forearms and hands.

Her manner announced that she was the leader of the Giants.

Both Stave and Galt bowed deeply, honouring the ancient respect of the *Haruchai* for the Giants; and Stave said, 'We are timely met, Giant. Unexpected aid is twice welcome. And we' – he flicked a glance at Galt – 'I did not anticipate your return to the Land.'

The woman ignored Stave and the Humbled. To Linden, she said brusquely, 'You would do well to extinguish your flame. In this dire wood, darkness is less perilous than power.'

Linden swallowed heavily, struggling to clear her throat of relief and dismay and memory. The Giant's air of command and obvious prowess reminded her poignantly of the First of the Search. This woman's countenance did not resemble the First's. Nor did her armour. Nonetheless she seemed to have emerged from Linden's distant past, bringing with her Linden's love for the First and Pitchwife, for lost Honninscrave and doomed Seadreamer.

And Linden had failed against the *skurj*. She was adrift in recollection, bereavement, inadequacy. Because she could not find any other words, she said dully, 'You killed it.'

She had done little more than slow the monster. Soon it would have consumed her—

The Staff's light was all that kept the Giants from vanishing.

'For a short time,' the Giant replied. 'Its death and your magicks will soon draw others of its kind. They will devour its remains and multiply. When they have feasted, two or three will become four or six. With each death, their numbers increase.

'Again I ask you to quench your flame. Then we must depart with as much haste as we may. These creatures – knowing nothing of them, we name them *were-menhirs* – are not laggardly. Ere long they will assail us in numbers too great for our strength.'

Linden stared in chagrin. With each death—? The *skurj* reproduced by eating their own dead? Trembling, she clung to Earthpower and Law; to herself. Without fire, she would be at the night's mercy.

What in God's name were the Giants *doing* here? And why did one of them want to kill her?

'You're a Swordmain,' she murmured as if she were stupefied. All of the Giants were Swordmainnir. Even the madman– 'Like the First of the Search'.

They could have been a war party—

Grimly the Giant answered, 'And you are Linden Avery, called Chosen and Sun-Sage' – she grinned like a threat – 'if the tales of our people have not been excessively embellished. As the Master has said, we are timely met. But if you do not—'

Sudden relief shook Linden. With a convulsive effort, she stifled her fire; let herself fall into darkness. She was known: these Giants knew her.

She did not need to fear facing them without light.

The survivors of the Search had carried stories of their adventures back to their people. The Giants loved such tales; told and retold them in eager detail. And their lives were measured by centuries rather than years or decades. They would not have forgotten her. Or Covenant. Or the love for the Land which the First and Pitchwife had learned in Andelain.

For a moment, she was lost; blinded. The intense mephitic stench and sickness of the monster's corpse overwhelmed her senses. She required other dimensions of perception in order to distinguish the figures around her, Stave, Galt and Mahrtiir as well as the Giants.

Unsteadily she said, 'I don't know how to thank you. I couldn't stop that thing.' It was only *one* of the *skurj*– 'Kevin's Dirt is worse than I thought. We would all be dead if you hadn't found us.'

'Linden Avery' – the Giant's tone was iron – 'our cause for gratitude is no less than yours. We must exchange tales. Yet our foremost need is for distance from this beast's remains.'

'Chosen,' Stave said at once, 'the Swordmain speaks sooth. We have now no guard to the east, and the *skurj* surely draw nigh. We must gather our companions and make haste.'

'Companions?' asked the woman sharply. 'You are not alone?'

'Only some of us are here.' Linden's voice still shook. 'We have—' She was about to say, —a madman of our own to worry about. But the injustice of comparing Anele to the Giant who had tried to hack her down stopped her. 'We have an old man with us. The others are protecting him.'

'They approach,' stated Galt flatly. 'Though you do not acknowledge our presence, Giant, you hear us. Watch to the west.'

'The unwelcome of the Masters is not forgotten,' the woman rasped. 'We—' Then she halted: Linden felt her stiffen. 'Stone and Sea! Your companions are a beacon, Linden Avery. Surely every *were-menhir* – do you name them *skurj*? – within a score of leagues speeds hither.'

At once, the leader of the Giants shouted, 'Quell your power, stranger! You summon a peril too swift to be outrun!'

Glimmering among the benighted trees, Liand's Sunstone shone like a star.

'Linden?' he called in the distance; and Bhapa added, 'Ringthane?' Then they fell silent. A moment later, the radiance of the *orcrest* winked out.

Linden felt them now, all of them: Liand and Anele, Bhapa and Pahni, Clyme and Branl. They were less than a stone's throw away. She might have descried them sooner if the dead *skurj* had not occluded her health-sense.

Presumably Branl or Clyme had commanded Liand to obey the Giant. If so, Linden was sure that the Humbled had not deigned to explain why.

To reassure her friends, she shouted, 'Hurry! The *skurj* is dead. We've met some people who might help us. But we have to get away from here!'

'You presume much, Linden Avery,' growled the Giant; but she did not sound vexed. Rather she conveyed the impression that she was grinning fiercely. 'How do you conclude that we may be inclined to aid you?'

Thinking of Giants who grinned and laughed, Linden grew calmer. 'Because you know who I am. The Giants of the Search were my friends. Grimmand Honninscrave and Cable Seadreamer died protecting Thomas Covenant and me. The First and Pitchwife went into the Wightwarrens of Mount Thunder with us. Remembering them gives me hope.

'You saved my life. And if that isn't enough, one of you just tried to kill me.' She had mentioned Seadreamer. After a severe blow to the head, he had gained what his people called 'Earth-Sight', a vision of a terrible danger abroad in the world. The mad Giant had also been hit hard. Now he wanted her dead. If he, too, were guided by Earth-Sight— Weakly she finished, 'The way I see it, that makes you responsible for me.'

The Giant barked a harsh laugh. 'We are too well known to you. All doubt that you are in good sooth Linden Avery, Chosen and Sun-Sage, is thus dispelled. Accept my name in token that Longwrath's sufferings do not define our goodwill. I am Rime Coldspray, the Ironhand of the Swordmainnir. Though I am far from the mightiest among us, I am so honoured' – again her tone suggested a grin – 'for my many years as for my low cunning.'

The Giants guarding the madman chuckled as if Rime Coldspray had made a familiar jest. Apparently his name was Longwrath.

In response, Mahrtiir proclaimed, 'The giving of your name honours

us. I am Mahrtiir, a Manethrall of the Ramen. Two of those who draw
nigh are my Cords. Though we are unknown to you, we have some
knowledge of you. In the distant past of our race, we were acquainted
with your lost kindred, the Giants of Seareach. They were much loved,
for they were mirthful and kind, leal and compassionate, in spite of their
bereavement.

'I have no eyes, yet I behold you well, Rime Coldspray, Ironhand. I
do not hesitate to avow that you will find naught but friendship among
the Ramen.'

His stern courtesy dignified the darkness. Hearing him, Linden felt
obliquely reproached. He may have been trying to compensate for her
comparative impolitesse.

'We are likewise honoured by the gift of your name,' replied the Giant.
'Having known Giants, you are doubtless aware that we find much
pleasure in courtesies. Nor do we turn aside from fulsomeness in praise
or thanksgiving.' The Ironhand's companions chuckled again; but she
continued darkly, 'For the present, however, we must delay further joy.
Your followers arrive, and our circumstances require haste.'

As Coldspray spoke, Linden heard her friends. The Cords and the
Humbled did not make a sound in the dense undergrowth; but Liand
stumbled occasionally, and Anele shuffled his feet as if he were feeling
his way, reluctant to come near the dead *skurj*.

As the group emerged from the trees above the watercourse, Linden
tasted Liand's astonishment, Anele's confused apprehension and relief.
The wonder of the Cords was vivid as they saw ancient tales come to
life before them. But Mahrtiir did not allow them an opportunity for
questions or explanations.

'Cords, guide us,' he commanded. 'We require a path suitable for
Giants. We must proceed towards Andelain, but more urgent is our need
to elude the coming *skurj*.' With an edge of asperity in his voice, he
added, 'Doubtless the Humbled will guard our passage. Their caution
will suffice.'

Without hesitation, Bhapa swallowed his amazement and disappeared
back into the forest, heading south and west from the stream. Pahni
was younger; too young to contain her emotions so promptly. After a
moment, however, she turned to follow Bhapa.

To Rime Coldspray, the Manethrall said gruffly, 'The Ramen are skilled in this. Their guidance will speed us. And the arrogance of the Masters is matched by their discernment and prowess. They will do much to ensure our safety.'

Galt, Branl and Clyme appeared to consult with each other. Then they withdrew into the night on both sides of Bhapa's heading. If they took offence at the attitude of the Ironhand, or at Mahrtiir's assumption of command, they did not show it.

At a gesture from Coldspray, the Swordmainnir guarding Longwrath pulled him to his feet. Others retrieved the bundles and bedrolls dropped by Linden's companions. 'Two matters remain,' the Ironhand told Linden and Mahrtiir roughly. 'Shackled, Longwrath cannot hasten. Yet I dare not unbind his legs with the target of his madness so near at hand. Five of us will accompany him at his pace, both to ward him and to preserve you, Linden Avery. The rest will follow the Manethrall's Cords more swiftly.

'However—' She surveyed Linden and Mahrtiir, Liand and Anele. 'Giants are not formed for stealth. Yet we pass with ease over or through obstacles which would deter you. And the clamour of our movements does not attract the *were-menhirs*, the *skurj*. They appear deaf to ordinary sound.

'Linden Avery, Manethrall Mahrtiir, will you permit us to bear you and your companions?'

Perhaps out of courtesy, she did not mention Mahrtiir's blindness, or Anele's.

'Linden—?' asked Liand in a congested voice.

Linden had nearly exhausted herself against the *skurj*. On foot, she would not have been able to keep pace with Liand and Anele and Stave. The Giants would leave her far behind.

She looked at Stave. When he nodded, she said to the Ironhand, 'If you don't mind. That's probably a good idea.'

Rime Coldspray gestured again; and four Giants strode forward. As one, effortlessly, they swept Linden, Mahrtiir, Liand and Anele into their arms, holding her and her companions upright so that they sat on the forearms of the women. In that position, they could lean against the Giants' chests and watch where they were going.

Anele may or may not have understood what was happening. But he appeared comfortable in his seat. Perhaps the well-meaning strength of the Giants reassured him.

Skirting the ground polluted by the *skurj*, Coldspray led her Swordmainnir out of the watercourse and into the jungle while the remaining Giants gathered to herd Longwrath along more slowly. Stave joined the Ironhand, trotting smoothly through the brush.

At first, Linden felt helpless; vaguely vulnerable. She did not know how to hold the Staff so that it would not catch on branches or vines. But gradually the oaken steadiness of the Giant calmed her. Coldspray was right: the Swordmainnir were not stealthy. They crashed through brush and boughs, leaving a tumult of frightened birds and animals in their wake. However, they were protected from thorns and jutting branches by armour and tough skin. In addition, they seemed to need as little illumination as the *Haruchai* or the Cords. And Bhapa and Pahni guided them well. In relays, so that one led the way while the other searched ahead, the Cords found a relatively clear route. The Giants were able to move with surprising speed.

—deaf to ordinary sound. Linden considered the idea. The *skurj* were creatures of the Earth's deep lava. What need did they have for organs of hearing? They had other senses.

Certainly Kastenessen did. So why had he sent just one of his monsters against her? To be sure of her location? Probe her power? Measure the effectiveness of Kevin's Dirt? In every case, the outcome of his gambit would please him. And his next attack would be more vicious—

Aiding Linden, the Giants had accepted a greater hazard than they knew.

At present, however, she caught no hint of Kastenessen or the *skurj*, or of any malevolence. And the solidity of the woman who carried her inspired a familiar trust. The mere presence of the Swordmainnir comforted her. By degrees, the pressure in her chest loosened.

While Giants and Ramen and *Haruchai* cared for her and her friends, Linden sank into herself. Resting, she tried to think about the challenge of finding the elusive mental or spiritual door which opened on wild magic.

She knew now that she could not confront the *skurj* with her Staff and live: not unless she first freed the Land from Kevin's Dirt. As matters stood, she needed Covenant's ring.

Time passed, undefined except by the long strides of the Giants, the sharp breakage of branches and undergrowth. Pahni and Bhapa guided the company with unflagging stamina and woodcraft. No one spoke until Rime Coldspray asked abruptly, 'Why do you accompany me, Master? Your comrades ward our way. Why do you not join their vigilance?'

Breathing easily in spite of the pace, Stave replied, 'You have honoured us with your name, Ironhand. Intending honour, I offer mine. I am Stave of the *Haruchai*, outcast by the Masters of the Land for my service to Linden Avery the Chosen.

'The others are the Humbled, maimed to resemble the ur-Lord, Covenant Giantfriend. It is the task of the Humbled to affirm and preserve the commitments of the Masters. They ward us because they mistrust the Chosen. They consider that her powers and needs may compel her to commit Desecration. I do not. For that reason, I have been spurned by my kindred.

'I accompany you because I have claimed a place at her side, as have the Ramen and the Stonedownor – and also the old man, after his fashion.' The Giants of the Search had known Sunder and Hollian. Presumably these Swordmainnir would recognise Stave's term for Liand. 'I have learned to fear many things, but I no longer oppose any deed or desire of the Chosen's.'

Coldspray strode forward sternly for a moment. Then she said, 'Permit me to comprehend you, Stave of the *Haruchai*. Have I heard you aright? Were the choice yours, would you welcome the return of Giants to the Land?'

In response, Stave made a sound that was as close as Linden had ever heard him come to laughter. 'Rime Coldspray,' he answered, 'Ironhand of the Swordmainnir, since the Chosen's coming I have been humbled both profoundly and often. I no longer deem myself wise enough to discourage the friendship of Giants.'

To Linden's ears, Stave seemed to be indulging in a peculiarly *Haruchai* form of humour.

'Then, Stave of the *Haruchai*,' replied the Ironhand gravely, 'I am indeed honoured by the gift of your name. Among us, the tales of the *Haruchai* are many and admirable. We have long been grieved by the dissuasion of the Masters, for we love friendship wherever it may be found. Take no offence when I ask if these Humbled are trustworthy to watch over us.'

Stave did not hesitate. 'While they encounter no discrepancy among their commitments, they remain *Haruchai*. They will preserve any life with theirs, if doing so does not betray their opposition to Corruption, or to the corrupting use of Earthpower.'

Coldspray considered his answer. 'And is this force which the Chosen wields not a "corrupting use of Earthpower"?'

'The Masters are uncertain. Therefore the Humbled guard against her, but do not demand the surrender of her powers. In our present straits, they will grant to her – and to you – their utmost service.'

'"Powers",' Coldspray mused. But she did not question Stave further.

The Giants of the Search must have taken back to their people stories of Covenant's victory over Lord Foul, of Linden and her Staff – and of white gold. The First and Pitchwife had seen Covenant exert wild magic. They had seen Linden claim his ring when he was gone. Rime Coldspray and the other Swordmainnir would know everything that their ancestors had done and witnessed.

Longwrath must have learned that history as well. It may have shaped his insanity—

Linden sighed to herself. At least she would not have to explain how she intended to fight the *skurj*.

Belatedly she realised that she did not know the name of the woman who carried her. Weary and fearful, and troubled by her unpredictable relationship with Covenant's ring, she had paid scant attention to the people around her.

One way or another, their lives were in her hands.

But she could not think of a way to address the woman without sounding brusque and graceless; too stilted to be polite. Like the courtesies of the Ramen, those of the Giants exceeded her.

While she groped for an approach, the dense canopy of Salva Gildenbourne opened unexpectedly. By starlight and percipience, she saw that Bhapa and Pahni had guided the Giants into a small glade. For some reason, the quality of the soil here discouraged trees. Instead wild grasses and brush flourished, interspersed with the piquant promise of *aliantha*.

The Cords awaited the Giants in the centre of the glade. There Clyme had joined them. When Coldspray and her comrades stopped to consider their surroundings – unrelieved jungle on all sides, dark as midnight – the Master said, 'Even Giants rest betimes, though their hardiness is beyond question. Ranging widely, we have found no sign of peril. If you will accept our counsel, you will abide here until the dawn. And if you will not sleep, mayhap you will find succour in your tales.'

The Ironhand's posture stiffened. 'The Masters mislike our tales,' she said coldly: an old grievance.

'For the present,' replied Clyme impassively, 'we find no harm in them.' His lack of inflection seemed to suggest that he did not expect Linden or her companions to live long enough to speak of what they heard.

Coldspray glared at him for a moment. Then she turned to Stave. 'What is your word, Stave of the *Haruchai*?'

His manner conveyed a shrug. 'In this the Humbled counsel wisely. The Chosen and the Stonedownor require rest – aye, and the Ramen as well, though it would be foolish to doubt their fortitude or resolve. And we would be well served by an exchange of tales.'

Rime Coldspray looked at Linden. 'Linden Avery?'

Linden nodded. 'Please.' She was tired of being a burden. 'I need time to think. And we really have to talk. I want to know what you're doing here,' at this precise point in Lord Foul's machinations, with a deranged man who craved her death. 'You may not realise how much trouble you're in.

'If we rest for a while,' she added, 'the others can catch up with us.'

Then she said quickly, 'But be careful with Anele.' She pointed at the old man. 'Strange things happen to him when he stands on grass. This glade isn't like any place that we've been before.' The grasses were wilder, tasseled like wheat, with thin, sawing blades. 'Blankets seem to protect him, but stone would be better.'

'There is no stone, Ringthane,' Bhapa observed. 'Here the loam lies deep.'

Coldspray studied Anele: his blind, staring eyes, his tangled hair and beard, his emaciated limbs; his air of madness and secret power. 'Will any manner of stone suffice?'

Before Linden could answer, Anele announced, 'He has no friend but stone. The stone of the Land is unkindly. It remembers. Yet it preserves him.'

The Swordmain chuckled humourlessly. 'Then I will offer you stone which is not of the Land. Perchance it also will preserve you, and hold no remembrance.'

First she unslung her sheathed glaive from her shoulders. Then she undid the hidden clasps which secured her armour. When she set the heavy curved plates on the ground, they formed a kind of cradle. If the stone had not been moulded to fit her, Anele could have stretched out on it.

The Giant bearing Anele lowered him to the armour. At the same time, Linden, Liand and Mahrtiir were placed on their feet. Immediately Liand moved towards Linden, brimming with questions. But the Manethrall told Bhapa and Pahni to gather deadwood from the forest. 'Fire will comfort the darkness of our straits. In this, I do not fear the *skurj*. Their hungers are too vast to regard such small fare.'

Both Coldspray and Clyme indicated their agreement. When the Cords headed obediently for the trees, Liand shook himself, shrugged, and joined them. Holding Pahni's hand, he let her lead him into the darker night of Salva Gildenbourne.

The Ironhand faced Linden again. 'As I have said, Longwrath's shackles hinder him. Some time will pass before my comrades join us. Yet I hold little fear for them. Of necessity, we have grown adept at discerning the evils which you name *skurj*. I have caught no fresh scent of them. And it appears that the Masters who ward us concur.'

'It is the word of the Humbled,' Clyme insisted, 'that there is no imminent peril.'

Coldspray seemed to ignore him. 'Therefore, Linden Avery, I deem that the time is apt for tales. By the light of the stars, and with a fire for warmth, let us each account for the strange fortune of our encounter.'

Now that she was no longer held by the heat of the Giant's arms, or shrouded by the warm vitality of the forest, Linden found that the night had turned cold. A breeze seemed to flow down into the glade from the heavens, sharp and chill.

Hugging the Staff to her chest, she said, 'I agree.' Then she asked, 'But don't you have any supplies? I haven't seen your people carrying anything.'

The Ironhand chuckled again, still without humour. 'You approach the conclusion of our tale. We are Giants, and love the journey from a tale's birth to its ending. You observe truly that we bear neither sustenance nor unworn apparel. If our weapons fail us, we have no others. However, at need we are able to endure some measure of privation.' A brief spatter of laughter arose from the other Giants; but Coldspray did not pause. 'And in this glade, none need fear hunger. Informed by tales, we know the virtue of *aliantha*. Neither our pleasure nor our solemnity will be hindered by inanition while we hold our Giantclave, seeking the import of our encounter. We must clarify our path towards a future which appears as tangled and trackless as this wood.'

'Solemnity, ha!' muttered one of the other Giants. 'In her lifetime, Rime Coldspray has never drawn a solemn breath.'

The woman's companions laughed softly again.

'You forget, Frostheart Grueburn,' retorted Coldspray, 'you who laugh at all jests and comprehend none, that I am not merely immeasurably aged and wise. I am also ripe with cunning. And while I retain my sight, I have not grown deaf. I hear you when you scoff at me.'

Now the Ironhand's comrades laughed outright, and one of them punched affectionately at the shoulder of the Swordmain called Frostheart Grueburn. With a shiver, Linden realised that Grueburn was the woman who had just carried her for several leagues through Salva Gildenbourne.

These Giants had rescued her from both Longwrath and Kastenessen's monster; and she had barely thanked them—

While she searched herself for graciousness, Liand returned laden with firewood. As he crossed to the centre of the glade, an unnamed Swordmain produced a pair of rocks and a pouch of tinder from a pocket covered by her cataphract. When he had dropped his burden, she built a small mound of twigs, leaves and bark, sprinkled them with flakes of tinder, and began striking sparks with her stones.

Brushing debris from his jerkin and leggings, Liand came to stand beside Linden. 'Giants, Linden?' he asked in a whisper. 'Are these indeed Giants? You have made no more than passing mention of such folk, and I did not think to query Pahni concerning them. Yet it is plain that you know them well.' His tone did not reproach her. 'When I beheld Sandgorgons, I conceived that the wide Earth held no greater wonder – aye, and no greater terror – for they were mighty and fearsome beyond my imagining. Now, however, I have felt the terrible puissance of the *skurj*. And I have been borne kindly by a Giant, when I had not grasped that such folk walked the world.

'Linden, I—' Liand's eyes echoed sparks. 'Perhaps my wits are sluggish. Only now does it occur to me that I do not comprehend how you are able to bear such knowledge. I am filled to bursting, and I have neither spoken with ancient Lords nor given battle in the depths of the Earth. We have witnessed powers which surpass me utterly, yet they revolve about you as moths do about a lamp – and with as little effect.

'I do not ask why you have not spoken more of Giants. They will soon speak of themselves. I ask how you contrive to endure all that you have known and done. You exceed forces and beings whose sheer magnitude turns my heart and mind to dust.'

The Ironhand drew closer as he spoke. 'Do not be dismayed, Stone-downor,' she advised him. 'There is no mystery here. She is Linden Avery, Chosen and Sun-Sage. Our tales say that she is merely magnificent.'

At the fringe of the jungle, Pahni's slim form stepped out of deeper blackness. She, too, carried a load of dead branches.

'No,' Linden protested uncomfortably. 'You're thinking of Covenant. I'm just me.' Then she faced Liand. 'And I'm not the only one who *exceeds*.' If she had ever done so. 'I'm not the one who gave those Woodhelvennin their health-sense.'

Flames had begun to bloom from the mound of twigs and tinder. The Giant put away her pouch and stones, feeding larger bits of wood to the fire as it took hold. Aching for warmth and reassurance, Linden moved closer to the small blaze.

'It's Jeremiah, Liand,' she murmured. 'He's how I do it. I would have fallen apart days ago, but I can't afford to. I can't let anything stop me. Lord Foul has my son.'

He's belonged *to Foul for years.*

But if she found the *krill*– If she could evoke Thomas Covenant—

'And you do not forgive,' Stave remarked. 'There is strength in ire, Chosen. But it may also become a snare.'

With the Staff in the crook of her arm, Linden held out her hands to the flames. Tell that to Kastenessen, she thought bitterly. Tell the Despiser. But she kept her retort to herself.

Pahni added her wood to Liand's pile, then went to stand beside him. A moment later, Bhapa approached with his arms full. When Mahrtiir had studied the supply of firewood as though he could see it, he nodded. 'You are weary,' he told the Cords. 'Gather *aliantha* and rest. As more wood is needed, perhaps Stave will guide me to obtain it.'

Pahni and Bhapa started to obey; but Coldspray stopped them. 'You have laboured much, and are indeed worn, Ramen. Permit us to perform this service.' She motioned for two of her comrades. 'Stormpast Galesend and Onyx Stonemage have ears to hear. They will not be denied our tales while they gather treasure-berries.'

In response, Mahrtiir bowed. 'Centuries have passed into millennia,' he pronounced, 'but the Giants remain considerate and compassionate. Gladly we accept the honour of your courtesy.'

Rime Coldspray smiled. 'In appearance, the Ramen are a nomadic and brusque people. Yet their politeness would grace a courtly kingdom. Were the Masters as gracious, much that now lies fallow would flourish.'

Both Stave and Clyme gazed at her without expression, and said nothing.

When the Manethrall had seated himself near the fire, Bhapa sank to the ground beside him. Pahni linked her arm with Liand's. In a more formal tone, the Ironhand continued, 'Linden Avery, it is unmistakable that you are the intersection of our tales. Yet mayhap this truth is not evident to you. Therefore I will speak first, though we are far from Home, and beset by perils which we cannot comprehend. When you have heard of our ventures, you will be better able to determine how you may account for our needs as well as your own.'

Linden edged a bit closer to the crackling fire. Its dancing illumination cast light and shadows across the faces of the Swordmainnir. At one moment, their strong faces seemed grotesque and suspicious, and at another, fraught with mirth.

'Thank you,' she said as clearly as she could. 'We just met a few hours ago, and already I haven't thanked you enough. The Giants of the Search were my friends. I loved them. I hope that when we've talked, we'll be able to face our problems together.'

She wanted the help of these women.

Coldspray nodded soberly. 'A worthy desire. Thus I begin.'

She remained standing, tall against the heavens, while Frostheart Grueburn and the Giant who tended the fire sat cross-legged nearby, and Galesend and Stonemage wandered the glade, picking *aliantha*. Anele had curled himself into Coldspray's armour as if he had lost interest in everything except the touch of her stone. But Linden, Liand and Pahni rested on one side of the fire, and Mahrtiir and Bhapa squatted opposite them. Stave remained near Linden. After a moment, Clyme drifted into the night, presumably to join Galt and Branl as they watched over the glade. He must have trusted Stave to relay the story of the Swordmainnir.

'Giants live long, as you know,' began the Ironhand. 'This is well, for we are not a fecund race, and our children, whom we treasure, are too few to content us. Thus we account for our restless roving of the Earth. Our hearts seldom find fullness among our families.

'It was with wonder, joy, and astonishment that we greeted the return of the Search, led by the First and her mate, Pitchwife. It was with mingled delight and weeping that we heard their tales, narratives of bitter loss and brave triumph, cruel suffering and dear friendship. But in the succeeding years, our happiness and amazement were multiplied when the First of the Search, Gossamer Glowlimn, gave birth to a son, and then to a second, and then in her later years to a third. This we deemed nigh miraculous, and our celebrations – which I will not describe, for one night is too brief – endured for decades.

'Yet wonder was compounded upon wonder, and joy upon joy, for as the centuries turned, the youngest son of Pitchwife and Gossamer Glowlimn, who was named Soar Gladbirth, found love and a mate in Sablehair Foamheart, called by all who knew her Filigree for her delicacy and loveliness. And in the fullness of time, Filigree also gave birth to sons, first one and then another. That alone would have made Glowlimn and Pitchwife a treasury of tales and pride, for across the millennia it has been rare and precious that two Giants were so blessed with descendants. Yet Filigree and Gladbirth were not done. When some decades had passed, they received the gift of a third son.

'Now our exultation knew no bounds. The Giants have ever lived their lives on the verge of diminishment. Our seafaring ways are in themselves hazardous, the loss of the Giants who became the Unhomed of the Land was rue and gall to us, and our children are not numerous, as I have said. In the sons of Filigree and Gladbirth, we felt that we had been granted an augury of hope, a promise that the seed of the Giants had regained its lost vitality.'

Firelight shed fraught shadows across Coldspray's features. 'Linden Avery, the third son of the third son of Glowlimn and Pitchwife was Exalt Widenedworld. But now the Giants of Home name him Lostson, and among the Swordmainnir he is called Longwrath.'

To herself, Linden groaned for Pitchwife's sake, and for the First's. But she did not interrupt the Ironhand's tale.

'The fault is mine,' continued Rime Coldspray, 'if indeed the notion of "fault" retains its meaning in such matters. Rare among our men, Widenedworld was drawn to the Swordmain craft. In jest, we say that our men are too soft of heart for battle. However, the truth is merely that their passions flow differently. All Giants love stone and sea, "permanence at rest and permanence in motion", but the adoration of our men is more direct. They are drawn to the fashioning of ships and dwellings intended to endure. Perhaps because the joy of birth and children is both uncommon and fleeting, our women seek skills and purposes which are likewise fleeting. So it occurs that we are women, as you have seen.'

While the Ironhand spoke, Galesend and Stonemage returned to the fire with their huge hands full of *aliantha*. In silence, they shared treasure-berries liberally among Linden and her companions. Linden accepted her portion and ate, although she scarcely noticed her own hunger, or the piquant nourishment of the fruit. All of her attention was focused on Rime Coldspray.

'Yet Exalt Widenedworld wished to join the Swordmainnir,' Coldspray said without pausing, 'and so he was made welcome. Thereafter his training revealed that he was prodigious in both might and aptitude, born to the sword and all weapons. Were our present plight a Search, and he whole in mind, I do not doubt that he would be the First.'

Briefly she bowed her head. Then she raised her countenance and her courage to the disconsolate stars. 'However, this is no Search. It is not guided by Earth-Sight. It is a journey of sorrow, and after our fashion we are as truly lost as Lostson Longwrath.

'When Widenedworld had mastered our more familiar skills, it fell to me to teach him cunning. Often we speak of cunning mirthfully, but the refinement of which I speak is no jest. It is the quality by which skill is transformed to art. I am the Ironhand, not because I am the mightiest of the Swordmainnir—'

'It is certain that she is not,' put in Grueburn affectionately.

'—but because,' Coldspray explained, 'I am able to best those who are mightier. Therefore the teaching of Exalt Widenedworld became my particular task.

'Gifted as he was, and exuberant of heart, within brief decades I found myself hard pressed to master him. And one day, by doom or ill chance, I misjudged his growth in our craft. With cunning rather than strength, I caused what I believed to be a breach in his self-defence, and into that breach I struck, intending to slap his forehead with the flat of my blade, blunt stone which the Swordmainnir wield in training. However, he had in some measure foiled me. By his own cunning, he had drawn me beyond my balance, and there he strove to turn my blade. Sadly either too little cunning or too much betrayed him. Because he had unbalanced me, I struck with too much force. And because he turned but did not deflect my blade, I struck with its edge.'

Liand winced, and Pahni stifled a sigh. But they said nothing. Like Linden, they were held by the Giant's tale.

'You have beheld the extent of his wound.' An undercurrent of self-recrimination troubled Coldspray's tone. 'At that time, we did not. We saw only that the bone of his visage had been broken. Therefore we tended him. Of necessity, the Swordmainnir study healing as well as warcraft. And Giants are hardy. We were grieved by the severity of his wound, but we did not fear for his life. Nor did Filigree and Gladbirth dread that he would perish, though they were likewise grieved.

'Now we have learned that death would have been a gentler fate.'

The Ironhand accepted a few *aliantha* from Galesend; ate them without haste; discarded the seeds. Then she resumed.

'His recovery was slow and arduous, and even in delirancy he did not speak. Remembering Cable Seadreamer, whose gift or affliction of Earth-Sight resulted from a similar wound, and who was rendered mute by visions, we considered that perhaps Exalt Widenedworld would also display signs of Earth-Sight. But he did not. Rather he arose one day from his bed, seemingly without cause or alteration, and announced his intention to "slay" some nameless "her". Then he struck down or forced aside the Giants tending him and hastened towards our harbourage, apparently seeking a vessel to bear him.

'The Swordmainnir captured him. What else might we have done? And when we discovered that we could not relieve his purpose – that no strength or kindness, no speech or expression of love, no medicament or *diamondraught*, calmed his violent resolve – we bound him. We had no recourse. Unrestrained, he harmed all who warded him. Again and again, he sought the harbour, and his mad wrath was terrible to those who opposed him.

'At first, his only words were, "Slay her". Later he inquired if we were fools. And no binding held him. Mere rope he parted as though it were twine. So great was his strength that he sundered hawsers. Fetters of wood became kindling on his limbs. Finally we were compelled to fashion shackles of heavy granite. Unwilling to end his life or cripple him, we knew no other means to contain his fury.

'Thereafter we gathered in Giantclave to choose what we must do. And while we debated together, he whom none now called Exalt Widenedworld shattered his bonds. With his fists, he battered senseless Soar Gladbirth his father and caused the death of Filigree his mother. When his escape was discovered, he had already taken to the sea in a small craft, a *tyrscull*, apparently intending to sail alone to the ends of the Earth in search of the "her" whom he desired to "slay".'

Mahrtiir's hands clenched each other as though he gripped his emotions in a garrote. Stave listened without expression.

'We recaptured him. Again we bound him in stone, he raving, "Slay her!" all the while, and, "Are you fools?" Only Swordmainnir stood guard over him, risking no other Giants.

'Now the disputes of the Giantclave had ceased to be, "How may we relieve his madness?" They had become simply, "How may we prevent further harm?" And our dilemma was this. We are lovers of stone. We are not cunning in ironwork. We disdain none of the metals of the Earth. Much we have acquired in trade and seafaring. But our hearts are turned elsewhere. Yet it had been made plain that we required iron to bind Lostson Longwrath. We could conceive of no other means to constrain his wildness.

'Therefore we resolved to convey Longwrath to the land of the *Bhrathair*, where iron is artfully forged – and commonly traded, for the *Bhrathair* meet the many needs of their inhospitable home with commerce. We ten of the Swordmainnir were given a compact *dromond* which we christened Dire's Vessel. A crew was chosen so that we need not be distracted from Longwrath's care. Grieving and baffled, we set our sails for *Bhrathairealm*.'

Linden held her breath without realising it. She felt neither the chill of the night nor the warmth of the fire. Long ago, she had visited *Bhrathairealm* with Covenant and the Giants of the Search. Kasreyn of the Gyre had tried to destroy them. Both Hergrom and Ceer had been slain.

'I will not consume the night with tales of our voyage,' Rime Coldspray promised, 'though it was much beleaguered, and for a time we wandered, helpless, in the toils of the Soulbiter. I am content to say that at last we found our course to known seas. Among the fading storms of summer, we gained shelter in *Bhrathairain* Harbour.

'Our sojourn there was protracted for several causes. The shackles which we required could not be quickly fashioned. And the *Bhrathair* bargained stringently, perceiving the scale of our need. Their need also was great, for a fearsome calamity – or perchance an extraordinary redemption – had befallen them.

'Some centuries past, the eldritch prison of Sandgorgons Doom had frayed and failed. By unguessed means, the Sandgorgons of the Great Desert had achieved their freedom. Yet their bestial savagery was but rarely turned towards *Bhrathairealm*. Against all likelihood, the *Bhrathair* were left in peace for decades together. When they were struck, the damage was slight.

'But no more than a moon or two before our arrival, the Sandgorgons appeared to conceive an unprecedented assault. United by some unknown force, a considerable number attacked the Sandwall of *Bhrathairealm* in a bayamo of immeasurable strength.'

Remembering how Sandgorgons had slaughtered Roger's Cavewights, Linden bit her lip.

'The *Bhrathair* feared extermination. However, it transpired that the Sandgorgons had another purpose. They did not wage warfare. Rather they merely bludgeoned a path through an obstacle. When they had breached the Sandwall, maimed the Sandhold and torn passage across the heart of *Bhrathairain* Town, they disappeared into the sea. To the wonder of the *Bhrathair*, an uncounted host of Sandgorgons had departed.

'Therefore the ironworkers of *Bhrathairealm* bartered greedily. They craved the service of Giants to restore the Sandwall, to secure the remnants of the Sandhold and to clear the debris from *Bhrathairain* Town.

'Even discounting our need to bind Longwrath,' Coldspray admitted, 'we would have aided the *Bhrathair* willingly, loving as we do both stone and friendship. But our stay among them was prolonged by another cause also. While we laboured, awaiting the preparation of shackles, we found that we were unable to imprison Longwrath. His madness appeared daily to increase his might. Or mayhap he gained aid by some unknown theurgy. Time and again, he escaped the donjons of the *Bhrathair* and our own vigilance. Time and again, we recaptured him in *Bhrathairain* Harbour while he strove to claim a vessel.

'Still he would say only, "Slay her", and, "Are you fools?"'

'Aye,' muttered the Giant who tended the fire, 'and we came to abhor the sound of those words in his mouth. We were not inured by repetition. Rather each utterance appeared to augment the meaning of his derangement. As by accretion, he acquired the authority of Earth-Sight.'

Coldspray nodded. 'Soon the *Bhrathair* grew fearful of his violence. They hastened the making of his shackles. And when he was bound in iron, we thought him helpless at last. His bonds he could not break. While we watched over him, he remained passive. Therefore we attempted to complete our promised service. By increments, the Swordmainnir became complacent. *I* became complacent. Trusting iron, we joined the Giants of Dire's Vessel in our agreed labours.

'However, we were indeed fools, as he had named us. During our absence from his donjon, he escaped his bonds, leaving them unopened and undamaged.'

Joan, Linden thought. Oh, God. For weeks, Covenant's ex-wife had slipped repeatedly, impossibly, out of her restraints.

'And now he eluded us,' Coldspray stated grimly. 'We found no sign of him, neither at the harbour nor aboard any ship, nor along the length of the Sandwall. We discovered only that he had breached the armoury of the Sandhold, beating aside its sentries to claim a sword. Thereafter it appeared to us that he had disappeared into the sea, as the Sandgorgons had done.

'When all our searching had proven fruitless, we elected to depart, thinking Longwrath lost and our purpose unmade. Approval was granted without demur, for the *Bhrathair* had learned to consider our presence costly. As the Harbour Captain escorted us aboard Dire's Vessel, however, we found Longwrath there before us, though earlier we had sought him assiduously. He stood like a heading near the prow of the *dromond* with his new blade sheathed at his back. And he did not resist when we affixed his shackles. Yet he struggled frantically when we strove to move him from his place. When we attempted merely to withdraw his sword, he fell into frothing frenzy. Therefore we left him as he was, bound and armed and calmed, with his gaze fixed before him.

'Ere we set sail, the Harbour Captain informed us that Longwrath faced in the direction taken by the Sandgorgons.'

Of course, Linden sighed, bleak in the darkness. Of course. Hugging her Staff, she faced Rime Coldspray and tried to contain her apprehension. Lord Foul was calling in his allies.

Joan had become calmer, if not more reactive or accessible, when Linden had 'armed' her by returning her ring.

'Linden Avery,' the Ironhand said with regret, 'we were entirely mystified – and felt entirely witless. Though Earth-Sight occurs seldom among us, it has never taken the form of murderous rage. Yet we had failed to manage our charge. We had failed dramatically. Indeed, we could not in good sooth name him our prisoner, for his madness or his theurgy had exceeded us.

'Therefore we took counsel together, the Swordmainnir and the

Giants of Dire's Vessel. After much debate, we determined to put aside our opposition for a time. While we could, we would set our sails to the heading of Longwrath's desire. Thereby we hoped to learn the meaning of his madness.

'Thus Lostson Longwrath became our lodestone.

'The season was now winter,' Coldspray explained as if she spoke for the gravid dark. 'In those seas, the gales of winter possess a legendary virulence. Yet we were neither beset nor becalmed. Guided by Longwrath's gaze, we encountered naught but favourable winds and kind passage. The shackles did not fall from his limbs. While he retained his sword, he accepted food and care, and offered no harm. And soon it became clear to even our crudest reckonings that his face was turned towards the Land.'

Liand and Pahni held each other with growing comprehension in their faces. Bhapa sat with his head lowered and his eyes covered as if he endeavoured to emulate Mahrtiir's blindness. The Manethrall gripped himself fiercely. Only Stave remained unmoved.

Acknowledging the reactions of her audience, Coldspray said, 'Then did we truly question the wisdom of our course. That we were unwelcome in the Land we knew, but the attitude of the Masters did not alarm us. For centuries, they have proffered only discouragement, not resistance. No, our concern was this. If indeed we traced the path of the Sandgorgons, as the Harbour Captain had suggested, we feared that a grave peril gripped the Land, and that we fared towards havoc which we were too few to oppose.

'Thus among us the words "slay" and "her" and "fools" gained new import.'

She sighed. 'And as winter became spring, we found new cause to debate our course, for it grew evident that Longwrath directed Dire's Vessel towards the noisome banes of Lifeswallower, the Great Swamp. There we were unwilling to follow his rapt gaze. The foulness of Lifeswallower dismayed our senses. Also we remembered the tales of the Search, which warned of the lurker of the Sarangrave, and of the lurker's servants, the corrosive *skest*.

'Therefore we turned aside from Longwrath's hunger. Sailing northward along the littoral of the Land, we sought a safer harbourage in The Grieve of the Unhomed.

'We did not doubt our choice,' Coldspray stated in sadness and defiance. 'We do not question it now. Yet we learned at once that the ease of our voyage was ended. Contrary and unseasonable winds opposed our course, compelling us to beat ceaselessly against them. And Longwrath emerged from his quiescence to rave and struggle. Had we permitted it, he would have hurled himself, iron-bound, into the sea. No less than three Swordmainnir were needed to restrain him – and five if we touched his blade. Yet we were also required among the sheets and canvas, for Dire's Vessel was sorely tried, and every element conspired to thwart us.

'Still we are Giants, not readily daunted. Our race has striven with sea and wind for millennia. We ourselves had endured the travail of the Soulbiter. We persisted, exerting our skill and strength to their utmost. At last, we gained anchorage in *Coercri*, ancient and ruined, The Grieve of the Unhomed.'

The Ironhand paused as if to acknowledge what she and her comrades had accomplished. When Coldspray fell silent, however, Linden's attention drifted. She remembered too much. In *Coercri*, Covenant had given a *caamora* to the Dead of the Unhomed. She needed him. And she did not have to hear the rest of the Swordmain's story to know where it was going.

She had been warned often enough—

After a moment, Coldspray resumed, 'There we deemed that we might rest. We wished to mourn for our lost kindred. And some of their dwellings remained habitable, defying long centuries of storm and disuse. But as we slumbered, believing Longwrath secure, he slipped again from his unopened shackles and fled.

'When his escape was discovered, we held a last, foreshortened Giantclave. We elected to separate, the Swordmainnir pursuing Longwrath while our friends and kin preserved Dire's Vessel for our future need.

'At another time' – Rime Coldspray looked in turn at each of her smaller companions – 'tales will be made of our urgent, maddened and maddening chase. Few Giants have crossed so many leagues so swiftly, for we ran and ran, and still we ran. Traversing Seareach southwestward, we skirted the foothills of the Northron Climbs to pass through Giant Woods and enter the perils of Sarangrave Flat. There, however, we scented faintly the ancient evil of the lurker. While we were compelled to caution, Longwrath continued to elude us. Yet he made no secret of his path. When every hint of the lurker had fallen behind us, we were able to gain ground in spite of our weariness.

'Finally we caught him, for we are more fleet than he.' Again she sighed. 'At the foot of Landsdrop, we shackled him once more. And for a handful of days thereafter, he ceased his escapes. Perhaps because we followed the path of his madness, or mayhap because the ascent of Landsdrop and the obstructions of this woodland hindered him, he permitted us to remain his captors. Thus we were granted a measure of rest.

'Yet our fear increased, for now when he spoke of "slay" and "her" and "fools", we heard eagerness as well as fury. By this sign, he revealed that he drew ever nearer to the object of his wish for murder.'

'Indeed,' murmured Onyx Stonemage. 'I am a Swordmain and deem myself valorous. Yet I knew such dread at his pronouncements that I am shamed by it.'

At Stonemage's side, Stormpast Galesend nodded. 'Though he uttered only, "Slay her", and "Are you fools?" his enflamed and avid vehemence prophesied ruin as much as death.'

Touched by an ire of her own, Coldspray said in a voice of metal, 'It was then that we first encountered the *were-menhirs*, which you name *skurj*. They were two, and they did not threaten us. Indeed, they appeared ignorant of our presence. We might have passed by in safety, as Longwrath clearly wished.

'Yet when we had witnessed their devouring of this great wood, their carnage and savagery, we could not refrain from combat. We are Giants and Swordmainnir, and our love for the living world is not limited to stone and sea. Though Longwrath howled in protest, we gave battle to the *skurj*.

'Tales will one day be made of that struggle, as they will of our pursuit of Longwrath, for we were unacquainted with our foes, and their monstrous fire and ferocity hindered our efforts to learn how they might be slain. Nevertheless at last they lay dead. And still Longwrath suffered himself to remain among us, bound and armed.

'In our ignorance, we sought to ascertain that the *skurj* were indeed lifeless by severing them into less ominous portions.' She snorted a bitter laugh. 'However, our error was soon made plain to us. Two were dead

– but in a short time, five more came to consume the fallen, and by that means their numbers became ten.'

Linden shivered in spite of the campfire's warmth.

'Then in dismay we fled, though we are Giants and Swordmainnir. We had met a foe which we could not defeat. Still guided by Longwrath's greed for bloodshed, we ran.

'Since that day, we have once more fought the *skurj*, though not by our own choosing. In some fashion which we do not comprehend, they have become aware of us. After our first battle, they did not appear to seek us out. When we chanced to draw near them, they paid no heed. Yester eve, however, we found ourselves hunted deliberately, with cunning as well as hunger. By some means, three *skurj* contrived to pass unsensed through the earth, emerging beneath our feet to catch us unprepared.

'It was there, Linden Avery, that we lost our supplies. While we gave battle, Longwrath slipped his shackles once more. Having stricken me to the ground' – she indicated the bruise on her cheek – 'he escaped. What food, raiment and weapons were not devoured by our foes, we of necessity abandoned. And it is well that we did so. Had we delayed to gather our burdens, we could not have pursued Longwrath swiftly enough to forestall the fulfilment of his madness.'

Again the Ironhand paused to regard Linden and her companions. Then Coldspray concluded, 'Thus our tale ends, though I have refrained from telling it as Giants do, fully, exploring each inference. The time is strait, and hazards await every heading. Therefore I ask. Do you now grasp how it is that we have come to be in this place at this time, and how we may be certain that happenstance has played no part in our meeting? Do you recognise that your own tale has become as necessary to us as breath and blood?

'Linden Avery, you have attained the stature of legends among the Giants. Had the Search not informed us that time flows otherwise in your world, your presence – aye, and your comparative youth – would surpass belief. You have been a redeemer of the Land, and mayhap of the wide Earth also. Yet now Lostson Longwrath craves the sacrifice of your life upon the altar of his derangement. Across a year of the world and thousands of leagues, he has pursued your death. If you do not grant us comprehension, we will remain as lost as he, and as bereft.'

Linden swallowed heavily, trying to clear her throat of implications and dread. She understood too much as well as too little, and her heart trembled. Instead of answering the Ironhand directly, she murmured, 'I don't think that they're aware of you. I think that they're being commanded.'

The *skurj* had attacked the Giants because Kastenessen wished it. So that Longwrath could elude his guardians. Now the creatures held back so that the mad Swordmain could get close to Linden again. Kastenessen meant to help him carry out his *geas*.

Liand shook himself as though he were rousing from a trance. 'Aye,' he whispered. 'It must be so. The *skurj* would not otherwise act as they have done. They are appetite incarnate. Hunger rules them, as Longwrath also is ruled.'

Like Joan, Linden thought. Joan's despair was a kind of hunger. And *turiya* Raver tormented her, urging destruction.

Kastenessen and Longwrath, Joan and Roger and Lord Foul: they all sought the same thing.

Apart from the claiming of your vacant son, I have merely whispered a word of counsel here and there, and awaited events.

Understanding too much, Linden knew that her need for the aid of the Swordmainnir was absolute, if only so that she might reach Andelain and Loric's *krill* alive.

And she could not tell them the truth. Not all of it: not the one thing which she had never revealed to anyone. If she did, they might turn their backs on her. Even Stave, Liand and Mahrtiir might prefer a doom of their own making. The Humbled would oppose her with all of their great strength.

He did not know of your intent.

While Linden attempted to sort her conflicting priorities, Stave said, 'A question, Rime Coldspray, if you will permit it?'

Unsteady flames made Coldspray's grin look crooked; broken. 'I would "permit" questions to any Master, Stave of the *Haruchai*, regardless of their unwelcome. But you stand with Linden Avery as Brinn, Cail and others of your kind did with Thomas Covenant. You require no permission of mine.'

'Then I ask if you have encountered Masters in your pursuit of Longwrath.'

The Ironhand shook her head. 'We have sighted none. But I cannot say that we have not been sighted. Our haste' – she scowled up at the stars – 'has precluded care. Apart from forests and the *skurj* and Longwrath, we have observed little. If any Master discerned us at a distance, he did so without our notice.

'Indeed,' she added, 'we pray that we have been observed – that even now some Master bears word of us, and of the *skurj*, to mighty Revelstone. The folk of the Land must be forewarned.

'Yet even a mounted Master will require many days to convey his tidings westward. For good or ill, your kinsmen will know naught of what transpires here until events have moved beyond their power to thwart or succour.'

Stave bowed gravely. His flat mien concealed his reactions. But Mahrtiir said gruffly, 'It is well. I doubt neither the valour of the Masters nor their dedication to the Land. Yet it is evident that no human flesh can withstand the *skurj*. Only Giants will serve here. The Masters would merely perish.' He turned his bandaged face towards Stave. 'As will the Ramen, and indeed the Ringthane herself, if these Swordmainnir do not accompany us – and if the Ringthane does not call upon powers other than Law to preserve her.'

Linden took a deep breath. 'Mahrtiir is right,' she told Coldspray. 'We need you. When we're attacked again, I'm going to try using Covenant's ring.' These Giants had heard the tales of the Search: they knew that she had claimed his wedding band. 'But I haven't exactly mastered it. And I don't know how many *skurj* I can face at once.'

Still hugging her Staff for reassurance, she began.

'Here's the short version. I want to reach Andelain. I hope to talk to the Dead.' She yearned to find Thomas Covenant among the Land's attending ghosts— 'And I need to locate Loric's *krill*.' The Giants of the Search would not have neglected to mention High Lord Loric's eldritch weapon. 'I'm too weak the way I am. We've all seen that. The *krill* might let me use my Staff and Covenant's ring at the same time.'

Coldspray stared at her. 'In that event,' the Ironhand said cautiously, 'your strength will exceed comprehension.'

'I hope so,' Linden responded. 'I need to be that strong.'

Then she told her story as well as her secret intentions permitted.

She glossed over those details which the Giants might already know. For Stave's sake, she said nothing of the ancient meeting of the *Haruchai* with the Insequent. And she did not dwell on the frightening similarities between Joan and Longwrath. But for herself, she omitted only the personal ramifications of her trials in the Land's past, and of her experiences with the Mahdoubt. Everyone that she had encountered, everything that she had learned or done, since Roger had first taken Jeremiah from her, she endeavoured to explain.

While she spoke, the night grew deeper. Darkness gathered close around her, relieved only by firelight and the faint silver gilding of the stars. During her tale, the rest of the Giants arrived with Longwrath still shackled in their midst. When he saw Linden, he tried to roar around his gag; began to struggle feverishly. But the Swordmainnir quelled him with as much gentleness as possible. And she did not pause for him. She had to finish her story.

Her friends listened uncomfortably. Until now, events had prevented her from telling them how Kevin's Dirt inhibited the power of her Staff. And doubtless they knew her well enough to recognise – or guess at – some of her elisions. But they did not protest. Perhaps they had grown accustomed to the ways in which she did not allow herself to be fully understood. Although that possibility grieved her, she valued their silence. She had her own reasons for truncating her story, and some of her intentions were honest.

After she was done, the Giants murmured together for a time, clearly troubled. Their firelit bulk seemed to fill the glade with apprehension. Then Rime Coldspray met Linden's gaze across the erratic dance of the flames.

'It is an extraordinary tale, Linden Avery. Your gift for brevity discomfits us. There is much that you have set aside. At another time, perhaps, we will ask more of you concerning the Insequent, Esmer, Kastenessen and halfhands. Certainly we wish to grasp how it is that you remain among the living when you have been slain.'

She glanced around at the rest of the Swordmainnir. When Stonemage, Grueburn, Galesend and the others nodded, she faced Linden again.

'However, the night grows short, and we cannot foretell how Kastenessen will direct his *skurj*. Therefore we must give precedence to a different concern.'

Linden tightened her embrace on the Staff. She knew what was coming.

The Ironhand appeared to select her words with care as she said, 'We cannot do otherwise than surmise that Longwrath's craving for your death bears upon your purpose in some fashion. Do you dispute this?'

Linden shook her head. 'Lord Foul seems to be everywhere these days. He told me that he hasn't done anything himself. He just gives advice and waits to see what happens. But even if he's telling the truth, he has a whole list of surrogates who could have twisted Longwrath's mind.' Or his madness might be a distorted form of Earth-Sight— 'One way or another, the Despiser wants to stop me.'

'Then, Linden Avery,' Coldspray pronounced distinctly, 'Chosen and Sun-Sage, it behooves me to observe that you have not named your purpose.'

Linden feigned incomprehension. 'What do you mean? I told you—'

'You wish to speak to the Dead,' countered the Swordmain. 'You desire their knowledge and counsel. This we acknowledge. But you also seek the *krill* of Loric – and you have not justified your need for its immeasurable magicks.' Her voice had a whetted edge. 'What use will you make of such vast puissance?'

'I thought that I was clear,' Linden insisted. 'I want to find my son. I want to free him from the *croyel*. I might have to fight my way through the Despiser to do that. I'll certainly have to deal with Kastenessen and Roger – and the *skurj*. And I want to do as much as I can for the Land.'

In that, she meant what she said.

'Does your intent end there, Chosen?' asked Stave quietly. 'Do you not also seek retribution?'

I do not forgive.

Linden rounded on him. 'So what?' He did not deserve her anger, but she made no effort to restrain it. 'That comes last.' She had too much to conceal. 'If I want to pay back some of my *son's* pain after I've rescued him, what do you care?'

Coldspray folded her arms across her chest. 'Linden Avery, you are not forthright.' Her eyes caught a combative glint from the firelight. 'Your words have another meaning which you do not name. It is audible.

'Will you not reveal *how* you propose to accomplish your ends? The power which you seek will not in itself uncover your son's hiding place. It may defeat Kastenessen and his *skurj*, but it will not halt the ruptures which you name *caesures*, or silence the madness of Thomas Covenant's lost mate. Nor will it reveal the machinations of the Despiser – or of the *Elohim*. It will merely enable the riving of the world.

'Why do you wish to wield illimitable might? What will you accomplish with Loric's *krill* that does not serve the Despiser?'

Linden resisted an impulse to duck her head, hide her eyes. Coldspray searched her, and she did not mean to be exposed. The Waynhim believed that *Good cannot be accomplished by evil means*. Instinctively she agreed with them. Therefore she had to trust that her intended means were not evil. Nonetheless her desire to protect her secret was inherently dishonest: it compelled her to tell lies of omission.

Yet some of her intentions were honest. She clung to that, and held the Ironhand's probing gaze.

'I'm sorry,' she said carefully. 'I know this is hard. But I'm not going to tell you. I won't say it out loud.' If she did, the granite of her heart might crack open, spilling more rage and terror and shame than she could bear. 'I need your help. I want your friendship. But I'm not going to answer you.'

Within her she holds the devastation of the Earth—

Long ago, she had learned the cost of escape. If she told the truth, someone here would try to stop her. Even her friends might oppose her. The Humbled would attack her without hesitation. Then she would be spared the burdens that she had chosen to bear – and Jeremiah would be lost to her – and she would not be able to endure it.

Liand, Pahni and Bhapa stared at her openly. Mahrtiir's stiffness suggested surprise. Apparently they had not thought so far ahead: they had focused their attention on the hazards of Linden's journey rather than on its outcome. Only Stave betrayed no reaction. He may have recognised her need to avoid the enmity of the Humbled.

Surely Galt, Branl and Clyme would not have left the glade if Stave had not agreed to let them hear what he heard?

'You prick my curiosity,' remarked Coldspray, poised and casual, like a woman ready to strike. 'Do you seek to encourage our doubts? Is that your intention here?'

In spite of his gag, Longwrath fought to make himself heard. Linden was sure that he wanted to howl, *Slay her!*

How quickly, she wondered, could the Ironhand reach her glaive? Coldspray would not need it. None of the Swordmainnir would need their weapons. Linden was too small; too human. Any blow of their heavy fists would kill her.

Trust yourself. The Giants of the Search had become her friends long before the *Haruchai* had learned to respect her.

'Yes,' she answered as firmly as she could. 'I need you to doubt me. If you don't decide to help me for your own reasons instead of for mine, I'm doomed anyway. I don't know how else to explain it. This is as close as I can come to the truth,' as close as she could afford to come. 'I've told you what I want to accomplish. If you aren't satisfied, you should walk away.'

Coldspray considered Linden for a long moment while Longwrath writhed in protest and stars thronged the cold sky. One by one, the Ironhand looked into the eyes of each of her comrades. In the moving shadows spread by the fire, some of them appeared to glower. Others grimaced.

Then she cocked her fists on her hips, threw back her head and began to laugh.

Her laughter was as rich and open-throated as an act of defiance. At first, Linden heard strain in it, effort and constriction: a difficult choice rather than humour. Almost at once, however, two or three and then more of the other Giants joined her; and her laughing loosened until it became untroubled mirth, full of gladness and freedom. Soon all of the Swordmainnir laughed with her, and their voices reached the heavens.

Liand laughed as well, as if he had been released from his cares. Pahni and Bhapa smiled broadly, and Mahrtiir grinned below his bandage. Anele stroked the smooth stone of Coldspray armour and crooned as though he were being cradled. For a time, Longwrath ceased his struggles: his gagged rage fell silent. Stave surveyed them all impassively; but the firelight in his eye hinted at relief.

Linden, too, would have laughed, if she could. The unfettered pleasure of the Giants reassured her. But she did not know what it meant.

Gradually Rime Coldspray subsided. Still chuckling, she said, 'Stone and Sea! We are Giants indeed. Though we live and die, we change as little as the permanence that we adore. In spite of our many centuries, we have not yet learned to be other than we are.

'After our children,' she continued, speaking more directly to Linden, 'tales are our greatest treasures. But there can be no story without hazard and daring, fortitude and uncertainty. Events and deeds which lack peril seldom enthrall. And joy is in the ears that hear, not in the mouth that speaks. Already you have supplied our most exigent need. You have allowed us to see that our seemingly lost and aimless voyages in Longwrath's name are but the prelude to a far larger tale.

'Linden Avery,' she proclaimed while her comrades went on laughing, 'it is enough. Seeking the import of our many labours, we will accompany you. If Stave of the *Haruchai* stands at your side, joined by the courteous and considerate Ramen – and likewise this wide-eyed Stonedownor and the anguished son of Sunder and Hollian – the Swordmainnir can do no less. Indeed, I name you Giantfriend, both for your known love towards the Giants of the Search, and in token of our own esteem.

'I have spoken.' Chuckling again, she asked, 'Does our doubt content you? Will you now accept our comradeship, come good or ill, joy or woe?'

At Coldspray's words, some of the fear lifted from Linden's heart. Although she could not laugh, she smiled warmly. '*Thank* you. The First and Pitchwife would be so proud—' The Giants may have had few children – too few – but they bred true. That was their birthright. 'Meeting you is the best thing that's happened to us since we left Revelstone.'

Her voice broke as she finished, '*God*, I've missed you.'

She believed now that none of her many enemies would be able to prevent her from reaching the Hills of Andelain.

Chapter Ten:

Struggles over Wild Magic

During the remainder of that night, Linden slept little. Her story was strange to the Swordmainnir: it raised more issues than it explained. Although they expressed concern for the weariness of their new companions, the Giants needed to talk.

They asked nothing more about Linden's intentions. For a while, they discussed the actions of the Sandgorgons, pondering what those creatures would do now that they had satisfied their ancient "gratitude". Then, with elaborate delicacy, Rime Coldspray indicated the bullet hole in Linden's shirt and inquired about the relationship between death in her former world and life in the Land.

Linden could not explain it: she could only relate what she had experienced. Like the lightning which had taken Joan, bullets were too violent for doubt. Therefore Linden could only assume that she, Jeremiah, and Roger had perished in the instant of their passage to the Land. In some sense, their presence here was permanent: they would endure until they were slain.

She had seen her son's wounds, and Roger's; but she did not want to remember them.

Clearing his throat, Mahrtiir turned towards Stave. Softly, as if he were prompting the *Haruchai*, he said, 'There are tales better known to the Bloodguard—'

Stave nodded. To Coldspray, he said, 'Thomas Covenant the Unbeliever was not the only man of the Chosen's world summoned to the Land. In the time of the new Lords, when Elena daughter of Lena was High Lord of the Council, a man named Hile Troy appeared, invoked by Atiaran Trell-mate. He it was who led the Warward into Garroting Deep, bartering his soul to Caerroil Wildwood in exchange for the ruin of *moksha* Fleshharrower's forces. Thus he ceased to be himself, for he was transformed, becoming Caer-Caveral, the last Forestal. For more than three millennia thereafter, he endured as the guardian of Andelain.'

In spite of her fatigue, Linden listened closely. Long ago, Covenant had told her about Hile Troy and Caer-Caveral; but Stave offered details which were new to her.

'The First of the Search and Pitchwife were present,' remarked Coldspray. 'We know their tale. If we understand events aright, Caer-Caveral's final sacrifice did much to enable Covenant Giantfriend's victory over the Despiser.'

Stave shrugged. 'It may be so. The Masters and all *Haruchai* distrust violations of Law. We are not persuaded that the ur-Lord would have failed to achieve his victory by some other means if the Law of Life had remained unmarred.

'However, it is of Hile Troy that I would speak, rather than of Caer-Caveral.'

The Manethrall murmured his approval. Liand and the Cords listened as they had since the tales began, rapt and troubled.

With his usual flatness, Stave said, 'She who invoked him, Atiaran Trell-mate, perished when she had completed his summons. By the common understanding of the Lords, the death of the summoner ended the summons. So it transpired three times for the ur-Lord, the Unbeliever. Yet when Atiaran Trell-mate died in fire, Hile Troy remained.

'The Council of Lords believed that his summons was not undone because in his own world his death preceded that of his summoner. Therefore his spirit could not return to its former life, and his place in the Land was fixed.

'I cannot know if Hile Troy's example is pertinent to the plight of the Chosen and her son. Their summoner yet lives, though she is tormented and possessed.

'Nonetheless,' the *Haruchai* stated with an air of increased concentration, 'there is hope in Hile Troy's tale. The woman Joan wields wild magic. With High Lord Loric's *krill*, the Chosen may be able to confront her, and yet remain among us. If so, the Land will be spared much, and perhaps Linden Avery's son also.'

The Giants considered Stave's assertion for a long moment. Then their leader chuckled grimly.

'You are cunning as well as valorous, Stave of the *Haruchai*. Indirectly you seek to allay both our doubts and those of the Humbled. At another time, perchance, my comrades and I will applaud your service to Linden Giantfriend. For the present, however, we can do no more than acknowledge that the magicks which rule the passage between worlds lie beyond our comprehension.'

The Ironhand's expression tightened as she continued. 'Of other foes and powers, we know only that they do not appear to threaten us here. But the peril of Kastenessen and his *skurj* is immediate and urgent. If Linden Giantfriend seeks the *krill*, Kastenessen must oppose her. And I do not doubt that he will strike with all the ferocity he may command.'

He hasn't brought very many of them down from the north yet. But he can get more whenever he wants them. Roger had lied about any number of things – but occasionally he had told the truth.

A score of those monsters would devour Linden's entire company as easily as breathing.

'By my reckoning,' said Coldspray, 'Andelain lies perhaps eight or nine leagues distant. But we cannot know whether Andelain has been overrun with *skurj*. If the *krill* has been neither taken nor unmade, it stands beyond the Soulsease. And Salva Gildenbourne's abundance hinders us. I foresee frantic battle and desperate flight ere we may hope to approach our goal.'

And while the company fought, Longwrath would strive for Linden's death. Two or three Giants would have to guard him at all times, regardless of the scale of Kastenessen's attacks.

'Linden Avery,' the Ironhand pronounced formally, 'Chosen and Giantfriend, you have spoken of white gold. We have no other clear hope. If we cannot trust to the Staff of Law, then only wild magic may preserve us.'

Linden felt the focused attention of the Giants. Even Longwrath paused to listen. While her friends watched, she reached under her shirt and drew Covenant's ring into the firelight.

Trying to be precise, she said, 'It isn't literally true that Covenant gave this to me, but it's probably fair to say that he left it for me. I've certainly claimed it.' And used it. 'You might think that I already have enough power to accomplish almost anything. God knows I've astonished myself—' She still did not understand how she had saved herself and Anele from the collapse of Kevin's Watch. 'But it doesn't come easily. I have to work hard for it.

'Maybe I'm afraid of it.' Covenant had taught her that wild magic tended to surge out of control; that with each use it grew more rampant and ungovernable. 'Or maybe I don't really have the right to wield it.' According to Roger, only the person to whom white gold truly belonged could call forth its full strength. 'All I know is that I can't chance it when I'm holding the Staff. Apparently Law and wild magic are antithetical.'

She believed this even though she had once exerted both argent fire and Earthpower. With Covenant's ring, she had melded Vain and Findail to form a new Staff of Law; her Staff. Then she had wielded both wild magic and Law to remain in the Land while she ended the Sunbane, began healing its ravages, and restored her friends. And since that time, her Staff had been annealed in EarthBlood; refined with runes. Caerroil Wildwood had granted her new possibilities which she did not fully comprehend.

Nonetheless Esmer and Stave together had assured her that no ordinary flesh could withstand such forces. In Kiril Threndor, when she had taken up Covenant's ring, his spirit had protected her. His love and her own grief had enabled her to perform feats which should have been impossible. And her summons to the Land had already been half undone: she had not been entirely corporeal. Now her health-sense insisted that she was simply inadequate – too human and frail – to contain or manage Earthpower and white gold simultaneously.

Like her struggles under *Melenkurion* Skyweir, the Forestal's runes had not made her strong enough to overcome the hindrance of Kevin's Dirt.

'On top of that,' she finished bitterly, 'I'm helpless whenever Esmer decides to put in an appearance. I don't know how he does it, but his presence blocks me. I can't touch wild magic while he's around.'

Abruptly Anele spoke from the cradle of Coldspray's armour. Stroking the rock, he murmured, 'This stone is unaware that Kevin's Watch has fallen. The knowledge is too recent – and too far removed. The stone believes. It will hold, ignorant of ruin.'

With Liand and Pahni, Linden stared at the old man. She wanted him to say more – and to say it so that she could understand him. *Seek deep rock. Only there the memory remains.* But he ignored her yearning. Nestled in the cataphract, he lapsed into incoherence again.

Oh, hell. With a sigh, Linden turned back to face Coldspray.

The Ironhand was grinning, but her eyes were empty of humour as she said, 'Take no umbrage, Linden Giantfriend, when I observe that you do not nurture confidence. Considering your many uncertainties, do you yet insist that you must gain Andelain and the *krill*?'

Linden glared up at the Swordmain. 'Lord Foul has my son. I'm certain of *that*.' She had been fused to her purpose: her heart held no room for doubt. 'If you don't want to risk it, I'll go by myself.'

For the second time, Coldspray and her comrades laughed joyfully. Linden might have thought that they were mocking her; but they were Giants, and their laughter held rich affection rather than scorn.

'Ah, risk,' the Ironhand said as she subsided. 'Linden Avery, *life* is risk. All who inhabit the Earth inhale peril with each breath. Though some hazards inspire more alarm than others, the truth remains, as sure as stone and sea. We are Giants and adore life. We do not baulk at mere risk.'

Comforted, Linden sighed again. 'I know. I just forget sometimes. Covenant might say something about laughing yourselves to death. Me, I'm just glad that you're here.'

At that moment, Longwrath's desire for her blood seemed a small price to pay for the warmth and aid of Giants.

Later Liand and the Cords opened the bedrolls so that Linden's company could try to find a little sleep before dawn. As she stretched out in her blankets, however, the Stonedownor squatted beside her. 'I wish rest for you, Linden,' he said softly, 'but I also fear it. The Giants are mighty, and they fill me with gladness. But if we are assailed by more than two or three *skurj* together—'

'Why do they not attack now? If Kastenessen directs them, does he not grasp that delay is perilous to him? Surely he must harry us while we remain far from the *krill*.'

In the background of his voice, Linden heard that his concern was more for Pahni than for himself. Like Linden's, his passage through Salva Gildenbourne had been comparatively easy, while Pahni's efforts had tested her Ramen toughness.

'I don't know, Liand.' Linden lay holding the Staff, although it did not reassure her. 'He's waiting for something, but I have no idea what.' Roger and Cavewights? *Moksha* Raver and *kresh*? Sandgorgons? 'Maybe he just needs time to gather more *skurj*.' Or maybe Lord Foul had other plans for Kastenessen. She had been given hints which revealed nothing. 'I can't worry about it right now. I'll just paralyse myself.'

Face it, Covenant had once told her. *Go forward. Give yourself a chance to find out who you are.* But he had also said to Liand through Anele, *I wish I could spare you.* Yet Liand was more afraid for Pahni, Linden, and the others than for himself.

His courage was less conflicted than Linden's.

For a while, he considered her and the campfire and the sharp night. Then he said through his teeth, 'Indeed.' A moment later, he surprised her by adding, 'When our need is upon us, I pray that you will entrust the Staff of Law to me, as you did when we fled through time to counter the Demondim.'

Before she could respond, he left her and went to lie down on his own blankets beside Pahni.

She could not read his thoughts, but she recognised the character of his emotions. He had reached a decision, one which resembled his determination to offer health-sense to the Woodhelvennin.

He had conceived of another extravagant use for his *orcrest*.

That prospect troubled her until weariness overcame her, and she drifted into an anxious sleep, fretful and unresolved.

Dawn came too early: Linden was not ready for it. But she forced herself to arise when Stave spoke her name. Jeremiah needed her. All of her companions needed her. Befogged by too little rest and too many dreams, she stumbled towards the campfire to warm the chill from her bones.

The Giants must have kept the flames burning all night.

She had made no attempt to wield wild magic since she had created the *caesure* which had carried her to Revelstone after she had recovered her Staff. Now she was not sure that she knew how to find the pathway to power hidden within her.

The Swordmainnir were all awake and moving, as were the rest of Linden's friends. Under Mahrtiir's blind supervision, Bhapa, Pahni and Liand prepared all of their remaining viands so that the Giants could each have one or two mouthfuls to supplement their breakfast of *aliantha*. While Linden rubbed her hands over the fire in the dim, grey morning, Stave informed her that the Humbled had discerned no danger during the night. Kastenessen was still waiting– She nodded inattentively: her thoughts were elsewhere. She could feel her health-sense leeching from her, sucked away by Kevin's Dirt.

As always, she felt an almost metaphysical pang of bereavement. Without percipience, she could not gauge the condition of her companions. And she could not see into herself. She had never tried to wield wild magic under the bale of Kevin's Dirt. She might be entirely unable to access Covenant's ring. She would certainly not be able to control its force.

But if she restored herself with Earthpower, she would attract the *skurj*.

When she had eaten a few treasure-berries, and their tonic vitality had begun to lift the brume of fatigue and dreams from her mind, Linden looked around for Rime Coldspray.

The Ironhand was with Longwrath. While Onyx Stonemage and another Giant held him, shackled but ungagged, Coldspray interrupted his harsh demands by pushing *aliantha* into his mouth. He chewed the berries reflexively, swallowing the seeds as well as the fruit. They seemed to feed his rage.

Beckoning for Stave to join her, Linden approached Coldspray through grass heavy with dew. As soon as the Ironhand greeted her, she said, 'Coldspray, we need to talk.'

Without hesitation, Coldspray asked another Giant to take over her task. Then she faced Linden and Stave, towering over them like a buttress against uncertainties and fears.

'I didn't ask you last night,' Linden began. 'Have any of your senses changed since you came to the Upper Land? Do they seem diminished?'

Coldspray shook her head. 'They do not. I behold your concern, Linden Giantfriend. I see that it swells within you, though I cannot hear its name. And we retain our acuteness to the evil of the *skurj*.'

'Good. You're like the *Haruchai*. Kevin's Dirt doesn't affect you. But the rest of us—' Linden dropped her gaze, irrationally ashamed of her weakness. 'We're being numbed. All of our senses are fading. And it's getting worse. Soon we'll be' – she fumbled for an adequate description – 'stuck on the surface of everything. We won't be able to see anything that isn't right in front of us.'

'We will preserve you,' Coldspray replied gruffly. 'Stave and the Humbled will do the same.'

Linden shook her head. 'I know you will. That's not the point. The point is that I can't use power,' any power, 'without my health-sense. Liand can't use his *orcrest*. The Ramen will lose some of their effectiveness as scouts.'

Coldspray started to object, then stopped herself and waited for Linden to go on.

With an effort, Linden raised her head again. 'We can solve the problem. Temporarily, anyway. But we can't do it without Earthpower – and that draws the *skurj*.' Bracing herself on granite, she concluded, 'Before we put you in any more danger, you should have a chance to think about it. If you have a better idea—'

Her voice sank away like water in sand. She could not imagine any response to the threat of Kastenessen and his creatures except wild magic.

Stave consulted the rising dawn. 'The Humbled distrust any exertion of Earthpower. However, they can offer no alternative. They are certain that stealth alone will not ward us from our foes. And they remain in doubt concerning your purpose. They have not yet opposed you. They will continue to refrain.'

'And you, Stave of the *Haruchai*?' asked Coldspray with a glint of morning or humour in her eyes. 'What is your counsel?'

The former Master gave a slight shrug. 'I have said that I no longer oppose the Chosen's deeds and desires. Also there is this to consider. Some use of *orcrest* or the Staff of Law may provoke a premature reply.

Should Kastenessen strike before his forces have been fully prepared, he will grant us an advantage which we could not obtain otherwise.'

The Ironhand chuckled. 'My friend,' she said, slapping Stave lightly on the shoulder, 'your cunning grows ever more evident. If it should chance that you weary of being *Haruchai*, know that you will be made welcome among the Swordmainnir. Lacking the good fortune – and also the stature – of our blood and bone, you will become a Giant by acclamation rather than by birth.

'Linden Avery,' she continued more seriously, 'my thoughts follow Stave's. We cannot hope to conceal our presence from the discernment of an *Elohim*. Therefore we lose naught, and may gain much, if Kastenessen answers the cleansing of your senses.'

Linden ducked her head again. When she raised her eyes, she tried to smile. 'Thank you,' she said unsteadily. 'I must have spent too much time alone. I keep forgetting what it's like to have friends. Stave and Liand and the Ramen are doing their best to teach me, but I'm out of the habit.'

Coldspray and the Giants around Longwrath replied by laughing as though they were delighted. 'Linden Giantfriend,' the Ironhand explained, 'that tale is too sad for tears. "Out of the habit".' She laughed again. 'And its dolour is made more cruel by brevity. We are Giants. If we do not laugh, we will be compelled to insist upon the full tale of your years and loneliness. The very blood in our veins will require it.'

'Slay her,' remarked Longwrath. 'Slay. Her.' For the moment, at least, he sounded strangely casual. He may have been affected by *aliantha*. Or perhaps the mirth of his people eased his turmoil.

'Oh, well,' Linden sighed, feigning sorrow or disappointment while her heart lifted. 'I haven't forgotten *everything*. I do remember Giants.' Then she called over her shoulder, 'Liand! Are you ready?'

At once, the Stonedownor bounded to his feet. 'I am.' His piece of Sunstone was already in his hand, and his face was bright with eagerness.

Quiescent, his *orcrest* seemed both translucent and empty, as if it formed a gap in the substance of his palm.

An oblique memory caught Linden. Millennia ago among the Dead in Andelain, High Lord Mhoram had urged Covenant to *remember the paradox of white gold.* Covenant had described that occasion to Linden days later, after he had rescued her from the Clave. *There is hope in contradiction.*

In Garroting Deep, the Mahdoubt had said the same thing. *Upon occasion, ruin and redemption defy distinction.*

Then Liand tightened his grip; and the Sunstone began to shine. Its light was whiter, purer, than the argent cast of wild magic. And it did not burn or flame: it simply emitted an immaculate radiance. Soon it filled the glade.

While the Giants watched in wonder, Liand bathed Pahni in whiteness until she, too, shone as if she had been transfigured.

Linden knew that the young Cord was afraid for Liand: Pahni dreaded the implications of his power or his fate. Nevertheless she made no attempt to conceal her gladness as her health-sense was renewed.

Linden ached to share in that restoration. Her nerves hungered for it.

Fortunately experience had made Liand adept. Although his people had been denied their true birthright for millennia, his entire being responded to the Sunstone. He needed only a few moments to cleanse Mahrtiir's perceptions, and Bhapa's. Then he turned his light on Linden as if it were chrism.

Earthpower could not heal her emotional hurts. It could not relieve her anguished yearning for Jeremiah – or for Thomas Covenant. Still it made her feel whole again; capable in spite of her many limitations. When Liand was done, she was once again the Linden Avery who had beaten back Roger and the *croyel;* the Linden who could tear open time—

Trust yourself. Do something they don't expect.

I can't help you unless you find me.

The Giants observed in mute joy, as if they were witnessing an exaltation. Then as one they began to cheer.

There is hope in contradiction.

At the same time, Longwrath's rage returned. 'Slay her!' he demanded. '*Slay her!*'

Liand ignored the other Swordmainnir. Linden saw the brilliance of *orcrest* echo like daring in his eyes as he strode towards Longwrath. Days ago, she had witnessed the Sunstone's effect on Anele. Clearly Liand intended to try a similar experiment with the damaged Giant.

Through his madness, Longwrath appeared to understand Liand's purpose. As the Stonedownor approached, Longwrath hunched suddenly forward, jerked his guardians off balance. Then, roaring, he pitched himself backwards with such vehemence that he broke free.

He landed on his back; flipped over to pull his feet under him. As he sprang upright, the shackles dropped from his wrists and ankles. An inarticulate howl corded his throat as he snatched his sword from its sheath.

Quickly Liand retreated. Quenching the Sunstone, he hid it behind his back. Chagrin burned in his face.

Linden feared that Longwrath would harm one of the Swordmainnir; but they recaptured their comrade with practised ease. Coldspray stepped in front of him and engaged his flamberge with her glaive, compelled his attention, while four women circled swiftly behind him. As soon as Coldspray created an opening, another Giant kicked him in the small of his back. The shock of the blow dropped him to his knees; and immediately the women swarmed over him. In a moment, they had twisted the sword from his grasp and pinned his arms.

Muttering Giantish curses, the Ironhand retrieved Longwrath's shackles and secured his wrists and ankles. Deceptively gentle, she replaced the gag in his mouth; returned his sword to its sheath. Then she left him to the care of Galesend and another Swordmain.

Linden sighed with relief – and regret. 'Well, *that* didn't work.'

'Forsooth,' growled Coldspray trenchantly. To Liand, she said, 'I do not doubt that your attempt was kindly meant, but you must not hazard it again.' He nodded, openly dismayed, as she continued, 'I fear that Longwrath poses a greater threat than any *skurj*. He will free himself and strike when we are least able to oppose him. Do not provoke him further.'

The thought made Linden's stomach clench. 'Then what should we do? He's going to get people killed, and there are too few of us as it is.'

The Ironhand scowled around the glade, considering her choices. 'We will separate once more,' she announced. 'Surely Kastenessen does not desire the death of one who desires yours. While Longwrath lags behind us, he will be spared. I will ask three of my comrades to accompany him.' Clearly she meant, To guard him. 'If Stave and the Manethrall of the Ramen have no better counsel, the remainder of our company will hasten towards Andelain with such speed as Salva Gildenbourne permits.'

Stave deferred to Mahrtiir. The Manethrall cleared his throat. 'My Cords will again scout our path. Their task will be to seek clear passage for long strides. It falls to the Humbled to ward us against peril.' Then he turned his bandaged face towards Bhapa and Pahni, locating them by scent and sound and aura. 'But you must also seek rocky ground. Surely vestiges of the former plains remain, bouldered and barren, where the ancient litter of scarps and tors hinders the trees. If it can be done, we must stand among an abundance of loose stones when Kastenessen strikes.'

He did not explain himself; but Linden assumed that he thought her companions would be better able to defend themselves if they were not obstructed by jungle and brush.

Bhapa swallowed heavily. 'We hear you, Manethrall. If your command can be met, we will meet it.'

Pahni gave Liand a quick hug, then clenched her teeth and left him to stand beside Bhapa.

With fierceness in his voice, Mahrtiir replied, 'I do not doubt you. Trust to the Humbled, and fare well.'

However, Bhapa and Pahni did not set out immediately. Instead they waited to hear what the Ironhand and Stave would say.

'Stave of the *Haruchai*?' asked Coldspray.

Stave shrugged. 'The Manethrall is wise and farseeing in the ways of strife. The Humbled approve his counsel. And I do not fear for them. It is their word that they are much healed. While they live, they will ward us.

'Rime Coldspray, I inquire only if you will bear the Chosen and her slower companions, as you have done before.'

'We will.' The Ironhand snorted a laugh. 'Indeed, we insist upon it.' Several of her comrades nodded. 'As stealth will not serve us, we must have speed.' Then she looked to Linden.

'Linden Giantfriend, what is your word?'

Linden took a deep breath; tightened her grip on the Staff. With as much confidence as she could summon, she said, 'All right. Let's do it. Just take care of Anele. And keep Liand near me.'

Chuckling, Frostheart Grueburn stepped forward and lifted Linden into her arms. 'You misgauge us, Linden Avery,' she said with a grin. 'Though we are large and for the most part foolish, we know a stick when it jabs our eyes. Any man as blighted as your old companion compels our esteem. Already we prize him.'

Stormpast Galesend chortled at Grueburn's jest as she picked up Anele; cradled him gently against her stone-clad chest. While the Ironhand donned her armour, Grueburn continued more seriously, 'As for the Stonedownor, we have heard you. He must bear the Staff of Law when the time has come for wild magic. Salva Gildenbourne permitting, Onyx Stonemage will run at my shoulder. At worst, she will be a stride before or behind me.'

Stonemage bent down so that Liand could sit on her forearm. Then she carried him to Grueburn's side. Both Giants appeared to be stifling laughter.

A Swordmain who introduced herself as Cirrus Kindwind bowed to Mahrtiir gravely before she presumed to take him in her arms. Her manner revealed an instinctive sensitivity to his emotional straits. Being carried as if he were a child galled his combative spirit. Hidden deep within him was a dumb snarl of anguish and frustration. Kindwind had not known him before he lost his eyes. Nevertheless she appeared to recognise – and respect – his denied distress. She supported him on her forearm as if he were a visiting dignitary, and her posture conveyed the impression that she bore him with pride.

As Coldspray finished securing her cataphract, three Giants pulled Longwrath to his feet. The rest gathered around the Ironhand. At a nod from Mahrtiir, Bhapa and Pahni ran south across the glade. Abandoning the blankets and bundles that Linden's friends had brought from Revelstone, seven Giants and Stave followed the Cords towards the knotted shade of the jungle.

Behind them, Longwrath protested through his gag. But he made no effort to break free. His shackles remained in place. For the moment, at least, he seemed willing to shuffle along in the wake of the woman he wanted to kill.

Then Rime Coldspray and Stave led Grueburn, Kindwind, and the others at a brisk trot into Salva Gildenbourne. The thick gloom of the trees closed over Linden's company, immersed her in darkness. The early light could not penetrate the canopy. While her eyes adjusted to the shifting weight of shadows, she felt herself hurtling towards a future which might become an abyss.

Branches slapped at Grueburn. A few flicked Linden's head and shoulders. The path of the Cords left no room for Grueburn and Onyx Stonemage to run side by side. Stonemage was compelled to follow Grueburn. Nonetheless it was obvious that Pahni and Bhapa had found a route along which the Swordmainnir could travel easily. While Bhapa scouted farther ahead, Pahni stayed near enough to guide the Giants. To Linden, they seemed to flit among the massive old trees and the younger saplings.

Because she felt helpless and wanted reassurance, she called softly, 'Stave, where are the Humbled?' She did not trust herself to raise wild magic suddenly. She would need warning—

Stave's voice filtered back to her through the leaves. 'Galt and Branl match our pace to the east, where we are certain of the *skurj*. Galt ranges ahead while Branl wards our rear at the outermost extent of our speech. To the west, Clyme watches. When the *skurj* approach, we will be fore-warned while they are perhaps a league distant.'

A league, Linden thought; but the word told her nothing. She could not estimate distances in the constricted and bestrewn jungle. And she had no idea how swiftly the *skurj* might come. She only knew that tree trunks and boughs, fallen deadwood and swarming vines, rushed past her with disorienting quickness; that she crossed low hills and swept through shallow vales before she could count them; that Grueburn's breathing was deep and hard, but far from desperation, and that her strength ran like valour in her veins. All of the Swordmainnir gave the impression that they were as fleet as Ranyhyn.

If they could sustain this pace, would they reach the boundaries of Andelain by noon?

Whatever happened, Linden would not have much time to prepare herself for Kastenessen's attack.

Still she was too distracted to concentrate. Grueburn's steps shook her; and the woodland inundated her senses with a cacophony of growth and decay. Sunlight began to glitter in the treetops. Around her, the forest seemed to unfurl endlessly, rumpled and unruly; manic with untended life. From the jouncing perspective of Grueburn's arms, Salva Gildenbourne appeared impenetrable. The Swordmainnir should not have been able to move so rapidly. But at every twist and angle of the earth, every place where the trees clustered to form a barricade, every obstruction of vines and deadwood, the Cords found a path that allowed the Giants to run unhindered.

Hills and more hills. Swales and streambeds. Unexpected swaths of open grass bedecked with wildflowers. Small marshes like puddles in the jungle.

Every stride brought the need for wild magic nearer; and still Linden was not ready.

Snagged occasionally by snarls of brush, the company pelted down a long slope. Whenever Grueburn missed her footing and collided with a tree, she wrapped her free arm protectively around Linden; accepted the impact with her shoulder and ran on. Held against the woman's armour, Linden felt the jolt as if she had been punched. But the branches that plucked at her face and arms only scratched her rarely; slightly. She kept her grip on the Staff.

She did not know how Mahrtiir's Cords contrived to stay ahead of the Giants. She was familiar with the immense stamina of Coldspray's people. And Stave was *Haruchai*. But there was nothing preternatural about the Ramen, except perhaps their communion with the Ranyhyn. Being smaller, Bhapa and Pahni had to sprint while the Swordmainnir trotted. Surely even their hardiness would not enable them to continue like this indefinitely?

At the bottom of the slope, the Cords led the Giants into a ravine like a jagged wound in the flesh of the terrain. There the ground was complicated with boulders, and the Giants were forced to move more slowly. In that respite, Linden cast her health-sense ahead; tried to catch a hint of Pahni's condition. But the ravine twisted: the mossed granite of its walls blocked her view. The thick odours of damp, mould and cold stone crowded her nose. She was tossed from side to side by Grueburn's passage around and over the boulders. And the Giants in front of her filled her percipience. When she concentrated on Mahrtiir, Liand and Anele, she could see that they were well. But she failed to detect Pahni's presence.

'Mahrtiir?' she asked anxiously. 'I'm worried about Pahni and Bhapa. How long can they keep this up?'

Over Kindwind's shoulder, the Manethrall answered, 'You have not been long acquainted with the Ramen, Ringthane. At need, we are able to run briefly with the Ranyhyn. And our inborn endurance is rigorously trained.

'My Cords will perform all that is asked of them.' After an instant's hesitation, he added, 'Yet it is plain that they near the limits of their strength. I do not wish them driven beyond themselves, if that may be avoided.'

As one, the Giants slowed their strides. Through the labour of their breathing, Linden heard Coldspray ask, 'Stave?'

'The Cords have guided us well.' Stave did not sound winded. His voice betrayed none of his exertions. 'We will sacrifice the benefit of their aid if we ask more haste than they can sustain.' To the Ironhand's unspoken question, he replied, 'The Humbled sense no peril.'

'Very well.' At the head of the company, Coldspray slackened her pace further. 'In all sooth, we also are weary. We have known no true rest for many days, and even Giants must tire.

'I gauge that we have traversed four leagues. Doubtless our foes gather against us. If the Manethrall's Cords discover a favourable battleground, perhaps we will do well to await our doom there rather than hazard exhaustion.'

'Aye,' answered Mahrtiir. 'Rime Coldspray, you possess wisdom as well as cunning. If Kastenessen desires to prevent us from Andelain, he must strike soon. Therefore speed is no longer our greatest requirement.'

Covered in omens of shadow, the Ironhand's aura seemed to imply a wish for confirmation. Again she asked, 'Stave?'

Stave's tone resembled a shrug. 'If the Chosen does not gainsay it, I concur with the Manethrall.' After a moment, he added, 'As do the Humbled. The time has come to seek terrain which may aid us.'

'Linden Giantfriend?' Coldspray inquired. 'Do you consent?'

Four leagues? wondered Linden. Halfway to Andelain? She had no idea how much time had passed. Sunshine spangled the leaves in tiny flecks far overhead, but the sides of the ravine hid the sun. If the Giants had indeed covered four leagues—

Coldspray, Mahrtiir and Stave were right. Kastenessen would attack soon. She needed to prepare herself.

What in God's name was he waiting for?

Perhaps he was not waiting. Perhaps he had already prepared an ambush in Andelain.

The possibility that the *skurj* were feasting among the Hills of Andelain made Linden feel sick. But she swallowed her trepidations.

'You're probably right. In any case, I don't have a better suggestion. I could use the rest. And I need a chance to pull myself together.'

At once, the Ironhand sent one of her unburdened comrades ahead to talk to Pahni and Bhapa. Stave and the other Giants continued along the depths of the ravine.

Vaguely Linden wondered how much ground Longwrath and his guards had lost – and how long he would delay before he tried to kill her again. But she could not afford to distract herself with such concerns. The Swordmainnir would protect her. She needed to focus her attention on power and the *skurj*; on Thomas Covenant's ring and his illimitable resolve. Not for the first time, her circumstances pressed her to surpass herself.

A grieved and frightened part of her insisted that she was not Covenant, she was *not*. She had never been his equal. It was folly to pretend that she could match his capacity for extravagant and unforeseen victories.

But if Roger and the *croyel* had given her time to think in the cave of the EarthBlood, she would have said the same; and by doing so, she would have helped them to destroy her. At least in part, she had succeeded against them because they had left her no room for self-doubt. Jeremiah's wounded helplessness and the *croyel*'s cruelty had made her certain.

That certainty remained deep in her, as unshaken as buried stone. As long as she did not dwell on her inadequacies, she would be able to fight for what she loved; oppose what she loathed. She would find a way.

She had done so after the destruction of First Woodhelven.

Resting in Grueburn's arms, Linden searched herself for scraps of Covenant's power.

Gradually the walls of the ravine slumped away, releasing the company into a wide valley bordered on the south by an overgrown escarpment, high and thick with trees. Glimpsed through the jungle, the skyward thrust of the scarp looked too sheer to be climbed. But Bhapa and Pahni found a path upwards by angling across the rise, bracing themselves on tree trunks and clinging to bushes. The roots of the trees and brush were deeply knotted in the escarpment's fissured bones: they held the Swordmainnir as easily as the Ramen. Linden's company made the ascent with less difficulty than she would have thought possible.

Beyond the crest, Salva Gildenbourne lost elevation by slow increments; and the Giants quickened their pace. Here the soil lay more thinly over its bedrock. Wider spaces separated the trees: undergrowth no longer clogged the ground. At irregular intervals, rocks mantled with grey-green lichen jutted among Gilden, sycamore and oak. For the first time since dawn, Linden could look around her and see all seven of the Swordmainnir. When she glanced at Liand, he smiled to reassure her.

Pahni remained out of sight ahead, hidden by broad-boughed trees and the heavy shoulders of the Giants; but now Linden caught hints of the Cord with her other senses. Although Pahni moved fluidly down the gentle slope, she emanated an unmistakable pang of fatigue. Linden could feel the Cord's muscles trembling.

Soon, Linden thought. Bhapa would have to find a place that suited Mahrtiir soon.

Abruptly Stave's head jerked. An instant later, he announced to Coldspray, 'The *skurj*, Ironhand. Galt has discerned them.'

Fear clutched at Linden as the Swordmain asked, 'Is he able to count their number?'

'He cannot. They blur at the limit of his senses. However, they advance as though they are certain of us. And their pace exceeds ours. Soon Galt will endeavour to number them.'

Coldspray glanced back at Mahrtiir and Linden. 'Shall we run, then? Is there hope in flight?'

Presumably the Giants could carry Pahni and Bhapa.

'Galt deems that there is not,' replied Stave flatly. 'Trees and terrain do not hinder the *skurj*. And they appear capable of great speed. Can you outrun them at need? Can you do so until we have gained Loric's *krill?*'

The Ironhand shook her head. 'We have run too much. Already weariness weighs upon us, though we are Giants, and proud of our strength. If it can be done, we must abide by the Manethrall's counsel.'

'Then my Cords must be forewarned,' growled Mahrtiir. 'They cannot hear the minds of the Humbled.'

'Cabledarm!' Coldspray called to one of the Giants. 'This falls to you. Overtake the Cords. Aid them in their search.'

'Aye,' Cabledarm responded. 'Who else?' She bared her teeth in a willing grin. 'When wisdom and cunning exhaust themselves, simple strength must prevail.

'Observe and learn, Linden Giantfriend!' she shouted as she broke into a run. 'It is with good cause that Cabledarm is acknowledged as the mightiest of the Swordmainnir!'

Assisted by the slope, she seemed to bound after Pahni.

'Mightiest, ha!' muttered Grueburn to her comrades. 'I claim that title. Free my arms, and I will "acknowledge" any might that strives to prove itself against me.'

Several of the Giants chuckled; but Coldspray commanded sternly, 'Quicken your strides, Swordmainnir. Haste now may earn a measure of respite ere the *skurj* assail us.'

The women picked up their pace. Linden expected them to race after Cabledarm, but they did not. Instead the Ironhand held them to a swift walk. After a moment, Linden realised that Coldspray did not want to overrun the Cords' search for *an abundance of loose stones— —the ancient litter of scarps and tors—* When – or if – Bhapa found a place that satisfied Mahrtiir's requirements, Coldspray wished to head towards it without needing to double back.

Trembling as if she, too, had run for leagues, Linden touched her pocket to confirm that she still had Jeremiah's racecar. Then she drew out Covenant's ring.

Irregular splashes of sunshine caught the small metal circle as the sun rose towards midday. Whenever Covenant's wedding band flared silver in her hand, Linden winced involuntarily. Please, God, she prayed without hearing herself. Please. The ring looked puny against the pale skin of her palm; too little to encompass either hope or contradiction.

Wild magic is only as powerful as the will, the determination, of the person it belongs to. The rightful white gold wielder.

With it, Covenant had mastered Nom; faced Kasreyn of the Gyre; denatured the virulence of the Banefire. Wielded by the Despiser, its savage ecstasy had exalted Covenant's spirit to secure and sustain the Arch of Time. And Linden herself had caused a *caesure*. *In the wrong hands, it's still pretty strong.* Nevertheless this immaculate instance of white gold was not hers.

It doesn't really come to life until the person it belongs to chooses to use it.

Roger could have been lying; but she did not think so. Too much of what he had said matched her memories, her experiences.

Damn it. She clenched her fist around the ring. She had created one *caesure*: she could form another; catch the *skurj* in a mad whirl of instants and send them hurtling towards an imponderable future. If she were willing to take the risk—

When she had asked Roger about Falls, he had replied, *Eventually they'll destroy everything.*

On that subject as well, she could believe that he had told the truth.

All right, she promised herself grimly. No more *caesures*. I'll try something else.

But she did not know what she would be able to attempt.

In the distance ahead, she felt Cabledarm reach Pahni; felt the Giant sweep Pahni into her arms and go on running. They sought Bhapa, but they passed beyond Linden's range without finding him.

Moving at Coldspray's side, Stave spoke so that Linden and the Manethrall could hear him. 'Branl reports no threat. It appears that Longwrath and his escort will not be assailed. And Clyme also descries no presage of harm. Therefore he and Branl come to join our defence.

'Galt will do likewise. However, he intends first to number the *skurj*. At present, he perceives less than a score. If he discovers no increase in their force, he will endeavour to learn if they may be made to turn aside.'

Linden flinched. One of those monsters could swallow Galt whole—

'Then he is a fool,' snapped the Ironhand.

Stolidly Stave replied, 'He is *Haruchai* as well as Humbled, neither slow of wit nor weak of limb. He will not sacrifice himself except in our direct aid. Rather he will seek only to determine whether the *skurj* may be slowed or diverted.'

Coldspray started to respond, but a distant shout interrupted her. Muffled by trees and foliage, Cabledarm's bellow was barely audible.

'A place is found! Alter your heading somewhat eastward!'

Eastward– Closer to the *skurj*.

The Ironhand stopped; turned to face Mahrtiir. 'Manethrall,' she said tensely, 'our esteem for the Ramen grows ever greater. To say that your Cords have served us well is scant praise. We cannot delay for true gratitude. Know, however, that we are honoured to claim the friendship of a people who possess such fortitude and skill.'

Before he could answer, she spun away and began to run. At once, her comrades followed, angling slightly to the left as they rushed between the trees.

Linden did not know how far they ran. Fears confused her. Repeatedly she caught herself holding her breath. Nevertheless the pace of the Giants made it obvious that Salva Gildenbourne's verdure was growing thin. As the soil lost its richness, it exposed new sheets of stone and older out-croppings of bedrock stained by weather and time and lichen. Few shrubs and saplings obstructed the strides of the Swordmainnir. Gilden, ancient oaks and occasional, brittle birches stood farther apart, allowing swaths of sunlight to reach the ground. The Giants flashed through incursions of brightness as if they flickered in and out of predictable reality.

Ahead of them, the trees opened briefly. Through the gap, Linden spotted a rocky tor, high and rounded like the burial-mound of a titan. Then the Giants ran into full sunshine, brilliant as Staff-fire; and she found herself staring at a formation like a volcanic plug so immeasurably ancient that the eons had worn it down to rubble.

It seemed tall to her: she could not have thrown a pebble to reach its crown. Yet it stood lower than the surrounding trees. Without Bhapa's guidance, and Pahni's, the Giants might easily have missed it.

Boulders as big as dwellings supported its sides, but the rest of the mound was composed of broken rocks in all sizes and shapes. From Linden's perspective, the crest looked wide enough for all of the Giants to stand together and wield their weapons.

Mahrtiir's eagerness suggested that the tor was exactly what he wanted.

But Linden was not convinced. If her companions chose to defend themselves atop the mound, they would have no line of escape.

Bhapa stood, panting urgently, at the foot of the knuckled slope. But Cabledarm had carried Pahni up the tor. The Swordmain waved dramatically as her comrades emerged from the forest. 'I recant my vaunt!' she crowed: a shout of delight. 'Skill may accomplish much which lies beyond the reach of muscle and thew! The Manethrall's Cords have humbled me. *I* would not have stumbled upon this admirable redoubt!'

'It will serve,' muttered Mahrtiir, peering at the mound with senses other than sight. 'Here even Ramen may oppose Kastenessen's vile beasts.'

Linden blinked in the sunlight; shook her head. Bhapa's condition alarmed her. He gasped as if he were still running, on the edge of exhaustion. Dehydration made his limbs tremble. Apparently he had not paused for treasure-berries or water while he searched. After the battle of First Woodhelven, he had refused Mahrtiir's place as Manethrall. Perhaps in compensation, he had nearly prostrated himself to prove worthy of Mahrtiir's trust.

By finding this tor? Linden did not understand. The *skurj* devoured granite. She had assumed that the Cords sought an open rock field where the Giants could dodge and strike and flee. If they mounted the rocks, they would be trapped.

But the Ironhand did not seem to share Linden's concern. 'Serve?' she retorted as if Mahrtiir had made a jest. 'It will do more than serve. It will concentrate our foes where the advantage of elevation and stone is ours. If Linden Giantfriend does not falter, we may yet hope for our lives.'

If Linden did not falter—

'Galt hastens towards us,' Stave announced. 'The *skurj* pass beneath him. He has failed to deflect their course. Therefore he will endeavour to outrun them. He descries eighteen of the creatures. If others follow, he cannot yet discern them.'

'And the distance?' asked Coldspray.

'Less than a league.'

The Ironhand nodded sharply. 'Then we must ascend now. Linden Avery may ready her power while we prepare ourselves.'

Coldspray's comrades responded quickly. As Grueburn and Stonemage confronted the piled boulders, the last unburdened Giant lifted Bhapa into her arms and began to climb.

Supporting herself with her free hand, Grueburn worked her way upwards. Time and weight had made the tor more stable than it appeared. And the Giants were intimately familiar with stone in every manifestation. None of them slipped on their way to the crest of the mound.

There the rocks were jagged and dangerous. Cracked granite and slick basalt protruded everywhere, as raw-edged as teeth: an invitation to twisted ankles, scraped shins, snapped bones. Combat would be difficult here. The Giants would have to watch where they placed their feet as closely as they studied their assailants. However, the crown formed a rough circle broader than Linden had guessed, perhaps thirty paces from edge to edge. Her defenders would have more than enough room to fight.

Grueburn set her down carefully. Bracing herself on uneven angles and splits, Linden looked at Pahni to gauge the young Cord's condition. Like Bhapa, Pahni was close to the end of her strength – and seriously dehydrated. And she lacked his years of training and stamina. In spite of her Ramen pride, she sagged against Cabledarm.

As soon as Stonemage released him, Liand sprang over the rocks towards Pahni. He seemed careless of the treacherous surface, but his Stonedownor heritage must have guided his feet. He reached her in a moment; caught her in his arms. When he had held her for a few heartbeats, he panted, 'Water. She is hardy, but she must have water.'

'As must Cord Bhapa,' muttered Coldspray distantly. Her gaze searched the eastward expanse of Salva Gildenbourne as if she sought to see past or through the trees. 'We have none. And I will not risk one of my comrades to seek out a stream.' Then she glanced at Liand, smiling to reassure him. 'Yet we would be abject indeed, unworthy of ourselves, if we had failed to secure some meagre store of *diamondraught*.'

Liand stared, uncomprehending and frightened; but Linden's anxiety for the Cords eased. She remembered *diamondraught* well. It was a potent liquor distilled to suit Giants. But it had virtues in common with *aliantha*: it would restore Bhapa and Pahni for a while.

Grinning, Grueburn and Stonemage reached under their armour and brought out stone flasks that looked small in their massive hands. By some application of Giantish lore, the flasks had been fashioned flat and slightly curved so that they fit comfortably inside the shaped armour.

Grueburn gave her flask to Liand; let him care for Pahni while Stonemage tended to Bhapa.

Relieved, Linden turned to consider the state of her other companions.

The Giants were visibly tired. They had been under too much strain for too long: their huge vitality had begun to fray like overstressed hawsers. But they still had reserves of endurance. And a few swallows of *diamondraught* appeared to lift their hearts.

At need, they would fight with the force of gales.

When Galesend released him, Anele moved, blind and sure-footed, towards the centre of the crown. There he sat down, wedged into a snug crack between boulders. Bowing his head, he began to stroke the stone and hum as if he wished to soothe it.

Less certain than Anele, Mahrtiir felt his way around the rim of the crest, apparently examining the stones. Then he said to Stave, 'You comprehend the worth of this vantage?'

'I do,' replied Stave impassively. 'As will the Humbled. I honour your foresight, Manethrall.'

'I merit no honour, Stave of the *Haruchai*.' Mahrtiir continued his scrutiny of the mound. 'I will be of scant use in these straits.' Then he bared his teeth. 'Yet I am gladdened that my devotion to the lessons of struggle and combat has been of service.'

'Manethrall,' Rime Coldspray put in like a reprimand, 'your tales are as mournful as Linden Avery's, and as bitter in their concision. Do not speak of them here.'

'Aye,' Mahrtiir growled under his breath. 'I hear you.' His bandage obscured his eyeless mien.

Muttering empty curses, Linden scanned the region around the tor.

When she looked to the west, she saw Clyme emerge from the forest. He ran easily; flung himself at the steep sides of the tor without obvious difficulty. She saw at a glance that he had told Stave the truth: his injuries were almost entirely healed.

A few moments later, Branl approached from the northeast. He sped to join Linden and her companions, unhampered by the rugged climb, as if he were as much an acolyte of stone as the Giants. He, too, was nearly whole.

Linden felt Galt's absence like a burr in her mind. She wanted to wait for him; to hear his report on the movements of the *skurj*. To postpone as long as possible the moment when she would need to concentrate on white gold. Every life around her depended on her ability to wield Covenant's ring. Fearing failure, she hesitated to make the attempt.

For that very reason, however, she could not afford to procrastinate any longer. She could *not*. Her companions had trapped themselves, and her. The *skurj* did not yet impinge upon her health-sense, but they were near. Kastenessen was not the Despiser. If Roger had described him honestly, his driving agony would make him impatient, intolerant of delay. She did not know why he had waited so long—

Now, she commanded herself. Do it now.

Liand still hovered over Pahni. Nevertheless Linden called his name as if she were callous to his apprehension. When he turned towards her, she said simply, 'Here,' and handed him the Staff of Law.

Instant possibilities flared in his eyes. He had asked her to do this. Perhaps he thought that holding the Staff would enable him to channel more Earthpower through his *orcrest*.

Linden nodded to him, accepting the promise of his nascent excitement. Then, half cowering as though she felt naked without her Staff, exposed to shame and inadequacy, she clambered awkwardly towards a flat sheet of basalt within ten paces of the crest's eastern rim. There she seated herself cross-legged, folded Covenant's ring in both hands as if she were praying, and tried to think her way to wild magic.

Around her, the Giants drank small sips of *diamondraught*; talked quietly among themselves; adjusted their armour and readied their weapons. Clyme and Branl watched the east for Galt and peril. Stave waited, apparently relaxed, beside Linden. At Mahrtiir's command, the Cords gathered to protect Anele.

Two or three paces beyond the old man, Liand stood alone with the Staff and his unspoken desires.

For the first time, Linden noticed the breeze that gusted over the tor, rustling like whispers among the treetops on all sides. Its touch made her aware of tiny lines of pain like damp streaks on her cheeks and forehead.

She had been scratched during the rush of the Giants through Salva Gildenbourne. Bits of scab crusted her small hurts.

But some of the branches must have caught at her shirt hard enough to snag and tear the red flannel. Minor rents were scattered over her shoulders and down her arms. A few of them held droplets of dried blood. Like the bullet hole over her heart – like the cryptic grass stains on her jeans – the tears and plucked threads seemed trivial; meaningless. They did not reveal her doom.

Jeremiah needed her. She needed Thomas Covenant. Nothing else mattered.

The door that opened on silver fire lay within her somewhere. She only had to find it.

But when she reached inwards, there was no door. Instead a twist of nausea squirmed in her stomach.

Oh, *God*! Sudden terror thudded through her. That's *it*! *That's* what he's been waiting for!

Hardly realising what she did, Linden dropped the ring. It dangled, useless, from its chain as she sprang to her feet—

—and Esmer materialised in front of her as if he had created himself out of wind and sunlight.

Kastenessen's grandson, by theurgy if not by blood. *I serve him utterly. As I also serve you.*

Without hesitation, Stave stepped between her and Cail's son; the son of the *merewives*. Shouting in surprise, the Giants wheeled. Their ready blades hissed across the breeze. Branl moved towards Stave. Undisturbed or simply uncaring, Clyme continued to watch for Galt and the *skurj*.

'Mane and Tail!' Mahrtiir snapped. 'Esmer, *no*! This is not mere betrayal. It is Kastenessen's triumph, and Fangthane's.'

If Liand reacted, Linden did not hear or feel it.

Esmer's presence precluded wild magic. Beyond question, this was what Kastenessen had been waiting for.

Yet Linden's terror became dismay as she stared at Esmer. Unconsciously she had expected him to heal himself; to appear immaculate and severe, poised for power. But she was wrong. His graceful cymar hung in tatters, fouled with dirt and blood. And the wounds which he had suffered in his bizarre struggle with the Harrow, Roger and the Demondim-spawn remained. His flesh had been burned and torn because he had declined to defend himself. Now his hurts stank of filth. Some of them were festering.

The green seethe of his gaze resembled weeping seas. Dolour and gall twisted his countenance. He looked like he had come to ensure Linden's death; to make certain that both the Staff of Law and Covenant's ring fell to Kastenessen – or to Roger and Lord Foul, if Kastenessen disdained such powers.

Coldspray stood behind him. 'Is this indeed Esmer?' she asked through her teeth. 'Then I will dismiss him.' Raising her stone sword, she demanded, 'Turn, caitiff cateran, and make the acquaintance of my glaive.'

Without glancing away from Linden, Esmer cried, 'Hold!' The word was a yelp of chagrin.

Sharply Stave said, 'Do not, Rime Coldspray. His powers are unfathomable and virulent. Should he so choose, he will shatter this mound, sweeping us into the maws of the *skurj*. Your strength will merely provoke him. You cannot prevail.'

Coldspray hesitated, but did not lower her sword. 'Linden Avery—' she began; then stopped as if in shock.

Until Mahrtiir barked her name, Linden did not see that the peak of the tor teemed with ur-viles and Waynhim.

In silence, they swarmed like shadows around the far taller Giants: several score of them, all that had survived the Harrow and Roger and the weapons of the Cavewights. Once again, their lore had enabled them to divine Esmer's intentions. And they had veiled their presence until he manifested himself. Now they massed around Linden and Cail's son, encircling Stave and Branl.

'Linden Avery—' Coldspray repeated. With an effort, she quenched her surprise. 'What is your will? Are these the creatures that have aided you? The Demondim-spawn? Why then do they now ward Esmer? We cannot oppose him without harming them.'

In response, the Waynhim and ur-viles began to shout, raucous as wild dogs. Their yipping howls and harsh coughs filled the air. They seemed to cast a pall over the tor as if their inherent darkness obscured the sunlight.

None of them brandished weapons. Even the loremaster did not.

Coldspray tried again. 'Linden—'

Esmer cut her off. Suddenly disdainful, he rasped, 'They do not ward me, Giant. That is the import of their speech.

'You possess a gift of tongues obtained from the *Elohim*. By my will, it is withdrawn. At no time will you be permitted to comprehend these creatures.

'However, they command me to inform you that they serve the Wildwielder. They acknowledge Giants. They have known the Unhomed, for good or ill. If you strike at them, they will not guard themselves. For her sake, they will raise neither hand nor theurgy against you. Yet you play no part in their desires.'

Coldspray glanced around at her comrades, then shook her head in bafflement. By my will— Apparently Esmer had the power to enforce his word.

Linden had made a promise to the ur-viles and Waynhim. *If you can ever figure out how to tell me what you need or want from me, I'll do it.* Now Esmer had erased her only chance to understand them.

'But they also wish you to apprehend,' he continued less scornfully, 'that their lore will not slow the *skurj*. They cannot preserve you.' An emotion that resembled remorse troubled his gaze. 'They intend only to ensure that I may harm neither you nor any of the Wildwielder's companions. If they mean to proffer some further service, they do not speak of it.'

The Ironhand's shoulders sagged. As if in defeat, she dropped her glaive back into its sheath. 'Then we must perish, son of malice. Kastenessen's beasts are too many. We cannot defeat them without wild magic – and we are informed that your presence prevents any use of white gold.

'Is that your purpose? Will you impose our deaths?'

'It is my nature.' Hauteur fumed like spray from Esmer's eyes, but his voice winced. 'I am made to be what I am. I do not command the *skurj*. Like them, I am commanded.'

Fierce with alarm and granite rage, Linden wanted to retort; but Stave spoke first. Facing Esmer impassively, he said, 'You are swift to cast blame, Esmer *mere*-son. It is your word that because of the *Haruchai* "there will be endless havoc". Yet is it not sooth that you fault Cail your sire and his kindred for your deeds rather than for theirs? The "havoc" will be of your making, not ours. When we fall' – his tone sharpened – 'we fall by your hand, Esmer, not by any act or reticence of the *Haruchai*.'

Esmer flinched. But he did not respond. And he did not withdraw.

Before Linden could voice her own accusations, Clyme announced, 'Galt approaches.' His voice carried, blunt as a fist, through the clamour of the Demondim-spawn. 'The *skurj* follow. They do not hasten, but they come.'

Involuntarily Linden imagined a path of blight and withering in Salva Gildenbourne's abundance, formed by the fiery passage of Kastenessen's monsters.

'Are they eighteen?' asked Coldspray tensely. 'Does that remain Galt's count?'

'It does,' Clyme answered. 'He has discerned no others.'

Branl's lack of expression suggested a sneer as he turned abruptly away from Linden, Esmer and Stave. The ur-viles and Waynhim parted for him: their barking subsided as if they had given up demanding translation. A few of them watched Branl join Coldspray and Clyme. Others shifted their attention towards Anele and Liand.

'Eighteen.' The Ironhand bowed her head. 'It cannot be done.' But then she raised her chin, bared her teeth. 'Nevertheless we will attempt it.'

Her eyes flared dangerously as she began positioning her comrades to defend the tor.

Linden had tried before: she tried again. But she found no wild magic within herself. The door was gone. The sick clench of her stomach confirmed its absence. She could not pierce the barrier imposed by Esmer's proximity.

And she could not oppose the *skurj* effectively with her Staff: not while Kevin's Dirt held sway.

Nevertheless she was not beaten. She refused to accept it. *Aid and betrayal.* Esmer's presence was a betrayal. Therefore he was vulnerable. His divided nature would compel him to help her, if she could ask the right questions, insist on the right answers; find the right lever—

You must be the first to drink of the EarthBlood.

His gaze remained fixed on her as if none of her companions existed. He ignored the Demondim-spawn. In a voice that steamed with pleading, he asked, 'Wildwielder, why have you come to this place?' His wounds seemed to ooze concern like pus. 'What madness drives you? Have you not been told that you must not enter Andelain? Do you hear neither friend nor foe?'

Linden shook her head. 'Damn it, Esmer,' she countered, 'can't you even *heal* yourself? Is this *really* what Kastenessen wants?' Or Lord Foul?

She intended to put as much pressure on Esmer as she could. And she was not going to reveal her underlying purpose: the bedrock on which she had founded all of her actions since *Melenkurion* Skyweir.

His manner stiffened. 'I have inherited many gifts. There is no healing among them.'

Cruelly Linden insisted, 'Your own grandfather wants you like this?' Flagrantly wounded, suppurating with pain. 'He doesn't want you whole?'

Esmer squirmed. 'Delivering the Demondim-spawn to this time, I displeased him. Defending them against the Harrow, I displeased him greatly. His wrath is boundless. Therefore I am here.'

Behind him, Galt appeared on the rim of the mound. The Master's chest heaved, demanding air, but he did not look weak or hurt – or troubled. 'They come,' he informed Coldspray and the other Giants. 'Strength alone will not avail against them. Yet we will strive to create opportunities for your blades.'

The Ironhand nodded grimly. 'Aye. Some few of them we will slay, with your aid. Then we must pray that they do not pause to feast upon their fallen and multiply.'

'That also,' replied Branl, 'we will endeavour to prevent.'

'As will I,' Mahrtiir promised gruffly. 'Blindness will not hamper my aim.'

Linden clenched her fists until her knuckles ached. Her palm and fingers missed the ciphered warmth of the Staff. 'All right, Esmer,' she said through her teeth. 'So Kastenessen is mad at you. So what? Give me something to count against this betrayal. Tell me why no one wants me to go to Andelain.'

She did not have much time.

His eyes bled anger and self-castigation. 'I know not how to serve you, other than by preventing you from ruin.'

'That doesn't make sense,' she retorted. 'I'm not going to ruin any-thing. If you go away – if you let me use wild magic – I won't threaten the Arch. I can't. I'm not the ring's rightful wielder.' Roger had insisted on that. She believed him despite his many falsehoods. 'I don't have enough power.'

Esmer drew himself up. 'You are mistaken.' Now he seemed to seethe with squalls as if she had insulted his intelligence. 'There are *two* white golds. Each alone may damage Law. When both are wielded, their peril swells.'

Covenant had told her to be careful with wild magic. *It feeds the caesures.*

'Kastenessen's desires are not the Despiser's,' Esmer continued harshly. 'He cares naught for the Arch of Time. Rather he yearns for the destruction of the *Elohim*. Yet he is but one against many. And the *skurj* are merely the *skurj*. He cannot sate his hunger by direct challenge. However, your white ring, and the other, may accomplish his desires. The ending of life within the Arch will achieve it. It will consume his true foes. Therefore Kastenessen commits his creatures against you. Your efforts to withstand them will commingle with the madness of the other Wildwielder. Your puissance will conduce to the end of those who Appointed him to bereavement and agony.'

Again Linden shook her head. 'No. That still doesn't make sense. If Kastenessen wants me to use wild magic, why are you here? Didn't you say that you were commanded?'

Esmer made a show of patience while his eyes frothed and his wounds wept. 'The attack of the *skurj* is a blade with two edges. Because of my presence, you will perish. Then your ring will fall into the hands of some other being. Kastenessen does not covet it for himself. No *Elohim* truly desires white gold. For such beings, its peril transcends its promise of might. But lesser wights crave it avidly. Should Thomas Covenant's son or the Harrow gain possession of your ring, they will evoke wild magic sufficient to feed Kastenessen's hunger.

'However, my grandsire is wroth with me. He execrates my wish to serve you. Therefore I am commanded here, as both a punishment and a snare. My presence ensures your death – and his triumph. Yet should you discover some means to sway me, so that I am induced to betray him, you yourself will provide his triumph.'

Abruptly the entire tor trembled. While Linden spread her feet to keep her balance, a scream of fire erupted beyond the eastern edge of the crest. Virulence shocked her senses as the *skurj* broke from the ground. From where she stood, the rim blocked her view of the beasts; but she recognised that they were many. Each roar exacerbated the others until the very air seemed to shriek with pain.

She closed her mind to the sound. She could not afford to quail. She *would* not. Therefore she chose to believe that the Giants would contrive to hold back the creatures.

'So either way Kastenessen wins,' she rasped at Esmer. 'All right. I get that. But you still haven't told me why you're here. Since he can't lose, why do you bother to do what he tells you? Why do you care?'

He ducked his head. His manner changed as unpredictably as wind-torn waves. 'It is my nature. I must strive to serve you.'

'Then tell me how I can get enough Earthpower from my Staff to hold off those monsters.'

'You cannot,' he said as though he feared her in spite of her help-lessness. 'That is the true purpose of Kevin's Dirt. My grandsire and I laboured long and assiduously among the fouled depths and banes of Gravin Threndor to procure this outcome.'

You? Linden thought, aghast. *You* did that?

'We have been aided,' Esmer admitted. 'The extremes of Kastenessen's excruciation madden him. His thoughts do not cohere. But he has been counselled by *moksha* Raver. Jehannum serves him, winning connivance from Thomas Covenant's son as from Cavewights and other powers. At the Raver's urging, my grandsire severed his hand to exalt Thomas Covenant's son. The magic to raise Kevin's Dirt from the roots of Mount Thunder was Kastenessen's, and mine. But the ploy was *moksha* Jehannum's.'

Linden swallowed her dismay. Esmer was helping her: she knew that. He had told her where to look for Kastenessen – and perhaps how to end Kevin's Dirt. He had revealed how her disparate foes had been induced to work together. But he had given her nothing that would thwart the *skurj*.

If he answered her questions in order to betray Kastenessen, he was doing his grandsire no harm.

'You're just talking, Esmer,' she said, deliberately dismissive. 'You can say whatever you want because you know that I won't live to do anything about it. If you want to prove that you're worthy of your father,' of Cail, whose courage had been as boundless as Kastenessen's rage, 'tell me something useful. Tell me why no one wants me to go to Andelain.'

Without warning, the first of the *skurj* reared into view.

The sight staggered her; broke her concentration. Even in full daylight, the beast seemed to dominate the sky. Its heat washed over the tor, terrible and chancrous: its massive jaws gaped, blazing with repeated rows of fangs like magma shaped and whetted until the teeth resembled kukris. Heat shouted from the monster's deep maw as if it articulated the Earth's quintessential hunger.

The ur-viles and Waynhim huddled around Linden, apparently cowed. Their subdued chittering sounded like whimpers.

Rime Coldspray confronted the creature with her sword held ready. Yet she did not strike. She might have been immobilised; stricken with terror; helpless before the lambent ineluctable fangs of the *skurj*. But she was not. She was waiting—

The beast towered over her, savouring her death. Then the tremendous kraken jaws pounced for her head. If it caught her, it would bite her in half.

Branl interrupted the creature's strike. Before it reached Coldspray, he flung a heavy rock down the throat of the *skurj*.

Reflexively the monster paused. It closed its jaws to swallow; concealed the sick radiance of its fangs.

In that instant, Coldspray swung her glaive. With all of her Giantish might and her Swordmainnir training, she cut into and through the heavy muscles at one hinge of the creature's jaws.

The *skurj* fell into a convulsion of pain. Yowling through a spray of vile blood, it plunged out of sight.

Dear God— *An abundance of loose stones*. Now Linden understood. The mound was not a trap: it was an armoury. Her companions could use the autonomic reactions of the creatures against them. Branl, Galt and Clyme – even Mahrtiir – could force the *skurj* to pause.

Any interruption would create openings for the Giants.

But Coldspray's blow appeared to infuriate the rest of the *skurj*. Their roaring lashed the air: their heat stank like gangrene. Eight or ten of them charged upwards simultaneously. The others were close behind. Threats of slaughter scaled into lunacy as the creatures arched above the tor to crash slavering towards the Giants.

In the space between heartbeats, one small sliver of time, Linden whirled towards Stave. 'The Seven Words!' she panted. 'They affect the *skurj*!'

The Giants believed that the monsters could not hear. But Linden had seen one of them hesitate before the implicit theurgy of the Seven Words.

Stave acknowledged her with a nod. Then he sprang away, shifting easily among the Demondim-spawn to inform her companions.

Around the entire rim of the crown, battle exploded.

'Wildwielder!' Esmer shouted. 'Forswear your purpose in Andelain, and I will depart!' A cryptic desperation edged his voice. 'Do as you will with the Harrow. Others will oppose your efforts to retrieve your son. I will not!'

Pallid with strain, Linden faced him again. The horrid gaping of fangs made his features ruddy and lurid: it seemed to fill his hurts with disease. A bloody sunset shone in his eyes. Her companions were fighting for their lives; everyone who had aided her; her friends—

There was nothing that she could do to help them.

'That's not an *answer*, Esmer.' If she turned her back on Andelain – on Covenant and the *krill* – she would sacrifice her only chance to save the Land. Terror and evil would rampage wherever they wished. 'The Harrow isn't *here*.'

'If I depart, he will come.' Esmer's mien was rife with supplication. 'He will remove you from this doom. Your death would complicate his desires.'

Should you discover some means to sway me—

The Giants were too few. The Humbled and Mahrtiir were fewer still. Kindwind tried to stop a *skurj* by jamming her sword past its teeth into the back of its maw. She hurt it; drove it back. But it clamped its jaws as it pulled away, taking her sword and her hand and all of her forearm with it. Blood fountained from the severed stump.

Guided by percipience, Mahrtiir heaved stones bigger than his fists between the fangs of the beasts. He yelled the Seven Words with such ferocity that the tor itself quivered. *Skurj* after *skurj* was forced to pause and swallow – or to falter. But that was the limit of what he could accomplish. If he touched one of the creatures, its hide would scald the flesh from his bones.

One of Clyme's rocks interrupted a flash of fangs and incandescence. In that instant, Grueburn ducked beneath the *skurj* and drove her sword upwards through its hide behind its jaws; buried her blade to the hilt. Somehow she struck a vital nerve-centre, perhaps the monster's brain. Spasming frantically, the *skurj* toppled down the stones. When its bulk collided with another creature, that beast tumbled as well.

Giants began to shout the Seven Words: a cacophony of invocation.

It was not enough.

Grinding her teeth, Linden demanded, 'And if he does? If the Harrow offers me a bargain that I can live with? Will he save my friends? Can he rescue all of us?'

Esmer snorted contemptuously. 'Doubtless he is able to do so. He will not. He need not. He cares naught for your companions. Knowing where your son is imprisoned, he requires no other suasion. He will not hazard himself for any cause other than white gold and the Staff of Law. If you insist upon the salvation of your companions, he will merely await a later opportunity to acquire your powers.

'The might of wild magic will be diminished if it is not ceded voluntarily. That he will regret. Nevertheless this plight serves his ends also.'

Bhapa and Pahni hovered uselessly over Anele. When they could, they threw stones at the *skurj*. The old man made mewling noises deep in his throat. His hands clutched at granite and basalt as if he thought that the broken rocks might redeem him.

Emulating Grueburn, Onyx Stonemage ducked under a blaze of fangs and thrust her sword like a spear behind the beast's jaws. But she missed her target. In a vast roar of pain and blood, the *skurj* struck at her; slammed her to the jagged stones.

For a moment, her armour blocked the monster's bite. At the same time, however, the beast's fury twisted her blade within its wound. Before her cataphract failed, her thrust became a killing stroke. The *skurj* recoiled, seized by death. Its blood drenched her, stinking like offal, as the creature fell.

Two *skurj* were dead. At least one had been badly wounded.

Too many remained.

Stave joined the Humbled. Together they hurled a barrage of rock. Risking her whole arm, Cabledarm succeeded at chopping one huge maw into a grin that could not close by cutting through the muscles at both corners of the jaw. With a volcanic howl, the *skurj* lurched away. A froth of vile blood spattered the tor.

'But he knows where Jeremiah is,' Linden insisted, panting urgently. 'Isn't that why you tried to suck him into a Fall? To keep him from helping me rescue my son?'

Esmer groaned. 'It is. It was.' His pleading became a kind of frenzy. 'Your son is beyond price. But if you will forswear your purpose in Andelain, the threat to Kastenessen is diminished. Therefore your son's worth declines. The Harrow will serve Kastenessen's desires, though he intends only his own glory. It cannot be otherwise when wild magic and Law are wielded by greed and aggrandisement.'

Kastenessen's desires are not the Despiser's.

Others will oppose your efforts to retrieve your son. I will not!

The ruddy hue of burning over the tor began to change. It grew pale. White brilliance reflected in the seethe and misery of Esmer's gaze. Through a fever of concentration, Linden felt Earthpower rise behind her.

The ur-viles and Waynhim jerked up their heads, scented the fraught air. Barking fervidly, they left Linden and Esmer. On all fours, they scampered to surround Liand.

The Stonedownor was calling up the light of his *orcrest*. He would draw the *skurj* to him; distract them—

But he was doing something else as well. Linden's attention nearly snapped when she realised that he was also summoning power from the Staff. Or summoning the Staff's strength through the Sunstone. By instinct or health-sense, he had tuned the Staff's resources to the specific pitch and possibility of his *orcrest*.

The Staff appeared to give him only a small portion of its potential. He lacked Linden's organic relationship with the runed black wood; and he had no experience. But in a mere handful of days, he had become intimately familiar with his piece of *orcrest*. Now he used Linden's Staff to feed the Sunstone, enhance its distinctive theurgy – and to reinforce his stone so that it would not be shattered by the magicks which he demanded from it.

Linden did not know what he had in mind. He had told her nothing. Nevertheless she understood that he was not merely trying to attract or disturb the *skurj*. He meant to attempt something far more ambitious—

Kevin's Dirt would hinder him as it did her.

Liand! Fearing the hunger of the monsters, she nearly shouted at him to stop. But she fought down the impulse. All of her companions were about to die. Her own death was no more than moments away. She could not afford to reject any gambit that might confuse or slow the *skurj*.

All who live share the Land's plight. Its cost will be borne by all who live.

She had to let Liand take his own risks.

Perhaps the Demondim-spawn would protect him—

Like an act of violence against herself, Linden closed her mind to Liand. Instead she told Esmer, 'Then you still have to answer my question. Why don't you want me in Andelain? I'm not going to "forswear" anything until I know what's at stake.'

'Because you are not *needed*!' Esmer cried in stymied supplication. 'There is no *peril* in Andelain! The *skurj* cannot enter among the Hills. Kastenessen himself cannot. *Caesures* do not form there. When Thomas Covenant's ring returned to the Land, Loric's *krill* was roused from its slumber. Its might wards the Hills. And other beings also act in Andelain's defence. The *skurj* are turned aside. Kastenessen is shunned. Disturbances of Time dissipate.

'Andelain is preserved,' Esmer asserted frantically. 'It has no *need* of you.'

Linden heard him with a surge of joy and despair. Andelain was safe—! If she and her companions could cross four more leagues, they, too, would be protected.

But the distance was too great. They would die on this pile of rocks. None of them would leave its crown alive.

Behind her, the ur-viles and Waynhim growled an indecipherable incantation. Her nerves felt a streak of dank power, black and vitriolic, as the loremaster produced a dagger with a blade that resembled molten iron.

One dagger. The dark lore of all the Waynhim and ur-viles combined could not make one dagger potent enough to ward Liand.

What did he hope to accomplish?

Unable to jump back quickly enough, Galesend dived under an attack; pitched herself headlong down the tearing rocks of the mound's slope. The creature's jaws tried to follow her. But Mahrtiir was screaming the Seven Words. And while the beast hesitated, Stave threw rock after rock into its gullet, coercing it to swallow, and swallow again.

In that respite, Galesend regained her feet. Battered and bleeding, she plunged her sword into the monster's hide to cut an opening. Then she shoved her arm to the shoulder into its fire. Though she cried out in pain, she probed within the *skurj*, seeking some essential organ or artery which her fingers could crush.

Coldspray seemed to hack in all directions. Cabledarm, Grueburn and the other Giants fought like titans; delivered an avalanche of blows. Even Kindwind gave battle, kicking heavily while she clutched her severed arm to slow the bleeding. Stave and Mahrtiir and the Humbled laboured everywhere, hurling rocks and interruptions.

Still monsters mounted the tor, as unrelenting as seas.

'That still isn't an answer!' Linden shouted, nearly wailing in frustration and terror. Come *on*, you sick bastard! Tell me something I can *use*! 'It doesn't explain why you and Kastenessen and Roger,' and Sunder and Hollian, 'don't want me to go there.'

Find me, Covenant had urged her. *Find* me.

Remember that I'm dead.

Esmer writhed as if he were being torn apart. 'Are you *blind*, Wildwielder?' Excoriation and horror bled from his eyes; his wounds. His shredded cymar fluttered in a kind of ecstasy. 'Do you comprehend *nothing*? We *fear* you.

'We fear what you may attempt with the *krill*. All the Earth fears it, every discerning or lorewise being among the living and the Dead. Even those who crave the destruction of life and Time fear it. The Harrow fears it, though doubtless he will feign otherwise. *We cannot perceive your purpose*. We know only your grief and your great rage. Thus we are assured that your intent is dreadful beyond any estimation. It will be no mere Ritual of Desecration. With Loric's *krill*, you will strive towards an end too absolute and abominable to be endured.

'Therefore you must forswear your purpose,' he finished in a harsh whisper. 'If you do not, I must incur your death, though Cail's blood in my veins demands to serve you. You will extinguish hope forever in the Earth.'

Esmer had answered her. But he gave her nothing.

And she did not believe him: not entirely. *Linden, find me.* She was convinced that Esmer and Kastenessen – and Roger – wanted to prevent her from reaching Thomas Covenant among the Dead.

The one Swordmain whose name she did not know went down: Linden could not tell whether she would stand again. Somehow the remaining Giants, the four *Haruchai* and Mahrtiir prevented the *skurj* from swarming over the crest. But with each strike, their incinerating crimson fangs reached deeper among the defenders. Bhapa, Pahni and Anele had all been scorched with foetid blood.

And Linden could not fight for them. She had no power. Esmer stood in front of her like a mute wail, quelling any possibility of wild magic.

While she reeled, helpless to save herself, helpless to save anyone, she heard a massive concussion like a crash of thunder.

She had not seen the sky grow dark; had not noticed the daylight failing until only incandescent fangs and the *orcrest*'s pure radiance illuminated the battle. But when raindrops splashed her face, she looked up and saw thunderheads boiling overhead.

Elsewhere there were no clouds: only the vicinity of the tor was covered in storm. Nevertheless the thunderheads were swollen and livid, flagrant with lightning and wind and violence—

—and rain.

When she spun towards Liand, saw him standing with the *orcrest* clenched over his head, she realised what he had done.

Stave had confirmed that the Sunstone could be used to cause *weather*—

Liand held the Staff in the crook of his elbow. His other hand gripped the hand of the ur-vile loremaster palm to palm. Both his human skin and the loremaster's black flesh were crusted with blood.

Oh, God, Linden thought, oh, *God*, remembering how the ur-viles shared their strength and clarity. The loremaster must have cut its own palm as well as Liand's; mingled its blood with his; infused him with its weird lore and puissance.

With blood, the Demondim-spawn had shown him how to create a storm. They had made him able to do so, in spite of their own suffering in proximity to the Staff.

Rain! Water– It was a *weapon*. Wind and thunder and lightning meant nothing: those elemental forces could not deter the *skurj*. But *rain*—!

As soon as she understood what Liand was doing, Linden knew that he would fail. He had already surpassed all of his limits – and his Sunstone had not shattered. But no mere shower would cool or daunt the terrible fires of the *skurj*. He had achieved more than she could have imagined. Nevertheless he simply did not have enough power—

The Staff did not belong to him. It was hers: she had made it. Caerroil Wildwood had incised it with unfathomable implications, and had returned it to her.

'*Liand!*' she yelled as she scrambled over the rocks towards him. 'That's brilliant! You're brilliant!

'Give me the *Staff*!'

Esmer made a sound like keening or exultation; but he did not leave the mound.

She feared that Liand would not hear her. He had immersed himself utterly in his efforts; in his *orcrest* and her Staff and the loremaster's blood. He may have gone beyond hearing.

But as she neared him, he unfolded his elbow to release the Staff.

Suddenly one of the monsters toppled, yowling, as if its serpentlike body had been cut in half. With a rage as loud as the massed thunder, Longwrath climbed onto the crest.

Anointed and annealed by the gore of the creature that he had slain, his flamberge steamed in the gathering fall of rain.

Without hesitation, he sprang at Linden. His great size and strength carried him towards her in three strides. His sword wheeled to send her head spinning far from the tor.

In the same instant, Stave hurled a large rock that struck the side of Longwrath's head. The impact staggered the mad Swordmain. He missed his footing; fell involuntarily to one knee with the tip of his blade inches from Linden's face.

Desperately Grueburn and Coldspray converged on Longwrath. Grueburn grappled for his sword-arm while Coldspray kicked him in the jaw.

Linden heard a snapping sound that may have been Longwrath's neck; but she did not falter. She was already shouting, '*Melenkurion abatha!*' as she snatched the Staff from Liand. '*Duroc minas mill!*' At once, Earthpower and Law poured through her as though she had uncapped a geyser. '*Harad khabaal!*'

With every ounce of her passion and purpose, she reached for Liand's storm. Wielding her fire like a scourge, she flailed at the rain until it became torrential.

Between heartbeats, she transformed Liand's showers. At once, they became a downpour so heavy that she seemed to have torn open an ocean in the sky. Water pounded the stones with such force that it nearly knocked her from her feet. Everything around her was inundated, hammered, bludgeoned, as if she stood directly under the cascade of the Mithil's Plunge.

Now there was no light at all apart from the fire of the Staff and the laval gaping of the monsters' fangs. Liand had collapsed. The loremaster held him while a Waynhim retrieved his quenched *orcrest* and returned it to its pouch at his waist.

Linden could no longer hear thunder: the torrent was louder. Rain swept the voices of her companions away. Only the furious consternation of the *skurj* pierced the downpour. They were creatures of magma and fire, stone and earth. They would not have survived if they had been dropped into the Sunbirth Sea. The whipped weight and ferocity of Linden's rainstorm did not kill them. But it erupted into steam in their mouths. Crimson fume burst from their teeth. Explosive gouts of superheated vapour tore at their fangs, their flesh, while their necessary heat cooled. When they swallowed, they swallowed water as if it were poison.

The sheer mass of the rain forced them to close their jaws. Then it drove them to eat their way into the ground, seeking an escape from the pummelling torrents.

Linden's fire was all that remained to light her companions.

She could not blink fast enough to keep her vision clear. She could scarcely hold up her head. Through a cataclysm of water, she barely saw two of Longwrath's guards clamber onto the crest. She heard nothing while the Giants yelled at each other, making swift decisions. She was focused heart and soul on the Staff and the storm. If Esmer remained or vanished, she did not notice it. She was only distantly aware that the Waynhim and ur-viles had scattered. She had no attention left for anything except rain.

If she could sustain this downpour—

Without disturbing Linden's concentration, Grueburn lifted her from her feet. Stonemage cradled Liand like a sleeping child. Galesend carried Anele while Cabledarm bore Pahni. Still gripping the stump of her lost arm, Kindwind squatted so that Mahrtiir could climb her back, cling to her shoulders. One of Longwrath's guards took Bhapa. The other and Coldspray supported Longwrath between them.

Leaving one Giant dead on the peak and another presumably lost to Longwrath's madness, the Swordmainnir and the *Haruchai* descended the tor in a perilous rush and ran south.

Chapter Eleven:

The Essence of the Land

When the company had passed out from under the downpour into the ambiguous shelter of the trees, the Giants paused – briefly, briefly – so that Linden could shift her attention to healing.

Kindwind's arm was the most urgent of their wounds, but their hurts were many. Galesend had been nearly hamstrung by raking fangs. Coldspray, Cabledarm and Stonemage bled from gashes like latticework on their arms and legs. And one of Longwrath's guards wore fractured bones in her cheek: he must have struck her when he broke free to pursue Linden. Only Grueburn and the Swordmain who aided Coldspray with Longwrath's unconscious bulk had avoided serious harm.

In addition, the Humbled, the Ramen, Stave, Liand and Anele had all been burned by splashes of gore. Among Linden's original companions, she alone had escaped any physical hurt. Her injuries were more spiritual, and she had borne them longer.

As soon as the Giants stopped, she withdrew her scourge of Earthpower from the thunderheads. Gritting her teeth against her fear of the *skurj*, she transformed her fire to more gentle flames and spread them over her friends. Rapidly she sealed Kindwind's severed arm; stopped the bleeding of the Giants; sent a quick wash of Law and balm to soothe the Ramen, Liand and Stave. But she did not offend the Humbled by offering to ease them. And she did not risk triggering Anele's self-imposed defences. She already knew how fiercely he would fight against healing and sanity.

Then the company ran again, dragging Longwrath with them. None of them knew when the *skurj* would attack again, and Liand's storm clouds were beginning to scatter.

Grueburn's arms seemed as certain as the Earth's bones. The senses of the *Haruchai* were preternaturally acute, and the Giants could see far. Surely they would know it when Kastenessen rallied his monsters?

The *skurj* had vindicated Linden's visions during her translation to the Land. If Lord Foul kept his promises, she would eventually have to face the Worm of the World's End.

In spite of her dreads, however, her efforts with the Staff had drained her. Fatigue blurred her attention for a time. Like the torrents which she had left behind, she frayed and drifted until only Jeremiah remained. Her son and Covenant.

Within the Andelainian Hills, Loric's *krill* summoned her like a beacon.

Esmer had not rescued her or her companions. But the lodestone of his presence had drawn the Demondim-spawn. And he had answered some of her questions.

Aid and betrayal.

Her foes were right to fear her.

Slowly Liand regained consciousness, although he rested with his eyes closed in Stonemage's embrace. The Humbled had already scattered to search for signs of pursuit behind or snares ahead. Mahrtiir watched over the company fervidly without his eyes. Alert for threats, Stave sped a few paces ahead of Grueburn.

Later the sound of Grueburn's stertorous breathing began to trouble Linden. The Giants had been under too much strain for too long. Their reserves of stamina were wearing thin. And they had lost two of their comrades. They needed to grieve.

But ahead of her, Salva Gildenbourne relapsed to thick jungle. Once again, it became a tangle of thickets, vines, draped ivy, crowding trees and deadwood monoliths like fallen kings. Without the guidance of the Cords, the Giants could not run unhindered; and they had no time to seek an easy route. They had to brunt their way by plain strength.

The *skurj* could move faster than this; much faster. The fact that the Humbled detected nothing did not reassure Linden. It may have meant only that Kastenessen had received new counsel, and had begun to devise a surer assault. She did not believe that the furious *Elohim* would cease his efforts to prevent her from reaching Andelain.

The company needed speed, but the Giants were too tired.

Apparently Coldspray shared Linden's concerns. Muttering Giantish obscenities, the Ironhand left her comrade to bear the burden of Longwrath alone. The woman draped his arms over her shoulders so that she could drag him on her back. Meanwhile Coldspray moved ahead of her people and began to hack a passage with her glaive. Arduously the Giants improved their pace.

Linden's percipience was focused behind her, northward towards the *skurj*. Too late to give warning, she felt Longwrath plant his feet and heave against the Giant supporting him. He moved so suddenly that Linden feared he would break the woman's neck.

But the Swordmain must have sensed his intent. She caught his wrists before his hands struck her throat. Holding him, she ducked under his arms and spun in an attempt to wrench him off balance, flip him to the ground.

He countered by kicking her hard enough to loosen her grasp.

The Giants heard that instant of struggle. Bracing themselves to protect their burdens, they turned quickly to face their comrade and Longwrath. Stave sprang to Grueburn's side as Longwrath reached for his flamberge.

But its sheath was empty. His sword had been left behind among the rocks and desperation of the tor.

For a moment, he gaped at Linden, apparently torn between his hunger for her death and his need for his weapon. Then, howling, he wheeled and raced away, back towards the battle-mound.

In the scales of his madness, his flamberge outweighed Linden's blood.

The Giant who had been carrying him started to give chase; but Coldspray called her back. 'Permit him, Latebirth,' the Ironhand commanded sadly. 'You are needed among us. And I deem that he is in no peril. While he covets Linden Giantfriend's death, our foes will not harm him. He will return when he has retrieved his blade.'

Cursing, Latebirth acquiesced. 'The fault of Scend Wavegift's death is mine, Ironhand,' she proclaimed loudly, bitterly. 'Halewhole Bluntfist and I held Longwrath's arms to aid him against the constraint of his shackles. Wavegift followed at his back. But I allowed my concern for your fate to loosen my clasp. When his shackles dropped from him, Bluntfist held him, but my grip was broken. With the hand that I should have restrained, he struck down Bluntfist. I endeavoured to grapple with him, but I stumbled, unable to avoid Bluntfist's fall. While I floundered, he confronted Wavegift.

'She was armed. He did not draw his blade. Therefore she hesitated. Doubtless she believed that Bluntfist and I would regain our feet swiftly to join her. But we hindered each other. While we rose, he slapped Wavegift's blade aside and contrived to snap her neck. Then he ran. Though Bluntfist and I gave chase, we could not catch him.

'With clumsiness and inattention, I have shamed the Swordmainnir as well as myself. Henceforth I will name myself Lax Blunderfoot. When our journey has come to its end, for good or ill, I will lay down my sword.'

Stop, Linden wanted to say. We don't have time for this. It doesn't do any good. But she bit her lip and did not intervene. She understood Latebirth too well.

'We will speak of your name in Andelain,' retorted Coldspray. 'Our present straits forbid recrimination. We must have haste. Let your shame become anger, and aid me in shaping a path.'

'Aye,' Latebirth muttered. 'I hear you.' Drawing her sword, she stamped past Grueburn, Stave and Linden to join Coldspray at the head of the company.

With pity in his eyes, Liand watched the woman pass. Like Linden, he said nothing; but she could see that his emotions were kinder than hers.

Together Rime Coldspray and Latebirth attacked the worst of the jungle's impediments. In a kind of shared outrage, they cut vines, ivy and deadwood aside, driving themselves past their fatigue so that their comrades could move more rapidly.

Fortunately the knotted underbrush and trees soon thinned as the terrain became a declining slope littered with moss-furred rocks and fallen leaves. There clusters of elm and sycamore stood back from solitary Gilden, and few shrubs and creepers found enough soil for their roots. As the Giants trotted downwards, their feet stirred up a haze of insects and the damp mould of fallen leaves.

And at the bottom of the slope, the company found a stream turbulent with new rain. The invoked torrents of Liand's storm filled the rushing current with silt, torn leaves, snapped twigs. Nevertheless the Swordmainnir paused once more so that the company could drink.

When he had eased his thirst, Bhapa asked Mahrtiir's permission to lead the Giants once more. But Coldspray shook her head before the Manethrall could respond.

'While this stream tends southward, we need no guidance. And we are Giants, agile on rock – aye, even on slick stones concealed by debris. I cast no doubt on your skill, Cord, when I say that your aid will not quicken us here.'

'Heed the Ironhand,' instructed Mahrtiir. His tone was unexpectedly gentle. 'You and Cord Pahni have won my pride. I do not doubt your resolve. Yet some further rest will harm neither you nor this company. When your aid becomes needful, you will be better able to provide it.'

If Bhapa or Pahni replied, Linden did not hear them. The Giants were already running again.

Now their long, heavy strides raised a loud clatter of water. They splashed forward with extraordinary speed, sending spray in all directions. Within moments, Linden's clothes were soaked, so wet that she shivered against Frostheart Grueburn's stone armour.

Here Stave could not keep pace: he sank too deeply into pools and holes that barely reached the Giants' knees. Unwilling to fall behind, he left the stream and made his way among the trees, flickering through patches of sunlight as he dodged past trunks and tore through the undergrowth.

Surely, Linden thought, surely this stream would lead the Giants into Andelain? But she could not credit that she and her companions had outrun the *skurj* – or Kastenessen's savagery. Her enemies could not afford to let her reach her goal. If they failed to thwart her themselves, *moksha* Jehannum would suggest other tactics; summon other foes.

The scraps of *samadhi* Sheol's dark spirit wielded some form of influence among the Sandgorgons. And they had repaid their self-imposed debt. *They are done with you.* If the *skurj* could not catch her in time, and Roger's resources proved useless in Salva Gildenbourne, *moksha* Raver might reach out to his rent brother—

Linden had made too many mistakes. Acknowledging that the Sandgorgons had honoured their debt was only one of them.

Still Stave reported that the Humbled discerned no sign of pursuit. They saw no dangers ahead.

How far had Grueburn carried Linden from the tor? She could not gauge the distance. The rapid stutter of trees and brush, shade and sunlight, along the western side of the stream confused her. And the foliage occluded any landmarks which might have defined the company's progress. She was sure only that the sun was falling past mid-afternoon – and that the Giants could not continue to run like this much longer.

The ragged labour of Grueburn's respiration was painful to hear. Linden tried to close her mind to it, and failed. She was barely able to stop herself from counting the frantic beats of Grueburn's heart.

By degrees, however, the current slowed as its flood dissipated. At the same time, the hills on either side gradually seemed to acquire a kind of gentleness. Flowing through softer terrain, the stream became more direct. Still it tended southward across bursts of afternoon sunshine.

Then Linden noticed that Salva Gildenbourne's unkempt extravagance was changing. By degrees, the constricted throng of trees modulated into a more stately forest, and the undergrowth gave way to unexpected swaths of grass. Stands of twisted jacaranda and crowded mimosa were replaced by comfortable chestnuts, austere elms, nervous birches. The rich gold leaves of the Gilden caught more sunlight and shone like resplendence. At last, the Giants were able to leave the stream and travel unobstructed by water or unseen rocks and holes.

And ahead of the company—

In faint whiffs and suggestions, evanescent savours like caresses, Linden's nerves found their first taste of Andelain.

She sat up straighter; leaned forward with instinctive eagerness. Was it possible? Had she and her companions come *four leagues* since their battle on the tor? Without being attacked? She did not know how to believe it: it surpassed all of her expectations. Instinctively she distrusted her senses – and strained to confirm them.

The Andelainian Hills. In some sense, consciously or unconsciously, she had been striving to reach them ever since she had first heard Thomas

Covenant's voice in her dreams; ever since she had begun to imagine that he walked among the Dead.

Linden, find me.

She could be wrong. Surely she was wrong?

Careless of the danger, she drew Earthpower from the Staff to sharpen her health-sense. Her heart swelled with supplications which she could not utter: anticipation, hope, doubt; desire as acute as exultation.

Allusive and enticing, scents came to her: greensward and munificent verdure, air as crisp and sapid as *aliantha*, wildflowers luxuriating in their abundance. No, she was not wrong. More and more, Salva Gildenbourne became a cathedral forest, solemn and sacral. With every step, the trees verged closer to transubstantiation. Ahead of her, they implied a bedecked panoply clinquant with Gilden sunshine. Grueburn carried her through splashes of declining light towards a woodland vista so numinous and vital that every line was limned with health.

Long ago, during her first approach to the Hills of Andelain, she had feared them. They had appeared to nurture something cancerous, a disease which would destroy her if she walked among them. Later, however, she had learned the truth. Her initial perceptions had been distorted by the Sunbane. Immersed in relentless evil and unable to control her sensitivity, she had seen sickness everywhere. As a result, she had failed to discern the real source of her dread.

Even then, the Hills were not ill. They could not be: the last Forestal protected them. Her trepidation had arisen, not from Andelain itself, but from the presence of the Dead. Because the Law of Death had been broken – and because Earthpower suffused the Hills – spectres walked in Andelain's loveliness. Confused by the Sunbane, she had felt their nearness as if they were evil.

Now she knew better. High Lord Elena's abuse of the Power of Command had made it possible for Covenant's Dead to speak with him; counsel him. Without their aid, he would not have been able to save the Land. Linden herself had met the shade of Kevin Landwaster and quailed; but even in his unrelieved despair, he had not been evil.

There is hope in contradiction.

Since that time, the Law of Life had been damaged as well. The Land held new possibilities, for good or ill. If the breaking of Laws enabled

Joan to spawn *caesures*, it might also free Linden to accomplish her unspoken purpose.

She approached Andelain with yearning because she had learned to love the Hills – and because she hoped to gain something more precious than reassurance or counsel.

Around her, her companions also beheld what lay ahead of them. Excitement shone in Liand's eyes, and he gazed past the Swordmainnir eagerly. Near him, Pahni glowed as if her weariness had become a form of enchantment. Even Stave appeared to lift more lightly from stride to stride, strengthened by the prospect of Andelain's distilled beauty.

As one, the Giants slowed their steps. As if in reverence, they set aside their haste, assumed a more condign *gravitas*. When they left the last fringes of Salva Gildenbourne and crossed into Andelain, they did so as if they were entering a place of worship. Here was the Land's untrammelled bounty, as essential as blood and as profound as orogeny. And they were Giants: instinctively they revelled in largesse.

Together they ascended partway up the first slope and surcease of Andelain's welcome. There Clyme awaited them calmly, certain that they had passed beyond peril. And there the Giants set down Linden and her friends so that they could walk at last, and feel the air freely, and be eased.

—*Loric's* krill *was roused from its slumber. Its might wards the Hills. The* skurj *cannot enter– Kastenessen himself cannot.*

Joyfully Bhapa and Pahni threw themselves prostrate on the lush grass, doing homage to Andelain and escape. Mahrtiir knelt with his head bowed to the earth as if he were praying. Liand flung his arms wide and spun in circles, crowing with delight. 'Andelain?' he cried. 'Oh, Linden! This is Andelain? I could not have believed—!'

Linden wanted to share their joy. She felt as they did, and would have celebrated. But her first concern was for Anele.

Amid the long verdure of the Verge of Wandering, the old man had spoken to her in Covenant's voice. Among the rich grasses of Revelstone's upland plateau, he had offered her friends rue and advice. And here every aspect of the tangible world was *more*—

The hillside glistened with grace, green and lavish. The air was a cleansing ache in her lungs, and the springtime daisies, forsythia and columbine were as bright as laughter. Every tree spread its leaves in wealth and majesty. The late sunlight offered warmth to soothe the chill of Linden's damp clothes.

She did not know how Anele would respond. The tonic atmosphere might comfort him. Or he might feel threatened by the inherent health on every side. Or he might be possessed—

Galesend had already lowered him to the ground. Now, however, the company had no blankets to protect him.

Suppressing her own reaction to escape and glory, Linden approached the old man. Softly she murmured his name.

For a moment, he seemed unaware of her. His moonstone gaze wandered the southward expanse of the Hills, and he stood stiffly erect as if he were awaiting the acknowledgment of an august host. But then a subtle alteration came over him. As he turned towards Linden, his posture loosened. Studying her, he seemed to peer outward through veils of madness.

'Ah, Linden,' he sighed. His voice was his own; but it was also Hollian's, light and loving, and as poignant as lamentation. 'You should not have come. The hazard is too great. Darkness consumes you. The Despiser has planned long and cunningly for your presence, and his snares are many.'

Anele paused, swallowing grief. He blinked at tears which were not his. Then he continued to speak words bestowed by his long-dead mother.

'Yet the sight of you gladdens me. I pray that you will be able to bear the burden of so many needs. There is more in Andelain – and among the Dead – and in your heart – than Lord Foul can conceive.'

The old man started to withdraw. But before Linden could cry out to him – or to Hollian – he faced her again. 'Be kind to my beloved son,' he said, quietly imploring. 'His vision of his parents is too lofty. He torments himself for faults which are not his. When your deeds have come to doom, as they must, remember that he is the hope of the Land.

'This, also, the Despiser and all who serve him cannot imagine.'

Abruptly Anele turned to the south. While Linden floundered in silence, shaken and unsure, he strode away from her. After a moment, he began to run deeper into Andelain as if he could hear Hollian and Sunder calling for him.

'Linden?' Liand asked. Apparently Anele's voice and her distress had pierced his jubilant astonishment. 'Linden? Shall I follow after him? Will he be lost?'

Liand's concern seemed to rouse the Ramen. Mahrtiir rose to his feet: his wrapped head moved like a hawk's as he scrutinised his companions. At once, Bhapa and Pahni stood. The young Cord's mien promised that she would accompany Liand if he pursued Anele.

Linden's eyes burned, but they were dry. 'No.' The stone of her purpose was too hard for weeping. 'Let him go. He's safe here.' *When your deeds have come to doom—* 'If we don't catch up with him, he'll wander back to us eventually.' *—as they must—* 'In the meantime, maybe he'll find a little peace.'

—remember that he is the hope of the Land.

After an instant of hesitation, Liand nodded. The angle of his raven eyebrows showed that he was more troubled on Linden's behalf than Anele's. But she had nothing more to say to him. She was not prepared to explain why she intended to ignore Hollian's warning.

While Anele ran, Branl and Galt emerged from the trees near the boundary of Andelain. Like Clyme, they seemed confident that they had passed beyond danger. Without obvious hurry, they trotted lightly into crystalline cleanliness. Soon they joined Clyme amid the wildflowers and the casual hum of feeding bees.

Rime Coldspray had gathered her Swordmainnir around her. For a few moments, they spoke together in low voices. Then the Ironhand turned to address the Humbled.

'We are Giants,' she said formally, 'and have not found pleasure in the unwelcome of the Masters. But the time has come to set aside such affronts. In the name of my comrades, I thank you for your many labours. You are the Humbled, Masters of the Land. But you are also *Haruchai*, and have done much to ensure our lives. I hope that you will honour us by accepting our gratitude.'

The Humbled faced her impassively. In a flat tone, Branl said, 'There is no need for gratitude, Rime Coldspray, Ironhand of the Swordmainnir. The unwelcome of which you speak was not meant as unfriendship. We were concerned only that your open hearts and tales might undermine our service to the Land. Now you have accomplished that which we deemed impossible. With the aid of this unlikely Stonedownor' – he indicated Liand – 'you have wrested the lives of Linden Avery's company from the jaws of the *skurj*. Together we acknowledge your deeds. When the time comes to speak of you before the Masters assembled in Revelstone, we will speak with one voice, and will be heeded.'

Sure, Linden thought dourly. Of course you will. The Humbled had as much authority among their people as Handir. But Branl had not revealed what he would say to the Masters.

She intended to pursue the question with Stave later, when she had a chance to talk to him alone.

Nonetheless Coldspray inclined her head as if Branl had satisfied her. Only her frown and an oblique timbre of anger in her voice suggested otherwise as she continued, 'Yet our gratitude remains. Therefore we ask your counsel. We are Giants. We must grieve for those whom we have lost. For that reason, we require a *caamora*. We wish to gather wood from Salva Gildenbourne, that we may express our sorrow in fire. Will your Mastery gainsay us? Will our flames offend the spirit of Andelain?'

If the Humbled felt any reluctance, they did not reveal it. Instead Clyme replied, 'Ironhand, we have no heart for sorrow. Yet here we would not oppose any need or desire of the Swordmainnir. And Andelain is the soul and essence of the Land. As the Land has known grief beyond description, so the Hills themselves are familiar with mourning and loss. Your flames cannot give offence where their meaning is shared and honoured.'

'That is well,' said Coldspray gruffly. 'Accept our thanks.'

With a gesture, she sent Cabledarm and Latebirth back down the slope towards the darkening forest.

Linden still did not know the name of the Giant who had died on the tor.

Doubtless Cabledarm and Latebirth were safe enough. If they sensed the *skurj*, or any other foes, they could return to Andelain quickly. While Mahrtiir instructed Bhapa and Pahni to forage for treasure-berries, Linden drew Earthpower from her Staff again; but she did not do so to protect the Giants. Rather she turned her attention and the Staff's flame, as yellow and lively as buttercups, to healing.

The Swordmainnir needed better care than she had given them earlier.

Now she treated their many wounds with more diligence. Walking slowly among the women, she tended severed nerves and blood vessels, ripped flesh and muscles. Gently she cauterised bleeding, burned away sepsis, repaired bone. The Giants were hardy: their wellsprings of health ran deep. Nevertheless the virulence of the poisons left by the fangs and blood of the monsters shocked her. Already every wound oozed with infection. The most severe hurts required a delicate balance of power and precision.

Kindwind's condition was the worst. Septicemia had polluted her bloodstream, and her long exertions had spread its taint throughout her body. Linden could not cleanse away the infection until she had searched the marrow of Kindwind's bones with percipience and strict fire.

By comparison, repairing the structure of Bluntfist's cheek was a simple task, easily completed. The burns suffered by Liand, the Ramen and Stave responded well to their given healing.

Linden expected her own weariness to hamper her efforts, but it did not. Andelain's air was a roborant, restoring her reserves. It dimmed the effects of Kevin's Dirt. Every glance around the ineffable Hills strengthened her. And the grass under her boots sent a caress of warmth and generosity along her nerves. While she worked, she found that she was capable of more than she had imagined.

The *krill* was in Andelain. Esmer had said so. The Hills themselves might make her strong enough to fulfil her intentions.

As she tended the Swordmainnir, their wonder and thankfulness gathered palpably around her. The tales of their people had not prepared them for what could be accomplished with health-sense and Earthpower. Even the First and Pitchwife had never seen her wield the Staff as she used it here.

If these women ever found their way Home, they would tell long tales about Linden's efforts. Like the other Giants whom she had known, they relished small miracles as much as grander achievements.

When Cabledarm and Latebirth returned, they bore huge stacks of deadwood. For a moment, Cabledarm bowed over the spot where she meant to build a fire as if she were asking the grass and ground to forgive her. Then she readied a small pile of twigs and kindling, took out her pouch of tinder and stones, and began to strike sparks.

As the wood smouldered into flame, Linden cared for Cabledarm and Latebirth with the same attentiveness that she had expended on Coldspray and her other companions.

In the west, the sun was setting among the tallest trees. Long shadows blurred by distance streaked the hillside while darkness accumulated in the margins of Salva Gildenbourne. A soothing breeze wafted like beneficence among the Hills. Pahni and Bhapa brought back an abundance of *aliantha* to nourish the company. And water was plentiful nearby. The stream which had led the Giants here ran eastward along the foot of the slope until it found its own course into Andelain.

Within the borders of the Land's essential health and bounty, Rime Coldspray and her comrades formed a circle around Cabledarm's fire and began their ritual of grief.

They were Giants: they took their time. Dusk and then night covered the hillside. Slowly stars added their cold glitter to the subdued dance of the flames. In the numinous dark, the Swordmainnir raised their voices as if they addressed Andelain and the wide heavens as well as each other.

First the Ironhand spoke sternly of 'fault'. The previous night, she had accepted some responsibility for Longwrath's condition. Now she claimed a similar blame for Scend Wavegift's death. Certainly Latebirth had erred. She was mortal: she could be taken by surprise, or suffer mishap, as easily as any being defined by birth and death. But she had not caused Longwrath's plight – and the deed of Wavegift's end was his, not Latebirth's.

Then Coldspray assumed the fault – if fault there was – for Moire Squareset, who had been slain by the *skurj*. Responsibility belonged to the Ironhand, whose decisions led the Swordmainnir. Like Wavegift's, Squareset's blood was on Coldspray's hands or no one's, for even Longwrath could not be held accountable. While she lived, she would both accuse and forgive herself.

When she was done, she knelt beside the fire and reached into the heart of the flames with both hands as though she sought to burn them clean.

Her flesh refused the harm of fire, but it could not refuse the pain. Her act was a deliberate immolation: in flame and willing agony, she surrendered her bereavement and remorse. This was the Giantish *caamora*, the articulation of their grief. In some sense, Linden understood it, although it filled her with dismay. Coldspray kept her hands in the fire while Cabledarm stoked it with more and more wood. A scream stretched the Ironhand's mouth, but she did not permit herself to voice it. The flames spoke for her.

The Ramen watched with their fists clenched and a kind of ferocity in their eyes. Long ago, their ancestors had known the Unhomed. Ramen may have witnessed a *caamora*: they had certainly given the story to their descendants. But millennia had passed since any Ramen had seen what transpired here. Their legends could not have prepared them for the intensity of Coldspray's chosen excruciation.

Liand stood near Pahni, but he did not touch her. He needed his arms; needed to clasp them across his chest with all of his strength in order to contain his horror and empathy, his protests. Unlike the Ramen and Linden – and the *Haruchai* – he had nothing except his health-sense to help him comprehend what he was seeing.

Finally Coldspray withdrew. As she regained her feet, her arms trembled, and tears spilled from her eyes. But her hands were whole.

Cirrus Kindwind was the next to speak. In careful detail, alternately grave and humorous, she described Moire Squareset's training and initiation among the Swordmainnir. Kindwind herself, with Onyx Stonemage and two other Giants, had been charged with developing Squareset's skills, and she remembered those years with loving vividness. She knew Squareset's strengths and weaknesses intimately, and she gave them all to the night.

Then she took her turn in the flames. The harsh silence of her pain and rue was so loud that Linden did not know how to bear it.

When Kindwind was done, Stormpast Galesend told similar tales of Scend Wavegift. She, too, thrust her hands into the fire. Grueburn, Bluntfist, and the rest of the Giants related their experiences with Wavegift and Squareset, their shared love and laughter, their memories of blunders and triumphs and longing. Each in turn, they offered their grief to the flames, and endured agony, and were annealed. Separately as well as together, they gave the ambergris of their woe to the dead.

But Linden turned away long before the Giants were done. She could not release her own tears and fury: they had been fused, made adamantine, by Roger's betrayal and Jeremiah's immeasurable suffering. She, too, yearned for a *caamora* – but not like this. Her heart craved an altogether different fire.

When she had gained some distance from the firelight and the Giants, she spent a while studying the vast isolation of the stars. In the expanse of the heavens, only the faintest glimmer of their mourning reached her – or each other. Yet she heeded their infinite lament. They could not burn away their loneliness without extinguishing themselves.

In that aspect of their limitless sojourn, she understood them better than she did the Giants. They calmed her as if she were in the presence of kindred spirits.

Gradually she let her attention return to Andelain, to the gentle embrace of health – and to the reasons that had compelled her here. But she did not rejoin the Giants, or listen to their stories and pain. Instead, certain of Stave's notice, she beckoned the former Master towards her.

He came to her softly, more silent than the drifting breeze. Under the stars, he asked in a low voice, 'Linden?'

It was the second time that he had called her by her given name.

His friendship touched her – and she did not want to be touched. More brusquely than she intended, she asked, 'What are the Humbled going to say when they get back to Revelstone?' We will speak with one voice— 'What will they tell the Masters?'

Stave made a small sound that may have been a snort. 'They remain uncertain. The Giants threaten the defined service of the Masters. It is their nature to do so. With tales alone, they wield power to overthrow millennia of dedication and sacrifice. Yet in all ways they merit admiration. Therefore the Humbled withhold appraisal. They will adjudge the Giants according to your deeds rather than theirs.'

Oh, good, Linden thought mordantly. That's perfect. It galled her to think that the attitude of the Masters towards the Giants depended on her. But then she swallowed her vexation. Whatever the Humbled decided was their problem, not hers. She could not make their choices for them. She would simply have to live with the consequences.

Sighing, she said, 'This is Andelain, Stave. You might think that here, at least,' if nowhere else in the Land, 'it would be acceptable for the Giants to be who they are.'

'Yet Andelain is not free of peril,' he returned stolidly. 'It may be that Kastenessen and the *skurj* cannot enter. Nonetheless the fate of the Land is the fate of Andelain as well. I do not concur with the Humbled, but I comprehend their doubt. In some measure, I share it.'

You share—? He startled her. In dozens of ways, he had declared his loyalty.

'Chosen,' he explained, 'you have not revealed your deeper purpose. You have not named your hopes for the unfathomable theurgies which the *krill* of Loric Vilesilencer will enable. By your own word, you desire those around you to know doubt.

'I do not seek to question you,' he stated before she could respond. 'I am content in the knowledge that you are Linden Avery the Chosen, Sun-Sage and Ringthane, companion of Thomas Covenant the Unbeliever. To me, you are "acceptable" in all things.

'Yet I am constrained by doubt to inquire if you also are uncertain. Have you not found cause to reconsider your intent?'

Linden stared at him in darkness. The stars shed too little light to unmask his features, and her health-sense could not reach into the mind or emotions of any *Haruchai*. She was barely able to discern the new skin where she had healed Stave's burns.

Without inflection, he continued, 'We stand now within the safety of Andelain. Here choices may diverge. Other paths lie before you. If you must confront your Dead, you do not require Loric's *krill* to do so. And Gravin Threndor may be approached without risk, though hazards wait within the Wightwarrens. It is there – is it not? – that Kevin's Dirt has its source. Are not Gravin Threndor's depths conceivable as a hiding place for the Unbeliever's son, and for your own?'

Linden wanted to cover her face. Jeremiah had built an image of Mount Thunder in her living room, as he had of Revelstone. Eventually she would have to go into the catacombs under the mountain: she knew that. But not yet—

Not while she was still so weak.

'I'm not Covenant,' she answered softly. 'I'm not Berek, or some other hero. I'm just me. And I could be wrong. Of *course* I could be wrong. This whole thing might turn out to be a monumental exercise in futility.' Or something worse— 'That's possible. It's absolutely possible.'

The breeze seemed to pause as if it wanted to hear her. Andelain itself appeared to hold its breath. In the distance, the voices of the Giants withdrew to a nearly inaudible murmur.

She needed to be doubted because she could not afford to doubt herself.

'But I have to have more power. Covenant's ring is useless whenever Esmer decides to interfere. Kevin's Dirt hampers Earthpower. If Jeremiah' – oh, my son! – 'stood right in front of me, I might not be able to save him. I don't know how to kill the *croyel* without killing him. I'm just not that strong.

'And look at who wants to stop me.' She gathered force as she spoke. 'Look at who wants to help. Kastenessen and Roger and the Ravers have tried hard to kill us. The ur-viles and Waynhim are *united*, for God's sake, even though they're the last, and too many of them are dead. The Mahdoubt gave up everything to protect me. I must be doing something right.'

'Chosen—' Stave tried to interrupt her, but she was not finished.

'Lord Foul has my *son*. I'm going to get him back. But first I need *more power*.'

'Chosen,' Stave said again more firmly. 'Longwrath approaches Andelain.'

Oh, shit. Wheeling, Linden projected her senses towards Salva Gilden-bourne.

Almost immediately, she felt Longwrath's unbridled rage. It was lurid in the darkness, a cynosure of hunger and desperation. The last trees still shrouded him, but he was heading straight towards her with his flamberge in his fists. Evanescent glints like phosphorescence wavered along the edges of his blade as though the iron had been forged to catch and hold starshine.

For the first time, Linden wondered whether his sword might be an instrument of magic. If his weapon had been formed with theurgy as well as fire, however, the effects were no longer perceptible. They had been attenuated by too much time – or they had been designed for circumstances which no longer existed.

The Swordmainnir seemed unaware of Longwrath. They were not done with their *caamora*: it held them like a *geas*. The Ramen and Liand remained transfixed by what they witnessed. But the Humbled were already moving, silent as thought.

Surely three *Haruchai* would suffice to restrain Longwrath until the *caamora* ended?

Nonetheless Linden tightened her grip on the Staff. Stave walked a little way down the slope to place himself between her and Long-wrath.

But Esmer had told her the truth. *Andelain is preserved.* Suddenly a small piece of night appeared to condense as if something blurred or invisible had come into focus; made itself real. Without transition, a yellow light like the delicate flame of a candle began to dance along the grass. As precise and self-contained as a single note of song, it bobbed some distance beyond the Giants. Yet it conveyed the impression that the distance was irrelevant. If the flame had shone directly in front of Linden, it would have been no larger – and no less vivid.

She recognised it instantly. It was a Wraith: one of the Wraiths of Andelain. She had seen its like before, during that cruel and necessary night when Sunder had slain Caer-Caveral with Loric's *krill* so that Hollian could live again. Wraiths had appeared then, dozens of them, hundreds, to mourn the passing of the last Forestal's music, and to celebrate what Sunder and Hollian had become.

The sight compelled an involuntary gasp from Linden. For a moment, she forgot Longwrath and every peril. The Wraith incarnated Andelain's eldritch beauty: it entranced her. Its beauty reminded her of loss and resurrection; of broken Law and death that enabled life and victory. And it made Thomas Covenant live again in her mind, her saviour and lover, whose consternation and courage had ruled him as severely as commandments.

I can't help you unless you find me.

Everything for which she had struggled since her escape from *Melenkurion* Skyweir was contingent upon him.

Then the moment passed – and the Wraith was not alone. Another appeared near Linden, and another among the Ramen. Exquisite candle flames pranced over the hillside, more and more of them, until at least a score had become manifest.

They seemed to cast a spell over the *caamora* as they swept down the slope towards Longwrath. Even the Humbled paused as if they were amazed.

As soon as Longwrath's foot touched the palpable demarcation between Salva Gildenbourne and Andelain, the Wraiths arrayed themselves in front of him. Together they gyred and flared as though they meant to ensorcel his madness.

Linden held her breath. At the edge of the stream, Longwrath hesitated. Yellow warmth illuminated his confusion. *Other beings also act in Andelain's defence.* Although they exerted no magic that Linden could detect, the Wraiths formed a barrier against Longwrath's craving for death.

Then he roared in defiance and charged at the lucent denial of the flames—

—and staggered as if he had collided with a wall. In some fashion that baffled Linden, he was shoved back. Each Wraith was a note, and together they formed a lush chord of rejection. As they danced, they looked small and frail; easily plucked from the air. Yet they refused Longwrath despite his size and strength.

His rage scaled higher as he charged again. The Wraiths took no visible notice of him. They merely swirled, bright and lovely, and self-absorbed as stars, as though they had no purpose except to be themselves: the simple fact of their existence summed up their significance. Nonetheless they repulsed Longwrath so firmly that he nearly fell.

Now he cut at them with his sword. His flamberge wove and slashed among the flames as if its dance might equal theirs. But his vehemence could not touch the Wraiths. They only flickered and burned, and were unharmed.

His fury became a scream that threatened to tear his throat; his lungs. Still the Wraiths did not permit him to advance. They made no discernible effort to elude his blade, yet their chord remained inviolate.

Then one of them swooped closer to alight delicately on the scar that disfigured his visage.

At once, his scream rose into a shriek. He plunged backwards, pounding at his face with fists that still clutched his sword. An instant later, the Wraith danced away; but he continued to strike and flounder after the flame was gone.

Finally he appeared to realise that he was no longer threatened; and his cry turned to rent sobs. Stumbling to his feet, he fled back into the forest. Behind him, dismay and horror seemed to linger in the air. When they faded at last, he had passed beyond the reach of Linden's percipience.

Shuddering, she began to breathe again.

After a moment, Stave observed quietly, 'Andelain is indeed warded. Yet the Wraiths refuse none but Longwrath. Perhaps the shades of Sunder Graveler and Hollian eh-Brand are mistaken.' *Darkness consumes you. Doom awaits you in the company of the Dead.* 'Perhaps there is no peril in your craving for Loric's *krill* – or in your chosen ire.'

The Wraiths had permitted Anele. They had permitted Linden herself. By forbidding Longwrath, they had countered Stave's doubt.

Until she concentrated on Stave's voice and understood what he was saying, she did not realise that the flames had scattered. Somehow they had wandered away without calling attention to their departure.

The Despiser has planned long and cunningly for your presence, and his snares are many.

Simultaneously bemused and troubled, Linden began to take notice of her companions once more. Around the fire, the *caamora* of the Giants had ended. At first, she did not know whether they had finished grieving. But the mood of their ritual had been broken – or the time for it had passed. They moved slowly, glancing around with a dazed air as if they had been dazzled by the Wraiths. Liand and the Ramen seemed to rouse themselves from reveries or dreams.

Then Linden looked at the Swordmainnir more closely and saw that they had relieved their sorrow. Although some sadness remained, they were ready now to bear Moire Squareset's death, and Scend Wavegift's.

They had assuaged their bereavement with fire. Long ago, Covenant had done the same for the Dead of The Grieve.

In her own way, Linden intended to follow their example.

The company talked for a while, eating treasure-berries and considering what lay ahead of them. The Humbled said nothing; but Stave offered the unsurprising information that the Masters knew the location of Loric's *krill*. The eldritch blade remained where Linden had last seen it after

Caer-Caveral's passing and Hollian's resurrection. Doubtless the Masters had taken pains to ensure that the *krill* was forgotten; that Andelain itself was forgotten. And the Earthpower of the Hills had prevented the Land's enemies from removing or using High Lord Loric's weapon.

However, the desultory conversations did not last long. All of Linden's companions were profoundly weary. And in every respect, Andelain comforted their strained nerves, their burdened hearts. The air filled their lungs with relaxation: their bodies absorbed reassurance from the grass: the scents of flowers and fruit trees and *aliantha* promised sanctuary. Even the darkness had a hushed and reverent timbre, a tone of reified consolation.

Soon Pahni and then Bhapa drifted into slumber. When Liand stretched out beside Pahni on the soft hillside, he fell asleep almost immediately. One by one, the Giants did the same until only Coldspray, Mahrtiir, the *Haruchai* and Linden remained awake.

Confident that the Humbled, Stave and perhaps Mahrtiir would keep watch when the Ironhand finally slept, Linden let herself lie down on the long balm of the grass. Reflexively she confirmed the presence of Jeremiah's racecar in her pocket and Covenant's ring under her shirt. Because her clothes were still damp, she wondered idly whether the spring night would grow cold enough to trouble her rest. Yet mere moments seemed to pass before she was awakened by sunlight rising beyond the tall monarchs of Andelain and Salva Gildenbourne.

Now she wondered if she had ever slept so deeply here, or felt so refreshed. Her previous nights among the Hills had been troubled ones. Involuntarily she remembered the spectre of Kevin Landwaster. Tormented by despair, the former High Lord had implored her to *halt the Unbeliever's mad intent.* Kevin had believed that the Despiser's cruelty had broken Covenant.

His purpose is the work of Despite. He must not be permitted.

Similar things had been said about Linden.

Yet Kevin had been wrong. Covenant's surrender had secured the Arch of Time. With sunshine on her face and Andelain's beneficence like chrism in her veins, Linden could believe that those who feared her capacity for darkness were also wrong.

She can do this. And there's no one else who can even make the attempt.

The Hills were safe. She and her friends had survived to reach this place of luxuriance and health. Now she was ready for the outcome of her choices. When she reached the *krill*—

Around the ashes of the *caamora*, some of the Giants were awake. The others stirred, roused by the quiet murmurs of their comrades. Liand still slept; but Pahni and Bhapa had risen to walk the greensward with their Manethrall, gathering treasure-berries. Stave and the Humbled guarded the rest of the company from perils which no longer threatened them. They looked as poised and vigilant as ever, like men who did not need rest and had never experienced fatigue. One night in Andelain had healed their lingering hurts.

There was no sign of Longwrath. If he remained hidden near the border of Salva Gildenbourne, Linden could not detect him. Like Anele, apparently, he was terrified by anything which endangered the hermetic logic of his madness. Therefore he feared the Wraiths. If their touch amended his insanity, he would remember the consequences of his deeds.

Sighing, Linden set the ramifications of Longwrath's dilemma aside. Anele had not been refused by the Wraiths. That meant more to her than Longwrath's desire for her death. She could hope that Anele might find a measure of solace among his Dead.

When Stonemage saw that Linden was awake, the woman nudged Liand. His eyes sparkled with anticipation as he sat up.

Escorted unnecessarily by Stave, Linden walked down the slope to drink from the stream. Then she washed her face and hands and arms. The water ran cleanly now, free of the tumbling detritus of the previous day's storm; and its chill tang sharpened her senses.

A handful of *aliantha* completed her preparations. While her companions ate enough to sustain them, she asked Stave how long it would take to reach the *krill*.

'In two days, we will gain the Soulsease,' he replied, 'if you are borne by the Giants, and they do not weary themselves running. Loric's *krill* stands little more than half a league to the south of the river.'

Linden frowned. She was more than ready: she was eager. And Jeremiah had already spent far too much time in torment. 'Damn it,' she muttered. 'Isn't there some way that we can go faster?

'Don't misunderstand me.' She included Coldspray in her appeal. 'I'm grateful to be here. I'm grateful for everything that you've done. I can't remember the last time that we weren't in danger. This is Andelain. We ought to relax and enjoy it.

'But I need my son.' She needed Thomas Covenant. 'I have to be able to save him. And for that, I need *power*,' a weapon which would transcend her inadequacy. 'I don't know how I can stand waiting for two more days.'

Coldspray's chagrin was plain as she contemplated more haste. The Swordmainnir had already run most of the way from The Grieve. And they had lost two of their comrades: they had lost Longwrath. Protests clouded her gaze as she searched for a reply.

But Stave held up a hand to forestall the Giant. Instead of answering Linden, he turned to Mahrtiir.

For a long moment, he and the Manethrall appeared to study each other, although Mahrtiir had no eyes and one of Stave's was gone. Then Mahrtiir cleared his throat.

'Ringthane—' he began carefully. 'We parted from the Ranyhyn in order that they might be spared from the *skurj*. It is well that we did so. But now that danger has passed. And they are Ranyhyn, capable of much which defies comprehension. They could not have borne us safely in Salva Gildenbourne. Yet you cannot question that they are able to rejoin us in Andelain.

'Then it will not be we who slow the long strides of the Giants. Rather it will be they who limit our pace.'

The Ranyhyn— Caught by astonishment, Linden stared at him. Hyn! God, yes.

She yearned to arrive by nightfall, when the Dead might walk among the trees and copses and lucent rivulets of Andelain.

'Linden,' Liand put in, 'is this wise? We did not quit the Ranyhyn solely to preserve them from the *skurj*. We sought also to spare them an arduous passage through Salva Gildenbourne. And we have been less than two days separated from them. Surely they—' He faltered, then finished more strongly, 'They are Ranyhyn, but they are also flesh and bone. If you summon them, will they not suffer in the attempt to answer?'

While Linden hesitated, Mahrtiir said gruffly, 'Do not speak when you are ignorant, Stonedownor. The Ranyhyn are beasts of Earthpower, as precious to the Land as Andelain.' Beneath the surface, he appeared to wrestle with the pain of knowing that he would never again gaze upon the great horses. 'If they are summoned, they will find a path and come, ready to bear those riders whom they have chosen.

'Also,' he added, 'the Ringthane has good cause to seek swiftness. Her own need is exceeded only by the plight of her son, and by the Land's doom.'

For a moment, Liand seemed unconvinced. But then Pahni tucked her arm through his, held him tightly. When he saw her reassuring smile, his apprehension eased.

Rime Coldspray peered down at Mahrtiir and Stave; at Linden; at Liand. 'Limit your pace?' she growled. 'That I will not credit until I have witnessed it – and even then I will require corroboration.'

Two or three of her Swordmainnir chuckled.

Slowly a combative grin bared the Ironhand's teeth. 'Are we not Giants? And do we not welcome wonders? The Manethrall of the Ramen has inspired in me a wish to behold these Ranyhyn. If they merit the service of the Ramen, they are worthy indeed.' She glanced around at her comrades. When they nodded, she said, 'We are loath to hasten in Andelain, where every view is balm to the worn of heart. But we have endured much to come so far. One day more will not daunt us.'

Linden's heart lifted. Quickly she urged, 'Stave? I can't whistle the way you do.'

He complied with a bow. Facing Andelain and the west as if he had turned his back on a silent debate among the Humbled, he put his fingers to his mouth and let out a piercing call.

Three times he whistled. Then he fell silent.

For moments that seemed long to Linden, she heard no reply. She had time to doubt herself and feel the first pricklings of alarm. Soon, however, a distant whinny carried through the crystal air, followed by the muted rumble of hooves on deep grass.

When the horses appeared, they seemed to gallop straight into the glory of the sun. Its light blazed like heraldry in the stars on their foreheads. They were ten, and they ran as though they were the rich heart of the Hills made flesh.

Linden recognised them all: Hyn and Hynyn and Rhohm; Narunal, Naybahn and the others. Even Hrama had answered.

Nevertheless her immediate joy faltered as she realised that all of them were hurt; desperately tired; nearly undone.

Their injuries were superficial: scratches, jabs and bruises caused by a hurried passage through the jungle. They showed no sign that they had encountered the *skurj*. But their weariness was altogether more serious. Sweat stained their coats like blood: froth splashed from their muzzles. Two or three of them stumbled at intervals, and their long muscles shuddered.

God, Linden thought. Oh, Christ. What have I done?

She could not even begin to guess how many leagues they had crossed, or how many obstacles they had overcome.

Yet they grew stronger as they approached. The change was slight but unmistakable. Andelain's vitality buoyed them along. With every stride, they absorbed energy from the ground, sucked renewal into their heaving chests. They remained near the edge of their endurance. But with a few hours of rest – with water and abundant nourishment – their exhaustion would fade. They would be ready to bear their riders.

Still Linden blamed herself for their condition. Every living thing that supported her paid too high a price for doing so. She ached to protect them all. As the Ranyhyn lurched to a halt before the glad appreciation of the Giants and the sharp empathy of the Ramen, she unfurled healing from the Staff of Law and threw it like a blanket over the great horses.

There was no danger. In this place, any exertion of Law was condign. And the Hills' benison diminished Kevin's Dirt. Nothing hindered her as she poured strength into the depleted stamina of the Ranyhyn.

By their very nature, they participated in Earthpower: they were apt vessels for her magic. They drank in flame as if it were the potent waters of Glimmermere; inhaled fire as if it combined the benefits of *amanibhavam* and *aliantha*. And as they did so, their fatigue fell away. When she was done – when she had banished their hurts and dried their coats and offered them her deepest gratitude – they gleamed with life.

Some of them nickered in delight and relief. Others tossed their manes, whisked their tails, stamped their hooves. Sunshine gleamed on their coats. While the *Haruchai* spoke their ancient ceremonial greeting, and the Ramen bowed their heads to the earth in homage, Hyn came prancing towards Linden.

First the mare bent her forelegs and bowed her head as if in obeisance or thanks. Then she nuzzled Linden's shoulder, urging Linden to mount. Her eyes were full of laughter.

In the horserite, Hyn and Hynyn had laughed at Stave with the same affectionate kindness that Linden saw in Hyn's soft gaze. To him, they had revealed their amusement at the presumption of the Masters – and their willingness to serve her utterly.

But her own experience when she had shared the mind-blending waters of the tarn had been entirely different. Hyn and Hynyn had offered her neither laughter nor affection. Instead they had shown her visions of such horror—

They had portrayed her to herself as if she were High Lord Elena, misguided and doomed. And they had superimposed images of both Linden and Covenant on Jeremiah. In the nightmare of the horserite, her efforts to redeem Covenant and her son had brought forth the Worm of the World's End.

Linden might have quailed at the memory; but she was spared by the fond mirth of Hyn's gaze. *See?* the mare's eyes seemed to say. *I am here. We are here. And we stand with you. We have only given warning. We have not prophesied that you will fail.*

'All right,' she replied like a promise. In her own way, she strove to emulate the Wraiths; to repel horror and doubt as they had refused Longwrath. She had come too far to falter, and the stakes were too high. She required a conflagration so mighty that it would shake the foundations of Lord Foul's evil. *You're the only one who can do this.* 'All right.'

While the Giants voiced their approval, Linden vaulted onto Hyn's back. And when she had settled herself on the mare's immaculate acceptance, she raised high the Staff.

'It's time!' she called to her companions. Andelain and the Land's future lay open before her. 'I'm done waiting. Let's do this!'

In response, the Ramen surged up from the grass. Nickering like horses, they seemed to flow onto the backs of their Ranyhyn. Even Mahrtiir mounted Narunal without uncertainty or fumbling. Stave and Liand followed their example. While the Ironhand gathered her comrades, the

Humbled surged to sit astride their Ranyhyn. In moments, only Hrama lacked a rider; and he reared as if he were eager to find Anele.

'Coldspray!' Linden urged. 'Set a pace that you can keep. Stop when you need rest. We'll stay with you.' Somehow she would restrain her impatience. 'All I want is to reach the Soulsease by sunset.'

'"All"?' Coldspray responded, chuckling. 'That is "all"? Then we must give thanks that it is not more. Already we have run for days without number, until we feared that our souls would break, Giants though we are.' After a moment, she added, 'I have a better thought. When we crave rest, lave us in fire as you have bathed these Ranyhyn. With such sustenance, we will surely accomplish your desire.'

'I'll do that.' Leaning forward, Linden nudged Hyn into motion. 'Remind me later to tell you how glad I am that you're here. I'll make a speech.'

Then she whirled the Staff around her head; and the Swordmainnir began to move, chortling as they spread out behind the Ranyhyn and stretched their strides to a brisk trot. At a canter, the horses bore Linden's company up the hillside into the burgeoning splendour of spring in Andelain.

Throughout the day, Linden revelled in swiftness, and in the munificent landscape, and in the prospect of culmination. The Ranyhyn could have travelled faster; much faster. Galloping, they could have outdistanced the best speed of the Giants. But she did not wish for that. She was already fond of Coldspray, Grueburn and their comrades. Their readiness to laugh with delight or appreciation in spite of their exertions nourished her spirit.

And the Hills nourished her as well. Although she remembered them vividly, her mind was too human to retain the full health and majesty of the woodlands, the shining of Gilden anademed in sunlight, the comfortable spread of sycamores and elms and oaks, the almost lambent sumptuousness of the greenswards. Or perhaps during her previous time in Andelain her senses had been tainted by the Sunbane, too troubled by *wrongness* to absorb so much beauty. As if for the first time, she saw hillsides and vales encircled by torcs or chaplets of wildflowers, *aliantha*, profuse primrose and daisies. When she swept past proud stands of spruce and cedar or copses of wattle, she immersed herself in their tang and redolence as though she had never known such scents before. The friendly chatter of brooks and streams bedizened with reflections greeted her like loved ones long lost.

As she rode, Linden felt that she was absorbing and storing the essence of the Land; the ultimate reason for everything that she endured or craved. If she had not seen the Hills corrupted by the Sunbane after the passing of the last Forestal, she might not have found the strength, the sheer passion, to form and wield a new Staff of Law. And without Thomas Covenant and Giants, without Sunder and Hollian – without Andelain itself, treasured and vulnerable – she would not have become the woman who had given so much of herself to her chosen son.

Beyond question, she would not have loved Jeremiah if Covenant had not first loved her – and if her soul's response to Andelain had not taught her to love the Land.

On Hyn's strong back, Linden rode among the Hills as if they answered every objection to her purpose. In the life that she had lost, Jeremiah had been her Andelain. His fey creative constructs and helplessness echoed Andelain's frangible loveliness. And the use that Lord Foul now made of her son was as bitter and unforgivable as the Sunbane.

If *Good cannot be accomplished by evil means*, then she would believe that her means were not evil.

Three times, the company paused. The first was for Anele. Apparently his blind destination was the same as Linden's. She had scarcely begun to worry about him when she found him directly in her path. He was talking to himself in a variety of voices – too many for her to distinguish – and walking at an erratic rate, alternately slowed and spurred by a chaos of fractured communication. But he noticed the riders as soon as they drew near. At once, he scrambled at Hrama's sides as if he knew that his mount would protect him. When Galesend lifted him onto Hrama's back, he fell silent at once. Moments later, worn out by indecipherable utterances, he fell asleep with his arms dangling on either side of Hrama's neck.

Andelain had healed the burns inflicted by the blood of the *skurj*.

Later, as the sun reached noon, the company halted beside a lazy rill to water the Ranyhyn and let them crop the grass. The Ramen and Liand gathered treasure-berries while Linden restored the flagging stamina of the Giants. And later still, in the middle of the afternoon, they stopped again for the same reasons.

In spite of the pressure driving her, Linden felt calm and sure; content with the company's progress. Andelain nurtured a tranquillity as pervasive as mansuetude. She would reach the Soulsease when she reached it. If night fell, darkness would not prevent her from locating the *krill*.

The Wraiths had allowed her to enter among the Hills.

Bemused by thoughts of acceptance and vindication, Linden mounted Hyn once more. When the Giants were ready, she rode on as if Andelain had healed all of her fears.

And as the sun neared the treetops in the west, casting long shadows like striations of augury across her path, she caught her first glimpse of the river through the gold leaves of Gilden and the warm flowers of fruit trees.

Tossing his head with an air of hauteur, Hynyn greeted the sight with a clarion whinny; and Hyn took a few dancing steps in a horse's gavotte. 'Stone and Sea!' panted Coldspray. 'When you tell the tale of your journeys, Linden Giantfriend, you must credit what we have accomplished in your name. Weary as we were, and are, I would not have believed—' She cut short her wonder and pride to catch her breath. Then she said, 'You voiced a desire to gain the Soulsease River ere nightfall. We have done so. The achievement of your purpose is at hand. We will pray for the Land's healing. Thereafter we will expend entire seasons in celebration.'

In a rush of excitement, Linden urged Hyn to quicken her strides. The Soulsease—! Conflicted by confluences in the west, and polluted in the east by its turmoil within the belly of Mount Thunder, the river was untrammelled and placid while it ran through Andelain: gentle as a caress, and warm as a vein of life. Millennia ago, she and Covenant had followed the course of the Soulsease towards their confrontation with the Despiser. Now she was less than a league from the place where they had left Loric's *krill* after Hollian's resurrection.

The sun had only begun to set, and already she was within a Giant's shout of her goal: the justification for everything that she had suffered and done since she had learned the truth about Roger Covenant and the *croyel*.

The other Ranyhyn kept pace with Hyn. Behind them, the Giants ran in spite of their protracted weariness. Swift with anticipation, the company rounded a last hillock, passed through a grove of stately Gilden, and reached the river.

Here the Soulsease tended quietly northeastward. Between its broad banks, however, it opened a gap among the trees. Although the sun was sinking, its light still lay along the water; and its farewell fire burnished the river, transforming the current to ruddy bronze like a carpet unrolled to welcome the advent of night.

As the company halted, Linden recognised the satisfied pride of the Giants, the calm confidence of the Ranyhyn. She tasted Liand's pleasure and that of the Cords. Indeed, Pahni's and Bhapa's gladness was dimmed only by their Manethrall's clenched, contained sorrow. Linden sensed the depth of Anele's dreamless slumber, the solidity of Stave's presence, the ungiving impassivity of the Humbled. But now she shared none of their reactions. Her attention had already gone past the Soulsease.

On the far side of the river, she saw the Harrow.

His relaxed poise as he sat his destrier made it obvious that he was waiting for her.

Linden's heart thudded as Stave said quietly, 'Chosen,' warning her.

What I seek, lady, is to possess your instruments of power.

A moment later, she felt a surge of alarm from Liand. 'Heaven and Earth,' he breathed. 'He is *here*? Does he dare to meditate harm in Andelain?'

What I will have, however, is your companionship.

Under his breath, Mahrtiir muttered Ramen curses.

'Mayhap he does not,' suggested Stave. 'The Wraiths have permitted him.'

The Harrow could unmake Demondim-spawn with a gesture; an incantation. Did he have the same kind of power over the Wraiths?

Linden shook her head. No. The ur-viles and Waynhim were unnatural creatures. *I have made a considerable study of such beings.* But the Wraiths were avatars of Earthpower: they flourished among Andelain's organic largesse. The Harrow's ability to destroy artificial life did not imply a comparable threat to the Wraiths.

They had accepted his presence as they had accepted Linden's.

I am able to convey you to your son.

The sight of him transformed her certainty to confusion.

Gritting his teeth, Mahrtiir answered the surprise of the Swordmainnir. Two nights ago, Linden had told them about the Harrow. Now Mahrtiir identified the figure, dun with dusk, on the south bank of the Soulsease. Grimly he repeated what he knew of the ornately caped and clad Insequent.

While the Manethrall spoke, Liand nudged Rhohm to Hyn's side.

'Linden,' he whispered urgently, 'what will you do? He covets both your Staff and the white gold ring. Yet he has forsworn coercion.' The Mahdoubt had given up her life to wrest that oath from the Harrow. 'And he claims that he can bear you to your son.

'If his word holds, how will he obtain his desires? Will you bargain with him to gain passage to your son?'

Esmer and Roger had fought to stop the Harrow; to kill him if they could not remove him from this time. Linden assumed that *moksha* Raver's *kresh* had attacked for the same reason. They wanted to prevent her from reaching Jeremiah.

But Kastenessen could not enter Andelain. The Despiser would not. Perhaps Esmer himself had no power here. Presumably even Roger did not pose a threat. The awakened *krill* and the Wraiths warded the Hills.

The Harrow was safe. As safe as Linden.

She had nothing to bargain with except her Staff and Covenant's ring. Could she trade them away now? Abandon her purpose? For Jeremiah's sake?

What would that accomplish? Without Earthpower and wild magic, she would have nothing to free him from the *croyel*—

The prospect scattered her thoughts like a gust of wind in dried leaves. She had experienced imponderable rescues, miracles of hope. Caerroil Wildwood had completed her Staff. The Mahdoubt had retrieved her from the Land's past. And Anele had named other mysteries. Two days ago, he had told her that *Morinmoss redeemed the covenant, the white gold wielder. The Forestal sang, and Morinmoss answered.*

She needed to believe that she was not done with wonders; that she could accomplish what she had come here to do. That she might find Jeremiah without surrendering any of her strengths. Otherwise she would be helpless to refuse the Insequent.

Now those days are lost.

Instead of answering Liand, Linden turned to Stave.

'Do you know what Anele was talking about?' she asked. 'In Salva Gildenbourne, before the Giants found us, he said that Morinmoss "redeemed" Covenant. It was a long time ago. Do you remember? Can you tell me what he meant?'

All vastness is forgotten.

If her query surprised Stave, he did not show it. 'There is a tale,' he said carefully. 'Some of its aspects are not known. The ur-Lord himself could not recall them clearly. Having eaten *amanibhavam*, he was held by delirancy for a time, and retained only fragments of what transpired.'

Beyond the trees, the sun sank lower. Its light left the Soulsease, shrouding the Harrow in gloom.

'In the unnatural winter which High Lord Elena had imposed upon the Land,' Stave continued, 'wielding the Staff of Law in Corruption's service, the Unbeliever sought sanctuary in a Ramen covert. But the covert was beset, and he fled. Freezing and alone, he confronted another servant of Corruption. Aided by a Ranyhyn, Lena mother of Elena saved his life. In the attempt, however, Lena perished, and the ur-Lord's ankle was broken.

'He would not consent to ride the Ranyhyn. Rather he freed them to escape that dire winter.'

'Aye,' Mahrtiir assented. He and the whole company listened to Stave. 'So the tale is told among the Ramen.'

'At first,' Stave explained, 'he wandered, lost. Yet in some fashion he was guided beyond the Roamsedge into Morinmoss. It appeared to him that he was called by the song of a Forestal – a song which summoned him to the care of an unknown woman.

'There memory failed him. He did not return to himself until his hurts had been healed, both his ankle and his *amanibhavam*-stricken mind, and the woman lay dead.

'If it is sooth that he was drawn into Morinmoss by a Forestal, and that he was restored at a Forestal's urging, then it may truly be said that he was "redeemed" by the power of wood and sap and song. Also he was later aided by the brief awakening of the Colossus when he confronted High Lord Elena and was powerless.'

The Giants harkened to Stave with fascination, the Ramen with acknowledgment and approval. The Humbled paid no apparent heed to anything except the crepuscular loom of the Harrow. But Liand chafed at Stave's explanation. As soon as the former Master was done, he protested, 'Linden, I do not comprehend. Often Anele has revealed much which others can not or do not discern. Yet how does this tale pertain to the Harrow?'

Linden felt an obscure relief. Her confusion was fading; dripping away like wave-tossed water from a boulder. *There is more in Andelain – and among the Dead – and in your heart – than Lord Foul can conceive.* Once again, she discovered that Anele's eerie utterances had substance. *Remember that he is the hope of the Land.*

'It doesn't,' she told Liand. 'Not directly.' Everything pertained, the doom of the One Forest and the passing of the Forestals as much as the Mahdoubt's ruin and Esmer's conflicted betrayals. 'I'm just trying to imagine what a bargain with the Harrow might cost.' She intended to redeem her son at any price – but she also intended to choose that price. 'The Wraiths refused Longwrath. But they're ignoring *him*. That must mean something.'

There is hope in contradiction.

The Law of Life had been broken in Andelain. Elena had broken the Law of Death among the roots of *Melenkurion* Skyweir. On both occasions, Covenant had found a way to save the Land.

Rime Coldspray's voice was a low rumble. 'In this, we cannot counsel you. Among us, children are precious beyond description. Both the Swordmainnir and the Giants of Dire's Vessel have hazarded their lives for Longwrath's unattained redemption. But you have not named your purpose. Ignorant of what you will attempt, we cannot gauge the import of the Harrow's presence.'

A moment passed before Linden realised that all of her companions were waiting for her decision.

'All right.' She had already made up her mind. 'I want to hear what he has to say. But I'm not going to agree to anything until we reach the *krill*. I don't trust him. I won't take any chances until I know more.'

The *krill* responded to wild magic. She had the Staff of Law. And if she found Thomas Covenant among the Dead—

One way or another, she meant to end Jeremiah's suffering.

Her answer appeared to satisfy Liand, although he did not relax his distrust of the Harrow.

'So how do we get across?' she asked Stave and Mahrtiir. 'Can the Ranyhyn carry us? Is there a ford?'

She was already familiar with the prowess of the Giants. The weight of their armour and swords would not hinder them.

The Manethrall snorted at the mere suggestion that the horses might not be able to bear their riders through the river; and Stave said, 'In Andelain, the current of the Soulsease is gentle. There will be no difficulty.'

As if to demonstrate his assertion, he sent Hynyn down the riverbank and into the water. For a few strides, Hynyn kept his footing. Then the stallion began to swim strongly.

Galt followed at once. Crossing the river, the company would be vulnerable. Clearly he and Stave meant to gain the south bank so that they could protect Linden and the others if the Harrow contemplated an attack.

'Swordmainnir!' called the Ironhand with a laugh. 'Here is opportunity for refreshment. Never let it be said that Giants shun clear water and cleansing!'

At once, she plunged into the Soulsease with her comrades behind her, chuckling as they forged ahead. Without warning, Grueburn threw a splash of water in Cabledarm's face. Stonemage responded by drenching Bluntfist. But their play did not slow them. In spite of their mirth, they carried their swords drawn.

Mahrtiir and Narunal entered the river after the Giants. Bhapa and Pahni, and then Clyme and Branl, positioned themselves around Linden, Liand and Anele as they followed the Manethrall.

When the water hit Linden's legs, she caught her breath. The Soulsease was colder than she had expected. But it did not resemble the winter which she had experienced with Roger and the *croyel*. The river was distilled springtime: the eagerness of fertility and flowing after winter's long sleep. Its touch conveyed hints of the world's renewal. And Hyn passed through it easily, thrusting ahead when her hooves could find the bottom, swimming with her head held high when they could not.

Surging up from the watercourse, Stave and Galt greeted the Harrow. If he granted them a reply, Linden did not hear it. Motionless on his destrier, he did not so much as incline his head to the *Haruchai* – or to the Swordmainnir when they splashed out of the river and surrounded him. 'This is an un-looked-for meeting,' Coldspray announced. 'Declare yourself, stranger.' But the Harrow's answer – if he gave one – did not reach Linden. Encircled by swords, he appeared to do nothing except wait for the arrival of his desires.

A fading glow still held the sky as Hyn gained the riverbank; heaved herself and her rider out of the Soulsease. The evening was too early for stars. And the Harrow had placed himself beneath the outspread shadows of a broad oak at the water's edge. Linden saw him as little more than a deeper blackness in the coming night. His leather apparel seemed to muffle or diffuse his aura; mask his intentions.

His destrier was more tangible. The beast was a gelding as massive and tall as Mhornym. It champed at its bit and fretted while its master sat without moving. Occasional quivers ran through its muscles like small galvanic shocks, jolts of excitement or terror. But its tension did not trouble the Harrow. Instead his mount's disquiet only made him look more unpredictable and dangerous.

Stave and Mahrtiir moved to escort Linden as she advanced. The Soulsease had carried her eastward: she faced the Harrow with the last of the sunset in her eyes. Some of the Swordmainnir stepped aside to watch over Liand, Anele and the Cords, but Coldspray, Grueburn and Stone-mage continued to confront the Insequent with their weapons ready.

Poised for battle, the Humbled regarded him impassively. He had already defeated them once. He had done so without difficulty. Yet Linden recognised that his physical strength did not equal theirs. His prowess was external in some fashion: an expression of acquired theurgy rather than of innate might. He wore his magicks like a form of raiment, as elaborate and distinctive as his leather garb.

When she reached the verge of the oak's shade, she asked Hyn to stop. She wanted to keep her distance. She could not see his eyes, but she was sure that he could see hers – and those of her companions. He had vowed that he would not make a second attempt to swallow her mind. He had called on his fellow Insequent to ensure that he kept his word. However, he had not promised to refrain from threatening her friends.

Mahrtiir and Anele were safe. The intransigence of the *Haruchai* might protect them from a fall into the Harrow's bottomless gaze. Even the Giants might be able to resist. But Liand, Bhapa, and Pahni had no defence. If the Harrow wanted leverage—

Time seemed to stretch as though it might tear. The darkness under the oak became all darkness despite the faint light beyond the shadows. The Giants shifted their feet, waiting for Linden to speak. The destrier stamped one hoof restively.

Linden secured her grip on the Staff. With one hand, she touched Covenant's ring through the fabric of her shirt.

'Say something,' she demanded. 'I'm here. It's your move.'

The Harrow laughed softly. 'Be welcome in Andelain, lady.' His voice held the fertile depth of damp loam. Unlike Esmer, he had suffered no apparent damage in their earlier struggle. 'You will find much to delight and surprise you in this bourn of peace.'

He may have been mocking her.

'Don't play games with me,' she retorted. '"Peace" isn't one of your strengths. Get to the point.'

He laughed again, a low rustle like the sound of canvas sliding over stone. 'Is it not sufficient that I am able to enter Andelain? Must I refrain from the enjoyment of loveliness because Kastenessen and the *mere*-son and your perished love's scion cannot share my pleasure?'

Linden started to reply, then stopped herself. Roger was blocked from Andelain? And Esmer? She had hoped for that, but Esmer had not said so explicitly.

Then why did the Harrow hold back? He was in no danger of any kind. Why did he taunt her instead of bargaining?

Implied threats scraped across her nerves. At that moment, however, her certainty was greater than her alarm. She was so close to her goal—

Apart from Stave and the Humbled, all of her companions were taut, apprehensive; braced for danger. In spite of their concerns, she forced herself to relax her shoulders and breathe more slowly.

'All right,' she said as if she had become calm. 'I'm confused. I know why you're here. What I don't know is *how*. Why didn't the Wraiths stop you? Or the *krill*? If they can forbid Kastenessen, how did *you* get in?'

The Harrow did not answer. His emanations suggested that he was not paying attention.

Linden thought that she heard a distant sound which did not belong to evening in Andelain. But it was too elusive to be identified; and then it was gone.

'Mayhap, Chosen,' Stave offered, 'he was not prevented because he is not a being of power. His theurgy is that of knowledge. It does not reside within him.'

Even Longwrath was possessed by a kind of magic: the ability to slough off his shackles whenever he wished.

Linden felt the Harrow's gaze return. 'Lady, I have promised my companionship, and the word of any Insequent is holy. Lacking such fidelity, knowledge erodes itself. I have striven too long, and have learned too much, to be made trivial by unfaith. Therefore I am here. No other justification is required.'

He still seemed to be mocking her.

Goaded by what he had done to the Mahdoubt, she said angrily, 'And you think that just showing up occasionally makes you honest?' But then she caught herself. 'No, forget that. I don't care how you justify yourself. Tell me something else. I want to understand this.

'Anele has power. Why didn't the Wraiths refuse him?'

Was it possible that the Wraiths had allowed the Harrow to enter Andelain because he did not serve Despite?

Something that she could not define seemed to snag his notice. It was not birdsong or breeze or the soughing of the Soulsease, although it resembled those sounds. Still she felt his posture shift; felt him probe the twilight behind her. Again he did not answer.

Stave appeared to shrug. 'The old man desires no harm. And his power is that of Andelain. Here he was transformed in his mother's womb, and given birth.'

'Then what about Longwrath?' Linden insisted, aiming her questions at the Harrow in spite of his inattention. 'Is he possessed?' She did not think so. If a Raver — or some similar entity — ruled him, she would have sensed its presence. But she wanted to be sure. 'Did the Wraiths stop him just because he's trying to kill me?'

The Insequent faced her. 'I would do so in their place.' His tone continued to jeer at her, but his manner implied boredom or distraction. 'Have I not said that your might becomes you? Others may desire your death. I do not.

'However, concerning this Giant who craves your blood—'

He paused as though he expected an interruption. But Linden waited, and her companions were silent. After a moment, he resumed.

'His blade holds some interest. It was forged at a time millennia past, when Kasreyn of the Gyre feared the Sandgorgons, having not yet devised their Doom. He hungered for a weapon puissant to slay those feral beasts. Therefore he wrought the flamberge, aided by the *croyel*. It was fearsome in the hands of a knowing wielder. Yet its purpose ended when the Sandgorgons were bound to their Doom. Deprived of use, its theurgy fades.'

Staring, Linden asked, 'Is that what attracted the Wraiths? His *sword?*'

'Lady,' replied the Harrow sardonically, 'I have said that his blade holds some interest. It does not fascinate me. And the Wraiths are of no consequence. They merely articulate the might of Loric's *krill*. Born of Andelain, they nurture its beauty. Far greater beings walk the Hills, among them one of vast arrogance and self-worship.'

She shook her head, trying to rid herself of an innominate whisper. Far greater beings– Was he referring to the Dead?

Stubbornly she returned to her essential question. 'I know what you want. You tried to force me, but you failed. So now I'm supposed to need your help.' *I am able to convey you to your son.* 'That way, you can "demand recompense". All right. Let's get on with it. Isn't it time for you to offer me a bargain? Isn't that why you're here?'

'It is,' he replied, 'and it is not. For the present, it would be bootless to barter. One comes who will preclude my desires without qualm. I do not relish the indignity of being thwarted. I will await a more congenial opportunity to speak of your son.'

Linden scowled. Hints of sound became more persistent, in spite of her efforts to dismiss them. She could almost—

An instant later, she realised that she was hearing the delicate music of bells or chimes: a soft ringing, at once beautiful and imprecise, as allusive as the scent of an exotic perfume. She nearly gasped as she recognised the tones. She knew them well.

Instinctively dismayed, she wheeled Hyn away from the Harrow.

'Linden?' Liand asked in surprise. Stave and the Humbled looked around, alert for danger. Muttering Giantish oaths, the Swordmainnir did the same.

They could not discern what Linden heard: she knew that. Long ago, this same chiming had filled her with turmoil and confusion – and none of her companions had been aware of it, not Covenant, not the Giants of the Search, not even the *Haruchai*.

Behind her, the Harrow said with rich sarcasm, 'Be at peace, lady. Your concern is needless. No powers will contend in this place.'

Linden ignored him; ignored her friends. At once alarmed and angry, she watched a portion of Andelain's dusk concatenate and flow as if the soul of the Hills were taking form.

Adorned with the tang and piquancy of tuned bells, a woman stepped out of the twilight and became herself.

She was tall and supple, lovely and lucent; bright with hues that glowed like the light of gems. Her raiment may have been sendaline, or it may have been composed of diamonds and rubies, its glitter and incarnadine woven together by the illimitable magic of dreams. The regal lustre of her hair seemed more precious than jewels: it shone like her ornate cymar and her sovereign eyes; like a sea entranced by the moon. Her chosen flesh spread gleams that caused or resembled her chiming. When she moved, every line and curve was limned in exaltation.

And in her gaze and her mien, an imperious disdain struggled against pleading and sorrow.

Linden knew her. She was Infelice. In some sense which Linden had never understood, she was the leader or spokeswoman or potentate of the *Elohim*. Among her people, she embodied what they called 'the Würd of the Earth', although in their mellifluous voices 'Würd' might have been 'Wyrd' or 'Word' or 'Weird'.

Her simple presence commanded humility: it urged abasement. In spite of Hyn's unflinching calm, Linden felt a blind impulse to kneel, abashed, before Infelice.

Her reaction was echoed by Liand and the Ramen. Their faces reflected Infelice's radiance. Even Mahrtiir was stricken with awe and chagrin. Scowling, Anele refused to turn towards her. And the Giants, who had been acquainted with the *Elohim* for millennia, scrambled to put away their weapons and bow deeply. Only the *Haruchai* showed no reaction – the *Haruchai* and the Harrow.

Thousands of years ago, the uncompromising dedication of Stave's ancestors had offended the *Elohim*. More recently, Linden had learned from the Theomach that his people resented the hauteur and power of the *Elohim*. The Vizard had tried to encourage Jeremiah to imprison them.

In the *Elohimfest* where Linden had first seen Infelice, her people had betrayed Covenant because they distrusted his possession of white gold. They had believed that Linden should wield wild magic. Even then, they had been certain that Covenant's efforts to defeat Lord Foul would ultimately fail.

Facing Infelice, Linden feared suddenly that her straits, and the Land's, demonstrated that the *Elohim* had been right all along. The Despiser's repeated return to strength demeaned Covenant's victories. They might as well have been failures.

Infelice did not walk on the grass. Instead she moved through the air at the height of the Giants. She may have wished to look down on Linden and the Harrow.

Her voice wore a penumbra of bells as she said, 'The Insequent speaks sooth, Wildwielder.' Around her, night thickened over the Hills and the Soulsease as if her appearance absorbed the last of the light. 'No powers will contend in sacred Andelain. Conscious of his littleness, and embittered, he faults us for arrogance and self-worship. Yet he declines to acknowledge that the quality which he deplores, the certainty that we are equal to all things, preserves his petty machinations as well as his life. Our unconcern spares smaller beings. Were we less than we are, we would have taken umbrage in an earlier age and extinguished the Insequent for their meddlesomeness.'

'You vaunt yourself without cause, *Elohim*,' retorted the Harrow. 'Was not your Appointed Guardian of the One Tree defeated by the Theomach?'

'He was,' admitted Infelice in a tone that conceded nothing. 'And in his turn, the Theomach was defeated. Though he strove to affect the Würd of the Earth, he fell before one mere *Haruchai*. Thus our present peril is in part attributable to the Insequent. Had the Theomach refrained from aggrandisement, much which now threatens the Earth would not have occurred, and I would not have come to counter your gluttony.'

The Harrow laughed, mocking Infelice as he had mocked Linden.

'You are clever, *Elohim*. You speak truth to conceal truth. Did you not also come to prevent the lady?'

Infelice did not waver. 'I did.' Nevertheless expressions molted across her face, ire and grief and alarm commingled with a look that resembled self-pity. 'If the Wildwielder will heed me.'

Their exchange gave Linden time to rally herself; step back from the brink of consternation. She did not trust the Harrow: she knew the intensity of his greed. And she was painfully, intimately familiar with the surquedry and secrets of the *Elohim*: she could not believe that Infelice wished her – or Jeremiah – well. As a people, the *Elohim* cared only for themselves.

The Theomach had enabled Berek Halfhand to fashion the first Staff of Law. He had made himself the Guardian of the One Tree. Then his stewardship had become Brinn's. But Linden did not understand how such things contributed to Lord Foul's designs.

'No,' she said before the Harrow spoke again. 'You can talk around me as if I'm not here some other time. Tonight is mine.'

'Stave. Mahrtiir. Coldspray.' Deliberately she turned away from Infelice. 'We're going. I need the *krill*.' And the Dead. 'If Infelice and the Harrow want to come with us, I don't mind. They can answer a few questions along the way.'

The Harrow laughed. A flare of anger burned in Infelice's eyes. Almost immediately, however, he cut short his scorn, and she quelled her indignation.

Out of the new dark, Wraiths came skirling like music, the song of pipes and flutes. Dancing and bobbing, they appeared as if in response to Linden's declaration, more and more of them at every moment: first a small handful, then a dozen, then one and two and three score. And as they lit themselves from their impalpable arcane wicks, they joined together in two rows to form an aisle leading southward.

Involuntarily Linden gasped. The Giants exclaimed their astonishment. 'Linden,' Liand breathed, unable to contain himself. 'Heaven and Earth. *Linden*.' The Ramen stared as if the Cords and their eyeless Manethrall were bedazzled.

'Sunder my father,' Anele panted between his teeth. 'Hollian my mother. Preserve your son.' A tumult of distress ran through his voice.

'Preserve him. Anele is lost. Without your forgiveness, he is damned.'

The Wraiths had come—

—to welcome Linden. For reasons which she could not fathom, they meant to escort her like an honour guard to Loric's *krill*.

Their presence filled her with hope as if they had opened her heart.

Unable to speak, she urged Hyn into motion. With a stately step and an arched neck, the mare entered the avenue of Wraiths as though she had accepted an obeisance.

Quickly the Swordmainnir arrayed themselves around Linden and Hyn. Prompted by an instinctive reverence, they drew their swords and stretched out their arms, pointing their blades at the first faint stars. A moment later, Stave guided Liand, Anele and the Ramen into formation behind Linden. None of the Humbled went ahead of her. Instead they rode down the aisle at the rear of the company as if to distance themselves from her intentions.

Without hesitation, the Harrow joined Linden; but he did not presume to precede her. Instead he rode his destrier beside one of the Giants. After an instant of outrage and chagrin, Infelice came to accompany Linden between the Wraiths. She, too, did not take the lead, but chose rather to float opposite the Harrow, placing her light in contrast with his darkness.

—*hope in contradiction.* Although they shared a wish to preserve the Arch of Time, the Insequent and the *Elohim* seemed to cancel each other.

Along a path defined by flames and implied melody, the riders, the Giants, and Infelice crossed a rounded hill and moved into a lea swept with night. Gradually stars began to peek out of the heavens, glittering dispassionately as the final remnants of daylight frayed and faded.

Old elms dotted the lea. Amid trees and Wraiths, the Harrow remarked quietly, 'In an ancient age, this night would have been *Banas Nimoram*, the Celebration of Spring. We might perchance have witnessed the Dance of the Wraiths of Andelain.' Every hint of mockery had fled from his deep voice. 'Millennia have passed since they last enacted their rite of gladness. Yet they remain to signify the import of our deeds and needs. Did I not say, lady, that here you would find delight and surprise?' After a pause, he added, 'No other Insequent has beheld such a sight.'

Linden made no reply. The voiceless entrancement of the living fires held her. Doubtless the *Haruchai* and the Ramen had memories or tales of *Banas Nimoram*: she did not. Yet she understood that every swirl and glow and note of the Wraiths accentuated the meaning of her presence.

Then, however, Infelice said in a tone of careful severity, 'Wildwielder, we must speak of your purpose here.'

With an effort, Linden set aside her hushed awe. She needed to ready herself for what she meant to attempt. More to occupy her conscious mind than to resolve any lingering uncertainty, she countered by asking, 'Did you really come all of this way just to stop the Harrow from taking me to my son?'

The *Elohim* made their home far to the east beyond the Sunbirth Sea. Infelice had crossed many hundred of leagues, leaving behind the rapt self-contemplation of her people.

'In part,' she admitted with a faint suggestion of disdain or revulsion. 'But I will not speak of the Harrow, or of his unscrupling greed, or of your son. We must address your intent.'

Linden refused to be distracted. 'I would rather talk about meddling.' The *Elohim* had Appointed Findail and Kastenessen: they had sealed Covenant's mind and tried to imprison Vain. They had sent one of their number to the aid of the One Forest, and another to warn the Land. 'Even though you're "equal to all things",' *the heart of the Earth*, 'you sometimes take matters into your own hands. You're here to block the Harrow. You want to interfere with me. So tell me something.

'According to the Theomach, if he hadn't disrupted Roger's plans to destroy the Arch, you would have intervened. Is that true?'

Haughtiness and pleading bled together in Infelice. 'It is. Much of the Despiser's evil does not concern us. His ends are an abomination, but often his means are too paltry to merit our notice. When he strives to unmake Time, however, our existence is imperilled. This alone we share with the Insequent. We do not desire the destruction of the Earth.'

Softly, as if in the distance, the Harrow began to sing. His low voice followed the inferred tune of the Wraiths as if he had deciphered their minuet.

'The ending of all things is nigh.
    Both grief and rue will pass away,
Both love and gratefulness; and why?
    No one will stand to offer, 'Nay.'

'This chosen plight is chosen doom,
    A path unwisely, bravely found
Which leads us to a lonely tomb,
    A sepulchre of ruined ground.

'Some fool or seer has made it so:
    That life and lore give way to dross
And so preclude our wail of woe.
    No heart remains to feel the loss.

'And so this way the world ends,
    In failure and mistaken faith.
We dream that we will make amends,
    Yet ev'ry hope is but a Wraith,

'A touch of soon extinguished flame,
    A residue of ash and dust.
We ache to save our use and name,
    And yet we die because we must.'

He seemed to be smiling as he sang.

But Linden did not heed him. 'Then is it also true,' she continued stubbornly, probing the *Elohim*, 'that the Insequent are the "shadow" on your hearts?'

Other *Elohim* had referred to a *shadow upon the heart of the Earth*. It justified their distress that Linden did not wield Covenant's ring, their betrayal of Covenant, and their efforts to neutralise Vain.

Divergent emotions chased each other across Infelice's lambent features. 'Wildwielder, the Insequent are filled to bursting with boasts. They vaunt their might and efficacy. Yet among them, only the Theomach has achieved an effect upon the fate of the Earth. Thoughts of them do not darken our absorption.'

'Then,' Linden insisted, 'what *is* it? What is the "shadow"?'

All who live contain some darkness, and much lies hidden there. But in us it has not been a matter of exigency – for are we not equal to all things?

Infelice sighed; but she did not decline to answer. Apparently her desire to sway Linden compelled her.

'For a time which you would measure in eons, it remained nameless among us. Later, we considered that perhaps it was cast by the Despiser's malevolence. But then we grew to understand that it was the threat of beings from beyond Time, beings such as yourself and also the Timewarden – beings both small and mortal who are nonetheless capable of utter devastation.

'By his own deeds, the Despiser cannot destroy the Arch of Time. He requires the connivance of such men and women as the Timewarden's son and mate. He requires your aid, Wildwielder, and that of the man who was once the Unbeliever.'

Linden winced; but she did not relent. 'Is that why you wanted me to have Covenant's ring? Is that how you justify closing his mind?'

'It is,' assented Infelice. 'Had wild magic been yours to wield in millennia past, you would have posed no hazard to the Arch of Time. The Unbeliever's white gold would have answered your need. But his ring was not yours. Constrained by incomplete mastery, you could not have summoned utter havoc. Yet you were the Sun-Sage, empowered with percipience to wield wild magic precisely. Had you rather than the Unbeliever confronted the Despiser then, his defeat would not have been what it was, both partial and ambiguous. The Earth would have been preserved – and you would not now aim to achieve the ruin for which the Despiser has long hungered.'

Achieve the ruin—

Linden refused to listen. She could not heed the *Elohim*: not now. Instead she concentrated on more immediate details. The dampness of her jeans. The water in her boots. The strict and comforting sensation of the Staff in her hand. Aflame, the Wraiths wove her way among the copses and greenswards. On her behalf, they held back every darkness. Their fires were too little to dim the thronging stars; but still the Wraiths gave a processional dignity to the night.

And so this way the world ends—

Everyone except Linden's friends expected calamities. And even they were not impervious to doubt. The Giants had expressed their concern. Earlier Stave had asked her to consider turning aside. Days ago, Liand had admitted, *It is possible that your loves will bind your heart to destruction—* The Theomach himself had warned her. *If you err in this, your losses will be greater than you are able to conceive.*

Now, however, Linden felt no reaction from her companions. Apart from the Harrow, they walked or rode in stillness. As far as she could tell, they were ensorcelled by the Wraiths and heard nothing. Infelice was certainly capable of making her voice, and Linden's, inaudible to others. By his own means, the Theomach had performed a similar feat in Berek's camp.

Speaking of Linden's capacity for darkness, Liand had also said, *I am not afraid.*

When she had steadied herself, she realised that Infelice's pronouncements made her stronger. Opposition confirmed her choices. The fact that she inspired fear in beings like Roger and Kastenessen, Esmer and Infelice, demonstrated that she was on the right path.

'You *Elohim* amaze me,' she remarked almost casually. 'You always have. After all of this time, you still don't realise that you're wrong.

'I'm not like Covenant. I never was. If he hadn't beaten Lord Foul, I would have broken.' She lacked his capacity for miracles. 'Lord Foul would have *won*, and none of us would be here to discuss whether Covenant and I did the right thing.'

'No, Wildwielder,' insisted Infelice with a flush of heat and pleading. 'We are not in error. Your thoughts are inadequate to comprehend ours. It was not for the Despiser's defeat that we sought to impose the burden of wild magic upon you. Had you indeed "broken", as you believe, both the Land and the Earth would have suffered great harm. That is sooth. But Time would have endured. Deprived of its rightful wielder, white gold is not puissant to destroy the Arch.

'Also there would now exist no Staff of Law. Its benisons are many. Nonetheless it constrains the Timewarden. By wild magic, he came into being – and by your deeds, he was made weak.'

If you hadn't taken my ring and made that Staff, I would have been able to fix everything—

'And we are the *Elohim*,' Infelice continued, 'equal to all things. Across the centuries, we would have healed much. Perhaps the Despiser's blight upon the Land would have remained, but the Earth we would have preserved and restored.'

With a strange calm exasperation as unexpected and luminous as her passage through Andelain, Linden asked, 'Then what was it all *for*? If you didn't care about the outcome – or the Land – why did you try so hard to force me to take Covenant's place?'

To himself, the Harrow chuckled scornfully.

Guided by Wraiths like candle flames, Linden rode under a broad Gilden and crossed the lip of a shallow vale – and saw her goal. It had always been there. Esmer had told her so: Stave and the Masters knew its location. Nevertheless it seemed to come into existence suddenly, as if it had manifested itself in response to her need. Between instants, the night was cast back, and silver fire shone from the bottom of the vale.

Dancing, the Wraiths moved ahead of her down the gentle slope and spread out to encircle the *krill* of High Lord Loric, son of Damelon, father of Kevin. There they bobbed and grew brighter, apparently bowing – and feeding, drawing sustenance from the blade's incandescence.

Here was the source of their power to preserve Andelain. The *krill* was powerful in itself, able to cut stone without being dulled, and to sever the lives of eldritch creatures like the Viles and the Demondim. But its greatest strength – the chief accomplishment of Loric's lore – was as a channel for other magicks. Made active by the mere presence, quiescent and extravagant, of white gold, the blade protected the Hills. Yet Linden had seen it accomplish more. With the *krill*, Sunder had slain Caer-Caveral, although Sunder was no more than a grieved Stonedownor, and Caer-Caveral was the last Forestal, powerful enough to preserve Andelain against the Sunbane. And in the release of Caer-Caveral's music, the *krill* had enabled Sunder's yearning to tear apart the fabric of Law so that Hollian lived again.

Loric's weapon was a two-edged dagger almost as long as a short sword. At the intersection of its blade, its straight guards, and its ribbed hilt, it had been forged around a clear gem, mystic and immaculate: the focal point of its power. There the gem blazed with condensed argent like contained wild magic, at once potent and controlled; ready for any use.

It remained exactly as Linden remembered it: a cynosure of vindication and loss deeply embedded in the black, blasted stump of a ruined tree which had once been Caer-Caveral and Hile Troy.

Goaded by memories and exigency, a purpose as desperate as the last Forestal's, she urged Hyn into a swift canter. Graceful as water, Hyn carried Linden through the acknowledgment of the Wraiths towards the bottom of the vale; towards dead wood and shining and culmination.

Behind her, Infelice called urgently, 'It was for *this*! *To avert this present moment.*' Dread and supplication squirmed through her voice. 'Broken or triumphant in the past, you would not have returned to the Land. You would not now hold white gold and the Staff of Law. Nor would you approach Loric's *krill* in Andelain accompanied by Wraiths. You would not be driven by mistaken love to bring about the end of all things!'

Linden wanted to laugh like the Harrow. As she swept closer to her destination, she answered in derision, 'Does it bother you at all that you're completely insane?'

Then Hyn led Linden's companions into the expanding circle of the Wraiths. There Linden dismounted. With the opulent grass of the Hills beneath her sodden boots and stained pants, she hugged the Staff of Law to her chest. It was *here*: Loric's *krill* was *here. —that which will enable her to bear her strengths—* And Covenant's ring hung under her shirt. Jeremiah's racecar rested in her pocket. She had gained everything that she required – except the Dead.

The *krill* had been driven deeply into the wood: she was not sure that she could remove it. And she remembered its heat. She was not Covenant, the rightful white gold wielder, numb with leprosy: if she touched the dagger with her bare skin, it might burn her. Instead she stood before it as though it were the altar of Caer-Caveral's sacrifice.

Liand and the rest of her friends arrived after her. Only Stave and the Humbled dropped to the ground: the other riders remained aback their Ranyhyn as if they were caught in dreams, bespelled by the Wraiths. Even the Giants appeared to wander entranced, lost in mysteries. Coldspray and perhaps Grueburn seemed to struggle against their amazement, but their comrades gazed upon the circling of the Wraiths and did not awaken.

Like Liand, Anele and the Ramen, the Harrow remained mounted at a distance from Linden and the *krill*. The bottomless holes of his eyes considered the fiery gem hungrily.

Floating, Infelice drifted to the ground near Linden. The intensity of the *krill* dimmed her raiment, robbed her of lustre. She sounded almost human – almost petulant – as she said, 'I have heard you, Wildwielder. Have you heard me? We stand now at the last crisis of the Earth. If you do not turn aside, you will be broken indeed. Your remorse will surpass your strength to bear it.'

Linden did not answer. Instead she spoke softly to the waiting night.

'I'm here. It's time. You know why I've come. You know what I have to do.' When Covenant had entered Andelain without her, his Dead had given him gifts to aid his efforts to redeem the Land. *Linden, find me. I can't help you unless you find me.* 'The Harrow says that this is *Banas Nimoram*, and you called me here. I can't save anything' – not Jeremiah, not the Land, not even herself – 'without you.'

Around her and the Wraiths, the darkness seemed to hold its breath. The Harrow murmured quiet invocations which meant nothing to her. Infelice fretted as if she were inconsolable. The Swordmainnir shifted restlessly in their trance, and Anele jerked his head from side to side, watchful and frightened, like a man being hunted. The stars grew still in their stately allemande.

Linden could not know that she would be heeded. Yet she felt no doubt. In dreams and through Anele, Covenant had reached out to her across the boundaries of life and death. She no longer considered it possible that she might be mistaken.

Then the night gave a low sigh; and beyond the Wraiths two figures came forward from the rim of the vale. They were portrayed in silver as though they were made of moonlight: they shone with phosphorescence like a gentler manifestation of the *krill's* argent blaze. But they were at once more definite than moonshine and less acute than the blade's echo of wild magic. Although they walked with formal steps, they appeared to drift like wisps over the grass, as evanescent as dreaming, and as allusive.

Linden knew them. They were Sunder Graveler and Hollian eh-Brand, Anele's parents.

When they had passed between the reverent flames, they stopped partway down the slope. They seemed strangely commanding and penitent, and their moonstone eyes gleamed with austere compassion. Linden's heart surged at the sight of them; but they did not glance in her direction or speak. Instead they gazed at Anele as if they were full of suppressed weeping.

He must have been aware of them. With his hands, he covered his face. But then he seemed to find that his fingers and palms were too thin, too frail, to protect him. Flinging his arms around his head, he ducked low over Hrama's neck like a child who hoped to hide from chastisement.

Now Linden saw tears in Hollian's eyes and sorrow in Sunder's. Yet they beckoned to their son, summoning him towards them with the certainty of monarchs. In life, their courage and love and Earthpower had earned them the stature of Lords.

Anele did not react to their mute call. But Hrama responded. As if both he and his rider belonged in such company, the Ranyhyn carried Anele towards his Dead.

Sunder and then Hollian bowed to Hrama, silent and grave. Gesturing, they invited the Ranyhyn to walk between them. Solemn as a cortège, they turned to escort Hrama and Anele away from Loric's *krill*; out of the vale. Linden felt her heart try to break – try and fail – while Sunder and Hollian departed with their son. But they said nothing; and so she could not. A cry of abandonment sounded within her for a moment. Then it relapsed to stone.

As Sunder, Hollian and their son passed away among the flames, Linden lost sight of them. In their place, another ghost strode down the slope.

She knew him as well, grieved for him as much.

He was Grimmand Honninscrave, the Master of Starfare's Gem. In measureless agony, he had contained *samadhi* Sheol so that the Sandgorgon Nom could kill him in order to rend the Raver. Thirty-five centuries later, anguish still gripped his face. As he moved, he seemed to shed droplets of moonlight like blood.

He also stopped midway between the Wraiths and the dead stump of Caer-Caveral's sacrifice. He also did not speak. And he did not spare a glance for Linden, in spite of their friendship. His ancient pain conveyed the impression that he feared her as he summoned the Swordmainnir.

They obeyed without hesitation, sheathing their weapons as they strode towards the Dead Giant. Around Honninscrave's moonstruck figure, they stood for a moment in silence and awe. Then they accompanied him away from Linden, leaving her to face her choices without their encouragement, their strength, their laughter. Together they followed Honninscrave past the Wraiths until he and they had faded into the night.

Of Linden's friends, only Stave, Liand and the Ramen remained.

'Do you behold this, Wildwielder?' Infelice hissed with the urgency of a serpent. 'Do you *see?* These are your Dead. Their love for you is not forgotten. Yet they shun you. They seek to spare their descendants the peril of your intent. If you will not heed *me*, heed *them*.'

The Harrow countered Infelice's appeal with a jeer, although he kept his distance. 'She is Infelice,' he told Linden scornfully, 'suzerain among the *Elohim*, and blind with self-worship. Yet there is insight in her disregard. You also have been made blind, lady.' His disdain became veiled supplication. 'There is a Kevin's Dirt of the soul as there is of the flesh. The Earth would have been better served if you had not cast away the Mahdoubt's name and use and life.'

Linden might have wavered then. But she had not come here for Honninscrave, or for Sunder and Hollian. Covenant's ring hung, untouched, under her shirt, and Jeremiah's racecar was in her pocket: she was still waiting. If all of her friends were taken from her, she would stand where she was until Covenant appeared.

Through her teeth, she repeated, 'I'm here. It's time.'

I need you. I need you *now*.

But if any ghost among the Hills heard her, it was not Thomas Covenant. Instead ten stern spirits walked like wafting down into the vale, and she saw that they were *Haruchai* whom she had known: Cail, Ceer and Hergrom, as well as others who had fought against the Clave in Revelstone. When she recognised Esmer's father, she had to bite her lip to stifle a groan. In spite of his long devotion, he had been beaten bloody by his kinsmen because he had failed to resist the seduction of the *merewives*. Forlorn, he had later left Lord's Keep to seek the Dancers of the Sea once again. He could not forget the passion and cruelty of their siren lure. The denunciation of his people had left him no other path.

Now he and his Dead company entered the vale severely, as if they had come to repay judgment with judgment.

They, too, halted on the slope of the vale. And they, too, did not speak. With moonlight in their eyes and authority in their gestures, they beckoned Stave and the Humbled towards them. If they addressed the living *Haruchai* mind to mind, Linden felt nothing.

But neither Stave nor the Masters obeyed.

The Dead insisted, upright and uncompromising. The argence of the *krill* reflected in Stave's eye, and in the eyes of the Humbled, echoing the glow of the Dead. Still none of the *Haruchai* left their places with Linden.

'Stave?' she breathed. 'What do they want? What are they saying?'

Stave shook his head. He did not glance away from Cail, Ceer, and Hergrom. 'This night holds no enmity,' he said as if to himself. 'The Dead neither spurn nor oppose you. Rather they seek to make way. Other spirits inhabit Andelain, spectres which may not be denied. While Loric's *krill* burns, their might requires compliance. They will come to affirm the necessity of freedom.

'The Insequent and the *Elohim* honour no power but their own. They remain because they fear for themselves. Yet they dare not contend. If they offer strife, they will be expelled in spite of their theurgies. And they cannot sway you. You hold no love for them. Therefore you cannot be misled.'

Be cautious of love. There is a glamour upon it which binds the heart to destruction.

Stave's quiet voice seemed to rouse Liand and the Ramen from their imposed reverie. They stirred as if they were awakening; turned their heads and looked around them. Linden felt their attention sharpen. Mahrtiir lifted his garrote in his hands.

After a time, the Dead *Haruchai* appeared to accept that they had been refused. Cail's expression was radiant sorrow; but Ceer and the others glowered in disapproval. Their movements were stiff with reproach as they withdrew.

'Stave?' Linden asked again. She believed that she understood Cail's sadness. But Hergrom, Ceer and the others were the ancestors of the Masters. If they were alive, surely they would have stood beside the Humbled?

Stave frowned. 'Be still, Chosen,' he said in a constrained hush. 'The Dead have no words for your ears. They are forbidden to address you. In this place, your deeds must be your own, unpersuaded for good or ill by the counsel and knowledge of those who have perished. So it has been commanded, and the Dead obey.'

Other spirits inhabit Andelain—

Who but Covenant had the stature to command the Dead?

The answer came towards the vale from four directions. As the Dead *Haruchai* faded past the dancing adulation of the Wraiths, vast doors seemed to open, rents in the fabric of the night, and four towering shades strode forth.

They were tall, prodigiously tall, not because they were Giants, but because their spirits were great. Their brightness emulated the blaze of the *krill*.

One of them walked out of the west. With a shock, Linden saw that he was Berek Halfhand. But he was not the Berek whom she had met, em-battled and weary, baffled by nameless powers. Rather he was High Lord Berek Heartthew, limned in victory and lore. Under the Theomach's tutelage, he had transcended himself. His eyes were stars, and he gazed upon Linden with sombre gladness, simultaneously concerned and grati-fied.

From the north came another mighty spectre whom she knew, although she had only met him briefly as a young man. He was Damelon son of Berek, now High Lord Damelon Giantfriend. In his time, he had both discovered and guarded the Blood of the Earth. As he aged, he had put on girth: Dead, he implied the bulk of mountains against the background of Andelain's darkness and the black heavens. To Linden's shaken stare, he replied with a beatific smile.

The figure approaching from the south was a man whom she had not encountered; but he could only be Damelon's son, High Lord Loric Vilesilencer. He was gaunt with striving and mastered anguish, and the dark pits of his eyes held the intimate ache of despair. Yet he gazed upon the *krill*, his handiwork, with an air of profound vindication. When he looked at Linden, he nodded in approval, as if he were certain of her.

But Kevin Landwaster entered the vale from the east. She knew him too well. He had confronted her once before in Andelain, ordering her to *halt the Unbeliever's mad intent*; prevent Covenant from surrendering his ring. *We are kindred in our way – the victims and enactors of Despite.* In torment and outrage, High Lord Kevin's ghost had implored or commanded her to kill Covenant if she could find no other way to stop him.

Living, he had fashioned and hidden the Seven Wards to preserve the lore of the Old Lords for future generations. He had greeted the *Haruchai* with respect, inspiring them to become the Bloodguard. And he had saved them as well as the Ranyhyn, the Ramen and most of the Land's people from the consequences of his despair. But his last act had been to join with Lord Foul in the Ritual of Desecration. And when Elena had broken the Law of Death to summon him, he had defeated her, turning the Staff of Law to the Despiser's service. Now he wore the cost of his deeds in every tortured line of his visage.

When evil rises in its full power, it surpasses truth and may wear the guise of good—

His presence made Linden tremble. *Good cannot be accomplished by evil means.* He had been wrong about Covenant. He may have been wrong about Despite. *There is hope in contradiction.* But she could not affirm that he was wrong about her. Too many people had tried to caution her—

Like the other Dead, the four High Lords were silent. And they did not enter the wide circle of the Wraiths. Instead they stood, august, etched in light, beyond the flames as if they had come to bear witness as Linden unveiled the Land's fate.

But of Covenant himself, who had called Linden here, there was no sign anywhere.

'Now, Linden,' Stave said distinctly. 'The time has indeed come. Act or turn aside, according to the dictates of your heart.'

Her sudden anguish resembled both Kevin's and Honninscrave's. 'Covenant isn't here. I *need* him. He's the reason I came.'

He did not know of your intent.

'Then summon the Law-Breakers,' Stave answered. But he did not explain. Instead he stepped back as if to abjure her.

For a moment, she could not understand him, and she nearly broke. His apparent disapproval hurt her worse than Cail's mute departure, or Honninscrave's, or Sunder's and Hollian's. She loved them all, but she had accepted their deaths. Stave was alive; as mortal as she was, and as much at risk. He was her *friend*—

But then her mind was filled with luminescence like the stringent shining of the High Lords. Of course, she thought. Of *course*. The Law-Breakers. The Laws of Death and Life. If Covenant could not hear or answer her directly, who else might invoke him from his participation in the Arch of Time? Who except the Law-Breakers, those who by their unique desperation had made possible the triumph of his surrender to Lord Foul?

Fearless again, and beyond doubt, Linden raised her head to the stars. 'Elena!' she called firmly. 'You were Lena's daughter, but you were also Covenant's. You drank the Blood of the Earth. Now I need you.

'Hile Troy! First you sacrificed yourself to save the army of the Lords. Then you became Caer-Caveral and sacrificed yourself again. I need you, too.'

As she spoke, the darkness trembled. Around her, the substance of reality seemed to ripple and surge like shaken cloth. Kevin Landwaster glared with unassuaged bitterness. An eager scowl clenched his father's moonlight face. Damelon continued to beam, but Berek gnawed his lips anxiously.

Beyond the *krill* and the Wraiths, three ghosts appeared at the rim of the vale.

One was a man, eyeless as an ur-vile, and fretted with commitments. He wore the raiment of a Forestal, apparel that flowed like melody even though the song of his life and power had been stilled; and in his hand, he carried a gnarled staff like an accompaniment to his lost music. To Linden, he was Caer-Caveral: she had not known him as Hile Troy. She would never forget his final threnody.

Oh, Andelain! forgive! for I am doomed to fail this war.

Near him walked a woman; surely Elena? But she was not the High Lord whom Covenant had described as one of his Dead, a figure of love and loveliness. Rather she appeared as she must have been when Covenant had destroyed the original Staff of Law, Berek's Staff, tearing loose her last grasp on life; exposing her soul to the horror of what she had done.

Her hair was rent with woe: bleeding galls marked her face as if she had tried to claw away her failures. As she entered the vale and paused with Caer-Caveral, her form flickered, alternately lit and obscured as though clouds scudded across her spectral moonshine.

The Law-Breakers, dead and broken; doomed. The ghosts of all that the Land had lost.

But Linden scarcely saw them. Instead she stared at the man who walked between them, silver and compelled, as if he had been brought forth against his will.

He was Thomas Covenant: he had come to her at last.

And he was more than the Dead, oh, infinitely more: he was a sovereign spirit, suffused with wild magic and Time. In one sense, he was unchanged. Wreathed in argence, he wore the same pierced T-shirt, the same worn jeans and boots that she remembered. The scar on his forehead was a faint crease of nacre. Even his soul had lost the last two fingers of his right hand. When he met her gaze, he searched her with the same strict and irrefusable compassion which had made her who she was; taught her to love him – and the Land.

But in every other respect, he had gone beyond recognition. He was no more human than the stars: a being of such illimitable loneliness and grandeur that he both defied and deified understanding.

Briefly the *krill* seemed to grow dim in his presence. Then it blazed brighter, alight with rapture and exaltation. And Linden blazed with it. She did not hear herself cry out Covenant's name, or feel the stone of her heart torn asunder. She only knew that when Caer-Caveral and Elena stopped, Covenant continued on down the slope, striding like a prophet of ruin and hope until he had passed among the High Lords, through the ecstasy of the Wraiths, and reached the bottom of the vale, where Linden could see him clearly.

On the far side of Loric's embedded blade, he halted. There he stood with his arms folded like denial across his chest.

'Oh, Covenant.' Linden verged on weeping. 'God, I need you. Lord Foul has my son. I don't know how to save him without you.'

I can't help you unless you find me.

Only Covenant could stand up to the forces arrayed against her.

Just be wary—

His eyes bled nacre on her behalf. But he shook his head. Harsh as a blow, he raised his halfhand to cover his mouth.

She understood in spite of her dismay. He, too, accepted the command of silence. No matter how she yearned for his guidance, he would not speak to her. His gaze begged her to make the right choice.

In this place, your deeds must be your own, unpersuaded for good or ill—

With every nerve, Linden ached to hear his voice; his counsel; his love. But the mere fact that he had come told her everything.

Trust yourself.

Ever since her battle with Roger and the *croyel*, she had striven towards this moment.

Do something they don't expect.

Holding the Staff with her left hand, she planted its heel in the grass. With her right, she reached under her shirt and drew out Covenant's ring. Deliberately she pulled its chain over her head. Then she closed the ring in her fist.

Either alone will transcend your strength, as they would that of any mortal. Together they will wreak only madness, for wild magic defies all Law.

But the gem of Loric's *krill* could hold and focus any amount of power.

With her arms outstretched in welcome or supplication, Linden Avery the Chosen confronted her purpose.

'Wildwielder!' Infelice gasped. '*Do not.* I implore you!'

Linden did not glance at the *Elohim*. 'Then free my son. Give him back to me.'

Are we not equal to all things?

Infelice made no answer. Instead the Harrow said disdainfully, 'They will not. They can not. They fear your son more than they fear you. Though his worth to the Despiser is beyond measure, his gifts taint the self-contemplation of the *Elohim*.'

—a shadow upon the heart—

Specific constructs attract them. Jeremiah could make a door to lure the Elohim in and never let them out.

When he was little more than a toddler, he had been touched and maimed by Lord Foul.

That I do not forgive.

'Then leave me alone,' muttered Linden. 'I have to concentrate.'

First health-sense and Loric's gem: then wild magic: then Earthpower and Law.

But before she could begin, Galt stepped in front of her.

'Linden Avery, no,' he said flatly. 'This we will not permit. Uncertain of you, we have withheld judgment. But now we deem that the peril is too great. Such extravagance is not wisdom. Nor is it seemly or salvific. You will unleash havoc, to the measureless delight of all who loathe life and the Land. Similar extreme passions performed the Ritual of Desecration, marred the Laws of Death and Life, and invoked the Sunbane.

'If you do not turn aside, we will wrest both Staff and ring from you because we must.'

An instant of absolute fury gathered in Linden, but she did not utter it.

The Humbled could not hear Stave's thoughts. While Galt's assertion lingered in the air, Stave charged into him; bore him thrashing to the ground.

At the same instant, Mahrtiir sprang from Narunal's back. Flipping his garrote around Clyme's neck, he wrenched the Master off balance.

Even sight would not have made the Manethrall a match for Clyme. But Bhapa and Pahni followed less than a heartbeat behind Mahrtiir. Pahni grappled for Clyme's legs: Bhapa snagged one of Clyme's hands with his fighting cord and heaved. Together the three Ramen pulled Clyme from his feet.

Simultaneously both Rhohm and the Ranyhyn Naybahn surged between Branl and Linden. Naybahn's chest struck his rider's: Rhohm collided with Branl from the side.

The great horses had *declared themselves utterly to the service of the Chosen.*

As Rhohm opposed Branl, Liand snatched out his *orcrest*; held it shining in his hand. 'Do you dare, Master?' he shouted. 'Will you accept the test of truth? If you refuse, you declare yourself unworthy to oppose the Chosen!'

The Masters ignored Liand. But Rhohm and Naybahn countered Branl's speed as if they were herding him. Bhanoryl stood ready to intervene if

Galt broke free of Stave. Mhornym and Hynyn circled Clyme's struggle with the Ramen. Hyn guarded Linden.

Infelice turned away as if she scorned the indignity of physical combat. The Harrow remained apart, laughing bitterly. From near the rim of the vale, Elena and Caer-Caveral watched with anguish and ire. The High Lords contained their reactions, although Kevin's jaws clenched and strained.

Covenant regarded them all with yearning and pity in every limned line of his form; but he did not move or speak.

The actions of Linden's friends were like Caerroil Wildwood's runes: they articulated her resolve. Grateful and ready, sure of her allies, she closed her eyes. In darkness, she began to tune her percipience to the precise splendour of the *krill*. When she opened her hidden door and found wild magic, she intended to release it in only one direction, using Loric's gem to manage its possible devastation.

There. She could not imagine how Loric had forged his blade, but she saw its nature; its unconstrained potential. With her Staff warm in her hand, she felt every eldritch quality and significance of the gem, and of its position in the dagger. She descried how the edges and guards and hilt contributed to the complex purity of the stone. She sensed the meaning of its many facets. Immense lore and ineffable skill had provided for the shaping of the gem, designed the form and function of the dagger. There were no defined boundaries to the forces which could be wielded with Loric's weapon.

Nothing intruded on Linden's attention now. Perhaps the will of the Ranyhyn had thwarted the Humbled. In every age, the *Haruchai* had treasured the horses of Ra: no Master would strike at a Ranyhyn. And Stave and the Ramen and even Liand would fight without compunction.

The Harrow's laughter had fallen silent. Infelice did not speak. The Dead remained still.

When Linden was confident of the *krill*, she turned her health-sense inwards.

Proximity to the gem's incandescence aided her; guided her. Brilliance led her through her human concealments, the secret implications of old doubts. And when she found the door, white fire responded eagerly to her desires. At her call, wild magic grew and branched within her like an image of the One Tree in purest argent, its boughs emblazoned with stars. During the space of two heartbeats, or three, flame accumulated until she held enough power to rive the night; alter the heraldry of the heavens.

When she released it, it became a ceaseless blast of lightning, a bolt which struck and flared and crackled between her right fist and Loric's gem.

She had been assured – repeatedly – that she could not damage the Arch of Time. Not alone. She was not the ring's rightful wielder: therefore her ability to use white gold was limited. But she did not *feel* limited. Her conflagration stopped the night: it seemed to stop the movement of one moment to the next. While her lightning rent the air, she possessed unfathomable might. Her choices and desires could shape reality.

Jeremiah, she thought: an uninterrupted blare of wild magic. I'm coming. The only way I know how.

Her fire became so extreme that she saw everything with her eyes closed: the Humbled and their opponents frozen in shock or chagrin or astonishment; the terror on Infelice's face, the frightened calculation in the Harrow's gaze; the scrutiny of the High Lords, solemn and alarmed. She saw Covenant consider her as if he were praying.

She had gone beyond fear – beyond the very concept of fear – as she reached out for the blessed yellow flame of her Staff.

At once, Earthpower and Law responded as though they had come to efface every darkness from the Hills of Andelain. Strength as blissful as sunshine, as natural as Gilden, and as capable as a furnace erupted from the Staff, pouring like the incarnation of her will into the heart of Loric's *krill*.

Briefly she seemed to feel herself battling in the depths of *Melenkurion* Skyweir, wielding the Power of Command and the Seven Words while Roger Covenant and the *croyel* strove to extinguish her. But wild lightning exceeded the frenzy of her earlier struggles. It lit the vale as if it could illuminate the Earth. Together argence and cornflower flame and the dagger's incandescence swallowed any possibility of opposition or malice, drowning mere inadequacy in a vast sea of power.

Now instinctively she understood the runes with which Caerroil

Wildwood had elaborated her Staff. They were for *this*. The Forestal of Garroting Deep had engraved the ebony wood with his knowledge of Life and Death. Indirectly he had given her a supernal relationship with Law. For a moment, at least, his gift enabled her to commingle wild magic and Earthpower without losing control of one or falsifying the other.

She could have raised or levelled mountains, divided oceans, carved glaciers. She had become greater than her most flagrant expectations: as efficacious as a god, and as complete.

It should have been too much. *Either alone will transcend your strength—* Human flesh had not been formed to survive such forces. Yet Linden felt no danger. She was hardly conscious of strain. Perhaps her mind had already shattered. If so, she did not recognise the loss, or choose to regret it. Loric's gem drew immeasurable might away from her mortal blood and nerves and bones. Caerroil Wildwood's runes imposed a kind of structure on potential chaos. Her beloved stood before her, radiant in the admixture of theurgies and his own innominate transcendence. And she did not doubt herself at all.

She could imagine that the Swordmainnir knew the location of Covenant's human bones. The First and Pitchwife had carried his body out of the Wightwarrens for burial. And they had told the tale. Rime Coldspray and her comrades might know where to find the last time-gnawed residue of his life. Linden could have summoned them to her with a thought.

But she did not need any lingering particle of his ordinary flesh. His spirit stood before her, as necessary as love, and as compulsory as a commandment. She had wild magic and Earthpower, Loric's *krill* and Caer-Caveral's runes. She had her health-sense. And the Laws of Death and Life had already been broken once. They were weaker now.

She knew of no power with which she could cause the immediate release of her son. Jeremiah was hidden from her; beyond her reach. Covenant's ring and her Staff did not enable her to scry, or to search out secrets, or to foretell the effects of malevolence.

But that which she could do, she did without hesitation.

Now, she said in fire and passion. **Now. Covenant, I need you. I need your help. I need to get you back.**

She had demonstrated again and again that she could not save Jeremiah alone. Without Covenant, she was inadequate to the task.

Gazing steadily through her eyelids at the Land's redeemer, she murmured his name in an exultation of fires. Then she brought her hands together, wild magic and Earthpower.

A blast that seemed to quell the stars erupted from Loric's *krill*. Deliberately she invoked a concussion which compelled conflicting energies to become one.

This was not culmination. It was apotheosis. Power shocked the bedrock of the world: it strove to claim the sky. Convulsions like the earthquake under *Melenkurion* Skyweir cast reality into madness.

Around the vale, the Wraiths scattered suddenly; fled and winked out. They may have been screaming. Someone wailed or roared: Elena or Kevin, Infelice or the Harrow. Emotions trumpeted from the High Lords. But Linden heeded nothing except Covenant and her own purpose.

Through the gem, her powers took hold of him as if she had chosen to incinerate his soul.

An instant later, the sheer scale of the forces which she had unleashed overwhelmed her; and the world was swept away.

Covenant's agony must have been terrible to behold. His cry of protest may have deafened the night. But Linden was no longer able to see or hear him. Absolute vastness stunned every nerve in her body, every impulse in her mind. For a moment, her detonation left her entirely insensate, unable to feel or think or move. She did not know that she had dropped Covenant's ring as if it had scalded her. Her fingers were too numb to realise that the Staff had slipped from her grasp. Her eyes might as well have been charred away: she did not see the *krill*'s coruscating puissance rupture and vanish, blown apart by fundamental contradictions.

She did not recognise what she had done until darkness reasserted her mortality, and the frantic labour of her pulse began to force new awareness into her muscles and nerves.

When she opened her eyes, she saw Covenant's resurrected form standing, twisted with pain, on the far side of the blank gem, the dead stump. Theurgies flared and spat from his arms, his shoulders, his chest. Linden had burned him as badly as Lord Foul had burned him in Kiril Threndor. But she had burned him to life instead of death. The fading energies of his transformation wracked him as though he had emerged from a bonfire.

Like Joan, he bore the consequences of too much time.

Yet he was alive. In some sense, he was whole; unmarked except by his old wounds. Even his clothes were intact. Linden could see the rent in his T-shirt where he had been stabbed for Joan's sake. His hair was tousled silver like reified white gold.

Fires flickered up and down his body. They were the only light in the vale; or in Andelain; or in the Land. Slowly they exhausted themselves and went out.

While the last wisps of power streamed from his eyes, Covenant forced himself to straighten his back and look at Linden.

He took one step towards her, then another, before his legs failed and he plunged to his knees. Still upright, he gazed at her with such dismay that her throat closed. She could not breathe.

'Oh, Linden.' His first words to her were a hoarse gasp. 'What have you done?'

'*Done*, Timewarden?' Infelice snapped viciously. '*Done?* She has roused the Worm of the World's End. Such magicks must be answered. Because of her madness and folly, every *Elohim* will be devoured.'

Abruptly the *krill*'s gem began to shine again. Its light throbbed like a heart in ecstasy, as if it echoed Joan's distant excitement – or Lord Foul's.

Hyn's dolorous whickering reminded Linden that the Ranyhyn had tried to warn her.

Here ends
Fatal Revenant
Book Two of
The Last Chronicles of Thomas Covenant.
The story continues in Book Three
Against All Things Ending.

COMBINED GLOSSARY FOR
THE CHRONICLES OF THOMAS COVENANT

A

Abatha: one of the Seven Words

Acence: a Stonedownor, sister of Atiaran

Ahamkara: Hoerkin, 'the Door'

Ahanna: painter, daughter of Hanna

Ahnryn: a Ranyhyn; mount of Tull

Aimil: daughter of Anest, wife of Sunder

Aisle of Approach: passage to Earthrootstair under *Melenkurion* Skyweir

a-Jeroth of the Seven Hells: Lord of wickedness; Clave-name for Lord Foul the Despiser

ak-Haru: a supreme *Haruchai* honorific; paragon and measure of all *Haruchai* virtues

Akkasri: a member of the Clave; one of the na-Mhoram-cro

aliantha: treasure-berries

Alif, the Lady: a woman Favoured of the *gaddhi*

amanibhavam: horse-healing grass, dangerous to humans

Amatin: a Lord, daughter of Matin

Amith: a woman of Crystal Stonedown

Amok: mysterious guide to ancient Lore

Amorine: First Haft, later Hiltmark

Anchormaster: second-in-command aboard a Giantship

Andelain, the Hills of Andelain, the Andelainian Hills: a region of the Land which embodies health and beauty

Andelainscion: a region in the Center Plains

Anele: deranged old man; son of Sunder and Hollian

Anest: a woman of Mithil Stonedown, sister of Kalina

Annoy: a Courser

anundivian yajña: lost Ramen craft of bone-sculpting

Appointed, the: an *Elohim* chosen to bear a particular burden; Findail

Arch of Time, the: symbol of the existence and structure of time; conditions which make the existence of time possible

arghule/arghuleh: ferocious ice-beasts

Asuraka: Staff-Elder of the Loresraat

Atiaran: a Stonedownor, daughter of Tiaran, wife of Trell, mother of Lena

Audience Hall of Earthroot: maze under *Melenkurion* Skyweir to conceal and protect the Blood of the Earth

Aumbrie of the Clave, the: storeroom for former Lore

Auspice, the: throne of the *gaddhi*

aussat Befylam: child-form of the *jheherrin*

B

Bahgoon the Unbearable: character in a Giantish tale

Banas Nimoram: the Celebration of Spring

Bandsoil Bounds: region north of Soulsease River

Banefire, the: fire by which the Clave affects the Sunbane

Bann: a Bloodguard, assigned to Lord Trevor

Bannor: a Bloodguard, assigned to Thomas Covenant

Baradakas: a Hirebrand of Soaring Woodhelven

Bargas Slit: a gap through the Last Hills from the Center Plains to Garroting Deep

Bareisle: an island off the coast of *Elemesnedene*

Basila: a scout in Berek Halfhand's army

Benj, the Lady: a woman Favoured by the *gaddhi*

Berek Halfhand: Heartthew, Lord-Fatherer; first of the Old Lords

Bern: *Haruchai* slain by the Clave

Bhanoryl: a Ranyhyn; mount of Galt

Bhapa: a Cord of the Ramen, Sahah's half-brother; companion of Linden Avery

Bhrathair: a people met by the wandering Giants, residents of *Bhrathairealm* on the verge of the Great Desert

Bhrathairain: the city of the *Bhrathair*

Bhrathairain Harbour: the port of the *Bhrathair*

Bhrathairealm: the land of the *Bhrathair*

Birinair: a Hirebrand, Hearthrall of Lord's Keep

Bloodguard, the: *Haruchai*, a people living in the Westron Mountains; the defenders of the Lords

bone-sculpting: ancient Ramen craft, marrowmeld

Borillar: a Hirebrand and Hearthrall of Lord's Keep

Bornin: a *Haruchai*; a Master of the Land

Brabha: a Ranyhyn; mount of Korik

Branl: a *Haruchai*; a Master of the Land; one of the Humbled

Brannil: man of Stonemight Woodhelven

Brinn: a leader of the *Haruchai*; protector of Thomas Covenant; later Guardian of the One Tree

Brow Gnarlfist: a Giant, father of the First of the Search

C

caamora: Giantish ordeal of grief by fire

Cable Seadreamer: a Giant, brother of Honninscrave; member of the Search; possessed of the Earth-Sight

Cabledarm: a Giant; one of the Swordmainnir

Caer-Caveral: Forestal of Andelain; formerly Hile Troy

Caerroil Wildwood: Forestal of Garroting Deep

caesure: a rent in the fabric of time; a Fall

Cail: one of the *Haruchai*; protector of Linden Avery

Caitiffin: a captain of the armed forces of *Bhrathairealm*

Callindrill: a Lord, husband of Faer

Callowwail, the River: stream arising from *Elemesnedene*

Cavewights: evil creatures existing under Mount Thunder

Ceer: one of the *Haruchai*

Celebration of Spring, the: the Dance of the Wraiths of Andelain on the dark of the moon in the middle of spring

Center Plains, the: a region of the Land

Centerpith Barrens: a region in the Center Plains

Cerrin: a Bloodguard, assigned to Lord Shetra

Chant: one of the *Elohim*

Char: a Cord of the Ramen, Sahah's brother

Chatelaine, the: courtiers of the *gaddhi*

Chosen, the: title given to Linden Avery

Circle of Elders: Stonedown leaders

Cirrus Kindwind: a Giant; one of the Swordmainnir

clachan, the: demesne of the *Elohim*

Clang: a Courser

Clangor: a Courser

Clash: a Courser

Clave, the: group which wields the Sunbane and rules the Land

clingor: adhesive leather

Close, the: the Council-chamber of Lord's Keep

Clyme: a *Haruchai*; a Master of the Land; one of the Humbled

Coercri: The Grieve; former home of the Giants in Seareach

Colossus of the Fall, the: ancient stone figure guarding the Upper Land

Consecear Redoin: a region north of the Soulsease River

Cord: Ramen second rank

Cording: Ramen ceremony of becoming a Cord

Corimini: Eldest of the Loresraat

Corruption: Bloodguard/*Haruchai* name for Lord Foul

Council of Lords, the: protectors of the Land

Courser: a beast made by the Clave using the Sunbane

Creator, the: maker of the Earth

Croft: Graveler of Crystal Stonedown

Crowl: a Bloodguard

croyel, the: mysterious creatures which grant power through bargains, living off their hosts

Crystal Stonedown: home of Hollian

Currier: a Ramen rank

D

Damelon Giantfriend: son of Berek Halfhand, second High Lord of the Old Lords

Damelon's Door: door of lore which when opened permits passage through the Audience Hall of Earthroot under *Melenkurion* Skyweir

Dance of the Wraiths, the: the Celebration of Spring

Dancers of the Sea, the: *merewives*; suspected to be the offspring of the *Elohim* Kastenessen and his mortal lover

Daphin: one of the *Elohim*

Dawngreeter: highest sail on the foremast of a Giantship

Dead, the: spectres of those who have died

Deaththane: title given to High Lord Elena by the Ramen

Defiles Course, the: river in the Lower Land

Demondim, the: creatures created by Viles; creators of ur-viles and Waynhim

Demondim-spawn: another name for ur-viles and Waynhim; also another name for Vain

Desolation, the: era of ruin in the Land, after the Ritual of Desecration

Despiser, the: Lord Foul

Despite: evil; name given to the Despiser's nature and effects

dharmakshetra: 'to brave the enemy', a Waynhim

dhraga: a Waynhim

dhubha: a Waynhim

dhurng: a Waynhim

diamondraught: Giantish liquor

Din: a Courser

Dire's Vessel: Giantship used by the Swordmainnir to convey Longwrath

Doar: a Bloodguard

Dohn: a Manethrall of the Ramen

Dolewind, the: wind blowing to the Soulbiter

Doom's Retreat: a gap in the Southron Range between the South Plains and Doriendor Corishev

Doriendor Corishev: an ancient city; seat of the King against whom Berek Halfhand rebelled

drhami: a Waynhim

Drinishok: Sword-Elder of the Loresraat

Drinny: a Ranyhyn, foal of Hynaril; mount of Lord Mhoram

dromond: a Giantship

Drool Rockworm: a Cavewight, leader of the Cavewights; finder of the Illearth Stone

dukkha: 'victim', Waynhim name

Dura Fairflank: a mustang, Thomas Covenant's mount

Durance, the: a barrier Appointed by the *Elohim*; a prison for both Kastenessen and the *skurj*

durhisitar: a Waynhim

During Stonedown: village destroyed by the *Grim*; home of Hamako

Duroc: one of the Seven Words

Durris: a *Haruchai*

E

EarthBlood: concentrated fluid Earthpower, only known to exist under *Melenkurion* Skyweir; source of the Power of Command

Earthfriend: title first given to Berek Halfhand

Earthpower: natural power of all life; the source of all organic power in the Land

Earthroot: lake under *Melenkurion* Skyweir

Earthrootstair: stairway down to the lake of Earthroot under *Melenkurion* Skyweir

Earth-Sight: Giantish power to perceive distant dangers and needs

eftmound: gathering place for the *Elohim*

eh-Brand: one who can use wood to read the Sunbane

Elemesnedene: home of the *Elohim*

Elena: daughter of Lena and Thomas Covenant; later High Lord

Elohim, the: a mystic people encountered by the wandering Giants

Elohimfest: a gathering of the *Elohim*

Emacrimma's Maw: a region in the Center Plains

Enemy: Lord Foul's term of reference for the Creator

Eoman: a unit of the Warward of Lord's Keep, twenty warriors and a Warhaft

Eoward: twenty Eoman plus a Haft

Epemin: a soldier in Berek Halfhand's army, tenth Eoman, second Eoward

Esmer: tormented son of Cail and the Dancers of the Sea

Exalt Widenedworld: a Giant; youngest son of Soar Gladbirth and Sablehair Foamheart; later called Lostson and Longwrath

F

fael Befylam: serpent-form of the *jheherrin*

Faer: wife of Lord Callindrill

Fall: *Haruchai* name for a *caesure*

Fangs: the Teeth of the Render; Ramen name for the Demondim

Fangthane the Render: Ramen name for Lord Foul

Far Woodhelven: a village of the Land

Father of Horses, the: *Kelenbhrabanal*, legendary sire of the Ranyhyn

Favoured, the: courtesans of the *gaddhi*

Fields of Richloam: a region in the Center Plains

Filigree: a Giant; another name for Sablehair Foamheart

Findail: one of the *Elohim*; the Appointed

Fire-Lions: living fire-flow of Mount Thunder

fire-stones: graveling

First Betrayer: Clave-name for Berek Halfhand

First Circinate: first level of the Sandhold

First Haft: third in command of the Warward

First Mark: Bloodguard commander

First of the Search, the: leader of the Giants who follow the Earth-Sight; Gossamer Glowlimn

First Ward of Kevin's Lore: primary cache of knowledge left by High Lord Kevin

First Woodhelven: banyan tree village between Revelstone and Andelain; first Woodhelven created by Sunder and Hollian

Fleshharrower: a Giant-Raver, Jehannum, *moksha*

Foamkite: *tyrscull* belonging to Honninscrave and Seadreamer

Fole: a *Haruchai*

Foodfendhall: eating-hall and galley aboard a Giantship
Forbidding: a wall of power
Forestal: a protector of the remnants of the One Forest
Fostil: a man of Mithil Stonedown; father of Liand
Foul's Creche: the Despiser's home; Ridjeck Thome
Frostheart Grueburn: a Giant; one of the Swordmainnir
Furl Falls: waterfall at Revelstone
Furl's Fire: warning fire at Revelstone

G

gaddhi, the: sovereign of *Bhrathairealm*
Gallows Howe: a place of execution in Garroting Deep
Galt: a *Haruchai*; a Master of the Land; one of the Humbled
Garroting Deep: a forest of the Land
Garth: Warmark of the Warward of Lord's Keep
Gay: a Winhome of the Ramen
ghohritsar: a Waynhim
ghramin: a Waynhim
Giantclave: Giantish conference
Giantfriend: title given first to Damelon, later to Thomas Covenant and
    then Linden Avery
Giants: the Unhomed, ancient friends of the Lords; a seafaring people
    of the Earth
Giantship: a stone sailing vessel made by Giants; *dromond*
Giantway: path made by Giants
Giant Woods: a forest of the Land
Gibbon: the na-Mhoram; leader of the Clave
Gilden: a maplelike tree with golden leaves
Gildenlode: a power-wood formed from the Gilden trees
Glimmermere: a lake on the plateau above Revelstone
Gorak Krembal: Hotash Slay, a defence around Foul's Creche
Gossamer Glowlimn: a Giant; the First of the Search
Grace: a Cord of the Ramen
Graveler: one who uses stone to wield the Sunbane

graveling: fire-stones, made to glow and emit heat by stone-lore

Gravelingas: a master of *rhadhamaerl* stone-lore

Gravin Threndor: Mount Thunder

Great Desert, the: a region of the Earth; home of the *Bhrathair* and the Sandgorgons

Great One: title given to Caerroil Wildwood by the Mahdoubt

Great Swamp, the: Lifeswallower; a region of the Land

Greshas Slant: a region in the Center Plains

Grey Desert, the: a region south of the Land

Grey River, the: a river of the Land

Grey Slayer: plains name for Lord Foul

Greywightswath: a region north of the Soulsease River

griffin: lionlike beast with wings

Grim, the: (also the na-Mhoram's *Grim*) a destructive storm sent by the Clave

Grimmand Honninscrave: a Giant; Master of Starfare's Gem; brother of Seadreamer

Grimmerdhore: a forest of the Land

Guard, the: *hustin*; soldiers serving the *gaddhi*

Guardian of the One Tree, the: mystic figure warding the approach to the One Tree; formerly *ak-Haru Kenaustin Ardenol*; now Brinn of the *Haruchai*

H

Haft: commander of an Eoward

Halewhole Bluntfist: a Giant; one of the Swordmainnir

Halfhand: title given to Thomas Covenant and to Berek

Hall of Gifts, the: large chamber in Revelstone devoted to the artworks of the Land

Hamako: sole survivor of the destruction of During Stonedown

Hami: a Manethrall of the Ramen

Hand: a rank in Berek Halfhand's army; aide to Berek

Handir: a *Haruchai* leader; the Voice of the Masters

Harad: one of the Seven Words

Harbour Captain: chief official of the port of *Bhrathairealm*

Harn: one of the *Haruchai*; protector of Hollian

Harrow, the: one of the Insequent

Haruchai: a warrior people from the Westron Mountains

Healer: a physician

Heart of Thunder: Kiril Threndor, a cave of power in Mount Thunder

Hearthcoal: a Giant; cook of Starfare's Gem; wife of Seasauce

Hearthrall of Lord's Keep: a steward responsible for light, warmth and hospitality

Heartthew: a title given to Berek Halfhand

heartwood chamber: meeting-place of a Woodhelven, within a tree

Heer: leader of a Woodhelven

Heft Galewrath: a Giant; Storesmaster of Starfare's Gem

Herem: a Raver, Kinslaughterer, *turiya*

Hergrom: one of the *Haruchai*

High Lord: leader of the Council of Lords

High Lord's Furl: banner of the High Lord

High Wood: *lomillialor*; offspring of the One Tree

Hile Troy: a man formerly from Covenant's world; Warmark of High Lord Elena's Warward

Hiltmark: second-in-command of the Warward

Hirebrand: a master of *lillianrill* wood-lore

Hoerkin: a Warhaft

Hollian: daughter of Amith; eh-Brand of Crystal Stonedown; companion of Thomas Covenant and Linden Avery

Home: original homeland of the Giants

Horizonscan: lookout atop the midmast of a Giantship

Horse, the: human soldiery of the *gaddhi*

horserite: a gathering of Ranyhyn in which they drink mind-blending waters in order to share visions, prophecies and purpose

Hotash Slay: Gorak Krembal, a flow of lava protecting Foul's Creche

Hower: a Bloodguard, assigned to Lord Loerya

Hrama: a Ranyhyn stallion; mount of Anele

Humbled, the: three *Haruchai* maimed to resemble Thomas Covenant in order to remind the Masters of their limitations

Hurn: a Cord of the Ramen

hurtloam: a healing mud

Huryn: a Ranyhyn; mount of Terrel

husta/hustin: partly human soldiers bred by Kasreyn to be the *gaddhi's* Guard

Hyn: a Ranyhyn mare; mount of Linden Avery

Hynaril: a Ranyhyn; mount of Tamarantha and then Mhoram

Hynyn: a Ranyhyn stallion; mount of Stave

Hyrim: a Lord, son of Hoole

I

Illearth Stone, the: powerful bane long buried under Mount Thunder

Illender: title given to Thomas Covenant

Imoiran Tomal-mate: a Stonedownor

Inbull: a Warhaft in Berek Halfhand's army; commander of the tenth Eoman, second Eoward

Infelice: reigning leader of the *Elohim*

Insequent, the: a mysterious people living far to the west of the Land

Interdict, the: reference to the power of the Colossus of the Fall to prevent Ravers from entering the Upper Land

Irin: a warrior of the Third Eoman of the Warward

Ironhand, the: title given to the leader of the Swordmainnir

Isle of the One Tree, the: location of the One Tree

J

Jain: a Manethrall of the Ramen

Jass: a *Haruchai*; a Master of the Land

Jehannum: a Raver, Fleshharrower, *moksha*

Jevin: a healer in Berek Halfhand's army

jheherrin: soft ones, misshapen by-products of Foul's making

Jous: a man of Mithil Stonedown, son of Prassan, father of Nassic; inheritor of an Unfettered One's mission to remember the Halfhand

K

Kalina: a woman of Mithil Stonedown; wife of Nassic, mother of Sunder

Kam: a Manethrall of the Ramen

Karnis: a Heer of First Woodhelven

Kasreyn of the Gyre: a thaumaturge; the *gaddhi*'s Kemper (advisor) in *Bhrathairealm*

Kastenessen: one of the *Elohim*; former Appointed

Keep of the na-Mhoram, the: Revelstone

Keeper: a Ramen rank, one of those unsuited to the rigours of being a Cord or a Manethrall

Kelenbhrabanal: Father of Horses in Ranyhyn legends

Kemper, the: chief advisor of the *gaddhi*; Kasreyn

Kemper's Pitch: highest level of the Sandhold

Kenaustin Ardenol: a figure of *Haruchai* legend; former Guardian of the One Tree; true name of the Theomach

Kevin Landwaster: son of Loric Vilesilencer; last High Lord of the Old Lords

Kevin's Dirt: smoglike pall covering the Upper Land; it blocks health-sense, making itself invisible from below

Kevin's Lore: knowledge of power left hidden by Kevin in the Seven Wards

Kevin's Watch: mountain lookout near Mithil Stonedown

Khabaal: one of the Seven Words

Kinslaughterer: a Giant-Raver, Herem, *turiya*

Kiril Threndor: chamber of power deep under Mount Thunder; Heart of Thunder

Koral: a Bloodguard, assigned to Lord Amatin

Korik: a Bloodguard

Krenwill: a scout in Berek Halfhand's army

kresh: savage giant yellow wolves

krill, the: knife of power forged by High Lord Loric; awakened to power by Thomas Covenant

Kurash Plenethor: region of the Land formally named Stricken Stone, now called Trothgard

Kurash Qwellinir: the Shattered Hills, region of the Lower Land protecting Foul's Creche

L

Lake Pelluce: a lake in Andelainscion

Lal: a Cord of the Ramen

Land, the: generally, area found on the map; a focal region of the Earth where Earthpower is uniquely accessible

Landsdrop: great cliff separating the Upper and Lower Lands

Landsverge Stonedown: a village of the Land

Landwaster: title given to High Lord Kevin

Latebirth: a Giant; one of the Swordmainnir

Law, the: the natural order

Law of Death, the: the natural order which separates the living from the dead

Law of Life, the: the natural order which separates the dead from the living

Law-Breaker: title given to both High Lord Elena and Caer-Caveral

Lax Blunderfoot: a name chosen by Latebirth in self-castigation

Lena: a Stonedownor, daughter of Atiaran, mother of Elena

lianar: wood of power used by an eh-Brand

Liand: a man of Mithil Stonedown, son of Fostil; companion of Linden Avery

Lifeswallower: the Great Swamp

lillianrill: wood-lore; masters of wood-lore

Lithe: a Manethrall of the Ramen

Llaura: a Heer of Soaring Woodhelven

Loerya: a Lord, wife of Trevor

lomillialor: High Wood; a wood of power

Longwrath: a Giant; Swordmainnir name for Exalt Widenedworld

Lord: one who has mastered both the Sword and the Staff aspects of Kevin's Lore

Lord-Fatherer: title given to Berek Halfhand

Lord Foul: the enemy of the Land; the Despiser

'Lord Mhoram's Victory': a painting by Ahanna
Lord of Wickedness: a-Jeroth
Lord's-fire: staff-fire used by the Lords
Lord's Keep: Revelstone
Lords, the: the primary protectors of the Land
loremaster: a leader of ur-viles
Loresraat: Trothgard school at Revelwood where Kevin's Lore is studied
Lorewarden: a teacher in the Loresraat
loreworks: Demondim power-laboratory
Loric Vilesilencer: a High Lord; son of Damelon Giantfriend
lor-liarill: Gildenlode
Lost, the: Giantish name for the Unhomed
Lost Deep, the: a loreworks; breeding pit/laboratory under Mount Thunder where Demondim, Waynhim, and ur-viles were created
Lostson: a Giant; later name for Exalt Widenedworld
Lower Land, the: region of the Land east of Landsdrop
lucubrium: laboratory of a thaumaturge
lurker of the Sarangrave, the: monster inhabiting the Great Swamp

M

Mahdoubt, the: a servant of Revelstone; one of the Insequent
Mahrtiir: a Manethrall of the Ramen; companion of Linden Avery
maidan: open land around *Elemesnedene*
Maker, the: *jheherrin* name for Lord Foul
Maker-place: *jheherrin* name for Foul's Creche
Malliner: Woodhelvennin Heer, son of Veinnin
Mane: Ramen reference to a Ranyhyn
Maneing: Ramen ceremony of becoming a Manethrall
Manethrall: highest Ramen rank
Manhome: main dwelling place of the Ramen in the Plains of Ra
Marid: a man of Mithil Stonedown; Sunbane victim
Marny: a Ranyhyn; mount of Tuvor
marrowmeld: bone-sculpting; *anundivian yajña*

Master: commander of a Giantship

Master, the: Clave-name for Lord Foul

master-rukh, the: iron triangle at Revelstone which feeds and reads other *rukhs*

Masters of the Land, the: *Haruchai* who have claimed responsibility for protecting the Land from Corruption

Mehryl: a Ranyhyn; mount of Hile Troy

Melenkurion: one of the Seven Words

Melenkurion Skyweir: a cleft peak in the Westron Mountains

Memla: a Rider of the Clave; one of the na-Mhoram-in

mere-son: name or title given to Esmer

merewives: the Dancers of the Sea

metheglin: a beverage; mead

Mhoram: a Lord, later high Lord; son of Variol

Mhornym: a Ranyhyn stallion; mount of Clyme

Mill: one of the Seven Words

Minas: one of the Seven Words

mirkfruit: papaya-like fruit with narcoleptic pulp

Mistweave: a Giant

Mithil River: a river of the Land

Mithil Stonedown: a village in the South Plains

Mithil's Plunge, the: waterfall at the head of the Mithil valley

Moire Squareset: a Giant; one of the Swordmainnir; killed in battle by the *skurj*

moksha: a Raver, Jehannum, Fleshharrower

Morin: First Mark of the Bloodguard; commander in original *Haruchai* army

Morinmoss: a forest of the Land

Morninglight: one of the *Elohim*

Morril: a Bloodguard, assigned to Lord Callindrill

Mount Thunder: a peak at the centre of Landsdrop

Murrin: a Stonedownor, mate of Odona

Myrha: a Ranyhyn; mount of High Lord Elena

N

na-Mhoram, the: leader of the Clave

na-Mhoram-cro: lowest rank of the Clave

na-Mhoram-in: highest rank of the Clave below the na-Mhoram

na-Mhoram-wist: middle rank of the Clave

Naharahn: a Ranyhyn mare; mount of Pahni

Narunal: a Ranyhyn stallion; mount of Mahrtiir

Nassic: father of Sunder, son of Jous; inheritor of an Unfettered One's mission to remember the Halfhand

Naybahn: a Ranyhyn; mount of Branl

Nelbrin: son of Sunder, 'heart's child'

Nicor, the: great sea-monster; said to be offspring of the Worm of the World's End

Nom: a Sandgorgon

North Plains, the: a region of the Land

Northron Climbs, the: a region of the Land

O

Oath of Peace, the: oath by the people of the Land against needless violence

Odona: a Stonedownor, mate of Murrin

Offin: a former na-Mhoram

Old Lords, the: Lords prior to the Ritual of Desecration

Omournil: Woodhelvennin Heer, daughter of Mournil

One Forest, the: ancient forest covering most of the Land

One Tree, the: mystic tree from which the Staff of Law was made

Onyx Stonemage: a Giant; one of the Swordmainnir

orcrest: a stone of power; Sunstone

Osondrea: a Lord, daughter of Sondrea; later high Lord

P

Padrias: Woodhelvennin Heer, son of Mill

Pahni: a Cord of the Ramen, cousin of Sahah; companion of Linden Avery

Palla: a healer in Berek Halfhand's army

Peak of the Fire-Lions, the: Mount Thunder, Gravin Threndor

Pietten: Woodhelvennin child damaged by Lord Foul's minions, son of Soranal

pitchbrew: a beverage combining *diamondraught* and *vitrim*, conceived by Pitchwife

Pitchwife: a Giant; member of the Search; husband of the First of the Search

Plains of Ra, the: a region of the Land

Porib: a Bloodguard

Power of Command, the: Seventh Ward of Kevin's Lore

Pren: a Bloodguard

Prothall: High Lord, son of Dwillian

Prover of Life: title given to Thomas Covenant

Puhl: a Cord of the Ramen

Pure One, the: redemptive figure of *jheherrin* legend

Q

Quaan: Warhaft of the Third Eoman of the Warward; later Hiltmark, then Warmark

quellvisk: a kind of monster, now apparently extinct

Quern Ehstrel: true name of the Mahdoubt

Quest for the Staff of Law, the: quest to recover the Staff of Law from Drool Rockworm

Questsimoon, the: the Roveheartswind; a steady, favourable wind, perhaps seasonal

Quilla: a Heer of First Woodhelven

Quirrel: a Stonedownor, companion of Triock

R

Ramen: people who serve the Ranyhyn

Rant Absolain: the *gaddhi*

Ranyhyn: the great horses of the Plains of Ra

Ravers: Lord Foul's three ancient servants

Raw, the: fjord into the demesne of the *Elohim*

Rawedge Rim, the: mountains around *Elemesnedene*

Reader: a member of the Clave who tends and uses the *master-rukh*

Rede, the: knowledge of history and survival promulgated by the Clave

Revelstone: Lord's Keep; mountain city formed by Giants

Revelwood: seat of the Loresraat; tree city grown by Lords

rhadhamaerl: stone-lore; masters of stone-lore

rhee: a Ramen food, a thick mush

Rhohm: a Ranyhyn stallion; mount of Liand

rhysh: a community of Waynhim; 'stead'

rhyshyshim: a gathering of *rhysh*; a place in which such gathering occurs

Riddenstretch: a region north of the Soulsease River

Rider: a member of the Clave

Ridjeck Thome: Foul's Creche, the Despiser's home

rillinlure: healing wood dust

Rime Coldspray: a Giant; the Ironhand of the Swordmainnir

Ringthane: Ramen name for Thomas Covenant, then Linden Avery

ring-wielder: *Elohim* term of reference for Thomas Covenant

Rire Grist: a Caitiffin of the *gaddhi*'s Horse

Rites of Unfettering: the ceremony of becoming Unfettered

Ritual of Desecration, the: act of despair by which High Lord Kevin destroyed the Old Lords and ruined most of the Land

Rivenrock: deep cleft splitting *Melenkurion* Skyweir and its plateau; there the Black River enters Garroting Deep

Riversward: a region north of the Soulsease River

Rockbrother, Rocksister: terms of affection between men and Giants

rocklight: light emitted by glowing stone

roge Befylam: Cavewight-form of the *jheherrin*

Rohnhyn: a Ranyhyn; mount of Bhapa after Whrany's death

Roveheartswind, the: the *Questsimoon*

Rue: a Manethrall of the Ramen, formerly named Gay

Ruel: a Bloodguard, assigned to Hile Troy

rukh: iron talisman by which a Rider wields the power of the Sunbane

Runnik: a Bloodguard

Rustah: a Cord of the Ramen

S

Sablehair Foamheart: a Giant, also called Filigree; mate of Soar Gladbirth; mother of Exalt Widenedworld

sacred enclosure: Vespers-hall at Revelstone; later the site of the Banefire

Sahah: a Cord of the Ramen

Saltheart Foamfollower: a Giant, friend of Thomas Covenant

Saltroamrest: bunk hold for the crew in a Giantship

Salttooth: jutting rock in the harbour of the Giants' Home

Salva Gildenbourne: forest surrounding the Hills of Andelain; begun by Sunder and Hollian

samadhi: a Raver, Sheol, Satansfist

Sandgorgons: monsters of the Great Desert of *Bhrathairealm*

Sandgorgons Doom: imprisoning storm created by Kasreyn to trap the Sandgorgons

Sandhold, the: the *gaddhi's* castle in *Bhrathairealm*

Sandwall, the: the great wall defending *Bhrathairain*

Santonin: a Rider of the Clave, one of the na-Mhoram-in

Sarangrave Flat: a region of the Lower Land encompassing the Great Swamp

Satansfist: a Giant-Raver, Sheol, *samadhi*

Satansheart: Giantish name for Lord Foul

Scend Wavegift: a Giant; one of the Swordmainnir; killed by Longwrath

Search, the: quest of the Giants for the wound in the Earth; later the quest for the Isle of the One Tree

Seareach: region of the Land occupied by the Unhomed

Seasauce: a Giant; husband of Hearthcoal; cook of Starfare's Gem

Seatheme: dead wife of Sevinhand

Second Circinate: second level of the Sandhold

Second Ward: second unit of Kevin's hidden knowledge

setrock: a type of stone used with pitch to repair stone

Seven Hells, the: a-Jeroth's demesne: desert, rain, pestilence, fertility, war, savagery and darkness

Seven Wards, the: collection of knowledge hidden by High Lord Kevin

Seven Words, the: words of power from Kevin's Lore

Sevinhand: a Giant, Anchormaster of Starfare's Gem

Shattered Hills, the: a region of the Land near Foul's Creche

Sheol: a Raver, Satansfist, *samadhi*

Shetra: a Lord, wife of Verement

Shipsheartthew: the wheel of a Giantship

shola: a small wooded glen where a stream runs between unwooded hills

Shull: a Bloodguard

Sill: a Bloodguard, assigned to Lord Hyrim

Sivit: a Rider of the Clave, one of the na-Mhoram-wist

skest: acid-creatures serving the lurker of the Sarangrave

skurj: laval monsters that devour earth and vegetation; long ago, the *Elohim* Kastenessen was Appointed (the Durance) to prevent them from wreaking terrible havoc

Slen: a Stonedownor, mate of Terass

Soar Gladbirth: a Giant; youngest son of Pitchwife and Gossamer Glowlimn

Soaring Woodhelven: a tree-village

soft ones, the: the *jheherrin*

Somo: pinto taken by Liand from Mithil Stonedown

soothreader: a seer

soothtell: ritual of revelation practised by the Clave

Soranal: a Woodhelvennin Heer, son of Thiller

Soulbiter, the: a dangerous ocean of Giantish legend

Soulbiter's Teeth: reefs in the Soulbiter

Soulcrusher: Giantish name for Lord Foul

South Plains, the: a region of the Land

Sparlimb Keelsetter: a Giant, father of triplets

Spikes, the: guard-towers at the mouth of *Bhrathairain* Harbour

Spray Frothsurge: a Giant; mother of the First of the Search

springwine: a mild, refreshing liquor

Staff, the: a branch of the study of Kevin's Lore

Staff of Law, the: a tool of Earthpower; the first Staff was formed by Berek from the One Tree and later destroyed by Thomas Covenant; the second was formed by Linden Avery by using wild magic to merge Vain and Findail

Stallion of the First Herd, the: *Kelenbhrabanal*

Starfare's Gem: Giantship used by the Search

Starkin: one of the *Elohim*

Stave: a *Haruchai*; a Master of the Land; companion of Linden Avery

Stell: one of the *Haruchai*, protector of Sunder

Stonedown: a stone-village

Stonedownor: one who lives in a stone-village

Stonemight, the: a fragment of the Illearth Stone

Stonemight Woodhelven: a village in the South Plains

Storesmaster: third-in-command aboard a Giantship

Stormpast Galesend: a Giant; one of the Swordmainnir

Stricken Stone: region of the Land, later called Trothgard

Sunbane, the: a power arising from the corruption of nature by Lord Foul

Sunbirth Sea, the: ocean east of the Land

Sunder: son of Nassic; Graveler of Mithil Stonedown; companion of Thomas Covenant and Linden Avery

Sun-Sage: one who can affect the Sunbane

Sunstone: *orcrest*

sur-jheherrin: descendants of the *jheherrin*; inhabitants of Sarangrave Flat

suru-pa-maerl: an art using stone

Swarte: a Rider of the Clave

Sword, the: a branch of the study of Kevin's Lore

Sword-Elder: chief Lorewarden of the Sword at the Loresraat

Swordmain/Swordmainnir: Giant(s) trained as warrior(s)

T

Tamarantha: a Lord, daughter of Enesta, wife of Variol

Teeth of the Render, the: Ramen name for the Demondim; Fangs

Terass: a Stonedownor, daughter of Annoria, wife of Slen

Terrel: a Bloodguard, assigned to Lord Mhoram; a commander of the original *Haruchai* army

test of silence, the: test of integrity used by the people of the Land

test of truth, the: test of veracity by *lomillialor* or *orcrest*

The Grieve: *Coercri*; home of the lost Giants in Seareach

Thelma Twofist: character in a Giantish tale

The Majesty: throne room of the *gaddhi*; fourth level of the Sandhold

Theomach, the: one of the Insequent

Thew: a Cord of the Ramen

Third Ward: third unit of Kevin's hidden knowledge

Thomin: a Bloodguard, assigned to Lord Verement

Three Corners of Truth, the: basic formulation of beliefs taught and enforced by the Clave

thronehall, the: the Despiser's seat in Foul's Creche

Tier of Riches, the: showroom of the *gaddhi*'s wealth; third level of the Sandhold

Timewarden: *Elohim* title for Thomas Covenant after his death

Tohrm: a Gravelingas; Hearthrall of Lord's Keep

Tomal: a Stonedownor craftmaster

Toril: *Haruchai* slain by the Clave

Treacher's Gorge: ravine opening into Mount Thunder

treasure-berries: *aliantha*, nourishing fruit found throughout the Land in all seasons

Trell: Gravelingas of Mithil Stonedown; husband of Atiaran, father of Lena

Trevor: a Lord, husband of Loerya

Triock: a Stonedownor, son of Thuler; loved Lena

Trothgard: a region of the Land, formerly Stricken Stone

Tull: a Bloodguard

turiya: a Raver, Herem, Kinslaughterer

Tuvor: First Mark of the Bloodguard; a commander of the original

Haruchai army

tyrscull: a Giantish training vessel for apprentice sailors

U

Unbeliever, the: title claimed by Thomas Covenant

Unfettered, the: lore-students freed from conventional responsibilities to seek individual knowledge and service

Unfettered One, the: founder of a line of men waiting to greet Thomas Covenant's return to the Land

Unhomed, the: the lost Giants living in Seareach

upland: plateau above Revelstone

Upper Land, the: region of the Land west of Landsdrop

ur-Lord: title given to Thomas Covenant

ur-viles: Demondim-spawn, evil creatures

ussusimiel: nourishing melon grown by the people of the Land

V

Vailant: former High Lord before Prothall

Vain: Demondim-spawn; bred by ur-viles for a secret purpose

Vale: a Bloodguard

Valley of Two Rivers, the: site of Revelwood in Trothgard

Variol Tamarantha-mate: a Lord, later High Lord; son of Pentil, father of Mhoram

Verement: a Lord, husband of Shetra

Verge of Wandering, the: valley in the Southron Range southeast of Mithil Stonedown; gathering place of the nomadic Ramen

Vernigil: a *Haruchai*; a Master of the Land guarding First Woodhelven

Vertorn: a healer in Berek Halfhand's army

Vespers: self-consecration rituals of the Lords

Vettalor: Warmark of the army opposing Berek Halfhand

viancome: meeting place at Revelwood

Victuallin Tayne: a region in the Center Plains

Viles: monstrous beings which created the Demondim
vitrim: nourishing fluid created by the Waynhim
Vizard, the: one of the Insequent
Voice of the Masters, the: a *Haruchai* leader; spokesman for the Masters as a group
voure: a plant-sap which wards off insects
Vow, the: *Haruchai* oath of service which formed the Bloodguard
vraith: a Waynhim

W

Ward: a unit of Kevin's lore
Warhaft: commander of an Eoman
Warlore: Sword knowledge in Kevin's Lore
Warmark: commander of the Warward
Warrenbridge: entrance to the catacombs under Mount Thunder
Warward, the: army of Lord's Keep
Wavedancer: Giantship commanded by Brow Gnarlfist
Wavenhair Haleall: a Giant, wife of Sparlimb Keelsetter, mother of triplets
Waymeet: resting place for travellers maintained by Waynhim
Waynhim: tenders of the Waymeets; rejected Demondim-spawn, opponents and relatives of ur-viles
Weird of the Waynhim, the: Waynhim concept of doom, destiny or duty
were-menhir(s): Giantish name for the *skurj*
Whane: a Cord of the Ramen
white gold: a metal of power not found in the Land
white gold wielder: title given to Thomas Covenant
White River, the: a river of the land
Whrany: a Ranyhyn stallion; mount of Bhapa
Wightburrow, the: cairn under which Drool Rockworm is buried
Wightwarrens: home of the Cavewights under Mount Thunder; catacombs
wild magic: the power of white gold; considered the keystone of the

Arch of Time

Wildwielder: white gold wielder; title given to Linden Avery by Esmer and the *Elohim*

Windscour: region in the Center Plains

Windshorn Stonedown: a village in the South Plains

Winhome: Ramen lowest rank

Woodenwold: region of trees surrounding the *maidan* of *Elemesnedene*

Woodhelven: wood-village

Woodhelvennin: inhabitants of wood-village

Word of Warning: a powerful, destructive forbidding

Worm of the World's End, the: creature believed by the *Elohim* to have formed the foundation of the Earth

Wraiths of Andelain, the: creatures of living light that perform the Dance at the Celebration of Spring

Würd of the Earth, the: term used by the *Elohim* to describe their own nature, destiny or purpose; could be read as Word, Worm or Weird

Y

Yellinin: a soldier in Berek Halfhand's army; third-in-command of the tenth Eoman, second Eoward

Yeurquin: a Stonedownor, companion of Triock

Yolenid: daughter of Loerya

Z

Zaynor: a *Haruchai* from a time long before the *Haruchai* first came to the Land